FOR THE SAKE OF ALL LIVING THINGS

ALSO BY JOHN M. DEL VECCHIO

THE 13TH VALLEY

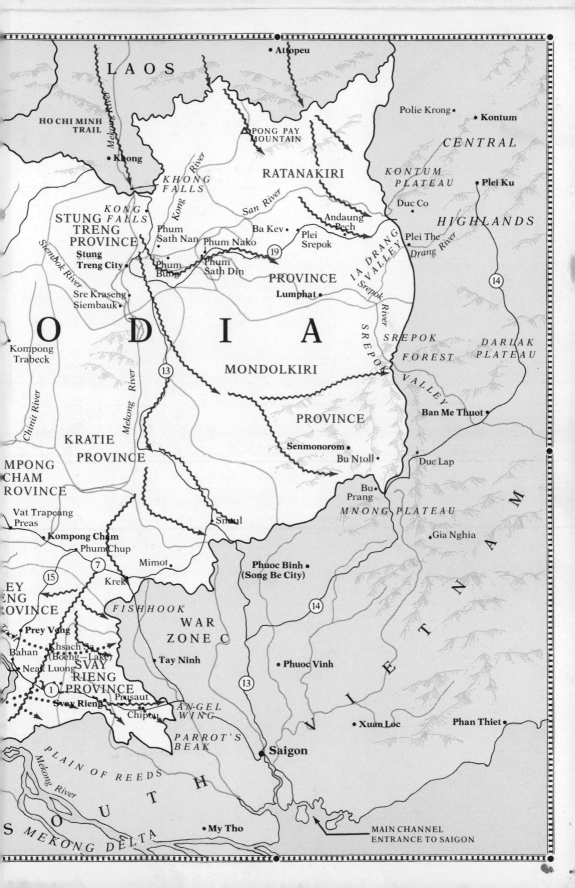

FOR THE SAKE OF ALL LIVING THINGS

JOHN M. DEL VECCHIO

BANTAM BOOKS
NEW YORK · TORONTO · LONDON · SYDNEY · AUCKLAND

FOR THE SAKE OF ALL LIVING THINGS
A Bantam Book / March 1990

Grateful acknowledgment is made for permission to reprint from
previously published material:
While Six Million Died: A Chronicle of American Apathy by Arthur Morse,
copyright 1967 by Arthur D. Morse, published by the Overlook Press,
Lewis Hollow Road, Woodstock, New York.
The Prestige Press and the Christmas Bombing by Martin Herz,
copyright 1980 by Ethics and Public Policy Center, Washington, D.C.
Cambodia: Starvation and Revolution by Gareth Porter and
George C. Hildebrand, copyright © 1976 by George Hildebrand
and Gareth Porter, reprinted by permission of Monthly Review
Foundation, New York, NY.

Library of Congress Cataloging-in-Publication Data

Del Vecchio, John M., 1948–
    For the sake of all living things / John M. Del Vecchio.
        p.   cm.
    ISBN 0-553-05742-1
    I. Title.
PS3554.E4327F6 1990
813'.54—dc20   89-28066
                                                                 CIP

Published simultaneously in the United States and Canada

*Bantam Books are published by Bantam Books, a division of Bantam
Doubleday Dell Publishing Group, Inc. Its trademark, consisting of the
words ''Bantam Books'' and the portrayal of a rooster, is Registered
in U.S. Patent and Trademark Office and in other countries. Marca
Registrada. Bantam Books, 666 Fifth Avenue, New York, New York 10103.*

PRINTED IN THE UNITED STATES OF AMERICA
RRH   0   9   8   7   6   5   4   3   2   1

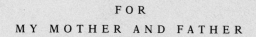

FOR
MY MOTHER AND FATHER

ACKNOWLEDGMENTS

This book was originally intended as a story about American veterans of the Viet Nam War which would also include segments on Viet Namese and Cambodian soldiers and their families. The Cambodian section took on a life of its own about three years into the writing. I would like to thank all those many people who assisted me in reaching an understanding of the American experience. The original story has not been abandoned—only temporarily put on hold.

In addition I would like to thank Sisomouth Bilavarn, F. C. Brown, Jim Catlin, David Chandler, Ronald E. Cowart, Sam Deibbler, Frank Del Vecchio, Ahmed Delvean, the Venerable Maha Gosshananda, Harry Hayes, Thanvy Kouk, Mike Kukler, Ben Cai Lam, Bill Laurie, Ned Leavitt, Marcus Leddy, Bob Ledlelaytner, Ron Mullins, Ven Nguyen, Doug Peacock, Bob Platte, Elena Rusnak, Ed Ruminski, Al Santoli, Mary Scully, Teddy Shpak, Mel Simensky, Shelby Stanton, and Tom Taylor.

I would also like to thank F. X. and Rebecca Anne Flinn for their inspiration.

And a very special acknowledgment to Jeremiah who was there every day, through every word of every rewrite, until the very last.

I shall become enlightened
for the sake of all living things.

— A BUDDHIST VOW

CAMBODIA:
Factions, Influences and Military Disposition

HISTORICAL SUMMATION
Part 1 (to mid-1968)

Prepared for
The Washington News-Times
J. L. Sullivan

April 1985

The Cambodian holocaust has not ended and we remain skeptical and uncertain if or how the "problem" will ever be resolved.

One in ten Cambodians was killed in the multiforce fighting between 1967 and 1975—600,000 to 700,000 of 7.1 million—approximately half to the civil war and half to various invasions, pogroms and purges. From April 1975 to January 1979 more than two million people were killed, starved to death or died of epidemics caused by government policies. In the twelve months after the Viet Namese conquest of January 1979, an additional 600,000 to 700,000 Khmers were sacrificed to the policies of this new regime. And ten years later, amid talk of new superpower détente and Viet Namese withdrawal from Cambodia, the cruelty, enslavement and murders continue.

How did it happen? What were the conditions and events that drove an unwitting people to the threshold of extinction? Was Cambodia a gentle land or the heart of darkness? A sideshow or an inextricable theater of the Southeast Asian war? A fertile lacustrine basin or an inevitable killing field?

By midsummer 1968 Cambodia was a nation set on a course of destruction, yet only a decade earlier Cambodia had been experiencing a period of unprecedented prosperity and optimism.

BROKEN PROMISES—BROKEN LEADERSHIP

In 1946, as Viet Namese nationalists were battling the reestablishment of French colonialism, France granted Cambodia internal autonomy. Three years later, as France foundered in Viet Nam and America sent its first anti-Communist aid to Southeast Asia, Cambodia gained de jure independence. Full independence was granted to the Royal Government of the Kingdom of Cambodia in November 1953—six months before the defeat of the French at Dien Bien Phu, eight months before the Geneva Agreements divided Viet Nam into Communist and non-Communist halves.

The excitement of independence drove Cambodia but the new state never expunged the weaknesses of colonialism or the underlying feudal structure. King Norodom Sihanouk abdicated his throne to become prince and head of state. Using his early popular mandate, partially based on a belief in the divinity of the monarch, he reduced his critics to states of impotence. Sihanouk became a neomandarin, a leader unable or unwilling to understand or direct his people. Under his growing cult of personality, contrary views had no outlet. Elements of the political right and left faded into urban back alleys or into the forests and jungles that cover three quarters of the country. Hidden, the disenchanted joined or formed revolutionary parties.

In the decade and a half following independence, there was no development of democratic institutions or of an independent bureaucracy to run the daily business of the government. Sihanouk delegated almost no authority. No ministers of the cabinet, no representatives in the legislature, no officers in the army, and no intellectuals at the university were allowed to mature into leaders. From 1955 Sihanouk ruled as if he were the government, overriding all institutions at his personal whim, suffocating all those subordinate to him. By 1960, he had established near-total dominance over all means of mass communication.

He seemed blind to the dynamic changes surrounding him. From 1945 to 1968 the population doubled. Half of all Cambodians were under fifteen years of age. In the six years 1962 to 1968, the population of the core areas around the major cities increased by 30 to 50 percent. Phnom Penh grew from 394,000 in 1962 to nearly 550,000 in 1968. The move to urban centers was coupled with the establishment of a large secular block which began to shed its Buddhism and its belief in the divinity of the monarch.

Outside the capital, the underlying feudal structure of barons, warlords and powerful landowners severely hampered the development of a modern state, and Sihanouk's monarchy did little to lessen the power of that traditionally corrupt class. His control of the national government and his influence over the regional barons was nearly absolute, but he was a man of contradictions. He pressed for universal primary education and encouraged secondary and university study. If the nation were to grow, he believed, it would need an educated class. Yet he was afraid that those with education would become prominent and powerful, potential enemies. Sihanouk and the ruling class undercut the institutions and blocked graduates from gaining employment, thus rendering them powerless. By 1968, protest and criticism were being dealt with by the jailing of teachers and students without charges being filed and without families being notified. These and other human rights violations were rampant.

Sihanouk also controlled the national "Buddhist-oriented system of voluntary contributions"—that is, taxes. To earn merit and achieve a better station in the next life, a Buddhist must be charitable. Sihanouk argued that because the rich were all devout Buddhists their contributions would support the poor and the state. In reality, the rich gave little to the poor and almost nothing to the state. The merchant or middle class, though taxed, was tiny, and state income from it amounted to little. This left only farmers to support the state, and they were heavily taxed, even though farmers as a percentage of the population had shrunk from nearly 80 percent to about 50 percent. Payment from them was usually in rice, which the government sold on the export market. By 1966, two thirds of the peasants were burdened by indebtedness, loans which carried interest rates of 12 percent *per month*. The new population pressures, the tax-caused indebtedness and the feudal order combined to create unstable land tenure conditions. In 1950, only one in twenty-five Khmer farmers rented his land. By 1968, the figure was one in five.

Without broad-based taxes the government had no capital with which to modernize the state, to improve or maintain the transportation and telephone systems or to raise, equip and train a viable national army. Cambodia, from 1954, was an ever-increasing low-pressure area—a power vacuum—a nation unable to ensure domestic tranquility, much less the integrity of its borders.

ELEMENTS, ARMIES AND FACTIONS

By 1968 this power vacuum had attracted, nourished or allowed the imposition of seven nongovernmental forces with seven different political agendas, each, at times, set against Sihanouk's poorly equipped Royal Cambodian Army.

Not yet on Khmer soil but of influence were two major forces: the ARVN (Army of the Republic of Viet Nam) and the Americans with assorted allies, including those from the Republic of Korea and Aus-

tralia. In the northeast border region of the highlands and Srepok
Forest (from the Mekong River east to the crest of the Annam Cordil-
lera) was the Mountaineer organization FULRO (French acronym for
the United Front of the Oppressed Races) struggling to maintain the
autonomy of their region, the old Crown Dominion Lands, from Viet
Namese and Khmers, from Communists and non-Communists.

There were four major Communist factions operating in Cambodia
in the late 1960s—the Viet Cong (indigenous South Viet Namese
rebels), the North Viet Namese, the Khmer Viet Minh, and the Khmer
Krahom. The Viet Cong operated from bases along the border and
concentrated their efforts on their war with the ARVN and the Americans in South Viet Nam. This was not so for the North Viet Namese
Army (NVA). By 1968 the NVA, by far the strongest force in Cambodia, had transformed the Northeast—Ratanakiri, Mondolkiri and portions of Stung Treng and Kratie provinces—into their own uncontested
base area. In a different manner, they also controlled large portions of
the South and Southeast. There they were entrenched—through bribery,
through corruption, through threat of force and through assassination—
in every area along the Sihanouk Trail from Kompong Som (Sihanoukville)
northward to Phnom Penh and eastward, along coastal Highway 3
through Bokor and Kampot, to the border regions. Indeed, in many of
the villages in Svay Rieng, Prey Veng, Kandal, Kompong Speu, Takeo
and Kampot provinces, the North Viet Namese maintained at least a
parallel governing administration to that of Sihanouk's government. In
portions of the southeastern provinces, especially along the border,
they controlled the economy so completely they printed their own
currency and forced local inhabitants to use it instead of the Cambodian
riel. In addition, the NVA had established a front headquarters just
outside Angkor Wat in Siem Reap Province in the Northwest.

THE KHMER COMMUNISTS AND NORODOM SIHANOUK

The two Cambodian Communist factions, the Khmer Krahom (KK) and
the Khmer Viet Minh (KVM), trace their lineage back to common cadre
trained by Ho Chi Minh between 1925 and 1930 at the Hoang Pho
Military Academy in Canton, China. In the early 1940s the forerun-
ners of these movements were functionally operating as anti-Sihanouk,
anti-French organizations. In 1943 these movements proclaimed an
end to the monarchy and, fearing retaliation, disbanded. Some rebels
remained in the wilds of Cambodia, others went into exile in China.

The term *krahom* was never picked up by the ethnocentric free-
world press and seldom used by Allied military intelligence. But the
distinction between the two factions is important. Without an understanding of the differences, one cannot understand what took place in

Cambodia. Those rebels who stayed in the Cambodian wilderness established the Krahom. *Krahom* is Khmer for "red," a designation used long before Sihanouk gave all insurgents the monolithic label "Khmer Rouge." It was the Khmer Krahom, Pol Pot's faction, which came to power in 1975.

In 1947, more than a year after France granted internal autonomy to Cambodia, Ho Chi Minh tapped the externally exiled cadre to establish a second front for his revolution. This marked the birth and became the core of the KVM. In the 1960s and 1970s, the KVM, sometimes called the Khmer Hanoi, was commanded by Le Duc Anh, a North Viet Namese politburo member and head of Hanoi's Central Office for Kampuchean Affairs (COKA).

The internally based Krahom necessarily wrapped itself in a tighter cloak of secrecy than did the externally based KVM. Also, the KK, untainted by the Viet Namese, attracted the Paris-educated Marxist extremists and the supernationalists.

From 1954 to 1968 Sihanouk's Royal Government *selectively* increased its harassment of the internal Communists, the KK, while pandering to the sponsors, the NVA, of the KVM—a fact that bred Krahom resentment toward the KVM.

Independence, in 1953, was a severe political setback for the Communists though the event had little military effect on the small bands of armed guerrillas. During the early 1950s, the exiled KVM fell more and more under the control of Hanoi, while the Krahom, under the covert guidance of Communist China, grew steadily in number and evolved ideologically. Saloth Sar, using the name Pol Pot, was among the leaders of the Krahom. He established relations with and became a disciple of Mao Zedong at the time when Mao was formulating the ideas that led to the Great Leap Forward, a major social experiment of 1958 to 1960.

During those years, Sihanouk, attempting to walk a tightrope between all the internal and external elements, squandered much of the goodwill of his own people. Sihanouk feared Ho Chi Minh and North Viet Namese hegemony. At Geneva in July 1954, the North Viet Namese had attempted to have a KVM area designated in northeastern Cambodia—patterned on the Pathet Lao zone they were able to secure in Laos. This amounted to an attempt to have Cambodia partitioned into Communist and non-Communist halves, like Viet Nam.

After the Geneva Agreements of 1954 Ho Chi Minh ordered the fledgling Cambodia-based KVM to maintain their jungle hideouts and to form an infrastructure that would eventually carry on *his* Indochinese revolution. At this time he also ordered these rebels to conscript and bring to Hanoi as many as 10,000 Mountaineer and Khmer boys to be trained as teachers, political agents and medical technicians. Hanoi strategists had determined very early, as NVA chief General Vo Nguyen Giap stated, "To sieze and control the highlands is to solve the whole problem of South Viet Nam." It was this perception which led the North Viet Namese to establish sanctuaries and bases—at whatever cost to the mountain peoples—on the Cambodian side of the border.

Over the years there was a growing animosity between the KK and KVM, yet both benefited from the established bases and the protection of Viet Namese Communist armies. Though an overt spirit of cooperation existed, each sought advantage over the others.

The Royal Cambodian Army had 30,000 to 35,000 troops—11,000 in combat units and the remainder in public works detachments doing road repair and like jobs. While rebel factions were building their military forces, Sihanouk, who feared a strong army would seize power and discard him, kept the Royal Army weak.

Western historians have referred to the insurgent forces in Cambodia in 1968, particularly the KK, as insignificant. The Krahom, Pol Pot's group, had an estimated 4,000 to 5,000 regular fighters plus a large contingent (Pol Pot claimed 50,000, though reality would probably be closer to 10,000) of irregular guerrillas and urban spies. The KVM had between 4,000 and 12,000 soldiers and cadre trained and stationed in North Viet Nam. The Viet Cong (VC), for whom figures vary drastically, had perhaps 20,000. The North Viet Namese, according to Royal Cambodian Government intelligence estimates, had 40,000 soldiers on Khmer territory. Thus the Khmer Communist movements, by 1968, had 8,000 to 17,000 combat troops to attack a Royal Cambodian Army, top-heavy with rear-echelon soldiers. Plus, the Khmer Communists had the backing of at least 60,000 Viet Namese Communist troops. This would be the equivalent of an insurgent force in the United States of 127,000 armed and organized troops, with a well-equipped reserve force in Canada of perhaps 254,000 political and combat cadres, plus an allied hostile force, stretching from Texas to California along the Mexican border, of 1.7 million troops. That can hardly be called insignificant. These figures are from May 1968, ten months before secret U.S. bombings began. Obviously, neither the KK nor the KVM was born out of the inferno that U.S. bombing created.

REGIONAL WAR—THE AMERICAN PRESENCE

To see the war in Southeast Asia as having occurred in South Viet Nam or Cambodia or North Viet Nam or Laos leads to conclusions which are necessarily untrue. To see the war in Cambodia as having spilled out of South Viet Nam is equally erroneous.

In January 1959 Hanoi directed its army to establish operation bases at Tay Ninh on the Cambodian border and in the Central Highlands east of Ratanakiri Province. By May large-scale infiltration forces were tramping out the Ho Chi Minh Trail in eastern Cambodia. By August 1960, NVA assassination teams were killing 100 to 200 local officials in South Viet Nam each month. The figure rose to between 300 and 350 each month in 1961 and to 1,000 each month in 1962. That element of the war also spilled onto Khmer territory.

1962 marked the beginning of the full-scale NVA buildup *on Cambodian territory*. This early heavy buildup was characterized by the bribing of local officials, local and national military leaders, *and* the royal family. Sihanouk, who, like Diem in South Viet Nam, would stand for no internal opposition, was not only acquiescent to Hanoi, but clearly accepted them as partners. With that acceptance, however, came the de facto forfeiture of Cambodian territory and the lessening of control over the population in areas where the Royal Cambodian Army continued to maintain a presence.

Relations between the United States and Cambodia deteriorated throughout the 1950s. In 1959, out of Bangkok, Thailand, a right-wing coup attempt was foiled by Sihanouk's secret police. The Prince implicated the American CIA, resulting in Sihanouk's increased suspicion of the United States, Thailand and South Viet Nam. The Prince severed relations with Bangkok in 1961 and with South Viet Nam in 1963. In November 1963, after the death by assassination of Ngo Dinh Diem, Sihanouk, declaring that the CIA was targeting him next, ordered the U.S. AID office in Phnom Penh closed. At that time, Cambodian defense minister Lon Nol and economic advisor Son Sann advised Sihanouk to proceed with caution and to allow the Americans to remain.

On 17 March 1964 the American National Security Council decided to allow the U.S. Air Force to retaliate against NVA/VC sanctuaries in Cambodia. This resulted in incidents, charges and countercharges between the two countries. On 10 April 1965 four RVNAF (Republic of Viet Nam Air Force) jets strafed two Cambodian villages, leading Sihanouk to break diplomatic relations with the United States and to establish formal relations with North Viet Nam and with the National Liberation Front (NLF), the political arm of the Viet Cong.

Attempting to cover his flanks, Sihanouk, in October 1964, entered into a mutual declaration with Red China in which the Chinese vowed to work tirelessly to strengthen Sino-Khmer friendship. Sihanouk received a military assistance agreement and China's affirmation of Cambodia's territorial integrity (that is, lands in the Northeast that the North Viet Namese had claimed in 1954 for the KVM). In exchange, he gave his formal agreement to allow NVA/VC forces full access to and use of eastern Cambodia.

When U.S. bombing slowed traffic on the Ho Chi Minh Trail in

Laos, Zhou Enlai personally asked Sihanouk to allow materials to be landed at Sihanoukville (Kompong Som) and to be shipped overland to Communist forces along the border. This route became known as the Sihanouk Trail. A tacit side agreement gave one third of all arriving supplies to the Prince.

Over the next few years a Chinese company, Haklee, trucked over 22,000 metric tons of arms and ammunition up Highway 4 from Kompong Som to Phnom Penh, or along coastal Highway 2 via Bokor to the VC/NVA border sanctuaries. Exactly how much was handled by Sihanouk's army, still called neutral, is not known.

During 1965, the Krahom set up new guerrilla bases next to the North Viet Namese sanctuaries in Ratanakiri, Mondolkiri, Stung Treng and Kratie provinces. Yet, citing "lax protection and ambiguous support," the KK split with the NVA and established a series of independent bases. By 1966 Krahom literature was calling for total social revolution. Historian Ben Kiernan reports the following translation of KK leaflets:

> Today's society is corrupt and won over by the cult of the individual, which must be abolished at all cost. We live in a sick society. . . . All brave and honest children . . . must join the revolutionary party in order to move the country toward Communist socialism. . . . The masses live in misery, bled by [the capitalists]. . . . The aim of the revolution is the liberation of the people. . . . To succeed it is necessary to resort to force.

During this period the war hit Cambodian Mountaineers en masse, bringing about the March of Tears. Villages were burned, rice destroyed, bronze gongs stolen, livestock slaughtered or taken. Thousands of Jarai, Mnong, Rhade and other tribal people, fleeing the onslaught of the North Viet Namese and the growing bands of KVM and KK, marched out of Ratanakiri and Mondolkiri provinces—a long, starving, destitute procession, heading into the southern Srepok Forest of Kratie Province. There they were forced to halt because the area further south was heavily populated with long-established Khmers. Where they stopped was where the indigenous South Viet Namese rebels, the Viet Cong, had long-established sanctuaries.

In the wake of Allied operations in War Zone C, a territory of South Viet Nam west of Saigon near the border, these same Viet Cong sanctuaries were rapidly expanding. The destitute Mountaineers became the first massive refugee movement in Southeast Asia to be ignored.

In the strange turn of the political process, President Lyndon Johnson, on 21 December 1965, ordered American commanders not to pursue NVA or VC units into Cambodia, and then further ordered

General William Westmoreland and the American Military Assistance Command, Viet Nam (MACV), to be silent regarding the sanctuaries in Cambodia. This one act, more than any other, set up the "credibility gap" which came to haunt Johnson and every American administration since.

On 11 December 1967 LBJ recanted the latter part of this decree. The United States had reached a tacit agreement with Sihanouk— Cambodia agreed to request the VC to leave Khmer territory; America agreed to avoid acts of aggression against Cambodia and, further, to supply Sihanouk with information on the sanctuaries. But Sihanouk either did not try or was unable to force the VC to move.

CIVIL WAR AND TET 1968

Each year Cambodian disillusionment increased. Each year more and more people criticized the Prince for self-indulgent behavior improper for a devout Buddhist. By 1966 Cambodia was on the brink of civil war. On 11 March 1967 a peasant uprising erupted in Battambang Province in the village of Samlaut. The farmers were angry with high interest rates, high taxes, high inflation and low government-estalished prices for their crops. The system had led them into debt, and debt had meant foreclosure and the loss of their fields to the land barons. More riots broke out in Kompong Chhnang, Kompong Thom, and Kompong Speu provinces. The rioting spread to all the major and many minor population centers in government-controlled Cambodia. Sihanouk declared martial law, and placed the nation under a state of siege. Movement within the country required official passes, which meant new fees. Sihanouk decreed the nationalization of all import and export businesses, a process he had begun in 1963 but now extended to complete control. And he nationalized the internal distribution of goods.

On 18 January 1968 new riots broke out in Samlaut. Sihanouk accused bandits of instigating the riots and sent army troops and national police to incite Khmer villagers to attack the "rebels." Many resettled ethnic Viet Namese and Mountaineers were clubbed to death. Villages were burned. Some "rebels" escaped into the southern Cardamom Mountains. Sihanouk labeled them Khmer Rouge and unleashed his troops on their lands. His Royal Cambodian Army forces burned fifty villages, killing hundreds of peasants and arresting thousands. His soldiers clubbed women to death and beheaded men, and the government paid the soldiers a bounty on each head. All across Cambodia, thousands of teachers and students exiled themselves to the forests!

On 22 January 1968, with the nation in disarray and with the second rebellion at Samlaut but four days old, Norodom Sihanouk announced to the world that he was siding with North Viet Nam and the National Liberation Front. Two months earlier he had sent Royal troops onto the basalt plateau of Ratanakiri Province. There, where they had not ventured for over a year because of NVA control of the area, they rendezvoused with the provincial forces of Governor Thang Nhach. Together these units attacked six Rhade villages, slaughtering the leaders and driving the villagers off their land. This was done, according to Sihanouk, so that he could use the land to establish new rubber plantations—the rubber ostensibly being needed for export to help offset the trade deficit. But this logic is faulty. First, Sihanouk's forces needed the permission of the NVA even to set foot on the plateau. Second, if he had actually wanted to establish plantations there, he would likely have desired the labor of the Mountaineers. And third, there is a far more sensible explanation for this action.

The heavy troop movement was a diversion. It masked other heavy troop stagings and maneuvers—that of the NVA divisions which on 30 January crossed the border along Highway 19 and assaulted Kontum and Pleiku in South Viet Nam. Was Sihanouk an active party in the 1968 Tet offensive? He prattled about Cambodian *neutrality,* but his speech of 22 January and his military actions put him entirely in support of the NVA. After the ARVN, American forces and South Viet Namese local militias repelled, counterattacked and destroyed much of the VC and NVA attacking force, Sihanouk backpedaled to verbal neutrality. On 1 May 1968 he appointed the pro-Western general Lon Nol as defense minister. In June the KK attacked the Northern Corridor town of Baray. In July Lon Nol was promoted to deputy prime minister. In August, Sihanouk did an overt about-face and blamed "foreigners" (the NVA) for the uprisings in the northeastern provinces. At first the Prince called the insurgents Pathet Lao. Later he charged they were Khmer Rouge. In December, Lon Nol was again promoted, now to acting prime minister, but by then the Royal government had lost control of 60 percent of Cambodia's land to the KK, the KVM or the NVA.

An aside to the Tet offensive: According to KK propaganda, the NVA attempted, even while the KK was launching its most sweeping attacks ever in Cambodia, to assassinate the leaders of the KK and to unite all Khmer Communist activity under Hanoi's rule.

THE CHINESE INFLUENCE

The significance of Chinese influence on the Krahom cannot be overstated. It is more reasonable to see the Cambodian holocaust of 1975 to 1979 as the culmination and apex of the Chinese Great Leap

Forward and the Great Proletarian Cultural Revolution than to see it as the result of a society driven insane by American B-52 bombings.

As noted, Pol Pot associated with Mao Zedong during the planning phase for the Great Leap Forward. The Great Leap Forward led to approximately 30 million deaths in 1960 alone. Perhaps a million people were killed outright. 29 million were sacrificed to drastic land tenure policies. Essentially, the Chinese were driven from established, fertile fields into forest areas to establish new farmland. Without proper tools, without preestablished, engineered plans, with nothing but their *will* as decreed from Peking, they were set to work. The first year they cut the forests down but were unable, without established irrigation, to raise a significant crop. They began to starve. Then heavy rains came. The newly stripped lands eroded. Silt clogged established irrigation canals and killed productive paddies downstream. A dry year followed and 29 million people starved to death. Fifteen years later the same policy infected Cambodia.

The Great Proletarian Cultural Revolution which began in 1966 was also a model for Cambodia. The policies were less agrarian "reform" than a stripping away of China's traditional culture. The war on culture envisioned turning traditional allegiances on their head—the primacy of parents, family, village and culture was replaced by the monolithic party-state and its inviolable interpretation of realities. Children became Mao's political instruments, his foot soldiers in the "Liberation and Struggle." Indeed, 1966 is considered a "Children's Crusade."

Nightly, youth, peasants, anyone that could be coerced, sat through political indoctrination sessions or self-criticism sessions known as "struggles." In Cambodia such sessions would be called *kosangs*. To own a book became a crime. To own a Western book was punishable by death. Libraries across the country were ransacked and books burned in huge bonfires. Similar policies, along with mass atrocities, were being used in Cambodia by the KK by 1968.

ANGKAR

In 1968 Krahom *yotheas*, soldiers, referred to their faction as "the Movement," or "the Organization." It was common for Southeast Asian Communists to call their parties "organization" while proselytizing, in order to hide their Communism from the masses. In Khmer, "organization" is *angkar* or *angka*.

PART ONE

THE KINGDOM OF CAMBODIA

If genocide is to be prevented in the future, we must understand how it happened in the past, not only in terms of the killers and the killed but of the bystanders.
—Arthur Morse,
While Six Million Died

CHAPTER ONE

Worry furrows creased Cahuom Chhuon's forehead. He was trapped, held in an amorphous iridescent blue, almost black, dream. Images parted, blurry, as if he were looking through deep water, as if he were at the bottom of a great basin. To one side a massive fuzzy maw stretched mechanically open, bit down, then slowly opened, rhythmically, like the breathing of a fish in a stream, the mouth pulsing, open closed open closed, not breathing but biting, ingesting all which entered the current. To the other side the basin floor rose. Colors, people emerged. They were all there by the side of the river. His entire family, Sok, Vathana, Yani and the boys, all, but much younger, even his father, strong, large, powerful. There too were distant relatives, neighbors, friends from the far reaches of Cambodia, even the Mountaineer, Y Ksar from Plei Srepok, all gathered as if for a great celebration. But the occasion was not happy.

His worry rose. He felt besieged. People were in small groups, some in the shade beneath the trees, some in the sun at the edge of the road leading back to Phum Sath Din, some at the river's edge. Only his older brother spoke to him, listened to him, but it was as if he, Cahuom Chhuon, were not really there but only a body like his and that body spoke a foreign tongue. He tried to call his brother, to explain, to warn. . . . He did not know of what. Something. Something very important. Something to be done. The people looked to him, to that body? He felt responsible but he was not there? Why? Why could he not reach them? Why was his brother resisting? He must reach them.

They milled around behind his brother, milled, not as a mob but more as if guests at a wedding, yet without happiness, without laughter, without the traditional feast. Behind them the river was brown. The sky turned mist green, green from the lush forest growth through which he watched. Dusk was upon them. Chhuon shuddered, stiffened. The waters of the Srepok, swollen by monsoon rains, roared over rapids. To his nose came the rancid aroma of river mud. Then a terrible, foul stench which made him retch. Then, on the river, in the river, all fallen into the quick current, frightened, not fighting the flow, riding the rushing water—Sok, Vathana, whole families fallen into the stream, sucked down current. From one bank tigers slashed mighty claws, from the other crocodiles slithered. Then, in the water, elephants, massive, swimming down upon them, coursing more quickly than water flow, overtaking him, them all, crushing them beneath their immensity, smashing them into rocks, into banks in their frenzy, he popping up like a cork, riding the empty water. Alone.

Phum Sath Din, Stung Treng Province, Cambodia, 5 August 1968—The sound of a heavy truck struggling through mud woke Cahuom Chhuon from his restless dreaming. He lay on his back on the sleeping mat. It was very dark in the house. Chhuon's children lay side to side on a second mat. Chhuon listened. The truck was close, just across the river. He raised his arms, crossed his forearms over his face. Every day, he thought. The truck passed. Chhuon brought his arms to his sides, folded his hands over his navel. He thought deeply, meditated, attempting to resee the dream, attempting to sink back into the restless disturbing journey. Later, he thought, if I can recall it, I will tell the *khrou,* or perhaps the monk. He dozed.

"ssst," Samnang hissed to Samay.

"ssshh," the older boy hushed his brother.

"ssst," Samnang whispered again. Chhuon coughed in his sleep.

"ssshh," Mayana whispered to both. "you'll wake papa."

"he talks in his sleep," Samay said.

"i know," Samnang hissed. "i was awake. i never sleep."

"ssh!" Vathana's hiss was quick, terse. "it's not time to get up."

Very quietly, so the girls couldn't hear, Samnang whispered to his brother, "samay."

"eh?"

"does the devil really have a great ledger for recording all the evil deeds we do?"

"you think of things like that at this hour, eh? go back to sleep. look how you disturb papa."

"samay," Samnang whispered again. "why can't a monk and a girl come in contact?"

"sleep," Samay ordered. "if you didn't put bad thoughts into your head, you would sleep like peou."

Again all was silent.

At six o'clock Chhuon rose quietly, moved to the door of the bamboo, wood and thatch home. His mother snored quietly in her small area of the central room. Snuggled next to her was Sakhon, Chhuon's three-year-old son. Ever since the death of his father three months earlier Chhuon's mother had withdrawn into deep lamentation, reaching out only to this youngest grandchild. Chhuon's wife, Neang Thi Sok, lay asleep on her mat against the near wall. I should wake her to start the fire, he thought, but he did not disturb her. The other children slept along the far wall. Chhuon looked at them: Vathana, lovely, tiny, not five feet tall, eighteen, arranged to be married to the second son of his brother's associate, a wealthy shipper with a section of pier on the Mekong at Neak Luong; Samay, his eldest son, fifteen, ready to leave the family for two years Sangha study with the monks; Samnang, almost twelve, a smart, agile though distant boy who Chhuon determined should follow him in business; and Mayana, Yani, eight, the image of her mother. Chhuon looked again at his mother and Sakhon, whom they called Peou, a nickname which simply designates last child. He lifted a tiny statuette of Buddha which had been carved from one of his father's teeth. It hung from a cotton cord about his neck. He kissed the Buddha seven times, once for each of his children, and he thanked the Blessed One for having spared five of the seven.

In the 1950s and early 1960s Cambodia's infant mortality rate was nearly fifty percent, higher in the rural provinces. Chhuon whispered another prayer, a special prayer to Buddha for having seen Samnang through his terrible illness. In the faint light Chhuon could just see the slim boy's form behind the mosquito netting and beneath his blanket. They had nicknamed him Kdeb (pronounced "Kay"), Spanky, because as a toddler he had chugged about so happily, eyes shining, before he could speak always cooing, later chattering without shyness to everyone. At six years old Kdeb fell ill to jungle fever, remained ill for half a year, changed from happy, chunky boy to frail, sullen child. His mother, father, eldest sister or a grandparent coddled him continually until Samnang, in an un-Khmer flourish of independence, revolted, as if, to his six-year-old mind, the illness was a betrayal, as if the pain were tied to the very people who cared for him. He became withdrawn, distrustful. By eight he had seemingly recovered, yet he harbored a coldness which pooled at the back of his eyes. Chhuon felt it, deep, hidden, a painful secret a father could never acknowledge. By nine Samnang again seemed happy, yet he was prone to sporadic bursts of uncontrolled behavior. In school other children shied away from him. Only in the mind of Chhuon was this boy still Kdeb.

Chhuon said another prayer for his family. He lit a cigarette, closed his eyes, took a deep drag, held the smoke, exhaled. Perhaps, he thought, after we return I'll see the monk and seek his analysis of the dream. Perhaps the *khrou*, the fortune-teller. He leaned his shoulder against the doorjamb, closed his eyes and replayed the dream in his mind to ensure he would be able to recall it. Such a strange dream, he thought. He contemplated the water, the colors. He began to say another prayer but his mind slid to the dream. A chill skittered up his spine as he recalled the entrapment by crocodiles, tigers and elephants while in the rushing current.

He felt old, older than his forty-three years. It was a custom in his family, as in many Khmer families, to discuss dreams and to analyze them in relationship to family problems. On this cool morning Chhuon felt stiff, sore, worn down by the struggle which was his life. He was aware that had he had this same dream ten years earlier, or were he more traditional, he would postpone the trip. The awareness increased his disturbance. Again he exhaled slowly. The smoke from his breath mixed with the morning mist and hung in a cloud before him. Is it an omen? he thought. A message from Papa's spirit?

Chhuon finished his cigarette. He wrapped a yellow checked *krama* about his neck, the long ends falling to his waist, then descended the few stairs to the muddy ground. He was a short man, short for Cambodian, five three, yet he was strong with muscular chest and legs. He bent, removed his sandals, then stood, straightened his back, rolled his shoulders attempting to loosen the stiffness. It had rained every night for three months and the village streets were saturated. He squatted to loosen his stiff knees, stood and looked into the dark morning sky, into the graying mist, patchy amid the village buildings and orchards, thick in the surrounding forest. He could hear the river rushing. The sound made him tense. Everything was telling him to cancel the trip. I'm becoming like a Frenchman, he thought. Maybe worse. Maybe like a Yuon or even an American. First the khrou, he thought. Then the monk. Ah, but first the trip. I'll bring Kdeb and Yani with me. Their uncle and Y Ksar will like seeing them, and a day away, it will settle him. Ah, deliveries must be made, eh? Despite dreams.

Chhuon stepped to a small house on a post before his home. He reached inside, removed an incense stick, lit it, placed it back into the house. He said a short prayer to the angel spirits asking them for a peaceful journey and a peaceful life.

"This is the Cambodia of 1968," Chhuon seemed to hear his older brother, Cheam, say. "We're a growing nation. No longer can we indulge ourselves with the old ways."

It's true, Chhuon thought. People are slowed by old beliefs. Ah, but on this morning, it would be good, eh? to fall back on tradition. Ah, to tell the fortune-teller, the healer, the monk! Sok . . . what will she say?

For much of his life Chhuon had followed traditional patterns. All the people, even the simplest rice farmer, consulted the khrou, the monk, or the lay priest, the *aacha*, if they had a disturbing dream. Cheam's imagined voice whispered again, "Younger Brother, I've a dream of good rice and good fortune; you, a dream of disaster. Yet it's the same day and the same business. One dream must not be true. Besides, we've promised deliveries. If we are to run our own country we must learn from the Chinese merchants. Commerce waits for no man."

Chhuon took a deep breath. "Older Brother," he muttered into the mist, "are we to be so removed from custom you do not even shave your head when our father dies?"

Like his parents, grandparents, siblings and children, Cahuom Chhuon had been born, raised and educated in Phum Sath Din. His father had been a rice farmer as had his uncles and most of his cousins. The village had changed little in Chhuon's four decades—even though the nation had changed dramatically. The population of Phum Sath Din had decreased from just over 500 to about 420. Both of Chhuon's sisters, with their husbands, moved away, Voen to Phnom Penh and Moeun to Battambang. All children who came of age and who were able to pay the *bonjour*, the kickback, for advanced studies moved first to the provincial capital, Stung Treng City, then, if qualified, to Phnom Penh.

In 1957, with proper "donations" from their father to local and provincial authorities, Cheam had left Phum Sath Din and founded a delivery service seventeen kilometers east in the provincial capital. Chhuon had joined his brother in 1960 and had taken the task of supplying and educating local farmers, and later mountain peoples, in new varieties of rice and other crops which were being developed in China and in the West. In the years since he'd begun his small personal campaign, rice production in his area had increased from less than one to just over 1.25 metric tons per hectare. Amongst the small farmers Chhuon was held in great esteem.

Phum Sath Din remained essentially a private community separate from the state. People left but few came. The four families which had founded it three hundred years earlier were still the four families who owned the land and worked the fields. Chhuon knew every resident, each knew him. They knew one another's history, finances, strengths, aspirations and fears. Of his siblings, only Chhuon remained in Phum Sath Din, remained with his parents because he alone saw the village as the best of Cambodia. To him it was a neat, well-administered small town without corruption, without the bastardization of generations of French colonial rule. To Chhuon the villages were the heart of a new, emerging Cambodia, were a peaceful link between the traditional kingdom and a forward-looking, independent, Buddhist-socialist state. Yet with Cheam in Stung Treng the Cahuom family entered Cambodia's tiny middle class and with that entry, traditions wobbled, fell and shattered.

Chhuon opened the hood of the small Japanese-built pickup truck. He tapped the dipstick seven times, then withdrew it to check the oil. He replaced the stick, gently closed the hood, wiped the headlights. He smiled at the truck, his brother's truck, one of only two trucks in Phum Sath Din. He looked down the graveled muddy main road of the village which ran parallel to the river. At the middle of the village he could see the silhouette of the pagoda's roof jabbing up through the mist. The decagonal temple or *vihear* and the adjoining hall or *sala* were the community's house of worship, school and focal point for all village celebrations and rites. They were Chhuon's anchor to the continuity of life from past generations through present. He whispered another prayer, then told himself, When we return I will bring the monks sugar and tea from Stung Treng, maybe cloth from Lomphat, and an ebony block from Plei Srepok.

Again a chill skittered on his spine and caused him to stiffen. His eyes darted toward the river. In the midseventeenth century the first pagoda in the village had been erected by Chhuon's ancestors just outside the walls of the settlement at the confluence of the San and Srepok rivers. A hundred years later the settlement had been lost to Viet Namese control. Ancestral tablets in the pagoda recorded the history of the Cahuom family through most of these times. Chhuon turned back to the village. Before his ancestors arrived, as early as the turn of the millennium, Khmer warriors had defeated Chams in bloody battles along the rivers and the Khmer Empire extended over most of Indochina. Permanent settlements were few in the heavily forested regions. The site of Phum Sath Din was occupied by Mountaineer tribesmen perhaps once every twenty years, a camp in their rotational nomadic hunting. Then came the Cahuoms, then the Viet Namese, the Khmer reconquest, and the loss of political decree to French colonialism though no Frenchman ever administered in the tiny settlement. Japanese occupation and new French rule had had little effect inside the community.

Chhuon walked to the back of the truck. The bed of the cargo box had been covered with wood planking for animals which Chhuon frequently carried. He checked the hemp ropes he used to tie his loads, then he pulled his krama more tightly about his neck to ward off the chill. He squatted, checked the tires, scooped the mud from beside one to ensure that the sidewall had not been cut when he'd driven into a deep pothole. He squeezed the mud into a ball, worked the ball in his hand.

A child's scream pierced the mist. Chhuon whispered a prayer. He was well known for his patience, well respected for his adherence to the Eightfold Path of moral behavior: right belief, aspiration, speech, doing, livelihood, effort, thought and meditation. Again the scream. Peou, Chhuon thought. He stood. For a man to be known as patient with his children was a great accolade. Chhuon breathed deeply.

In the house Samnang addressed his father. "Peou wants to come with us," he said.

"Then we'll make room for him," Chhuon answered.

"There's no room," Sok, Chhuon's wife, said.

"Papa, if you wish me to stay home," Samnang said, "Peou can have my seat." A simper flicked to his face, then vanished.

Chhuon looked approvingly at Samnang. The boy's behavior was proper. His own cheeks wrinkled with a thin smile, so slight it did not betray his thought: This son, whom others think odd, behaves perfectly.

Peou screamed again. "I won't go! I won't go! I want to stay with Grandma."

Chhuon nodded. "You stay," he said gently. The boy ran to where his grandmother was sitting, plopped onto her and hugged her lap.

Vathana handed her father a bowl of hot rice and pepper soup. "Papa . . . ," she said. All about them was activity. ". . . last night, when you told of Samdech Euv's system of voluntary contributions . . ."

"Eh. He thinks he can raise a national budget . . ."

"But it *should* work, shouldn't it?"

"Um." Chhuon nodded. "But it doesn't. The state has no money. It can't modernize. And the roads! Our poor truck."

"Or the army," Samnang piped in. He came from behind his sister and stood between the two. Vathana put an arm over his shoulder and gave a gentle hug. The boy's shoulders jerked.

Chhuon slurped soup from the bowl. His mind was not on their conversation of the night before but on the day's trip. Thoughts of the dream faded. "What do you know of the army, eh?" He chuckled.

"Only that you said it is poor. Will we see soldiers today? You said it's too small to guarantee security. I heard Mama's cousin say it can't hold the border."

"You," Sok called over from the table, "have big ears for a little boy."

"Yeah, big ears," giggled his little sister, Mayana.

Vathana hugged Samnang with both arms. "You hear all you can," she whispered.

Chhuon finished his soup. He looked at the two children, the beautiful young woman and the frail, yet beautiful small boy. "Learn," he said. "Learn all you can. But it is not always wise to tell all you know, eh!"

"Yes, Father," Samnang muttered.

"One day all the young will live in the cities and only the old will work the land, eh, Sok?" His wife smiled her assent.

"Oh Papa"—Vathana's voice was frivolous—"you'll never be old."

"Even when Yani was born," Chhuon said, "it was different. Now you will marry and move away. Then Samay. Then . . ." Chhuon looked at his middle son's face. The large dark eyes were turned down. He wanted to call him Kdeb but he said, ". . . Samnang."

"Papa," Vathana said, "could you buy a photograph of Samdech Euv?" She used the loving appellation referring to Prince Norodom Sihanouk. "When I go to Neak Luong I should bring the best photograph." Her smile was easy and radiant. With a slight, conscious pout she added, "There are none here. Near Uncle Cheam's there's a store that has the very best."

Chhuon winked at her. Though delicate, Vathana was nearly as tall as he, and to him she, with her almond-shaped eyes and long black hair tied back in a scarf, was so beautiful he whimsically wondered how she could have been born to him and his also short and stocky wife. A perfect bride, he thought. A perfect wife. Not just beauty but intelligence, with high respect for learning, able to talk of business, politics or religion. How she will help her husband. What honor this marriage brings to our family. "I'll ask Cheam to get the very best in all of Stung Treng."

Chhuon moved to where Sok sat at the central table. He

spoke quietly as she gathered the few dishes. Samay sat across from them. He had not eaten. His head was buried in a book and he was unaware of anyone about him. As the time for him to enter Sangha monastic training approached he prepared himself by practicing concentration, self-control and self-denial. Soon he would renounce his family and all material aspects of life.

"It's time we go," Chhuon announced. "We'll eat in the city while the truck's being loaded."

"Take this with you," Sok said. She handed Yani a basket with fruit and cooked rice. "One never knows what may happen on the road."

"Yes, Mama," Yani answered sleepily. She held her head down but glanced up to Vathana, wishing her older sister were coming instead of Samnang.

Before Chhuon, Samnang and Mayana left the house, Chhuon went to his mother. The old woman, with Peou in her lap, was praying before a small altar, a low table with a painted wooden Buddha in the center. Above the statue was a framed picture of Buddha in repose beneath the bodhi tree. A small picture of Prince Sihanouk, the symbol of the repository of merit for all Cambodia, was to one side. Pictures of the family were to the other. Ancestral tablets, fresh flowers, incense and candles completed the altar. Chhuon knelt and bowed his head to the floor before his mother and spoke softly, asking the old woman's blessing. She in turn placed her feet upon his shaved head and uttered a prayer.

Ground mist wrapped the village and foothills in a coal-gray blanket. Chhuon started the truck. Beside him, Yani lifted her jacket collar and sleepily tightened it about her neck. She snuggled against her father's side. Chhuon lit a cigarette. The smoke hung in the humid air, condensed on the windows making it almost impossible to see. Slowly Chhuon backed the truck onto the village street, shifted, then nursed the vehicle over the muck surface toward the bridge. Samnang sat against the passenger door. He stared blankly out the side window. At school the day before there had been another incident. Chhuon felt Yani's body sag limp in sleep.

"Papa," Samnang said quietly, "is Grandma ill?"

"No, just tired. With all that's happened . . ."

"When Grandpa died, I had terrible dreams. I'm afraid . . . Grandma . . ."

"Everyone dies, son. The Blessed One said there shall always be birth, old age, death, sorrow, grief and despair. But he also enlightened the path to the cessation of misery. You've discussed the dreams with your grandmother, eh?"

"Yes." Samnang was reluctant to continue. He'd brought the subject up more as diversion than as conversation. They were silent as the truck crossed the rickety wood bridge over the Srepok River. Chhuon's eyes searched the water, the bank. His dream rushed back to mind. He offered an inner prayer to the spirit of the river and another to the spirit of the forest. Samnang squeezed the armrest. With Yani asleep he feared his father would bring up his, Samnang's, school problem.

Beyond the bridge the road split, the main road continuing south. Chhuon turned right. The side road was rough, unsurfaced. He'd driven the back road to Stung Treng many times and he knew every rock, every soft spot which might mire the truck, anticipated every turn, recognized every peasant hut, every field. It descended steeply beside the surging, swirling river, not much more than a riverside trail completely canopied by the jungle. Chhuon concentrated on the path lit by the truck's headlights. He felt the tires slowly descend into each groove, roll over each boulder.

"Papa?" Samnang said.

Chhuon did not take his eyes from the path. "Yes?"

"Why doesn't the government attempt to harness the river?"

"Someday it will," Chhuon said. He tried to speak to his children in an educated manner, almost as equals, keeping in mind the importance of setting a good example. "Someday we'll build hydroelectric dams—one on the San, one on the Kong. Perhaps with the Laotians a giant one across the Mekong. Then all this territory will have abundant electric power and we'll be able to regulate the flow of the water for the farmers to irrigate new lands. Someday, Cambodia will be a very wealthy nation."

"Not the Srepok?" Samnang asked.

"No. The valley's too broad on this side of the border. South of Lomphat where it crosses into Viet Nam, there's a hydroelectric dam. Just west of Ban Me Thuot. You know that city?"

"Yes. When Samay enters Sangha, will he study about the land or only about religion?"

Chhuon glanced at Samnang. Perhaps, he thought, Samnang will feel that loss more than any other family member. "I don't know. Do you think someday you'll follow him?"

"No way!" Samnang said.

"No way!?" Chhuon repeated the Western idiom which had crept into use with schoolchildren.

"I mean, 'No, Father.' I don't believe a religious life is for me."

"Every generation of our family has had at least one son follow the path into the monastic life," Chhuon said. "My eldest brother left our home when I was six. It's a noble calling. Only within monastic life can perfect awareness be gained. Only then can people learn from the monk the path to deliverance from suffering."

"Oh Papa, people will continue to suffer. You're the holy man. Your work feeds more than all the monks."

"Ha! Who tells you that?"

"You're educated. You read. You travel. The village farmers look up to you."

The words embarrassed Chhuon. "We're talking different kinds of suffering," he said. He was pleased that his son respected him, yet he was upset that Samnang was so secular. His own son seemed a symbol of the transitions occurring within Cambodia. "Life is suffering," Chhuon said. "Birth is suffering, aging is suffering, death is suffering. The presence of material things we hate is suffering, and to be separated from objects we desire is suffering. For our wishes not to be met is suffering. Suffering ceases only when we no longer crave . . ."

Samnang hung his head. Chhuon's sermons made him shrink. At his father's next pause he said simply, "I don't think I should become a monk."

"Follow your heart," Chhuon answered. "My soul is filled with joy at Samay's choice. Though I . . . I'll miss him."

"Papa," Samnang said sharply, "I don't understand why, when a boy enters the Sangha he must renounce his family. Why do people say he's no longer a family member? I don't understand why the bonze can't be both."

"It's a deep question," Chhuon said. "This is something we should ask Maha Nyanananda. I know only when a boy approaches manhood, he must renounce his family. It's always been that way. In two years if he doesn't follow the monastic life, he may rejoin them."

Samnang did not answer and Chhuon let the conversation stop. They descended out of the hills. The road surface became smoother though softer and Chhuon wove the truck back and forth to avoid potholes. The road leveled onto the broad floodplain of the lower Srepok. The jungle thinned, the tunnel of vegetation giving way first to sparse forest, then to intermittent brush and grass, then to cultivated rice fields stretching as far as Samnang could see into the mist. Buildings and villages increased, though were still few and far between. Mayana curled tighter in against Chhuon, pulled her jacket tight and continued dozing.

After a period Chhuon said, "In seven days it will be one hundred days since my father died. When we return home, I want you to see Maha Nyanananda. Arrange for me to meet with him. Bring him six cans of milk."

"Papa," Samnang's voice was again sharp, "why don't the monks have food like other people? Why must someone—every day—bring them food?"

"Holy men aren't allowed to accumulate wealth or possessions," Chhuon said. "Thus material goods can't tarnish their spiritual work."

"But Father! Some monks don't work at all."

"Eh?" Chhuon pursed his lips. "You've spent many days at the pagoda. Do the monks work?"

"Only . . . I mean . . . well, Maha Nyanananda. He's always busy. But even he doesn't work like the farmers. Not even like you."

"They administer to our minds, our souls. Because you don't see them stoop in the paddies or load trucks doesn't mean their work's not hard. I seldom load or unload anymore, does that mean I no longer work?"

"But you do work with the farmers."

"Only as a teacher," Chhuon said modestly. "Every year there is new rice and each variety must be separately tended. That's my work: to teach the farmers about the new rice and to help them guard their fields. Monks teach people to guard their spirits. That's their work. Each new rice has its own weakness, so we plant a little and watch it. Each new day presents challenges to our weaknesses. Those too must be watched." Chhuon glanced at his son. If the boy was to follow him into business he should be taught everything Chhuon himself had learned through long hours of study. And if his spirituality was to grow, that too must be nurtured.

Chhuon stopped the truck in the center of the road and rolled his window down. Beside him Yani opened her eyes, yawned, looked about and seeing that they were only halfway to their destination, closed her eyes again. "The new IR 8 is semidwarf and resists lodging," Chhuon said. "That means the farmers will lose less of their crop to the wind. Look at this field. Cambodia grows eight hundred varieties of rice. Most of it, when the grain fills, and that during the windiest part of the monsoons, gets top-heavy. When it lies down like those plants," Chhuon pointed to an entire paddy where thousands of rice stems made horizontal line patterns indicating the wind direction of the day before, "the plants die and the grain rots."

"And semidwarfs prevent that?" Samnang asked.

"Yes," Chhuon said. He rolled his window back up, leaving it open several inches to clear the fog from the windshield. "Not completely though. And there are other problems—more pests, more plant disease. Uncle Cheam says in a few years we'll receive a new variety, IR 24, which is semidwarf and grows so fast that the grain will fill before the heaviest winds. The farmers will harvest in August, plant a second crop and harvest again in November. Instead of just the late harvest. Uncle Cheam is very optimistic, but I've read in French journals that the double cropping requires fertilizer."

"And we sell that," Samnang said happily.

"Yes. But most of our farmers can't afford commercial fertilizers."

"Then what will happen to the crop?"

"If it wears out the paddies the next crop will be poor, eh? There has to be a balance between what the land receives and what it gives. Just like a person's spirit, eh? A balance. American scientists are experimenting with a rice that produces three crops a year. That's fine in rich nations, but here . . . maybe only those who can afford fertilizers will be able to grow rice. Maybe the peasants will borrow money to buy chemicals. Maybe the price will come down. Maybe they won't pay back what they borrow. Maybe they lose their land, eh?"

The conversation lapsed. They drove in silence for several kilometers. Then Chhuon said, "We should talk about what happened yesterday."

Samnang looked at his lap. He glanced to see if Yani was still asleep. "Yes, Father," he said. "I . . ."

"I'm concerned about your schooling," Chhuon said. "If you're to be accepted into secondary school you must do well now. You cannot learn if you're not in class."

"The boys teased me again, Father."

"You're smart." Chhuon looked toward his son. "Very quick. I wasn't that way. You'll go further with your education than me. Today everyone goes to school, eh? You'll go to the university. But . . . how do you think your teachers look upon it?"

Samnang's voice was faint. "They called me 'girlie.' They say I should have been a girl."

"They know you were ill, eh?"

"They still tease me."

"And you . . . ," Chhuon began. It was hard for him to see his Kdeb in pain.

"I screamed at them. I wanted to hit them. Then I cried." He was on the verge of tears.

"Did you hit one?"

"Yes."

"And that's when they stole your pants?"

"Yes." Samnang's head was down, his voice weak.

"And you didn't go back into class?"

"No! Some of the girls already saw me because Khieng and Heng held me. They said they'd show the girls I really was a boy. If Kpa hadn't stopped them, I would've jumped into the river and never come back. I'll never forgive them."

The road smoothed as the small pickup neared Stung Treng. Two boys on Honda motorbikes whisked by in the opposite direction. Chhuon tensed. He watched the bikes in the mirror until they disappeared. Mayana moved restlessly. Without looking up she asked, "Are we there yet?"

"Soon," Chhuon answered. The clouds lifted, the mist became drizzle. Below the raised-dike roadway paddies glowed green. The road narrowed to one lane. Chhuon strained to see through the film-covered windshield.

"Oh! Stop!" Samnang shouted. "There's a . . ."

"I see." Chhuon's voice was calm. He tapped the breaks. A squad of soldiers had set up a roadblock. Two soldiers were on the road. Six were visible on the north side, two more on the south. Roadblocks were becoming more and more frequent. Since January, with the incidents in Ratanakiri Province and the rioting, troops had increased their vigilance.

Chhuon stopped the truck. He flashed the headlights, then advanced. Someone shouted. Several soldiers scampered from the north embankment to the south. "They're crazy," Chhuon muttered in the cab. "They see me every week." Yani scrunched up tighter to her father. Samnang rolled his window down. "Roll it up," Chhuon ordered harshly.

"Father!" Samnang said, shocked at the tone.

"Roll it up," he repeated.

Samnang raised the window. "I just wanted to see the soldiers."

Chhuon proceeded to a point twenty meters before the barrier. He stopped the truck, opened his door. "Hello," he called out. "You know me."

"Is that you, Professor?" one of the soldiers shouted back.

"Yes," Chhuon called. "I've my children with me."

"Advance and be recognized," a sergeant commanded.

Of course, Chhuon thought. He pulled the door shut, shouted from the window, "Now, Brothers?"

"One minute, Professor," called the soldier who had first shouted. The soldier and the sergeant spoke briefly, too quietly for Chhuon to hear. Samnang's heart raced. "Come forward . . ." the soldier called. "Slowly, Professor."

Chhuon put the transmission in first gear, slipped the clutch until the truck rolled, then feathered the clutch to keep the pace slow. Ten meters from the soldier and the sergeant he stopped the truck and turned the engine off. "Father ..." Samnang's voice shook. Chhuon glanced at him. Then, without a word, he got out of the truck and stood in the muddy road. Samnang looked down the embankment. The government soldiers looked motley. The sergeant before the truck wore an impeccably tailored new uniform.

The soldier came forward, his weapon slung across his back. He put his hands together and bowed slightly to Chhuon. Chhuon returned the *lei,* a salutation common in Cambodia. "Cautious today, Brother, eh?"

Quietly the soldier said, "I'm sorry, Professor. He's a new sergeant. From Phnom Penh ... doesn't know country courtesy. He wants me to inspect the truck."

Samnang watched his father. The new sergeant stood a short distance before the truck, his carbine at the ready. Samnang bit his lower lip. "Do soldiers always stop Father?" Yani asked her brother.

"Yes," Samnang said. "I think. But they don't make him get out. He pays them and they let him pass."

Chhuon led the soldier to the rear of the truck. "Are you carrying new rice, Professor?"

"We're going in for short-season rice," Chhuon answered.

"And what have you seen on the road?" The soldier rummaged through the hemp ropes.

"Nothing," Chhuon said. "A few boys on motorbikes."

"No bandits?"

"I hope not."

"May I see your papers, please?"

"They're inside."

"First, lift the boards," the soldier said.

Chhuon lifted the boards from the truck bed and the soldier glanced under them. "You inspect the pig platform?" Chhuon asked, smiling.

"Because of the explosions," the soldier said. "The sergeant thinks explosives are brought in by merchants. Now we inspect all the trucks."

"What explosions?" Chhuon asked. He led the soldier back to the cab. The drizzle was coming harder.

"Two this week. Since May, more and more. This week seven people are killed."

"That's terrible," Chhuon said. "I haven't heard a word."

"Hello little brother. Hello little sister," the soldier addressed the children. "Step out, please." To Chhuon he said, "They wish to keep it secret."

Yani looked at her father, who nodded for her to come to him. Samnang followed. He stared at the sergeant. The sergeant turned away. The soldier bent forward, made a cursory search of the cab, then called to the sergeant, "This truck's clear."

"Step back," the sergeant commanded. Behind him, several of the other soldiers were rolling their eyes upward and making gestures to one another and to the first soldier, indicating the sergeant was insane. "You," the sergeant said roughly to Chhuon, "open the hood." Chhuon smiled and bowed to the sergeant. He unlatched the hood and opened it. "Step back," the sergeant said. He pointed his carbine into the engine compartment. "Come here." Chhuon approached, slipped the sergeant ten fifty-riel notes. "Now it's clear," the sergeant announced.

The sergeant looked at Samnang, flashed a very large smile, and said, "You want to be a soldier like me?"

Samnang looked at his father, then to the sergeant. "Captain," Samnang said, "if I were a soldier could I carry a rifle like yours?"

The sergeant laughed. "I'm not a captain. I'm just a sergeant."

"If I were a sergeant," Samnang said, "I would have a uniform as beautiful as yours."

"Good," the sergeant said. "Someday the professor's son will be a soldier."

Now Chhuon laughed. "And I'm not a professor," he said. "I sell seed. Sometimes a few animals."

"Mister Cahuom," the soldier said to his sergeant, "brings new rice. He studies the grains and instructs the farmers. My brothers say he is a great teacher."

"Then, Teacher," the sergeant said, "be on your way."

After the roadblock Chhuon barely spoke. He drove quickly past the last fields, the airport, the ferry landing, the river choked with barges and sampans. He did not wish to show his anger but it manifested itself in his driving, a gentle man who lovingly tended his vehicle speeding like a cowboy until a fish truck pulled from a side alley and caused him to jam the brakes.

Chhuon broke his silence. "Samnang," he said. A line of women carrying baskets of goods crossed the road before them.

"Yes, Papa?"

"If I forget, remind me to ask Uncle Cheam to arrange for the wedding rice."

"Yes, Papa. And the photograph of Prince Sihanouk?"

"Yes. And the photograph."

Samnang smiled. As they passed through the riverfront market area he heard the high-pitched cackle from the stalls, studied the two- and three-story buildings rising on the left and, on the riverside, the fruit and vegetable stalls heaped with bananas, melons, sugarcane, sweet potatoes, tobacco and fish. They passed a dance hall and several cafes. Samnang envisioned himself in the city as a student, perhaps dancing with a girl. Mayana felt overwhelmed, it was her first visit in more than a year, but Samnang was bursting to be part of the city. Stung Treng fascinated him. As the most northern Mekong River market in Cambodia, Stung Treng was the heart of the Northeast. The port handled all river traffic to 120 kilometers south where rapids at Kratie disrupted continuous river transport. Fifty kilometers from Laos, and at the edge of the Srepok Forest, the wharves of Stung Treng handled nearly all of the nation's meat trade between Cambodia and its northern neighbor, all hardwood trade between mountainous Ratanakiri Province to the east and the rest of the nation. The city was more than a market, it was the regional center for culture, education, provincial government, finance and the Royal Army. And here people did not know Samnang, did not know the humiliations known to all in Phum Sath Din. Even at eleven years old he could sense that someday he would make a new start and he hoped it would be in this exciting city.

"Papa?" Samnang said.

"Yes."

"I'd like to go to the secondary schools here. I could live with Uncle Cheam."

"Yes, I hope you will."

Chhuon slowly worked the truck through other trucks, cars, bicycles, motorbikes, carts and *samlos* (bicycle-drawn carriages). Above the stone levee merchants were preparing their stalls. Barefoot boys and girls in straw hats ran among parked farm carts. A stallkeeper bowed politely to a city policeman. Two young boys carrying transistor radios wandered aimlessly. Chhuon spotted them and thought, Everything is changing. We're being Westernized. Samnang saw the boys, grinned inwardly and thought how grand it would be to wander amongst the wharves. From the last pier of the line Samnang could see the Mekong still to the west, a yellow water channel two kilometers wide, and the Srepok beside them, its red-brown mouth a kilometer wide, the waters mixing like fluid art.

Chhuon parked before the last warehouse. He pulled his Buddha statuette from his shirt, kissed it seven times and gave thanks.

"Good morning Uncle Cheam," Samnang called. He used the formal Khmer appellation which indicated not simply "uncle" but "my father's older brother." Cheam, like Chhuon, was stocky and muscular, though as he'd aged, his barrel chest had slipped to his waist. Samnang liked him. He saw his uncle as more aggressive than his father, perhaps as less Buddhist, less prone to passivity, though not less honest or less concerned for others.

"Nephew," Cheam grunted politely. Immediately he became stern. "I must speak with your father." The boy's face fell, became expressionless. To Chhuon, Cheam said, "Mister Pech Lim Song is here. We've much to discuss. But first . . ." Cheam stopped. He looked at Samnang and Mayana. "Children, go see your aunt. There's noodle soup for this cold morning. Younger Brother, come with me."

Samnang and Yani followed the stone path along the side of the warehouse. At the back of the building there was a modern wood and brick home with a tile roof and a porch overlooking the paddies which dropped west to the Mekong. Samnang led his sister to the house but he stopped, let her go to the stairs alone. "Come, come, little niece," their aunt called, seeing Mayana on the steps. "Have they started talking politics? That's all they talk anymore."

At the front of the warehouse Chhuon held his older brother's sleeve. "I know," Chhuon said. "Mister Pech can provide the very best rice for the wedding days. That's all the more reason I must supply the most beautiful—the whitest ever seen in Cambodia. Good rice is so hard to find."

"Uhm!" Cheam shook his head. "You worry too much. It's my honor to provide the rice for Vathana's wedding. We trade in rice. Don't you think we have connections?"

"You. Not me. I thank you deeply. This marriage is so important. Mr. Pech's second son will be my son-in-law. My daughter his daughter. The Wheel of Life . . ."

"Not the Wheel of Life." Cheam laughed brashly. "The Wheel of Commerce. Vathana will be the daughter of our chief supplier."

"You've arranged a fine union," Chhuon said sincerely. "Again, thank you. Vathana asked, would it be possible to purchase a large portrait of Samdech Euv."

"Uhm." Cheam grunted again. "I'll bring one as my wedding gift." Chhuon released his brother's sleeve, stepped toward the outer door to the office. But now Cheam held him. "Did they stop you again?" Cheam asked.

"Yes."

"How much?"

"Five hundred riels. Each time they ask for more. Last night I had a terrible dream. I dreamt the ancient dream of all Cambodia. We were being forced to choose between being eaten by tigers, devoured by crocodiles, or trampled by elephants."

"Ooh! You and your dreams! Younger Brother, you have dreams because you listen to old ladies. All the dream is is a folktale. Next you'll tell me you're going to the khrou. Better you should study finance."

Samnang returned to the warehouse and entered through a small back door. Quietly he walked the length of the large dark room, running a hand along the racks on one wall where rice sacks were stacked to the roof. His eyes skimmed the bins on the opposite wall full of ebony, mahogany, rosewood and teak blocks for statues. Outside the office he peered into the small rack for experimental rice seed. He could hear his uncle's voice. Then Mister Pech's. The men spoke of rice, fertilizer, hardwoods and breeding stock. Samnang listened but the words didn't interest him. He ran his hands over the cold metal of a gas-powered forklift truck parked in the center of the floor. He wanted to sit in the seat but was afraid to without permission.

Mister Pech's voice came strong into the warehouse. "He's a proper son," the older man said. "A little lost right now, like all the university boys, eh?" Chhuon answered but Samnang couldn't hear the words. Mister Pech continued. "He'll come around. He'll be a good husband. He comes from good stock, eh?" The men laughed loudly and Samnang laughed quietly.

Then Samnang heard his uncle say, "Who's printing these?"

Cheam's voice was so harsh, so uncharacteristic of Khmer society, in which overt expressions of hostility are considered reprehensible, that Samnang twitched. The boy crept forward to peek into the room. Cheam held a handful of fifty-riel notes. "This is what you brought."

Samnang squatted by a pallet of sacks they would later take to Lomphat and Plei Srepok. He listened quietly.

"There's a problem, Older Brother?"

"These are fake." Cheam did not disguise his disgust.

"Fake?!" Chhuon responded.

"Counterfeit!" Cheam shouted. "The bank won't take them. Even street vendors recognize them and refuse to accept. These are the notes you brought last trip."

"I received money from Mister Keng and Y Ksar. They're honorable . . ."

Cheam scowled. "Y Ksar's too stupid to counterfeit."

"Mister Keng's a farmer," Chhuon defended him. "He wouldn't print fake money."

Cheam turned from his brother. "But who? All the money you

brought last time . . . all of it is the same. It's worthless. Where do they get it?"

"I don't know," Chhuon said.

"Ask. Today, you ask. Look at these. See here, this is how you tell if they're fake. Corruption—everywhere!" Cheam slapped a stack of notes into his palm. "Bribery—everywhere! This"—his voice sank to conspirator level—"is what we'll do." Samnang strained to hear. Before he could decipher the words, Cheam exploded again. "I can't even send out a damn empty truck without paying hoodlums."

Chhuon hung his head, did not answer. In Khmer culture for a man to contradict another of equal or higher station caused both terrible humiliation. Yet his brother's tone disgraced him before Mister Pech. He sat quietly. Chhuon believed both Cheam's and Mister Pech's authority came to them as divine incarnation, that their rank reflected how much merit they'd earned in earlier lives. The first belief was a vestige of the Hindu base of Khmer society, the latter came from Buddhism's emphasis on personal salvation through the earning of merit. Both led Chhuon, at times, to extreme obedience.

In the shadows of the warehouse Samnang suffered his father's weakness. He recalled once overhearing his mother explaining his uncle's behavior, "It's because he has no children." Samnang didn't care. He wanted to storm the office, attack his uncle, tell his father to stand up.

"La sale guerre," Mister Pech Lim Song said in French. "It is this dirty war that causes you these problems." He spoke in a way which absolved Chhuon of his brother's charge and yet did not offend Cheam. "I think it's the Prince's fault," Mister Pech continued in French. "His love for power keeps him from stopping corruption. He's bound to our feudal heritage. He'll never carry out the reforms needed to unify our country, to keep it safe from Viet Namese hegemony."

Cheam also spoke in French. "Khmers are warriors," he said with passion. "Always we've fought for our people, for freedom and independence."

"Fighting is none of our business," Chhuon said in Khmer. In his home, with his family, Chhuon's speech was refined, lyrical Khmer full of sound redundancies, alliterations and rhymes. In business, he changed to a more technically based Khmer with a smattering of French. He was fluent in that language, used it liberally with officials in Stung Treng and Lomphat, but he detested it because it was non-Khmer. "Leave war to the politicians. It does nothing but serve the Prince of Death."

"Don't be fooled, Brothers." Mister Pech switched back to

Khmer. "This is not something to ignore. It's there whether we wish to see it or not."

"The country's a mess," Samnang heard Cheam say. "Mister Pech was telling me what he's discovered about the attacks in Ratanakiri." Now Cheam began to rant. "It's not enough to nationalize imports and exports, to nationalize the internal distribution of goods . . . but we're paid in counterfeit notes. And now this!"

"Now what?" Chhuon began.

"Corruption and foreigners," Cheam blurted. "The Chinese control business, the Viet Namese labor. I won't abandon commerce to the Chinese and I won't hire a Viet Namese. They work hard but I don't trust them. They work until they're in just the right position, then, bam, they take over. Ingrates. There, Brother, are your crocodiles."

"The country *is* a mess," Mister Pech repeated. "What the Royal Army did in Battambang Province last year . . . you know of the murders."

"I've heard rumors," Chhuon responded.

"Riots in seventeen of nineteen provinces," Mr. Pech continued. "Thirty thousand Royal troops internally yet no one to protect the borders. And this in the highlands."

"What in the—" Chhuon began again but Cheam interrupted him.

"He thinks he can push everyone around." There was anger in Cheam's voice. "Brothers, we must respect the rights of all Cambodians, Khmer or not. The Holy One says that, eh? Tribal people are people, eh? If Samdech Euv wants to build a rubber plantation on their land . . ."

"Is that what you were telling?" Chhuon asked.

"I have a friend, Colonel Chlay," Mister Pech said. "He tells me for two years his officers in Lomphat and Senmonorom have reported exact Yuon locations, exact units, exact strengths. The Prince has done nothing. Worse. He cut ties with America to earn respect from Hanoi and Peking. Now, who knows? Maybe he changes again. But he lets the yuons have the province, and he kills Mountaineers."

"The attack at Veunsai, eh?" Chhuon said.

"I can no longer support the Prince." Samnang heard his uncle's vehement whisper.

"It came one week before the North Viet Namese launched their New Year's offensive against the South," Mister Pech said. "The yuons haven't tolerated Royal troops in those mountains for a year. Now, *now*?! I have heard"—Mister Pech hesitated—

"the troop movement was a guise. My friend tells me it masked Viet Namese staging for their attacks on Pleiku and Kontum."

"He would not do that," Chhuon said.

"How can I support him?" Mister Pech said. "His troops supported the Communist offensive. He was a party to their Tet!"

"ssshh!" Cheam said. "Mister Pech! The walls have ears."

Chhuon drove south on Highway 13. The road climbed quickly out of the floodplain, away from the rice fields, into the forest. On the uphill stretches Chhuon dropped to second gear so the small truck could pull its load. Under a tarpaulin in the bed of the truck were the dozen forty-kilogram sacks of rice and four sacks of fertilizer which Samnang had squatted beside as he listened to his father, uncle and Mister Pech. In a separate plastic bag were two ten-kilo sacks of experimental seed. On top of the load two small black breeding pigs were being soaked by driving rain.

Chhuon leaned forward, wiped the windshield with a cloth. The moisture and smoke residue smeared. He wiped harder. "Damn," he muttered in French. "Maybe one more trip before the rain makes the roads impassable."

"Papa," Samnang said in Khmer, "why do all educated Cambodians speak French?"

"Hum?" Chhuon said. He squinted, trying to see the familiar landmarks which would tell him he was nearing the junction with Highway 19.

"France is eleven thousand kilometers away," Samnang said.

"Yes," Chhuon said. They were approaching the turnoff. Mayana squirmed restlessly in the seat beside him. "Yes," he repeated. "France is far away. It would be better to learn Jarai, Rhade or Mnong, but the educated look down on the mountain peoples."

"I can speak Jarai," Samnang said.

"You cannot," Mayana challenged him.

"Can too," the boy shot back.

They spoke intermittently. Chhuon again was gentle with the truck. On downhills where the wet brakes had diminished effect he slowed to a crawl and let the engine control the speed. As he drove he thought, How can I ask Mister Keng about these notes? What will I do if the soldiers recognize them? I should have seen the khrou. With such a dream how could I travel? Mayana and Samnang began playing a hand-slapping game and Chhuon felt relieved he didn't have to entertain them.

Highway 19 ran east over a small set of hills, then turned

north and descended into the valley of the Srepok River. As they emerged from the forest Chhuon kept the truck in second gear, then shifted into third as the road leveled and the forest gave way to more paddies. They passed several poor hamlets where peasant families tilled their half-hectare plots, raising rice and vegetables. Too poor to afford fertilizer, they jealously reserved their own excrement, a source of nitrogen, for the family garden.

They approached the river. Chhuon again said a prayer to the water spirit. Then spontaneously he said, "He who controls the water, controls life. Rivers flow like life flows, like ancestry, like rice in its rhythmic reproduction. In my great-great-grandfather's time," he continued, "Cambodia covered all the Ca Mau Peninsula to north of Saigon. Saigon was Prey Nokor, 'the Forest Home.' Cambodia covered the Bolovens Plateau of Laos all the way to Luang Prabang. Even much of Thailand. All because we controlled the water."

"What happened?" Samnang asked.

"Yuons, Thais, they invaded. They destroyed the irrigation because they were jealous." Chhuon's tone was didactic, without anger.

"What happened to your great-great-grandfather?" Yani asked.

"My father told many stories of the ancestors," Chhuon said. "He said yuons killed him. And my grandfather. But my Uncle Choeu says no. He once showed me on the tablets that great-great-Grandpa lived eighty years. Choeu said Grandfather was killed by the French."

"The French?" Yani asked.

"During the uprising of 1885. They were fighting to keep all the fields in the name of the king because in those times everyone worked the land and kept most of their rice. They didn't worry about someone taking their fields. The French thought that was barbaric and insisted all land was private property. That's when farmers began to lose the land."

"Yuons killed your great-great-grandfather?" Samnang said.

"I don't know," Chhuon repeated.

"If yuons killed him, I shall hate them forever," Samnang blurted.

Chhuon was aghast. Sternly he said, "One must exorcise traditional hatreds. We must tolerate all people who live beside us."

The conversation stopped. Samnang tensed. Hadn't he just overheard Mister Pech describe the treachery of the Viet Namese?

Chhuon drove on. He did not know how to handle his son's animosity. Highway 19 consisted of long stretches of uninhabited dirt and gravel ridge with deep shoulder gullies to carry away the heavy rains. "At one time"—Chhuon began a story he felt would ease their talk—"rice grew wild. It had very large, very white grains and it had the fragrance of cow's milk. A single grain would fill a hungry man. Men were good. Then they became selfish. They learned to lie, to steal and to possess. The rice grain deteriorated. The aroma faded. Now rice alone cannot sustain."

"Will we get the good kind for Vathana's wedding?" Yani asked.

"We'll get the most beautiful that grows," Chhuon answered.

"Father," Yani's little-girl voice giggled, "is Vathana the prettiest girl in Cambodia?"

"To me"—Chhuon smiled—"my daughters and their mother are the prettiest girls in all the world. But it's their compassion that's important."

"But Vathana really is the prettiest, isn't she?" Yani persisted. "When all Teck's uncles and aunts came to our house, and his parents, I loved them right away. They're so gentle. I wish, when I'm eighteen, a kind and handsome man is found for me."

"We've some time before we concern ourselves with that." Chhuon laughed.

"Shouldn't Mister Pech work for you?" Yani asked. She then announced, "When I get engaged, my betrothed shall work for you for a year."

"Little Yani"—her voice warmed Chhuon—"that custom has lost favor. Except amongst some farmers."

"Will they live with us?"

"No. They'll live in Neak Luong. Pech Chieu Teck is in business there with his father. They're a good family. This will be the most spectacular marriage. Through their children we'll be linked to all generations, for all generations."

Again they rode in silence. The land dipped and the forest gave way to uncultivated marshland or to small rice or sweet potato farms. Under the low monsoon clouds and heavy rain the land appeared unpopulated. "The Holy One," Chhuon broke the silence, "has taught the responsibility of each man to do good works."

Samnang had been slowly seething since his father's call for toleration. "But," he said dryly, "Buddha also fought dishonesty and deceit. He fought against privileges of one class over another."

"Man is born," Chhuon said. "He lives, grows old, dies. Buddha teaches that man is then reborn to live again. The cycle continues. Life means suffering . . .'' Samnang clenched his teeth. He hummed to himself. "If one is to alleviate suffering, one must renounce evil and pursue good. Only through good conduct can a man ease his burden; only through good deeds can one lighten his karma until he has no karma at all. Then he will enter the state of nirvana where there is no physical existence.

"Keep the right thoughts," Chhuon continued. "Anger produces anger. Gentleness produces gentleness. Aggression produces aggression. Generosity produces generosity."

"Papa . . ." Samnang's voice was cold. "Why do you support Samdech Euv though he allows yuons to run rampant over our country? Though he allows corruption and lets the army attack farmers?"

"Who told you . . . ? You were in the warehouse, eh?"

"Yes, Father." The boy pressed. "What did Mister Pech say happened in Battambang? I heard him on Ratanakiri."

Chhuon hesitated. He glanced at his son and daughter. He wanted to say to Samnang, I can't tell you before Mayana, but he was sure the boy would take it as another shun. For a minute he was silent. Then he told them what he'd heard of Samlaut and the riots. Then he said, "If it weren't for Mister Pech and Uncle Cheam we'd never know. The Prince tries to protect us by keeping these things hidden. Just as I try to protect you."

Chhuon stopped. He looked at his children. Mayana's mouth was open, Samnang's eyes glared. "Is this what you want to hear?"

"Yes, Papa," Samnang said. "I should know these things."

"Yuk." Yani broke from her trance. "Why do you want to hear that?"

"Men should know these things," Samnang said to his sister. He leaned forward to talk directly to his father. "Why don't we riot?"

"There's been too many arrests, too many exiles, too many teachers have run to the forests. Khmers must talk to Khmers. It's a national flaw. If we don't agree, we don't talk. If we disagree, we are enemies forever."

The small truck entered the high plateau north of Lomphat. Chhuon made an ever-increasing number of detours over temporary culverts, around washed-out sections. Then the road split. Chhuon turned onto the lesser road and headed south down the mountains. The grade was steep. He forced the transmission into first gear. He said nothing as the truck descended but prayed silently. After half an hour of curves and drops the road leveled onto the floodplain of the upper Srepok River.

"Isn't there a better road?" Yani asked.

"Always—" Chhuon began.

A warning burst of rifle fire cracked over them. Samnang jerked. Chhuon scanned left and right. A small plastic lean-to at the road's edge protected four or five soldiers from the rain. A corporal stood by the road's edge. Behind his carbine he smiled broadly. The soldiers didn't even look up. Two rifles lay on the pavement as if abandoned. Not far off the road three smaller huts of plastic had been set up amid a cluster of trees. Women and children, the families of the soldiers, were busy collecting firewood and cooking.

"Your papers," the corporal said. Chhuon had never seen him before. He handed the corporal his pass and smiled ambiguously. The soldier studied the form, then said, "From Stung Treng you come this way? Everyone out!" The soldier jerked the door open. Other soldiers surrounded the truck. One jumped into the bed and threw the pigs off. Hanging by their tethers they kicked and squealed. Another soldier ripped the tarpaulin back. Mayana clutched at her father. Samnang froze, unable to move.

"Hey," Chhuon said. "Brothers, my papers are in order. I'm to make two deliveries." A soldier stabbed his bayonet into one of the rice sacks. "Stop. What do you look for?"

"Silence!" the corporal yelled.

Chhuon pulled a wad of counterfeit riels from his pocket. He peeled off ten fifty-fiel notes and shoved them at the corporal who quickly stuffed them into his own pocket. "As you know, Brother"—the corporal's manner softened and he again smiled—"this is a toll road." To his squad he yelled, "Cover that rice. Pick up the pigs." Then to Chhuon, "Have the children get back in. There's no reason for them to get wet. The charge for road use is five hundred riels."

"Five hundred?!" Chhuon feigned shock.

"Bandits raided the road," the corporal said. "If it's to remain open, eh? we must collect a road tax. Otherwise"—he shrugged—"there'll be no money for protection. Then you would be robbed."

Again Chhuon removed a wad of riels. This time the soldier placed the bills on a clipboard. Don't, Chhuon ordered himself, look at the money. He turned, looked beyond the road at the plastic huts. "This must be a very hard job," he said.

From the corner of his eye he could see the corporal studying the notes. "Eh . . ." the man groaned, "yes. You may go."

"A very tough and very important job, Brother," Chhuon said.

Samnang was shaken. His respect for his father increased. Why, he trembled inwardly, do I freeze? He felt humiliated. He might just as well have broken down and cried or screamed like a girl—like the girl Khieng and Heng said he really should have been. In the truck he was silent, sullen.

"It's okay," Chhuon said to them. "It's okay now. In a few minutes we'll see the tall building of Lomphat. It's okay to be scared. I was scared myself."

"Father," Yani cried. Tears were in her eyes and on her cheeks. "You're so brave."

Chhuon hugged his daughter. Brave, he thought. Stupid maybe. I shouldn't have them with me.

It was one in the afternoon when Chhuon pulled the heavily laden truck into Lomphat. The town was different from primarily Khmer Stung Treng. Its ethnic makeup was a mix of Khmer and Cham plus a number of minorities, including a substantial Viet Namese district, a small Chinese business district and Lao, Brao, Rhade, Jarai and Mnong sectors. The short main boulevard through town was dotted with cafes and dance halls and there was a provincial government office building. On a rise south of the main road was the governor's villa. "Can we stop?" Yani asked.

"For a minute," Chhuon answered.

"Buy me a cola?"

"Yani," Chhuon warned, "Mister Keng will be insulted if we don't eat with him." Chhuon parked before a small cafe. "Be quick," he said.

Behind the counter a thin woman bent over a crude sink. She did not look up, did not really notice Chhuon or the children. In Viet Namese she asked for their order.

"Three colas, please," Chhuon said in Khmer. The woman straightened, gave them the bottles, took a counterfeit note and gave change without saying a word.

Mister Keng bowed with his hands touching before his very round and very large head. He greeted Chhuon with a farm idiom which would translate literally as "Have you had rice today?" but in essence meant "Good afternoon."

"Mister Keng," Chhuon returned his client's greeting with a gracious *lei*. Samnang and Mayana also bowed. Keng Sambath ushered them into the central room of his small home. Immediately a servant brought the men a hot curry lunch. Keng's wife, to Samnang's umbrage, pushed him and Yani out the door and to a small lean-to kitchen at the side of the house. There they ate a simpler lunch, and each was treated to a single sweet rice cake.

Inside, the men's speech was animated. This was a happy occasion, good friends meeting after not having seen one another for some time. They spoke of irrigation problems and new rice, of how, where and when to plant the new seed, how much seed they would plant directly in the paddy, how much they would germinate and replant. And they asked after each other's family. Then Mister Keng asked about the explosions in Stung Treng.

Outside, Samnang could hear the early talk, but then it quieted. The men finished, sipped tea and nibbled on watermelon seeds. Samnang fidgeted. He wanted to hear. For a long time he had been curious about his father's business and with what he'd overheard earlier, his insides were tense. "Ssshh!" He hissed at his sister each time she spoke.

Chhuon had become contemplative. Prince Sihanouk's own intelligence reports indicated that the Viet Namese, soldiers and civilians, were becoming increasingly hostile to the Khmer people and governmental authorities in the border provinces. Because Chhuon thought Sambath held similar beliefs to his own he ventured, "Some say Samdech Euv is selling out to the yuons."

"The North Viet Namese," Mister Keng countered hard and loud before his wife and servants, "and the Viet Minh treat us with more respect than our Royal troops. It's rightist factions that cause this evil. If Samdech Euv listened to someone other than that fascist colonel, the army wouldn't treat us so."

Chhuon, with a most enigmatic smile, answered, "If I may broach this subject, Mister Keng, may I ask, from whom do you receive your largest cash sums?"

For a split second Mister Keng's face showed shock, then he too smiled. "I sell my rice to those who wish to purchase it," he said.

"Dear Honorable Sir," Chhuon addressed his host in the most formal fashion, "I would not ask you this if it were not for a problem I have had. Please, Brother, I do not question your honesty for one second, but please . . ." Chhuon removed from his briefcase an envelope containing the order from their last transaction plus 400 fifty-riel notes. He spoke very softly as he fanned the notes and pointed to the defect. "Someone, Dear Brother, has paid you in counterfeit riels. These are the notes you paid with last."

Outside, Samnang heard none of the quiet talk. Suddenly Mister Keng's voice blurted loudly, "There is a problem developing with an insect I've never seen before. Come to the paddy. Examine the new plants."

Alone the two men walked the dikes to the far corner of one field where a small area had been sectioned off by a temporary low, narrow dike. "Mister Cahuom," Keng Sambath began. He spoke very differently in the field than he had in the house. "I love my country very much. I love Samdech Euv. He's a gentle king. I don't know how to say this. One must be discreet, eh? Our problems are serious. I've no choice. I sell to the Viet Minh. They pay world market prices instead of the low rate set by the government. At first they bought only a little and I was happy to receive such a price. Then they asked to buy more. Still they paid a fair price. Last year they purchased half of what I produce. I told them they ate too much. I needed to sell more to state merchants. They told me they would need even more this year. And they told me . . . they told *me* how much I must produce. The Viet Minh say each hectare must produce one-point-two tons. They say I *will* harvest twenty-one tons. They say five tons will keep the government happy.

"Dear Chhuon, I don't wish to deprive the Prince or my country of profit it should make from exporting rice but I have no alternative. You know better than anyone, I don't reap one-point-two tons on every hectare. My yield's seventeen, maybe eighteen tons. Now you tell me they pay with fake money. It used to be so easy to live. I've always believed the rice yields were good because Samdech Euv had accumulated much merit. The Viet Minh say the Prince is surrounded by evil. By men who won't protect us but still collect taxes. I've heard say the Prince hoards gold and has many women. I don't believe it. When it's time for war, I'll stand with my king against all invaders. But why doesn't the government help us?"

CHAPTER TWO

The Communists have developed *a new kind of aggression in which one country sponsors internal war within another.* Communist-sponsored internal war is clearly international aggression, but a form of aggression that frequently eludes the traditional definitions of international law. It means the use of native and imported guerrillas to serve the interests of Communist nations.

> —From the Foreword
> by Roger Hilsman to
> *People's War: People's Army*
> by Vo Nguyen Giap

Again they were stopped. From Lomphat they had traveled north and northeast, back onto the plateau, across flat, barren, crumbling red ledge, then into dense double-canopy mountain forest. This time the troops were neither motley, undisciplined nor rough. Chhuon got out. Samnang sank low in his seat, torn between curiosity and fear. Yani knelt and spied through the rear window. The officer seemed gracious. Yani nudged her brother and both children poked their heads up.

Quietly the soldier accepted the papers Chhuon presented. He asked for a donation. Chhuon handed him ten fifty-riel notes. The man flipped the notes over. "You are much generous," he said in broken Khmer. "Allow me give back you donation. No we need for hard work money. You donate rice."

As his father pulled back the tarpaulin Samnang winced. Four laborers came. "Our kind friend has offered us two sacks of rice," the officer said in Viet Namese. "Help him." Two men hefted each sack.

Samnang wanted to jump out, yell, kick the soldier. He wanted his father to take the rifle. "They can't do that," he stammered to Yani. Then he slapped a hand against the seat. The officer started, spun, glared at him. The boy withered under his eyes.

When the small truck was again under way Samnang blurted angrily, "Damn them. Damn them all."

"It's not proper," Chhuon said, controlling his own irritation, "for one to show anger. It only makes others angry."

"But . . ."

"It's difficult, but it's something one must do."

Samnang had heard the admonition many times. To his eleven-year-old mind he understood it to mean, not control one's anger, but don't get angry. He repressed his anger, denied the emotions, pouted. Since early morning they had been on highways and back roads of northeastern Cambodia, passing through two major cities and by many villages, hamlets and isolated farms. Samnang had begun to see his country as a patchwork of different peoples, like contiguous rice fields separated by dikes and canals, forests and rivers. He saw them struggling, some prospering, some withering. It confused him and this too he repressed. With all that had happened in the past few days he felt like a powder keg.

If going to Lomphat was like stepping back in time, going to Plei Srepok was a leap into time suspended, into an Iron Age tinged with technological sophistication. Cahuom Chhuon maneuvered the small truck up the last rutted incline. He watched the beautiful country of high mountains and deep valleys unfold under lightening monsoon clouds. By midafternoon the sun had broken through and was glistening in the wet canopy. Chhuon unwrapped his checked krama from his neck. He wiped his shaved head. They drove southwest into a jungled thicket, then arced west and northwest into the mouth of a tapering canyon created by mountainous fingers descending from a high peak. Four kilometers west a main branch of the Ho Chi Minh Trail intersected Highway 19 near Ba Kev.

"Yani," Chhuon said, "this is a very different place."

"Boy! I'll say," Samnang said.

Chhuon glanced at him, noticed him rocking in the seat, smiling. He'd accompanied his father to this and other Mountaineer villages numerous times. "Yani," Chhuon said, "to speak another language is to enter a different world. Words influence thoughts. The Mountaineers not only dress differently, they think differently. Some Khmers call them *phnongs*, just as yuons call them *mois*. They are our friends. My friends. I expect them to be treated with the very highest respect."

"I know . . ." Mayana began.

"Forty, fifty years ago," Chhuon said, "many of the tribes degenerated and acquiesced to the fate forced on them by lowland majorities and colonial powers. For them life stopped. They sat in their longhouses, smoked their pipes, drank from the jars. Then came the resurgence. They're good-hearted people. Don't be alarmed if you don't understand. They'll never allow harm to come to you."

"But Papa," Mayana protested, "I know. You've told us their stories. Doesn't Mister Y Ksar have a daughter my age? And don't most of them speak Khmer? I bet I could talk to her even if she doesn't."

"You don't know anything," Samnang snapped nastily.

Chhuon ignored his behavior. To Mayana he said, "I bet you could. Mister Y Ksar is very old. His son Chung married into the Draam clan and lives with his wife's family. Chung and Draam Mul have a daughter, oh, a little older than you. About Samay's age. Maybe thirteen."

"Y Bhur's my age," Samnang said. "He showed me how to fire a crossbow."

The dense vegetation opened abruptly onto a vacant dry-rice field. Without the trees they could see the breadth of the valley, perhaps three hundred meters. Ahead, the road reentered the jungle. Above the canopy they could see the cliff which terminated the canyon and the mountain rising into broken clouds. They crossed a log bridge surfaced with woven bamboo mats. Beneath them the waters of the O Kamang Chong, the canyon stream, were dark. At first Samnang thought the stream still, then he noticed a single piece of grass moving quickly with the glimmering surface. Chhuon's eyes darted everywhere. The emptiness caused eerie chills to rise up his back. Again the trees closed, the trail remained level, the ridges rose. Light filtered through the foliage. Chhuon felt as if he were driving directly into the mountain. Not a breath of wind stirred.

Suddenly the revving whine of small motors surrounded them. Yani snapped about. Three gray Honda 90 motorcycles, each with two warriors, appeared. Chhuon laughed. "By the way children," he said, "remember, here men think, eh? Women work." Chhuon laughed happily. He waved his krama out the window at the riding soldiers. "Hello," he clucked in Jarai.

Immediately there were two heavy thunks at the bed of the truck. Mayana popped to her knees. A chestnut-colored man dressed only in loincloth and open vest flashed a gigantic filed-toothed grin at her. "Oh!" She gasped.

"Hello," Samnang clucked out his window.

The small truck entered another clearing, now carrying four soldiers, two in the bed plus one on each front fender. Mayana tried to see everything at once. Chhuon drove across another log bridge and up to a gate in a high bamboo picket fence. The escort motorcycles raced ahead as Chhuon chatted briefly in

Jarai with the gate guard. High thatched roofs could be seen over the treetops of a mango grove.

"If I believe," Chhuon said to the children as he drove into Plei Srepok, "that one should speak Khmer in Stung Treng because it's our country, then mustn't I attempt to speak Jarai on Jarai land?"

Samnang ignored the question. In an excited voice he said, "I hope Y Bhur'll let me shoot his bow again."

The village before them consisted of eleven longhouses in four parallel tiers rising up the east hillside which had been notched like the notched logs that served as stairs into the homes themselves. The houses, sitting on four-foot-high stilt platforms, varied from fifty to as much as 120 feet long, though in other dimensions they varied little—width twenty feet, walls three feet, and immense thatched roofs like A-frames without windows beginning from below the height of the short walls and rising twelve to fifteen feet to cover the ridgepoles. Between and under the houses children played and bare-breasted women coated with sweat pounded grain, wove cloth or split wood. Samnang tried not to stare at the women, tried not to let his father see him staring. Older men in loincloths sat in the shade of small ritual verandas talking and smoking crooked pipes. Young men clad in Western-style shirts or partial military uniforms busied themselves with their motorcycles or rifles. The smell of cows mixed with the strong aroma of cinnamon.

Chhuon pulled the truck up to Y Ksar's longhouse. Chickens scattered, runt pigs squealed. "Eh! Look! Look at that!" Before them, across from a large vegetable garden, was a structure of a type Chhuon had never seen in a mountain village. Samnang looked about furtively, hoping to see Sraang, Y Bhur's older sister, hoping, she, like the old women, would be clad in only a black sarong skirt.

"I'll be," Chhuon said. Before them was a large, round, adobe-brick structure with a few small windows and a high, intricately woven, spearhead-shaped thatched roof. Beside its wide entry there was a raised platform and before that a swept courtyard with several low log tables.

Mayana slid across the seat, out the door. She stood close by her father as a horde of villagers, men and children mostly, came to greet them. Samnang slithered out his side window and immediately was lifted by the soldier who had ridden the right fender.

"Hey! Hey! Hallo! Hallo!" An old man leading the procession called out joyously in heavily accented Khmer.

"Hello, My Brother," Chhuon clucked back in Jarai.

"Hello, Uncle." Samnang ran to Y Ksar. "What's that?"

"Come, come inside and I'll tell you everything." Y Ksar laughed gaily. "Come, we shall open a jar and get drunk."

The common room of Y Ksar's longhouse was hot and dark, the still air thick with humidity and smoke. To one side, on a raised hearth a large caldron sat on inverted iron cones embedded in hot embers. Chhuon paired off with Y Ksar; Samnang, accepted as an adult, paired with Y Bhur. On the floor between them was a five-gallon earthenware jar. Mayana, her eyes tearing from the smoke, squatted with Sraang, her grandmother Jaang, and other women, sisters and aunts, near the hearth. By the door, Draam Chung, Y Ksar's eldest son (in the village Y Ksar was known as Ama Chung, "father of Chung," as it was the tradition to call a parent after the firstborn), held a live chicken by the neck. At the back wall, on an elevated pallet which ran the length of the room, were sixteen more huge jars.

"To you, Y Chhuon, father of Samnang, my newest brother," Y Ksar began a buoyant, poetic invocation:

> You have brought us rice.
> You have brought us fat breeding pigs.
> You have honored the Spirit of our Door.
> May your body be cool,
>   sleep deep
>   snore loud.

Y Ksar presented Chhuon with an elaborately woven winnowing basket heaped with glutinous rice and topped with bananas and slivers of chicken. He dipped his hands into the basket and lifted a sticky mass of food to Chhuon's lips. From a second basket Y Bhur followed suit, offering Samnang both friendship and sustenance. Y Ksar continued with the sonorous coughing prayer:

> May our young brothers and our old brothers
>   catch no sickness.
>   May you again return in peace to your village
>   and again to ours.
>   May your truck tires remain plump.
>   May no one stop you on the road.

Samnang took his cues from Chhuon. When his father raised his head from Y Ksar's hands, the boy raised his from Y Bhur's. He felt uneasy yet proud. Chhuon scooped up a large handful and held it up for Y Ksar. In Jarai he attempted:

Spirit of the Mountain watch over all men, all things,
   watch over those who live in Plei Srepok,
   I command you, watch over the high villages and the low.

At that moment Draam Chung slit the chicken's neck. Blood
spurted, then dripped into a neckless jug. Y Ksar, finished with
the exchange of food, broke the seal on the large jar before him.
His rich voice chittered gaily.

   Rice beer be dark and ripe and strong as the nightstar,
May all be in unison and full of joy.
   I command all here in my home
     to eat your fill of chicken
     to drink your fill from the jar
   May your bodies be cool
   Do not let me hear an angry voice
   Do not kill me with your words.

As he recited the verse, Jaang stuffed the jar with lalang grass
to keep the thick bran at the bottom. Then the jar was topped
off with water. Y Ksar tipped the jar as he inserted a four-foot-
long straw to the bottom. Properly, a few drops of beer spilled
onto the floor. He incanted:

   May the Spirit of the Belly of the paddies
     make the rice grow,
   May the pigs get fat and have many piglets,
   Let us do as the ancestors did in bygone days,
     as the Mother of Yesterday did in bygone days,
   Let us eat chicken until we are full,
   Let us drink rice beer until we belch,
   Soul of this food and drink do not fear us,
     so we may again eat food and drink *numpai.*

With those words the women and other villagers began to eat,
but Draam Chung's bellowing voice halted them:

   May the magic of the elephant plant strengthen all
   May the snake slither away before you step on him.
   We are about to anoint my brother's feet
     with chicken blood and rice alcohol.
     May the tiger stay in the forest,
     May the crocodile stay on the shore
     May our bodies be cool,
       sleep deep
       snore loud.

Chhuon, his body hot and sticky with smoke and mist, shivered. He felt his heart pause, then overfill and contract. A giant pulse flooded his body. He did not turn to look at Chung, but in himself said, May I not fall into the river.

With the straw tip at the bottom of the jar Y Ksar sucked up the fermented-bran numpai as the others again began to eat. It was difficult to pull the numpai up through the long straw. For young men it was considered a test of their manhood. As he swallowed, Y Ksar slipped his thumb over the mouth end of the straw to keep the wine-beer from falling back. He drank for some minutes, then thumb-covered the straw. "Measure," he called out. Sraang came with a smaller jar and a measuring cup. She knelt before the large jar, filled the measuring cup with water from the small, then poured the water into the large, measuring and pouring until the large jar was again full.

"Ha ha." Y Ksar laughed his spirited laugh. "Six plus a half." Carefully he passed the straw to Chhuon, still not allowing air to drive the numpai back into the jar. Chhuon smiled, knowing he was expected to match the feat of six and a half measures. Y Ksar looked at Chhuon's eyes and laughed and laughed. Then he began to tell stories, some in Jarai but most in Khmer. He was a lively, witty storyteller, chanting long embellished tales. Jaang and Sraang brought more food. Chung joined in the circle and invited Mayana to sit just behind him. Y Ksar told tale after tale. He joked and laughed at the jokes himself and he made everyone else, especially Mayana, laugh too.

"Uncle," Mayana asked in her little-girl voice, "why do you live up here? How did the mountain people get here?"

Y Ksar winked at her. "According to ancient legend," he said, "long, long ago, after forty days and forty nights of rain caused the waters to cover the earth and after the waters receded and the mountains could again be seen, Giong, great-grandson of the Spirit of Time, soared above the earth in a kite. From the kite he could see the coast and the plains and the mountains, and all the people begged him for land. To the Khmer and to the Lao, Giong granted the valley of the great river. To the Viets he gave the coastal plain. But the Mountaineers, they did not plead. They did not even listen because they were busy eating sugarcane." Y Ksar laughed, rolled back and stomped his enormous right foot. "Ha! Niece and nephew, we mountain people never knew which land was ours so we have roamed here and there and scattered into a hundred tribes and settled by a source of clear water. And now you shall be Mountaineers with us. We shall call you Y Nang and H Yani. You are my grandchildren. My children, as your father is my brother."

After he had eaten, Y Ksar lit his pipe. Mayana went with Sraang and other women to the village watering spot. Draam Chung returned to work on his motorcycle. Only Y Bhur, Chhuon and Samnang remained about the jar with the old man.

"Your trip was good?" Y Ksar asked Chhuon as Chhuon continued to suck on the straw. If a man could be from two different milieus simultaneously, Y Ksar was such a man. Long ago he had filed his upper teeth to nubs and painted the lowers with ebon lacquer. His hair, what was left, was pulled tight to his head and tied in a chignon, his earlobes held fat ivory plugs. His clothing was an ornate length of cloth wrapped between his legs and about his waist. Had time run back a thousand years and dropped him in the mountains of the Srepok Forest, the inhabitants would have welcomed him as a contemporary. Yet, if one could see within his mind, Y Ksar was a tenth- and nineteenth- and twentieth-century man. Very early in his life he had become the village blacksmith, forging swords and lances, bushhooks and hoes, from imported iron ingots. In 1926 his older brother had been ordered by French colonial authorities to report for militia duty. In his stead he had sent Y Ksar. For fifteen years, Y Ksar assisted in the "pacification" of the Srepok region. He learned to handle Western weapons, to dress in Western dress, to use the colonial monetary system. For fifteen years Y Ksar traveled—from Ban Me Thuot to Stung Treng, from Kontum to Phnom Penh. He learned to speak French, Khmer, Viet Namese, Bahnar and Rhade. For fifteen years he was away from his village and people. Then, in 1942, he became canton chief, the highest governmental post allowed to one of a minority race. In 1947 he was appointed a member of the district council of the French colonial government. After the devastation caused by Viet Minh and French conscription and by cholera, in the early 1950s, Y Ksar quit his post and led many villagers on an escape march to a hidden valley where they remained until 1954. Then, with the help of the Mountaineer movement, even though all major political powers ignored it, Y Ksar, his sect and the people of Plei Srepok attempted to establish an autonomous region.

"We were stopped by a North Viet Namese patrol very near here," Chhuon said, breaking from the jar, indicating to a house girl that he wished the jar to be measured.

"Yes," Y Ksar said. "We're used to them now. They camp in the Cloud Forest, where the mist and drizzle never stop, where the Spirits live. The yuons force us to sell them rice, which is why we buy rice." He laughed. "No rice, no rice beer. Ah, how well now they pay. At one time they simply took it."

Chhuon glanced at his old friend. He was not sure how to respond. He was not sure if Y Ksar was being shrewd, knew the riels were counterfeit, but was not letting on, or if he truly did not know. He decided not to confront the old man. Instead, he imagined himself reporting to Cheam that the soldiers at the NVA roadblock had demanded ten of the twelve bags. He himself would pay for two and all would be accounted for. "Are there many soldiers in the forest?" Chhuon asked.

"Yes," Y Ksar said. "There are many. Thousands, but not all at one time. They flow like the river. Sometimes they pool deep. Always there are puddles. I'm told they've a large hospital in the forest—and a sports arena. Ha! Every evening our scouts see their columns. For a time we coexisted. This changes. The Mountaineers switch allegiance."

"Switch allegiance?!" Chhuon said.

"That's what the village commonhouse is about."

"The brick building?" Samnang asked, astonished.

"Ah-doh-bee," Y Bhur pronounced the Spanish word slowly.

"But from where . . ."

"My Brother." Y Ksar laughed. His old eyes were bright, his back straight. "We have a brick press from my sons in the Jarai village at Duc Co. American Special Forces gave them the press and taught them to make granaries. Our grain's better stored in the *xum*, but look what we've done. Now when we have a large sacrifice the whole village can sit in the courtyard. Or inside."

"From the Americans?" Chhuon asked.

"Yes. And we've brought our children to them. Draam Wah was very sick and the shaman said he might die even though Ama Wah sacrificed all his chickens and his pigs and two buffalo. Y Ko heard of it and directed Ama Wah to bring the boy to the Duc Co Special Forces camp. I wasn't there but I was told the phalang medic wasn't concerned Wah was not from his village. He treated Wah. Wah is better. They treat us like people, not like dogs as yuons and Khmers. They treat my people like you treat my people." *Phalang* was Khmer for "white foreigner."

"And the yuons?" Chhuon protested. "They must . . ."

"We've carried their supplies for ten years," Y Ksar said. "We've fed them. Now we tell them, 'no more.' Are we beasts of burden? They steal my pigs. For them three of my sons have been guides across the border. All are dead. We were approached by a Jarai man from Duc Co. 'The Americans want to hire you.' The Oppressed Races Front agreed. Seventeen of my people are with CIDG [Civilian Irregular Defense Group].

"This is our land," Y Ksar continued. "We've told the yuons

no more will we be a part of their war. Once we saw the Communist soldiers as allies. Then we see they think this is their land. This is Mountaineer land. Giong granted it so. We don't want Sihanouk's soldiers; we don't want Viet Namese. I've sent them all word: Stay away! Get away! Ha! The Americans pay better too."

"You are very wise," Chhuon said to Y Ksar. The rice beer was making his heart beat in his head. "Anyone who harms you, who harms your crops, your people or your belongings, is your enemy. It makes no difference if they're Viet Minh, North Viet Namese, South Viet Namese, American or even Khmer."

"Especially Khmer." Y Ksar laughed. "Understand, the North Viet Namese threaten us, 'Be on our side.' Sihanouk threatens us, 'Be on my side.' Side? This is our land. They want us to be their slaves. At least when the French were here, we were autonomous. Now everybody's a liberation armed force. Liberation for whom? To me they're slave masters."

"They're evil." Chhuon was drunk. "There's nothing good in them. Not a single organ."

Y Bhur drank three measures of numpai and passed the straw to Samnang who immediately let the straw drain and had to work to get the fluid back up.

"Here we are," Chhuon continued. "Khmer and Jarai, part of Cambodia, but often our children go undernourished, our debt grows. The elite in Phnom Penh grow fortunes in paddies of corruption. Our sweat, our blood, are their fertilizer. North Viet Namese tax you. Viet Minh tax us."

"Not just tax," Y Ksar said. "Attack. And across the border South Viet Namese troops attack Jarai saying they help the enemy. American reconnaissance teams ambush us. Death to them all! A typhoon has swooped down upon the mountains. In one lifetime we have moved from separate villages that have never known outside control, never a mountain kingdom, to villages everyone from the outside wants to control. Now in FULRO we're as the fibers which make a single tree. We must have autonomy. Freedoms we knew in isolation are gone. To be free in a forest of foreign armies, we must be strong.

"My Brother," Y Ksar went on, "here we want what all Khmers have. We want our schools to be the same system as the rest of the country. Not frontier schools. We want the rights of citizenship; passports if we want. We want the province officials to be Mountaineers, not Khmers. We want our defense forces to be recognized as semiautonomous. We'll support Phnom Penh if they supply us. Let us keep foreign armies off this land.

We want to be able to trade with merchants from Lomphat and Stung Treng and Pleiku because that will bring us a better life.

"Royal troops are the same as yuons. NVA attack one village, Sihanouk another. They want nothing but to slaughter us. But we will grow back ten times as strong."

While Y Ksar gave an embellished account of the government attack to rid the basalt plateau of Mountaineers, Samnang worked to raise the rice beer. Finally he swallowed a large mouthful. He forced back the impulse to vomit and held his breath as he heard his father say, "Evil. They'll be destroyed. They must be destroyed." In his entire life Samnang had never heard his father say anything so blasphemous.

"Our soldiers protect us," Y Ksar said. He too was feeling the numpai. "Americans make fools of the yuons." The old warrior laughed loudly. "They send SOG teams. Ha! The yuons think they're safe in Cambodia. They say, 'International law will protect us.' Ha! Jarai and American teams ambush the yuons. Ha! International law! This is a Mountaineer nation. Umph! What international law protects us? Not a single nation recognizes us. Upon ourselves only can we rely."

"That's best," Chhuon said emotionally. "The best way for a man, a family, a village, a nation. Self-reliant. Anyone who harms you or your village is evil. How can anyone ever forget what Royal troops have done? For all eternity our blood will call for revenge. Blood for blood."

"To forgive them," Y Bhur piped up, "would be a sign of weakness."

"It's better to ignore the fact they're human," Chhuon said. "To act the way they have acted is to renounce their humanity."

Samnang passed the straw to Y Ksar. Never before had he drunk alcohol. Never had he seen his father more than sip from the jar. Much later he would become very cruel to anyone caught drinking alcohol and he would never again drink himself. But he also would never forget Y Ksar's tale of how Royal troops and yuons treated and slaughtered Mountaineers. And he would never forget his father's words.

Late that afternoon, with the truck unloaded, Chhuon prepared to leave Plei Srepok, alone, for a trip halfway down the mountain, back toward Lomphat. From a small Rhade village sawmill he would buy a truckload of rough-sawn teak blocks which would eventually be made into either busts of Norodom Sihanouk or statuettes of Buddha.

It's quarter to five, Chhuon thought as he checked the truck's tires. I can be to Buon O Sieng by five-thirty, loaded by six.

Then back here by six-thirty, no, quarter to seven. . . . That's too late. I must be there by five-fifteen, leave by five-forty. Then I can be here to pick up Kdeb and Yani by six-fifteen. We'll leave by six-thirty. I must drive quickly if we're to reach home before dark. . . . The yuons will have a roadblock. Maybe they won't keep me long. The Royal troops will have pulled back and probably be asleep. Stress is bad for children. Another roadblock and Yani'll become ill. Y Ksar's wise. I'll leave them here, then drive back all the way on 19.

"Children," Chhuon called.

"Yes Father," they both answered.

"You must be ready when I return."

"Yes Papa."

"And . . . and . . ." Chhuon reached out and pulled his offspring to him. He hugged Mayana and then Samnang. He held his boy at arm's length and said, "Take care and watch over Yani. Never forget our family legacy or the Path of the Elders. Remember our family, our village and our people." Chhuon untied the yellow-checked krama from about his waist and pushed it into Samnang's hands. "If anything should happen to me . . . remember how you want to go to school in Stung Treng. Become all you're capable of becoming. Whatever happens—*do not cry.*"

Y Bhur pulled Samnang back under the longhouse. The sun had begun its descent yet cloud-filtered sunlight still streamed in from the southwest and filled the canyon. The air was heavy with the smell of cinnamon and pig shit.

"No," Y Bhur said. At twelve years old he was only one year Samnang's senior but he was both large for his age and the product of a culture where boys take over men's duties earlier than in Khmer society. "That's backwards. Let's retie it."

Samnang put his crossbow on the ground and unwound the long strip of cloth. Earlier he had removed his sandals and clothes and had tied the loincloth as he thought it should be tied. As he had emerged from beneath the house the cloth had begun to unwind.

"Between your thighs like . . . yes, that's right." Y Bhur tugged at the cloth in back. "Around you it goes three times." He chuckled. He made sure it was tied properly before they emerged again to where Mayana sat with Sraang. Each girl had a quiver of arrows and a bushhook, a short-bladed scythe with a three-foot bamboo handle.

"Ha," Y Bhur laughed good-heartedly. "You almost look Jarai—but you're too thin."

Samnang hefted the crossbow and smiled back. He said nothing. He felt strange and exposed in the tribal dress and he felt uncomfortable before Y Bhur's sister, Sraang. Sraang was as tall as he. Her black hair was combed straight and it caught the southwest sun and glistened. She had adorned herself with additional bracelets and a bead necklace which lay at the top of her breasts, and Samnang wondered if she had added the ornaments for him.

Mayana remained in Khmer dress. She tugged at her brother's arm and said, "We have to be here when Papa comes."

"Don't worry," Samnang reassured her. He drew himself up to full height and puffed out his chest. "We'll return from our expedition long before Father does."

At that the small force set out. They crossed through Jaang's garden and through the courtyard of the adobe commonhouse to the village watering spot which was a small natural pool at the base of the canyon-terminus cliff. There, long ago, Jarai women had pounded thick bamboo tubes into the cliff at head height. The natural hydrostatic pressure within the mountain released into the tubes. Instead of water trickling down the rocks or bubbling up from a spring below the pool, a shower flowed continuously from the bamboo.

Playfully Y Bhur led his patrol through the water, across the shallow ford and up the east slope to a small plateau. Older, sweat-shiny women bent over dry-rice stubble, their bodies and hand scythes swinging monotonously. Y Bhur gazed upon the women with an air of disdain. To him their sweat was a totally undignified condition, at least for a Jarai man. Samnang looked at the field. "One moment, Brother," he said to Y Bhur. He walked into the field, knelt. The stubble felt sharp against his bare feet, feet not unaccustomed to going without shoes but not peasant feet used to such rough walking. He inspected several uncut rice stalks. "With more nitrogen," he said authoritatively, "the stalks would be stronger and the grain fuller."

"Ha," Y Bhur laughed, and smiled in his sincere yet jocular, hillbilly manner. "Just like your father."

They continued their climb up a narrow path to a second plateau where village buffalo and cattle were grazing. Y Bhur led, followed by Samnang, Sraang and Mayana. "When we return," Sraang said, "we must herd the animals back to their pens."

"Can't they stay here?" Yani asked.

"Oh no," Y Bhur answered for his sister. "If we leave them their smell will attract the tiger."

"Or the yuons?!" Samnang said it softly, hesitantly, both as a statement and as a question. They continued to climb, now into the forest, along a steep trail. Y Bhur halted on a false peak. The trail ended. He looked into the forest then back down the trail. The vegetation was thick. Through breaks he could see the roofs of the longhouses below. Samnang was thirty feet back. He had stopped to give his hand to Sraang who feigned finding one steep rock difficult to negotiate in her long skirt. Yani was another twenty feet below, spunkily trying to keep up, afraid of being alone in this unknown forest yet telling herself, Afraid of nothing.

"Here we must stay close," Y Bhur said as the column closed. "We should have a chicken to sacrifice to the Spirit of the Forest." He spoke solemnly. "Here the Cloud Forest begins. Here the Spirits live."

"Is it here where the yuons camp?" Samnang asked quietly.

"Yes," Y Bhur said. "But the Cloud Forest is vast. They camp at the Canyon of the Dead Teak, which is half a day's walk. We'll walk the ridge and I'll show you where to find small game. Now that you're Jarai, you must be a good hunter."

Again they set out. Below them the longhouses fell to shadow but on the west slope of the east ridge, light remained. Above them, the mountain peak alone was shrouded in mist. Y Bhur led them deeper and deeper into the Cloud Forest. As they walked Samnang first pretended he was hunting roebucks, then tigers. Then he imagined he was leading Sraang to a beautiful valley which was theirs. Finally, as they entered the lower mist, he saw himself as a soldier out to kill the hated yuons or the corrupt Royal troops. For all eternity, he thought, our blood will call for revenge.

"ssshh." Y Bhur held up his hand. He stopped. Ahead there was a clearing. He crouched. Froze. His eyes did not blink, did not for an instant leave the scene before him.

Almost by instinct the other children also stuck fast in their tracks. Slowly, ever so slowly, eyes still fixed, Y Bhur backed to Samnang. Samnang said nothing, whispered nothing. Without moving his head he scanned the vegetation about the small clearing, about his own position. Sraang silently crept up behind him. Two uniformed soldiers were setting up aiming stakes before a metal tube. They made little effort to be quiet. Mayana, immobilized with fear, remained fifteen feet back. She had not, could not, see the clearing but was certain they had come upon a tiger. Her face puckered, squinched. Her eyes shut tight. Inside she whispered a prayer to the Blessed One. Then Sraang tapped her hand. Mayana's eyes opened wide. She was about to speak but Sraang's look strangled her as effectively as if someone had tightened a noose about her neck.

Sraang tapped lightly and pointed to the quiver of arrows Yani carried for Y Bhur. Yani blinked. The arrows and Sraang were gone. She blinked again and the Jarai girl was leading her silently back toward the village.

Quietly, ever so quietly, the boys settled back and watched as the soldiers and their porters set up a radio and a landline telephone. Y Bhur recognized the tube but he did not know its name. He counted the soldiers—only four—and the porters, who seemed to number at least eight. He counted the rounds of ammunition as best he could but he lost count at forty-five. He looked for other weapons but saw only one rifle and one pistol.

Samnang squatted just behind his friend. He did not count. At first he was afraid to notice anything, but the longer they sat the more comfortable he was watching the soldiers and the more secure he felt they could not see him. He noticed other details. The uniformed men spoke Viet Namese. The coolies, the few who spoke, spoke an unfamiliar mountain dialect. He was sure it was not a language of any of the tribes of the Srepok Forest. Perhaps, he thought, they are Lao. Perhaps . . . His thoughts wandered. One moment he imagined he was watching fish in a basin; the next he looked at the sky and thought, Even if we leave now, it will be dark before we reach the village. If I'm not there when Papa returns, I'll disappoint him. I always disappoint him.

Y Bhur cocked his crossbow. He glanced at his lowland brother. Suddenly Samnang's arms shook. His chest tightened, his legs felt leaden. Y Bhur's right hand slipped a second arrow from Samnang's quiver. He turned it up in his hand indicating they should fire, reload and fire again. Samnang, as if the fibers and fragments of this day had finally spun into a single strand, understood. He cocked his crossbow. Y Bhur raised his weapon, aimed. Samnang raised up the stock. The bow ends caught in branches to his sides. His arms shook. He forced the stock up. It leveled and the man with the pistol was small at the tip of the arrow. He shut his eyes, heard the cord of Y Bhur's bow spank forward. He squeezed. He fumbled for the second arrow. Rifle shots cracked.

The village and canyon were dark with shadow but overhead the clouds were still gray. Y Ksar pulled his blanket more tightly about his neck and shoulders, sucked harder on his bent pipe. Where are the children? he thought. Chhuon will be here soon. He looked at the sky. A lone blackbird swooped down from the cliff, effortlessly glided the length of the village street, winged over, flapped and glided back to alight on the roof of Y

Ksar's longhouse. The bird cawed loudly once. Then it seemed
to jump from the roof and slide through the air to the roof of
the new commonhouse. Then it disappeared. Y Ksar shook his
head. Everything which blooms . . . his thoughts began, but
before they could be completed they were halted by Sraang's
and Mayana's shouting from the cattle pasture.

The girls were breathless as they ran to the courtyard. Y
Ksar, Jaang, Chung, Mul and two dozen villagers gathered about
them.

"Breathe deep," Y Ksar said. "Then your words will come."

"There are soldiers . . ." Sraang gasped in Jarai.

"A tiger . . ." Mayana exhaled in Khmer. She did not understand Sraang's words.

"No . . . in the Cloud . . . Forest . . ."

"Stop. Breathe deep," Y Ksar repeated.

Chung put his blanket over his daughter's shoulders. "Women
should winnow rice," he said angrily in Jarai, "not meander in
the woods."

"Y Bhur . . ." Sraang began again. "Y Bhur and Samnang . . .
There are many soldiers just over the ridge. They stayed to see
while we came to warn . . ."

"What is this of a tiger?" Y Ksar said in Khmer to Mayana.

"We're running from a tiger," the little girl said.

"No," Sraang interrupted. "Not tiger. Soldiers."

"I thought . . ."

"Okay," Y Ksar said. He questioned Sraang but she knew few
details.

"I'm certain they were yuon," Sraang said.

"Perhaps," Y Ksar said. There were now seven young men
listening, watching, as Y Ksar transformed from village old
man to village chief, from Iron Age Jarai to modern tactical
leader. "Perhaps," Y Ksar repeated. "Warn the children," he
said to his wife. "Y Tang, Y Tung, follow the path into the
forest. Djhang, ride to Plei Pang and prepare them to reinforce
us or to defend themselves. K Drai, ride to the airfield at
Andaung Pech. Tell them we're being attacked. If they aid us
we'll know the attackers are yuons. If not, perhaps the attack
comes from Royal Khmer."

Immediately the two soldiers jumped on their Hondas and
sped from the village. Others ran from house to house rousing
the people. Still others sounded a village-specific alarm pattern
on the gongs—an eerie dirge which to the uninitiated could
mean the sacrifice of a pig or the announcement of some social
event but to the people of Plei Srepok meant return from the
woods and fields immediately.

For a quarter of an hour men, women and children scurried—men with rifles to defensive positions along the village stockade, women to the communal center to prepare a secondary defense, and children into concealed holes beneath granaries or chicken coops. Then all was silent.

Before the first mortar rounds exploded the early evening was quiet and peaceful. Chhuon was feeling particularly good. On the trip from Plei Srepok to the sawmill at Buon O Sieng, he had made excellent time. Two FULRO troops on gray Hondas had escorted him to the edge of the Cloud Forest where he was met by an NVA roadblock. But the Viet Namese did not search him, did not even slow him but waved him on as if they knew his truck was empty and he in a hurry. He had kissed his Buddha statuette seven times and said a prayer of thanks. Then at Buon O Sieng he again had luck. The men at the mill wanted to leave quickly to check their fish traps and thus loaded the truck without the usual formalities or haggling, and by five-thirty Chhuon was again on the road to Plei Srepok. With luck, he thought, I will be at the village gate by only a few minutes past six.

Chhuon hummed a tune as the small truck struggled to raise the heavy load of fresh-cut teak up the mountain road. He hummed as he laid out in his mind consecutive images of the remainder of his journey. Certainly another roadblock. He checked the roll of counterfeit riels in his pocket. And he told himself to make it appear painful to part with the money. Then he saw the soldier inspecting the top fifty-riel note and fear flashed through him. He stopped the truck. From beneath the seat he removed an envelope and from it took a single good bill. Chhuon rehid the envelope, wrapped the good note around the wad of counterfeits, then drove on thinking, humming, seeing himself with Kdeb and Yani speeding from the high plateau, crossing the bridge to Phum Sath Din.

Chhuon reached into his shirt and grasped his statuette of Buddha. He lifted it to his lips, kissed it seven times. The higher onto the mountain he drove the lighter the cloud cover seemed, yet with the setting sun the light lessened. The vibration of the small truck seemed constant. The road seemed to stretch on forever yet not move at all. For one moment he felt as if physical movement were an illusion, as if he, everything, were standing perfectly still. He tried to make the truck go faster.

He checked his watch. It was only three minutes since the last time he'd checked yet he felt he had been driving for an hour. He was still a few kilometers from the turnoff to Plei Srepok.

The road dropped into a shallow valley, then rose. As he crested the second knoll a squad of soldiers blocked the road.

"Hello," Chhuon called out. He stuck his head and left arm out the window and waved. "Hello. May I pass. I have . . ."

"Halt!" a soldier yelled. He raised his rifle and aimed through the windshield. Other rifle bolts snapped, pointed at him from behind log fighting positions beside the road.

From the third round, Y Ksar knew the mortar barrage would not, was not meant to, destroy the village. The first round impacted just beyond the village gate. The second, nearly a full minute later, also exploded outside the village. The third landed in the cornfields west of the road. Plei Srepok had no artillery to answer the attack. KkkaRrump! KkkaRrump! Back and forth across the canyon just beyond the bamboo stockade.

He stood before his house and listened carefully. The sky was late-evening dark. His scouts had not returned. From his messengers no word, no signal. The village warriors, with an assortment of rifles and two machine guns, had deployed along the front stockade and the treeline above the dry-rice fields on the slope of the east ridge. Nothing had been heard from Y Bhur and Samnang. More explosions jarred the fields before the gate. The mortars were firing from at least two positions, of that Y Ksar was certain. Who was firing, of that he was not sure.

Flash!KkkaRrUMP! A shout. One, two, three rounds landed on the stockade, blowing bamboo slivers, earth and blood into the mango orchard and the first line of longhouses. Then the barrage ceased. Y Ksar called for a runner. ". . . to each position," he instructed the young man. "We're no match for their arms. Tell all not to fire until they're on top of us." Now, he thought, the assault will begin. Now we'll know.

For a time nothing happened. Then from the east ridge small-arms fire erupted. Several short bursts. Then several more. A pause. More firing. Then from the west ridge. Repeat burst. From the high cliff. Longer bursts. Consistent, methodical, lower and lower as the cordon tightened on all sides. In it all Y Ksar could hear the buffalo and cattle lowing, falling. He could see muzzle flashes and tracers, green light balls seemingly floating down from the blackness, stinging the periphery of the village, carefully avoiding firing into the people. Closing down. Not yet presenting a target he wanted his soldiers to engage. A village defender fired off a single round. Six weapons fired onto the muzzle flash. Two RPG, rocket-propelled grenade, rounds exploded near the village well. The U-shaped cordon tightened but the enemy stayed unseen in the trees on the slopes above the village.

On the road to the village there was great clatter. The road's sealed, Y Ksar thought. We're trapped. He saw headlights. They're good, he thought. They cannot be Royal troops. Let them get closer before we fight. A single jeep drove up, stopped fifty meters before the gate. Oh, for a few rockets, he thought.

Mayana and Sraang had come from their concealed hole near the well. Sraang's left arm was badly scraped and bleeding. Before Y Ksar could tell them to go back, a powerful spotlight mounted on the jeep illuminated the village road all the way to the adobe building.

"PEOPLE OF PLEI SREPOK," an announcement in Jarai blasted from bullhorns beyond the jeep. "WE MEAN YOU NO HARM. ALL MEN, WOMEN AND CHILDREN, ASSEMBLE IN THE COURTYARD BEFORE THE COMMONHOUSE. STACK ALL WEAPONS ON THE ROAD BEFORE THE LONGHOUSE OF Y KSAR. NO ONE WILL BE HURT."

The light went out. "Stay where you are," Chung, Y Ksar's son, shouted. A few women jumped from their secondary fighting positions within the village and advanced to reinforce the stockade.

Again the bullhorn blasted, repeating the demand to assemble and the promise that no one would be hurt. No one moved. Y Ksar felt satisfied at their performance. The spotlight again came on. There was the clatter of tank treads in the blackness beyond the jeep. A second light crossed the first and its beam flooded the tiers of longhouses.

"WE WANT ONE MAN. ONE MAN WHO HAS COMMITTED THE MOST GRIEVOUS CRIMES AGAINST HIS OWN PEO-PLE. ONE INGRATE WHO HAS INSULTED US. YOU SHALL BE THE JUDGES. TRY Y KSAR BEFORE YOUR VILLAGE COUNCIL. TRY Y KSAR WHO SENDS BOYS INTO THE FOR-EST TO HUNT US DOWN. GRANT HIM A FAIR TRIAL AND NO ONE WILL BE HURT. WE WILL LEAVE YOU IN PEACE."

Again the lights went out. The night was very black. "What boys?" The shout, a woman's voice, came from the mango grove.

"Quiet," Chung ordered.

"What boys?" the woman called out again. It was Draam Mul, wife of Chung, mother of Y Bhur and Sraang.

Lights again. Three now. "Tell them to shoot the lights out," Chung whispered to his father, but as he spoke a man, trussed at the elbows, shackled at the ankles, was thrust before each light.

"Y TUNG IS DEAD. HE DIED LIKE A COWARD ABANDON-ING HIS COMRADES, Y BHUR, Y NANG, Y TANG. WE WILL EXCHANGE THESE BOYS FOR Y KSAR."

"Release them. Withdraw your troops, and I will come forward," Y Ksar shouted in Viet Namese. He laughed, chuckled. Beneath his breath he cursed the yuon dogs.

Trussed before the jeep light, a white bandage wrapped about his left thigh, Y Bhur stood straight. Before one tank light Samnang cowered; before the other Y Tang's head dropped stiffly to one side, the result of muscle spasms from being beaten.

The lights went off. There was no answer. Draam Mul began to wail. Someone began to play the gongs. The jeep light flicked on. Eight soldiers advanced behind the vehicle. Behind them the sound of two hundred soldiers moving filled the canyon. "Y KSAR, WE SHALL SEND IN A DELEGATION WITH Y NANG. TELL ALL YOUR PEOPLE TO STACK THEIR WEAPONS AND ASSEMBLE IN THE COURTYARD."

"Uncle! Uncle!" Mayana reached for the elder. "Don't! Don't go."

"It's all right, Daughter," the old man said in Khmer. "Everything which blooms, perishes. The rice withers. The mango falls."

Y Ksar stepped into the center of the road, faced the brilliance of the lightbeam.

"Don't let them in," Chung ordered from the shadow of a pigsty. "Stay put." One villager rose. Then another. The dignity of Y Ksar walking into the lightbeam mesmerized them. Soon many villagers were milling about at the edge of the lighted swath behind Y Ksar.

"Let the boys go." Y Ksar smiled at captors unseen behind the light. Both tanks closed upon the village, clicked on their lights.

"TELL YOUR PEOPLE TO ASSEMBLE TO TRY YOU OR THE BOYS WILL BE SHOT! NOW!"

A few of the milling people moved toward the courtyard. "Stop!" Chung commanded.

Immediately a rifle cracked. In the light before one tank Y Tang's head jerked. His body collapsed. Again the gongs. More women wailed. A defender sprung from his trench before the tank, threw his rifle down, ran to his brother's body. Of all days for the crow to land on my house, Y Ksar thought.

"WE WILL KILL THESE TWO IF EVERYONE DOES NOT ASSEMBLE IMMEDIATELY. DRAAM CHUNG, DRAAM MUL, IS THAT WHAT YOU WISH FOR YOUR SON? RAM SU, ELDER OF THE EBING CLAN, WILL YOU STAND BY AS CHUNG ORDERS HIS OWN SON'S DEATH AND THE DEATH OF THE VILLAGE MUTE, Y NANG? NAY SAH, ELDER OF THE H'MAT

CLAN, ARE YOU TO BE HELD RESPONSIBLE FOR THESE DEATHS CAUSED BY Y KSAR? STACK ARMS. ASSEMBLE."

The tank light went out. Where Y Tang had stood there was the sound of scuffling. Naming the village elders had great effect on their descendants. The milling crowd drifted toward the courtyard. Y Ksar could not find it in himself to order the defenders to hold the line when indeed it seemed the NVA wanted only to punish him. One by one the defenders rose. Some abandoned their weapons, others carried theirs to the road before Y Ksar's longhouse and dropped them. On the east ridge a resister was shot. The incident was radioed to the men at the jeep and the details were broadcast into the village. From houses, holes, trees, fields, the villagers converged on the courtyard. Only Y Ksar stood his ground at the entrance to Plei Srepok.

Chhuon brought the truck forward a few more meters. Then he stopped. Beyond the blockage, stretching for several hundred meters, he saw milling groups of soldiers, jeeps, trucks, a tank. A whole army seemed to be before him. He opened the door and stood with his hands up. With a big smile he said in Viet Namese, "I go Jarai village. Get son. Get daughter. Go home."

"No go," the soldier answered in Khmer. "No village here."

"My son and daughter are there," Chhuon said in lyrical Khmer. "They're there waiting for me to get this wood for statues of Buddha. We live . . ."

"No go," the soldier said again. He did not smile. "Go back," he said. "No village here."

"Oh yes," Chhuon said. He reached slowly into his pocket and pulled out the wad of riel notes. Before his face he peeled off ten bills. "Five hundred," he said in Viet Namese. "Must go get children at Plei Srepok."

"No go," the soldier shot back.

Chhuon peeled off ten more bills. "One thousand," he said nervously. He held out the whole wad in his left hand, waved his right as if to block the barrel of the soldier's weapon. "More hidden," he said frantically. "Much more. Rice too."

"Go back," the soldier ordered. "No money."

"Plei Srepok," Chhuon pleaded.

"Plei Srepok, *chiet*! Dead!" The soldier swept his hand down as if it were an airplane diving. "Boom! Boom! Phalang!"

"No. *No!*"

"Go back." He dove his hand again. "More boom!" Then he raised his rifle and aimed it at Chhuon.

Chhuon dropped his hands. He felt the blood drain from his face. His breath seeped out but did not return. He shook his head, turned to the truck. His knees became rigid. He glanced at the soldier. Tears welled in his eyes. He climbed in, started the truck, turned it around. How could he go? How could he stay?

Again there was no motion. His cheeks, chin and neck were wet. He drove, lost in darkness, confusion, despair. "Yani," he whimpered. "Kdeb," he cried. "I've abandoned them! Kdeb! My Kdeb. My Kdeb."

In the courtyard the villagers were ordered to arrange themselves not by clan but by age and gender. The first seven careless rows facing the front of the adobe edifice were comprised of the village children, boys to the right, girls to the left. Behind the girls were the mothers with infants, behind the boys, young men. In the last rows, according to the new order, stood the elders. Surrounding the assembly was an entire platoon of formally uniformed NVA soldiers, square belt buckles with stars, heavily armed. Other soldiers were going through the longhouses, flushing out the stragglers, herding them into the cluster.

To one side of the adobe the Viet Namese had stoked, fed and bellowed the fire of the village forge. A jeep had been positioned behind the villagers, its light switched to flood. The entire arena was illuminated, flat and pale. At the adobe entrance there was a small platform. To one side Y Bhur and Samnang were tied, still trussed and shackled, to stakes. A very large Mountaineer had been directing the villagers, chatting, forcing many to drink from the jars he had had placed like a low fence on the platform before him. Whispers abounded. "It's Bok Roh, the Giant." Fear spread at the repetition of his name. He was infamous for his cruelty. Bok Roh lectured them on the evils of alcohol as he forced the elders to drink more and more. He harangued the elders for their lack of courtesy and loyalty. Between each verbal explosion he consulted with a uniformed North Viet Namese political officer and a black-clad Khmer.

At the stakes a soldier cuffed Y Bhur on the jaw. "Keep your head up," he scolded as if disciplining a naughty child. Samnang watched. He had been playing mute ever since capture, acting out of terror the soldiers would discover he was Khmer and not Jarai. The soldier who had hit Y Bhur cocked his hand before Samnang. The frail boy trembled, bewildered, shrank back against the stake. "He's a mute. An idiot," Y Bhur said in Jarai. The soldier didn't understand. The villagers did.

"Y Ksar with the Large Foot . . ." Bok Roh shouted. A hush fell over the assemblage. The elder village chief had not been seen since guards had grabbed him by the village gate. Sraang and Mayana, seated on the ground before Draam Mul, both were crying softly. *"Silence!"* Bok Roh bellowed, his immense voice echoing off the cliff, reverberating down the canyon. "Y Ksar," the giant seethed angrily, "you are accused of collaborating with the enemies of the people. You have, in your life, served the French against your own people, and now you conspire with imperialist running dogs and bring a phalang invasion deep into the land of your people. You have aligned yourself with renegade Mountaineers. And"—Bok Roh turned toward the staked boys and laughed a guttural chilling disgusted laugh— "you have sent these ants, a boy and a mute, to fire arrows through our radios. *Bad elements must* be punished. Thoughts which veer from the true course of liberation for all oppressed peoples must be exorcised. Come forth. Make your plea."

At that moment, from inside the adobe, four soldiers carried out a large wooden X-frame. To it was tied a naked, bruised old man. Immediately a murmur rose from the audience. Immediately voices of protest rose.

"Silence!" Bok Roh's voice exploded louder than artillery. Even the NVA soldiers jumped back, glanced furtively at one another.

"Is this building"—Bok Roh, standing before Y Ksar, whipped his large arms at the adobe—"not proof of collusion with the running dogs who have invaded our land? Have you"—Bok's angry voice spit from his hate-contorted mouth—"have you not even this very day, conducted illicit business with a lackey of Pech Lim Song? A lackey liquidated by the people."

"No!" Samnang screamed in Khmer. He strained his small wiry body against the wires and the stake. "No! No, my father ... Papa ... Papa ..." He dropped his head. His body wilted.

"Well ..." Bok Roh smiled delightedly. He conferred with the NVA officer and the black-clad Khmer. Then, "So, Y Nang, you are not mute."

"Stop it!" Now Chung stood. Another Jarai man leaped up, jumped forward.

Two guards fired. Five AK rounds slammed into the second man, twisted him, threw him.

"Bring him here!" Bok pointed at Chung. He conferred again with the officer. "Who is this?" Two armed guards held Chung by the hair, one held a bayonet at his back. Chung's eyes reached his father's. "You don't need to tell me. I know. Our intelligence on this village is perfect ... Draam Chung." Bok Roh gestured with his head. The soldiers pushed Chung into the adobe with the tips of their bayonets while they held him back by the hair so he was forced to walk with his groin thrust forward, his back arched. From the dark adobe interior, kicks were heard.

"Y Ksar with the Large Foot," Bok Roh mocked, "why," he shouted in Y Ksar's face, "are you at war with us?"

"We shall be at war with anyone who defiles our land," Y Ksar said. His voice was soft. Gentle.

"And you and all your people will meet death," Bok Roh hissed.

"I am accustomed to death," Y Ksar said. He addressed the village. "We are not frightened by death of the body. We are men of dignity."

"You are an enemy of the people. Plei Srepok must stop relying on old organizations." Bok Roh turned to the villagers. "You must move forward within the new framework. You shall convict this man. And"—again four soldiers brought out a naked beaten man tied and splayed on a large X—"and this one. Traitors must be denounced. Their heads must be bowed. *Denounce them!* Or . . . everyone will be punished. Who is that crying? Bring her up."

Bok Roh pointed to Sraang. Two soldiers descended upon her. They grabbed her and immediately wired her elbows together. "Silence!" The large man screamed. "Do you hear me? *Silence!*" He grabbed her skirt and ripped it from her. Sraang's cries became shrieks. She tried to collapse to the ground but a soldier behind her lifted her by the wires, cutting her already scraped arm. "*Silence!* You don't hear!" She continued to shriek uncontrollably. "No! You don't want to hear." The big man clamped the sides of her face with his large hands and twisted her head up to look at him. From behind, a soldier placed a chopstick in each ear. Then the soldier behind grabbed her, held her up by the wires and her hair, and the big man before her let her head go. "*For not hearing me,*" Bok Roh screamed. He extended his arms far to his sides, then slapped them toward each other, catching the chopsticks and driving them into Sraang's brain. She fell, withered, twitching, contorting, rasping her head horribly on the ground.

A deluge of cold fear froze the assembled as totally as if they had been physically frozen in ice. From the forge a soldier emerged with a glowing steel machete. "Y Ksar, you have been convicted by your own people." Bok Roh touched the blade ever so lightly to the old man's lower lip. Y Ksar did not flinch, did not move. His skin blistered, burned, stuck to the red metal. "You are sentenced to death by decapitation." Now Bok Roh stood perfectly still as smoke and odor from the blade and Y Ksar's burning flesh rose and spread.

In the frozen scene, Sraang's head still madly raked against the ground. Then, from the row of girls, Mayana stood and as simply as if on a stroll to pick flowers, she walked to Sraang and pulled the sticks from her ears. Sraang collapsed, still. Mayana looked blankly up into the eyes of the giant. He turned his face on her. His mouth opened in tense horror. Mayana's childlike naiveté was destroying Bok Roh's control. From the row of old women in back, Jaang, Y Ksar's wife, rose feebly. From her skirt she raised a .45 caliber pistol, aimed . . .

"Yiii—" Bok Roh swung the machete up—"KA!"—down, cleaving the small girl in two.

Jaang's weapon fired. Immediately she was shot. Her body crumpled as if it were not supported by a skeleton of bone but only by a spirit. Her fired round lodged in the adobe wall.

"Burn the village," the NVA political officer said. He said it matter-of-factly, then turned and spoke to the black-clad man. To Bok Roh the officer said, "Save those boys for me. Kill the rest."

CHAPTER THREE

The brotherhood of suffering is
a bond, power is a drug.
—Theodore H. White,
China After The War

The night was dark. Samnang's lips were cut. Dry. His throat rasped. He coughed dryly. The pain in his arms and shoulders would not subside, would not dull. His hands pulsed numb, tingled on the stretched surface. The soldiers had wired his elbows tightly together before the march from Plei Srepok. In the blackness he could hear voices, mostly Viet Namese, some Khmer. He tried to hear, to concentrate on the voices, to listen so as to forget his lips and throat and arms. He tried to force himself to lie on the ground without moving and listen but each moment he lay still his mind shot to his shoulders, elbows, to the pain, to the terror. He did not yet question why they had taken him, why they had not killed him, what they were going to do with him. The terror was numbing. He shook violently yet was hardly aware of his tremors. He did not realize or understand the magnitude of the scene carved onto his mind.

He moved. The noise of his motion masked the voices and he missed part of what was said. It did not matter. From the Khmer he ascertained the men were bartering over something. The Khmer man spoke with the sarcastic formality of an educated city dweller. Samnang laughed to himself, amused, realizing the Viet Namese soldiers didn't know, couldn't understand, the sarcasm, the antagonism held in the Khmer idioms the man used graciously.

The pain grabbed him, he fidgeted, the noise again blotted out the voices. He took a deep breath, held it, counted to four and let it out.

"Nuoc?" a guard asked him.

He stared into the blackness. There was nothing there. Again the guard asked, *"Nuoc?"*

Samnang cleared his parched throat. He tried to speak but no sound came. He licked his lips. His tongue was dry. He could taste the faint saltiness of blood. The soldier clicked on a flashlight and poked the beam into his eyes. *"Nuoc!"* The light was blinding. The soldier held a canteen cup in the beam. Samnang nodded and the soldier gently allowed him to drink. Then he turned the light off and left.

As his eyes readjusted Samnang looked to see if Y Bhur were near. He could not tell. The Khmer man who had been bartering with the Viet Namese left. From somewhere in the darkness came a staccato female radio voice. He picked out the words "Radio Hanoi." The radio seemed nearby, perhaps less than ten meters. The broadcast was sad, soulful songs. Samnang rolled. He rolled gingerly, afraid of hurting his hands. His hands no longer felt like overfilled balloons. There was no feeling at all. Now his chest screamed. The radio noise was soothing, giving him something on which to focus but his mind couldn't hold it in his body's agitation. He rolled again. Images of the night flashed subliminally in his mind, yet again, in the agitation caused by pain, he couldn't hold a single image, not of Y Ksar, not of Sraang, not of Yani, not of the tremendous conflagration and its sucking wind.

Several Viet Namese soldiers began arguing. He recognized the voice of the political officer, understood a few phrases, did not understand the context of the argument. Then he heard the voice of Bok Roh. Samnang's body went rigid. Urine squirted into the loincloth he still wore. Without emotion the giant told the Viet Namese, in Jarai, he wanted to keep the Jarai and sell the Khmer. Again there was argument in Viet Namese. Samnang tried to pray but his teeth chattered so violently he could not.

The camp was quiet. Not because the soldiers were practicing noise discipline, in the sanctuary area it wasn't necessary, but simply because most were asleep. A rustling noise came from below, approaching. Samnang rolled. A group of men with flashlights came toward him. He could not make out how many or who. When they reached him one guard passed a beam up and down his body and face. Samnang turned away, jammed a heel against the earth, breathed hard. He began to whimper. A guard said something and a second soldier rolled the boy and loosened the wire at his elbows. Immediately relief swept him from head to foot. His shoulders and chest, which were near spasm, relaxed. His hands pulsed, ached. In a moment they felt cold and hot, clammy, partially numb, stiff, flashed hot. After no feeling, the sensation was wonderful, terrible. He did not notice when guards deposited Y Bhur beside him. He slipped into a drowsy haze, not sleep, not consciousness, a protective limbo in which his mind blocked the horror.

Again the Khmer man was talking with the Viet Namese officer. Samnang did not know how long it was from the time the guard had eased the pain by loosening his bonds but the forest was still dark. Perhaps it was minutes, perhaps hours. He didn't think about time. The man was speaking in more pleasant tones and phrases. Or perhaps, Samnang thought, he was still dozing. Dreaming. "Then it is decided," the Khmer man said. "We will have that one also. You'll keep the rice and we'll see that the supplies which have reached Kratie continue unimpeded."

"The other speaks Khmer and Jarai," he thought he heard the Viet Namese political officer say. "I would keep him but just now we're moving too quickly."

"He would never serve you," the Khmer said. "Not after seeing you eliminate his people. You'd have to kill him sooner or later."

"Still," the Viet officer said, "a sly boy like that could be made an asset."

Thus did Cahuom Samnang become a conscript of the Khmer Krahom.

For three nights and three days he marched in file behind a boy younger than he. The column avoided main roads and paths, using animal trails and, in the few populated areas they traversed, the smallest dikes. For three days he was kept trussed. The pain in his arms, shoulders and chest came and went according to the tightness of the bonding wires. The tightness was related to how well he followed orders. When he spoke to Y Bhur who limped behind him his bonds were tightened. When the pain caused him to cry to the boy before him the bonds were tightened again. When he stumbled, walking the hill trails without being able to use his arms to counterbalance his gait, the wires were raised and tightened until his upper arms were drawn together, his elbows crossed, his lower arms and hands flapping behind like dead wings.

They paused often. Each time a guard came, separated him and Y Bhur, and loosened the wires. "Have some tea," the guard would say. "We'll be there shortly. Eat rice. What was your village? Ah! Tell me later. We must move again."

At the next pause the same black-clad guard came and loosened the wires that had been tightened again by his comrades during the move. "I would like to be your friend," the guard said in Khmer. He spoke well, yet in a rural dialect which

Samnang could not place. "I'm Met Hon," the guard said. "You are Met Nang."

"I'm called Cahuom Samnang." Samnang was bewildered, frightened, yet so exhausted, so surrounded by alien behavior, he could barely react beyond numbness.

"No," the guard said. "Met Nang. Comrade Nang. We are all comrades in the Movement. Look about. There is only the Movement. There is no other past."

Samnang looked forward, back, at the resting column. He saw nearly twenty guards, all young boys only slightly older than him. He looked at Hon. He didn't wish to offend him by looking into his eyes but he had to see. Was Hon sincere? "What movement? Where are you taking me?"

"Ah. You'll see, Met Nang," Met Hon said. "Oh, I like that. Nang, 'Lucky'; Comrade Lucky. When a coin falls, you shall always receive the head. There is a place where the rice grows, where you'll learn to live without corruption, where all live in perfect self-reliance. That is the Movement." Hon spoke simply. He neither smiled nor scowled. The words came from him as from a man in total tranquility. "Now, Met Nang, eat the rice the Movement has provided. It will nourish you for the journey ahead."

"Older Brother . . ." Samnang began to address Hon with the formal appellation a young boy uses with an older male friend.

"No." Hon snapped harshly. "Not 'Older Brother.' 'Met.' 'Comrade.' No 'Older Brother,' 'Little Sister' anymore. 'Met.' Now stand. We must go before an enemy discovers us."

By the third night fatigue had pushed Samnang to a state of apathetic delirium. He barely knew when he was resting, when he was walking. Constantly he heard Met Hon address him in gentle yet unfamiliar terms. He began to think of himself as Met Nang, of Y Bhur as Met Ur, but his thoughts, like the questions where? and why? and the images of Plei Srepok, had not congealed but were like globules of fat floating in a hot chicken broth.

His feet were sore. He'd been barefoot since disrobing beneath Y Ksar's longhouse. Behind him, always, was Y Bhur. They were not allowed to speak, nor was Samnang allowed to speak with the other conscripted boys or with other guards. His confusion increased. He did not, could not, think of Y Bhur except for the clump-drag limping noise made by Met Ur, who was wounded and probably crazy with fever.

Of himself? What? *Thlak tuck chet*. His heart could no longer speak to his mind. His desire to behave, to adhere to the Eightfold Path, to his belief in right thoughts, right mindfulness, right meditation, evaporated and dissipated like the mist following the last monsoon before the dry season.

That night they covered his eyes, packed him in a coffin full of soft dirt so he could not move, and they buried him. His only connection to the outside world was a thin reed through which he had to suck in air to keep from suffocating.

In dark early morning mist and rain Cahuom Chhuon stood on the steps of the decagonal pagoda in Phum Sath Din. It was the one hundredth day since the death of his father, the seventh day since the attack at Plei Srepok. No one had yet risen. Even the monks were asleep. Chhuon let the rain drench him, let it run from his shaved head, stream with the tears from his eyes, dribble diluted salt into and from his mouth. For three days he had wailed like an old woman. For three days he had sat perfectly quiet, perfectly still, breaking neither to eat nor to relieve himself. In the wet darkness he turned, faced north, then west, south and east. Four directions, he thought. Four Noble Truths: hardship and suffering are elements of life; suffering is caused by the passion to possess that which has no permanence; suffering can be defeated by overpowering one's passions; to control one's passions one must strictly follow the Eightfold Path. He repeated to himself the second Truth. He repeated it again and again. He lay the Truth, as if a three-dimensional jigsaw puzzle part, onto the image he held of the events of the past seven days, seventy days, forty-five years. Somehow it should fit, should fall in if turned just so, set at the exact angle which would allow the shape to mesh. He thought of his truck, his most prized possession, and he thought he would never again touch it. His desire to possess, yes, that was where it would fit, to possess goods which have no permanence, yes, not the goods themselves, but the desire for he himself to have them as if he were alone, as individual, apart from all others, yes, his passion for the *glories* Westernization was bestowing upon him, upon Phum Sath Din, upon all Cambodia . . . he wished he could explain it to Cheam . . . here was the pain, the passion which caused the pain . . . which . . . The anguish in his heart welled up in his throat and behind his eyes . . . I have yielded to my passion for worldly goods and for this the spirits have taken Kdeb. Have taken Yani. I am the source . . . Chhuon pulled the statuette from his soiled shirt. He squeezed it. He prayed to the spirit of his father. In midprayer his thought transformed to a prayer of homage to his father's spirit on its hundredth day of liberation from its earthly vessel. Chhuon returned home.

Midday, two days after Chhuon had returned from Plei Srepok without his children, a FULRO messenger had arrived with word of the destruction of the Jarai village. K Drai, the messenger dispatched by Y Ksar to the airfield at Andaung Pech, had returned from the government post without reinforcements. From a position on the canyon's escarpment he had witnessed the ceremonial trial and the slaughter. On foot he had raced through dense forest to a small Mountaineer outpost and from there the commander had sent word of the attack in every direction. Thus had Chhuon and all Phum Sath Din learned of the death of Samnang, Mayana and 317 Jarai villagers, and the conscription of two tribal boys.

When Chhuon returned to the wat he was washed, dressed, composed. Under his left arm he held a white satchel. Behind the pagoda, under the trees by the river, a score of village men milled in groups of two, three or four. Chhuon felt their eyes keep pace with his approach. He bowed his head, climbed the steps and entered the vestibule, removed his sandals, entered the main hall.

For several weeks village women had been preparing for the hundredth-day ceremony for the dead. When word of the children's fate arrived, a rite for their spirits was added. Relatives and neighbors had cooked elaborate meals and now the bowls, dishes and platters covered three long tables. Sweet pungent smells of curried foods mixed with earthy odors of boiled greens and steaming mist from hot soups and rice. The scent of mint garnished the aromas. At the far end of the hall on the altar to Buddha the smoke from a hundred incense sticks rose and mixed with the fragrance of baskets of flowers. Young children darted behind groups of eating, chattering women, playing hide-and-seek and peekaboo with their cousins. The atmosphere was light, happy even in its solemnness, gay, the occasion bringing together nearly the entire village, bringing together an extended loving family in their best and whitest clothing, taking them from fields and the confines of their homes to celebrate the journey of the spirits.

Chhuon approached the altar. To one side Vathana and Samay held their grieving mother. Chhuon knelt before the altar, said a prayer, advanced. He lit several joss sticks and stuck the ends into cans of rice to support them. From the carefully packed satchel he removed two red candles which he lit and placed on the altar so that Samnang's and Mayana's ghosts would be able to find their way home. In his heart he feared their ghosts would be disoriented and bewildered. Any ghost, in its first days, could have trouble adjusting to the state of death, and the

ghost of a child violently killed far from home needed guidance
lest it return to frighten or harm its own family.

Chhuon removed a lacquered wooden box containing the ashes
of his father. Sok joined her husband. She brought a bowl of
fresh fruit and sweet rice cakes. Chhuon eyed her as she arranged the fruit on the altar. He wished with all his heart he
could find comfort in her presence, but he could not. He looked
at Samay who now held Peou in his arms. Then he looked at
Vathana. He could not but believe that they blamed him, as he
did himself, for the death of the children. Sok retreated without
a word.

Chhuon placed his father's ashes on the altar. In this act there
was joy. Though he was distraught over the children he was
proud to be able to provide properly for his father. Then
hopelessness seized him. He would never have the ashes of
Samnang or Mayana. Never be able to place them at the altar
of the village wat. Their spirits would never find peace and the
path to rebirth. Behind him the room had filled.

"It's their strategy," Chhuon heard a male voice. Then another, "Eh? The yuons?" "The Communists," the first answered.
"If they rid the mountains of the tribals they have no opposition." A third voice said authoritatively, "Ten thousand have
been pushed from the land. Tens of thousands killed. They're
marching south. Why'd Chhuon go up there?" The second voice
piped, "It's one thing to kill himself, eh, but his own flesh?!"

Chhuon removed from his satchel a comb, shirt, pack of
cigarettes and a small roll of twenty-riel notes and placed them
with his father's ashes. For Mayana he left a scarf which had
been Vathana's and which the younger daughter had always
admired. In the scarf were pieces of cellophane-wrapped candy
and a pack of gum. For Samnang there was a new pair of pants,
a book of maps, two ballpoint pens and an order pad. Chhuon
closed his eyes, stepped back, then stopped. He opened his eyes.
He reached into his pocket. He had not planned the action but
suddenly he felt he must. From his pocket he withdrew the wad
of counterfeit fifty-riel notes. He stared at them in his hand.
"For what possible reason," Chhuon muttered, shaking, suddenly shaking violently, unable to control his arms or body,
throwing the wad on the new pants, "could you possibly want
these?"

"Brother," Cheam said, "the monks have arrived. Come."
Cheam led Chhuon to their family mat where Vathana was
again supporting her mother, where Samay and Sakhon knelt.
All the food had vanished in deference to the monks who could
not eat for six more hours. Maha Nyanananda climbed onto a

raised pallet by the altar, sat, tucked his feet beneath him.
Chhuon barely noticed. Then the saffron robe caught his eye. He
looked up and tears welled. About the old monk were several
assistants, the *aacha*, and several of the village leaders. Through
Chhuon's swollen eyes all his people in their best and whitest
clothes looked gray, like apparitions. The apparitions brought
their hands together and bowed their heads to the floor three
times. The monotonic chanting in Pali reached his ears but did
not enter his head. He knew the prayers but he could not utter a
sound. An urge to rise swept over him but he forced it to pass
through him and on. In its wake he yet wanted to rise, wanted
to address his family, neighbors, wanted to explain why he had
left the children, wanted to make them understand. The *aacha*
sprayed perfume into a bowl of water, the monk dipped a white
chrysanthemum. Maha Nyanananda flicked the flower toward
the kneeling congregation and over the clothes and gifts, conse-
crating them for the dead. Later he would give them to the
poor. The chanting continued for hours though the young children had long since departed and again was playing hide-and-
seek in the vestibule and on the grounds about the pagoda.
Chhuon forced himself to repeat the prayers, the suttas shielding his consciousness against the tragedies that had befallen
his family, forced his eyes to close, to hide in blackness, forced
his body into a state of numbed trance. Again and again his
mind escaped from the prayers to think, first, if it is not the
fate of a person to remain with the living then this must
be accepted. Then with great anxiety, to think of the Samsara,
the Wheel of Life, which connects all generations, and to
project the ramifications of his deed, his loss, his unheeded
dream.

In the first days that followed, Chhuon appeared calm. After the
days of wailing and the days of silence the sudden change was
welcomed as a sign of moderation of his grief. But within days
his wife, his brother, all the villagers, again became concerned
for him and said prayers for him.

"Mama," Vathana whispered, "what can we do?"

"In time . . ." the older woman began, but she did not finish.
How strong she seemed to her daughter, and how affected
seemed her father. Yet Vathana knew her mother was not so
much stronger, only she did not show her grief.

"I'm so sad, Mama," Vathana said. "I'm sad for Yani and
Samnang, and I'm so sad for you and Papa."

"In time . . ." the older woman repeated. "In time. Now we
must plan for your wedding."

"I won't go now," Vathana said compassionately. "I'll stay with you and Papa."

"No," Sok said quietly. "You will go as planned. I will take care of the things your father should do . . . until he comes awake."

On the surface Chhuon was spiritless, apathetic about Vathana's wedding plans, despondent. "Please!" Sok pleaded. "Talk to the monk. Talk to the khrou." "It was fate," Cheam said. "Had you taken the trip, had you not, exactly what was fated to occur came to pass." "Say another prayer," his cousin Sam advised. "I pray to the spirit of your home," Sam's wife, Ry, added. "You have three children alive. You're a very lucky man."

But inside, under his despondency, like a planted grain of rice sprouting, flourishing, blooming, spreading its seed, resprouting, multiplying in tranquil paddies under darkened still skies, in him like the wave of snowmelt rushing down the mighty river, building momentum unstoppable, a mantra directed at the yuons rumbled, repeated, doubled with each repetition:

blood-for-blood!
blood-for-blood!
Blood-for-Blood!
Blood-For-Blood!
BLOOD-FOR-BLOOD!
BLOOD-FOR-BLOOD!

After three days and nights of bound, painful forced march the cool earth and light restraints of the box were a welcome relief. Samnang was frightened yet too exhausted, too confused, too disoriented for the reality of his burial to seize him. For twelve hours he slept. For twelve hours he dreamt nothing, felt nothing, thought nothing. Then, slowly, the earthy facts of capture, rite, witness, march and burial oozed into the emptiness like lava seeping under pressure into a sealed underground chamber.

He tried to open his eyes. Dirt particles fell into the slits. He jammed them shut. They had bound him loosely, only enough to keep his hands and legs still. When they had told him to lie in the dirt in the box, he had done so without the slightest resistance. They had tied his arms at the wrists to loops of vine about his upper thighs. They had wrapped his hands, each finger separately, in soft cloth. Carefully they had packed dirt over his body, enough to fill the box and hold him motionless though not enough to crush him when they shut the lid. Then they fitted a reed through a cloth over his face and pushed it into his lips. They aligned the other end with a hole in the lid, packed his head, neck and face in dirt, closed the lid and buried

Samnang's coffin in a shallow grave. Only the reed tip broke the surface.

When he woke he tried to move his right hand, then his left. A dull force kept them at his side. He wiggled his jaw side to side but was able to open his mouth only a half inch. Immediately fear of losing the reed grasped him and he tightly snapped his lips. He tried his feet, his legs, every joint. Each he was able to move only slightly. Each fractional movement assured him he was alive, whole. His shoulders and arms ached where they previously had been bound. His feet itched at a hundred abrasions. He tried to breathe through his nose. The vacuum in his head made his ears ache. He breathed quickly through the tube. He could hear nothing but his own blood pulsing. His mouth was dry. Suddenly images flooded in. Images of home, family. He pulled violently at the restraints about his wrists but he was unable to budge his arms more than the width of the vine, unable to raise his shoulders or flex his elbows. Immediately he was gasping for air through the narrow reed. He tried to squeeze his hands, to grab his thigh, touch his own skin. He could not feel even one finger against the next. He tried to yell. His voice peed tiny spurts into the tube: "hey! help! help me! help me!" With each effort the dirt on his chest and abdomen fell and constricted and the effort required to suck in enough air to raise the dirt terrified him.

I must pray, he thought. I shall pray. I shall pray like Papa. He tried to clear his mind, to practice perfect attention, but the complete emptiness, the total void, instead of making it easier allowed thousands of thoughts to slip loose of their moorings and cascade into his consciousness. The rapid bombardment of images horrified him. A thought stuck and he leaped for it. Bodies are made of water, earth, wind and fire. He chanted it within his mind. Water earth wind and fire. Water earth wind and fire. He chanted it silently again and again. In thought he offered the Enlightened One his own body, his own water earth wind and fire. For hours he repeated the chant and offer into the constant cool black void.

He slept again. Woke again to nothingness, to total sensory deprivation. No pain. No feeling. No time. He thought of his father. ". . . a lackey of Pech Lim Song," Bok Roh had screamed. "A lackey liquidated by the people . . ." He tried to cry. He could feel his eyes jittering beneath their lids, beneath the cloth and the weight of the soft earth. Dirt particles ground his eyeballs as they skittered below the lids. He could not cry. He cried inside for not being able to cry. He attempted returning to the chant but he could not make his mind hold the words. He saw images of home, wat, school, friends. He saw his mother, Vathana, Samay, Peou. Then the series of roadblocks replayed and that released images of Plei Srepok. Water earth wind and fire. Water earth wind and fire. He did not wish to see Plei Srepok. "Come here," his father says. "Take care and watch over ..." "Yiii ..." the giant screams. Waterearthwindfire. Waterearthwindfire. "Never forget our family legacy ..." father says. His voice blends with the perfect constantness of the void. "... or the Path of the Elders." Waterearthwindfire. Fire. Total village immolation. Total blackness surrounding immense flames within his eyes. Within his eyes, head ears scraping naked body. He is blind. He believes he is blind, has been blinded by the sight he has witnessed. Nothing could be so totally black. Empty. He cowers. Tied. Tied to the stake of Plei Srepok. Mute. Dazed. "For all eternity our blood will call for revenge." Yes Father. "Do not cry." Yes Father. "Become all you are capable of becoming." Yes Father. "... watch over Mayana." Yes ... "Yiii-KA!"

Water. Earth. Wind. Fire. Blackness. Trembling. Complete emptiness. Isolation. Void. Nothing. He urinates. The urine feels warm but soon cools and blends with the zero, the hunger, the disorientation, the mystical acceptance. Nang sleeps, wakes. I've disappointed Papa, again. Papa, don't leave me. It wasn't my fault at school. Please don't blame me. I won't disappoint you ever, ever again. Please don't go. Don't leave me. Samnang cries, bawls, whimpers himself to sleep. Nang wakes totally numb, totally lost in space, time, emotions. Totally acquiescent.

"What does he say?" Voen whispered to Vathana. Everything inside the Cahuom home was being washed, polished, straightened or freshened.

"I ... I haven't asked." Vathana hung her head concentrating on the flower arrangement. "He's been so ..."

"I know," Voen said. "Your poor mother. She endures the loss and she has to endure his silence. Still, he is your father. Ask him."

"But Auntie ..." Vathana began, stopped.

"When we were little our father used to make him concentrate on his lessons. More than any of us. 'Chhuon,' Pa would say. 'You're not the oldest. You're not the strongest or the biggest. You must be the smartest.' And he would be silent and think his deep thoughts for weeks. Then he'd come out of it with some new understanding and Pa would shower him with attention."

"Auntie ..." Vathana murmured.

"Um."

"Would you . . ." Vathana's fingers worked nervously at the arrangement, ". . . ask him for me?"

"No, Vathana." Voen came, stood behind her, gently straightened Vathana's hair with her hands. "This is something you must do."

Vathana said a prayer for her father, her sister and brother. Then she entered the second room. "Father," she called sweetly. It was the day of the third and last gift-giving ceremony. Mister Pech and his wife had arrived in Phum Sath Din the day before with an entourage of aunts and uncles, brothers and sisters. And with Pech Chieu Teck, second son of the wealthy merchant, Vathana's betrothed. The village was alive with the news, alive with the rumor that the bride's father had not greeted the lesser guests. Vathana had never been so anxious. How she wished she could again whisper with Yani, giggle about this man who some said looked like the Prince, tell her little sister how she, Vathana, was now afraid to talk to their father.

"Um," Chhuon grunted. He sat on a sleeping mat, staring at a blank spot on the wall. His grief had not tempered. He was withdrawn, argumentative, irritable. Only a month had passed from the ceremony for his father and young children to the occasion of the first gift-giving, and only two weeks more. For days he had stooped silently in paddies, weeding, moving handfuls of mud meaninglessly. With his hands in the mud he had felt he could almost touch his son. Inside he screamed. Nights he dreamt of Kdeb and Yani. Mayana was at peace. He could sense it. Kdeb's spirit was hurt, lost.

"Teck's sister and brother have brought bolts of English linen and Thai silk. Mama, Grandma and Aunt Voen have prepared a very special meal and everyone is dressed so beautifully. Even cousin Sam and Ry and Great Aunt Moeun have come. Please Papa, smile. For me."

"Yes." Chhuon's answer was simple. A smile wrinkled his face. He looked up at his daughter.

"*Papa!*" Vathana cried.

"We'll have a good talk," Chhuon said. "We'll plan everything as it should be. When we're finished eating I'll come and ask you to meet our guests. You know how very distinguished Mister Pech is, eh? Ah, but I think still, you're too beautiful for his son."

Vathana laughed, at first a small titter, then a bigger giggle, then a sustained gleeful laugh. It was the first time in seven weeks Chhuon had joked with her, with anyone, had given her any indication he was aware of the wedding plans. Vathana went to him, knelt beside him. She grasped his callused hands. Chhuon squeezed her hands briefly then said, "Now go. Let me get ready."

Blossoms and candles made the central room of the Cahuom home feel as elegant as the dining room of the best French restaurant in Neak Luong. Mister Pech and his wife were expected within the hour for the *connecting-word ceremony*, a serious conversation about the couple's future, a bountiful meal, and a time for Vathana to meet, for the first time, her betrothed. On the morrow the four parents would go to the khrou for advice on picking a lucky day for the wedding.

That Vathana had never spoken to Teck was not unusual. Nor was it unusual that he had seen her only in a photograph. Uncle Cheam had made the preliminary arrangements and he was trusted by all. Pech Lim Song knew that Cahuom Chhuon's family was a good family, if rural, and Chhuon knew that the Pechs were of excellent ancestry. To the parents, nothing more need be of concern.

Chhuon washed, dressed in his best clothes. He stopped every few minutes to kiss his statuette of Buddha seven times. His hair had grown an inch long since the hundredth-day ceremony for his father. One did not shave one's head for the death of a child. To keep the bristles from standing straight out, Chhuon oiled them lightly and combed them to one side. He could not help but feel empty as he checked himself in a mirror, and he could not rejoice at the thought of Vathana's wedding. Tiny Phum Sath Din, he thought, raising children to populate the cities. Samay had moved to the monastery to begin Sangha training. Vathana would move to Neak Luong. No . . . he could not repeat their names again. Only Peou will be here, he thought. Only Peou.

After three days, Met Hon lifted Nang from the coffin. He hugged him. He held the boy for a long silent moment. Nang's body hung limp in his arms. "Tonight you've been reborn," Met Hon whispered. "You are as an infant in my arms. We will care for you and nurture you all the days of your life." He lay Nang on a sleeping mat over soft earth, untied his wrists, unwrapped his fingers. The boy's body was cool, cold, clammy. His eyes seemed disconnected within their sockets, falling to different angles in the dim light of late dusk. Met Hon left. A pang of fear whisked through Nang's chest, his only emotional capacity. Met Hon returned with hot tea, lifted the boy's head and gently let him sip the liquid. "You shall be one with the Movement," Hon whispered, "and we shall usher in an age more remarkable than that of the Angkor kings."

Hon pulled the boy onto his lap and held him for an hour. His body heat warmed Nang. Slowly the stiffness dissipated from the boy's limbs. He moved his shoulders, then fingers, ankles, knees. "I'm hungry," he said.

"Then you shall feast," Met Hon answered. He helped Nang roll to his knees and stand. The boy wobbled. "You are very strong," Hon praised him as he led him to a small bamboo table at the center of the camp. "You must obey all orders of the Movement. Then you'll be allowed whatever you need." On the table were sandals, fresh clothes, a sleeping blanket, and three beautiful bowls of food—a noodle dish with chicken, a river fish cooked in banana leaves, and a huge rice pot.

"Tell me your name," Met Hon whispered quietly.

"Cahuom Samnang," the boy said.

"No!" Hon barked viciously.

Samnang startled, trembled, fell to his knees cowering.

"Tell me your name," Met Hon hissed angrily.

"Nang?" the boy whimpered.

"Met Nang," Hon corrected.

"Met Nang," Nang said.

"You may dress. Eat your fill of rice." Hon spoke flatly, with neither respect nor ridicule. To a guard he said, "Take the other dishes away."

Nang scooped a handful of rice into his mouth. He dressed in the clothes of the Movement as he chewed, then he ate more greedily. After he stuffed himself, he retched. He rushed as quickly as his stiffness allowed from the table but vomited onto a muddy path which led through the camp.

Hon pounced on him. He screamed, grabbing the boy's slender shoulders, shaking him, "How dare you vomit food the Movement has provided. See what greed produces. Ingrate! Eat it!" Hon shoved Nang's face into the vomit and mud. "Eat!" he screamed. He held Nang roughly by the back of the neck as the boy licked the ground. "Good," Hon said, relaxing his grip but not letting go. "Ah, much better, Comrade. You see, you can obey the Movement. Tonight you shall rest. Eat as you wish. Prepare yourself. Strengthen yourself. At dawn we commence our march."

Nang was led back to his coffin and left. The guard gave him no instructions, no indication if he was allowed to stand, sit, lie, sleep, walk about. Again he was alone. He looked into the darkness hoping to find something, anything, on which to center himself, on which to pin this new, strange reality. He squatted beside the coffin, wrapped the sleeping blanket about his shoulders, shuttered in the cold night dampness and the residual chill from the grave. Again there was radio music. Two guards passed on the trail. In the light of their lantern he saw they were heavy, thickset, strong. He heard their speech and he thought, rural. From villages so isolated they must be without pagodas or schools. Their strangeness frightened him.

Nang thought carefully about what he had seen of the camp. The site repulsed him. The guards were slovenly. Except for Hon. Hon was immaculate, educated. Hon, he thought. He was no older than Samay, sixteen, yet he seemed to be in command. Who is Hon? he thought. In the darkness and stillness the question convoluted. Who is Nang? Quietly he began to sob. Nang, son of Chhuon who has been liquidated. He said a prayer for Chhuon's spirit and wished it a peaceful journey and quick progress to its next re-creation. Then he thought of escape, of Nang rising and walking silently into the jungle, but Samnang, he thought, has no knowledge of where he is, of where he should go, of how to survive in the wild. Nang has no light, he thought. Y Bhur would know. The name awakened images that made him tremble. Fighting back the nightmare he thought, Tomorrow I'll find Y Bhur, Y . . . No. Met Ur.

Nang lay on the coffin. Again he cried. He was alone, isolated now even from Hon, isolated by Hon's violent burst of anger. Alone, withdrawn, withdrawing, his only friend and companion the half-developed consciousness of an eleven-year-old boy which seethed in darkness behind eyes, which was repulsed and disgusted by the vile scenes its own core demanded to repeat . . . to repeat . . . to repeat the cleaving. He sees Samnang, tied, trussed, forced to watch. He sees Bok Roh swing, hears the giant scream, sees the massive cleaver enter, the head part, the right half fall on the shoulder of a body not yet realizing it has died, the left half for a fraction of a second looking like a drawing, for a fraction seeing the mystery before the surface seeps a thousand drops of blood and cloaks the drawing red, sees the machete wedge into the bone at the midback, sees the giant kick his sister's body from the blade. Sees nothing in the dark nightmist, nothing in the deepest of darknesses within.

First light penetrates the jungle canopy. Met Nang opens his eyes. He is surprised at the size of the complex, at the number of small shelters. He sits up. There are at least thirty two-man sleeping positions, perhaps more, plus a dozen hammocks, and half a dozen coffins. He does not move. From the coffin lid he can see a single delicate filament strung to a leaf perhaps ten feet away. Mist has settled on the web and formed a series of miniature pearllike droplets. They are beautiful, he thinks. He shivers. He is afraid to move. Others in camp are up. He stares at the pearls, stares into the jungle. There are thousands of filaments with minute morning pearls reflecting almost imperceptibly the hint of light beneath the vegetation. Whoever Nang is, he thinks, there is still the spider, the web, the glass beads. They can have him, he thinks. He does not think clearly, verbally. He sees his body as a mass of glutinous rice capable of being tamped and shaped by the blade of a knife. Nang's body rises, rolls the sleeping mat and blanket. Outside, he is obedient, withdrawn, pliable, yet at the core there is a being still intact. Whether, he thinks, the vessel is Samnang or Met Nang makes no difference.

For eleven days Nang marched with the long patrol, marched through jungle and over mountains, seemingly not in a single direction but in circles, or perhaps in an expanding spiral or simply in meandering curves with a general destination but no constraint of time, marched toward the first segment of his formal training. Each day Nang marched more easily, each day he ate better, each day he became stronger and each day Met Hon instructed him in hygiene, jungle and camp life, cooking, sanitation, even sleeping, resting, sitting on one sandal with feet on the other so as not to muddy one's clothes. Each day Hon instructed him in proper thought and action. Each day he punished him for improper behavior.

"No crying," Hon seethed the third night.

Nang had dreamed Chhuon's spirit was beseeching him. "But my father . . ." Nang began.

Hon snapped. "There is no father." He dropped his anger. "There is only the Movement. The man who sired you only did his duty for the collective good of Cambodia."

On the fourth day Nang asked, "May I speak to Met Ur?"

"He is ill," Hon answered.

"But he marches with us. I've seen him at the rear of the column."

Hon spit, disgusted. "Why do you concern yourself with him?"

"He's . . ." Nang's face contorted. "He's my friend."

"He's a burden to the Movement," Met Hon rasped. "The Movement is your only friend."

"I could help him. He'll help the Movement."

"Ah. So you're that strong, eh? Then you'll be responsible for him. If he doesn't keep up, you'll be beaten."

Y Bhur, Met Ur, was wretched, sick, pathetic. Nang himself felt dirtier than a sweat-coated mountain woman cutting dry rice in the hot sun, but Met Ur's countenance was vile, repugnant. Nang's smell was that of the unwashed; Met Ur's that of decay, mummification. Under Hon's eyes Nang forced himself to behold Ur, forced himself to near his friend, to touch him, to offer him a hesitant repulsed hug.

"Met Ur," Nang whispered, "we're . . . we're to march again. I've come to"—Y Bhur glared at the boy through sunken hollow eyes, the skin below them so drawn and the eyeballs so shrunken and glazed, Nang could see the yellow inner tissues of the sockets—"I've come to help you."

"May their spirits depart in peace," Y Bhur muttered in Jarai. "May they never return." Nang froze. He had lost his father and sister. He had not thought of Y Bhur's loss. "Spirits." Y Bhur coughed. "Do not retrace your steps."

"Stop him from muttering that cluck," Met Hon descended upon them. "Make him march."

Nang gripped the boy who had once been his friend, who had once been much larger than he, gripped his flaccid arms and pulled him up. "You can do it," he said. "You must . . ." He cowered beneath Hon's glare. "His . . . his leg's bad," Nang mumbled. "It should be treated."

"If the Movement wished to treat him," Hon scowled, "he would be treated."

Throughout the day Nang urged Y Bhur to walk faster, to try harder. "Do all you're capable of," he said as sincerely as his father had once said it to him. "Don't cry." When they came to steep inclines Nang half carried him. When they rested by a stream Nang unwound the leg bandage. The stench revolted him. The sight of the festering raw meat horrified him. He forced Y Bhur to sit in shallow rushing current where he, Nang, scraped the surface of the wound with a sharp stone as he'd once seen the khrou clean an abscess from his father's foot. Nang beat the swollen thigh with the butt of the rock until the oozing yellowgreen fluid turned red. Then he washed the bandage and reapplied it.

They moved again. Hon marched before them, several guards behind. "At our next rest," Nang turned and whispered to Y Bhur in Jarai, "I'll get you a walking stick."

He turned back forward into Hon's flying fist. The punch sent him sprawling. "Speak Khmer!" Met Hon spat angrily. "Or you'll be killed."

On the fifth day and again on the seventh and eighth the size of the column increased. Nang didn't know the extent of the unit but he'd seen five more who he took to be, like himself, conscripts. He estimated there were at least three guards for each newly selected child.

The school to which Nang was being marched was officially known as the Liberation School, but Khmer Communist cadres (and later Royal Cambodian intelligence reports, and later still Western documents) referred to it as the School of the Cruel.

"Come on," Nang tormented Y Bhur. "Get up. They won't wait." Y Bhur rolled to his side and pulled himself halfway up using the staff Nang had brought. He looked to Nang for assistance. They did not speak. In the five days since Nang had begun helping him his strength and condition had stabilized. He was sallow, limp, odorous and repulsive but the slide toward death had temporarily halted. Nang washed his bandage and wound only twice more, both on their second day. That night six guards beat Nang and for the next two days his rice ration was halved. "Damn it," Nang cursed Y Bhur like Met Hon had cursed him so many times. "March. March, Met Ur, or *I* shall beat *you*."

During marches Nang did not speak. He eyed Hon and the guards. Except for Met Hon all were humorless, faceless, hostile. Stupid, Nang thought. Underlings, he thought. Not crocodiles, not tigers. Dogs.

On the eleventh day they marched into the crotch of two blunt Laotian legs which jutted into Cambodia. They climbed beside a creek for several kilometers then rested and set up cooking fires. Met Hon motioned for Met Nang to come with him and Nang obeyed immediately. Hon led him nearly a hundred meters away from the others. Before he spoke he sized up Nang with his eyes. He spoke gently. "If you're to survive, Little Brother," he said, using the forbidden appellation, "you must learn to keep your mouth shut, your eyes closed and your ears plugged. You must forget everything from the past." He glanced up the mountain. "Pong Pay is the hardest training on earth." Nang looked up but could see little other than the vegetation of the canopy. "If you're going to become a comrade of the Movement, not just a soldier, you must be serious. You must do what you are told."

The cadres did not come for the conscripts until night had settled upon the temporary camp. At dusk the conscripts had been huddled together at the camp's center, had had their wrists tied behind their backs with vines, and then all their hands were tied together. If seen from above they would have looked like a human wheel, their hands the hub, their arms stretched behind their backs like spokes.

"No words! No movement!" Met Hon had ordered. Then he and the guards had backed into the jungle and vanished.

For ten minutes no one spoke. They stood quietly in the blackness. Fear descended upon them, ten boys trapped, trussed together, cold, alone, shaking. Y Bhur broke the silence. He was wired to Nang on his left and a Khmer boy he'd heard called Pah on his right. "Samnang," Y Bhur whispered. He spoke in Jarai. "My hands. I think I can get loose. We can run away."

Nang shuddered silently. Y Bhur's hands twisted at the hub of the wheel. The motion tightened the vines about the others' wrists. "Samnang, raise your hand. No, push it down."

On the far side a Mnong boy wept quietly, wrenched his hands distorting the circle. Another boy grunted. One groaned at the increasing pain. A third muttered in French, "Stop. You're cutting me."

"Be still!" Nang snapped. The boys quieted, quit pulling at the vines. Nang cowered—ashamed in the dark, ashamed of his voice, his order, afraid of alienating the others. Y Bhur again twisted. He pulled hard with his right hand and pushed with his left. The vines cut into the base of his right thumb. He pulled harder, twisting toward Nang. The vine slid. His hand deformed from the pressure, molded to the oblique circuit of liana. He pulled harder, gouging his flesh. The blood greased his skin. The vine began to slip. Nang raised his right foot. He cocked his leg behind him. "Be still!" he sneered. Then he whipped his knee into Y Bhur's wounded thigh.

"Aaaaahhh!" Y Bhur shouted. "Why . . . ooooph!" A club struck him in the chest. Another hit him. Then all of the conscripts were being wildly beaten by unseen attackers, bashed in the legs, the groin, the stomach. One cringing pulled another forward into a bludgeoning blow.

"Stand still!" The order came in Khmer from deep in the blackness. The blows softened to probes and jabs. Still the boys could not see their tormentors.

A club poked Y Bhur in the groin. "Fuck water buffalo," he hissed in Jarai.

"With your member." The tormentor laughed. He spoke Jarai.

Y Bhur lunged outward trying to butt his head against the source of the voice in the dark. The entire circle stumbled, the sides fell, the back toppled. Y Bhur, pinned at the bottom, screamed vicious obscenities in Jarai and Khmer and Viet Namese.

"Quiet!" The order came from nearby. The officer moved close. "You shall be as one," he said calmly. "You shall walk as one. School is two kilometers. If you walk as a team, we will be there shortly. If you walk as ten . . . Well, we have all night. You"—he reached down and grabbed a head by the hair and lifted—"you shall lead off. What's your name?"

"Met Nang."

A slap stung Nang's face. He shivered, tried to pull his face into his chest. "Nang," the cadreman said. "You don't merit to be called 'comrade.' If you last through school, then you'll be Met Nang. Now walk." Nang could feel the conscripts struggling to their feet beside and behind him. "Met Din," the cadreman said softly, "hook your rope to Nang's neck so he'll know the way."

The night was hard on the conscripts. For hours, tied, they stumbled in the dark attempting to negotiate steep, narrow mountain trails. When one fell, they all fell. When one collapsed, they all collapsed. The clubbings continued. If their progress was too slow the leader was jabbed in the stomach. Then the lead changed. At times the boys worked together, counting steps quietly to develop a rhythm, but more often they argued nastily, blaming one another, or one gave up, fell, cried like an infant, or tugged back when he felt another tug too hard. The guards laughed at the boys' pain.

As dawn broke they glimpsed the compound for the first time. Nang glanced furtively past Y Bhur. He looked down. Not until they had reached a point only two or three meters from the bluff did any of them realize they had finished their night's trek. They stood at the edge of a small cliff which formed one end barrier of the school. Ten feet below, and stretching for several hundred meters, Nang could see a huge, partially camouflaged compound sectioned like an egg crate into subcamps by high bamboo fences. The closest compound was empty except for a flagpole with a small red flag hanging limp. Other sections held a variety of buildings: one had small shells, another seemingly had longhouses and schools. Glimpses of hundreds of armed guards along the fences made him tremble.

A guard's laugh tore him from the view. The guard laughed hysterically. Other guards were pointing to different boys and giggling mean giggles. They placed wagers—this one will break, this one will die, this one will be good fertilizer. More guards appeared. They were dressed in black with red- or green-striped kramas about their necks. They were more solemn though they too laughed menacingly. The guards of the night stood back and gave wide berth to the new squad. The conscripts, still tied in a wheel, sensed a new phase had begun.

One boy, the smallest, to Nang's left, began sobbing. Nang jerked the hub, trying to shake the child. Two more black-clad guards appeared. Between them they carried a long, thick bamboo pole. They chuckled. The others laughed. The conscripts cowered, silent except for the littlest, spent, exhausted from days of fear and constant walking, and the night of the wheel. Nang knew what was coming. He sensed the meaning of the bluff even before the pole appeared, and he vowed inwardly to survive. The pole was placed tangentially against the circle, contacting at the waists of two boys with their backs to the bluff. The two touched by the pole stepped back, forcing the wheel to stumble a step closer to the edge. At each end of the pole, first one, then two, then three guards pushed the pole toward the small cliff. The wheel resisted. The guards pushed harder though not hard enough to force the wheel off the edge. Y Bhur faced the cliff. Below, the ground was barren red-orange hardpack. Nang, to his left, planted his heels as best he could. He crouched, pulled with his right hand, pushed with his left, trying to turn the circle. He did not want to be on the bottom when they hit. Y Bhur stood, offered little resistance. Some resisted violently, some spasmodically. The circle turned counterclockwise a full hour as the side opposite Nang fell back a step under the pressure of the pole. The guards giggled, keeping the pressure constant, not wanting to push the wheel over the cliff, which they could have easily done, but wanting to see the conscripts relent, slowly, to their sense of the inevitable. "Nooo," the smallest boy wailed. "No-aaahh." The far side stumbled back another step, the circle rotated. If the boy with his toes over the bluff's edge was at twelve o'clock, Nang was at nine. He judged that to be a good position. The guards forced the pole another inch. The heels of the boy at twelve skidded to the edge, he straightened, the edge collapsed, his feet shot out, his arms snapped up as the hub resisted, then slowly the sides collapsed, accelerating, Y Bhur to his right knee, off, others, then all. The wheel slapped down, a rapid thudding and three loud cracks. Guards cheered. Then the moaning began.

CHAPTER FOUR

For seven days they were beaten harshly. Their hair was cut, short on the sides, left thick on top. Their clothes were taken from them, even the clothes Nang had received from Met Hon after the coffin torture. Another break with the past, another barrier to even the minutest growth of security. The new issue of baggy, lightweight green utilities announced immediately to everyone they were plebes to be hazed, conscripts to be humiliated, boys with pasts that must be beaten, starved or terrorized out of them or who must die in the attempt.

For ten days they subsisted on reduced food and water rations until hunger and thirst became constant thoughts adding the fear of death by starvation to the fear of beatings. For fourteen nights they were locked, alone, hands tied, in tiny cages where lizards scurried about their bodies; or in twos, in leg stocks exposed to the elements in the open yard. One night, while Nang suffered in the stocks, Ur escaped from his cage. He did not attempt to escape from the camp. There was no possibility. He slinked to a water jug, stole the ladle and drank. Then, in the dark, he crept to Nang, then to the smaller boy, Pah. He dared not release them but he brought them water. Then he returned the ladle to the jar and himself to the cage.

Nang's first interrogation, before the beatings began, was the night of the day he was delivered to the School of the Cruel. He was instructed to sit in a chair at a small wooden desk in what looked to him like his Uncle Cheam's office, only much larger. An older man asked him his name. The man was gentle, well spoken. Nang hesitated. Guards lurked in corners and doorways. Other conscripts were seated at other tables with other men. "It's all right," the man said. "Call me Met Sar. In here you will always be safe."

"Nang," the boy answered. As the word seeped from his mouth he flinched, expecting to be hit.

"It's okay, Nang. No one will hurt you. We need to know more about you." Met Sar's voice was soothing. To Nang the man looked like Uncle Cheam. He even sounded like Nang's uncle when Cheam was not talking business or politics. "Nang, what was your village?"

The interrogator wrote the answer. He asked the boy about his schooling and they talked for some minutes about the pagoda in Phum Sath Din, the lay of the homes, the names of the families and of each member. Met Sar systematically recorded the information and filed different sheets in different folders. Then they talked about rice and irrigation. Met Sar was amazed at Nang's knowledge of the subject and made special note of it in his file. "One day, you will be a patriot and hero of Kambuja," Met Sar told him. He used the ancient name for Cambodia as though time had receded a thousand years.

Sar leaned back in his chair. "What of your family?" he asked.

Nang looked bitterly at the older man. "You killed my father. And my sister." He was vehement. His entire body trembled.

Met Sar placed his hands together and bowed in contemplation. "Tell me how this happened," he said.

Nang's face contorted. Tears ran from his eyes. His voice quivered. "The giant, Bok Roh . . . He chopped Mayana . . ."

"Bok Roh!" Met Sar interrupted with feigned astonishment. "He's not part of us. He . . . I know of him. He serves the yuons. Tell me . . . tell me! Tell me what happened."

For an hour Nang recounted the day at Plei Srepok, the village attack, soldiers, meeting, executions and fire. Nang described Bok Roh and repeated long passages of his rantings, he, Nang, did not know were in his mind. Met Sar urged him on, asked him to expand various parts. He interrupted various passages to explain, reexplain, to lead Nang to the knowledge that those responsible for his father's and sister's deaths were Viet Namese and a few bad Khmers who served their interests. "Bok Roh, eh?" Met Sar said. "He could have been a great warrior for Kambuja. But he was seized by the yuons at the time of the false independence. He spent a dozen years in camps north of Hanoi where they turned his mind against his own people. I too hate him. He and the yuons are worthy of your hate. We will teach you, systematically, how to avenge your father. You've much to learn."

Nang stared at Met Sar. The smile on the older man's lips was thin. His eyes sunk deeper into his skull. Nang glanced about the room. All the conscripts and interrogators were gone. Only a single guard remained at the far end where one wall was solid with files. "You must be trained," Met Sar said. "At times it will be very hard but everything is done with purpose. Once you are clean you'll be allowed special privileges. You've been abandoned by your family and all elders. The Movement is your salvation. I have no past. You have no past. There is no past. You have no name. For now you are Prisoner. The Movement will name you when the time comes. There is only the present and the future, and the future exists only in the Movement."

Nang was fed his last full meal then taken alone to an isolation section where the week of beatings and deprivation began. Again and again he was interrogated—not by Met Sar but by toughs, by dumb, brutal guards who forced absurd confessions from him then beat him for the lies. He was forced to learn catchphrases and creeds, was beaten if he stuttered, refused to answer or didn't know. Toward the end of the first week two very strong Khmer soldiers made him crawl into one of the isolated sections where beatings could be meted out without witnesses. They stood over him. Nang sat on the ground as he had learned. His legs were straight, his feet pointed, his back erect. He held his hands stiff, flat to the side of his knees. His chin was up. He stared forward in the posture of perfect attention.

"Ur . . ." one interrogator asked, "he is your friend, eh?" Nang did not answer. The interrogator spoke softly. "He does not have a proper attitude," the soldier said. "You'll keep an eye on him for us." Still Nang didn't answer. He concentrated all his energy into sitting perfectly still. "Prisoner, I said you'll watch him for me." No reaction. "Yes?" Nang's eyes darted to the dark figure. "In the village of Phum Sath Din there is a woman, Neang Thi Sok, with a mother-in-law, two sons, Samay and Sakhon, and a daughter, Vathana. They say the daughter has very soft skin." The soldier's face contorted into an eerie smile. "You'll spy on Ur. You'll tell me every word he speaks or Vathana will be brought here for interrogation." The guard laughed heartily. "Say yes."

"Yes," Nang answered.

"Say, 'I will spy on Ur.' "

"I will spy on Ur."

"If you kill yourself, Prisoner," the second guard said, "she will be brought here for torture. Now, report!"

Nang chanted as he had learned, "In rain, in wind, in health, in sickness, day or night, I will obey, correctly and without complaining, what the Movement orders."

*   *   *

"So," Louis said, "what is she like?"

The five young men sat beneath a large umbrella at an out-door cafe on the main street of Neak Luong. Louis and Kim sat with their backs to the road. Thiounn and Sakun bracketed Pech Chieu Teck, their backs to the cafe wall. "You know," Teck said.

"Ha!" Kim laughed. "Tell us."

"She's just a girl," Teck said sheepishly. They spoke French at the cafe, at school, whenever they were together.

"Sure!" Louis laughed. Teck was the first of their crowd to be arranged in marriage and the others had been teasing him for weeks. " 'Just a girl,' " Louis mimicked Teck. "Ha! I thought the Dragon Lady would have found you a boy! Ha!"

"That's not right speech," Thiounn said mock-seriously. "You can't call the madam 'Dragon Lady.' Her baby boy might feel hurt."

"Really!" Teck said. He sipped his cola and winked at the waitress who was serving at the next table. All the friends laughed.

"Ooo-la-la." Kim giggled. They were in excellent spirits. "Come on now, tell us."

"Well," Teck said, "she's . . . you know, she's a country girl."

"Ha!" Thiounn blurted. "You mean she has a round rump and a round face and . . ."

"No! No," Teck cut in. "She's very pretty. Really. You'll see."

"So what *does* your mother say?" Louis asked.

"You know her. She wanted my father to arrange something with that Phnom Penh family she likes, but Papa's so Republican . . . you know how he is. He arranged it because her uncle is very Republican, too."

"And you agreed, eh?" Louis said.

Teck leaned forward on his arms, looked away from his friends, out, across the street and across the river. "How could I do otherwise?" he said quietly.

"You can't stand up to him?" Thiounn said.

"No," Teck responded. "Besides, he's giving me a river barge as a wedding gift."

"So," Sakun said, "*that's* it!"

"What about the girl," Louis asked. "I want to know about her. Is she Republican?"

"Vathana?" Teck said. "I don't think she knows anything about politics. You know those ceremonies. We didn't get to talk much. Everything was very proper."

Thiounn nudged him. "What would her uncle say if he knew you were a socialist?"

"I'm not," Teck answered.

"No!?" Louis shooed Teck's answer away with a flick of his hand. "Your father thinks you still study your painting, but we know."

"I've been to a few rallies. That's all."

"You should be more serious," Sakun said. "Truly. Marriage is a sacred rite and the Wheel of Life . . ."

"God! You sound like my father," Teck said.

"Truly," Sakun repeated. "When you're married, you will have to change."

Teck slapped his fingertips on the table. "I will still come here," he said. "Just as always."

The conscripts were reunited. They were told they would move en masse to a far section of the camp. Guards from the old section herded them into one end of a long, narrow, covered, meandering bamboo maze, then closed the gate. They had been instructed to run. Nang led the group. Fear made him obey. In obedience there was security. Ur hung back. Nang had not seen him since the night he brought the water. He was horrified. Without treatment Ur's thigh wound had reinfected. He was ill, feverish. His nose had been broken. Bruises discolored his hands and feet. He had the look of being beyond fear. From the original wheel, only seven remained.

"Run with me." Nang came back, prodded Ur. He had moved just past the first turn and stopped. The others had run until the second turn, then fear overcame them and they halted, hesitated, virtually running in place, afraid not to run, afraid to proceed into the tunnel. Slowly, they began to advance, disoriented, feeling the sides, afraid of their own disorientation, not even sure after the fourth or fifth turn if they indeed were continuing in the right direction or if they had accidentally reversed themselves and were headed back to their old tormentors.

"Samnang," Y Bhur said. "We must escape."

Samnang, Nang thought. He turned, looked behind himself. The others were no longer in sight. Samnang, he thought again. It sounded very strange. He knew that once he had been . . . *"Run!"* The order roiled up out of him from somewhere he did not know, pushed by something he did not recognize, could not question. Nang grabbed Ur's shoulder and pulled, ran and pulled with all his strength, a reserve he did not know existed. In seconds they were at the back of the cluster of cringing conscripts. *"Run!"* Nang growled horribly, growled like a guard, with contorted face. The mob spurted, hesitated. Nang dragged

Ur crazily through, over the others, seething mad, pulled as if pulling the entire band until they burst forth from the tube.

Nang froze. Others cringed. A contingent of *neary*, girl soldiers, welcomed them with half coconut shells of water. Pah crept forward. Met Sar stepped before the ranks. To one side a double rank of green-clad cadets stood smartly at attention.

"Welcome." Met Sar's voice was so comforting Nang felt fear melt, flow from his face, through his shoulders, down his abdomen, felt it piss from his groin, trickle down his legs and seep into the earth. He hunched there like an animal, humiliated.

"From today on," Met Sar said loudly enough for all to hear, "you shall be known as 'student.' " To the seven he said quietly, "Stand up straight." He motioned them erect with both hands, palms rising. "In a line, please." The conscripts formed into a row. "You shall be Student Pah. You, Student Eng. You, Student Ur. The Movement will heal your wound. You, Student Nang." He continued down the line, then directed them to a dining area.

Training was rigidly structured and compartmentalized. Varying tasks were accomplished at dispersed locations in or around the compound. Their days began at first light with vigorous calisthenics, then breakfast, followed by classes from seven o'clock to eleven o'clock. More physical exercise, lunch, chores, then classes from two to four-thirty. The new conscripts were added to a group of thirty-nine to make a class of forty-six. Nang found this camp delightful compared to the reception area. Had he recalled his home he would have found it pathetic, an ensnaring wretched quagmire of pitiful shacks, poor-quality rice and vile living conditions where only the elite were allowed any material comforts. But he did not compare it to Phum Sath Din. He compared it to the Mountaineer village aflame, to the coffin, the wheel, the beatings. Each day he grew stronger, more sure, slyer. Each day he understood more. Each day he received instructions in the new revolutionary mentality, the politics of enlightenment, the necessity for obedience. He was taught jungle living, hygiene and survival; he learned which plants were edible, which toxic. He was sent to collect a week's food—leaves, roots, bark—set to prepare it, to exist on it. There was no time to think of earlier life. Each day the desire to earn a yothea's krama, a soldier's scarf, increased.

In religion class Nang sat mesmerized as the instructor said, "I bet you've been stuffed with Buddhist teachings, that you've heard your fathers talk of the evils of the upper classes and of Norodom Sihanouk."

Yes, yes, Nang thought. How did you know? He sat perfectly

still, though wishing to turn and speak to Student Eng beside him and tell him the teacher was right.

"The real Buddha is the People," the instructor continued. "The People are invincible. They can accomplish any task. But they have been told since birth to give their spirit to this Buddha. Habit in youth becomes nature in age. For generations babies have had heaped upon them Buddha, Buddha, Buddha! Habit became nature. But it is not true. Henceforth, anyone who meddles with the People will be eliminated. Buddha! Augh! He was not even Kampuchean. Five hundred years ago some crazed monk from Sri Lanka tricked a frightened feudal monarch into exchanging the wealth of our nation for a promise of salvation. The monarchy forced the People to become Buddhist and this false foreign doctrine has passed from generation to generation as Kampuchea has been bled from great empire to poverty.

"Dumb king. Not even in India do people worship this Buddha. Kings are dumb. Two centuries ago a king was tricked into giving a quarter of our land to an Annamite family as dowry for their daughter. Driven by sins of the flesh he gave them Prey Nokor. The yuons named it Sai Con; the French, Saigon. But it is Khmer. The Mekong Delta is Khmer. We will regain these lands."

Yes, Nang thought. I know this to be true. He sat, stunned, seized by the words, the thoughts.

"Not once, in two thousand years, has the monarchy been able to defend Kampuchea's territorial integrity. Again and again"—the instructor slammed his fists angrily on his small lectern—"the monarch has sold out Kampuchea."

"Yes," Nang jumped up, shouted. "That's true," he yelled. The class stared at him. The lecturer smiled inwardly, took note, stared Nang back into his rigid seated posture.

"Two years ago," the lecturer continued, "Sihanouk obtained statements from the government of North Viet Nam and the provisional government of the South expressing recognition and acceptance of Kampuchea's present territorial boundaries including the coastal islands off Kep and Kampot. What good is writing. No matter how fine the paper, no matter how elaborate the words, the yuons still have thousands of troops inhabiting our territory. It's collusion. Buddha and the monarchy. We shall rid the land of both and the yuons will flee."

Nang left the lecture elated. To Ur he said, "My father said those same things. We can avenge our families."

Ur stared into his eyes. "Your father said similar things. Not the same."

Nang turned to Pah and Eng. "We'll be soldiers."

"Yeah," Eng answered. "Real soldiers."

Pah looked at Eng and Nang. Then at Ur. He said nothing but he walked behind Ur.

In the new compound the beatings did not stop but now they were meted out for specific infractions. As often as not punishment was delivered, not immediately, but during self-criticism sessions. Immediate punishments were light. Nang had been slapped twice during the day following the lecture on Buddhism and the monarchy for humming without permission. Eng had been roughed up for singing. Ur had been beaten for showing disrespect.

Punishments in self-criticism sessions were harsh. On the seventh night the class was separated into four cells for *kosangs*, Khmer for construction, a ritual similar to "struggles" in China, to *kiem thao* in Viet Nam. Three guards sat behind a narrow split-bamboo table set in a small open-sided hut. A dozen students sat on the earth in proper posture before the table. The guard at the center, Met Din, spoke seriously, not loudly, not angrily, just harshly. "Student Ur will rise, come forward and kneel." Ur immediately obeyed. He did not know his offense or who had reported him. He knew only he would be punished for his infractions and the punishment would hurt. He did not understand why they had not allowed the infection to consume him, why they had treated him, tended his wound with powders, cleansed it daily, even given him extra rations, since, he was certain, had been certain since they marched from Plei Srepok, he was destined to be killed.

"The Movement wishes you to learn proper revolutionary attitudes," Met Din rasped in Khmer.

"I wish to learn also," Ur responded. In his nervousness before the panel he spoke in Jarai. Immediately a guard from the end of the table leaped at him, swinging full arm, slapping his face, knocking Ur to the earth. The students cursed him in Khmer. Ur scrambled to recover his posture. Met Din repeated his statement. Ur responded in Khmer.

"Last night you were heard committing a sin of the flesh." Ur stared at Met Din. "Answer."

He did not know what to answer. "In rain, in wind, in health . . ." he began.

"Damn savage," Met Din shouted. "You must confess. You will confess and promise to rebuild yourself a better person. You must promise loyalty to the Movement. You must learn to tremble. Masturbation is a sin against the People. Confess."

"Confess," screamed a student.

"Last night—" Ur began.

"Turn," a side guard shouted. "To the students. Not to me."

"Last night I—" Ur began again.

"You are scum," Met Din interrupted.

"Scum," Nang shouted. The word came out before his thought congealed.

"I will not do it again," Ur said.

"You are buffalo shit," Met Din screamed.

"He steals," Pah shouted. "Tell all. Tell them how you steal water."

"I am shit," Student Ur said. "I promise to rebuild myself a good and pure person."

"You are despicable."

"I am despicable. I will try to rebuild myself . . ."

"Try?! *Try?!*" Met Din screamed. "You may die trying."

"I *will* rebuild myself for the good of the Brotherhood of the Pure and the good of all Kampuchea."

Met Din shouted, "And the water . . ."

As the kosang progressed the students, boys ten to thirteen, became more and more aggressive, swearing angrily, spitting on Ur, jumping up and poking or shoving him. Two, three at a time they surrounded him, screaming insults and abusing him.

"The Movement wishes the offender to be punished," Din said. The students sat. "Those of you who wish to receive the great honor of becoming yotheas of the Movement will decide the appropriate punishment."

A silence fell over the kosang hut. Met Din sat motionless, unblinking, eyes fixed on the seated. No one spoke. No one moved. They had never gone this far and they were unsure how to proceed. Nang stared at Ur. He felt horrified. How, he thought, how could Ur have done such a disgusting thing? Behind Nang, Eng stood. He bowed, stood at attention, said, "Place him in the stocks for one night." Eng sat. The guards remained motionless. Student Kun in the first row stood. "No water or food for one day." Silence continued. Little Pah arose, "Ten lashes with the split bamboo club." He sat. There was silence. A pang of guilt flooded Nang's mind. Still silence. Then Kun stood again. "Two days in stocks without food or water." The quiet pauses between suggested punishments shortened. "Hang him by his feet." "Let us each flail him with the bamboo." "Slice his fingertips." "Club him." Nang had not spoken. Met Din stared into Nang's eyes. The guards converged their ghastly glowers. Nang's breath shortened. A quivering rolled up from his abdomen, up through his shoulders, out the nape of his neck. He stood. Words came out. He sat. He had not heard his own words: "Tear his genitals from his body."

Met Din stood slowly. He shook his head. "Savages." He smiled. "Student Ur." Ur stood, turned and knelt facing the table. He had heard. He expected the worst. "The Movement is just, lenient, kind. Do you hate imperialists?"

"I hate imperialists."

"Do you hate the monarchy?"

"I loathe the monarchy."

"Do you hate yuons."

"I despise yuons."

"Should your genitals be ripped from your body?" Ur looked at Din. He could not answer. Sweat broke from his brow, trickled from his temples. "Yes?"

"No," Ur said weakly.

Din smiled. "Of course not," he said. He glared at Nang.

Nang's eyes met his, darted to the others. He felt humiliated, not by the punishment he'd suggested, but because Din had singled him out with his stare and rejected his demand.

"Not," Din smiled again, "at the first infraction. The Movement yet has use for you."

Once fear had become permanent it took only mild guidance and the threat of punishment to lead the students to true cruelty, to the total enjoyment of seeing others in pain. Political-ideological indoctrination and military training served to direct their cruelty, to give them efficient means of performance. From the fourth week of school, under the guise of jungle survival, the students practiced capturing, torturing and killing various kinds of animals. "Those who hesitate go hungry," Met Din announced.

The fifth week their rations were suspended. "Eat from the forest," Din told them. The sixth week they received bayonets and were turned loose on Pong Pay Mountain. Nang became so proficient at catching mice he could have fed his entire class. Instead, he ate his fill and systematically tortured those left. He built small kindling piles and tethered the animals to branches at the center. Then he lit the piles and watched the desperate creatures leap, trying to stay above the flames, screech, then frantically try to dig below, finally, in agony, expire and sizzle. Every day he developed new variations to tell the guards about. Kindling circles with six, eight, ten mice tethered to a stake at the center. The mice would push and bite one another trying to escape from the heat. Nang found their cruelty to one another fascinating.

The school had a deep narrow crocodile pit into which monkeys could be thrown. The elation, the applause, was tremendously fulfilling if one could catch a monkey for all to watch. In their seventh week Nang and Eng captured a large monkey and presented it to Met Din.

"This is a fine animal," Met Din congratulated the students. "Today, you be the instructors. I'll watch with the class." Eng tied the monkey's arms behind its back. Nang hooked his rope about the animal's neck, hooked it exactly as he himself had been hooked in the dark the night he was brought to the school. The monkey shrieked, lunged, struggled against the restraints. "Make him run with you," a cadreman called, and Nang took off at a sprint. The monkey ran but soon stumbled facedown and screamed. Nang jerked it up, ran again. Again the animal fell and shrieked. The students laughed, the cadres applauded. The teasing continued, transformed to torture. At this point in their training, the only time students were permitted to smile or laugh was during torture. Many became addicted to sadism. The animal, expressing so much anguish, so uncomprehending, displaying such human traits, made the crowd guffaw.

"Hack off his tail," Kun yelled, and Nang immediately flourished his honed bayonet. For weeks their physical training had focused on hand-to-hand combat, jujitsu, karate and bayonet. Nang leaped, kicked the animal. As it sprawled Nang whisked off its tail and flung it to the crowd. Again the animal screamed.

"The pit! The pit!" the mob chanted. Everyone pushed in. Nang and Eng untied the animal to keep their cords. They held it head down over the crocodiles below. The monkey shook spasmodically, lurched to no avail. Then it let out an eerie low moaning the likes of which Nang had never heard. It disgusted and horrified him. It sounded like prayer. Nang's nostril's flared. He reared up whipping the monkey overhead, then snapped his arms forward, down, flinging the animal toward the crocodiles. About him giggles, laughs, titters, hoorahs. And from below the moan, the moan apparently unperceived by all except Nang.

Indoctrination never ceased. From the very highest levels of Khmer Krahom policymaking came this understanding and direction—the greater one's belief in a cause, the greater one's effort and sacrifice. Classes began with the chant: In wind, in rain, in health, in sickness, day or night, we will obey, correctly and without complaint, that which the Movement orders. Again and again, repeated endlessly for months. Classes closed with the call, "Victory to the Revolution!"

Lectures delivered by information cadremen were highly informative—usually ending in militant zealousness. "During the colonial period," they were told, "Cambodian money went to France for the purchase of manufactured goods neither desired nor needed by Kampucheans. Money which should have been used to develop the nation was diverted to the colonialists and imperialists. When the rubber plantations brought in French currency, even though the Khmer laborers were paid well, it was all to serve France. Those who tended the plantations were paid more than all other Kampucheans but they were charged more to live and their living conditions were poorer than those of any others in the nation. And their money forced prices up throughout the land and made all Kampucheans poorer."

As Nang listened he felt as if in his mind there existed an impervious bubble in which someone had told him these things before. Who the someone had been, he did not attempt to recall.

"During the nineteen-twenties, thirties, and forties, landownership was taken from the peasants by the banks. Ownership concentrated in the hands of the capitalists."

Yes, Nang thought. The triple exploitation.

". . . Sihanouk sponsored co-op lending, but with his feudal mentality he let the capitalists burden the People with 'whatever the market will bear.' Corruption is a remnant of feudal mentality . . ."

Yes. Colonialists. The monarchy. Imperialists.

". . . in his new government, the feudal power structure was left intact. Provincial governors continued to steal the wealth of their subjects."

I've been told this before.

". . . they have been corrupted by an economic system based on private profit. We must struggle to build a society unmarred by selfishness, unblemished by passions for material possessions, unfouled by privileges. We shall create a *new man, a new mankind.*"

Nang's eyes were fastened to the instructor's lips. Perhaps the words heard were those spoken, perhaps in his mind he dredged up old thought and added meaning under the new light of his indoctrination. "We shall obtain mastery over the waters," the words formed in his mind. "Cambodia covered the Ca Mau Peninsula because we controlled the water."

One evening Met Sar addressed Nang's class. "To achieve victory, to defeat the enemies of the People, you will have to withstand long periods of denial. You will be strong, powerful. You will not know fear. Death, injury, will be without significance. Rid yourselves of desire and passion and you shall be unstoppable."

The class rose as one, chanted in one voice, "I am desire not contrary to duty. I am the sacrifice. I will do whatever the

Movement asks. I am happy to serve. I will die for the Movement if it is so deemed."

In the years which followed Nang's indoctrination, much of the academic portion of the Liberation School training would be abandoned, swept away in the tremendous deluge of volunteers and forced recruits, but the early training would remain at the foundation of the Krahom myth and ideology as the early conscripts later became the core cadres of Angkar Leou and of the nation.

One evening Nang sat with Met Sar at a small table under a thatch roof held up by five posts. The older man had greeted him warmly and offered him tea. "Student Nang," he said, "I'm told often of your excellent progress. You wished to see me."

"Thank you, Met Sar. Yes." Nang sipped his tea. He did not smile. "I think I want to be a disciple of the Movement," he said slowly, "but I'm not sure. I'm trying to figure it out."

"Let the Movement help you," Met Sar said, his lips pulling into a thin smile. "Listen to the Movement. We're a select group. Expose your torment to the Movement. You, Nang, have the makings of one who could someday be at the inner circle." Met Sar spoke sincerely, gently. "The Movement is kind. The Movement's loving hands reach out to all, even amid pain and suffering and sorrow."

"Yes," Nang sighed.

"Has Student Ur spoken anymore of escape?" Met Sar asked. His voice remained as smooth as before. Almost hypnotic.

"Yes," Nang answered. "On three occasions he has approached me."

"And you . . ." Met Sar paused.

"I let him speak as you've instructed. I try to show sorrow to cover my disgust."

"You shall be rewarded. In the Movement you will be fulfilled. Your salvation shall be found in service to Angkar Leou."

"To . . . I do not understand."

"The Movement. Give yourself up to the Movement and you'll be free from these self-centered concerns. You'll be able to focus on the outer world of our people."

Late that night Nang prayed. He thought about all the things he had been told, all he had seen. He had seen the massive stocks of rice in the warehouse in Stung Treng and the misery of poor villages; he had seen the motley government soldiers at roadblocks, the brutal yuon massacre, the sellout of Kampuchea by the likes of Bok Roh.

Suddenly they seemed to crystalize, to be seen in a new light, the light of the Movement, and that light, like a beam in thin night fog, illuminated his future, his direction. He would follow the cadres and the rules of the Movement. He would become the fighter in his people's struggle for independence that the Movement was asking him to be. There would be much to learn but in that moment, that dark moment, he decided he would become everything he was capable of becoming. He would obey and avenge his father. He would become the Movement.

Punishment for infractions became more sophisticated. One morning Nang and Ur were spied resting under a tree while they were expected to be hunting. That night their ankles were clamped to the top of a foot-high iron post. Their arms were crossed before them, their wrists tied behind their necks. Behind their backs needle-sharp bamboo spikes had been driven into the earth. If they leaned back they would be cut. If they fell back they would be impaled. The night was not dark. Behind thin clouds the moon was full. They could see they were alone. Ur whispered to Nang, "You've sold out, haven't you?" Nang did not answer. "You've gone to them in your head," Ur accused. His physical strength was near restored but he had not accepted the treatment.

"I have, eh?" Nang finally answered. Now Ur was silent. It was difficult to speak and maintain the rigid posture necessary to keep one's stomach muscles from relaxing. "They're right," Nang said.

"Right?!" Ur hissed.

"They're fair," Nang said.

"You, a Buddhist, call them fair after what we must do to monkeys? Even in my village, when we sacrifice animals, we're not so cruel."

"I'm not Buddhist," Nang said. "Buddha was Indian. Just like Met Sar said." Ur hissed again but did not speak. "If you can kill the monkey," Nang repeated what the cadremen said, "when you face an enemy you'll not hesitate. You'll kill him. If you hesitate, he'll kill you."

Again a pause. "I hunt better than you," Ur said. "I stalk better than you. I kill better than you. I will not kill their way."

Neither boy spoke for over an hour. Screams came from the compound where the *neary* were trained. Nang memorized Ur's words. He would tell Met Din or Met Huk during the morning and Ur would endure another kosang. Nang laughed inwardly. The fool, he thought. Ur, too, memorized his words. He was certain now that Nang was a *chrop*, an informer. How quickly,

Ur thought, this Khmer boy changes. He wished to tell Nang to resist, resist one day longer, but he, Ur, no longer had the energy or the desire to devote to his onetime friend. He would listen. He would play along. But he would never convert.

Chhuon stood in the hallway of the apartment building in Neak Luong. He pulled the leaflet from his pants pocket and looked again at the photo. The merriment of the crowd in the new apartment irritated him. But for Vathana, he thought, I would barge in screaming. I would . . . what would I scream? Chhuon's lack of patience, today, and his recognition that the occasion was, as it should be, joyous, made him feel guilty and the guilt added to his irritability. He no longer sought to eliminate the impurities of his mind. Instead he hid them, hid his thoughts, operated outwardly in a nearly normal manner. At home, after the connecting-word ceremony, after Voen had returned to Phnom Penh and after the Pechs had left the village, Chhuon had returned to his withdrawn, spiritless state. In the months since the funeral, major shifts had taken place within him. At times he felt he no longer knew himself. The wailing had been followed by the first withdrawal and then the growing passion for revenge. Upon that broke a second wave of withdrawal mixed with feelings of helplessness and impatience as water washing a beach is mixed with seaweed and residue. The wave receded and the beach reverted to normalcy only to be inundated by a larger wave of emptiness and apathy. As those emotions ebbed he was left numb, encased, his shell impenetrable to feelings from without, incapable of allowing inner feelings to escape. Every night he dreamed of revenge. Every dawn he heard the trucks across the river and a portion of his dream returned. He did not see the khrou or the monk, and though he again served his farm clients he no longer read the agricultural journals, no longer strove to ensure that each rice experiment and each breeding animal was properly handled. He meditated on revenge, on death. He speculated on the causes of the slaughter of Kdeb and Yani. All the reassurance, all the comfort his Buddhism had given him in the past, all the strength it had bestowed at the death, during infancy, of two of his children, all the joy it had brought him after his father's death knowing he had properly provided for his father's spirit was dashed, was destroyed, was slaughtered with the distant violent slaughter of Kdeb and Yani, slaughtered beyond mitigation, slaughtered and aggravated because the earthly vessels of their spirits were unrecovered. Instead of reaching for religious significance he consciously courted revenge and hatred and xenophobic anguish. His grief and guilt, which should have been tempered by the making public during the rite for the dead, was instead tempered in the furnace of withdrawal.

The wedding feast was under way. The first two days of celebration had been, as Sok had whispered to Chhuon, "beautiful for a city wedding." Chhuon, like his wife, missed some of the traditional aspects which had been set aside. Usually the ceremony was held at the bride's parents' home and the first day was given to erecting a three-room bamboo house for the groom. Indeed, in Phum Sath Din, villagers did erect a groom's house, and they feasted and celebrated the village's most spectacular marriage, but in the heart of Neak Luong no one erected a groom's house. Instead Pech Chieu Teck, second son of Pech Lim Song, had arranged for the use of three apartments in the city's first modern concrete-and-glass building. Vathana and her family were given a fourth-floor, three-room apartment which the new couple would occupy after their marriage. Teck and his groom entourage moved into a third-floor unit and various relatives and guests shared a flat on the ground floor where much of the food preparation took place. But the vertical separation also meant that family and friends saw less of each other and that a certain traditional warmth which should have grown from the labor of the first day was stillborn.

Chhuon studied the leaflet photo. The paper was flimsy and greatly deteriorated. Folds had become cracks, cracks turned to powder, yet the unfolded picture remained clear.

Pech Lim Song's voice seeped from the apartment. "When Samdech Sihanouk became king," he said, "they made him take courses in military tactics. Ha, he didn't know the difference between a sergeant and a captain. He didn't even know which end of a rifle the bullet came out. He boasts that he got rid of the Viet Minh by saying to them, 'What the devil are you doing here? Get out!' He thinks they left."

The photo was of a mass of contorted, disfigured bodies. Six faces were easily discernible, one of an elder tied to a large X-rack, one of a girl with dry blood-rivers running from her ears. Four of Jarai youngsters in the center of the heap. The words in the fold were imprinted indelibly on Chhuon's brain: *This photograph is supplied as a service to families or relatives seeking missing children* ... Chhuon scoffed. Supplied to let us know, he thought, what you'll do if we resist you, or if our resistance is too weak to stop you. He thought to show the photo to his older sister, Voen, to ask her to look at the other faces, at those he, Chhuon, could not identify, but he knew he could not now confront her, could never confront her with such horror.

Another voice reached the hallway. "They're the ones who control the Northeast. But the Prince closes his eyes."

Chhuon did not recognize the speaker. This day's ceremonies had begun at dawn on the third floor with Teck, dressed in gold cape and loincloth, bowing to the rising sun, chanting traditional prayers. Then a priest had drawn a sword and led the groom and his male relatives to the fourth floor for the "open-house rite." A bridesmaid, Voen, Chhuon's sister, had come out to ring the gong Teck's brother had carried. Traditionally the bridesmaid should have been a young girl. To Chhuon, that meant Mayana. He folded the leaflet.

"I've heard there's a hundred thousand yuons in the mountains." Again the voice was the groom's father's. "They've a base at Siem Reap. Still he doesn't see them. They pay him, they don't attack. Mark my words, they'll take our country if we don't do something."

The bridesmaid had been followed by a young boy carrying a bowl of water to wash the groom's feet. Peou had compensated well for his age, Chhuon thought, but properly Samnang should have borne the offering and received the candy gift.

Chhuon knew that Sok, too, was pained by the conspicuous absence of the younger children. In the bridal chamber he had whispered to her, "Don't cry."

"Don't you cry," Sok had answered. It was their most gentle exchange in months.

"Yes," Chhuon had said. "We see the children and we cannot help but think of Yani and Samnang."

"Yes," Sok had answered dryly, and Chhuon had felt great guilt and humiliation and he'd dreaded seeing Vathana, sure she too would look at him, accusing him of his own thoughts.

Again the voice that Chhuon did not know spilled into the hall. "Samdech Euv could preserve our neutrality. He could raise a Khmer army capable of defending our borders. I know what's happening. I've seen with my own eyes. I have business in Sihanoukville. My trucks travel Highways 2, 3 and 4. He allows the Chinese to unload their guns and ship them to the border . . . secret bases . . . open use of the border . . . his army is nothing more than a palace guard. They've no training, no discipline. That's why they become thugs when they're used. Thirty-five thousand thugs."

Talk, Chhuon thought. It's so easy. But this man, he's a fool to let his voice travel places he cannot see.

Chhuon entered the room. He stood with his back to the wall, looking between heads, catching only slight glimpses of the ceremony. For him the rite known as "turning the candle" had always been the most beautiful of all the wedding rituals. Vathana and Teck sat stiffly side by side. The marriage was a contract, a religious relationship, not the union of two people "in love." That Vathana was beautiful was ostensibly of secondary importance to Teck. He did not look at her but he was aware of her beauty. He was both thankful and resentful his father had arranged this match. That Teck was physically flimsy upset Vathana. She had expected him to be strong like her father, like his own father.

Chhuon watched his eldest daughter from the back of the assembled crowd. While his eyes beheld her he felt peaceful. Voen rose, led four aunts, each holding a candle in a circle about the couple. The aunts blew smoke from their candles onto the newlyweds to give them strength. Uncles joined the aunts. The priests and the monk chanted prayers and everyone repeated them and a feeling of joy and holiness spread and grasped all in the room. Each uncle tied a thread to Vathana's wrist, then to Teck's. Chhuon should have been the first to tie the thread but his legs froze and he couldn't move into the center of the crowded room. Suddenly he felt revulsion. His eyes fell to Vathana's hips. This marriage to the second son of Pech Lim Song is wrong. It's not enough. She should've been married to a minister in Sihanouk's cabinet or to a wealthy man, not to the second son of a second-level entrepreneur. It's me. I am nothing. It rubs off on my children.

Chhuon breathed heavily, shut his eyes to attempt to contemplate the ceremony, to attempt to pray. He heard the whisper of the man with the loose voice and he opened his eyes. In the crowd before him he saw a man leaning to the ear of another. "Look what happened earlier this year. Not only did the people not rise up and join the Communists, they rose up and defended themselves and Saigon. How can he back the North?"

"Are you talking politics again?" The voice was Madame Pech's. "They'll be coming around to visit with each of us. Please leave your politics out there. Has anyone seen the bride's father? Did you see the rice? It's the whitest I've ever seen."

Before Nang's class could be used to spearhead the attack on the village of Phum Siembauk, certain changes had to be made.

In the tenth week of Liberation School the conscripts changed their uniforms from baggy green utilities to the heavier black cloth of the Khmer Krahom army. They were permitted increased freedom within the compound. Already they had guided two new wheels of recruits to the cliff; had learned to use the pole not to push them off but to guide them to the edge where the recruits would, themselves, in time, commit themselves to the fall; had cruelly beaten two groups at the barren reception area thinking how strong they themselves had become and how this would be for the good of these new boys; had welcomed six groups at the end of the bamboo corridor. Of forty-six who had begun, forty-one remained. One had accidentally been killed during bayonet drill. One had been killed by being beaten after his fourth kosang. Three had disappeared in the night. Those remaining were now teamed with a battalion of older, fully trained yotheas; teamed in preparation for their baptism by fire, teamed for the reeducation of a hamlet on the west bank of the Mekong, twenty-three kilometers south of Stung Treng City.

The class moved to a camp lower on Pong Pay Mountain. The pace and attitude of training quickened, became more intense, fanatical. For many, training had eliminated every outward vestige of human warmth and emotion other than approved hatred, official rage, and the delight of seeing others suffer.

The monsoon season was passing. Preparations for the main rice harvest were under way. The time for new offensives, and for new units to be unleashed, had arrived. Quickly, day and night without pause to think, the students prepared for the operation.

They were not let in on the overall plan but were instructed first in the basic principles of Khmer Krahom tactics, then in the specifics of their part in a raid. The principles were summarized much like the American Military Code of Conduct and, in similar fashion, memorized by every student, every yothea, every neary.

1. I will protect, defend and expand the front.
2. I will seal off the areas we control from the corrupting influence of the bourgeoisie.
3. When our front advances, everything captured will be sealed within so we may consolidate our victories. If we temporarily retreat, *everything* that can divulge anything about us to our enemies must be removed with us or destroyed. People, rumors and lies must not escape our sealed area.
4. All corrupt village leaders will immediately be shot.
5. All potential leaders will be led away for future liquidation.
6. All family heads will be removed for future liquidation.
7. One pliable elder shall be identified and used as a symbol of local leadership. He will be the conduit for rules from the Movement to the people. He will command the People.
8. No harm will come to the people.

"Nang, Eng, Ur, Pah . . ." Met Dy, the cadreman in charge of their unit, addressed each. They surrounded a precise sand-table model of Phum Siembauk and Hamlet 4. "These figures are you, these are your sampans . . ." Met Dy moved the small bamboo boats from the bank of a large midriver island to the west bank of the river. He moved the figures which represented each team across the floodplain and paddies to the berm which protected the hamlet. "Once you're in position, here, you'll wait until you hear the attack begin. Then you must move quickly.

"Ur, Kun, you will take your team and surround this house where an evil landlord, Kim Kamel, will be asleep with his whores. He must remain inside while you burn the building. Pah, Ka, your team will ignite the next house where the evil merchant Chen Qing lives. Eng, Nang, you will enter this house, of Doctor Leu Lahn Phal. He is an especially terrible man and must avow his guilt before the representatives of the People."

For a week the students practiced the attack, meditated through the attack, played it out on the sand table. "It is night," Met Dy said quietly to Nang's team. The students were gathered beneath a large tree by the creek at the base of Pong Pay two hours before sunset. "It is very dark," Met Dy said. The students sat, eyes closed, silent, listening. "You can hear the river. Your blood is coursing quickly, bringing you great courage. Your clubs are hammers. They are extensions of your arms. The signal arrives. See yourself rise . . ." Step-by-step Met Dy explained how each student would behave, how each would feel; described each obstacle and how it would be conquered, each sight and how they would react. Then they moved.

For two days and nights the Krahom battalion crept through the jungle. They stopped often, rested, reviewed the battle plan. At first the going was quick. The trails and secret roads running south from Pong Pay were well established and unhindered. Twelve miles north, in Laos, the same road network was being heavily bombarded. On 31 October Lyndon Johnson had announced the cessation of all bombing of North Viet Nam. Within two days, American B-52 crews had been redirected—tripling their tonnage on the Ho Chi Minh supply trails in Laos. No bombs interdicted the Krahom move. From Pong Pay they moved en masse to Phum Chuntong, then Phum Kha Panang and Phum Bang Hio, to the outskirts of Phum Sath Din. The unit disintegrated into three- to seven-man student teams led by a single hardened yothea.

Nang knew the forest here. A twinge formed in his gut, tensed about his heart. Instead of skirting, he wished to go through this village. He knew why, yet he could not recognize the reason. There was once a boy named Cahuom Samnang who lived in the village, lived there not particularly happily, as Nang recalled, for the boy was always very weak. So why wish to see this village? There were two friends there who needed a lesson, two lackeys of the Royal imperialists who had once ripped his pants from him. Nang did not focus on thoughts of Phum Sath Din, but instead meditated on his role in the coming battle. Still the twinge festered in him as he waited for it to be his team's turn to move.

Nang felt irritated, looked irritable. Met Dy told him to relax. "This raid will be as easy as swiping rice cakes from babies." As Nang waited the festering ate at him from the inside, gnawed horribly. If he could have identified the feeling he might have seen it as old values and beliefs, awakened by home, kicking and clawing to resurface, to reassert themselves, to topple new beliefs, new dogmas, new gods, but each kick was countered with the new mind's bludgeoning of less-than-subtle fear. He might have seen it as guilt for what he'd become, what he was about to do, but each clawing was countered with the new revolutionary mind's stabbing recall of pain endured. He might have thought of his father, but his father had been murdered by Bok Roh and the yuons and that, even repressed, was painful. The team circled Phum Sath Din, dropped to the bank of the Srepok River, rose, crossed the bridge. The gnawing waned, flickered out.

Mynah birds chattered in the trees. A light mist hung in the air. Slowly, quietly, Nang, Eng, the others followed the yothea to the edge of the treeline on the west of the large mid-Mekong island. The yothea vanished. Across the main channel they could just make out their target. Above and below them ferry docks protruded into the water. Other teams were slated to destroy them once the battle was joined; still others would destroy the docks and ferries on the far bank; and additional teams would deploy both north and south to ambush any relief forces which might come from Stung Treng or Kratie.

An hour before the attack the teams slipped their commandeered sampans from beneath thick overhanging vegetation. The battle at Siembauk 4 was designed from the outset to be an act of terrorism in a guerrilla war. The Krahom leadership did not intend to hold the hamlet but simply to destroy it. If the maneuver also closed the Mekong to river traffic from Kratie to Stung Treng, all the better. The last of the monsoon season supplies scheduled to be shipped north would be delayed, Stung Treng would wither slightly, sag slightly, until the dry season came and heavy road traffic on Highway 13 could again begin.

More important, Stung Treng and the Northeast would again be reminded of their precarious situation. The feeling, the belief, of insecurity would soften future resistance.

On the night of 6 November, as Americans were waking to the day they would elect Richard Milhous Nixon president of the United States, two river observation teams moved into positions approximately ten kilometers north and thirteen kilometers south of Phum Siembauk. Other squads had converged undetected east of Siambok, others west of town along the floodplain of both the Siambok and O Run rivers. That night supplies, ammunition and soldiers were infiltrated to additional staging sites. The next day the soldiers, hidden, rested, observed. By the night of the seventh, all units were in position.

They were armed with stout clubs and bayonets. Nang waited. Observing the river and the hamlet relaxed him. The mud-yellow waters were high, fast, but not raging as they could during the height of the monsoons and at the arrival of the Himalaya melt. Nang rose, checked the narrow sampan he and Eng had taken from an isolated farm north of Sre Kraseng. They would launch above their objective, let themselves be carried down as they propelled across. He watched the far bank. The hamlet at this distance looked exactly like the sand-table model. Every house, every shed, every tree was in place. He could walk through the village blind. As night fell Nang was amazed at how light the night was, and he thought vaguely that the nights in Phum Sath Din had never been this light. But then he thought, Perhaps it is that I am now accustomed to the night. I am now blessed by the Movement. Student Orn reached them, signaled the team. Thought ceased. Rote human automation replaced reasoning. The play began. They converged on the sampan, pushed off, glided into the current. Adrenaline rushed. Below them, Ur's team was already halfway across. Farther down current, Pah's team was struggling with the largest of the stolen boats. As Pah's team hit shore, the mortar team set up on the island dropped the first rounds into the tube. The thump of the round firing signaled all near units into action. The explosion a minute later signaled distant units. Three regular squads launched a diversionary rifle and grenade assault on the main town. Immediately four squads of regulars slipped into Hamlet 4 from the west. From the east Nang and three student teams charged across the floodplain into the hamlet. Smaller teams attacked the ferries and docks.

Doctor Leu was awakened by the explosions. He had not yet lit a lantern. His family slumbered. The hamlet attackers swept in like fog. The battle sounds came from town.

Eng dove through a side window. Nang, though the door was not locked, did not have a lock, crashed through and ripped the door from the jamb. Orn, then Nika, Chan and Buor followed him in. Doctor Leu leaped back from the kerosene lamp he'd just lit, froze. The older man stared at the boys in sleepy amazement and fascination. They were tiny, menacing with their clubs and bayonets, but small. The incongruity of the scene puzzled him. Behind him, his wife and daughters huddled.

Doctor Leu Lahn Phal said, "Welcome to my home." He bowed. "May I serve you?"

"Nang," Eng whispered. Nang was silent, unable to remember the condemnation speech. "Nang," Eng whispered again. Nika and Chan dropped back a step. Their fervor flickered in Nang's hesitation and Doctor Leu's calm command presence.

"Meayeat," the doctor said calmly to his wife, "tea." Then to the boys, "You will sip tea with me. You"—he looked kindly at Nang—"are thirsty, eh? Hungry? Let me get rice bowls and tea—"

"Halt!" Nang demanded. "You are accused of collusion"—Met Dy's words came from his mouth an octave too high—"with imperialists. You have . . ."

"My dear son," Doctor Leu forcefully interrupted, "I am a—"

"Silence!" Nang screamed, his voice hard, strong. The command broke the students' growing doubt. Three lunged to the children. Eng swung, smashed his club into the side of the doctor's knee, toppling him.

"What . . . ," he groaned, "what do you wa—"

"Silence! You cannot speak." Nang's words were loud, fast, full of his own fright. "Every thought, without exception, is stamped with the brand of your class. You will confess before the People. You will be severely punished. Your head must bow." Nang bellowed at Nika, "Bring her." Nang's eyes bulged. His nares dilated. With his left hand he squeezed his bayonet. In his right he gripped his club. The doctor began to rise. Nang swung, backhand, an ingrained, automatic response. His club smashed Doctor Leu's face. Nika lifted the tiniest daughter by her feet. In one motion he flung her at Nang, at his raised bayonet. Nang braced, stiff armed. At the instant the infant hit the point, Meayeat shrieking in terror, Nang withdrew and let the baby crash to the floor. From outside, cries, wails, screams mixed with barked orders. Light flashes hit walls before explosive booms reached the Leu home. To each side homes burst into flames.

"My God!" Doctor Leu's voice rumbled deep behind his smashed bleeding face. "What's happening? We've done nothing. Who are you?"

"Tie him," Nang ordered. Adrenaline fired Nang's fears. He was out of control, knew he was out of control. This scared him and the fear fired more adrenaline.

For half an hour, trussed and shackled, Doctor Leu endured pokes, prods and blows. They smashed his teeth, then concentrated on his feet and shins while his wife and daughters were forced to watch. Then Nang ordered Meayeat to wash her husband's face. She obeyed as Met Dy said she would. Everything moved as planned. As she squatted beside his still-bound frame, crying, gently washing away blood and picking tooth fragments from his mouth, Eng raised his club and bludgeoned her with such force her head splattered into her husband's eyes. In his pain his pinned arms lurched for her. Then, reduced to cowering, he whimpered before the boys. Nang laughed nervously. Encouraged by Doctor Leu's pacification Eng grabbed the man's hair, lifted his face, smiled hysterically, fanatically, the face of a shark in feeding frenzy. Nika and Orn dragged the daughters forward. The baby had fallen into sleep, driven to escape in sleep after wailing for an hour. The three-year-old was silent, withdrawn, in shock. The eldest, perhaps six, seemed to understand and accept, accept in horror, yet accept. Nang grabbed her from Orn. He took her thin shoulders in his palms and forced them back, back, together, while Orn methodically slit her shirt from neck to navel, then her chest with his razor-sharp knife. He stroked the incision with the blade. She screamed, struggled, shook. Nang, his mind shrieking at itself, afraid of its own uncontrolled fury, increased his pressure. Doctor Leu mumbled a prayer, closed his eyes. Chan grabbed his right eyelid, stretched the skin the length of his hand, then sliced. He repeated on the left. Orn continued stroking, the blade tip now working through the cartilage between sternum and ribs, slicing her until her chest burst.

The Khmer Krahom battalion held Siembauk Hamlet 4 from 7 to 10 November. The town of Siembauk, as if petrified, did not attempt to relieve the hamlet only three quarters of a kilometer north. Local government resistance can best be described as light. Perhaps they were not expecting the attack, perhaps those who knew it was coming had quietly evacuated. Perhaps it could be seen as a sign that by the end of 1968 local officials had given up all territory in the Northeast, but Siembauk 4 was on the west bank of the Mekong and was twenty-three kilometers south of Stung Treng. At the least, there should have been a real battle, but no battle materialized. In the first hour all resistance had been neutralized.

Royal Cambodian forces from Stung Treng and Kratie were ambushed on the river on 8 November. They engaged enemy forces equipped with rocket-propelled grenades on the eighth and ninth, until the enemy withdrew. On 10 November the flotilla reached Siembauk, rendezvoused with an armored column from Kompong Thom and surrounded a lifeless, abandoned community. One hundred and fourteen people were found beaten to death within their homes. Seven people, the entire Kim Kamel family, escaped. No corpses of children between nine and fifteen years old were found. Presumably those children were conscripted. Also notably missing from amongst the dead were two hamlet elders of minor administrative importance. Nine enfeebled elders were wounded but not killed. They were evacuated and resettled with relatives in the town. Presumably this was a Khmer Krahom tactic designed to increase the burden on Siembauk and hasten its economic decline.

"Perhaps he was too old," Met Dy whispered to Met Sar. The breakdown of order disturbed both men.

"Perhaps," Met Sar whispered back. "Or perhaps of the wrong ethnic group, but other Jarai have worked well." He paused, looked at the gathering of students before him and at the accused. The kosang had been in session for four hours. Met Sar and others, using the occasion as a class, had delivered long harangues: that which is rotten must be excised . . . soldiers must set an example of order and discipline . . . reactionaries must be disciplined . . . vigilance must be razor sharp or purity will be contaminated . . .

"I think," Met Sar's calm whisper began again, "it is neither age nor tribal origin per se. I think our mistake was to allow the Jarai to train with a Khmer class. He should have been separated and trained at Mount Aural with other eastern Mountaineers. Removed further from his old culture he would have been less apt to regress."

Met Sar stood. "You have contemplated the judgment long enough," he said. "Now it is time for sentencing. Team leaders stand and report. Student Pah."

"Let him attempt to escape." Pah snickered.

"Student Nang."

Nang stood ramrod straight, tall and proud. His team had been honored by the battalion of regulars. No other team had been singled out, except Ur's for disgrace, for violating the Krahom code, for subverting the operation. Student Ur had advanced to the home of Kim Kamel moments before the attack, had woken the seven people inside and had guided them to a hiding place at the village berm. From there they had escaped while Ur's team went through the motions of burning the house. Ur was despicable, vulgar. Nang had long since mentally abandoned him. "My team would like to be first hunters," Nang said.

"Student Kun," Met Sar called.

"We are the team he betrayed," Kun said. He spoke softly, yet his voice was full of hate. "Let us beat him until dead."

"So be it." Met Sar scowled. "Each sentence shall be carried out. Prisoner! Escape!"

Ur glanced at Met Sar. He was not bound though he was surrounded. He glared at his classmates. His breath came hard, his body tensed like that of a bull about to charge. There was no way out except through them. For a few seconds he froze, thinking perhaps it would be best to let them beat him to death where he stood, then he exploded forward crashing into little Pah, bowling him over, fist smashing Ka, breaking through the weakest team, sprinting toward the perimeter until Nang, chasing, flinging his club into Ur's legs, upended him. Immediately Eng and Nika clubbed him, subdued him, broke his ankles with splintering blows. Ur spun his legs away, his feet flopping. He growled like an animal. Nika backed away, laughed. Ur's eyes flashed daggers. The others surrounded him, though at a distance over which he could not strike. Nang scampered to the fore, retrieved his club. He tried to suppress his laugh, his delight. Ur locked eyes with him. Nang stared back. He felt the pressure of eyes, the look of Met Sar, of his own teammates. Eng swung from behind, breaking Ur's left elbow. Slowly, methodically, each student approached, swung, first at Ur's right hand, his last pathetic defense, until Ur could no longer hold the hand and arm up. Then from his feet they worked. They formed a line, each student with his ax-handle club, shouting, bouncing on the balls of his feet, waiting to be next, first in line, then shouting, "Traitor!" springing forward, ax handle raised then slammed down smashing a knee or hip until the bone was pulverized and Met Sar or Met Dy indicated a new bodily zone, each boy spinning after his hit, running to the end of the line, bouncing, shouting—Ur's body slowly transforming into a seeping sack of mush—running, THUNK, the head so mashed as to be unrecognizable.

Then the students returned to the body. Each grabbed a handful of brain or intestine or sliced a piece of liver or heart, then smeared the bloody tissue on his face and arms. They smiled at one another, brothers in blood, bonded in deed. Nang came last. Ur's head was scraped clean, his viscera empty.

Nang removed his bayonet. At Ur's left knee he made a deep incision, he looked to Sar and Dy for approval, then he proceeded to carve upward until he had removed the entire mashed quadriceps, the muscle wounded an age ago when Samnang and Y Bhur lost their boyhoods in the Cloud Forest above Plei Srepok.

"From this day forward," Met Sar announced to the gathered class, cadres, guards and yotheas, "these men shall be comrades of the Movement, brothers in the Brotherhood of the Pure." The final rite at the Liberation School was solemn. The students, eleven to thirteen years old, were mature and grave. In three months of cleansing, instruction and indoctrination, the shy, terrified conscripts had been reborn as *mets*, comrades, as yotheas, soldiers, of the Khmer Krahom. If any mind still harbored the possibility of reversal, that emotion would soon be extinguished by one last ritual, a confirmation of their status as soldiers of the Movement—a barrier designed to seal the possibility forever.

Met Sar stood before four large posters. Before the ceremony the new yotheas had stood below the portraits for a class photo—Karl Marx, Friedrich Engels, Joseph Stalin and Mao Zedong overlooking them. "The moment the imperialist dogs and their lackeys are defeated and the country is ordered," Met Sar announced, "we shall usher in an age of happiness. Everyone will be happy and will share in all the wealth of Kampuchea. Students, new comrades, come forward and receive your kramas. To you shall fall the responsibility of ridding our country of fascists, capitalists and reactionaries." The class, now thirty-three, marched in an orderly line before Met Sar's podium, received their scarfs, wrapped them about their necks and marched back. "You shall swear allegiance to the leadership of the Movement. You shall be disciples. You shall spread the message. 'All comrades,' " Met Sar quoted Ho Chi Minh, speaking the words as if his own, " 'from the Central Committee down to the cell, must preserve the unity and oneness of mind in the Party.' "

The ceremony was formal. Like Buddhist monks, like Christian monks, the new yotheas took vows of poverty, chastity, obedience and hard work. "Through these vows," Met Sar addressed the class, "you shall find a great burden lifted from your back. In loyalty to the Movement you will find the passage to inner freedom."

Nang looked upon Met Sar with elation exploding in his chest, with a fervor that can only be expressed by the term "love."

"We believe in the Movement," Met Sar said in his soft voice. The students repeated the line. Then in unison they continued:

We believe in what the Movement has done for us,
   and for all people and all eternity.
We believe the Movement is a gift to the People;
   we praise the Movement.
The better we serve and honor the Movement,
   the better we serve and honor the People.
We shall grow in the Movement as rice grows in fertile paddies.
We shall search in the Movement and our souls shall have stable
   homes.
We shall share in the Movement and our strength will be
   multiplied a hundredfold.
The way of the Movement is not easy, but it is righteous and perfect.
   We are desire not contrary to duty.
   We are the sacrifice. We are the offering.
The Movement is the People!
We are the Movement!
We are Kampuchea!

"Met Nang." Met Sar cornered the boy after the ceremony. "You and Met Eng have been chosen for special assignment. You shall go with Comrade Binh. He will brief you."

Nang looked at Met Sar. He did not speak though he wished to. Nor did he smile.

Met Sar beheld Met Nang. He stepped to the boy and put his arms about his waist. "Learn everything you can," Met Sar whispered. "Be cautious. You are going for international training to the camp where Bok Roh once trained. No one will recognize you. When you return, you'll be a great warrior."

CHAPTER FIVE

The international new year had passed (the Cambodian New Year falls in mid-April) and the dry season was upon the land. Cahuom Chhuon broke from his heavy labor. His pants were soaked with sweat and stuck in his crotch. He had eaten less and less each day for six months and his once stocky body was light, not frail but wiry. He mopped his brow with a rag, a worn krama Sok had begun to use for cleaning. When he'd grabbed it he'd felt a certain pleasure, a certain acknowledgment in the denial to himself of a new krama. For a month he'd washed it daily in the river when he'd broken from his chores.

Chhuon sat beneath a tree at the river's edge. The afternoon sun bore through the branches to bake him but he did not move. He'd rinsed in the current, washed the rag, wrung it and sat. Slowly he placed the rag over his head. He sat erect, perfectly still, cleared his mind. His breath came shallow. He could feel his face, his jowls, sag. The weight of his thumbs felt like thousands of pounds, his wrists drooped, his hands turned inward on his thighs, the sun burned their backs.

Peou must go to school. Sok must eat. His thoughts ran down his responsibilities as if he had a list. Cousin Sam needs help repairing his furrower. A cloud passed in front of the sun. Coolness enwrapped him. He shivered slightly but refused to respond. Seed must be distributed, his thoughts continued. I must write Vathana. The cloud cleared and again the sun burned into his hands, arms, body. And I must awaken my people, Chhuon thought. But how? Awaken them to the yuon threat. How? There must be revenge.

Vathana was unhappy.

Pech Chieu Teck was proper. His lovemaking was proper, his behavior and manners were impeccable. The luxuries he, his family, especially his mother, showered on the new bride were marvelous, yet in a month's time Vathana felt as if she'd been tethered to an elephant and was about to be trampled. She told herself it was natural, told herself, "Mama called them postwedding blues." Aunt Voen, in her intimate manner, had kidded Vathana before the wedding, "with all his money, you'll have nothing to do"—she'd giggled—"but the best thing." For a month Vathana clung to the thought that they, she and Teck together, were very proper.

Yet something was wrong. She hid her feelings from her husband, from everyone, blamed herself for feeling empty, felt guilty for having such thoughts. At the market she met a woman who lived in the same building two floors below and in a gush of desperation she whispered, "He's like cold rice. He never talks to me. He doesn't want me."

The woman mocked her. "It takes time to adjust," she said. "Rice doesn't grow in a day and cold rice is better than no rice, eh?" The guilt increased.

By the second month Vathana was very unhappy. Indeed, she had nothing to do. This man was nothing like her father. He was proper but he seemed to have no interests, no desires, no passions, no drives. Or at least none he shared with her. People seemed to mean little to him. He was neither friendly nor aggressive. Business did not interest him; of his studies he seemed apathetic. Despite the new appliances, the closets full of clothes, the apartment with furnishings even Aunt Voen with a home in Phnom Penh would envy, Vathana felt nothing. No intimacy, no spirituality.

She prayed. Her very first memories of her father were of him praying, teaching her to pray, teaching her to look inside herself even before she had reached the age of reason. Always he had taken her to the pagoda to pray, to ask the Holy One's blessing, to help the spirit of a recently departed villager. Always they had talked of things which concerned the family or the village, talked of business, politics, religion, of dreams, health and the beauty of growing rice. In the late fifties, when Vathana was eight or nine, before Chhuon had entered business with Uncle Cheam, she recalled him donating to the monks a portion of the little they had, not because he, Chhuon, wished others to know he donated, not even to earn merit and ensure his next life's status, but because he believed, without trappings, that it was right. It was his way. Now it was hers.

Teck was not like her father. After the ceremonies had ended, the guests had gone home, the food and presents had been repacked and stored, after they had settled in, alone, without family, without parents or siblings in a culture where solitude is almost unknown, Teck had called as many people as he could muster, his school friends, workers from the piers, peasants he knew in the city delivering farm goods, so they could witness him donating a few unwanted gifts and several hundred riels to the bonze. To Vathana, in their abundance, the gifts were meaningless, insulting.

And Teck didn't work. Mister Pech had given his son a river barge as a wedding present. The barges traveled the Mekong from My Tho, South Viet Nam, to Phnom Penh, under new license and the semicontrol of Sihanouk's nationalization of trade. Since September 1968, trade and banking were being gradually returned to private control. Both nationalization and denationalization had worked to Pech Lim Song's benefit. Under each change his profits increased. But whereas Teck's father managed every detail of order, purchase, transport and delivery, Teck appointed a barge captain and collected money due. Day after day she watched him sitting, listening passively to the radio. When she mentioned it, when she attempted to show affection, he shrank back, became defensive, then left for the dance halls to be with his idle pals from their student days. To Vathana the contrast between Teck's cool, seemingly frivolous behavior and both her father's and her father-in-law's constant, diligent work was bewildering. Daily she compared the three men, daily her resentment grew. Even in her father's withdrawal following the death of her siblings, she'd seen him labor harder and communicate more intimately than her new, wealthy husband.

Then everything changed.

"Madam, I must speak to your husband." It was the barge captain. He had come to their apartment house shouting the name Pech Chieu Teck loudly dozens of times until he was directed to the fourth floor, then down the hallway. He banged on the door, once, and barged in. "It's very urgent," he said in French.

"He's not here," Vathana responded, also in French.

"He must be!" The captain threw his arms in the air, looked up and down, into the doorways to the other rooms, arms flailing as if he could turn over the entire room and check under each object and thus produce the man he desired to see.

"He's not here," Vathana repeated. "He's . . ." She hesitated. ". . . dancing."

"Dancing? Dancing!" The captain exploded. He smacked a fist into an open palm. "The river burns and he's dancing!?"

"Please." Vathana's hands swayed gracefully toward a chair. "I can help. Tea? Have you had rice today?"

The captain sat momentarily, then sprang up and paced as Vathana brought out rice, tea, a plate of pickled fish. "We must arm the crew," the captain said, his arms flying in exasperation.

"Now," Vathana said calmly, "you will tell me all."

"The water's low this time of year," the captain said as if explaining to a child. "The river's not so wide. They attack us more easily."

"Who?"

"Who? Who knows? Bandits!" he shouted. "This morning, not twenty-five kilometers from here they rose up out of the swamps west of the channel. You know Phum Sambour? Just below. Where the river's very narrow. They wounded two crewmen. Good men."

"I beg you"—Vathana showed deep concern—"tell me how you run the barge."

"Madam, come with me. I'll show you."

For an hour the captain explained the incidents on the river as he and Vathana walked the deck, inspected the sandbagged wheelhouse, the hold and the damage caused by the rocket-propelled grenade which had wounded the men. For two hours he explained the operations of the barge, and of the tugs which were required at the ports. He showed her channel charts and explained why they had to hug one shore here, the other there. Then he resuggested armament.

"And the army?" Vathana asked.

"Useless." The riverman shook his head. "Across the border the ARVN river patrols come. Here, we radio the Royals and we must negotiate payment before they come. Madam," he said, "we must arm."

Vathana turned away, looked down the river. For the first time she felt she had some understanding of the business her husband failed to direct, felt she might have a reason to be in Neak Luong. Could she direct the business? She turned back, fixed the captain with her stare. Her stomach tightened. She had no breath to speak. Yes, she thought, I can. I can. "Do what you must"—she gasped, she gulped air, blurted: "to arm the men."

The captain locked his eyes on her. His stare was savage, challenging. Vathana stared back. "I want to know everything that concerns this vessel," she said firmly. "Where you go, when, the crew, exactly what you buy, what you fire off." She inhaled deeply. With her assertion came an unexpected calm.

"Fight only to defend yourselves," she said. "We're a merchant company, not an army."

Though Nang and Eng traveled with fellow Communists, they were outsiders. Their training, their age, their feeling of racial superiority alienated them. The Viet Namese were five to forty years older. Nang and Eng were but twelve. For Nang there was no trust, no solidarity with yuons. At times he spied Mountaineers, some soldiers but mostly coolies. With them he felt a kinship yet he did not approach. Amongst them he looked for the giant.

Nang, Eng, and Binh became a cell. Comrade Binh was Viet Namese, a lame combatant of the People's Army of Viet Nam (PAVN). He was their guide, their authorization to be on the trail. He made no attempt to be their friend. Nang was not sure where Binh was leading them; he had been told only that it was toward a camp at which Bok Roh trained others, a camp of international training. For thirty-four days they walked north, rode north, at times during the day, mostly at night. Each day Nang felt the removal from Kampuchea more deeply; each night he questioned this disruption of his mission.

The land changed drastically. For a time they traveled in steep mountains, for a time over relatively flat plateau. At one point the mountain paths were so steep that in a week they covered no more than thirty kilometers. It became cold, colder than Nang had ever known. The dry season was under way in Cambodia but here rains continued. Binh called them mountain rains. Most of the traffic they saw was heading south. To Nang, the vision of thousands of soldiers with thousands of bicycles and thousands of heavy trucks, more vehicles than he'd seen in his entire life, was intimidating. Gone was the security of Cambodia. Every night planes bombed or strafed distant sections of the trail; uncanny, Nang heard porters say, in their accuracy. Each night the planes destroyed huge amounts of materiel and many vehicles. Some soldiers were killed, some wounded, but personnel trails were separate from truck routes and only truck routes were bombed.

To have that power, Nang thought. Yet it's like trying to stop the flow of a river by tossing boulders into the current. They alter the course, even back the stream into pools, but eventually the water leaks through and flows on. Still, he thought, still . . .

Each night, antecedent to bombing, flares popped and lit the roadway. Invariably, second flares and second bombing waves followed. Nang came to enjoy the noise on the parallel trails. When the flares came he would sit, his arms squeezed tightly to his sides, his fists at his lowered chin, and he would wonder about the power. Then one night, in the last flat light before the second wave of explosions, Nang witnessed the severity of damage inflicted by bomb shrapnel on yuon torsos. The sight struck him. All that night he thought about the power, the ability to kill from such a great distance.

By the twenty-third day they had moved north of the bombing grids. There they rendezvoused with other pairs of Khmer boys, each escorted by a PAVN soldier. For five days they marched, their column ever increasing. Then, with hundreds of others, they were trucked out of the mountains, into beautiful tropical hills, and deposited at an immense training camp where armored vehicles, tanks, cannons and AA guns were in abundance.

China, Nang thought. China!

"Someone is bombing," Vathana said in French. They spoke only French in the apartment. "Also, I must tell you . . ."

"To you, always there is a crisis," Teck retorted. He looked at his wife with disgust, the same look his father gave his mother when they argued.

"Eh . . ." Her primary thought had been of personal news yet his words made her defensive. "Why can't it be true?" she said. "Does the captain lie?"

"Did he see them bomb?" Teck's voice was harsh. Ever since the betrothal he had been seething inside—angry with his father for attaching him to this peasant girl, angry with his culture for demanding obedience, compliance to the wishes of the elders, angry with himself for not being able to say he wanted more, wanted to go to Paris, to find an educated woman, to lead his own life as he pictured a French son would. "No!" he shouted. "Did any of the crew see bombings? No! I tell you if the South Viet Namese bombed as you say, Samdech Sihanouk would have been on the radio for five hours."

"Maybe he refuses to believe it. It could be . . ."

"It could be nothing." Teck stood, tense. "Why couldn't you just leave it alone," he yelled at her. "We were paid. We had a good captain. You order guns for them. You tell them when and where to load, to unload?! You and that damn monk. What does he know?"

"They've no reason to report untruths," Vathana said bitterly. "No reason." She reached to her chest, pulled out the statuette of Buddha carved from her grandfather's tooth that her father had given her the last day of the wedding ceremony. "The crew brought six children and their mother upriver. She said she was there. She said the ground trembled and many bombs tore the jungle where the Viet Namese had their camp. You could have talked to them. No, you have to dance."

"Stay out of this business. Why can't you believe like your father?"

"My father!?" Vathana caressed the statuette.

"My father says your father told him, 'War is for politicians. Not for us.' I believe that."

Vathana stared at her husband. He had never spoken so harshly to her, had never shown such emotion. She wanted him to talk but now she wanted to win the argument. "Two crewmen refuse to cross the border, refuse to even travel near the border. What politician will convince them to go?"

"You want to run the company?" Teck snapped the words. He spun, walked toward the door. Spun, strode back. "Let me do it. To hell with those two. Get a new crew. I'm going out."

"Out?" Vathana shook her head. "How can you do it? You're always out. We've reports of Khmer Rouge attacking villages above Kratie. Reports of bombings. Maybe South Viet Namese attack North Viet Namese on Cambodian soil. Samdech Euv's wife, she and her brother . . . your father says they collaborate in rice smuggling to the VC and NVA. Don't you listen to your father?"

"My father knows only money," Teck shouted. "There's nothing to worry about. In a short time all this will pass."

"Pass! A short time! It gets worse."

"You know what I hear? I hear the people in the countryside help the Khmer Rouge because they can trust the Khmer Rouge. I hear the Communists are good. Tell that to my father. I hear they help the farmers. My father talks of crocodiles. It's the Royal Army who are crocodiles. Ha! All the people in the city are afraid. He's afraid. You're afraid. You should be. Ha!"

"Teck! Stop it!"

"No! If the Khmer Rouge build a solid relationship with the peasants, why should I object? The government doesn't help them. You make believe you want to help people but you're just like my father."

"Your father's a good man. You should be half like him."

"I'm sick of being under his control. And of you controlling me for him. I'm going dancing." Teck steamed to the door. "Think"—he grasped the handle—"if the barge crew fires at anyone, it'll be Khmers they kill. Tell that to your monk and my father."

"I will," Vathana began, "and, wait, I've got to tell you . . ."

"You tell me nothing." Teck slammed the door.

". . . tell you that"—she hung her head, tears came to her eyes—"that I'm pregnant."

China! Nang thought. He stared at the soldiers before him. China! The concept stirred stories from his early youth, stories of adventure, of an exotic and rich land. Yet he yearned for Cambodia. Beyond the lush green rolling hills, over the mountains, down the trail, there was a people's war, a movement to liberate his homeland from the feudalism of Norodom Sihanouk, from the capitalism of the right, the imperialism of overseas Chinese and Westerners, and the invasion by the yuon armies.

Guoshen surveyed his new charges. "I'm here to teach you," he said. His smile flicked, his eyes set on Nang, his smile froze. Nang's eyes were the most animal he had ever seen. Guoshen welcomed Nang, then the others. "It's our duty to teach, to give you a strong mental foundation in politics and order. Others will teach you the mechanics of war. I will teach you the spirit of revolution. I will tell you *how* to convert others."

As Guoshen spoke, Nang sized him up. Round faced, Nang thought. Square bodied, quick tongued. Ha! Nang thought. Larger than me, larger than my father, but not Khmer, not pure. Nang felt superior, yet he was aware of an inferiority, a backwardness he sensed all Khmers, all third-world soldiers, must feel when surrounded by the military hardware of a superpower. Nang felt isolated, stuck in a foreign training camp where even other Khmers seemed alien. The front! He dreamed of it. He prayed for it. Let me go to the front, he thought. Let me be a soldier. Then he thought of Bok Roh. Let me see him, he thought. Let me see that face. Then let me go.

". . . we shall, as one, create new socialist men," Guoshen was saying.

Nang looked past the Chinese boy. Four Soviet PT-76 light tanks were crossing a field beyond what would be their first bivouac. The tanks were joined by six Chinese Type 59s, copies of the Soviet medium T-54. Within minutes the armor, with their huge 100mm guns, disappeared. Power, Nang thought, power.

". . . The goal," Guoshen quoted Mao, "is to demolish all old ideology and culture, to create and cultivate among the masses an entirely new proletarian ideology and culture. You and I are vehicles. Youth, those least poisoned by tradition, can wipe out feudalism, capit . . ."

Then let us go do it, Nang's thought broke in.

". . . all items of the past shall be flung into the fires which smelt the future. All people with problems of thought must be denounced, exposed and publicly humiliated . . ."

Again the tanks roared into view. Nang stopped listening. The PT-76s were followed by several armored personnel carriers and a dozen trucks trailing twin-barreled 23mm antiaircraft guns. Nang wanted to learn about the guns, about their firepower. Guoshen's ideology did not interest him.

"Met Nang!" A Khmer cadreman interrupted his wandering thoughts. "Later you'll be taught about them. Pay attention here."

For months Nang paid attention. The school, the People's Liberation Army Camp for Foreign Nationals north of the Lihsien River in southern China, trained soldiers from different nations, or different factions within a nation. Training was carried out with little contact between groups. Though boys and girls from Taiwan, the Philippines, Indonesia, Burma, India, Japan, Thailand, Laos, North and South Viet Nam, Bangladesh, Malaysia and Pakistan were all being trained, Krahom cadets had no contact with them, nor did they mingle with Khmer Viet Minh trainees. The staff was international consisting largely of Maoist Chinese or Red Guard Youth, and Chinese graduates of Moscow's School of Terrorism. It also included some Russians and Eastern Europeans and a dozen Cubans. Units were grouped into battalions, led by semipermanent cadres of their own countrymen who lived with them, cared for them, treated them like precious family, ensured that their needs, within the parameters of the training mission, were met.

Each day began with rigorous calisthenics followed by long, grueling hill runs and practice sessions in crawling, hiding, digging in and hand-to-hand combat. Then lecture, drill, review, rehearsal. Through the long months of training Nang changed. He had shed his flimsy appearance at the School of the Cruel, now, taller, he filled out, added muscle, developed a form like his father's.

Lectures were systematic. Each class began with one student reading the material aloud while the others followed in workbooks. Trainers demonstrated and summarized, then asked for opinions, which were mandatory. Every student responded either by rote or by paraphrasing. No deviations in thought or style were accepted. Nonconforming thought, political or military, was justification for a public self-criticism session. Repeated nonconformity was justification for washing out.

Nang learned pistol and rifle marksmanship. He fired SKS and AR-15 carbines, RPD and M-60 machine guns, RPG and

M-79 grenade launchers, Soviet and Chinese mortars. By February he could field-strip and reassemble a TT 7.62mm pistol, an AKH-47, and an M-14, all in total darkness. He learned about explosives, mines and booby traps, about target acquisition, approach and engagement. He learned to use radios, read maps, plan village attacks. With mock explosives he practiced tactics for destroying American tanks and APCs. With heavy machine guns and AA weapons he practiced blowing up small cutouts of Huey helicopters. He learned how to infiltrate and booby-trap fixed installations, which terrorist acts drew the most attention and thus were the most effective. And he learned to spy.

Through it all he received constant indoctrination. " 'Political work in the ranks,' " Guoshen quoted Vo Nguyen Giap, " 'is of the first importance. It is the soul of the army.' "

He was not there to learn a new political ideology, but to learn how to teach political ideology, how to indoctrinate, to establish propaganda networks, to teach others to teach. At the age of twelve, Nang was a soldier, a combat leader, a spy. Now he would be capable of being an instructor, a political officer. Of the seventy-eight Krahom boys in his company who began the training, by February forty had suffered self-criticism sessions, twenty had washed out. Nang suffered neither. He learned to be sly, obedient, a fanatically militant nationalist Communist.

"When you spy," Guoshen whispered to Nang, "you must smile. You've learned not to smile. That's for soldiers. You're the elite of the elite, a trained leader. Be flexible. When you mix with civilians in unliberated areas, you smile like them. That way you are invisible." Nang smiled for Guoshen. The Chinese boy trembled.

Throughout March and April Guoshen spent extra hours each day with Nang. "Don't think," Guoshen said to him one evening, "of only the war. Think beyond."

"How are men led to abandon their pasts?" Nang responded.

"The quickest way is to remove them from their pasts. In a blink of the eye, when a peasant is moved to a collective, he transforms. He ceases being absorbed with his self and his family and immediately recognizes a new allegiance to the collective and the Party."

"And"—Nang spoke quietly, for this question, if asked during class, would bring a criticism—"how can you tell that it works?"

"Nang," Guoshen whispered, "behind closed doors, some people will attempt to revert to old ways."

"Then," Nang said, "why not remove the doors?"

Another night, Guoshen and Nang discussed communism and the economics of rice first. " 'Revolution and production,' "

Guoshen repeated a slogan of the Cultural Revolution, " 'will solve all problems.' Peasants know how to grow rice." About South Viet Nam Guoshen told Nang, "Their leaders are too corrupt to hold off the North, and the Americans won't stay there forever." He produced a lesson sheet. "See. On 12 November last year, Clark Clifford, the American secretary of defense, declared that if the Thieu clique won't join the peace talks, the U.S. will conduct unilateral negotiations. Cambodia's only chance for true independence is to befriend China. Sihanouk knows, but he's fat. He splashes perfume on himself like a 'broken shoe.' "

"That's why we'll destroy him," Nang answered. An eerie glint possessed Nang's face. He was not thinking about Sihanouk or the Americans, but about yuons.

"Beware of American mercenaries," Guoshen went on. "They're savages! Ugh. They're hairy. And ugly with big noses. If they capture young boys they sell them to capitalist men for sex. I've seen pictures. And when their bombers are shot down and the pilots captured, they confess they search for hospitals to bomb. In Viet Nam they've been known to roast children alive, before their parents, and then eat them."

Nang's battalion went through three phases of training. At the end of the first and the second, sixty percent of the cadets remaining were graduated and returned to Cambodia. Of the several hundred boys, almost all products of Khmer Krahom training camps in Cambodia, who began the course, fewer than fourteen percent remained for the last phase. These boys were trained in escape methods, clandestine communication, sabotage and assassination. During a martial arts class Nang puffed himself up. "You are a chameleon," Guoshen noted. Nang looked stronger and older than the other Khmer boys. "A chameleon or a king cobra." Guoshen laughed. "Go small again." To Guoshen's delight Nang deflated, looked slight, impish, even frail. Again Guoshen laughed. Nang smiled pitifully.

The elite were trained in disguise and deception until each had a repertoire of possible acts—orphan, escapee from the liberated zone, cripple. Nang added to those his perfected act as a mute Mountaineer. He learned new techniques of torture. For learning he was promised new privileges. They need not have promised him anything.

He became more proficient at killing by knife, pistol and booby trap. He barely recognized he had a background or family. He owed no one other than the Movement, which Khmer cadremen were now calling the Organization, or Angkar. To the fraternal nations joined in the Communist International and to

Angkar, Nang owed total obedience and his life. He considered himself a Marxist and a Maoist, even while he knew he first was Kampuchean.

The last month of ideological training in China had emphasized the fraternal nature of all socialist movements. The section leader was a Chinese colonel, the executive officer a Viet Namese lieutenant colonel, the main lecturer a Khmer major. Each day a nationalist from a different country addressed the class about the struggle of his people.

In those final weeks Nang spent his evenings copying or paraphrasing sections of Mao's little red book, *On People's War*, into a notebook of his own.

War is the highest form of struggle . . .

Make wiping out the enemy's effective strength our main objective; do not make holding or seizing a city or place our main objective. Holding [territory] is the outcome of wiping out the enemy . . .

In every battle concentrate an absolutely superior force (two, three, four and sometimes five or six times the enemy's strength), encircle the enemy forces completely, strive to wipe them out thoroughly and do not let any escape from the net. . . . Although inferior in numbers we shall be absolutely superior in every specific campaign; this ensures victory . . .

Fight no battle unprepared, fight no battle you are not sure of winning . . .

The imperialists, headed by the United States, are attempting to invade and subvert socialist countries. Therefore, the revolutionary people of the socialist countries must conscientiously study Chairman Mao's theory of people's war and get a good grasp of this weapon, the sharpest of ideological weapons for smashing the schemes of capitalist restoration and for consolidating the dictatorship of the proletariat . . .

Then on the last day Nang bowed to the Viet Namese lieutenant colonel. "Where is Bok Roh, the Giant?" Nang smiled.

"Ah," the lieutenant colonel sighed, pleased the Khmer boy knew of the Mountaineer who aided the NVA. "Is he a friend of yours?"

"I have a gift for him," Nang replied.

"A lady chicken, perhaps," the colonel laughed, referring to the Jarai legend of the Giant, Bok Roh, from which the large Mountaineer had taken his name.

"Perhaps," Nang said pleasantly. The desire for revenge had not dissipated over the long months of training though it had changed. No longer was avenging his sister, Yani, or the tribal girl, Sraang, the main passion driving him. He was barely able to bring images of the girls to mind. His father's murder, too, was no longer paramount. Revenge had gained its own life, its own justification. Revenge for the sake of revenge.

"You just missed him," the officer said. "He's gone again to the South. You'll find him there."

In May 1969 Chhuon returned to fields he had not worked in a decade. Stooped, he slogged in the fertile mud planting new seedlings—backstep, plant; backstep, plant; row after row. The rains had begun again, two weeks late this year. The brown of the paddies slowly took a green tinge. By midmonth they were the wonderful fresh light green of new growth, new life, new promise. Stooped, Chhuon did not think. Stooped with the rich organic smell whelming his sinuses, he did penance. Stooped, his forty-five-year-old back, unused to long bent hours, ached yet he repressed the pain until his day's section was planted. Alongside his cousin and neighbor, Sam, he labored like Khmers of a hundred and a thousand years earlier. In his mind, he had returned to the very root of Khmer life. From there, he told himself, he would view the changes in his family, village, region and country; from there he would judge himself; from there he would discover how.

Since the planting of the last main crop Phum Sath Din had changed dramatically. The closing of the Mekong at Siambok in October had shaken the Northeast. Sok, her sister and the women of other families urged their husbands to abandon their homes, their villages, their ancestral interments and move south or west. Both Chhuon's sisters, Voen in Phnom Penh and Moen in Battambang, offered them space in their homes, yet Chhuon, like most of the men of Phum Sath Din, resisted, procrastinated, postponed the decision, lingering on reports, discussing the possible truth of rumors endlessly.

Each new thought seemed to produce a new rumor. Each real or imagined report of terrorism in the cities, or of entire villages being burned or simply falling behind the line of no information, or of isolated farms, like Keng Sambath's, being swallowed by an ambiguous advancing front propelled by anonymous aggressors, elevated the tension in the village. Entire families left. The population dropped from 420 to below 300. The pagoda school closed as the first to leave were those with young children. The marketplace dwindled. Stalls at the ends of the row never filled and the habit of daily purchase of perishables gradually faded, replaced by essential gatherings on the first and fifteenth of the lunar month. And yet Phum Sath Din remained without incident until Chhuon's brawl with the tinker.

At the end of the day Chhuon straightened his back. The pain was immense. He could no longer repress it. Nor could he suppress his thoughts, keep them from rising to consciousness. "Ahh," he sighed.

"It's been a long while since we worked together, eh?" Sam grinned. "Your back's not used to it."

"Each day it gets stronger." Chhuon smiled back.

"When I look at the paddy like this," Sam said, "I feel very good."

"I feel good too," Chhuon answered. "I could plant more rows. I could walk backwards until I fell on a yuon." Chhuon paused. He looked over the richness of the land, breathed deeply. "Why aren't you going?" he asked Sam, not looking at his cousin.

"The best paddies are now mine to plant," Sam answered. "Besides, where would I go? It's only Ry and me and her mother. The children are grown. So what if things change? But you, why don't you go? You still have Sakhon in your house."

"The best paddies are now mine, too." Chhuon laughed, yet mixed with the laugh was sarcasm. "Besides, someday they'll come to me."

The men walked the dikes to the edge of the village, then parted. Chhuon looked at the sky, the trees, the ground. As he passed the pagoda he did not lift his eyes but thought instead of his knees which were throbbing and tight with swelling. Before he entered his house he paused, glanced at the tiny angel spirits' house, now neglected. I must fix it, he thought. Tomorrow. He shuffled to the outdoor washing area where he cleaned himself, where Sok met him with tea. He smiled, again a mixed, charged smile. He thanked the old woman, four years his junior, in proper fashion, sipped the tea then moaned and lamented, "My knees are so bad tonight I think I'll need help up the stairs."

"And your back?" Sok whispered.

"Terrible," he said. Since he had returned full-time to the fields the household nightly ritual had become almost a game. Chhuon listed his ailments; Sok responded by silently assisting him; his mother sympathized, feebly attempting to get herself up until Sok laid a hand on her shoulder and told her to remain; and Peou withdrew to a corner of the central room to play with a small plastic John Deere tractor given to him by Mister Pech.

After a brief rest Chhuon rose, as he did each night, cringed, as he did each night, the pain in his knees and back rifling across his face. "And now," he said, "a bowl of rice for Kdeb. His spirit needs sustenance. I feel it. His spirit wanders."

"We should go," Sok said quietly. "Today I heard . . ."

"We can't go," Chhuon snapped. "How can we go? Kdeb's spirit . . ." He shuddered, twisted, a spasm of pain seizing his side.

Sok gave him a small rice bowl for the altar. "We received word today . . ." she began, but Chhuon interrupted her again.

"What do you put in my tea?" His eyes darted to her then away. He put a hand to his breastbone. "I'm burning up."

"Your passions are too hot," his mother said firmly. "The heat rises to your mouth."

"It's the damned yuons that rise to my mouth," Chhuon cursed bitterly. "The damned yuons who are . . . are . . . killing me."

Chhuon placed a small bowl on the altar and lit two incense sticks for Samnang. He tapped a heavy finger on the tabletop. Tapped it seven, eight, ten times. "Blood for blood!" he murmured. He turned, scowled, his face tightened, transformed to a mask. Sok rocked back, aghast. "Blood for blood!" Chhuon repeated louder.

"Vathana sent word . . ." Sok interjected. She knew it was the one name which could break his deepening trance.

"Yes?" Harsh, questioning.

A slight smile curled Sok's lips. "You're going to be a grandfather."

For a week Nang sat in a whitewashed cave awaiting debriefing. His trip south had not been easy. In the far north of Laos he'd been stranded for weeks when the NVA and Pathet Lao suddenly switched their effort from moving men and materiel south and diverted all their resources to the battle of the Plain of Jars. Despite heavy American air strikes and torrential monsoons the NVA offensive seized the government stronghold at Muong Soui on the western edge of the plateau. In rear areas Nang had listened to reports from soldiers returning from the front. They'd bragged of savage fighting, of victory, of pushing west and cutting Highway 13, of how they were now in striking distance of Vientiane and Luang Prabang.

The tales made Nang itch to be part of a battle, any battle. He'd questioned them with the little Viet Namese he'd learned.

How stupid they are, he'd thought. In youthful enthusiasm and naiveté he was certain he could do better. Had they better coordinated their infantry and artillery, they would have been even more successful. Had they used less explosive at each point but doubled the attack points . . . Oh, he'd thought, to be part of the great victory!

With the itch to fight strong, he'd picked his way down the Ho Chi Minh Trail. In southeastern Laos the trail bombings were so heavy they all but closed the route. Twice Nang was caught in areas adjacent to B-52 bomb boxes. As the ground trembled, fear, awe, vengeance had heightened his resolve. Now, too, there were rumors of American bombings of NVA sanctuaries in his country. To be there, he'd thought, to see yuons slaughtered, then to butcher the hairy American savages.

Nang had marched west, with a transportation unit, across the Bolovens Plateau below Saravan to the Mekong. At the river soldiers cut trees, fashioned crude rafts, stacked and tied crates of arms and ammunition, distributing the weight so the craft would have a chance in the rapids. At night rafts were released, unmanned, left to float to the Khong Falls at the border where other units would catch them, unload them, porter the goods around the falls. Then the materiel would be trucked, unmolested, 110 kilometers south to Kratie for further distribution.

Nang had jumped a raft. At Ban Mai a reconnaissance aircraft spotted him, radioed for clearance to fire. He'd slithered between crates, trying to hide. The aircraft flew off. Unknown to Nang, the next day, after eleven hours of seeking clearance, a second U.S. F-4 Phantom fighter-bomber searched the river, but by then Nang had reached Cambodia.

In Cambodia, the Krahom network aided by Khmer Viet Minh transport units expedited Nang's trip past Stung Treng, Kratie and Kompong Cham, through the outskirts of Phnom Penh, to Kompong Speu. There he waited in the whitewashed cave. Only the most trusted Krahom yotheas and cadre knew how to proceed to Krahom headquarters at Peam Amleang.

In the 1950s the KK established a secret regional headquarters in the craggy pocket on Mount Aural, Cambodia's highest peak—primary headquarters were in Phnom Penh. In 1963 the primary unit was shifted to the southeast where it coexisted with Viet Cong offices. In 1966 it was moved to Pong Pay Mountain, adjacent to the training school, and was known as the Central Committee at Ratanakiri. As tension between the Krahom and NVA/KVM mounted, the Central Committee headquarters was moved to the old southwest regional site. By 1969 Peam Amleang was a deep-tunneled, camouflaged complex from which the

Khmer Krahom military and political hierarchy, the Center, directed the revolution.

Met Sar had been promoted to general. "You shall be my eyes where my eyes cannot see," he said quietly. "You shall be my ears where my ears cannot hear; my feet where my feet dare not walk." A fine mist filled the early-morning mountain air. Nang had been brought up the mountain blindfolded, had been grilled by senior cadremen about the People's Liberation Army School for a week. Met Sar had briefly questioned him and a thin man named Nim had explained to him what had occurred in his absence.

"We no longer call ourselves the Movement," Nim had said. "We've adopted the name Angkar Leou so as not to be coupled with the Communists." Nim's voice was machinelike. "We can be more effective this way. Let them think we're Viet Minh. Or yuon. Or bandits. We've attacked in all nineteen provinces since the New Year but the yuons carry the brunt of battle. They die. We grow strong. Let it be."

"And the Royal forces?" Nang had asked.

"The Prince," Met Nim had said sarcastically, "is angry. The yuons have detached Ratanakiri. He's ordered his army to have an offensive spirit. Ha! An offensive spirit. Isn't that a joke? Not to go on the offensive but . . ."

"That's not the problem, Nim," the firm gentle voice of Met Sar had interrupted, and Nang had snapped erect.

"Oh! No. No, it's not," Nim had stuttered.

"Norodom Sihanouk has reestablished relations with cold-blooded imperialist aggressors," Met Sar had said. He'd read from a French newspaper quoting the Prince. " '. . . the Asian Communists are already attacking us before the end of the Viet Nam War.' This is a serious development." Met Sar had paced back and forth. Agitation crept into his tone. "Yuons move ever greater numbers into the interior," he said. "Americans bomb sanctuaries along the eastern border. As long as that's secret, the Prince approves. Augh! He too wants the NVA gone. But Hanoi . . . if they can break the secrecy . . . this is a nightmare! American escalation presages ground-force intervention. That"— Met Sar had slapped a wall map—"that must be avoided. At the same time, the NVA must be driven out! We need a greater presence in the East. We need spies, scouts. We need greater intelligence."

"Met Sar," Nim had addressed the new general, "why not allow them to murder each other?"

"Let them murder each other in Viet Nam," Sar had grumbled. He'd grabbed his chin, slid his fingers down to his neck.

"Hold no illusions," he had said. "A full-scale fight with the Americans will extend the war for years." Sar had shaken his head. "Keep them out. We must drive the yuons out . . . and we *must* keep out the Americans."

Nang had risen. "Met Sar," he'd said, "allow me to recon the front."

Sar had studied the boy. "Our people are blank posters," Sar had said quietly. "There will be but one chance to paint their future." Then he'd left. In a deep pensive mood he'd brooded for days while Nang and the cadre languished.

On 20 May, Sar called for Nang. They sat outdoors, under a canopy of woven branches and vines. "You shall be my eyes where my eyes cannot see," Sar repeated. "My ears . . . my feet. Met Nang, you shall walk all Kampuchea."

Nang looked at Sar, his mentor, his tutor, his guide and sponsor through the political and bureaucratic morass of the growing Movement. Nang's face lit, keen, infectious, bright-eyed. This man, he thought, this one man is the only man on earth I need to please. "I'm prepared for any sacrifice," he said pleasantly. "I wish only to be of service to the People."

"Good." Met Sar delicatedly peeled a banana, ate it. The chairs and table of the canopied-office were exquisitely crafted, the ground covered with bamboo mats woven in intricate patterns. Walkways to and from the office were made of bamboo tubes laid perpendicular to the path. Drainage was perfect; even in the heaviest monsoon deluge the feet of general staff officers never got wet.

From their seats Sar and Nang could see the valley below—the low south filled with white clouds, the middle thick with forest, the north end closing and running toward a great peak. A porter brought more tea and a bowl of fresh fruit then disappeared down a walkway into an underground cavern.

"Good," Met Sar repeated. "Once the country is organized you shall have a well-deserved position."

Nang puffed his chest like a bird.

"I have determined," the older man said, "that we can slice up or club to death those who need to be eliminated. Did not your friend Bok Roh do this?" Sar laughed as if he had told a great joke.

"My friend!" Nang was astonished by the officer's words.

"You remember." Sar laughed. "You told me all about him your first day at Pong Pay. He's now your friend, eh?"

"My friend!" Nang repeated. He felt Sar's power, the power of information, the power of knowing another's secrets. He

hated Sar for his power, yet he admired him, wanted to emulate his every strategem.

"Bok Roh . . ." Sar laughed. His eyes were riveted on Nang,
gauging Nang's response. "Do you know where to look for him?"

"No." Nang's voice was flat.

"He is not a soldier, you know." Nang did not speak. "He's a
tool." Sar laughed. He sensed Nang's tension. "They use him,"
Sar said. "He's very smart but he's only a smart tool. Your
story of him was not the first. Do you wish to get him?"

"I wish only to serve." Nang lowered his eyes to mask his
emotions.

"Ha!" Sar blurted. "It doesn't matter. We will not rely on
tools, or supplies, from anyone," he said. "It is the will of
Angkar Leou. Victory to the Brotherhood of the Pure."

"Victory," Nang repeated.

Again Met Sar said, "You shall be my eyes . . . my ears . . .
my feet. . . . You shall walk the entire country. Report to me
what you see, all you hear. That shall be your mission. You
have been trained to collect intelligence. You are an agent for
the Center. We must know all."

Nang's face lit, his eyes glistened.

"Sihanouk is stirring about Chinese supplies entering at
Sihanoukville. Go there first. See what is happening. Make your
report. Then find the sanctuaries. And if you find Bok Roh . . .
study him, eh? He may yet be helpful to us. But, Met Nang,
don't concentrate on just tools. Tell me, too, what the Americans are doing."

The main road of Neak Luong was a bustle of activity when
Chhuon arrived. Cars, trucks, buses and motorcycles vied with
bicycles and buffalo-drawn carts for rain-drenched space along
riverside quays or land-side construction sites. Old, traditional
wood-and-bamboo stilt houses were being replaced by structures of brick, block and mortar. The river, too, was crowded:
tugs, barges and large river freighters dwarfed small fishing
boats and sampans. Jacaranda trees, thick with clusters of blue-
purple flowers, seemed sad, trapped between machines and concrete beneath the leaden sky.

Chhuon walked hesitantly. He was eager yet timid. He had
come to Neak Luong with Cheam, the latter to see Pech Lim
Song on business, Chhuon to see his daughter. Outside the
four-story apartment building he stopped. He lit a cigarette,
inhaled, blew the smoke before him and rebreathed the cloud. A
young man, his head down in the rain, bumped Chhuon. As he

stepped around, he looked up at the man in rural dress and said, "Excuse me, Grandfather."

Chhuon smiled and bowed as the young man marched on. Grandfather, he thought. Yes. Soon. Pretty soon. Six months. Six months I haven't seen her. How she'll have changed.

"Un moment," Vathana called in French when Chhuon knocked. He could hear her talking on the telephone, all in French, about shipping schedules. Her voice sounded harried.

Chhuon let himself in. The apartment was impeccably decorated. Without the wedding crowd it was spacious. Chhuon stood by the door. Vathana sat at a delicate mahogany desk in what had been intended as a dining el but was now her office. Beside her were open file carriages, before her an open folder. She did not turn around but continued insisting that the price of something was much too high. Chhuon glanced into the kitchen. A radio was on the refrigerator. He looked through the doorway into the bedroom. There was a television set on a small stand by an immense Western-style bed. In the living room, on a rosewood table, there was a closed photo album. Chhuon turned back to Vathana. Above her desk was the large framed picture of Norodom Sihanouk Cheam had given as a wedding present. His eyes swept the room. Vaguely he approved the large photo, admired the well-organized desk and files, yet he felt much of the furnishings were material triviality. He glanced at the closed photo album then raised his eyes to his daughter's back. How beautiful, he thought. Then, She doesn't look pregnant. Then, Her hair is black as monsoon clouds. Finally, Still she wears the white dress of mourning. That pleased him. Others may have forgotten Samnang and Mayana but not Vathana. He watched, now with pleasure, as she pulled the Buddha statuette from her bodice and rubbed it between her thumb and fingers. It amused him that she had exchanged the cotton cord for a gold chain.

Vathana argued on. Chhuon stood by the door like a delivery boy waiting to be acknowledged by an important feudal lord. *"Oui. Oui. Adieu."* She closed the phone, turned and gasped. "Papa! I thought it was Teck."

"You are in good health?" Chhuon smiled broadly.

Vathana launched into an excited prattle of greeting and reacquaintance, as if she hadn't talked to anyone in months. As she chatted she prepared a buffet for her father who barely got in a word. She spoke French at first, a habit she'd fallen into in Neak Luong, but soon she switched to a beautiful Khmer full of sound redundancies which pleased Chhuon immensely. Finally she ran down. She hung her head low and whispered, "I'm pregnant."

Chhuon reacted to her tone. "But that's wonderful." His eyes sparkled as they had not since early August. "Your mother will come and stay to help."

"Papa," Vathana whispered. She pulled the statuette and massaged it. "I'm so afraid." It was difficult for her. Traditional belief held it unhealthy for a pregnant woman to talk of her worries. "I'm so vulnerable, but how can I stop this work?"

"Your uncle tells me you're the best businesswoman on the river," Chhuon said. It was an attempt to reassure her but also to divert the conversation from fears Chhuon himself did not know how to handle. "Better than all the men," he said. "Cheam says you're the only one who doesn't lie."

"Buddha forbids one to use words to conceal the truth," she said quietly. "But to be pregnant and to work. I'm so vulnerable to spirits. What if something should happen to the baby?"

"And Teck?" Chhuon's words hardened.

"He says he's an Epicurean."

"He's what?"

"His only concern is his own happiness."

"He ..." Chhuon clenched his fists. "... he cannot be that ... that. ... His father ..."

"Mister Pech is wonderful. I've learned so much. Especially who *must* be paid."

"Does his mother help?"

"She's like Lady Monique Sihanouk," Vathana said, an odd smile on her face.

"She's good to you?"

"She bought all the furniture. She buys Teck's clothes. She shops every day ... in Phnom Penh. She won't live here. And she doesn't approve of my running the company."

"Vathana"—Chhuon addressed her as an adult—"you must pay someone to ship, yes? Like I paid road donations?" Vathana nodded and Chhuon added bitterly, "Don't pay the yuons. Even five hundred riels is too much."

"Five hundred!? Papa! Try five hundred thousand in three months."

"Five hundred thous ..."

"Yes. And if I change from exporting rice to moving palm oil it will cost more. It will cost a large *bonjour* just to acquire the tanks. But there's more money in palm oil than in rice."

"You sound like Mister Pech," Chhuon said. A sharpness crept into his voice. "Does he tell you how to think about yuons?"

"Every day the radio's full of reports," Vathana said. "Every day Samdech Euv has new activities to report but his talk is so general, unless you have family or workers in those areas ..."

"Does he say what is happening to the Northeast? Do the people cringe? Are they as infuriated as I am?"

"Papa," Vathana said carefully, "no one cringes. No one knows. There are bombings in the East but no one seems to care. If you tell them, they don't believe you. I tell them I come from the Northeast and every day more of the country is lost. They look at me as if I were from another world. They say, 'Rice is fifteen percent more than last year. You merchants cheat us.' "

"They don't know?!" Chhuon was aghast.

"They don't want to know," Vathana said. "They're mostly like Teck. Teck says the war will soon end. He says it'll never reach here." She paused. She felt she'd said too much, revealed too much about her husband, her mother-in-law and her new city. She sensed that her father was very hurt. "But ... but Papa, you haven't told me how you are. Uncle Cheam says you work the paddies with Cousin Sam."

Chhuon dropped his face. His complexion seemed to pale before Vathana's eyes. "I no longer know the right way to live," Chhuon said. He might have said, "I fear I'm crazy," for in Khmer society the loss of way was considered borderline insanity. "Some days my body is like a stranger to me," he confessed. "On those days I work very hard so the pain will be very bad and I'll know that ..." He stopped, looked up. Vathana's eyes were tearing. I could tell her of the dream I had the night before the trip. He shook his head. "I feel like our family is no longer connected. Alone we have no meaning."

They sat quietly for some time. Chhuon ate from the dishes Vathana brought, though for herself she ate only the traditional foods for mothers-to-be. Chhuon felt more and more enclosed in the apartment as day passed to dusk. He sat for a while looking at the photo album—mostly pictures of the wedding—and he was surprised to find not a single photo of himself.

"Where's your husband?" Chhuon asked his daughter as darkness settled on Neak Luong.

"He's out," Vathana answered.

"Does he return?" Chhuon asked pointedly.

"Yes. He'll ... he'll ..."

"Does he hurt you?"

"Papa, how do I keep Teck from embarrassing himself and the family when he's without a self?"

Chhuon looked at his daughter but did not speak. He lifted his teacup, sipped, contemplated the question. He understood self to mean something different from what Westerners might. In Vathana's use, self first meant Teck's spirit interconnected with the family spirit encompassing past, present and future generations. For her to say he has no self did not mean he lacks physical existence or ego, but that his body is without a soul, spiritually adrift on earth. In Western terms, Teck had immense ego.

Vathana fidgeted as Chhuon sipped his tea. For Chhuon the role of sage was pleasing. In Phum Sath Din his family no longer brought him their fears and problems. He thought of his own father and drew strength from the thought. He thought of his grandfathers, especially his father's father from whom so many sought advice. "Someday," Chhuon began, "he will change. He is young, but he will change because he comes from a proper family. He will become like his father." Chhuon felt the explanation was inadequate. He was about to say it is a question of searching for the self and not a matter of embarrassment but he became confused and overwhelmed with thoughts of himself, adrift. He could not further answer his daughter. He shut his eyes and wished to pray but he could not pray. A terrible burning surged in his chest. Finally he answered, "When the yuons leave, Cambodia's self will return. Now I must go."

Nang crept forward like a rat. He froze, darted forward under the heavy pipeline which ran from the pier to the huge storage tanks, froze again. It was his seventh day in Sihanoukville. The air in the port city was clear below dark turbulent monsoon clouds. The water was greenblack. Until a week before Nang had never seen anything like the coastal city; never smelled anything like it. The entire southern coast was alien. Sea air, away from the oil refineries, smelled different from inland air, felt different. In such air sounds traveled in an unfamiliar way. The sight of distant hills dropping to paddies, then blending into Cambodia's most industrialized city, which in turn faded to beaches and they to endless water, confused him. The first two days he was not the eyes of Met Sar, not the hardened, highly trained terrorist agent of Angkar Leou, not even the bitter boy who believed his father had been killed by Viet Namese, but simply a rural Khmer child set agog by the sight of industries and luxuries he did not know, had never even imagined. Had his contacts not brought him back to reality he might have lost himself amid the ships and wharves and sought a totally different adventure.

From beneath the pipeline Nang counted the new ships in the harbor and at the piers. Two more Soviet and one Chinese freighter, he noted. Plus the tanker. And the ship with the blue triangle on a split white and red field. And one with no markings. "You can read their flags or their stacks," Met Ang, Nang's senior contact, had told him. "If you don't know the nations, remember the pattern. I'll know."

"You're easy on them." Nang had searched the young man's face.

"We live here. We do the job."

"How do you know what's unloaded?"

"Everyone knows," Ang had answered. "Ammunition is marked 'Goods in transit'; rice and fish for the sanctuaries are labeled 'For export to South Viet Nam.' "

Nang crept farther down the pipeline toward the pier. He carefully noted the pipe unions and moorings and mentally set charges where they would do the most destruction. The first day in the patrolled area the activity so dazzled him he saw only the movement of men and machines without cataloguing cargo. Now, as the giant crane at a far pier dipped into the hold of a ship and brought forth crates or pallets of bags or boxes, Nang estimated the contents and added to his mental inventory. He noted which pallets were placed before the crane for the massive forklift trucks to carry to large open warehouses; which pallets were placed to the side where men broke the wares down immediately and dispersed them either to smaller forklifts, which brought them to buildings where the doors opened only at their arrival, or directly into the backs of covered military trucks.

At another pier the side of a freighter was open. Empty trucks disappeared into the ship then reemerged laden with concealed cargo. "If the flag is red with five gold stars," Ang had said, "then we'll have the exact manifest and we'll take our share. But if it's Soviet, we need to count to confirm our lists."

"And the goods . . ." Nang had questioned.

"You watch. One third goes on Royal Army trucks. One third goes to Haklee warehouses where only the Viet Namese are allowed. One third goes directly to commercial trucks. It's easiest to bribe the Royal Army drivers. Then we supply ourselves. Yuons are hard to bribe. Commercial trucks, if they don't pay road fees, can be ambushed."

Nang put his ear to the pipeline expecting to hear fluid gurgling. Instead he heard the high-pitched hum of pumps. Below him, on the pier, were a few idle men. The pipeline was hooked to an offshore tanker via thick black hoses supported by a series of large floats. Nang noted the flag—three horizontal bands, red, white with three green stars, then black (Iraq). Ang will tell me, he thought, and Sar will know.

Through the afternoon and into the evening Nang remained beneath, beside, then atop the pipe. In the dull light he turned, looked up to the distant hills where huge villas shone like small cities. Nang contemplated the delivery system, the lax security of the port area, the obvious wealth of the royal officials in charge. It's safe, he thought, because all profit. He would put that in his report. He squatted on the pipe. In his mind he formulated a plan for disruption, for total destruction of the entire facility. That too he would send to Sar. Nang noted weak points, not only of the government security forces, the Chinese and the North Viet Namese, but also of the small squad of Krahom yotheas and spies led by Met Ang. Later, he knew, he would recommend Met Ang be eliminated.

Like a wraith Nang rose, walked barefooted, exposed, up the pipe to where it passed through the chainlink fencing. He jumped off, walked to the gate and exited, a rag-clothed child somehow misplaced on the pier.

"Hey, where you going?" A uniformed man emerged from the small guardhouse.

"I look for Bok Roh," Nang answered in Jarai-tainted Khmer.

"Who? What?"

"My father," Nang said, shrinking, looking no more than eight.

"Eh, you can't go in there, kid."

Instead of fleeing, Nang walked to the man. "Are those the trucks to Bokor?"

The guard eyed him warily.

"My father driver," Nang said.

As the sun set Chhuon followed his cousin into Phum Sath Din's nearly idle marketplace. In their left hands they carried their weeding hoes, in their right, curved-bladed rice knives. They walked slowly past the many stalls no longer maintained, past the few stalls with shabby common wares. Gone were the many food stalls with the vast variety of fish, chickens, vegetables, fruits and nuts; gone were the small tools and appliances; gone were the familiar faces of townspeople, peasants from surrounding farms and the tailor and doctor from Stung Treng who used to come twice a month, faces seemingly unchanged for a generation; gone all and replaced by a few suspicious outside vendors who posed as tinkers or weavers. In the market, food had become secondary. Beneath the pots and pans and hammers, the tinkers sold handguns and ammunition. If paid the right price, they could obtain nearly any small arm or crew-served weapon in use anywhere in Southeast Asia. Behind the bolts of cloth the weavers bought and sold information.

Chhuon stopped in the road before a tinker's stall. The man

was small, petite as a preadolescent girl. Chhuon watched as he nimbly stacked and crated his product. "They're like vultures," Sam whispered to Chhuon. "They appear when a village dies."

"Blood for blood," Chhuon answered quietly. His eyes glazed over as he spoke. He had never used the phrase outside his home, and there only once since the first time he'd shocked his wife. "Blood for blood," he repeated to Sam. He did not say it with the vengeance he'd used mentally ten thousand times, nor did he give it the charged emotion he felt. He said it almost apologetically. Still Sam understood.

Then Chhuon repeated it more loudly, boisterously. Two women shoppers stopped. The tinker turned and looked at him. The weaver took silent note. "Blood for blood, eh tinker?" Chhuon snickered. "Have you had a good day?" he asked in Viet Namese.

"A slow day," the petite man answered pleasantly in Khmer.

"You are Viet, yes?" Chhuon prodded in Viet Namese.

"My mother was half Viet Namese, half Chinese," the tinker responded so only Chhuon could hear. A little louder he said, "My father is Khmer from Kompong Thom."

Suddenly Chhuon shouted, "Your mother is a pig." Then he lunged at the tinker. Sam lunged, grabbed Chhuon. The tinker darted back. The women and other merchants startled as if shaken by a powerful concussion. "Yuons are pigs," Chhuon snarled, his voice harsh, low. Then he rocked back, laughed.

Sam let Chhuon go. "Let's get on." He pushed his cousin. "Viet or not, this tinker . . ."

"I want to look at him." Chhuon seethed. "I want to see if he killed my son."

"I'm just a tinker," the petite man said timidly. "From Kompong Thom. I know nothing of your son. I'm sorry if you had a great loss."

"Ha!" Chhuon's laugh was short, brusque. "The Prince of Death must be served, eh tinker!?" Sam put a hand back on Chhuon's arm. Chhuon flicked it off. "Eh, tinker?" he shouted. "I hope your wares serve the Prince well." The tinker again shied back. He did not know this man, nor did he know the local merchants, shoppers or other alien traders who had begun to cluster. Suddenly Chhuon thrust his hoe into the stall, crashing stacked pots to the ground. With a flick of his wrist he overturned a wooden box, exposing three pistols wrapped in clear plastic. He hooked one with the hoe, flipped it back to himself and caught it before the tinker could recover. Chhuon stuck his rice knife under his left arm, and while still wielding the hoe, tore the plastic from the pistol. He grasped the weapon— slowly, deliberately, he shook it as one might shake a threaten-

ing fist. "Let this kill yuons!" he snarled crazily. "Let this
honor the Prince"—he hacked the air with the pistol—"as it
mangles Viet Namese."

In the next stall the weaver smiled inwardly.

Before Nang was arrested on his second day in Bokor, before he
was beaten and led to the cliffs, he secreted himself in Ang's
hideout, wrote his report, sealed it and sent it by KK runner to
Met Sar.

"You'll find in Bokor," Ang told him while he wrote, "a
roadside soup stand before a house with four double pillars
holding the porch roof. Ask for red and blue crab soup. Met
Hout is senior. But be cautious. Bokor is owned by yuons."

"Might Bok Roh be there?" Nang had asked.

"Bok Roh!" Ang had stepped back, laughed as if the name
were a joke. "That's only a legend."

The town of Bokor, on Highway 3 between Sihanoukville and
Kampot, sat at the terminus of the Cardamom Mountains where
the ridge hooked south and dropped precipitously into the sea.
It was controlled by the NVA though a Khmer administration
coexisted. During the dry season huge villas, gleaming like
jewels set in the 3,500-foot cliff overlooking the town, were
crammed with North Viet Namese, Viet Cong, Red Chinese and
Soviet officials. Under monsoon skies the villas held only skeleton crews. Beneath the mountain, unseen, the NVA had a massive storage facility. Only bandits and the Krahom underground
existed outside the woven net.

"Red and blue crab soup," Nang said cockily to the woman in
the soup stand. He eyed an NVA soldier who openly directed
traffic at a nearby intersection. The woman nodded and disappeared. Nang laughed quietly. The trip had been easy. He had
stolen a bicycle and chased the Haklee convoy, coming forty
kilometers the first day. He had then settled into an elevated
jungle thicket from which he counted trucks for ten days. Every
day, often three times a day, the same truck convoys passed
east below him then returned west, empty. Eight to twelve
trucks per convoy, three convoys, two or three trips each day. In
the first seven days, 481 truckloads of arms and ammunition
passed below him. Then the trucks stopped. Nang waited. Nothing. A few cars. A light truck. Several students on bicycles.

Nang rode to Bokor, a young boy on a bike not unlike others,
entering the arms-rich resort as it reeled from new decrees. The
balance of power between competing elements, which only weeks
before had seemed stable, was now teetering on Norodom
Sihanouk's change of diplomatic tactics—a change perhaps moti-

vated by America's illegal show of willpower, the secret bomb-ings of border sanctuaries. By May 1969 the North Viet Namese and the Khmer Viet Minh presence in Cambodia was so great, Sihanouk took action. In the first week of the month he an-nounced that Cambodian MiG fighter-bombers had attacked NVA positions in the border area. Then he expressed his inter-est in reestablishing relations with the United States. Simulta-neously, Sihanouk *verbally* suspended Communist use of the port facilities at Sihanoukville and the first American troops were withdrawn from South Viet Nam. In June, under direct orders from Sihanouk and the prime minister of the new "last-ditch" government, Penn Nouth, Royal Army soldiers seized a large shipment of arms destined for the NVA/VC.

"Red and blue crab soup." The woman reappeared and whis-pered, "There's none here. Try the yellow house with two porches."

All day Nang was sent from one location to another. His frustration rose. He did not know what had happened at the national level, did not know what new orders had come from Phnom Penh. Finally a young woman whispered to him, "Met Hout has been seized. Go away."

"I can release him," Nang said quietly.

The woman looked at the boy and scoffed. "You?"

Nang's face went rigid. He was too tired to continue the guise. He straightened his back, grew in height to match hers, his shoulders widened, his chest bulged beneath his loose-fitting shirt until the shirt seemed ready to split. The woman's jaw dropped. She stepped back. "I am Met Nang of Angkar Leou," he announced. His eyes pierced her. "I am the eyes of Angkar Leou." Nang's voice came from deep in his chest. "I am the spirit. I am the sacrifice. Angkar Leou will be obeyed."

"Come in. Hide here." The woman flitted nervously. "I'll gather the others." She grabbed a market basket and fled.

Nang rifled the house for currency and food. His head jerked at every sound. He stood back from the windows, searched the outside from the dark within. He felt caged. Monsoon dusk settled upon Bokor. No one appeared. Nang needed to make contact, needed information, needed to send and receive word from Sar, from the Center. A feeling of abandonment swept over him. He stepped to a side window, deflated, slid out. Again he looked like an eight-year-old boy.

Night fell. Still no one appeared. "I am the sacrifice," Nang repeated to himself. "I am the will of Angkar Leou." His head nodded. He raised it, shook it. Nodded again. He did not wish to sleep. He recited successive creeds he'd learned at the School of the Cruel. He sat at perfect attention. Recited quietly. Nodded and fell asleep.

"Here!" the soldier shouted. "He's sleeping."

"Watch it," the sergeant warned. "He's probably armed."

Nang opened his eyes. The day had dawned gray. Then concussion and pain erupted at his abdomen as a soldier's kick connected. Then, before he could react, a second kick to his kidneys. Someone wired his wrists behind his back. Then he was blindfolded.

"That him?" he heard a soldier ask.

"Yes." He recognized the young woman's voice.

"You sure, Sister? He's just a little kid."

All morning Nang remained blindfolded and bound. At first they brought him to a building and made him sit, alone, on a cool concrete floor. Nang deflated himself to the total limit of his guise. He was not twelve, not eight, but five. At five he could cry, whimper, whine, talk such nonsense no one could take him seriously. He peed his pants.

"Augh, damn," a low-level guard said. "Why're they holding him?"

"They say he's Khmer Rouge," a second guard answered.

"If that's Khmer Rouge," the first said, "who cares?"

"I want my father," Nang whined. He cried loudly.

"Shit," the first guard said. "Why did Sihanouk have to disrupt everything?"

More hours passed. A squad of Royal soldiers pulled Nang from the concrete room, made him march, blindfolded, toward the mountain. He was expert at walking in blackness, at letting his feet guide themselves to firm footings, but he could not show it. Every few meters he stumbled, every few stumbles he fell. His shirt ripped on one fall, he split his forehead on another. Blood trickled down his temple, curled about his cheekbone, ran to his jaw then dripped from the tip of his chin. He cried like a terrified five-year-old. A guard grabbed his upper arm firmly, helped him up and led him. He stumbled again jamming his toes into a step and burst out with a horrible shriek.

"Eh," the guard grunted. "Listen, Little Brother, I'll take this off you if you promise to stop screaming." Then to the others, "I'm going to take the blindfold off."

Nang whimpered. The guard pried the knotted cloth up over the back of his head. Nang grimaced in pain. He made them stand still as he pretended to let his eyes adjust. Through his squint he counted and sized up the soldiers. It surprised him to see they all wore complete Royal Cambodian uniforms and all were armed with AK-47 assault rifles. They did not look at all like the ragtag national troops he'd seen in the Northeast. Sixty thousand North Viet Namese troops in Cambodia, Nang thought, and Norodom Sihanouk had his best troops chasing little boys. He laughed inwardly and thought, The guards think exactly the same.

The guards seemed somber, too somber for those thoughts. Nang walked grudgingly up the steep path. A faint deep moaning sound came from the mountain as if a syrup-thick wind was pushing through the trees, but there was no wind. They walked past the outer walls of the first villa, then onto a narrow road which wound inward and upward, away from the cliff, past two more villas, neither as expansive as the first. The faint low soughing continued. They followed the road as it curved back, upward, back to the highest and most magnificent villa at the edge of the highest overlook.

Before they reached the upper villa the guards reblindfolded him. They marched him to a small block structure outside the villa walls and threw him into a cell with a dozen blindfolded, bound men. This time Nang did stumble, over a body, and crashed down hard on his face. The door banged shut. Nang whined. "ssshh!" a voice whispered. "listen to see if they go." Nang froze. For a moment everyone was still. Then breathing began. Nang held his breath. He counted the breathing. Four, five, six. More. Then, from the whisperer, a faint exhale. Nang breathed. He righted himself and sat still. The cell smelled stale, foul. "ssst. don't remove your blindfold," the whisperer said. "they'll hang you for that."

"I want my father," Nang whimpered.

"who are you?"

"Y Bhur," Nang answered.

"ssshh. mountaineer? who's your father, boy?"

"Y Ksar," Nang answered. "He drives a truck. I came . . ."

"No talking in there!" The door screeched. Nang could feel the air first being sucked from the room then rushing back. "Grab that boy."

"better to die than submit."

"I want my father," Nang cried in Jarai.

"Take Mister Hout and those students to the cliff."

Inside the villa, Nang's blindfold was removed. The wires at his wrists were loosened, not about the wrist but extended between them. He looked quickly about. The room was sealed, saved one unbarred, unshuttered, unglassed window. Two guards stood by the closed door. A large round yellow man who looked to Nang like Guoshen's father stood near the window. The man bowed slightly. "They say you are called Comrade Nang," the man said in Jarai.

"I am Y Bhur," Nang whimpered.

"If you don't cooperate, you may be killed," the man said softly. He turned and looked out the window. "Come here," he said. Nang cowered. "Come here!" Nang approached two steps. Stopped. "I won't hurt you," the man said, "unless you refuse to cooperate." Nang stepped closer to the window. Outside, heavy afternoon rain had begun. Through the rain and mist Nang sensed the wall was an extension of the cliff face. He stepped closer. "Did you know Comrade Hout well?" The interrogator motioned at an angle through the window. Nang looked. The cliff rim formed a large U with the villa on the right and the sheerest and deepest face at the curve. Above the curve four men stood blindfolded and bound. A squad of soldiers stood behind them. The interrogator stuck his hand with a forefinger extended out the window, then flicked his wrist, pointing the finger down. At the cliff a soldier with a long bamboo lance jabbed one man in the back. The man lurched forward, dropped. He screamed. Then all was silent.

"You have committed war crimes," the interrogator said. "You are subject to punishment as a war criminal."

Nang's mind raced. At once he thought he could kill all three men and throw them from the window, confuse them with his child act, withstand any interrogation.

"They say you are Comrade Nang," the interrogator repeated in Khmer.

"I am Y Bhur, son of Y Ksar," Nang answered in broken Khmer. "I want my father. He drives a truck for Samdech Euv."

The interrogator strolled leisurely about Nang, stepped back to the window and flicked his wrist. Another man lurched, screamed. From below an eerie moaning gurgled up the cliff to the window.

"Remove his shirt," the interrogator ordered. A guard came forward, ripped Nang's shirt from his back. Even deflated, his hard wiry body could not be mistaken for that of a child. Harshly the yellow man rasped, "Comrade Nang, you will tell me who you are, what your unit is, where you are from. What's your mission?"

"Honest, Uncle," Nang pleaded in a mix of Mountaineer and Khmer words and phrases. "I'm not with any unit. I'm with my father. He's a driver. I'm Y Bhur. Please, Uncle."

"Don't give me that 'Uncle' dung. Your scars say you're a soldier." The interrogator grabbed Nang by the hair and forced his head out the window. The vertical drop was a hundred meters. The interrogator sliced his free hand horizontally through the air. At the cliff two soldiers grabbed a man as a third soldier slashed his abdomen open. In the gray of stones and rain and sky the student's belly burst red. A scream reached the window seemingly disconnected from the torture. "I want to be your friend, Nang. You must cooperate." Moaning now came from both below and across.

"I am Y Bhur," Nang answered in a firm voice. "Bok Roh killed my father, Y Ksar. I heard he's in Bokor. I've come to kill him."

"Bok Roh!?" The interrogator backed away. First one guard, then both, began to laugh. "Bok Roh is a fairy tale."

"Bok Roh is a yuon agent," Nang spat. "He killed my whole village."

The interrogator smacked Nang's face with the back of his hand. "You called yourself Met Nang," the round man said angrily. Again he grabbed Nang's hair, jerked him to the window smashing his head against the frame. "I don't have time for your games." He pointed out the window and flicked his finger again and the whisperer was jabbed. He fell to his knees at the rim. The lancer jabbed him repeatedly. He squirmed, blindfolded, bound. His right leg fell over. He kicked it up, swung it back toward his unseen attacker. Nang zoomed in on the struggle. The soldier caught the kicking leg with the lance point. On contact he thrust. The whisperer, his own force kicking against the lance, spun his torso onto the edge. Slowly, he slid backwards, seemingly trying to hook his heels on the rim, then he fell away. No scream. No moaning. In the last second Nang shifted his eyes to the squad at the cliff. Only the lancer watched. The others had turned away.

Nang was blindfolded again. The interrogator left. The two guards beat him with their fists, though they beat him lackadaisically for they saw him as he claimed to be, a young Mountaineer child searching for a fairy-tale character who had killed his father. Nang bore the blows without reaction, without sound. He had not been so beaten since the first Krahom school and he'd almost forgotten the pleasure of withstanding a beating, of beating the torturer with utter passivity.

They threw him back in the block cell outside the villa. He listened as they left, then counted the breathing of his cellmates. Eight.

"brothers, do any of you know where is bok roh?" Nang whispered in Jarai.

No one answered. He repeated the question in Khmer. A quiet answer: "i've heard he's on the border at bu ntoll."

Nang sat forward. He bent his knees, placed his eyes on the knees and began to rub the blindfold back and forth, up and down. The cloth was very tight. Slowly he was able to raise one corner enough so a crack of light entered. He worked the other side. The pressure hurt his eyeballs. He tilted his head back. He could see. Nang put his head down on his knees and rested. Then he forced his arms down, his buttocks up between his wrists. His back bent like a bow. He forced his wrists forward to under his knees. There he was able to loosen the wires.

"Bring them all," a voice commanded.

Bu Ntoll, Nang thought. Bu Ntoll, the border sanctuary. He slid his hands under his ass and back to position.

The nine prisoners were led to the edge of the cliff. Nang kept his head down. He stumbled. Was lifted, prodded forward. Ceremoniously each was read a short, identical statement finding each guilty of war crimes and condemning each to death. Nang was seventh. He kept his head down. He breathed with his mouth open so he could hear and place the others, prisoners and guards.

"Tuay Teng," the squad leader said.

"No!" The first man in line screamed. The sound of the lancer's lunge. Then "Aaaa . . ." a fading scream. Silence.

"Hang Houk." The lancer's jab. No scream. A dull concussion as meat formed to rock with force.

"Vouch Voen."

"Please." A woman's voice. "Please," the woman begged.

Nang lifted his head. It was almost dark. He turned toward the woman. Below the cloth he could see the guards' feet facing away, see the heavy vegetation and forest beyond. The lancer jabbed the woman in the spine. She shrieked.

Instead of knocking her forward, the soldier had impaled her with his spear. "Damn," the lancer muttered. A dirty kill. As he stepped forward, about to put his boot in her back and yank out the lance, Nang spun. He snapped his arms outward. The wire unraveled. Vouch Voen shieked madly as the soldier struggled with the lance. Nang sprang, a bound coil released, toward the forest. Guards caught turning back toward the entangled lancer and his victim first saw only a streak. Then one spun and opened fire. Nang dove half blind into trees, raced low on all fours deeper and deeper into the thickets. He ripped at the blindfold. The squad leader shouted. Shots cracked. The remaining prisoners were hurled off the cliff without hesitation. Screams. Silence. Moans filled the canyon. Nang slithered between, over, under vines and brush. Darkness settled. He raced on. There was no sound of pursuit.

Bu Ntoll, he thought. I will send the next report from Bu Ntoll.

"Madam, what would you have us do with him?"

"Why did you insist on showing it to her?"

"She insists on knowing everything we do. Madam?"

Vathana stared at the remains between the barge captain and the crewman. "Perhaps," the captain said in French, "I should have fed it to the crabs."

Vathana shook her head. "No," she whispered. "It is proper to have brought him here. You notified the authorities?"

"God!" The crewman cussed lowly, rolled his eyes to the sky. "No, madam. We didn't wish to be slowed."

"He tried to board?"

"There were eight. Plus those firing from the bank. The others fled when Sarath fired and killed this one."

Vathana bent to see better. The body was mangled. An arm was ripped off, both legs were broken and folded in horrifying positions. Flies swarmed above a ragged chest hole. Vathana straightened. "He's so young."

"They all looked young, madam. They all wore these checked kramas."

"He's not even as old as Samnang," Vathana said absently. Involuntarily she grimaced, squeezed her eyes tightly shut. She shuddered, scrunched her shoulders toward her neck, pulled her shawl tight against the heavy afternoon rain.

"Madam . . ."

Vathana took a deep breath, exhaled slowly, opened her eyes. "What did Sarath fire at him to cause this?"

"An RPG. Kot hit him too. With the machine gun. What would you have—"

"Wrap him in this." Vathana handed the captain her shawl. "Have Sarath and Kot take him to the pagoda." Without the wrap Vathana's abdomen bulged conspicuously.

"No good," Sarath whispered to Kot. He had retreated to the sandbag wall about the pilothouse. "The baby will be born like it."

"Maybe," Kot whispered.

"We'll go too," Vathana said to the barge captain. "We must pray for his spirit. And ours."

CHAPTER SIX

ON NEUTRALITY:
". . . as defined by international law, specifically the Hague Convention of 1907, which
states that, 'A neutral country has the obligation not to allow its territory to be used by
a belligerent. If the neutral country is unwilling or unable to prevent this, the other belligerent has the right to take appropriate
counteraction.'"

—Harry G. Summers, Jr.,
Viet Nam War Almanac

It was seven weeks before Nang laid eyes on Bok Roh. For seven
weeks the energy released from escaping death propelled him.
He had never felt freer, never as a Khmer boy, never as a
conscript, never as a yothea of Angkar Leou. As he approached
his thirteenth birthday he was free to live, free to die, free to
kill. He was strong and highly trained in all the survival arts—
mental as well as physical.

Before he reached the border camp at Bu Ntoll, Nang trekked
across the Southeast. At times he posed as a refugee, at times an
orphan, at times a mute. He walked most of the distance. In
Kampot he linked up with a Krahom guerrilla cell for several
days without identifying himself or his mission. East of Takeo
he discovered an NVA storage facility and shipping depot which
made the warehouse areas of the Ho Chi Minh Trail look paltry.
At Prey Lovea he was first assisted by an official of the Cambodian administration, then blocked by one from the parallel
North Viet Namese regime, then assisted by a Viet Namese,
then ordered into detention by Cambodians. All along the trail
he simply asked Khmer families for rice or shelter. In the
gracious tradition of Cambodians he was fed, often invited in.
On these occasions he found his quick smile, infectious laugh
and a simple story led him to be treated like a sibling. Each

night Nang listened to stories of bravado and hardship under the parallel regimes; stories of atrocities along the border; stories of skirmishes between clashing foreign armies. Almost every week he found a way to send word to Mount Aural of what he'd heard.

At Neak Luong he worked for two days cleaning river barges. The crewmen entertained him during the evening with imagined tales of private battles with bandits. "The lady owner has armed us with machine guns," one crewman told him. He produced an aged and worn AK-47. "She says, 'Shoot and run.'" The man laughed. He rubbed his hand over the wooden stock. "'Shoot and run.' Ha! Do you think you can make this old scow run?" Aside he whispered, "The captain's obtained rocket grenades and launchers."

"The lady owner, she says it's okay?" Nang asked in broken Khmer.

"She's too pregnant to think. Ha!"

"And the Prince's army, they say okay?"

"Eh? Are you crazy? The less they know, the better."

At Phum Chup, near the huge Chup Rubber Plantation Nang stole a Haklee truck and drove it for a mile toward the border before abandoning it in the quagmire of a paddy. From the back he stole an antitank mine which he quickly buried in the roadbed a dozen meters from the sinking truck. He waited, hidden across the road. In minutes a second Chinese truck and a sedan raced toward the stolen vehicles. The truck missed the detonator and stopped. Four soldiers jumped out, cussed, slogged into the paddy. Nang froze behind his concealment. The sedan parked behind the second truck. No one emerged. The windows were closed and dark. A soldier, dripping from the paddy, walked around the front of his truck. A rear window of the sedan opened and a man called out in Chinese. Nang was unable to understand the words. He imagined the man to be a bureaucrat with the Chinese Social Affairs Department, the ChiCom CIA, and he was delighted. The motor of the sedan churned, caught. The unseen driver edged back toward the road. The soldier stepped forward. Then, as if in one motion, the entire area lit, flashed yellow-orange-bright, a fireball roiling up, out. Then the concussion. It hit Nang, knocked him flat. Laughing, chunks of shrapnel crashing down about him, Nang fled across the paddy, down a dike path, running, laughing, free, easy, exhilarated.

For six nights he walked the road to Mimot and north toward Snuol. At Snuol Nang switched to forest trails. Where no inhabitants were supposed to live he stumbled into the midst of the putrid, loathsome camp. He stared in from the edge of the compound. Thousands of starving listless wraiths were rooted on the half-barren, gravel earthen hump. Most were old, toothless, wordless. They squatted or lay in shelters not suitable for pigs. A few infants lay in watery puddles of excrement. In spite of the torment there was no sound. Nang recognized the tribal dress of a few of the Mountaineers. An ancient Mnong man, the ivory plugs long fallen from his stretched limp earlobes, saw Nang, rose, fell and died. Three frail women cackled, dragged the body to the wooded edge, then returned, squatted, silent.

Nang circled the compound to where a score of Jarai elders lay in the shade of a flimsy blue plastic tarp. He emerged, hissed. No one turned. "Uncle," he clucked. "Uncle, who are you?"

An old woman turned. The bones of her neck jutted like horns on a lizard's back. She stared at the boy as if he were a mirage. "Great Aunt," Nang said in Jarai. He came forward and squatted beside her. "You are Jarai?"

"All Jarai are dead," the woman sighed.

"You are Jarai," Nang stated.

"We used to live in the great mountains." The woman's voice was light, breathless. "Look how few are left. I am death."

"Who killed you?" Nang asked.

"We've become accustomed to being dead."

"Who?" Nang persisted.

"Does it matter?" The woman's voice faded.

"Was it Bok Roh?" Nang insisted. The woman was too weary to answer. Those around her did not even look. Nang raged, "Bok Roh the giant?"

"We are the March of Tears," a second woman whispered. "Here the march ends."

"Was it Bok Roh?" Nang demanded.

"Yes," the second woman answered. "Bok Roh sent us here. He killed the others. Bombs killed many."

"Why don't you go to Snuol?" Nang pressed.

"Anyone who leaves is shot," the woman said. "Our land is empty. Our souls have been destroyed."

Nang crept out, circled the squalid settlement, staying at the treeline. He circled again twenty meters farther out. Twice he saw trip wires. Bu Ntoll, he thought. A restrained smirk curled his lip.

It was cold though the wind had slackened. The sky grayed. Nang sat in a crotch of tree trunk and limb at the fringe of the North Viet Namese sanctuary. The military complex at Bu Ntoll was built on a 3000-foot peak set in a V-shaped inclusion of

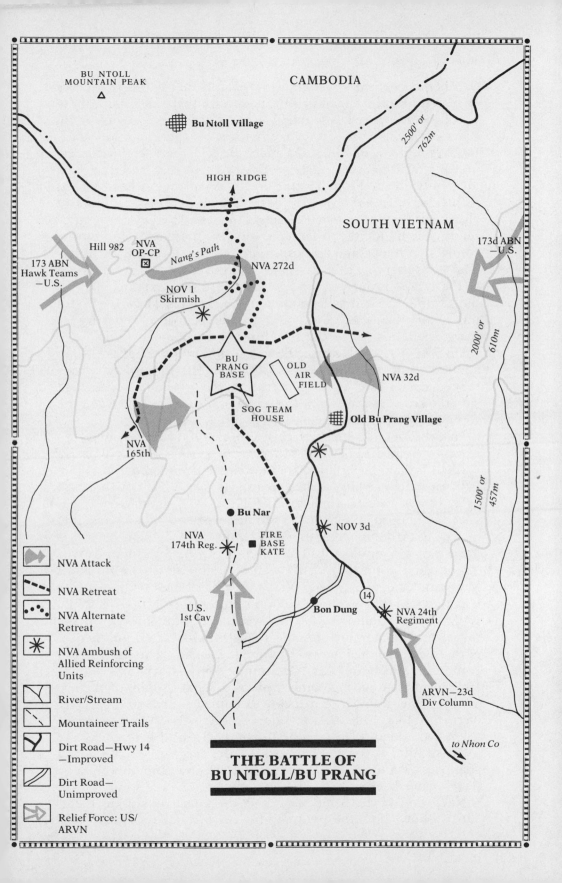

BU NTOLL MOUNTAIN PEAK △

CAMBODIA

⊞ **Bu Ntoll Village**

2500' or 762m

HIGH RIDGE

SOUTH VIETNAM

Hill 982

NVA OP-CP ☒

Nang's Path

NVA 272d

173 ABN Hawk Teams —U.S.

NOV 1 Skirmish ✳

173d ABN —U.S.

2000' or 610m

BU PRANG BASE

OLD AIR FIELD

NVA 32d

NVA 165th

SOG TEAM HOUSE

⊞ **Old Bu Prang Village** ✳

1500' or 457m

● **Bu Nar**

NVA 174th Reg. ✳

■ **FIRE BASE KATE**

✳ **NOV 3d**

U.S. 1st Cav

14

● **Bon Dung**

✳ **NVA 24th Regiment**

ARVN—23d Div Column

to Nhon Co

⬤▶ NVA Attack

- - - NVA Retreat

•••• NVA Alternate Retreat

✳ NVA Ambush of Allied Reinforcing Units

River/Stream

Mountaineer Trails

Dirt Road—Hwy 14 —Improved

Dirt Road— Unimproved

▷▷ Relief Force: US/ ARVN

THE BATTLE OF BU NTOLL/BU PRANG

Cambodian territory wedging into South Viet Nam. Nang had slithered into the encampment, a small bivouac at the perimeter of the multisited sanctuary, on the third day of August 1969. For two days he sat, trancelike, without eating, without sleeping, vigilant yet inanimate, a machine, a camera and recorder, viewing, waiting, seeking, expecting without reason the appearance of Bok Roh. From his tree-crotch concealment he observed nitpicking cadre thoroughly inspect four distinct elements of clean, well-equipped troops, inspect their mission-specific equipment, saw hundreds of *dan cong* porters prepare to follow the soldiers with food and ammunition; watched as captured American jeeps carrying officers snaked up the covered one-lane road to the camp, through the camp, on toward the next site. For two days Nang watched as Russian and Chinese trucks arrived with more equipment and new, young troops. They are preparing for battle, he thought. He knew nothing of the plans.

On 5 August, one year to the day from his conscription, Nang spotted, amid a passing unit, Bok Roh. His inanimate trance turned colder. His eyes, penetrating the blocking vegetation, saw the scope of the camp, the scope of his revenge. It was time to move.

Nang slithered from the tree, crept past the guards, out of the camp. Then he rose. Do not concentrate on tools, he thought. He turned, walked back, up to the sentries, surrendered.

It was tricky. Nang wished to appear dumb but not so dumb as to be assigned to a porter unit. He wished to appear experienced but not so experienced as to be suspected of being capable of spying or double-agenting. He could not tell them he was a local boy or a guide or a FULRO soldier. If he told them he was Khmer Viet Minh they easily would be able to check: Bu Ntoll Mountain had two Khmer Viet Minh base sites. If he said he was Krahom they would hold him suspect, turn him over to the KVM. That wouldn't do. That would separate him from his target and render him unable to accomplish his intelligence-gathering mission. Ideally, he thought, I can be assigned to a communal subcommissar. (Communal commissars were responsible for disseminating combat plans to local people just before or just as an ambush or attack was launched against an enemy element.) Nang felt secure, safe in age, in knowledge. I'll let them know I can translate, he thought. Then I'll hear plans.

"Take him to the field hospital," the sergeant of the guard snapped. "Tie him." To Nang, "What are you doing here? Your people have been told."

Nang bowed, held his wrists so the guard could tie them. "Just follow me," the guard indicated after the sergeant left.

"He thinks," he mumbled to another soldier, "this boy breeches security!?"

Nang told a doctor his name was Khat Doh. He told him he was from the Jarai village of Plei The more than a hundred kilometers north in the Ia Drang Valley and that he had been directed to Bu Ntoll by many people. The man accepted Nang's story because he did not care if the little boy was telling the truth or lying. Nang told a second officer he had traveled for a few weeks with a FULRO platoon which had come south to Ban Me Thuot but that they had had no food, few arms and no organization. The officer sneered as if to say, "Of course. They're ignorant *moi.*" Nang did not stop. He rattled on to his interrogator that he wished to kill the hairy meddling Americans who were behind the death of his father and the conquest of his village, that he wished to join the NVA in their attacks on the Americans. Nang clucked in Jarai, stammered in Khmer, butchered his few Viet Namese phrases. The officer noted it all.

On 6 August, Nang was briefly interviewed a second time, and on the seventh, a third. He was held aboveground in loose "camp arrest" where he was observed and lightly guarded. Had the attacks not been imminent Nang likely would have been handled differently, but with plans set and preparation for the offensive under way, there was no time to concentrate on the small Mountaineer who called himself Khat Doh, who wished to avenge his father.

"You may work at the hospital," the last interviewer told him. "Assist the nurses. Help them clean. Later we'll talk again."

At three A.M., 8 August, the NVA began to move out. Thousands of men climbed from the mountain's beehive of tunnels and caves to march down scores of narrow paths which led to secret border-crossing sites, fanned out and filtered into southern II Corps and northern III Corps.

In the underground medical station Nang paced, an animal in a cage. "Can't I go," he asked the section leader, a strong girl named Thi.

"No." She laughed. "You're still a baby."

"I am not," he said haughtily.

"You help me here." Thi smiled pleasantly.

"Bok Roh is my uncle," Nang said desperately. "I should find him. I could carry his pack."

Thi shot him a wary glance. "You help here," she said. "That giant needs no help."

"Nor do you," Nang countered.

"There's been little fighting," Thi said. "Now there'll be much. Besides, his company's just left. You keep oil in the lamps, bring the stretchers back up to the dispensary, help the soldiers with their food. When the giant returns, you'll see him."

Nang slunk glumly to a corner. He withered before Thi's eyes, no longer the ten-year-old Khat Doh, but now a six-year-old. Thi watched him for a few moments as she went about her chores. She felt concern, as one might for a sulking pet, but she thought better than to interfere with the savage's withdrawal. Thi turned from the boy, walked to a crate of wound dressings and began to unpack and organize them into shelves built into the earthen walls. When she turned again, her spare uniform shirt, a rucksack, a medical kit and the boy were gone.

Night was falling on the Mekong. To the east the sky was leaden, to the west pink, almost violet. Vathana stood by the pier. The barge had been pushed into the channel by a small tug and was now maneuvering into the wake of a freighter heading to Phnom Penh. Vathana rested her hands on her bulging tight abdomen. She was warm, content. The past month had been good. No incidents on the river, no fights with Teck. And the easing of trade restrictions had eliminated an entire layer of bureaucrats who needed to be paid *bonjour* before any cargo could be off-loaded at the capital. The barge turned in the current. The setting sun glinted in the water and reflected red off the wave wash on the barge side, making the cumbersome ark look as if it were dancing lightly on flames.

From the corner of her eye Vathana caught movement. She turned her head. Something darted. Crates of rotting vegetables were stacked four high in a haphazard wall at quay edge. She took a step away. Rats, she thought. She turned back to the barge. The sun dipped, the water became dull, the barge black, ugly. Again at the corner of her eye, a flashed blackness. She snapped her head. Not a rat, a hand. Gone!

"Oh!" She thought to hurry away. Quickly she back-stepped, began to turn. Again the hand, small. Vathana stopped, puzzled, stared. The hand darted into a crate, seemed to stick, then quickly withdrew with a handful of limp bean pods. Vathana moved slowly, quietly, forward. The sky was now deep gray. She walked to a point in the line of crates ten box lengths from where she'd seen the small hand. She laid a hand on a crate and leaned over. Her belly hit the middle box. She adjusted her stance, leaned between two stacks and looked down behind the wall. A small child was eating the garbage. At first Vathana did not understand what she was seeing. He should be home, she thought. What kind of mother would allow such a young one to play here at this hour? But the child was not playing. Vathana squeezed in farther to get a better look. She saw a second child. The sky was getting very dark. She squeezed out, walked down a few stacks, peered over. No one. She stepped down a few more, poked her head between. Still, no one.

"All right," she said in a motherly voice, "come out here." She waited. Nothing moved. For a second she felt very self-conscious talking to the crate wall of rotting plants. She started to go. She touched her belly, took a breath, then commanded, "Come out right now. This has gone on long enough." She paused, readied herself to plunge in. Suddenly a small face appeared. Vathana looked at the child sternly. "Come," she said. Her voice was firm, not harsh. "Bring the other."

A tiny boy, perhaps just three, emerged. He was thin, frail, a swollen stomach protruding from his ripped, dirty shirt. Awkwardly Vathana knelt down, held out a hand. Then a small girl, identical in size to the boy, appeared. "What are you children doing back there?" The children didn't answer. "Come now," Vathana said louder. "Why aren't you home?" The children cringed, their faces pinched, lower lips protruded, curled down as if they were about to cry. Still they were silent. Vathana leaned forward, braced herself on the pier with one hand, reached out to touch the little girl with the other. The child didn't move. Gently Vathana grasped her hand. Still kneeling she righted herself, bringing the girl to her side. "Do you live here?" No utterance. Vathana stood. She held the girl's right hand in her left, held out her right for the boy. Hesitantly he reached up, placed his small hand in hers. Vathana stepped slowly toward the main road. She looked first at one child, then the other. "We'll find your mom," she whispered. The little girl tugged, resisted. "What is it?" Vathana asked, again puzzled, now becoming tired, frustrated. Night had settled on Neak Luong.

Still the imps said nothing, but a new sound came. Something was crouched at the end of the wall, watching, wide-eyed. A shiver crossed Vathana's shoulders. She glared into the darkness at the new intrusion, straightened her shoulders, maternally protective, holding the hands of the little ones, challenging, intimidating the unseen. "Come along," she said very properly, attempting to ignore the potential danger.

The thing cried softly like a cat. Vathana looked at the children, then again into the shadow behind the crates. Again the cry. The little boy whimpered. The girl pulled, trying to loosen her hand from Vathana's.

"You come out too," Vathana ordered. "That's no place to play." Now a skinny girl, looking six, shyly emerged. "Are there any more?" The older girl shook her head. "Then come along. You looked starved. And you *certainly* need baths."

"What do you mean bringing those filthy urchins in here?!"

"I found them on the pier."

"I don't care if you found them in a . . . a cola bottle. I won't have them in my house."

"This one is Seta . . ." Vathana began.

"Stop! Get them out of here."

"Teck . . ."

"Give them to your monk."

"Teck, they . . . they stowed away on . . ."

"Then stow them back. You can throw 'em into the river for all I care."

"They're border children."

"They're what?"

"Orphans. From the border region. Seta said her . . ."

"Augh! Get them out of here. I'm going out. They're to be gone when I return."

Teck left the apartment. Furiously he leaped down the four flights of stairs, ran through the courtyard, stopped only when he reached the main road. He looked right. A few lights shone, the doctors', the pagoda, some at the garrison beyond. To the left, a few hundred meters down, began Neak Luong's small strip of cafes and dance halls. Teck slogged through the dim stretch, through his anger and bitterness and despair until he reached the rim of the first club's lights. Then he straightened, slicked back his hair and walked through the light, glancing in for friends. He passed two more establishments, entered the next.

"Teck," three young men greeted him.

"Hallo Sakun, Kim, Louis. You are all here."

"Where else?" Louis joked. "Just waiting for you." They all laughed silly laughs.

"Where's Thiounn?"

"His father has obtained a position for him," Sakun said.

"A position?" Teck pulled his head back with question. The four moved to a small table at the rear of the cafe. A waiter brought their usual, small cups of dark thick coffee laced with chocolate shavings.

"Some position," Kim muttered. "He won't be allowed to do a thing."

"He'll get to sit in an office and watch the pretty girls," Louis countered, and again they all laughed.

"What about you?" Sakun asked Teck. "Your father won't hire you?"

"I won't be hired," Teck corrected.

"And what about a teaching position? Can't the Ma-dame come up with something?"

"Oh come on!" Teck jerked his shoulders haughtily. "Mother thinks I'm very well situated now. She says to me, 'Why would you want to be in a room with all those foolish brats?' Besides, the Prince has seen to it that none of the *neak ches-doeng* will ever work. You know I've applied."

"Ha!" Louis chided him. "Maybe there's no opening for an expert on Monet." The young men giggled.

Teck pouted. "Paintings are important," he said firmly. "They enrich life. It's only Sihanouk's fears which makes for no openings."

The four friends talked and sipped their coffee. Louis nudged Teck each time the daughter of the owner emerged from the small kitchen. Each time Teck looked, the girl glanced shyly at him then immediately turned away. "She likes you," Louis teased Teck.

"She likes anything in pants," Teck whispered defensively.

"She doesn't look at Kim or Sakun," Louis baited him. "Well, maybe at me!"

"Ha! That's because she knows," Teck blurted the words between spitting snickers, "they've nothing *in* their pants."

Louis laughed and they all prodded one another and finished their drinks. Then Kim said, "Let's go in back."

Quietly the young men rose and followed Kim into a hallway with many doors. They shuffled in silence to a room Kim had rented. The cubicle was tiny, no bigger than a cell, windowless, airless, with but a single small low table with two candles burning. Teck locked the door. They sat. Now Louis opened a small sheet of aluminum foil exposing a cube about the size of a lump of sugar. He methodically crumbled the block into grains, curled the foil so the grains lay loosely in a trough. Very carefully, slowly, Louis passed the foil over one candle. Teck, Kim and Sakun leaned in tight. Back and forth, gently, Louis heated the foil until the heroin began to ooze heavy cream-colored smoke. Louis stretched his neck, his face forward, his nose in the smoke. He inhaled deeply, leaned back. The smoke swirled up in the rising heat, fell gracefully back upon itself as it cooled. Teck pulled a soda straw from his pocket. The smoke became thicker as the crumbs became hotter. Teck put the straw to his lips, put the open end in the thickest swirl, sucked it in and held it. He passed the straw to Kim. The straw went around three times. Then the young men leaned back, relaxed. "Never," Sakun whispered, "never will Sihanouk let us work." They all giggled.

They crossed the border. Monsoon thunder exploded above the peaks, trembled in the valleys. With each clap heavy rain crashed in sheets against thick vegetation. Nang fell in at the back of a column, behind a squad of ammo porters. The column wound slowly down trackless ravines where streams gushed. They climbed little, sought crevices below knolls, circled rises beneath thick canopy where humid air seemed as impenetrable as jungle growth. At each rest Nang moved up. Slyly he asked porters or privates details of the plan. By evening he knew he was with an element of the NVA 272d Regiment, that they had moved southwest from Bu Ntoll, crossed between American Special Forces camps at Duc Lap and Bu Prang, and were on schedule for a four-day trek which would take them nearly sixty kilometers to a staging area south of Phuoc Binh and Song Be City. There they would rendezvous with other infiltrating elements.

The sky darkened. Rain slowed to a constant patter on the leaves. From caves in Bu Ntoll, NVA gunners began firing 130-mm shells at Bu Prang. The column rose, followed the guides. Counterbattery artillery from Bu Prang answered the NVA guns. For an hour Nang's column meandered behind the scout, beneath cover of darkness, concealment of rain, diversion of artillery duel. NVA soldiers knew the imperialist forces—the American 173d Airborne Brigade, the South Viet Namese 23d Division, and the American Special Forces–led Mountaineer units—relied on seismic sensor devices near the border to detect liberation troop movements, yet they moved without concern. Porters told Nang the rain and thunder would interfere with detection. The column stopped. They entered a fortified, camouflaged way station hidden in dense bamboo groves. Night settled. The rain ceased. A chill wind blew above the camp swaying the bamboo. Nang lay awake, tense, planning.

"Take that boy to Major Bui," a lieutenant broke in an hour before first light. "How could no one know who he is? Get the giant to interpret. Don't trust these *moi* porters."

Nang started. He wasn't certain he understood but he thought he had heard mention of the giant. A soldier motioned him up. He bowed his head to the lieutenant. Sheepishly he dragged his feet. His mind raced with possible scenarios, possible lies.

The structure at the center of the way station was four low cornerposts with a vine-lashed ridge pole and bamboo joists covered with thatch. Beneath, in the glow of a small oil lantern, three men sat in large wicker chairs. Two wore NVA officer uniforms. One wore a simple unmarked khaki tunic.

"Excuse me, sir," Nang's escort interrupted. "We have a mountain boy who's been assisting the porters but who is unknown to them. Lieutenant Hoa thought he should be questioned by. Mister Bok."

Nang bowed before the three men. As he lowered his head he noted both officers had their pistols disassembled for cleaning. Between them lay a map. Then Nang saw Bok Roh. His heart leaped. He fought to keep his face empty, to deny his rage visible vent. Bok glanced up sleepily. He had an issue of *Nhan Dan,* Hanoi's newspaper, on his lap and a copy of *Paris Match* in his hands. "So, who are you?" Bok asked in Mnong.

Nang chirred, an odd yet specific Jarai sonant mannerism indicating confusion, but before Bok could rattle off a string of questions in that language, Nang asked in slightly broken Khmer if the officer spoke the Cambodian language.

"So, who are you?" Bok asked in Khmer. He reached a hand to his face, massaged his chin, glowered at the cowering boy. Nang repeated the lies he'd told earlier, embellishing with even more details. As he spoke he respectfully lowered his head. Inside he shuddered, confused. Could this truly be Bok Roh? Bok Roh the violent manic savage? Could this man, sitting in a wicker chair, reading a newspaper not unlike his father used to, be the target of his vengeance?

"He says"—the large man turned from Nang and spoke to the officers in Viet Namese—"that his father was French-Khmer and his mother Jarai, that both were killed by American bombs on the village of Plei The."

"Do you know the village?" one officer asked.

"I do. I don't. I know the area." Bok glanced back at Nang.

"When did he say they were bombed?" an officer asked.

Bok translated. To the officers he interpreted the answer, "Two years ago. Maybe three. He says he was very young."

The oldest officer shook his head. *"Tien su no!* Hell! Why do they bother us with these little problems?"

Nang bowed and stepped to the officer. Feigning confusion, absorbing as much detail as possible in the two-second glance, he shook his hand back and forth over one corner of the map and muttered Plei The.

"Tell him I don't care where it is," the officer snapped. "It's not on this map."

"Come here boy," Bok Roh said in Jarai. His voice was calm, gentle. "You look familiar," he said. He eyed him up and down.

"Maybe like I did when I was seven or eight." Bok chuckled, stood. Nang rolled his head back, feigning shock at the giant's height. "I could use a porter who's good at languages. These Viets won't stoop to learn. *Parlez-vous français?*"

"*Oui.*" Nang laughed. "*Un peu.*"

. In the distance, thunder exploded again. Bok Roh froze. He snapped his head toward the older officer. "*Tien su no!*" The man shook. The thunder rolled toward them without pause. The younger officer jumped. The older rose slowly, deliberately, snuffed the lantern. All about soldiers could be heard scurrying. The thunder grew. The earth trembled. Bok grabbed Nang, forced him to the ground. He covered the boy with his body as the first bomb flash erupted. The earth burst. Roar and concussion swept across the ground. Bamboo slivers shot like arrows into the hut. Steel shards sliced soldiers at the column's south point. Dirt clumps crashed about the center. Nang felt pinned, not safe. Bok's body covered him. Bok Roh who'd killed . . . was over him! A second concussion flattened the shack. Above, over a thirty-kilometer stretch of border, U.S. Air Force B-52 bombers computer-released their ordnance, eighty 500-pound bombs each. Fifty sorties, each designated for a half-mile-wide by two-mile-long bomb box, targets identified by electronic sensors and aerial infrared reconnaissance.

Another series of crashes. Closer. Erupting burning sucking the air from the graying sky, throwing them up, crashing down, earth banging like hammer-smashed anvil, smoke blackening the fog. Nang pushed up, gulped for air, wanting to see, hear, witness. Bok Roh held him. Then the giant lifted him like a football scooped in one hand tight against his side, crouched, ran. About them men screamed. The bombing stopped. Fires smouldered. Huge rings, craters, were blown clear, clean as new-plowed paddies. Nang's ears stung, hurt, hurt not only at the ear but all the way to the top of his throat. The sky lightened. Bok Roh halted. He seemed surprised to find Nang hanging from his hand. Nang was shocked, not witless, not dazed, but awed by Bok's power. He squirmed from the giant's grasp, dropped to the earth. Then he took the big man's hand and led him to a crater berm. "Come. Come," Nang whispered. "If they follow up with troops we'll need cover."

Bok Roh too was shocked. His face was burned, his left arm bloody. The concussion of the closest bomb had left him stunned. He shook his head violently, attempting to stop the roar though the bombers had long flown by. Then he started. Khat Doh's sense of survival rocked him. Beyond them sergeants snapped at men, organized, counted.

Then all was quiet.

Slowly jungle noises returned—birds chirped, a monkey whooped, a small enemy reconnaissance plane buzzed. Nang crept from the giant's side, squatted behind him, beneath tilted bamboo cover. A lieutenant approached, reported to Bok Roh. There were two dead, seven seriously wounded. The column would not move until the reconnaissance plane went off station.

"You must eat," Nang whispered to Bok Roh. He had gotten the giant's ration and his own, had eaten a third of the giant's. "You must eat," he repeated calmly. "They say we'll move shortly. There are Americans to the north."

Inside, Nang was bursting, frenzied. Again he was alive, unscathed, liberated from fear of harm, elevated by having cheated death, yet he was confused, enthralled with the giant, this new giant, a man who could kill him or save him at will.

"Let me change the dressing and clean your arm." Nang bowed.

"Khat Doh, you should learn Viet Namese," Bok said in Jarai as Nang unwound the first hasty bandage.

"Because they won't stoop to learn Jarai," Nang retorted.

"No, because they fight for us all," Bok Roh said. "Because their victory is inevitable."

"They would as soon destroy Jarai as Americans." Nang coughed the words out apologetically. Again, in the sky over the valley a small enemy plane buzzed.

"The American war is aggression against all the peoples of Southeast Asia," Bok said sadly. "The Americans violate our fundamental national rights. Ouch!"

"There's much dirt in the cut."

"It's not deep," Bok said, leaning over, eyeing the scraped skin below his elbow. Nang lifted Bok's hand, rolled his arm, forcing him to see the deeper jagged slash on the underside. Bok grimaced. The wound was not deep but looked nasty. Nang smeared on an antibacterial salve. "They escalate the war with these B-52s and their poison gases," Bok said. "These are crimes against our people. Defoliating crops so people starve is a crime."

Bok squeezed his hand into a fist, testing the arm. He watched Nang work. "Where did you learn this?" He spoke slowly in Viet Namese. Nang understood the words "where" and "learn" but he did not answer. Bok asked again in French.

"Around," Nang answered in Khmer.

Forcefully Bok Roh said, "You know too much not to learn Viet Namese. I'll teach you. You'll be my aide."

Nang looked up. A porter came with Bok's backpack and gear. Sheathed at the pack's side was a huge machete. Nang smiled.

Bok Roh was not a soldier of the North Viet Namese Army. Nor was he a member of the National Liberation Front, or of FULRO, or of the Alliance of National, Democratic and Peace Forces. He might have been labeled Khmer Viet Minh though even there he was not a soldier. He held a peculiar position, one which gave him the status of a middle-level diplomat or an officer—though he represented no government, commanded no troops, analyzed no intelligence, prepared no supplies and planned no operations. Indeed, the giant had no freedom. He was as much a prisoner, even if willingly, of the NVA as he would have been had he been held captive in a jungle jail. Bok Roh was incarcerated by his past, by conflicting brutal mercenary actions. He was trusted by no one, held outlaw by all, valued no greater than dust. Yet, with his massive physical stature and his mastery of thirty languages and dialects, he was also invaluable.

Bok Roh was pensive, lonesome, a man who buried his mental agitation in books, magazines, reports. Each day he pored over English, French, Chinese and Viet Namese newspapers. When at Bu Ntoll he studied Tolstoi in Russian, Mishima in Japanese and Marx, Engels and Hesse in German. His eye for the written word was nearly photographic; his ear for the spoken nearly perfect. Yet each year he found his talents of less value to others, of less pleasure to himself. He no longer wrote the speeches he delivered but relied on NVA political cadre to tell him exactly what to say. No longer did he question village raids or massacres, but abdicated total responsibility to NVA intelligence and operations officers.

A hundred meters above and several hundred meters south of the camp a white phosphorus marking round burst. Again there was scurrying, soldiers scratching the earth, forming depressions, jumping into fighting positions or hugging crater berms. Two hundred meters south of the way station six 105mm howitzer rounds exploded. Bok grabbed his pack, reached for Nang. The boy was down, shrunken to a ball like a hard-backed insect, shrunken into a small foot-deep depression. Six more rounds screamed in, exploded in succession. Bok dropped beside Nang, pulled his pack over them. Six rounds exploded at the camp's edge. Soldiers began running, fleeing north. The rounds, shot from Bu Prang, were being walked north in lines a hundred meters apart—three aerial bursts and three contact detonations in each salvo. Mortar rounds, dull thunks, dropped in behind the howitzer explosions. Again Bok reached to pull Nang under him but Nang sprung, sprinted from the giant's hand. The man raced behind the boy. To the east planes buzzed. Another salvo burst behind them. Soldiers screamed. Forty, fifty dashed, crashing through vegetation, north, fanning out east, west. The salvos chased them. A group broke east. Nang started to follow. Bok caught him, grabbed a shoulder of the running boy, threw him, dove with him into a stream, below the surface, to the side. There they forced themselves up, under a tree's overhanging root clump. Nang gasped, water cascaded into his mouth. Bok grabbed his head, forced him up. To the east claymore mines exploded, machine guns and assault rifles barked. Artillery rounds exploded north. Then farther north.

Late that evening word came that the remnant of the column of the NVA 272d Regiment should disperse, return to Bu Ntoll, forgo their planned part in the attack on Song Be City. Nang followed Bok Roh, backtracking to Cambodia. As he watched the large man's silhouette, he thought, I am going to learn from you, Mister Giant. I'll be your slave. Ha! And you'll be your slave's slave. Ah, what you can teach me, eh? But one day, you mutant *moi*, I'll have learned all you can give. One day you won't be surrounded by your lackeys.

From Ben Het in the North through Duc Co on Highway 19, south to Bu Ntoll and Snuol, farther to the Fishhook, Tay Ninh and the Parrot's Beak, east of Svay Rieng and west of Chau Duc and Tri Ton to the terminus at Ha Tien—all along the Cambodia–Viet Nam border, the summer of 1969 was marred with artillery duels and infantry skirmishes. Thousands of soldiers were killed. Nearly ten thousand were wounded.

A general offensive, mini-Tet II (mini-Tet I having occurred in May of 1968), was launched on 12 August. Communist forces attacked 150 cities and bases throughout South Viet Nam, setting off the heaviest fighting in three months. The city hardest hit was An Loc, the capital of Binh Long Province, fifty kilometers west-southwest of Phuoc Binh and Song Be City. Also hit hard were Quan Loi, east of An Loc, and Tay Ninh, fifty kilometers farther south. Ninety-seven Americans were reported killed and 523 wounded during the three-day offensive. ARVN casualties were 107 killed, 371 wounded; North Viet Namese casualties were estimated at 1,597 killed. Not included in the estimate were 64 NVA killed on 9 August by artillery from Bu Prang or by small arms fire when, fleeing the artillery, they emerged from jungle thickets into a fusillade from a unit of the 173d Airborne Brigade.

In Cambodia internal factors and border pressure caused Prince Sihanouk to appoint a "salvage government" headed by Prime Minister General Lon Nol. Lon Nol's first reports indicate there were, in August, thirty-five to forty thousand NVA soldiers on Khmer territory and that they were spreading west.

North Viet Nam's president, Ho Chi Minh, died on 3 September at the age of 79. Norodom Sihanouk, in Hanoi for the funeral, publicly called for the withdrawal of all Americans from South Viet Nam. Simultaneously he expressed Cambodia's support for the "just stand" of North Viet Nam.

On his return home, Sihanouk privately changed course. American B-52s had secretly begun bombing NVA/VC base camps and supply areas along the border of Cambodia on 18 March 1969. The first strike was called Operation Breakfast. Subsequent border bombings (also kept secret from the U.S. Congress and the American people) were labeled Lunch, Dinner, et cetera, and together became known as the "Menu" bombings. In mid-September Prince Sihanouk ordered his military chiefs to disclose to U.S. intelligence the known locations of VC/NVA sanctuaries. Additional secret bombings ensued.

For two months the North Viet Namese at Bu Ntoll planned and plotted a revenge attack on Bu Prang. For two months the two bases traded artillery shots across the border. For two months Lieutenant Hoa and many others nursed their wounds, first in the underground infirmary, then in surface patient dormitories. And for two months Nang, as Khat Doh, shadowed Bok Roh.

Khat Doh became the giant's aide, and to the giant, the mountain boy, awestruck by Bok's talents, size and apparent status, became his revival. In Nang's eyes Bok Roh saw admiration; in his impish smile he found levity. Nang smiled for Bok Roh. He smiled and he continued to think, I'll learn from you, Mister Giant. I'll learn.

"Coso khong?" Bok whispered in Viet Namese. Are you afraid? There had been another B-52 alert.

"Suc may!" Nang laughed. Hardly.

"Nephew," Bok Roh whispered. He switched to Khmer. "Tonight come with me. Skip Duc Lap."

"Uncle, why? Where? I wanted a view of the American dogs."

"Colonel Pham suggests I meet with the Dong Nai Regiment," Bok Roh continued in Khmer.

"I don't understand," Nang said in Viet Namese.

In Jarai Bok whispered, "Here, don't ask me."

At dusk Bok Roh and Nang climbed from the earth. The bombers had unloaded their ordnance ten miles to the south. "We squeeze into the earth like worms." Nang looked up at Bok Roh. "For nothing." Bok looked down. He almost held out his hand as a father would to a toddler son. "They're keeping to the other side of the border," Nang said.

"Here," Bok answered slowly. "Yes. But where we're going they're bombing both sides."

The jeep with Bok, Nang and four political officers lurched and jolted south down the narrow mountain road from Bu Ntoll to Highway 14, sped west, then south, on a comparatively smooth though rutted graveled roadway. For an hour they bounced and banged in the vehicle as it approached the border near Bu Jerman. Twice they passed through ghost villages: one bombed out, trees splintered, homes swallowed by craters; the second empty, villager-abandoned or inhabitants-exterminated without a trace. Bok Roh knew. Nang did not ask.

They approached the border. The jeep slowed, entered a one-lane passage. Without lights they bumped over heaves, crashed into potholes. A light flicked—on off on off. In the haze which packed itself between leaves, vines and fronds, Nang could not judge the distance to the source. Again, on off on off. Either a strong beam at a distance or a weak one very close. "We'll switch here," Bok said to him quietly.

Nang felt uncomfortable. He was unarmed. They left the jeep and immediately were directed to the backs of small, unseen motorcycles. The entire political entourage mounted up. Riders kick-started the bikes. A dozen muffled coughs sounded in the dark.

For an hour they rode, first down the side road through fields of sugarcane and manioc, then up and down a military trail which brought them to a small cottage. Bok Roh disappeared, reemerged in a black pajama uniform. "Follow me," he told Nang in Khmer.

"Where to?" Nang asked.

For half an hour they walked through the jungle on a narrow dirt path. With each step Nang tried to anticipate what lay ahead but the secrecy of the movement left him without even the flimsiest foundation upon which to build.

Again they halted at a lone jungle cottage. Nang could hear and smell chickens in a coop, could hear a stream babble, but in the dark he saw nothing.

Bok bent and spoke quietly. "Pham says you must also change."

"Where are we?"

"By the Song Be," Bok Roh answered.

"In Cambodia?"

"No. We haven't been there for two hours."

"Will we go much farther?"

"A little. This is the first security ring of the Dong Nai Regiment."

Nang emerged from the cottage dressed in identical black pajamas as Bok Roh and the others. He was escorted to a second cottage crammed with men he viewed as very old and overly polite. For hours the men talked in the dim light of a lantern. Bok Roh was often spoken to, directed, ordered. He was not part of the conversation. Nang curled up in a corner, pretended sleep, attempted to understand the security procedure, attempted to formulate a report for Met Sar.

"You are Hai Hoa Binh." Bok Roh nudged Nang.

"Eh?"

"Second Peaceful One," Bok said. "Because you sleep like a baby and you follow me. Come now."

Soldiers, officers, support personnel and cadres of the Dong Nai Regiment were assembled three hundred strong in a large, open-sided, temporary hall. Representatives of nine other Viet Cong units, plus dignitaries and leaders of the National Liberation Front (NLF), the Provisional Revolutionary Government (PRG), the North Viet Namese Army and the Central Office for South Viet Nam (COSVN) were seated at tables before a low stage. Draped behind the stage were two five-by-ten-foot red and blue flags with yellow stars in the middle. To one side a huge poster declared, NOTHING IS MORE PRECIOUS THAN INDEPENDENCE AND LIBERTY. Strains of "Liberate the South," the NLF anthem, played as the last of the dignitaries entered.

Nang sat with the soldiers toward the rear. His blood was aboil in the presence of so many yuons but his countenance was that of a sleepy child. Again Bok Roh had vanished.

The Viet Cong Dong Nai Regiment had been heavily wounded by the U.S. 1st Infantry Division early in 1969 when Alpha Company, 1st of the 26th, blew up the regiment's base camp along the Song Be River south of An Loc. The regiment relocated farther north where the U.S. 1st Air Cavalry Division destroyed their major food and materiel caches. Again they'd moved north, establishing a small camp on the Song Be twenty miles northeast of An Loc, eleven miles from the Cambodian border.

The rally was formal. Opening remarks by the Dong Nai commander were followed by briefings on the political, military and diplomatic status of the liberation effort, then by reports of specific activities by local units and urban front organizations.

Nang's attention wandered. Between reports he rose, excused himself, indicating he needed to urinate. The morning had dawned without rain, without mist. By nine the sun had dried exposed surfaces, the temperature had risen. Nang meandered; yet, aware of the numerous guards, he merely peered into the surrounding camp. He was surprised at the crude shelters. Compared to Bu Ntoll the camp was a slum; compared to Mount Aural it was a pigmire. He noted the soldiers, officers and dignitaries. All seemed in a state of semistarvation. One in ten seemed sickly, jaundiced, infected with malaria. He snooped further.

Unit morale was low. In 1967, 27,178 Viet Cong soldiers deserted the Communist ranks and rallied to the government of South Viet Nam under the Open Arms, or *Chieu Hoi*, program. In 1968 the figure dropped to 18,171. In 1969, by November, more than forty thousand had rallied. Communist field strength in South Viet Nam and the border sanctuaries was at least seventy percent North Viet Namese. Numerous traditionally indigenous southern rebel units were manned by upwards of ninety-five percent Northern soldiers. Nearly every Viet Cong unit shared command with or was commanded by NVA officers. Few North Viet Namese soldiers had defected: 284 in 1968, 302 to November 1969.

Nang returned to the hall. He noted the NVA officers with whom he'd arrived. The VC, he thought, must receive only half the Northern ration. Like Khmers, he thought. Opening their arms to Northern crocodiles who lure them with words and plans, who wish to devour them.

In the hall NVA officers wore dress khaki uniforms, dignitaries wore loose tan or light gray trousers and open short-sleeve shirts. Then Bok appeared. Nang's body turned to stone. A low chatter rippled across the audience. Bok was dressed in a white tropical suit, white shirt and narrow red tie.

In such dress it was impossible to tell Bok's ethnic or racial origin—he could have been Mountaineer or American Indian; Khmer, North Viet Namese, or Mongolian; Pakistani, Azerbaijani or Turkmenian. With his stature, his knowledge and his linguistic abilities he, in one man, could represent a quarter of the world's people.

Nang's eyes squinted, his face hardened, dagger beams slashed through jungle air piercing his mentor's heart. How dare he, how dare he . . . I am the chameleon.

Bok's head snapped to the beam as if directed by electronic sensors, his own beam clashing with Nang's, attempting to blast it back into the boy's head, two pairs of hate-seeking lasers in collision above the heads of the Dong Nai soldiers.

". . . please welcome Ba Bac." The regimental executive offi-

cer introduced him as Number Three Uncle, a Viet Namese
identity to which the weary troops could cling—could value the
man in white only slightly below Bac Ho, Uncle Ho. To establish his prestige further the XO had given Bok the title of
Political Affairs Officer, Extraordinary, and had explained that
he was the NLF's ambassador to the Khmer Viet Minh, an
organization the soldiers knew only as a supporter of their
cause.

Humbly Bok bowed his immense frame. He spoke a formal,
rhythmic Viet Namese. "In two days," Bok Roh began, "we will
fight again. In a week the general offensive will be under way.
Everything, *everything*, must be aimed at making the Americans
withdraw. That is the first priority for all Asians. In the South,
in the North, in Cambodia, all who seek to strengthen our great,
united solidarity must struggle ceaselessly to renew their moral
commitment during our country's most difficult period.

"We fight on four fronts. The military, the political, the diplomatic and the domestic front in the United States . . ."

Nang turned to the soldier beside him. The man, like Nang,
was less wrapped in Number Three Uncle's words than were
the mass of soldiers surrounding them.

". . . every military clash has consequences far beyond its
immediate and apparent outcome . . ."

The soldier glanced at Nang. "You're new?" he whispered.

"Yes," Nang answered.

". . . In the integrated whole, every act, every propaganda
appeal, assists our cause. Each battle is a psychological event.
Each negotiation strengthens our battlefield position . . ."

"You're very young."

"Not so young."

". . . *danh va dam, dam va danh* . . ." (Fighting is talking,
talking is fighting.)

"We'll talk later."

"A little."

". . . Your persistent military actions are impacting on America's perseverance. I want to tell you what else is happening to
positively affect your strong efforts. This past month, Premier
Pham Van Dong signed new agreements with China and the
Soviet Union guaranteeing an unceasing flow of food, arms and
ammunition. This past month American protestors demonstrated
their great wish for peace in a moratorium march on Washington. Within a week, Richard Nixon is expected to propose a
unilateral, a leopard-spot [units-in-place] ceasefire. The United
States has withdrawn twenty of every one hundred combat

soldiers. The *nguy* [puppet] army pales like a man who has lost
one fifth of his blood . . ."

"I've not seen Number Three Uncle before, have you?"

"I know him, a little."

"I'm Truong Cao Kiet," the soldier whispered. "I too am new
here."

Nang did not turn to look at the soldier but viewed him
intensely from the corner of his eye. He did not trust this man,
did not believe this was his name. Yet, with his attention split,
he made an error, one he recognized as the words slipped from
his lips. "They call me Hai Hoa Binh," he said, giving an obvious code name which would indicate to the soldier that he,
Nang, was not simply a soldier but someone whose identity
must be masked.

". . . when the American president announces the withdrawal
of a unit he tells his people it is a signal to us, a show of their
willingness to negotiate. In reality, Mr. Nixon is placating U.S.
public opinion . . ."

"We'll talk later," Truong Cao Kiet said.

"Perhaps," Nang said. Suddenly he felt like the boy he actually was. He could not think of a way to extricate himself from
suspicion without raising even more. He closed his mouth, concentrated on Bok Roh.

". . . We'll hit and run. We'll talk ceasefire but never stop
until we've unified the nation. As we continue the armed struggle in the countryside, our counterparts redouble their political
struggle in the urban centers. In Cambodia our partners solidify
their role in aiding our just cause. Our successes increase their
power. Their power feeds our successes . . ."

To Nang, as Bok Roh spoke he lost his magic. He became
another politician, a lecturer babbling without might. Soon,
Nang thought, soon, I will leave this miserable country. When
his attention returned to the words spoken he was surprised to
find Bok lecturing in terms of Marxist philosophy. The VC,
unlike the NVA, were seldom exposed to straight political ideology. To them their objective was to deliver the country from
foreign domination and the oppression of the Thieu regime.

". . . through these disguised organizations we can induce the
masses to respond to our struggle slogans. Through them we
will rally the masses, step-by-step, in accord with the directions
of the revolution. We will renew our effort to bring about the
general uprising . . ."

You yuon-loving fool, Nang thought. You know this talk is
the work of a dull Northern functionary. Look at these fools.

Why are soldiers dumb? He knows his words are just so much low wind.

"... In two days we shall roll back the Saigon lackey pacification program by striking the Chieu Hoi centers and the villages erected to house traitors. In a week, we'll attack American weak points. Everything must be done to make the Americans withdraw ..."

On the harried trip back to Bu Ntoll Nang whispered to Bok, "Why do you serve the Northerners?"

Bok eyed his young charge. The question was idolatrous. "The Northerners fight for all third-world people," Bok Roh said coolly in Viet Namese. "Their victory is inevitable because their cause is just."

"I spoke with Truong Cao Kiet. He was very worried and very unsure."

"He is a *nguy* agent. We know him. He'll be eliminated during the offensive."

"Kiet!?"

"Le. Tran Van Le. That's his name. You shouldn't listen to men like that."

"Uncle, he ... he ... he seemed to have so much hate for Americans."

"I don't hate them." The conversation irritated Bok Roh and he didn't hide his anger. "Le hates for show," Bok said. He put his hand on Nang's knee as a father might a small son. "I feel sorry at American deaths. They die young because of the Washington governing clique."

"You feel ... ! They kill without thought," Nang retorted.

"Their people mourn for the Viet Namese people. Americans carry a great burden. But their government ... I'm indignant at the losses, the destruction caused by America's war machine. They have their army on our land. There's not a single Viet Namese soldier on American soil. Ah, Khat Doh, you must learn to read as well as to speak."

"You've taught me to read."

"No. I taught you to recognize printed words. Now you must learn to read ... to expand your thoughts ... to know what happens each day."

"The Northerners forbid soldiers to read anything but what they provide. It's even forbidden to listen to any radio but Hanoi Radio."

"We're not Northerners," Bok said in Jarai. "We can get around that. I can tell you what President Nixon says in his speech. I can tell you if he promises strong measures, if the antiwar movement presses him with strong measures."

"All our fighting does, eh?"

"That's all you know because that's all you've been told. I can get you newspapers."

"Then why do you serve them?" Nang persisted.

Bok eyed him sharply. Should the question lead to a *kiem thao*, a criticism / self-criticism session? "I am devoted to peace. Real peace. Real freedom." Bok paused. Nang's eyes glazed with disbelief. "I fight to the end," Bok continued more powerfully. "Viet Nam is indivisible. Seventeen million Northern compatriots live with tightened belts to help us defeat the invaders. It's our duty to the Fatherland. Armed *dau tranh*, armed struggle, for the revolution is our supreme duty."

Nang beamed as if a religious truth had been revealed to him, but inside he thought, Bok Roh, you believe your own stupid propaganda. "Do you welcome," Nang asked sheepishly, knowing he was baiting his mentor, "the North's annexation of the South?"

Bok slammed his fist into his open palm. His nares flared, his mouth curled. "Premier Pham Van Dong calls that a 'stupid and criminal idea.' He has stated, 'The South will have its own policy.' And there will be a policy for Mountaineers."

"Do you welcome violence against villages which do not support either North or South?"

"There are times when violence is necessary. Violence which advances our political cause is imperative."

"Then, when we attack a village, it is imperative, yes? For political reasons?"

"There's a *ruup areak* in Phum Sath Nan," Sam said.

Chhuon nodded. The two men were in the treeline at the village edge overlooking the paddies. The rice harvest had just begun, and their stores were already a quarter full. In the moonlight the dry paddy stubble gleamed like gold. "I had a dream the night before . . ."

"You've told me," Sam said sadly.

"Is he competent?" Chhuon asked.

"The medium?"

"Yes."

"I don't know."

"I wish to know if my son's spirit is at peace. If this medium can contact him, I'll be ready to sit in the corner with the ancestors."

"Ssshh!" Sam put his hand on Chhuon's arm. He motioned into the paddies.

Chhuon stared. An entire armed platoon was moving noiselessly toward them. "quick."

The men, staying in their squats, spun, slithered into the shadows, then ran through alleys and streets rapping out the alert on doors and walls.

For months, ever since Norodom Sihanouk had seriously ordered his army to engage the NVA and halt the border erosion, military units had circled or passed through Phum Sath Din. At first they had been Royal forces on their way east—ragtag outfits dragging cannons and their families, camping on the road, twice passing through the middle of Phum Sath Din, twice shelling areas northeast of the village with antiquated howitzers set up in Chhuon's paddies. Then units and direction changed, NVA heading west—crack infantry units carried by truck and escorted by armor giving the village wide berth on their way to reinforce a buildup farther south—or Khmer Viet Minh units of Hanoi-trained hardcore Khmer cadres and a growing mix of volunteers and conscripts, Khmers, Mountaineers and Chams.

"wake!" Chhuon ordered his family. His breath came hard and fast. "wake," he hissed, shook his wife, Sok, then his mother and finally Peou, his last born. "quickly. to the shelter."

"I'll sleep on my mat," Chhuon's mother said calmly, with the dignity of age when death is not feared.

Chhuon looked briefly at the old woman. "they're coming. this time . . . they won't go by . . . they're entering now."

"And what would they want with this old woman?" As she spoke Sok and Peou rolled up their sleeping mats. "Better I stay and greet them," the old woman said. "Better they find a house with someone than with no one."

Chhuon kissed his mother. He turned to the altar. Already many of the ancestral mementos had been removed, hidden, buried in the orchard. He grabbed the bowl of rice he still filled daily for Samnang. He raced to the door, knees, pains unheeded, jumped down the steps and joined Sok and Peou as they skittered like mice through a hole behind the oven, then down into the tight, newly dug family bunker.

Peou slept on Sok's lap. Sok dozed sporadically, leaning against the cool hard earth, afraid to change positions, to set a mat behind her, afraid to wake Peou. Chhuon sat on his hams for hours, facing the covered hole, listening intently, staring like a raccoon trapped in a tree hollow by barking dogs. Yet there was no barking. Only silent darkness. Silence for hours.

In the morning Sam's wife, Ry, sat in the central room crying.

"They took them," she wailed. "Took them both. They've taken six."

Chhuon's hands squeezed tight but hung by his side—meaty, ineffective mallets.

"All young." Ry rocked back and forth. "Except Sam. But he's strong. And Mama! Why would they take an old woman?"

Chhuon paced in sorrow, in grief, in anger. "Why?!" he growled through gritted teeth. "Why Sam? Why Moeun? And who? Who are they?" He brushed a hand through his hair. His body tensed, quaked in anger, in grief, in guilt for again not having fought but for having hidden, in guilt for not being taken, for not even knowing who did the taking, for being left to survive, again, survive now without his last consolation.

For months Phum Sath Din had been filling with known and unknown families and workers, each claiming to be, most being, peasants from outlying isolated farms seeking the security of the village, pushed and prodded from behind by military forces, for tactical military and political reasons they neither knew nor understood. Within days of Sam's disappearance the influx blossomed, swelling the village to over a thousand inhabitants. Some families found vacant homes left by residents who had fled south or west months earlier. When all the houses were filled, the new families built makeshift abodes of bamboo, branches, thatch, built them without order about the old symmetrical quadrants of Phum Sath Din, built them touching one to the next, indeed the poorest built being lean-tos against the walls of the willing neighbor.

In the market Chhuon heard the voices of the new-people but he did not talk with them. Their words confused him, sapped him further of resolve. "When we're finally liberated," the voices repeated again and again, "everything will be better." Or, "The Royal troops attacked us, shelled our farm because we sell to the Viets. I hope they don't attack here." "Why should they attack here, Brother? We're all Khmers." "Why should they have attacked my farm?" "Don't they attack only when the NVA is there? Attack to keep the yuons from destroying villages?" "It's Royal troops that destroyed my village." "The monk here, he says we should assist the Royals to save the country. I don't trust him." "Maha Nyanananda is a very holy man, but . . . he's old. He's not a military man." "I'll tell you this, I'm against the NVA and the Royals."

Three weeks after Sam disappeared, Chhuon found an ally amongst the newcomers.

"Honored Professor Mister Cahuom," a young man addressed Chhuon in the most formal fashion. "Maybe you remember me,

Uncle. You assisted my father many times with seed and advice. Our farm's been ruined and my mother killed."

Chhuon looked into the young man's face. He did not recognize him.

"Hang Tung." The young man bowed. "We lived beyond Phum Sath Nan."

"Your father then is Hang Hak?"

"Yes. He's a year with the ancestors."

"Why didn't you seek shelter in Sath Nan? You've relatives there."

"They've all gone. It's a hard village now. Here the people are more compassionate."

For a week Hang Tung cultivated Chhuon's friendship. For a week he lamented to Chhuon about the rumors of pending Royal troop attack on Phum Sath Din. And for a week Chhuon assisted, advised and consoled his new friend who spoke about awakening the people to all threats. One evening Hang Tung said to Chhuon, "Tonight I'm going to set a trip wire and flare on the west approach to town. We'll know by the light if Royal troops are going to storm through. Will you come with me?"

"I'll come," Chhuon answered. "But I place no value in this forecast."

"Uncle." Tung changed his tone.

"Um."

"May I put my sleeping mat in your courtyard? I'm with a family of eleven. There's so little room."

"Of course, Tung. Stay in my house."

That evening the young man and the old set out on the trail which led west from town to Phum Bung and then north to Phum Sath Nan. Hang Tung carried a dilapidated haversack over one shoulder. To Chhuon he seemed tense, nervous, his smile and talk forced. They walked slowly, carefully into the jungle. The path surface, hidden from the sun by the canopy, was damp here, wet there. "For all the troubles that have befallen us," Chhuon explained quietly as he followed Tung, "this year's rice looks to be the best ever."

"Really Uncle? The newcomers have so little."

"There's so much to harvest and so few old families, my cousin and I had full granaries before half the paddies were cut." Chhuon paused. It was becoming easier to mention Sam though the thought was still painful. "We'll fill the vacant granaries with the surplus. And the pagoda's small room. We can't ship and sell as we used to." Again he paused. "Perhaps we can share with the newcomers, eh?"

"You're a good man, Uncle. Here, this is the spot." Tung

opened the haversack. From it he pulled not just tripwire and flares but two Chicom grenades.

"That's not necessary," Chhuon protested.

"No one's supposed to be here at night, Uncle."

"But what if a farmer is fleeing to our village?"

"No more farmers," Hang Tung said curtly. "All the farms are ruined. Only Royal soldiers or Viets will come this way."

"Tung! You said a flare. You . . ."

"Uncle Chhuon, when we return to your house I'll tell you what I know about their plans. They destroyed my farm. Killed my mother. Surely you understand."

At Chhuon's house seven old family elders sat in the central room awaiting his return. Sok had served the men tea and rice cakes as they grumbled bitterly. Chhuon's mother knelt before the family altar. She was crying loudly. Ry, Sam's wife, knelt beside her, repeating the prayer for the dead. Peou waited on the steps. He wanted to be first to tell his father the important news.

Horizontal light from the rising moon filtered through the low branches of the orchard as Chhuon and Tung entered the courtyard. "Father! Father!" Peou jumped up, ran to Chhuon, hugged his leg. "Father, Maha Nyanananda has been assassinated!"

The words hit Chhuon like a cloud of poison gas, surrounded him, enveloped him in a fog of disbelief. Peou repeated the words and others but Chhuon did not hear. Tung expressed appropriate grief for the community's spiritual leader though his voice splashed on the viscous cloud about Chhuon without penetrating. Inside the elders addressed him, bombarded him with theories, badgered him with suggestions. For an hour nothing penetrated. A burning sensation steamed from his stomach to his chest and mouth. His knees grew sore. His back ached. Then he heard Hang Tung say, "Yes, my uncle will organize the village guards. Tonight he himself led me out the Phum Bung trail where he set both warning flares and booby traps. If every quadrant of the village blocked and monitored the incoming trails in their sections, no one could come without all knowing."

"Cahuom Chhuon"—one old man smiled ironically—"you are an explosives expert now, eh?!"

"Not I . . ."

"Don't be so humble, Uncle," Tung interrupted. "Now's not the time for modesty. Now we need a strong leader."

"Then it is settled," a second old gentleman said. "Mr. Chhuon will be chairman of the new guard."

To the west, on the trail to Phum Bung and Phum Sath Nan, two blasts erupted. The sound rolled over the Cahuom household like the first thunder of an approaching monsoon season.

                              *   *   *

4 November—Nang sat atop Hill 982 with the NVA command
post looking down upon the Special Forces camp at Bu Prang.
For Nang, for the defenders of Bu Ntoll, for the remanned NVA
272d Regiment, revenge was near. For twelve days skirmishes
and minor assaults had bloodied the hilltop defenders yet yielded
nothing for either side except body counts. At midnight the
final attack would begin.

From the peak of 982, Nang, Bok Roh, and a contingent of
political cadre and artillery forward observers scanned the base
through scopes and binoculars. They checked the scale maps
produced earlier by reconnaissance teams. Every building, every radio antenna, every machine gun emplacement, the commo
and headquarters bunkers, supply points for ammo and POL
(petroleum, oil and lubricants), and the tiny airstrip were noted,
targeted, preregistered on the big guns at Bu Ntoll and with the
mortar and rocket units infiltrating to points closer to the base.

Earlier, at Ban Me Thuot, ARVN and U.S. intelligence reported four new NVA regiments, upwards of seven thousand
troops, descending onto the Dar Lac and Mnong plateaus from
Cambodian sanctuaries. Yet even with knowledge of the impending attack, U.S. and ARVN efforts to thwart it had been
miserable. For months the NVA meticulously planned and prepared the attack. Within the deepest caves at Bu Ntoll sand-
table models of the entire area had been constructed in minute
detail. Units rehearsed their roles. The battlefield itself was
methodically prepared—not simply the attack points but a nearly
200-square-kilometer area stretching from within Cambodia to
eight kilometers south of the base and to trails and groves seven
and ten kilometers west and east. Covertly, bridges had been
constructed four inches below water surfaces in order to conceal them from aerial reconnaissance, across rivers that were
along advance, primary and alternate withdrawal routes. Caches
of food, water, ammunition, weapons and medical supplies had
been hidden at strategic points. Ambush sites had been prepared, deep bunkers constructed, camouflaged and interconnected by trenches, fields of fire cut, guides, trail watchers and
"custodians" planted. Even the steep hillside approaches to the
Special Forces camp at Bu Prang had had stairs dug into the
narrow covered trails.

On 30 October the buried NVA guns of Bu Ntoll struck Bu
Prang, Duc Lap and Firebases Kate, Annie and Susan which
could offer the Special Forces base supporting fire. On the 31st,
thirty B-52s bombed the forested valleys northeast of Bu Prang.
The American contingent on the hilltop consisted of only twelve

advisors and a four-man Studies and Observation Group (SOG). Indigenous Mountaineers made up the bulk of personnel, four hundred Mnong with the advisors and 150 Stieng tribesmen with the SOG. SOG teams had reported the new enemy regiments and the construction of ambush sites and rocket launch pads; indeed, Allied intelligence knew essentially the entire NVA battle plan. Yet both ARVN and U.S. commands responded minimally. The ARVN 23d Infantry Division moved only a two-company potential relief force to Nhon Co, twenty-four kilometers south of Bu Prang. The U.S. command reinforced the Mountaineer howitzer battery with six cannons from the U.S. 1st Battalion, 92d Artillery. As proof of the success of Viet Namization, no American infantry or armored units were brought up.

Dusk settled on the border mountain. From the peak of Hill 982 Nang took last note of the camp's preparations. He thought of the report he would send to Met Sar. Barbed wire barriers have been restrung and tightened, he imagined writing. Foot traps and mines were laid along obvious approaches. Huge stocks of food, water and artillery rounds have been delivered and stored in open pits or in bunkers.

On 1 November, Firebases Annie and Susan had been abandoned after four thousand rounds of NVA heavy mortar, rocket and howitzer fire rendered them undefendable. More supplies had been brought to Bu Prang.

Every structure on Firebase Kate, seven kilometers south of Bu Prang, had been leveled by 1500 hours on the 1st yet the defenders had fought on. At 1530 hours the NVA artillery units in Cambodia switched to air-burst shells, raining steel shards into the foxholes. American and Mountaineer defenders tightened the perimeter. Two of their five howitzers were destroyed. All that night the NVA guns from Cambodia continued firing, blasting the small hilltop. On 2 November the Allied commands refused reinforcements. Two more howitzers were destroyed.

On Hill 982 Nang had heard Major Bui lament to Bok Roh, "Why don't they take the bait? Why?"

"What bait?" Nang had asked aside.

"We're the bait," Bok had explained. "We must entice the Americans and their lackeys from the lowlands to the border camps. With their troops in the mountains, we'll slip through the valleys and attack the pacification centers in the lowlands. We'll make the cities bleed."

"I want to join them," Nang had said.

"We'll see." Bok had laughed at the boy. "With those artillery bases destroyed, Bu Prang is vulnerable."

"What of the bombers?"

"They'll be needed elsewhere," Bok had said. "Elsewhere."

Early evening, 3 November, the NVA had offered the defenders of Firebase Kate a break. The surviving American advisors and Mountaineers pounced. Racing from bunker to bunker the officers and NCOs had quickly organized a withdrawal. Under cover of darkness the soldiers spiked the only working howitzer with a thermite grenade then crawled through the concertina wire and raced down the steep slope toward Bu Prang. Twenty seconds behind them, a regiment of NVA soldiers had swarmed the hill. The entire NVA force now was free to concentrate its destruction on the Bu Prang Special Forces camp.

Midnight arrived. The main assault was delayed. Around Bu Prang tunnels, trenches and bunkers were extended toward the camp. As planned, most of the B-52s were diverted elsewhere. Fifteen hours earlier, timed to coincide with Richard Nixon's television speech half the world away, NVA and VC units had shelled forty-five Allied bases and towns and attacked eight more outposts along the border and the coast.

At Firebase Ike, twenty-six kilometers northeast of Tay Ninh, in a two-hour pitched battle, U.S. helicopters killed forty-eight soldiers of the Viet Cong 9th Division; all but two were Northern replacements. At Firebase Ellen, southwest of Song Be, an element of the Dong Nai Regiment wounded sixteen Americans. Five kilometers away, at Firebase Burton, Dong Nai and NVA 88th Regiment troops breeched the wire and minefields but withdrew under immense firepower, leaving fifty-five bodies. Finally, at 0120 hours on 5 November, heavy shelling of Bu Prang began.

Vathana retched. She covered her mouth, forced the vomit back. She paused, leaned against the wall of her apartment building looking up at seemingly swaying concrete and glass. She panted. The pain eased momentarily. *I should have stayed at the pagoda,* she thought. *I must get home.*

Ever since the incidents with the border children and the dead boy on her barge she had spent an hour each morning at the wat in prayer. Even as she'd left the apartment for the quarter-mile walk she'd felt ill, but nothing compared with this horrible, nausea-producing cramping pain—at once constant and throbbing. She breathed slightly deeper. Her vision cleared. She stepped through the main door into the small courtyard and toward the stairs. Again she paused. The proximity of her apartment pulled her. The stairs looked formidable. She grasped the railing, forced back another heaving. Again her vision blurred, her hearing dulled as if her ears were stuffed down deep with wet clay, her sense of balance waned, she swayed, gripped the railing more tightly.

I must get there, she told herself. Must. Must. Up a step. Must. She squeezed the railing until her knuckles whitened. Someone come by and help me, she thought. Why, of all times, are the stairs empty? Up. Up. Must. Labor isn't like this, she thought. This is too early. Three more weeks. Mother was never so sick. Aunt Voen never said she was sick. Up. Must. Up. At her crotch she could feel warm liquid, a trickle. She squeezed her thighs together but her expanded pelvis held them so far apart the squeeze was useless. On the last flight the trickle reached her ankles. Up. Must. Only a little more. I have calls to make. Three more weeks. Oh, just one more week. The shelter. The barge. Mister Pech. The new oil tanks. Vathana lifted her skirt to see the fluid, the water. Her ankle was bright red. Blood oozed to the top of her foot. The sight shocked her. The pain surged. She vomited, the effluent gushing with such force its spatter splashed back from the few stairs yet to be ascended, splashed over her feet, against her skirt, blouse and shawl, tiny globs hitting her cheeks. The sight and smell disgusted her but much more was the fear. What's happening? I've been so careful. Not a thing have I stitched shut. Not a doorway have I lingered in. What's happening to me? What's happening to my baby?

"Teck." Vathana's voice was weak. Her foot smeared blood on the floor as she wobbled toward the bedroom. "Teck," she called. Her husband was still in bed. "Teck," she panted. "Wake up." Her voice was shallow, hollow, fearful. "Please wake up." She shook him. The agitation set off a burst of pain stabbing outward from her abdomen, reaching her entire body, splitting her face, forehead. Teck lay like a corpse, cool like a corpse. "Teck!" Vathana forced a wail. Still he didn't respond. "I need you," she whimpered. Tears flooded her eyes. "Why? Why do you do this? I need you."

She began to sit. How easy to let herself fall, let her knees fold, to collapse beside her husband in his deep heroin-slumber. She straightened. The pain throughout her abdomen was as if a vise were gripping her, the screw closing down with constant increasing pressure. She vomited again, dry bile phlegm. Her long black hair stuck in slithering coils to her sweat wet face like snakes of the Gorgon Medusa. Again she tried to wake Teck. Still he slumbered. The hemorrhaging flow increased as the placenta, in partial previa, split.

In adversity, in sorrow, in the presence of greed, corruption and evil, in the wake of the killing of the bandit boy by her barge crew and the turning out of the border children by Teck, Vathana had become more Buddhist, more giving, more concerned. With it came more business success, more business, more social responsibilities. Throughout the summer and fall there had been a steady trickle of refugees from the Northeast and border areas seeping into Neak Luong. Most had moved in with relatives, unnoticed, without social burden to the community or the government. Yet an increasing number arrived without money, without food, without shelter, without destination. They slept in parks, along byways, on riverfront piers. They ate by begging. In her fifth month of pregnancy Vathana, her skills sharpened through business, organized through the monks an assistance shelter supported by half a dozen local businessmen, staffed by a dozen volunteer women from apartments and homes. In two months the program had expanded to include a small house for orphans. Each day Vathana split her time between prayer, business and volunteer work. Each evening she remained alone as Teck went to dance halls or to share a pipe with his friends.

Vathana stared at the photo album. Teck was beyond waking. She concentrated on the album's cover as the pain overwhelmed her body. Her face felt swollen, her eyes forced to squint through puffed skin slits. She had made the call. Help would come. Now she could let go, let what would happen happen. Her eyes pushed closed. The album faded to a negative retinal image, then to nothing. Her hand groped, found the Buddha statuette at her throat.

Vathana woke with a needle and red tube in each arm. The pain had subsided. Her head was clogged. About her dozens of people were attending patients on steel beds in the cold clinic ward. Teck's face hung over her, looked down at her, seemingly suspended from the ceiling or floating in air. She closed her eyes.

She opened them again. One arm was plumbed with clear tubing. Teck had vanished. "Welcome back, Angel," a stout border woman whispered in French. Vathana could see tears in the woman's eyes but she didn't know why she was crying or who she was. "You've crossed the great ocean alone," the woman whispered. "You have a son. The grandfather has called him Pech Samnang."

"They were both Royal soldiers," Tung said to Chhuon. Chhuon sat on the ground. His legs were spread. He leaned forward and beat the ground rhythmically with his fists. Tears of despair seeped from his eyes. Do not kill the living creatures, he thought. Do not kill. Do not kill. It was a basic tenet of his Buddhist morality, of his righteousness. Through all the struggles he had been able to maintain his integrity, his inner purity. Perhaps he had transgressed on occasion but never had he killed a living thing. Never had he killed a human.

"Uncle, I think they were an assassination team. They would have killed another village leader had they not walked into your trap."

Chhuon continued to pound the earth with his fist. To him they could have been devils and the words would have made no difference.

"Blood for blood, Uncle," Tung said. "Blood for blood. Your own words."

Chhuon rocked farther forward. Had they been yuon, he thought, then it would have been just. "But," he cried, "they were Khmer boys."

"Just like those who killed my mother," Tung said bitterly. "Perhaps like those who killed the monk."

"We don't know who killed the monk."

"Uncle, I'm certain it was Royal treachery. It's Prince Sihanouk's wish to punish the Northeast."

"I can't believe it."

"It makes no difference, Uncle. In the eyes of the Royal army you now are a criminal. You can no longer stay in the village unless the village defends itself from the Prince's troops."

Nang carried ammunition for Bok Roh. The giant carried an assault rifle and a lightened pack. They moved quickly through tangled vegetation, off Hill 982, into the jungle to join troops poised for the attack. They crossed defoliated swaths, moved down onto narrow paths marked with short white stakes, down toward the river. They paused to rest with a three-man cell of infantry troops from the NVA 272d Regiment. From every direction, unseen in the night, cells moved forward, merged to form fire-teams, combined to form squads, converged to form platoons, rivers of men surging toward final staging, five thousand Communist troops coordinated for the clockwork attack, waiting for the signal.

The NVA plan was simple. The 32d Regiment would launch a broad frontal attack from the east, over Bu Prang's airstrip and POL storage points, attempting to pull in as many defenders as possible. Then the 165th Regiment would assault the southwest perimeter. Finally, when the defenders were bogged down, pinned down or dead, the 272d would concentrate a pinpoint force against the north berm, would blow through the wire and over-run the hill. From Bu Ntoll the 66th Regiment's heavy artillery would soften up the foe, and its 82mm mortar teams, dug in and supplied at five points about the camp, would support the infantry. The 40th Artillery Regiment with 120mm mortars could move to reinforce the 66th or deliver knockout blows. Support units included a company of elite *dac cong*, combat engineers or sappers, plus command and control posts, communication and transportation companies, and the ever-present custodian-guides. In reserve were the 24th and 174th Infantry Regiments.

Nang was shocked, frightened. Even with his exceptional training he had never seen a unit as well concealed and camouflaged as the new 272d. Had the guides not known their positions, Nang would have walked through without sensing their presence. The surprise infuriated him. How? he asked, how did I let them do this to me?

Heavy crashes, NVA shell explosions on Bu Prang, reverberated and shook the cool night air. To Nang the sound was beautiful, exciting. The tempo picked up. Nang's shock gave way to an anxious itch to experience the death of the hated Americans. Bok had encouraged him to remain at the observation post on Hill 982 but Nang had insisted and Bok had agreed he could accompany him to the *giua binh tram*, the midjungle post. With each kilometer Nang had expanded, until he no longer resembled the boy, the pet, the aide, but now appeared strong, hard, a midteen athlete-soldier.

An immense concussion rocked the camp on Bu Prang. Volcanic flames shot skyward, lighting the base and surrounding ridges. A 130mm shell had scored a hit, the POL dump exploded. Flames silhouetted bunkers and howitzers then swallowed themselves in billowing black clouds. Outgoing fire from Bu Prang shrieked.

Bok squeezed Nang's shoulder to indicate his joy. The shoulder was thick, hard, like a pick-and-shovelman's. Bok dropped his hand. Before thought could form, the sound of the 155mm battery at Duc Lap pulled his attention to what seemed coordinated salvos sent into Cambodia. The Bu Prang batteries, too, came to full life firing preset defensive targets far beyond the concealed regiments creeping toward their perimeter. Again and again and again for two hours Communist heavy guns scored, their projectile trajectories adjusted from Hill 982—walking the airstrip, the perimeter, trying to knock out Bu Prang's defenses.

The wap of helicopter rotors sounded above the valleys and over the peaks. "Wounded," Bok whispered. "They're for wounded."

Beside Nang a soldier raised his AK-47 as escort helicopters approached low, circling the camp below shell trajectories. Nang grabbed the man's wrist. "Don't fire," he whispered. "Only when they land." Bok overheard him and wondered who had taught him that.

Nang fidgeted, anxious for the infantry charges. Bok urged patience. The 32d, in place, surged up under a five-point 400-round mortar barrage. Six hundred Communist soldiers assaulted, their weapons blazing as they hit the edge of the airstrip. From the camp's perimeter hand flares streaked red like Fourth of July skyrockets. Fire from a hundred positions felled a hundred attackers. Mortar-launched flares popped high, hung, hissed, cast their eerie flat light over the hill.

In the chasm where Nang's heart pounded the light was diffuse, a glint, the shadowed outline of a face. The bark buzzing of automatic weapons was accented with sharp reports from howitzer outgoing and thick crunching explosions of incoming. Above it all, more helicopter noise, then in it, diving unseen in black sky, pulsating birds spewing red-snake streams onto the airstrip, loosing rockets, exploding not loud but whiter-flamed, throatier concussions than howitzer rounds.

Another immense continuous explosion, incoming detonating one of six ammo dumps within the compound. Bok clapped his hands quietly, recognizing the unmistakable chaotic concussive pattern. The fighting continued, the 165th struck from the west. Cannoneers of the U.S 1st of the 92d lowered their barrels and shot beehive rounds, 8,500 flachettes, nail-size arrows, the ultimate grapeshot, point-blank into the advancing wave of NVA bodies crashing against the wire.

Nang rose. It was time. It had to be time. Bok pulled him down. Helicopters swarmed and dove west, east. "Not yet." "Now?" "No." "Now?" "Soon."

The fighting waned, the sounds of rifle reports puttered to a trickle. The mortar barrage ceased. Outgoing fire from Bu Prang slowed. Choppers went off-station, to refuel, rearm. New birds arrived. Evacuation. Sporadic fire tinked on thin aluminum skins. Rhythmically, like waves crashing against a jetty, the battle established its own tempo. From east, west, attack, repulse, withdraw, regroup, attack, repulse, withdraw, regroup, attack, penetrate, entangle in the wires, die, kill, repulse, withdraw, regroup.

Heavy crashing footfalls smashed wildly before their concealment. Nang hefted Bok Roh's pistol. Bok signaled him to hold:
Americans don't pursue at night. Nang understood without a
word passing. Heavy frantic panting paused on the trail only
feet away. Nang sprung, cat silent, hit the soldier, clamped his
hands over nose and mouth, jabbed kidneys with his knees,
dropped the soldier, breaking the fall, only dull thumps being
made. Nang dragged the wide-eyed troop into their vegetation
pocket. The man tried to speak. His back, sides ached; his lungs
demanded all breathing effort.

Nang settled beside him. Bok hovered over both. In one hand
he held a huge machete. In their three months, Nang had never
seen it unsheathed. The cell of the 272d squeezed in. "I . . . I . . ."
the young soldier tried. Nang rubbed the heel of his hand
down the soldier's back, over the kidneys he'd kneed, pushing
the pain away, out. From the corner of his eye, he watched Bok.

"Your unit," Bok said.

"32d . . ."

"You're not wounded?"

"They're Viet Namese . . ." the soldier panted. Nang studied
him in the dark. He was young, not as young as Nang, in his
twenties like most of the NVA troops Nang had seen. Perhaps
eighteen. "They're Viet Namese," the soldier said again. "They're
not Americans."

"Who?" Nang asked. He quietly slid the boy's rifle from him
and laid it on his own lap. It felt new. Nang ran his hand up the
barrel to the flash suppressor. He forced his smallest finger into
the bore. The cool metal felt sticky, packing-grease sticky.

"Who!" the soldier blurted. "Them. On the hill. The ones we
. . . My friends Toai and . . . he killed. He was killed by a Viet
Namese."

Bok touched Nang's shoulder. Nang snapped, startled, froze.
Bok tapped him to step aside. "He's new," Bok said. He'd
resheathed the machete. "Brand-new. They don't tell them at
the training centers there are Southern lackeys."

"Who does he think—?"

"Only Americans. They tell them only Americans are the
enemy."

Nang returned to the soldier. The revelation of incompetence
delighted him. What intelligence, he thought. They're ignorant,
he thought. Weak. Nothing. Met Sar will be impressed. We
won't make that mistake.

The soldiers of the 272d were talking quietly to the boy from
the 32d. "You haven't fired your rifle," Nang interjected.

The others hushed. "I . . . Toai was hit on our first charge. I tried to carry him . . ."

"Into battle." Nang completed the sentence, turning it into accusation.

"He couldn't fight. I was going to the withdrawal path—"

"Before the signal to regroup?"

Bok tapped Nang. His aide's questions puzzled him. They were appropriate, should be asked during the *kiem thao*, the criticism session which would follow the battle. Only, Bok thought, how has Khat Doh learned this? How does he know what to ask? "He's disoriented," Bok whispered. "Let his cadre ask him."

Nang again focused on the boy. "I expected," the soldier was saying to the others, "to live in a barracks outside Saigon or Pleiku. Why are we in caves? We were told everyplace was liberated except the large cities."

It is time, Nang laughed to himself, time for Met Nang's return.

At 0430 hours Nang's unit crept, undetected, to the edge of the concealing vegetation. Before them were two *dac cong* weapons squads equipped with B-40 rockets and thirty feet of four-inch explosive-packed bamboo—a bangalore torpedo—to blow a passage through the wire, plus a dozen captured American LAWs (light antitank weapons). Behind them were three squads, each with the set task of taking out one of the three defending machine gun emplacements in their attack sector. Farther back was an entire company, 160 soldiers ready to charge through the hole to the center of camp. East and west attacks were in full renewed surge.

Nang crouched. Moved forward. Bok reached for the boy, missed, followed him. Nang moved smooth silent, a snake; froze, darted, a spider. Bok grabbed him. They were between the weapons squads. Back, Bok signaled. Forward, Nang motioned. He turned from his mentor, skittered by two RPG carriers. Others moved up, split to six clustered points, three for the machine guns, two between, weapons in a natural gully leading to the wire. Bok crept. Before him he could see defenders abandoning their posts to reinforce east or west, double-teaming attackers, leaving the north sector undermanned. Forward. Nang slipped in with the torpedo squad. He wanted to see how the torpedo was laid. His heart raced. Silhouetted by flare light every hilltop position was visible, running defenders were easy targets. He hefted the assault rifle he'd taken from the soldier of the 32d. Don't fire, he ordered himself. Don't fire. Conquer haste. Wait! Wait for the order: Charge! Go! Attack! A signal passed. The torpedo squad eased from concealment, blackened faces, camouflaged backs, burlap-wrapped tube. Nang prone, with the others, inched over defoliated earth, his nose on the heels of the man before him. Bok stretched out, grabbed Nang's foot. Kick. Loose. Turn. Signal, join me. Bok emerged. His sated enthusiasm for battle growing hungry, stimulated by Nang's verve, nerve. He crawled to Nang, past.

Nang grits his teeth.

Slow motion bushes, unseen, undetected by defenders, advance to the outer wire. Nang feels for mines, creeps, a pro, a vet. Bok flash-thinks, He learns too fast, knows too much. Who are you?

Red-star cluster to the right. Machine gun attackers detected.

Explosions. Full frontal blast of two claymore mines blow apart faces, bodies of half the squad. "Up! Up! Go!" Screams, orders left and right. More flares. Full charge. Five fire-spewing points focusing on the defenders. "Charge! Attack!" Answering fire. RPGs, LAWs explode at each machine gun emplacement. Two defender guns continue constant red-tracer lead streams. Two attack squads concentrate on bunkers. Between, hilltop riflemen spray rapid bursts, duck, spray, duck, reload. The noise is tremendous, nearness making it louder than five-hundred-pounders at half a klick. Claymore mines, tripwired and command detonated, explode sporadically as 272d troops lunge into the wire. Nang pushes a torpedo section. The *dac cong* are yet undetected, inching forward, hugging gravel clay hillside as riflemen squads attack. Inching faster, inchworming, knees to chest, reach, the tube end is through the first strands, through the rolls and tanglefoot. New helicopters on station. About Nang the squad attaches the second section, then the third. Nang is amazed at the defenders, at their tenacity, at their firepower, at their stupidity backlighting themselves with flare light. Mortar and 105mm rounds seeking attacker columns explode against the hillside. The NVA tighten in east, north, west, hugging the defenders, making it difficult or impossible for big guns or helicopters to identify clear targets in the flare-lit dark.

The fifth section clamps on, the torpedo is jammed forward. False dawn lightens the firmament. The *dac cong* begin their slow withdrawal, checking blasting-cap wire. Nang hesitates. He forces himself into the wire. Barbs scratch bloody furrows into his back. He shoves the tube a foot deeper where it reaches a third set of wire. Then he too withdraws. Firing tapers at each side. Nang shrinks back. In the gully wounded moan. Nang clamps his jaw, tries to shut out the noise. Word passes, a night relief column from Nhon Co, two mechanized companies from the 23d ARVN, has been ambushed, has withdrawn. Nang rolls to his back, gulps air. He is suddenly tired. About him additional hundreds of troops are surging, called up because the command sees a major victory in the making. He rolls back. New enemy howitzer and mortar barrages rain shrapnel on the north slope. "Attack!" Orders are barked. The torpedo is blown. A white flame expands as if parting a sea. Nang lurches. Falls. A mortar round explodes before him. Another to his side. He clings to the hill. His body refusing to obey mental orders to attack. He lurches, falls. Is swept by disgust as others race past. He has killed. He has enjoyed killing. He has escaped being killed. In his inner core he is a yothea of Angkar Leou, a disciple of Met Sar. Yet he has never fought a battle where the opponent is armed and fights back. His scuffles have been short. He is not looking for a fight, only for victory, only for defeated foes. It is one thing to lure, play, torture a weak victim, but with a strong enemy, the kill must be quick to reduce his exposure. Nang the boy, Khat Doh the pet, takes pride in the underdog role. It has never occurred to him that an opponent might be his equal, his superior. Again he lurches, trips over three dead, falls face-to-face with a man with no face. Up again, running forward, crazy, behind an entire company, into the gully, the alleyway through the parted wire. Defenders fire recoilless rifle flachette rounds into the trench. Scores fall. Rise up or are picked up, carried forward, wounded and able all firing. Nang cannot move. He is at the wire on his knees staring into the tempest flash-lit by explosions, flat-lit by flares. Silhouettes sprint, engage, fall. Hand-to-hand fighting. One shadow stands huge. In its hand a huge machete swirls. Defenders rush. The blade flies, decapitates.

Nang stands. His eyes widen. He steps forward as if there were nothing but he and the giant and the machete. "You mothafucka," a defender screams as he leaps at Bok, swings a shovel. The giant grabs it in midflight with his left hand. The GI freezes. Bok swings his right. The machete tip splits the man's face an inch deep. He falls, rolls. Bok raises the blade, begins his downward arc. Then Bok is upended. A Stieng tribesman's bullet shatters his calf. Nang fires. The defender crumples.

Suddenly, behind them, beyond them, the earth shivers, quakes. Nang can feel, cannot hear, the rumbling vibration below the maelstrom swirling in his visual plane. Again he fires. He runs toward Bok Roh. The first of twelve B-52s loaded for a "Menu" target has been diverted in late course. The day is dawning gray under thin clouds. On the yet dark earth surface eleven more long hells of 750-pound bombs fire-blast tangential swaths across the hills, jolting attackers. Then Hill 982 blows, a volcano peak erupting blasting outward, imploding, rubble collapsing tunnel complexes, command nerve center obliterated. Low lingering black haze from the petroleum fires darken the windward. Acrid bomb smoke-clouds coat Bu Prang. Hasty orders.

Disengage! Police up! Withdraw! Disperse!

With Bok Roh wounded, Nang had several alternatives. He had pulled, carried, helped the big man during the first frantic moments of withdrawal—a falling plunge down two hundred meters of mountainside into a small, hidden jungle pocket. Now he could call for the transportation unit porters who were assigned the job of policing the battlefield for wounded before final withdrawal, or he could assist Bok himself. The wounds were serious yet the man, with assistance, was ambulatory. Nang gave his "uncle" his hand, helped him to sit up. Quickly he removed his bayonet and split the side of Bok's trousers, exposing the shredded calf.

"Loosen the tourniquet," he whispered. Bok complied. Blood spurted from the descending artery. Immediately Bok tightened the cord at his upper thigh. "No!" Nang ordered. "No. Loosen it. It must bleed more to keep healthy." Again Bok complied. Again the spurt. Bok wheezed. His left hand was broken, swelling. His mouth hung haggard. The sprint fall through jungle away from Bu Prang, the blood loss, sapped him. His chest felt empty. To him his eyes seemed on the verge of caving in, falling behind his cheekbones. He could barely think. About them the battlefield was deserted except for the last of the dead, porters removing the dead, and rearguard snipers.

From their cover they watched a porter slip an ankle thong over dead shattered feet and drag the body away. The battle smoke had dissipated, the sky lightened further. American and ARVN soldiers were preparing a counterattack. NVA mortars sailed over them and exploded at the edge of Bu Prang.

"Do it later," Bok moaned. His voice was weak. "We must go. Get me to the porters."

"Relax," Nang said. "They know we're here. You'll be taken next."

"They're taking the dead," Bok hissed. "I should go first."

"Lie back," Nang whispered. "They're coming." Nang flicked the blade of his bayonet into Bok's wound. Bok collapsed, his body jerked. His breath came hard, quick, shallow. Nang stabbed the bone with the bayonet tip.

"AaaAh!" Bok screamed involuntarily. He clamped his mouth and controlled it. Above, leaves lay listless in still air. Bok focused on one clump, on one leaf, on one vein in the leaf. Nang stabbed the bone again. Bok's leg jolted but he did not scream. Sweat broke out in tiny beads on his face. "What are you doing? Where are the porters? Water."

"I'm afraid this is a very bad wound," Nang said. "I want to dig out the poison." He stabbed the bone again then laughed as Bok squirmed, moaned.

"Khat Doh!" Bok's voice was weak.

"Do you remember the village of Plei Srepok?" Nang asked in Viet Namese. Bok strained, raised his head. He stared at the boy. "That was my village. You tortured Y Ksar. Don't you remember? You killed my brother, Y Bhur." As he spoke he scraped the blade up the tibia wracking Bok with pain. "Don't you recall?" Nang asked calmly in Khmer. "Remember?" he said in French. Nang jabbed the bayonet into Bok's other calf.

Bok, screaming, rose to sit. To him Nang's words were unintelligible, meaningless. "Khat Doh . . ." Bok coughed.

Nang smiled. "I was Samnang," he said. "Once I was Samnang."

Then Nang leaped upon Bok's chest knocking his head back. Bok cussed. His hands shot for Nang's face. His right grabbed. Nang slashed it with his bayonet. The hand opened. The arm fell. Smirk faced, Nang thrust the blade into Bok's mouth slicing tongue muscles, epiglottis, soft palate, piercing the trachea and esophagus. He withdrew the blade, slowly dragging the sharp edge hard across the lower incisor until the tooth split. Blood burst from Bok's mouth. He rolled coughing, hanging his head, trying to breathe. Nang backed off, sat. Bok pulled himself to his knees, a dying buffalo, blood dribbling from his chin, unable to make a sound, blood spurting from his calf. He planted his broken fists on the earth, reared his shoulders, raised his one good leg as if to sprint-start. Deftly Nang stood, stood not as a frightened soldier facing an enemy's guns of an hour earlier, nor as the eight- or ten-year-old boy Bok had grown to love in three months, but as Met Nang of Angkar Leou, his entire being expanding, crystallizing into harsh angular force-lines, fluid and solid.

Bok leaped, dove with his massive bulk ready to crash, ready to crush the wasp which had stung him. Nang sidestepped, jump-kicked, smashing Bok's ribs with his heel, the huge body crumpling to earth like a great bag of sand, lying, writhing, retching.

Nang rolled Bok over. Bok's eyes clouded behind wet surfaces. His abdomen constricted as his body attempted to suck air through the blood-vomit-clogged airway. Nang removed an ankle-thong from his pack, dangled it over Bok's eyes, smiled a beaming, pleasant, impish smile at his mentor. "Don't you remember?" Nang clucked in Jarai. "For political reasons."

Fighting about Bu Prang continued for six days with much of the action being two miles south of the camp where four hundred troops of the ARVN Mobile Strike Force fought to stalemate nine hundred entrenched Northerners.

A two-day artillery duel erupted between Bu Ntoll, Duc Lap and Bu Prang, culminating with the first U.S. Air Force fighter-bomber strikes against the NVA complex in Cambodia.

Khat Doh, "seeking revenge" for his uncle, Bok Roh, took part in much of the early November fighting. On the 15th, six days after his thirteenth birthday, he was honored for heroic actions against imperialist forces. Major Bui personally congratulated Nang for destroying two armored personnel carriers and for killing one tank crewman escaping a disabled vehicle through the bottom emergency hatch. The honors were bittersweet. Medical section leader Thi, perhaps the only Viet Namese Nang had ever liked, along with six patients, was killed when a 250-pound bomb exploded and caved in the infirmary. That night Khat Doh disappeared.

On 31 December 1969 Met Nang, a.k.a. Khat Doh and Cahuom Samnang, reported, amongst many details, to his Krahom general, Met Sar: "Without our victory the North Viet Namese cannot win."

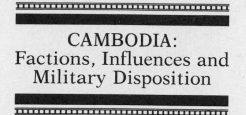

CAMBODIA:
Factions, Influences and Military Disposition

HISTORICAL SUMMATION
Part 2 (1969-1970)

Prepared for
The Washington News-Times
J. L. Sullivan

April 1985

With the Khmer economy in shambles, with industrial output and agricultural production at record lows, inflation and trade deficits at record highs, with ever more government-controlled area being lost, the North Viet Namese Communists accelerated their long-term plan, Campaign X, to conquer Cambodia. At the same time, American will diminished further over the outcry caused by President Richard Nixon's 3 November 1969 speech and the beginning of the exposé of the massacre at My Lai.

Entering 1970 Cambodia was a ship smoldering throughout its hold, though flames had not yet appeared in the portholes or smoke yet begun to billow from the deck—a ship tossed by international waves created by the shifting of two major opposing elements, like continental plates beneath an ocean. The violent jarrings reverberated through every faction.

By January the NVA had the military might—the supply lines, the troops and the political cadres—to force the collapse of Cambodia. Their only concern was how America would react. Throughout the American war years in South Viet Nam, the North Viet Namese generally chose when and where each battle would take place. It had been the sanctuary system along the Cambodian and Laotian borders which had allowed this unilateral decision making. Now they asked themselves, at this time of U.S. deescalation, would the Americans choose to ignore the Khmer nation that had been a thorn in the side of two administrations, or would the United States, in its self-perceived "world-police" role, feel it must stave off the fall of Phnom Penh?

Political purpose and military objective define the scope and intensity of any army's, or nation's, war effort. Under a dictatorial regime, or among guerrillas attempting to seize power, the cult of personality determines the political-military aim and thus the scope and intensity of the effort. The more absolute the control of the leadership, the more absolute its influence. The Hanoi-Politburo, led by Pham Van Dong, Le Duc Tho, Vo Nguyen Giap and the residue of the spirit of Ho Chi Minh, held near total control of their own nation and only slightly less control over the Laotian Pathet Lao and the Cambodian Khmer Viet Minh. In the battle for Cambodia, these men directed the largest and best-equipped military forces. They determined the scope and intensity of the war in this theater. American and South Viet Namese actions in regard to Cambodia would have a major impact on the North Viet Namese Communists, but 1970 was a year of such quick changes that many observers would never understand what happened. Some U.S. and ARVN actions affected the NVA and VC in ways exactly opposite to the usual interpretations.

The NVA campaign precipitated turmoil and crisis within the Cambodian government and produced what historian Ben Kiernan would later call "the second civil war." The NVA drive caused the explosive emergence of a new faction, the Khmer Rumdoah (Khmer for Liberation); filled Norodom Sihanouk's power vacuum and sucked in additional foreign armies; and led to enormous increases in recruitment by all Khmer factions, by forcing the polarization of Cambodian society. In the end it also produced factional fratricide amongst the Communists.

SIHANOUK'S ACTIONS

On 10 December 1969, sixty days after announcing his support for North Viet Nam's "just stand," Sihanouk publicly loosed FARK (Forces Armée Royale Khmère, the Royal Cambodian Army) in major actions against NVA positions. The shift from supporting the NVA / VC presence to resisting the continuing buildup resulted partly from the secret U.S. "Menu" bombings and partly from Sihanouk's fear that he had misjudged the strength and intentions of the North Viet Namese Communists.

In January 1970 Sihanouk commenced the execution of a go-for-broke game plan. Cambodia's head of state, with wife and entourage, flew from Phnom Penh to Rome to begin a round of alternate feasting and fasting at luxurious continental spas—an act the Prince saw as a personal physical and spiritual righting maneuver, much as he viewed the rest of his plan as a rebalancing of Cambodia's "neutrality" between the yin and yang of superior alien powers.

Sihanouk directed his now prime minister General Lon Nol to arrange in his absence a series of forceful anti–Viet Namese demonstrations. When the nation was in the grip of this Sihanouk-designed, government-manufactured crisis, the scenario went, the Prince would fly from Rome to Paris and then on to Moscow and Peking, with the precise plan of persuading the Viet negotiators in Paris and the Communist leaders in Moscow and Peking to bring pressure upon the North Viet Namese to withdraw from Cambodia or at least curtail their expanding activity throughout that nation. Upon his departure, he believed, the NVA had 35,000 to 40,000 troops in permanent positions in his country. In Rome he was presented with new Khmer intelligence estimates raising the total to 60,000 and indicating that the Viet Namese Communists were both organizing hundreds of villages to revolt against him and attempting to gain control of all Khmer rebel factions.

In addition to Viet Namese soldiers, 400,000 ethnic Viet Namese civilians lived in Cambodia at the beginning of 1970. About 200,000 are said to have been either North Viet Namese cadres, agents working in Cambodia, the families of those cadre and agents, or the families of NVA soldiers operating either from the border sanctuaries or along the Sihanouk Trail. For years, some say since the 1950s, the Viets, both legitimate and insurgent, had established home and/or neighborhoods within every major Cambodian city, the heaviest concentrations being in Phnom Penh (120,000) and in the southeastern cities of Takeo, Svay Rieng, Prey Veng and Neak Luong, and in the east central city of Kompong Cham.

KVM REPATRIATION

Coupled with the presence of North Viet Namese soldiers, agents and civilians was the repatriation of the Khmer Viet Minh who had been held in North Viet Nam.

Western historians disagree on when the Hanoi Politburo, through COKA, directed the repatriation of KVM soldiers and political officers, and on how many were repatriated. Some say 12,000 cadremen were repatriated between January and March 1969. Their activities, according to these accounts, threw the country into civil war. Others claim that only 4,000 to 6,000 were repatriated, all in mid-March 1970. A review of battle records suggests the repatriation was not a single wave but a constant moderate flow beginning in January 1969 and culminating in February or March 1970. At any rate, all of Hanoi's Khmer Viet Minh cadre were in position by mid-March 1970.

By the end of January 1970, the KVM buildup and NVA movements had touched off what would become ever-escalating rounds of Communist fratricide; touched this off even as Royal Government Forces began new tactical operations to, ostensibly, reassert Cambodian sovereignty, halt NVA expansion and force a political guarantee from the North Viet Namese that they would withdraw after their victory in South Viet Nam. Simultaneously, NVA and Krahom intelligence indicated to their respective leaders that American diplomatic efforts were pressing Sihanouk to formally sanction additional high-level B-52 "Menu" bombings. NVA historical accounts call these reports ominous. Perhaps the reports caused a feeling of urgency amongst the North Viet Namese leadership, a need to attack and conquer Phnom Penh before Sihanouk's approval of the raids—a need to achieve a fait accompli before the Americans could respond.

As Royal forces moved east along main roads toward the border, Communist forces moved west on prepared secondary trails. In the Southeast, in Kampot, Takeo and Kandal Provinces, NVA/VC and KVM units systematically attacked and destroyed a line of small, lightly defended government border posts. The NVA then drew additional units from South Viet Nam in February, reinforced, and attacked from and expanded their established positions along the Sihanouk Trail, about Phnom Penh, and in the West near Siem Reap.

By March the NVA had almost completed the move of its Central Office for South Viet Nam (COSVN) headquarters to a prepared position near Kratie. COSVN was operational and directing not only the Communist war in the southern third of Viet Nam but also in Cambodia (though much of the direction for Cambodia came from the COKA headquarters near Siem Reap). In every direction that Hanoi sent new KVM political cadre they also sent regular NVA military units.

This distribution of Viet Namese and Khmer Viet-sympathizers caused Sihanouk, in Rome, upon reviewing the more detailed intelligence reports of his staff, to sigh *"C'est fini!"* It is over. It also triggered virulent anti–Viet Namese hatred in the general public *and* amongst the Khmer Krahom leadership.

THE KHMER KRAHOM

The Movement, Angkar, Angka, the Khmer Krahom, the Khmer Rouge—whatever label might be used—was at this time a federation of six semiautonomous armies controlled by six semiautonomous parties, more or less directed by the Standing Committee of the Central Committee, the Center. Within each zone (north, northeast, east, southwest, northwest and special or central) the zonal central commit-

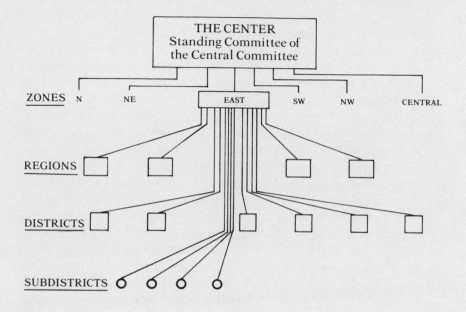

tee (ZCC) had near absolute power over its zone party cadre, army, descending committees and militias. Each ZCC had its own ideological and political slant. For example, the Army of the East was semifraternal with the Viet Cong; the Army of the Northeast was heavily influenced by the NVA and their attached Khmer Viet Minh. The Army of the North was the first to exhibit the terrible ruthlessness which became the signature of the KK.

The zones were responsive only to the Center and were essentially isolated from one another; regions, districts and even lower levels of organization reported to and were directed by the ZCC, not (except in the case of regions) by the next higher level. In this way, the rule of the ZCC was absolute and that of the Center was filtered through only one descending level, no matter how far down the organizational chart. In early 1970, with the KK in a period of rapid expansion, the Center was attempting to consolidate its control over the zones.

WORLD VIEW

Half a world away, fissures in American public opinion, partly reconciled in the post-Tet 1968 period by the election of Richard Nixon, again ruptured. On 3 November 1969 Nixon delivered to the American people his first major policy speech on Viet Nam. The President outlined a plan calling for gradual, though eventually total, withdrawal of American combat units and for an increased emphasis on Viet Namization (the Nixon doctrine, as applied to Viet Nam, of giving materiel and moral support, but no U.S. combat troops, to assist indigenous peoples in defending themselves from outside aggression). Though the immediate results showed that more than three quarters of all listeners favored the President's policies, versus only six percent opposed, strong dormant forces in the U.S. Senate were jarred awake. J. William Fulbright promised Senate hearings to educate the "real silent majority" to the facts of the war, and Senate majority leader Mike Mansfield denounced the policy as the new administration's adoption of Johnson's war.

This was followed almost immediately (12 November) by the first sketchy stories of the massacre of Viet Namese civilians by American troops at Song My village, My Lai hamlet. On 20 November, the Cleveland *Plain Dealer* published photographs of the massacre. Then, on the 25th, *The New York Times* and other newspapers confirmed the atrocity to many skeptical Americans with headlines announcing the Army's order that Lieutenant William Calley stand trial. By the beginning of 1970, My Lai had redivided the United States.

The effect of the Nixon doctrine announcement coupled with renewed American domestic turmoil was translated by Hanoi's America watchers as ambiguous U.S. support. This encouraged the Communist factions to commit additional men and materiel to the battle for Cambodia.

The covert North Viet Namese thrust into the interior of Cambodia, spearheaded by the repatriation of the KVM, sent tidal waves through the Krahom movement, as it did through the Royal Government and much of Khmer society. In a nation at war, in a culture under attack, every military setback or victory affects every individual —to the very essence of his or her being.

It is in this context that the battle of Chenla II must be understood, for each nuance of that battle touched the lives of every Cambodian. Chenla II was a tsunami which reverberated throughout the Khmer Basin, bouncing, as waves bounce, off the surrounding mountains, sending secondary waves crashing into and washing over each other in the central area known as the Northern Corridor (see map), a tempest slowly, violently splintering an entire nation, a storm which would have two eyes, the first resulting from gusting multiple engagements leading to the worst battlefield defeat of the war.

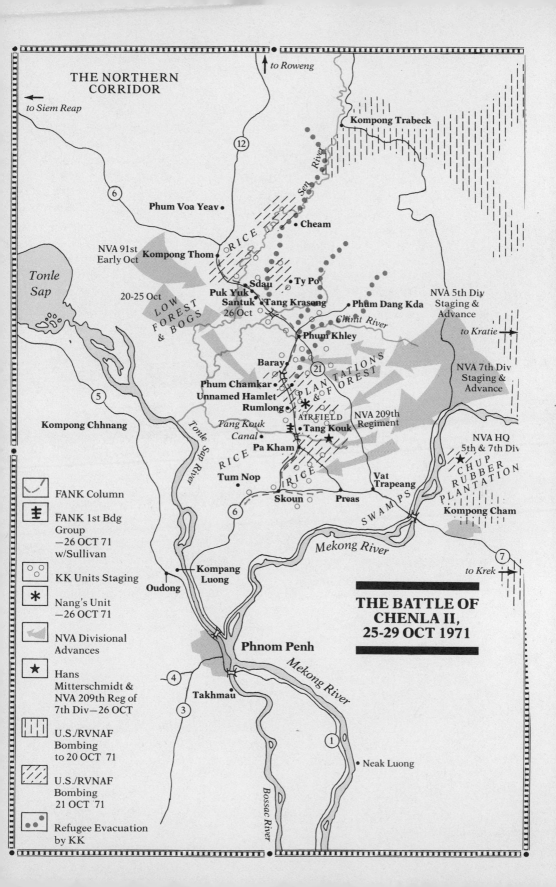

THE NORTHERN
CORRIDOR

← to Siem Reap

↑ to Roweng

Kompong Trabeck

⑫

⑥

Phum Voa Yeav •

Sen River

• Cheam

NVA 91st
Early Oct   Kompong Thom •

Tonle
Sap

20–25 Oct

Sdau •
• Ty Po

Puk Yuk
Santuk   • Tang Krasong
26 Oct

LOW FOREST & BOGS

RICE

• Phum Dang Kda

NVA 5th Div
Staging &
Advance

Chinit River

→ to Kratie

Phum Khley •

⑤

Baray •

⑳①

Phum Chamkar •
Unnamed Hamlet
Rumlong •

PLANTATIONS & FOREST

NVA 7th Div
Staging &
Advance

Kompong Chhnang •

Tang Kouk
Canal

AIRFIELD

• Tang Kouk

NVA 209th
Regiment

NVA HQ
5th & 7th Div

Pa Kham •

CHUP
RUBBER
PLANTATION

Tonle Sap River

RICE

Tum Nop •

RICE

Vat
Trapeang

⑥

Skoun   Preas

SWAMPS

Kompong Cham

FANK Column

FANK 1st Bdg
Group
—26 OCT 71
w/Sullivan

KK Units Staging

Nang's Unit
—26 OCT 71

NVA Divisional
Advances

Hans
Mitterschmidt &
NVA 209th Reg of
7th Div—26 OCT

U.S./RVNAF
Bombing
to 20 OCT 71

U.S./RVNAF
Bombing
21 OCT 71

Refugee Evacuation
by KK

Mekong River

⑦

→ to Krek

Kompang
Luong

Oudong

④

③

Phnom Penh

Takhmau

①

Mekong River

• Neak Luong

Bossac River

**THE BATTLE OF
CHENLA II,
25–29 OCT 1971**

PART TWO

THE REPUBLIC OF CAMBODIA RISING

Hanoi could easily devour both Cambodia and what is left of Laos if it were not faced with US opposition. There are enough North Vietnamese and Viet Cong troops in Cambodia today to seize [the] country.

> —C. L. Sulzberger, paraphrasing Norodom Sihanouk, in
> *The Indianapolis News,*
> 18 March 1970

CHAPTER SEVEN

"Are you hungry?" Nang spoke slowly to the children though his inner pace was frantic. After only one week at Mount Aural he had been sent to Stung Treng to help accelerate Krahom recruitment. "Don't be afraid," he said. "We guarantee everyone will share equally in the nation's food." It was not the assignment he'd wanted. Every day he asked why. Why had Met Sar sent him away so quickly, away to these children, away when so much was happening elsewhere? "Here," Nang said, "peasants work twelve hours a day. In Phnom Penh, government functionaries work two! They eat well. They pay no taxes."

"You see." Met Phan smiled. "Comrade Rang has been to the front. He knows victory is inevitable. He has killed enemy soldiers. He has blown up enemy tanks. He's not much older than you."

Nang bowed to the boys and girls. They sat elbow to elbow in the hot shack, sat in the posture of perfect attention as they had learned, sat in awe of Met Nang, to them Comrade Rang, a mysterious figure sent to them in their mysterious back-street hovel, sat in awe in the shadows as the January dry season sun baked the sleepy alley.

"Comrade Rang has been sent to us to teach us courage," Phan said. He sat with the children, sat in perfect egalitarian posture, eyes on Nang.

"The Americans," Nang whispered, "killed my uncle. He had been wounded in the leg and taken prisoner. While he still lived, they stabbed him in the mouth and cut out his tongue." Nang paused. He trembled at the recollection, at the sight which he forced himself to believe. "The imperialists have poisoned the mind of Prince Sihanouk. Royal soldiers killed my whole family. If we show fear they will kill us all, but if we have courage . . ."

The youngest child, a girl of seven, watched Nang with widening eyes. He spoke with such feeling and gentleness she wanted to touch his hand, yet his words carried such horror she fought to control the undefined terror gripping her. Behind her an untrained boy of eleven stiffened. His imagination placed him in this soldier's tale; his resolve to be courageous stiffened.

Each child had slipped away from a parent, each having been recruited because each had had a father or mother killed in the low-level guerrilla war of the preceding years. They were the core of Phan's Stung Treng Children's Brigade. Phan, a covert political officer of both the Krahom and the Khmer Viet Minh, had started the clandestine unit in 1967 with one boy whose father had been shot by government soldiers during an anti-government demonstration. Phan had asked the boy if he would like assistance in gaining reparation and the boy had followed him. "Tell me three of your friends," Phan had said at their second meeting. "Bring a friend," he urged during the third. Each child, once lured, hooked, sworn to secrecy, was required to recruit two friends. "One becomes three," Phan repeated the Communist axiom. "Three become nine." From early 1967 to mid-1969 recruitment had been difficult but tactics and the situation were changing. By 1970 Phan had nineteen cells of children, three to six youngsters per cell. Nang had come to bolster that recruitment.

"Children can be very courageous." Nang's eyes were soft. These children, he knew, would never be sent to advanced Communist training schools. They were not destined to become cadre; there would be no School of the Cruel, no ideological indoctrination. For them there would be only the underground school, the fetid back-alley shack, the brief afternoon classes in hate, the first all-night patrol, the first act of terrorism, and then death—death in the meat grinder of war, death to the naive, pushed knowingly into the funnel by ideologically secure cadres who not only would feed that grinder, but had justified in their minds their duty to feed it the most expendable, until the grinder itself ran down and the cadres could control it unilaterally.

Nang continued. "Children can turn the tide of battle," he said. "They can win wars. You know imperialists are trying to take the country from the people, eh? If you are a coward you will live your life in shame in a country owned by others. It's better to die with courage than to live with shame."

Nang paused. He lowered his head, closed his eyes. In the steaming motionless silence the little girl in the front and the boy in back leaned imperceptibly forward. Even Phan strained his ears to hear Nang's next utterance though Phan had sat through the show four times with four cells and would listen fourteen more times with perfect attention. "Once," Nang whispered, his eyes shut in pain, "we were caught in the crossfire of two American tanks. Met Peou snuck from his hiding place. He was so small. Only six years old. He didn't wear any pants. He ran forward crying as the tanks came toward us. Under his shirt he had dynamite. When he reached the first tank it stopped. The enemy stopped firing and one soldier came out. Met Peou pulled the cord under his shirt and killed the long-nose. Peou stopped the tanks long enough for us to capture them and kill the crews. He was my little brother. His life is better than mine. He had more courage and he has no shame."

Two girls wept. Nang let tears come to his eyes. He was pleased by the children's reaction. It deepened his belief in the cause, the just cause of the Khmer Krahom, his cause. And . . . the tears were not entirely fake. In his mind he saw his own little brother and he saw him explode. Nineteen times in Stung Treng, a hundred times in the Northeast, he saw that image and it grew to be true and he hated it and a hundred times he chased away the intrusive thought and asked himself why— why had Sar sent him back so close to home?

Then came the government announcement; then Nang's recall.

Vathana opened her eyes. Teck's head was curled down upon his chest. From behind him she could see only the skinny shoulder of a headless form protruding above the coverlet. Between them lay the two-month-old infant, Samnang, asleep, angelic, snoring a high thin infant snore. Vathana cupped the baby to her side. She looked up. The canopy of sheer white mosquito netting fell in graceful folds about them like a protective cocoon. Teck snorted, rolled to his back, arched, melted back into the mattress like a deflating balloon. "Sophan," Vathana called softly.

In the first weeks after Vathana's trauma and the birth of his son, Teck had been more attentive than at any time since their wedding. Grudgingly he'd stumbled through the intricacies of river-barge management, on one occasion actually talking to the captain on the wharf. During those weeks he neither went dancing nor smoked heroin, and to him Cambodia seemed to open itself, denude itself, stand before him in raunch corrupt ugliness without the filter of his mother or the firm control of his father. He cowered. He wanted to hide, to run. But he held together and for that his mother rewarded him. One evening, she brought him to Phnom Penh to a most fashionable party; a party where wines flowed and young women chatted softly in

French with handsome military men; a party where the under-current of conversation amongst the uniformed officers was of the Prince, the war, the rumor of the fabled white crocodile foreshadowing change, though on the surface no deep concern was expressed.

The dazzle of the party, of his mother's growing association with the haut monde, captivated Teck. Capriciously he resolved to have his father purchase for him a commission into the Royal forces. Then he returned to Neak Luong, saw his weary wife up, about, able if still frail, and his resolve dissipated. Slowly he slipped into former habits.

The infant wheezed. Vathana hugged him, kissed him, then slipped her arm from around him to tug the mosquito net from its tuck beneath the mattress. "Sophan," she called again. She rose.

A stout woman came and bowed. "Yes'm." Sophan bowed again. She was one of the hundreds of women Vathana had rescued, had taken into her expanding refugee center after their homes near the border had been destroyed. Vathana had not particularly noticed Sophan amid the border people, but Sophan had chosen her, had attached herself to Vathana because she no longer had a family. Whenever Teck had left Vathana unat-tended in the hospital, it had been Sophan who had cared for her.

"Take the baby and nurse him. Then swaddle him in the sunflower blanket with the emerald-green bunting. His grandfa-ther's coming."

Pech Lim Song burst upon the apartment like sun rays breaking through sluggish clouds. Teck was still in bed. Half the morning had passed. "Let me hold my grandson," Mister Pech said. His speech was light, his movements quick, gentle, his face radiant as he cooed to the infant and praised his daughter-in-law. Then Teck emerged. The clouds thickened.

"Crocodiles consume the countryside . . ." Mister Pech said sarcastically. He stood before Vathana's work desk eyeing the elegantly framed photo of Prince Sihanouk. ". . . while the na-tion's young men sleep."

"How is your health, Father?" Teck bowed though Mister Pech remained with his back to his son.

"They're closing in," Mister Pech said. "I quote the Prince. North Viet Namese armed penetration into Cambodia coupled with 'an energetic subversion campaign aimed at *my* peasants, workers, Buddhist monks . . . attempting to organize a "Khmer popular uprising" against the monarchy whom they accuse of selling out to French colonialism.' Yes! French! Those were his words! Nineteen fifty-three! 'Anti-Sihanouk propaganda . . . terrorism . . . assassination of Khmer loyalists, officials and civil servants . . .' Their objectives haven't changed but their ability has blossomed a hundredfold."

Teck glanced at Vathana. She had grasped the Buddha statuette at her neck and was whispering a prayer. "Father, you're always welcome here," Teck said to the older man's back, "but it's not good to speak such things before your grandson. He's vulnerable to ill will."

Mister Pech turned, looked beyond his son to Vathana and to Sophan with the listless infant tightly wrapped in a yellow blanket. "Someone's here, eh!?"

Teck's jaw tightened. "I can't do this," he mumbled beneath his breath.

"You're too young to understand when a man must stand," Mister Pech said. Still he did not look at his son. "Right action," he said sharply. "All holy Buddhists are anti-Communists."

"You wish me to die before yuon rifles?! That it, eh!?" Teck ground his teeth. "Or maybe under those damned American bombs?"

"I came with an amulet for Vathana and a toy for the baby," Mister Pech said, dismissing Teck.

"How much do you know about the American bombings, eh, Father? You know the generals. Do you encourage them? Do you tell them to urge the Prince to formally sanction them? That's what's happening, isn't it? It's the bombings that are forcing the Viets onto us. It's the bombings that deepen the crisis. Should we exchange the NVA presence along the border for an American invasion?"

Mister Pech turned, faced Teck squarely. "Who's talking invasion?" he snapped. "For centuries Khmers have been warriors. For our safety"—Pech Lim Song pointed to himself and then to Vathana—"we must defend ourselves. For our dignity we must repel the Viet Namese. As a Khmer, you're a disgrace."

"Humph!" Teck snorted. Though their argument had been continuous for a year, Teck was uncomfortable arguing with his father. "Shouldn't we clean our own house first?" He tried to control his tone. "The Prince hasn't stopped influence peddling. He hasn't stopped corruption. His wife engages in illicit trade with the Communists . . ."

"You want me to get you a commission, eh?!"

". . . the yuons, the Chinese pay her to keep him in line. And her brother, Oum Mannorine, secretary of state for surface defense. Ha! He collaborates in rice smuggling. You want me to support *them*? General Sosthènes Fernandez—you know him, eh? Mother does—national security secretary! He takes bribes from the arms shippers. My friends at the dance hall know. Street peddlers know. But you, you refuse to know."

"I don't refuse to know," Mister Pech said sternly. "I recognize it for what it is—an appendage of the Viet Minh conspiracy, a force we can't cope with because the young men are all in dance halls!" Mister Pech turned from his son. To Vathana, in a pleasant voice, he said, "I'm very busy today. I came only to see my grandson and to give you this." From his pocket he pulled a bracelet with a Buddhist prayer carved onto an ebony charm. "I don't have leisure time to waste on anti-Khmer talk." He smiled broadly. "I am a patriot. I would expect that of my son, but he . . . what does he call himself?—Epicurean. He cares not for the nation. I blame myself. Let this little one hear you talk, see you do business. Don't swaddle him like his grandmother did to . . . did until he's a twenty-two-year-old infant."

"Damn it! That's not true. Your cronies have power. They use it to bleed people."

Mister Pech's eyes shifted momentarily toward his son then back to Vathana. "Have you heard from your mother and father?" he asked sweetly.

"It's been a month," Vathana said. "There's no communication with the Northeast."

For three days the winds increased until finally blowing so violently huge palm fronds littered the streets of Phnom Penh and all Cambodia's cities, towns and villages. Then the monsoons burst upon the land, a mid-March—instead of April or even May—deluge. Dust-dry roads turned to ribbons of red muck stretching through paddies not yet green and jungles still covered with sand and grit. Dormant rills trickled, babbled, gushed as the saturated land attempted to shed the torrents. Streams became rivers, rivers escaped their banks and became mile-wide puddles. The Mekong, not yet inundated by Himalayan snowmelt, like a huge drain sucking the torrents from the land, seemingly searched for new ways to divert the deluge, new trenches, chasms, gorges, valleys into which to dump the excess wet. The whole country became precariously saturated and the heaviest rains were yet expected. And in every corner of the country, inside every political and military faction, in every household, and internationally, Cambodia was facing a precarious watershed. The once placid kingdom roiled in frantic power-grab waves.

"Viet Namese are snatching the country!" Met Sar, on Mount

Aural, was livid, was crazy with rage. "Viet Namese this . . . Viet Namese that!" He had been shouting continuously for an hour. Nang's friend from Pong Pay Mountain, Met Eng, trembled before the verbal storm. Nang had never heard Sar rant so, fume so. He stood beside Eng in rank with thirty top *yotheas* and cadremen, stood listening with the bastardized perfect attention the Krahom had transfigured from Buddhist culture.

"They roll through the countryside one hundred thousand strong. More! Two hundred thousand. Everywhere! Lon Nol, that lackey puppet, has declared the figures before the National Assembly. Viet Namese are preparing to take the capital. They steal the revolution from Angkar Leou." Met Sar banged his fists on a table; paced back and forth, looked not at his field leaders and agents but first up at the roof then down at the floor. "They outnumber Royal soldiers by at least three to one—outnumber the Royals in combat strength ten to one. They're better equipped, led, trained. They're more experienced! Sihanouk, that idiot! *Aekarcach-mochasker*," Met Sar shouted. "Independence and sovereignty. Without them, Kampuchea will wither like an orchid snatched from the earth."

Met Sar paused. No one moved. From Nang's position behind a comrade he could see the older man had gained weight in the two months since Nang had been sent to the Northeast, could see that Met Sar's jowls hung just like those of Norodom Sihanouk, could see that the leader's face was sweat-drenched and mottled, that he was suffering from the increased weight he carried, not just physically but mentally, politically.

"There is no détente with the Viet Namese. None with Khmer puppets. We must have rapid improvement of our position! Take control! Organize the people! Order! Order! Order!" Again Sar banged his fists. "Angka will control!" he boomed. "Angka will order! Angka will lead! Sihanouk wants anti–Viet Namese demonstrations. We shall lead!"

"We are isolated," Hang Tung shouted from the steps of the pagoda. "We need voluntary contributions to keep armies out." Chhuon stood beside him. Behind them were five of the seven elders who had assembled earlier in Chhuon's central room. Before them were a dozen armed guards, the core of Phum Sath Din's new militia. Beyond the guards the entire village population spilled back toward the river and down the street. From Tung's shrill call newcomers recoiled. To his words old families traded glances of resentment.

"My brothers and sisters," Chhuon addressed the village in a firm yet anguished voice, "our village is isolated . . . from our country. My nephew wishes to sell self-determination bonds to raise the money necessary to equip and maintain a guard."

From the audience came a lone call, "They're already equipped. Who are they?" Then an entire chorus, "Ssshh! Mr. Cahuom can be trusted."

"These men are here to raise money for a militia." Chhuon's voice was softened by the damp air. "We *are* isolated," he emphasized. "Viet Namese are to the north, east and maybe south. Crazed provincial troops are to the west. The village of Phum Sath Nan has been destroyed. Survivors have come to us for safety. Some say American soldiers are invading the country. We must defend ourselves. Against all armies. We are the best of Cambodia. When this crisis has passed we will regain our position in the country and all will return home. But now we must act. Each family head must register. All the land which has been abandoned will be redistributed to newcomers. Every family must contribute to the self-determination fund. It will be used to expand and maintain the militia."

From the middle of the crowd a man shouted, "How much must we contribute?"

Chhuon looked at the man. He looked remarkably like Hang Tung, but Chhuon did not recognize him.

"Brother," Tung shouted, "the tax will be small. Today you will receive land. We'll tell you then what is your contribution. Now that the village is liberated everyone will be better off."

Late that afternoon the land distribution commenced with all paddies, those abandoned and those still worked by long-time residents, divided amongst not families but new village quadrant committees for further distribution to village quadrant production teams. To many the assignments seemed just, approximately the same as the old system. A few old-timers grumbled. Others reminded them there *was* a crisis and the distribution was to be temporary. Others saw it as unenforceable. Most felt, with an abundance of land, there was no need to be concerned.

What did annoy almost everyone, however, was the announcement of the "voluntary contribution for self-determination bonds." Half of all existing rice stores were to be brought to the pagoda. One third of all new rice would be collected for the militia and for the village's "contribution to the effort against the imperialist aggressors." Each family was further required to write out a list of all personal property, "for their own protection," and as a basis for determining the monetary tax.

The dozen militiamen in the village grew to a platoon of forty green-clad uniformed soldiers plus four cadremen to organize the new village quadrant administrations. Within three days

Chhuon found he was answering to new masters, issuing their orders to the village in his name, under threat to the villagers themselves if he, Cahuom Chhuon, did not receive full cooperation.

"We must realize optimum production," a cadreman told Chhuon. "We are now on a war footing and every effort must be made during our country's most difficult period."

Chhuon understood. There was no room for questions.

"Plant every plot," the cadre said. "Plant early rice, late rice, ten-month rice. In their yards have them plant yams. Along the trails and roads they'll plant maize. An agronomist's dream, eh?"

Chhuon understood. Yet he did not fully understand. He had become an instrument in the takeover. Indeed, he, like most of the villagers, did not fully understand there had been a take-over. In the confusion Chhuon simply went along with what was ordered. There seemed to be no other course.

Thus did the Khmer Viet Minh, backed unseen by the North Viet Namese Army, almost bloodlessly take over the adminis-tration of Phum Sath Din. It had come not with a bang, barely with a whisper. Royal forces retreated from their thin, heavily perforated line in the Northeast, allowing the Communists to add all of Stung Treng Province east of the Mekong, with the exception of Stung Treng City, to their control, along with Ratanakiri, Mondolkiri, eastern Kratie and Kompong Cham provinces.

"Where do you think they'll send us now?" Eng asked Nang as they scurried through the tunnel to the planning room.

"I don't know, Met Eng," Nang said pleasantly. He was pleased to be with his old friend, to be assigned a mission with him, to see that Eng, like he himself, had advanced to be included in such an elite group. And he was pleased to be back from the Northeast.

"One small group," Met Ary, a staff officer of the Center, addressed the team, " 'with no resources at all, can free itself from the yoke of oppression' "—he paused for emphasis—" 'if it wants to badly enough.' "

"Chairman Mao," Eng said.

"Yes," Ary said. "We must want our independence and sover-eignty badly enough to sacrifice whatever need be sacrificed in order to be free."

"We are the sacrifice," Met Ty responded. Nang did not com-ment. He'd often taught the same lesson and Met Ary's remedial tutoring irritated him.

"Yes, we are the sacrifice," Met Ary said. "But we must now

be more. We must now be the guides. We must be willing to unite with whoever can help us without allowing them to change our course."

"Who would you have join us?" Nang asked.

"You are all young," Ary said. "You'll pass as orphans."

"Where?" Nang prodded.

"Though we've been united with the North Viet Namese in our struggle to oust Sihanouk, we now must unite with Sihanouk to oust the NVA and VC. But keep your lips sealed. Lead the people to terrorize our enemies. Then transform the people, step-by-step."

"Met Ary," Nang's voice sliced out. "Where? Who? When?"

"Phnom Penh. Tomorrow."

"How?"

"Riots. Government agents are right now baiting the students with tales of NVA barbarity and with documents proving their treacherous advance."

Nang smiled. "What should we do?"

Ary paused. "Rendezvous with the students," he said. "Once they have crossed the line, there will be no turning back."

"There's something wrong with him, isn't there?" Vathana whispered to Sophan in French.

"He's a good nurser," the wet nurse answered. "A very good nurser, Angel. He's a very beautiful boy."

"But . . ." Vathana sat beside the squat woman nursing her baby. She reached for the boy's chubby hand, hesitated, then gently seized it with thumb and forefinger. The infant's hand was a cool stiff fist hanging from a listless arm. Vathana pried the tiny fingers back. They opened and reclosed about her foreknuckle without significant pressure as if the tendons were lifeless elastic bands keeping constant tension on mechanical levers instead of spirited tiny muscles instinctively clamping, clinging to life.

"I'll work his hands," Sophan said. "You'll see, Angel. He'll come along fine."

Vathana groaned. She grasped the statuette at her throat, squeezed her eyes in prayer. "Why?" she lamented quietly. A bit louder she said, "There *is* something wrong with him."

"What?!" Teck had been lying in bed wondering what he would do this day, lying, wishing not to arise but vaguely wishing also for a reason to get up. "What did I hear you say?" He rolled his knees over, dropped his feet to the floor. Neither Vathana nor Sophan answered. He stood, his Parisian silk paja-mas hanging loose at his skinny hips. "There's nothing wrong with that child," he all but shouted. "He's a sleepy baby. That's all." It felt good to assert himself in his own home.

"My brothers and sisters were never so sleepy," Vathana cried back. "Never."

"You don't love your own child, woman," Teck snorted. He fumbled in the closet pulling out first a pair of white trousers, then beige, then light yellow. "What's all the noise out there?"

Vathana opened the bedroom door. Her eyes glistened with tears though she was not crying. From the street voices, shouts, could be heard though words couldn't be distinguished. "We should have him examined by the doctors in Phnom Penh," Vathana said.

"You're a worrisome farmer's daughter," Teck shot back.

"And you"—Vathana's tears burst—"you . . . you're more French than Khmer." In Khmer she added, "A Khmer man would never treat his wife or son so."

From outside a subdued crackling staccato of firecrackers or automatic rifles could be heard. Then loud shouts. Screams. "What's going on out there?" Teck boomed. The cacophony excited him, intrigued him. Not looking at Vathana, walking quickly past Sophan and the infant, Teck checked himself in the mirror then fled through the apartment door.

11 March 1970—Nang squatted in the doorway of a small shop on Monivong Boulevard in Phnom Penh. The early morning sky was heavy with dark clouds. In other doorways, behind fences, in courtyards, beneath blossoming trees, student leaders lurked, Krahom boys and girls waited patiently, government agents tensed and relaxed their muscles. Phnom Penh woke. Trucks clattered by, buses belched black clouds of diesel exhaust, motorbikes wheezed, and radios splashed their voices into streets unaware of those listening. Small battles, Nang thought—he did not wish to be sidetracked by the sights, noises, smells or opulence of the city—but promising successes.

Suddenly from behind, "What do you want?" a shopkeep demanded. Nang started. He had not heard the door unlatch. The man approached. Nang glared like a trapped cat, silent, wary. Then his face cracked in nervous eerie smile. "Go!" the shopkeep barked. "Get out of here!"

Nang slinked back. Jungle vigilance was easier than city, he thought. His neck stiffened. He leaned back against a wet concrete facade. Immediately water soaked through his shirt, chilled him. He raised his shoulders, pulled his elbows tightly to his sides. A truck horn blasted. Again he started. Evil, he thought. Cities are evil, just as Met Sar says. That woman. I bet she's one. City women sell themselves. City noise is evil. City air is evil. City dwellers are evil. It's our duty, our destiny, to establish order—for the good of Kampuchea. He shivered. The left corner of his mouth twitched.

Two students ran toward him. He tensed. Seemingly from nowhere young people began to seep onto the street, to flow slowly toward him, by him. "Come with us, Little Brother," one called, and Nang became part of the growing crowd. "You look frightened," the boy said jovially to Nang. Nang looked up with naive, trusting puppy eyes. "Little Brother"—the student was concerned—"have you eaten today? Are you hungry? Where do you sleep?"

"I have no home," Nang said sadly. "It was taken by yuons." He walked shyly, lagged behind the student.

"Where was your home?" The boy walked backwards, smiling, happy, hoping Nang would walk faster, not wanting to lose his friends.

"We lived in the Northeast," Nang answered.

"Hey, listen to this kid," the student called out, trying to slow his friends. "He's one of 'em."

"Come Tam," one friend called back. "We don't want to miss the speech."

"They murdered my family," Nang said, catching up to Tam.

"What?! Vanty! Chan! Listen!" Tam's face lost its cheerful gleam. "We've got to bring him with us. The yuons made him an orphan."

At each block the crowd grew in chunks as new marchers came from side streets. The occasion was festive though the sky remained ominous. Minor commotions erupted sporadically around student leaders, government agents and border refugees.

From one corner a chant began. "VIET NAM QUIT CAMBODIA! VIET NAM QUIT CAMBODIA!" Others picked it up. "VIET NAM QUIT CAMBODIA!" Through city center two thousand strong the demonstrators chanted. More joined. Several contingents of small motorcycles squeezed between walkers, the riders revving tiny motors in time with the chant. "VIET NAM QUIT CAMBODIA!" From Norodom Boulevard a second demonstration meshed with the first, a third came from the stadium, a fourth from the central market area. Ten thousand strong and growing they marched on the North Viet Namese and Provisional Revolutionary Government embassies. Throughout the crowd monks positioned themselves offering examples of controlled peaceful protest. Throughout the crowd Krahom children, government agents and soldiers pumped bellows on the fires of hate.

"When they came into our village," Nang whimpered to Tam, his friends and perhaps forty listeners, "they said they would help. But they're crocodiles. Samdech Euv gave them bases. He let them use the ports. He traded rice with them. But they're crocodiles." Nang paused. He felt the presence of someone hostile. Khmer Viet Minh, he thought. "We gave them rice. Then they took all the girls to their camp. They killed the elders. I ran to the forest. I saw the village burn."

"And they still keep coming," Tam shouted. "They'll kill us all. They keep coming."

"They've overrun Svay Rieng," someone shouted.

"They're in Prasaut," another called.

"Don't forget the provinces," called an angry third. "They've overrun the Northeast."

"They're in Kompong Thom. My uncle lives there. They demand rice. They'll murder all Khmers."

Each voice was angrier. Each harsher, louder, more full of hate. The chant began again, "VIET NAM QUIT CAMBODIA!" Now fifteen thousand, now eighteen thousand strong, angry, in a culture that doesn't condone anger, angry in a culture where anger is equated with madness, angry, angrily surrounding the elegant colonial-building embassies.

"QUIT CAMBODIA!" Nang joined in the shouting. "OUT! OUT! VIET NAM OUT!" Nang worked his way to the gate. From his pocket he pulled a stone. About him, amongst the masses, monks assuaged the people as if they were sponges capable of absorbing anger. Nang cocked his arm, threw the stone as hard as he could. A window crashed. A split second of silence swept the demonstrators—then—as if the window were a dam, they gave physical vent to seventeen years of placating neutrality, seventeen years of being slowly devoured. Hell broke loose. Stones, branches, bricks from the walls were hurled. Windows on every side of both buildings were shattered. In pressed the masses, ripping shutters, crashing the doors, crossing the line, ransacking the embassies wildly in a frenzy of frustration and hate.

Nang fled.

"Did you *really* ask the Ma'dam for a commission to the Royal forces?" Thiounn asked Teck. Since the time his father had obtained a position for him in Phnom Penh Teck had not socialized with his old friends. Because of the escalating government crisis, his office had been closed. He'd returned to Neak Luong that morning, 18 March 1970.

"Of course not," Teck said defensively. "Louis started that rumor. He . . ."

"I did not." Louis laughed. He nudged Sakun and Kim and they chuckled with him. "Hey," Louis said, "this is just like old times, eh? Five of us. We can do anything with five of us."

"Let's go out," Thiounn said. "The cafe's open."

"I . . . ah," Teck mumbled. "When Vathana gets back, eh? She won't be long. You know, she's taken Samnang to the doctor."

"A commission and now a papa!" Thiounn chided him. "If we go now, we'll get our old seats."

Kim smirked. "I'd rather stay here and see that wife of his."

Louis rocked back into the cushion of the sofa. "If she were mine," he said, "I wouldn't let her out alone. Ha! Do you remember what he said before we saw her. 'Just a girl!' Ha! The rest of us should be strapped to that kind of just-a-girl."

"Loui—" Teck began, but a loud crash outside the apartment cut him short.

"This is a serious time," Sakun said somberly. "Really. We shouldn't joke now."

"Oh, Sakun!" Louis flopped a hand at him. "You always get so serious."

"You know what I hear . . . ?"

"More news of the riots, eh?" Teck said.

"There's been no paper for four days, but I hear anti–Viet Namese demonstrations have hit every city and town in the country. I hear people are ransacking and looting their stores. Even burning their homes."

"Maybe . . ." Thiounn said quietly, thoughtfully, ". . . they deserve it."

"Thiounn!" Kim reared back in his seat. "You! You, a social-ist, say that?"

"I . . . I said maybe, eh? You've read the government reports. I've seen some of the evidence. Truly, why are there so many—so deep in the country?"

"Did you read this?" Sakun picked up a 13 March newspaper from the coffee table before the sofa. " 'Prime Minister Lon Nol,' " he read, " 'has extended formal apologies to the North Viet Namese and the PRG for the embassy attacks. Simulta-neously, he and First Deputy Prime Minister Sisowath Sirik Matak have canceled the trade agreements between the govern-ment and the Viet Namese Communists which allow the Viet Namese to purchase food and supplies in Cambodia. The prime minister has also announced the closing of the port at Sihanoukville to Communist arms shippers; and he has issued an ultimatum to VC and NVA forces demanding they leave Cambodian terri-tory within seventy-two hours.' "

"Seventy-two—" Teck blurted. "That's impossible. How could they—"

"That's only part of it," Thiounn interrupted. "You haven't followed the news, eh? Before I left the capital I heard Lon Nol had put the army on alert—to prevent Sihanouk from . . . well, I don't know, exactly, what he could do from abroad . . . but, so Sihanouk won't block the cabinet's orders."

Kim started. "Thiounn, what do you mean? I haven't heard . . ."

"Well, you know . . ." Thiounn began.

"No. Tell us. What have you heard?"

Thiounn looked at his friends. All except Teck were seated about the coffee table in the living room of Teck's apartment. Teck stood by the window scanning the empty street for his wife and child. "You've really not followed the news, eh?" No one answered. "The Prince, you've heard this? He has threatened to have all the cabinet officers shot."

"What!?"

"Oh, yes. From Paris, three days ago. He said he was very embarrassed by the embassy attacks. Some say a unit of Khmer Serei, returned from South Viet Nam, was responsible for the ransacking. That the CIA and Lon Nol were behind it! Even two days ago, after Lon Nol apologized, Sihanouk said the cabinet had broken faith with him. They would be shot. That's why the army's on alert. I thought you knew."

"You're not serious," Louis said.

"Yes. You know he's flown to Moscow, eh? And that the National Assembly has been in special session. My father says they were going to pass a constitutional amendment limiting the monarchy, but that's when Oum Mannorine, Sihanouk's own brother-in-law . . ."

"He's a Viet sympathizer, eh?" Sakun inserted.

Thiounn nodded, continued. "Yes. Well, he tried to take over the government but Lon Nol foiled the coup. I think it will be in all the papers tomorrow. I can hardly believe you haven't heard any of . . ."

"Oum?! He tried a coup? A coup d'état?"

"Yes. Truly. But the general's men exposed him—his dealings with the Viets and his arm's and rice kickbacks. The Republicans are furious. Teck, don't you talk to your father? He must know. The government is coming apart."

"Then, Doctor, there is something . . ." Vathana could not complete her sentence. She sat in the small cluttered office, her torso curled forward, her shoulders sagging. Sophan stood near the door, her strong square legs planted like old trees, clutching the swaddled infant as if to protect it from the doctor's words.

"We'll have to wait," the doctor said. He was a middle-aged man, younger than her father by perhaps four or five years. "The brain is a marvelous instrument. It has great capacity for rejuvenation."

"I still don't understand."

"Well, it's hard to say for sure. I think what happened"—the doctor paused, leaned on his small desk, shifted some papers as if trying to find the right words lying between paper clips and medical journals—"I think . . . You understand I wasn't there at the birth . . . when the fertilized egg implanted in the uterus it lodged very low . . . very low. And in such a way, well, the placenta, the tissue which nourishes the fetus, developed across the cervix and that partially blocked the fetal descent."

A loud crash was heard from the street. Then shouting. Sophan tightened her grip on the infant Samnang. Vathana slumped further, shutting out the noise. Doctor Sarin Sam Ol jumped, then settled again. Shouting in Khmer and Viet Namese continued. Then the wailing of police sirens approaching from a distance.

"Riots again, eh? This is the seventh day. Where do they find any Viet shops left to destroy? Oh . . . Where was I? Fetal descent . . . It's a condition known as placenta previa . . . not really all that uncommon. At the end of your pregnancy when the cervix was very thin and beginning to dilate, the fetus was blocked from falling into the birthing canal. With the pressure on the placenta and the expanding cervix, the placenta ruptured. That's when the mother hemorrhaged and lost so much of her bloo . . ."

"I'm the mother, Doctor," Vathana whispered.

"Oh yes. Yes. I mean . . . I'm sorry. It's these riots and all the talk of war and corruption. My own sons were caught in the rioting. Last night as I was plunged in meditation a great explosion shook my house. Next door a Viet Namese doctor . . . a very compassionate man . . . his family has fled toward the border even though they have lived here for three generations."

"Our center," Sophan broke in unexpectedly, "is overflowing with Khmers the yuons have uprooted at the border."

"Yes. I've heard these things. Still, Doctor Truong was . . . is very decent."

"Then . . ." Vathana's voice was small.

"Then?" The doctor looked pitifully at the young mother clutching an amulet at her throat. "Then . . . for five hours . . . you understand, I wasn't there . . ."

"I understand."

". . . for five hours you bled. The fetus was increasingly starved for oxygen. His brain wasn't receiving oxygen. Had the medical team not forced you open and pulled the fetus out . . . neither of you would have lived."

"I live, Doctor. With sorrow, with misery, with grief. With despair for what I have done to my son's brain . . . It can rejuvenate . . . ?"

"Yes. We don't know how much. All that can be done is to wait and see. Someday . . . he may be almost normal."

As Vathana and Sophan walked back through the streets of Neak Luong they avoided the debris left from the week of rioting, avoided not only walking through or over piles but avoided the thought by immersing themselves in talk of the doctor.

"The first Noble Truth should not be that hardship and suffering are part of life," Vathana said softly, "but that they invade most quickly when life is most joyful."

"Angel." Sophan's smile and tone were perfectly consoling. "Don't desire him to be perfect and you won't suffer. Accept him for what he is. You'll see. He'll be more than you could ever desire."

"Perhaps in his last life he was perfect. Perfect he will be again in his next."

Sophan caressed the infant's head as they walked. The baby cooed softly, then snorted. "He's perfect now," Sophan said gleefully. Her eyes twinkled, her entire face lit in impish smile. "Ssshh." She touched Vathana's arm. Very quietly she whispered, "He's perfect now but don't let anyone hear. If the spirit of his previous mother knows, she'll be jealous."

When they entered the apartment Teck was standing before Vathana's desk staring up at the framed portrait of Prince Norodom Sihanouk. The volume of the radio on the refrigerator was turned up high. Thiounn, Kim and Louis sat quietly on the sofa. Sakun squatted by the coffee table. His face was distorted and he wept openly. The young men did not turn as the women entered.

Unknown to Thiounn, to Vathana, to them all, two days earlier, North Viet Namese and PRG officials had met with high Khmer officers to negotiate an NVA/VC presence on Khmer lands. Also unknown to them were the mixed messages Lon Nol was receiving from America and South Viet Nam.

"What . . . ?" Vathana began.

Teck tilted his head toward the radio. Again the Phnom Penh station repeated the announcement:

In view of the political crisis created in recent days by the chief of state, Prince Sihanouk, and in conformity with the constitution of Cambodia, the National Assembly and the Council of the Kingdom during plenary session held on 18 March at 1300 hours have unanimously agreed to withdraw confidence in Prince Sihanouk.

As of 1300 hours 18 March, Prince Sihanouk shall cease his function as chief of state of Cambodia. Mr. Cheng Heng, chairman of the National Assembly, is entrusted with the function of chief of state in conformity with the national constitution.

CHAPTER EIGHT

"Ain't no way, L-T. I got me a fine young woman waitin and I don't mean to disappoint her."

"I only said think about it, Conk."

"Yeah, but you say 'think' and we always end up doin." The American sergeant pushed his floppy bush hat to the back of his head. "I'm short. Down to sixty-six and a wake-up. That's it for me."

"It's a big city, Conklin," the lieutenant said. "Besides, you guys trained some of them Cambos. No more being stuck in a little corner of the Delta. No more Major Travis. Phnom Penh, Conk. We could be in Phnom Penh."

Lieutenant John L. Sullivan, 5th Special Forces, leaned forward in his chair in the small operations bunker. He had been an advisor to a Viet Namese provincial force for almost a year. He passed Ian Conklin the Ba Muoi Ba beer the two had been sharing.

"Those dudes are ripe for disaster," Conklin said. "Coup . . . new government . . . God! It's chaos. What do they have? The Khmer Serei? Two or three thousand U.S.-trained troops. Those guys are goina be like foreigners in their own country. They've been in Nam too long. Ya can't go back, L-T. Just because they hated Sihanouk . . . that ain't good enough. What else does this Lon Nol got? No, thanks."

"They're going to reach out to us, Conk," Sullivan said. The lieutenant took a deep breath. He raised his hands to his face, cupped his mouth and nose and exhaled into his palms. Then he wiped his hands back over his freckled cheeks and up through his coppery hair.

"Sure, L-T. Sure. While Nixon's cuttin back he's goina commit to takin on the Cambos. Even suppose authorization does come down"—Conklin shook his head—"ain't no way I'd get picked. Or I'd accept."

The two men sat in silence. The night was relatively cool though the humidity was high. A hiss came from the radio, the one a.m. situation report from the PRU, the breaking of the radio's squelch by the Province Reconnaissance Unit, an eighteen-man Viet Namese force the advisors often worked with.

Sullivan began again. "Their minds . . . ," he said, " . . . they'll have to be disciplined to induce the habits of patient investigation. You've seen it work here." The young lieutenant rubbed skin flakes from his sunburnt nose. "It can work there."

Conklin didn't answer. Again they sat in silence. Again Sullivan broke it. "You know what's going to happen?" Conklin looked over. "It's Nam, Conk. Nam 1960. Or '56." Sullivan was adamant, intense. "They'll go nuts. Make a mess of it. They've got to be trained to conquer haste, to work methodically at uncovering the infrastructure . . ."

"L-T, you're beatin on me again."

"Naw." Sullivan switched tone. "Am I?" He smiled broadly.

"It's like Quay says"—Conklin readjusted his hat—"unless the South drops about a hundred thousand troops on Hanoi, there ain't no way in West Hello we're ever goina stop the attacks. Infrastructure or not."

"That's it!" Sullivan snapped his fingers. He sat up straight. "Exactly." He tapped the desk before him. "Cambodia is the opportunity. We can knock on Mister Charlie's back door. Serve him eviction papers. Follow it up with proper police procedures. That's the winning combination."

Conklin chuckled. "Ain't nothin goina stop em unless there's the firepower to back it up."

Sullivan got up. "What about Huntley?" he asked. "He worked with the Serei."

"He can't speak it."

"You can?"

"No. Some. Re or Quay always interpreted."

"Hum."

"There's no way, L-T. It's total chaos."

"Let's make a way."

"No one ever even said we're goin in!"

"We're going." Sullivan clapped his right fist into his left palm as one might do with a baseball glove. "You bet yer sweet ass we're going. Now it's up to us whether that front gets the best, which is us, or some dipped-in-shinola Saigon desk jockey who doesn't know . . . who doesn't understand and who has no quantitative skills. No ability to apply the system. Where's Huntley?''

"He's on ambush with the PRU.''

"Prince Sihanouk is gone,'' Chhuon lamented to Hang Tung in private.

"A shame,'' Hang Tung answered.

"Yes, I suppose,'' Chhuon said. He was confused. Bewildered.

There was no chaos in Phum Sath Din. In three weeks of Khmer Viet Minh control, life had changed little. Information flow in and out of the village had been further reduced, and the land tenure system, said to be temporary, was in flux, but activities in homes, the market, the pagoda remained as before. What was happening in Paris, Moscow, Peking was unknown, but that had been of concern to only a very few. The radio announcement that the Cambodian National Assembly, all members of the Prince's own political party, had voted ninety-two to zero to withdraw confidence in the monarch, that the monarchy, the entire governmental system, had been deposed, shocked all. Yet they did not react, could not react, were not allowed to react.

Phum Sath Din, which had never known as much as a one-man police force now harbored an eighty-man platoon. And with Khmer Viet Minh entrenchment the NVA set up a new base camp and way station in the forest to the northeast. The village, which had never had a formal government other than a council of elders and a part-time administrator, now had overlapping tripartite committees: four encompassing the village quadrants for work and defense; eleven, one for each of the basic cells (*kroms*, or family groups, with ten to fifteen families per group), for political indoctrination and social change; plus a village central committee consisting of the newly appointed chairman, Cahuom Chhuon, the new vice-chairman, Ny Non Chan (of the village's traditional Ny family), and a committee "member" from among the new people, Hang Tung.

"Now we have the yuons to deal with," Chhuon said.

"Yes Uncle,'' Tung answered with appropriate concern. "But you will see, they're here to help us, to defend us.''

Suddenly Chhuon threw his arms into the air. "Defend us?!''

"You'll see, Uncle.'' Hang Tung paused to size up the older man. "There are riots and killings in the unliberated zones. People are butchered. But not here. Here, everything is better.'' Tung spoke with quiet conviction. "You and I will persuade the farmers, teach them, make them conscious of the need for political and social change. Peasants can no longer be passive. You'll see. Within a month, two at the most, the People's Liberation Army will free Phnom Penh."

Chhuon stared at Tung. His fists were clenched, his arms tense as if to throw a punch. "What are you saying?" he screamed. For a brief moment everything seemed clear. "The country's lost its head! And . . . and you talk of . . . of what army?!"

"Our army, Uncle." Hang Tung remained calm. "You and I shall raise an army."

"Tung"—Chhuon felt crazy, out of control—"the North Viet Namese are here! There's the army!"

"They're here to help us, Uncle," Hang Tung said. "And we'll help them. We'll help them win the confidence and affection of the people. You and I. We'll achieve a perfect understanding between the people and the army."

Chhuon shook his head violently as if the words were slime which couldn't be shaken off. His shoulders quaked, his knees seemed to swell, to ache. The army that had killed his son and daughter, that had taken his cousin, that moved through the country at will—that was yuon—and he, Cahuom Chhuon, was being asked, asked the evening of the day his king was ousted, to help that army, to raise an army to aid the element he most despised.

"You'll see, Uncle," Hang Tung assured him. "You'll see. Tomorrow we'll gather all the villagers at the pagoda. We'll tell them what has really happened. You must help me so no one is hurt."

The rally did not take place on 19 March, nor on the twentieth. The village was isolated. The people waited, unaware of the explosive forces released throughout much of the country, aware of Lon Nol's denunciation of their Prince, aware of some up-heavals, of rumors that the American CIA was behind the coup, but unaware of the riots, demonstrations and fighting between the NVA with their Khmer Viet Minh allies and the national (no longer Royal) army, or between the KVM and the Krahom, who had based much of their propaganda on Sihanouk's sellout to the Viet Namese. Phum Sath Din waited, isolated, cut off. Chhuon did not leave his house, nor did he allow Peou to leave. Sok and Chhuon's mother prepared extra food which they hid in the family bunker. Only Hang Tung came and went.

On 21 March a Khmer Viet Minh armed propaganda team entered the village. With the militia, they requested for military reasons, cajoled with patriotic phrases, then demanded, searched if necessary, and confiscated every radio from every home. Still

Phum Sath Din waited, more isolated, as if floating, a tiny community in flux, alone.

Late on the evening of the twenty-second, propaganda team members knocked respectfully on Chhuon's door. "Tomorrow, Uncle"—Hang Tung spoke for the team—"we will have a very large rally. Tomorrow everyone will come to the pagoda. You will see that no one is absent."

Chhuon nodded. He felt lost. There was no alternative, no place to run, no way to fight. "I'll do what I can," he answered.

"No, Uncle," a team member said. "You'll have everyone there. For their own safety, Uncle. The Americans are going to invade. They must know the escape plans."

Chhuon closed his eyes. "Everyone will be present," he said.

"It has been a long time since we spoke," the bonze said softly.

"Yes. Since my son was killed." The two men sat in predawn dimness on the floor in the small pagoda room where Chhuon had found the monk praying. Respectfully Chhuon had deposited the gifts of sugar, tea and canned milk he'd meant to bring almost two years earlier. Respectfully he'd waited until Maha Vanatanda finished his meditation.

After Maha Nyanananda was assassinated the spiritual leadership of Phum Sath Din fell to this younger monk. From him Chhuon sought the advice he'd been unable to bring himself to seek from his old teacher—unable because of embarrassment, because he had become lax in the years he'd worked as a rice trader and agronomist, because he had lapsed further in the time following the destruction of Plei Srepok.

"And in your heart you have harbored an anger?" Vanatanda asked.

"Yes." Chhuon's voice was low, sheepish.

"Has anger helped your son or you?"

"I, ah . . . n . . . no."

"Has it blocked you from attaining proper recourse?"

"I . . . Yes. Yes it has." For an hour Chhuon related to the monk his dream, the trip to the mountains, the military columns and all the events since. Then he said, "I no longer care for my home. The village, my life mean nothing. I renounce their value. I free myself from the pain of witnessing their destruction."

Maha Vanatanda said nothing.

"I renounce control of my life. I'm *their* mouth. I give up my life freely. Still, I'm not straight."

"You have come for instructions on calming your mind." The

monk's voice was compassionate, knowing. Chhuon nodded carefully. "You are very agitated."

Chhuon said nothing.

"Chhuon, when one gives in to worldly desires," the monk said, "there is no struggle, no fire, thus no process to transform the inner world into unity. But to renounce worldly desires for the sake of austerity, for pride in that austerity, for masochism, this is not the middle path. You may sacrifice all worldly desires to punish yourself but then you have not sacrificed your suffering. If you sacrifice all worldly desires to free yourself, you shall also sacrifice suffering. To suffer to show yourself, or to show others, that you can bear the suffering is merely to demonstrate one's attachment to one's self. Do you desire to show everyone how badly you've been hurt?"

"I don't know, Maha Vanatanda," Chhuon lamented.

"If you crave to demonstrate your pain, doesn't the desire create its own image and isn't the image an illusion? Hasn't the craving created the illusion?"

Chhuon dropped his head. "There is something else."

"Yes."

"They want me to lead the village."

"The new administrators?"

"Yes."

"They will pass."

"They say if one cadre is injured, ten villagers will likewise be harmed. If a cadreman is killed, ten villagers will die. They've even drawn up a list which tells the order in which villagers will be executed. You . . . I thought to escape to the forest, to join the maquis, but they say if I go one hundred people will be executed. You are first on the list."

The monk smiled. "I should be honored to be thought of so highly."

"Should I surrender to their demands?" Chhuon asked.

"When a tree falls on a man his knees buckle and he surrenders to its weight," Maha Vanatanda said. "This is a surrender which is not a surrender."

A wave of anguish flooded Chhuon's mind. Maha Vanatanda has not grasped what I say, he thought. Vehemently Chhuon said, "They hold us prisoner."

"Time passes," the monk said. "Do not be trapped in time. This authority will pass as have all others."

"We're being enslaved!" Chhuon was exasperated. "We're prisoners!" He tensed. His knees flared with pain, his stomach burned.

"We hold ourselves prisoners," the monk said. "If our bodies toil for them, then our bodies are enslaved, but we are not our bodies. If we let them convince our minds we are slaves, then they have enslaved us."

"But"—the heat rose, hit the back of Chhuon's throat—"if we don't recognize the prison or the guards, how can we escape?"

"From which prison, Chhuon, do you wish escape?" The monk paused. "Come to your center," he said gently. "Let your desires fall away." He closed his eyes. "I vow," the monk chanted quietly, "to become enlightened for the sake of all living things. Do you remember the vows?"

"It's . . . it's been a long time." Chhuon hesitated. He clenched his teeth.

"I will cut my ties to delusive passions," the monk chanted. Chhuon breathed deeply. He hesitated. The monk remained silent. Lowly Chhuon repeated the prayer. "I will open myself to the supreme way of the Enlightened One," the monk droned.

"I *will* open myself to the way of the Enlightened One," Chhuon said. He would try, he told himself.

"Listen. Trust your heart. If you are in doubt, listen more closely. Do not be your desires, but that does not say, 'Do not be.' If doubt persists, pause. Actions which are necessary will come to you."

From the street the blare of loudspeakers interrupted them. "Trust your heart," the monk repeated.

From the steps of the pagoda Chhuon saw two jeeps mounted with speakers, thirty, perhaps forty village militiamen, a dozen North Viet Namese soldiers wearing pins with the usual picture of Norodom Sihanouk, and scores of village children grasping for the Sihanouk buttons being freely distributed. Chhuon's brow furrowed. He inhaled deeply, exhaled, inhaled deeply, exhaled. Trust your heart, he repeated to himself. Trust your heart. Among the children were Khieng and Heng who had stripped Samnang of his pants so long ago. Chhuon stood on the top step, alone, watching the grasping horde grow to include young adults, middle-aged women, old men, all reaching out for the trinkets. For illusions, he thought. On the far side of the village street, unreaching, watching, was the orphaned Mountaineer boy, Kpa, who as a toddler had been brought to the village to live with and help a childless couple, Kpa who had defended Samnang at school so long ago. Chhuon stared into Kpa's distant face and saw the reflection of his own Kdeb, asleep, peaceful, without tension, without aggravation. Chhuon looked up past the overhang, through the trees into the overcast. I shall become enlightened . . .

". . . I have been odiously calumniated and dishonored by the Lon Nol group . . ." The voice of Norodom Sihanouk burst from the loudspeakers. On 19 March, Sihanouk had flown from Moscow to Peking where over the next four days he had conferred with Zhou Enlai, Pham Van Dong and representatives of the Pathet Lao, Viet Cong and Khmer Rouge (both the Khmer Viet Minh and the Khmer Krahom). On the twenty-third the Prince announced to the international press his assumption of the role of leader in absentia of a Communist front (FUNK, an acronym from the French for National United Front of Kampuchea) comprising Khmer Rouge, Viet Cong, NVA and Pathet Lao forces to "liberate Cambodia from the right-wing dogs of Lon Nol."

". . . my people have lost everything . . ."—the speakers blasted the recorded message to the villagers—". . . peace, dignity, independence, territorial integrity . . ."

Chhuon's mind stopped. On the moment of clarity a thick haze descended engulfing past, present and future.

". . . my people are immersed in the worst suffering, the worst misfortunes and the worst catastrophe in their history . . ."

Chhuon's mind bolted, searching the fog for the patch of blue; then, as in an inner chess game, he juxtaposed a hundred pieces in imagined scenarios, played out each move in seconds, then brooded. There was no escape. He looked for Kpa but the boy was gone. He thought of the small angel house before his home which had fallen into disrepair and thought of the steps needed to repair it.

". . . I can only hope for total victory of the revolution . . . for total defeat of the reactionary and pro-imperialist . . ."

"Uncle." Hang Tung joined Chhuon on the pagoda steps.

". . . the American imperialists will be beaten by the Viet Namese and our Khmer People's Liberation Army . . ."

"I'm very happy to see that you are already here."

"I'm here," Chhuon answered flatly.

"You left very early this morning."

"The village is large," Chhuon said. "There are many people now. The committee requires their presence, eh?"

". . . in my name . . . the establishment of the government-in-exile . . . the National United Front of Kampuchea . . ."

"Then you've notified everyone?" Hang Tung asked.

"I have sent word for all to be notified," Chhuon answered.

Hang Tung's lips parted into a thin smile. He watched Chhuon as Chhuon watched the crowd grow. He will obey, Hang thought. He is Khmer, he is Buddhist. Khmer Buddhists obey authority.

". . . in my name . . ."—the Prince's voice boomed from the speakers—". . . I call on all those of my children, compatriots, military and civilian, who can no longer endure the unjust oppression, join the Liberation Army . . . raise up and oust the pretender regime, the treacherous Lon Nol, his lackey Sirik Matak and their masters, the American imperialists . . . rise up before the Lon Nol clique massacres all . . . join the maquis . . . engage in guerrila warfare in the jungles against our enemies . . . the People's Army . . . patriotic volunteers will provide you with rifles and ammunition. You will be provided proper military training . . ."

"It is our destiny, eh, Uncle?" Tung whispered to Chhuon.

"Is it?" Chhuon hid a sneer. He offered a slight smile. My body, he thought, you can imprison my body.

"Yes." Tung smiled. "Now we are a village under Prince Sihanouk, loyal to the Prince, protected by our own army."

"This is very good," Chhuon said, hiding his sarcasm. He now knew that to disagree would be dangerous.

"It is up to us to shape the village, to unite it, to rid it of tyrants." Hang Tung's voice was smooth. "When the country is liberated all Khmers will unite."

Chhuon smiled, his face an actor's mask.

For nine days North Viet Namese and Khmer Viet Minh armed propaganda teams played tapes of Sihanouk's speeches and pleas in Phum Sath Din and in Viet Namese–controlled villages and cities from Bokor to Battambang, from Preah Vihear to Prey Veng. Sihanouk broadcast his appeals via Radio Peking, Radio Hanoi, Viet Cong Liberation Radio, and Khmer Viet Minh channels urging the Khmer people to join the revolution against the republican government. The pleas of Samdech Euv, Prince Father, ignited in the rural and urban poor uncontrollable fires. These speeches were the primary stimulus for the growth of the maquis throughout the nation. Sihanouk's words gave the Communists a cloak of respectability which they had never achieved through terrorism, conscription, or proselytizing. In Phum Sath Din, Khieng and Heng were the first of many to join up. They, like most of the nearly seventy thousand volunteers who joined the rebels over the next year, thought they were joining a new faction, the Khmer Rumdoah. They saw themselves as Royalist, not Communist.

When the world outside seems to be disintegrating a man likes to establish a solid calm within his own family. So it was that Pech Lim Song invited his second son and son's wife to dinner on the evening of 27 March, invited them on a dual pretext; first to show them his new home and second to discuss the new national situation and its demand for new business policies. Yet the true reason was he sought reconciliation with Teck.

"The house is marvelous, Mother." Teck twirled, waving an arm at the vaulted ceiling, the chandeliers, the rosewood balustrades guarding the second-floor balconies. He tapped his feet on the tiled floor. "Absolutely marvelous, Father," he said in French. "It must have cost a fortune."

The new home was a modest villa set on a forested rise (Madame Pech called it a hill) on Highway 15 a kilometer north of Neak Luong. In the ballroom the chatter was light, happy. A servant offered hors d'oeuvres, a band played traditional music on a sailing vessel–shaped bamboo xylophone to which even Sophan swayed gaily, clutching Mister Pech's infant grandson as if the baby were a dance partner. Vathana stood alone in the darkened dining room. Through the French doors she could see the dim lights of the city reflected on the rumpled bottom of the night overcast. To the east over Boeng (Lake) Khsach Sa, the surrounding swamps and paddies, and the small but growing refugee shantytown, the night was an impenetrable amorphous black wall.

"Cost is not your concern," Madame Pech retorted gaily. "Of course with the riel's devaluation, why, it's forty percent less now than when your father began . . ."

Vathana stepped to the dining room door, grabbed the door handle for balance, squeezed her eyes closed then opened them and stared into the night. This talk, this opulence, she thought, it's not Khmer, it's . . . but before she could complete the thought Pech Lim Song's voice carried throughout the villa. "Let's dine," he said cheerily.

Vathana turned toward the ballroom. Two servants were leading the family toward her. She reached up, massaged her forehead briefly, then, smiling, stepped toward her father-in-law as the lights opened refracting and sparkling from crystal stemware and chandelier. "Outside," she said pleasantly, "the night is as dark as it was in Phum Sath Din, and in here, it's as lovely as the sun on the river."

"Did you see the whole house?" Teck asked, not recalling her presence during his mother's tour.

"Every corner." Vathana smiled.

"*Vin, Madame?*" A servant offered her a filled glass from a tray.

"*Oui. Merci.*"

Teck raised his glass. "To your good fortune and the good fortune of your home, Father," he offered.

"To the good health of our family," Mister Pech rejoined.

Conversation through the six-course continental meal was stilted, limited to details of house construction and banal chatter about the infant, Samnang. For an hour Vathana sat, uneasy, sure the topic would fall to politics. When it did she felt relieved.

"I hope he doesn't return," Teck said almost whimsically.

"I'm surprised you feel that way," Mister Pech said.

"You were right, Father. Under Prince Sihanouk the country was weak."

"It was a feudal kingdom," Mister Pech said sadly. "Warlords, barons, each governor with his own fiefdom. The coup has brought a new era, an era of justice which will cleanse the system of feudal corruption. And yet . . . I . . ."

"You, Father?!" Teck smiled sympathetically.

"I'll miss him. I won't miss the corruption." Pech Lim Song listed some of the more glaring mistakes of Norodom Sihanouk. After each item he said, "And still he was the monarch," or "Yet still there was no amendment limiting his powers."

Teck responded with conciliatory interjections of "He was a bore," or "How I hated his films," or "Those endless radio speeches." Then Teck smirked, taunted his father, "But Father, you paid *bonjour* to everyone. It's the traders who caused the bribes."

Mister Pech glared at his second son, who now lowered his eyes, seemingly intent on the food. Madame Pech watched her husband. Vathana's chest tightened. She was about to say business was impossible without *bonjour* when Sophan, who had been in the kitchen with the servants, approached and whispered to her. Vathana smiled. "Oh yes," she said to Sophan. "Yes." "It will take a few minutes, Angel." Sophan bowed and left.

"Perhaps," Mister Pech said when Sophan was gone, "you're right. I wish it hadn't happened as it has. I wish he weren't humiliating himself and disgracing all Khmers with his Communist babble. *La sale guerre,* eh?"

Teck did not respond. Mister Pech tried to control his irritation but the absence of reaction made him seethe. "He was like a father," Pech Lim Song said, "but a father who, though he sees to their needs, keeps his children locked in separate rooms so they neither mature nor unite. Now that he's gone the feudal system will pass. The children will be free."

"Free?" Teck blurted. "To mature? Are they prepared for that?" He smiled to soften his words. "Is the army ready for Lon Nol's 'holy war'? Are they ready to drive out the 'evil ones'?

If the new father is also a child, can the children become adults? Are *you* ready for it, Father?"

"I'm prepared to do what must be done," Mister Pech said flatly.

Lightly Teck slapped the table. "Father! The country still has a feudal regime."

"No," Mister Pech said firmly. "It has passed. The National Assembly's given only emergency powers to the prime min . . ."

"Sisowath Sirik Matak and Lon Nol!" Teck said the names as if they were an accusation.

"Yes," Mister Pech said. "Your mother's a Sisowath. This is good, eh?" Mister Pech cited the attributes of each man, then named other statesmen and listed their good deeds.

Teck countered each. "They instigated the coup . . . A bumbler. . . . He's of the old order. . . . He's as corrupt as Samdech Euv."

"Bumbling! Corrupt! Do you think anyone can come in"—he clapped his hands—"like that! Take over like that! Without difficulties! Certainly, they scramble for support. I've been assured Lon Nol has even sent the Prince a private memo requesting his return, asking him to assist in expelling the Viet Namese."

"Father"—Teck shook his head—"not one of those men has the intelligence, honesty or ability you have. If you ran the country, maybe there would be a chance for real reform. But you don't. You stop short of involving yourself. We've only traded one king for another, *and* this one, he's suspended the Bill of Rights. Now they arrest whomever they please."

"At least he's not aiding the Communists. He's not leading the Viet Namese takeover."

Vathana put her hand over her husband's. She had been silent during much of the discussion. Now, with the security of belief in her opinion, she said emphatically, "Under Prince Sihanouk our shelter was ignored by the government. In nine days of Lon Nol we have been requested to file forms for assistance. All month new refugees have come to us. They've been bombed and attacked by Viet Namese."

"They're bombed by Americans." Teck jerked his hand from under his wife's, embarrassing her.

"The rivermen feel safer, too," Vathana said. "If they call for help, someone responds."

"As Lon Nol says," Pech Lim Song said, bitterness creeping into his voice, "Sihanouk is a demon sent by the king of hell to destroy Buddhism."

"Lon Nol is an American agent." Teck did not disguise his anger.

"Well." Madame Pech laughed. She tapped her long finger-nails nervously on the table. "All we can really do is sit and wait to see what the Americans do, eh? If they decided to, eh? they could line up shoulder to shoulder on the western border and march east consuming everything like locusts. Or march east to west? Which is it? They do surround us, don't they, *mon cher?* Thailand and Viet Nam *are* their satellites . . . just as the Communists claim. Oh dear!" Madame Pech turned to her daughter-in-law. "I must admit though, I would love to meet some Americans. What about you, Vathana? I understand in Saigon they throw the most extravagant parties."

Softly Teck said, "Mother!"

"I mean with you, of course, dear. Just think of their wealth. Oh"—Madame Pech switched from French to English, which neither her husband, the young couple nor the servants under-stood—"to be as rich as an American!"

"You'll do well with an American presence," Teck said, ignor-ing his mother's foreign phrases. "They always bring lots of money."

"Then you also shall do well, husband," Vathana said. Her face was calm but inside she was tense, angry—deeply angry still at this man for his heroin slumber the day she couldn't wake him, the day she had nearly bled to death. "We're in the same business as your father."

"Talk of war and politics . . . it's such a bore." Madame Pech stopped the conversation. "Let's talk, instead, of wine."

"What is it, Mother?"

Aside to Vathana Mister Pech said, "There's South Viet Namese and American escorts on the Mekong. And there's talk of addi-tional American assistance."

"What!?" Teck yelped. Both Vathana and Mister Pech looked at him, alarmed. "American . . ."—he clapped his hands for emphasis exactly as his father had. From his throat burst a nervous titter—". . . Lon Nol's invited them, eh?"

"Better the Americans than the yuons," Mister Pech said.

"It was the CIA behind the coup," Teck snapped. "Better them!?"

"It wasn't the Americans," Mister Pech snapped back. "They supported the Prince. He'd moved much closer to them. This departure upsets the balance they established along the border."

"That's why it took them only hours to announce their back-ing for Lon Nol."

"More likely the Soviets and their Hanoi clients were behind it. That's who's benefiting."

"That's who's bene . . . !? The national army is seizing all Viet-owned property." Teck's voice cracked. "That's who's benefiting."

"Still, better we align ourselves with America than with Communists."

"Better neither," Teck said bitterly. "Agh, Viets are only Asian Americans. They're both expansionists. Both believe their culture's imposition on anyone is a gift. Both are organizers, and followers of organizers! Agh!" Teck shook his fists before him like a little boy in a tantrum. "Why should I care if Americans or Viet Namese come!? Why? I should care only to kill both, to free myself and our land."

"Humph!" Mister Pech scoffed. "How many yuons, or Americans, can you and that Louis kill from the cafes? Someday"— Pech Lim Song turned to Vathana—"he will grow up. Someday he will be like me."

At that moment Sophan reappeared with the infant, freshly bathed and swaddled for warmth. Talk ceased. The aroma of Tiger Balm salve wafted through the room. The infant cooed, gurgled. Vathana smiled. Mister Pech's eyes shined. "Watch," Sophan said proudly. She loosened the blanket, nudged an arm out and placed a bamboo rattle in Samnang's hand. The baby clumsily clutched it in a stiff hand then fiercely whipped it up and down and laughed an infant's high-pitched snorting laugh.

As the grandfather clapped, his first servant came from the hallway. "Sir." The old man bowed. "There's important news on the radio. Poland has closed its embassy and in Kompong Cham two demonstrators have been shot."

"Bring it here."

"Wouldn't it be wise," Madame Pech addressed the table as the butler went for the radio, "*not* to take sides? If the Royalists return, we'll live as before. If Lon Nol succeeds, well, so much the better. And if the Communists are victorious, you, my dear husband, should think of becoming commissar of transportation." Madame Pech paused. She winked at her son, returned to her husband. "You do have contact with the Communists, don't you, dear?"

Mister Pech did not answer. Vathana's smile at Samnang's antics drooped. Teck chuckled. "The Viet Namese call it *attentisme*. Fence sitting. Ha! I should have known."

"It may be prudent"—Madame Pech's voice was a sweet whisper—"to provide a little support to all sides, eh?"

"Here, sir," the butler said, placing the Japanese transistor radio before the head of the house and adjusting the dial.

". . . such a demonstration was, we are certain, the work of the Viet Cong who are masters of this kind of thing . . ."

"Who's speaking?"

"A government spokesman, sir," the servant replied.

". . . incited by the Viet Cong, the demonstrators sacked the courthouse, the provincial offices. Several trucks were stolen. Some of the demonstrators approached to within three kilometers of Phnom Penh . . ."

"Three kilometers of the capital!?"

"I didn't hear that before, sir. Only that a six o'clock curfew is now in force and that the army intercepted the demonstration."

". . . all patriots, especially the people of Kompong Cham, keep cool heads and remain calm . . . the army has been instructed to crush any further demonstrations . . ."

"Is that all?" Mister Pech asked as program music followed the announcement.

"Isn't that enough?" Teck said lowly.

"The government has announced the mobilization of all former servicemen," the servant answered. "Veterans are to report for duty. Sir, you're a former serviceman, aren't you?"

"I'm too old. What else did they say?"

"They said thirty-six hundred Communist soldiers are advancing on Phnom Penh. That they incited the riot. National assemblyman Trinh Hoan reported three Viet Cong columns of a thousand each have advanced to within fifty kilometers of the capital. All from the Northeast, sir. Plus six hundred from the Southeast. And sir, there is other news on VC Liberation Radio."

Mister Pech carefully rotated the tuner until the dial lined up with a mark he'd made earlier.

". . . we denounce the South Viet Namese attack into Kandal Province, which has killed fifty-three innocent people, as a heinous crime of war against the Khmer people . . ."

"Kompong Cham, Kandal, Phnom Penh," Vathana murmured. "We're surrounded by fighting."

". . . we warmly hail and actively support Norodom Sihanouk's plan to build a liberation army to overthrow the Lon Nol regime . . ."

"It . . . it will never reach us," Teck whispered.

". . . reports reaching this station from Kompong Cham say thirty thousand patriotic Cambodian workers and peasants bravely resisted Lon Nol's lackey army and liberated much of that city, even in the face of troops with heavy weapons raking the people with gunfire . . ."

*   *   *

"We"—Met Sar smashed his pudgy hand down hard causing papers and maps to leap from the table—"*we* are the rightful benefactors of the coup." Again he smashed the table. He leaped up. "It must be ours." In the empty warehouse his shout sent a whiplash of spittle slashing across the floor. "The exact stinging red ants against whom the coup was staged . . . the crocodiles . . . they profit because we are not properly organized."

He strode left, right. He stopped before a wall map of Kompong Cham then before a poster of Mao, stopped staring like a rabid rodent into Mao's eyes, swishing away, huffing so angrily as to choke on his words before the first syllables escaped his spit-wet lips. "Yuons!" Sar exploded. "Ingrates! Ally, humph!" He spun, crouched, as if ready to grapple with the first thing that moved. "North Viet Namese and lackey Khmer hooligans brainwashed in Hanoi! *Why!?*" He sat. Banged both fists on the report-strewn table. "Because they've got microphones. They've got speakers. They've got buttons!"

Met Sar untied the krama from his neck, wiped beads of anger-sweat from his high forehead. "That vindictive *anoupra-cheachon*, that subhuman king-father, Samdech Euv, siding with the very scum that led the coup, willing to destroy the country for his own vengeful pride." Met Sar cleaned his lips and chin of saliva, his eyes of tears, his hands of moisture he found odious. He straightened the table, his tunic, his hair. At the door he calmly said to an aide, "Fetch the agents. Keep the Chams in the bunker. This isn't for them."

Thirty-five air miles from the border, Kompong Cham (City of the Chams) held Southeast Asia's highest concentration of the ethnic remnant of the Kingdom of Champa, an Islamic-Hindu state which had flourished along the South China Sea until an expanding Viet Nam had wiped it out in fourteenth- and fifteenth-century city-by-city genocidal attacks. Throughout the late 1950s and into the sixties Kompong Cham was turbulent. A strong, if disorganized, Cham autonomy movement had been held in check by a ploy of Norodom Sihanouk and his Royal manipulators. They offered the ethnic masses meaningless local sovereignty while covertly prosecuting rising individual leaders who espoused ethnic unity. The Prince's image amongst the Chams had been that of a benign dictator, a benevolent protector who held in check the ruthless ethnic Khmers. Yet despite that image, the Chams lived in fear. To counterbalance superior Khmer numbers, they entered into an informal alliance with the Communist Viet Namese, whose long-established encampments in the surrounding forest impeded Khmer domination. Though the best-educated Chams (and Krahom and Khmer Viet

Minh proselytizers) had been aware of Sihanouk's ploy, prior to the coup they had been unable to sustain a movement amongst the Cham people. With Sihanouk's ousting, fear of ethnic Khmers increased. When government troops pulled down the last Sihanouk posters, the Chams, along with many local Khmers, went wild.

Met Sar rose like a prophet before the rank of agents. The Center had ordered him to come to Kompong Cham, to take direct command of the Krahom operatives, to infuse the nationalistic movement with a sense of urgency. Over the years, the Krahom had patiently built an extensive network of spies and proselytizers, yet here, in ten days of post-coup strain—ten days in which the NVA and the Khmer Viet Minh had overtly taken control of fully forty percent of the country, contested thirty percent and threatened what remained—even his closest and most trusted agents were cracking, turning.

Met Sar surveyed the agents with cool passion. A third, mostly older men, wore net masks to keep their identities secret; a third, mostly young men and women, stood boldly; a third, mostly boys trained on Pong Pay Mountain, stood armed.

"The Chams," Met Sar said in a fatherly voice, "are a river. The power of their flow is unstoppable yet the direction of the flow is controllable. Accommodate yourselves to their power while you struggle to direct the flow. Move rapidly before others establish levees. Only we have the good interests of Kampuchea in our hearts. *We*, not new government functionaries, not alien invaders. Do not group us with the Communists. We alone are the nationalists."

Met Sar paused. He stepped lightly to the first file and with his pudgy hands warmly grasped the hands of a masked agent. He moved down the line squeezing each man's or woman's hands in a bond of fidelity to the cause, the Movement. As he embraced his followers he said, "For each of you there are buttons with the portrait of Norodom Sihanouk. Flow with the river, lead the river, do not fight its power. Denounce anyone who denounces Sihanouk!"

"Denounce?" a young woman gasped.

"It is essential," Sar said so all could hear, "that everyone be conscious of the purpose of the riots. Lower the riverbed in the direction of desired flow. Let the Viets lower it where our desires are the same. They will try to move their people into key positions. They will try to conscript the young. We will use the same tools but at the last we will snatch away the prize."

As Sar worked the second row an armed yothea hissed, "They are pitiful snakes."

"Don't underestimate the yuons," Sar said. "Exploit their strength and we will achieve promising successes. Without us, their actions constitute a foreign invasion. They have accelerated their Campaign X, already proceeding throughout the nation. They invoke Sihanouk's name while they launch attacks against national forces. In the North, in the Northwest, their aim is to occupy as much territory as possible, to expand their so-called Khmer Viet Minh revolution. In the East and Northeast their goal is to protect and further entrench their supply lines and sanctuaries. They have pulled four divisions from duty in the South for combat in our fatherland. Do not underestimate them!

"With us, their actions become civil war. Lead them as well as the people. The regime must be destroyed. Then all enemies shall be crushed and we shall establish a true and pure nation of Khmer and Cham."

Met Sar's voice was soft, fervent, as if he alone possessed truth. He continued to the last man in the last line. There he stood before Met Nang. "We are the sole authentic representatives of Cambodia's people." Met Sar grasped Nang's hard hands. "Urge the people to demand their civil rights, to intensify their efforts in the name of the revolution. Whisper to them . . . tell them Hanoi sees the ousting as a rare opportunity to force the political collapse of Kampuchea. Tell those who are ready to hear that many NVA units, under the control of COKA—why should they have a Central Office for Kampuchean Affairs?— tell them Le Duc Anh, who heads COKA, tell them Le Duc Tho, who directs the Central Kampuchean Affairs Commission of the Viet Namese Communist Party's Central Committee, tell them these men have ordered their military units to focus on Cambodian targets. Tell them Hanoi exploits the Prince."

"What should we tell them of the bombings?" Nang's voice, like his hands, was hard.

"The bombings?" Met Sar was caught off guard.

"The American dogs are bombing more and more along the border. They extend the bomb line . . ."

"How far?"

"Sixteen kilometers into the interior. The yuons are using it in their propaganda. They're telling the people Americans are invading."

"Float in the river, Nang." Met Sar returned to the front of the room. "If the flow is strong, accommodate yourselves to it. It can only embarrass the Phnom Penh puppets to invite the imperialists. People will rush to join us." In the back row Nang twinkled under Sar's mention of him by name.

"We must struggle to serve the people," Sar continued. "Struggle to serve the revolution, to stimulate the contradictions of the feudal system, to establish the peasant-worker alliance. We must gain momentum, retake the leadership of the maquis. The people, only the people, can shape the course of our future."

The streets of Kompong Cham were littered with debris from the riots of 27 March yet the refuse was but a pitiful precursor of what was to come.

Nang squatted at the edge of a mob of two thousand. Quietly he snatched the pant legs of boys he felt he could influence. From outlying areas, from urban hovels, from the best homes, farmers dropped their hoes, fishermen left their nets, tradespeople abandoned their work and merchants their wares. First a thousand, then three, five, ten, pouring, again, into the streets, again, rising like the tide. Twenty thousand, thirty, Khmer and Cham, finally by midafternoon a floodtide of forty thousand people joyfully, tearfully waving placards of Norodom Sihanouk, chanting his name as they milled about the center of town. Then they broke, erupted, violently looted any home, any business without Samdech Euv's face displayed.

"Here, Brother, a button for you. Come with us."

"Eh?"

"Join us," Nang said. "You too, Brother. Come with me."

"Who are you?"

"Forget that kid. Come on. There's a government house in the next block."

"Let him go," Nang said to the first. "Come with us. Lon Nol's brother is near."

"Forget him. He's crazy." The two ran off with the mob.

About Nang thirty boys had gathered. "Are there riches?" one asked. He wore a white collarless shirt, like all Cham males, and a green and white checked turban. Others spoke quickly—six, eight, ten at once. "How can we do it?" "Is he sure?" "He's Khmer." "He favors Sihanouk." "I'm going to ride a Honda." "Why not?" "He says he can give us guns. I don't like that." "I do!"

"We'll use the guns," Nang said, "to smash the feudal apparatus and destroy the running dogs."

"How?" the boy with the checked turban asked. "We know nothing of fighting."

"One learns warfare through warfare." Nang smiled satanically.

"You know warfare?" a boy of sixteen challenged.

"I can teach you how to set explosives," Nang answered. His eyes gleamed. "I've blown up Viet Namese trucks, American tanks."

"Yeah, sure you have," the older boy mocked. "Come on," he said to the others. "We're missing the march."

Another older boy demanded, "Where are these guns?"

"He doesn't have any," the first said. "Come on!"

The older boys ran off to the main demonstration leaving the youngest, the most pliable, and the boy with the checked turban. Nang ached. Easily, he thought, I could have ripped out the older one's throat. That would show them all.

The nine-, ten- and eleven-year-olds followed Nang. They were small, so small that when Nang brought them to his cache of clubs the sticks seemed long and unwieldy in their hands. "You said guns," the boy with the checked turban snapped.

Nang could not hold back. He expanded before the boys, the chameleon transforming from ratlike urchin to apelike yothea, shedding the stoic exterior he had maintained at the earlier rejection, revealing to his charges piercing resentment, ready to pulverize the next challenger. "We're here to transform the country," Nang seethed. He raged hysterically about CIA and NVA collusion, about rightful benefactors. He warned his recruits of Viet Namese "sophisticated lying techniques." He told them stories of American atrocities.

"Now," he ordered, "follow me! We'll join the others."

Seven hundred strong, a battalion formed by forty agents, they merged with the mob, pushed the mob toward the new governor's house and set it ablaze, marched the mob to the government offices where civil servants either fled, rallied to the rebel side or were beaten to death. Students and teachers, blamed for Sihanouk's ousting, were hunted, dragged down, executed.

Attempting to escape, Lon Nil, brother of the new head of state, was captured and dragged by the feet behind his sedan, dragged over the rough roads as angry demonstrators kicked and stomped his broken body. Before the governor's house Nang lunged at the body. His small platoon surrounded him, cordoned off the area. From beneath his shirt Nang pulled a bayonet. Immediately he sliced the official's belly, then reached in, hacking at tissues and organs until he, Nang, held the liver, the seat of the human soul, high above the corpse.

"Follow me." Nang sprung through the cordon, his band trailing him, a merry snake dance to a roadside cafe.

"Cook it!" Nang ordered a quaking vendor. "Cook it!" the boys shouted. Nang leaped behind the stand, slapped the organ on the hot grill. The liver seared noisily. Nang shoved the vendor aside, slashed maniacally at the smoking meat. Then he scooped it onto a tray and darted amongst his boys distributing chunks to be eaten.

From the mob, "To Phnom Penh. To Phnom Penh." Wild chanting. "Long Live Samdech Euv!" Frantically, cars, buses, trucks, motorcycles were commandeered. For four hours, as the city smoldered, a manic mob fled, a ragtag convoy, a ten-mile-long column of enraged citizens parading by the city's inert west army garrison.

Two hours before midnight the column crossed into Koh Ky twelve miles from Phnom Penh. There the national military finally reacted. First the high screams then the explosions, 105mm howitzer shells rained down on the people. Then the horrible, loud growling T-28s strafed them. The multitudes scattered leaving sixty dead on the road. From Kompong Cham, finally with orders, west garrison soldiers caught the tail of the column. They drove into the stragglers, shooting, killing ninety, arresting hundreds. Nang gathered his shocked recruits, led them through paddies into the forest. The boy with the checked turban was dead.

Sullivan could not sit. Nor could Huntley. Conklin was hunched by the radios with his Viet Namese counterpart, Re. He was flipping through a three-week stack of newspapers and magazines he'd received that morning from his father. Major Travis, Quay and Lieutenant Hoa sat at the small field desk in the operations bunker perusing the stack of reports. Re adjusted the tuner for reports in Khmer. Takeo City, the provincial capital of Takeo Province, only twenty miles from the border, twenty-two miles from their position, was under heavy NVA attack.

"God damn it! Sit down, Sullivan." Major Travis wanted to sound as if he'd risen to the occasion.

"I can't," Sullivan snapped.

"Sit down," Travis snapped back. "We're all antsy. That damn pacing only makes it worse."

"How many have come in?" Sullivan stood between Lieutenant Hoa and Sergeant Quay. There were no more chairs.

"Many," Quay said. His voice was high-pitched. "A forty t'ousand."

"We must have ten thousand in our own compound," Travis said. "It's like a goddamned pipe burst. We're being absolutely inundated."

"Boy, those bastards are good," Sullivan said. He wiped a hand over his face, then through his hair. "Those Commie bastards're rolling that country up like ..." He snapped his fingers three times.

Huntley laughed. He lumbered toward the table. "Not accordin ta them, L-T," he said. "I seen the news. They still say they ain't got no units in ol' Cambo. No designs on the country."

"I knew it." Sullivan smacked his right fist into his left palm. "I told Conklin a month ago. A mess. They'd make a mess."

"And you wanted me ta go," Conklin piped up. "Me, thirty-three and a wake-up, with a fine young woman waitin. Hey, listen to this. 'The Vietnam Moratorium Committee, a leading antiwar organization, citing President Nixon's April 21 announcement that 150,000 more U.S. troops will be withdrawn by April 1971, has disbanded and closed its doors.' "

"They need our help," Sullivan said.

"Who?" Conklin looked up from his papers.

"The Cambodians," Sullivan said as if Conklin had gone off his track. "They're the key to the war, but without us . . . Damn! They're attacking Viet civilians, running from the NVA. They've got to be turned around. They need advisors."

"That's exactly what this report says." Major Travis flipped a few pages. " '. . . in the event negotiations . . .' "

"Na-go-tiations," Quay injected. "Humph!"

" '. . . fail, the NVA / VC will support the Khmer Rouge in guerrilla attacks against Lon Nol's . . .' No, that's not it. Wait one." Travis paged through the document. "Here it is. 'The NVA is in a position to collapse Phnom Penh and turn all Cambodia into enemy territory. Communist forces have taken or threaten sixteen of nineteen provincial capitals. They have cut, permanently or temporarily, every major road, rail line and waterway to Phnom Penh. If the President does not respond immediately, the Cambodian domino will fall.' "

"Back to square one," Sullivan said. "November '65. Back to the first battle of the Ia Drang. Shit!"

For an hour the men reviewed reports of Cambodian riots and battles. Antigovernment riots on 19 and 23 March, Prey Veng and Takeo provinces. Suspected VC instigation. Anti–Viet Namese riots in every major city. How would this affect South Viet Nam? Racial animosity was already high. This added a new, tangential dimension to the anti-Communist war. On 27 March three thousand NVA regulars attacked the Cambodian town and garrison of Svay An Dong in Prey Veng Province; other NVA units hit Prek Chrou in Kratie Province; and South Viet Namese Rangers, on their first cross-border assault (1.8 miles) raided a 300-man NVA camp at Vinh Xuong in Kandal Province, killing fifty-three enemy. On 29 March, NVA units again assaulted Cambodian army outposts along the southeastern border. The next three days, in conjunction with Cambodian national forces and with American tactical air support, ARVN units engaged major elements of the NVA 5th and 7th divisions near Mimot and Snuol and the VC 9th Division (consisting of ninety-five percent Northern replacements) along Cambodian Highway 7. More ARVN forays occurred on 4 and 5 April. More NVA attacks hit Cambodian towns: on the sixth, Chipou in the Parrot's Beak; on the ninth, FANK (the French acronym for Forces Armée Nationale Kampuchea, the government's forces) totally abandoned Svay Rieng Province to the NVA; on the nineteenth, Cambodian forces relinquished Saang in the heartland, closer to Phnom Penh than to the border; on the twenty-first Snuol fell as did several towns in Siem Reap Province in the far west, more than two hundred miles from Viet Nam. The North Viet Namese consolidated their total hold on Svay Rieng Province and their partial hold on Kampot, Takeo, Kandal, Prey Veng, Kompong Cham and Kratie provinces—adding those areas to the provinces of Ratanakiri, Mondolkiri and most of Stung Treng. In all areas where NVA units were reported to have seized district towns, they had allegedly expelled Khmer peasants and taken control of roads and waterways. In addition, manpower and materiel buildup estimates showed "the largest manpower move thus far of the Indochina war."

In response the ARVN launched its first significant thrust into Cambodia, Operation Toan Thang ("Total Victory") 41. From 14 to 18 April, two thousand South Viet Namese soldiers attacked NVA sanctuaries in the Angel Wing area, one mile from the border. On the twentieth, the ARVN again crossed the border (three miles) into Svay Rieng Province.

"That's not support for Cambodia," Sullivan said.

"No?" Lieutenant Hoa was surprised at Sullivan's comment.

"We're just extending our buffer zone," Sullivan said. "This isn't going to shore up Mister Lon's government."

"What do you want us to do?" Major Travis said.

"Exactly what our team does here," Sullivan said.

"Hey," Conklin broke in. "Here's a good one. 'Senate Democratic leader Mike Mansfield is leading the opposition to any extension of American military aid, *no matter what the form*, to Cambodia.' Let's see. 'Other opposition to Lon Nol's appeal comes from Senators Frank Church of Idaho and John Sherman Cooper of Kentucky.' Ah, Cooper . . . Cooper-Church . . . seeking a congressional ban on U.S. soldiers in Cambodia . . ."

"You've got to be kid—" Sullivan began.

"America wants much to go—" Hoa also began.

But Conklin continued, "'. . . a prohibition similar to one passed last year regarding Laos and Thailand.'"

"Sir," Sullivan addressed Major Travis. "When American advisors go into Cambodia, I want to be with the first team."

The team leader looked up into Sullivan's face. Before he could respond, Ron Huntley said, "Me too, sir."

The week-long early burst of monsoon rains broke and the evening air was no longer oppressive. Sophan squeezed the infant tightly to her bosom as the gawking mob pressed them against the piling at the end of the pier. "Please." Vathana used her back and shoulders to push back against a teenage boy. "Please! You'll force us into the river."

An hour earlier the pier had been deserted and only the chattering of river birds and the imposing beauty of the jacaranda trees thick with deep blue-red flowers had diverted their attention from the serenity of the Mekong. The two women, the slight young mother and the older, stocky wet-nurse, sat touching, holding each other's arms, massaging the infant's legs and arms, breathing full breaths of air as if they'd been locked away in a dank cellar and only just released—the younger woman pouring out her trepidations as the sun dropped into smoke-gray overcast, its rays first streaking through cloud clefts, then bursting like fire, refracting from the cloud base, glistening off leaves and buildings, barges and cross-river swamps, glittering like glass shards on the rippling surface of the brown river.

"We're an island now," Vathana had whispered. Her preoccupation with the events of the past month obscured her vision of the spectacular scene unfolding. "Worse. More like the over-crowded life raft of a sinking ocean vessel."

Sophan answered tenderly. "Yes Angel. An island. A lifeboat. An outpost. With Svay Rieng abandoned the front is less than twenty-five kilometers away. How can one trust that Lon Nol?"

"Sophan, the refugees. I can't keep up with them. Every day more. I can't even count them."

"Must they be counted?"

"Yes. It's the only way to get them food."

"What does your husband say? Oh. Look up there. All those birds."

"Like always. He says it won't reach us. The army, he says, is very strong at protecting enclaves. Enclaves! That's what we are. He says each day the army becomes larger. Seventy thousand have volunteered."

"Do you see the birds, Angel?"

Upriver, in the distance, a massive flock of gliding black dots circled and swooped. "Yes," Vathana said. "Mister Pech says if the Communists try to take any major cities, the Americans will come to our aid. Yet even now the Viet Cong hold the river-banks. I don't dare sail the barge."

"What's floating up there?"

Vathana strained to see the upriver flotsam or debris but could only make out a blackish gray clog in the brown water. She told Sophan of the most recent refugees as the wet-nurse cuddled the baby, cooed softly to him so his mother's fears would not be sensed and frighten the child. Vathana shook her head slowly. "I don't know what to believe," she said. "Some of the rice farmers say the Viet Cong expelled them. Some say they fled terrible bombings. Some want to help the Khmer Rouge. Some want the army to kill all the Viet Namese. Sophan . . . Sophan, you're so compassionate. I don't know what I'd do without you."

"Or I without you, Angel."

Vathana shook her head. "It becomes more difficult to buy rice just when we have more refugees to feed."

Suddenly Sophan shook. Her arms became rigid, her neck spasmodic. A shudder transformed her soft face into a ghoulish mask.

"Everywhere people say the North Viet Namese have set a course to capture Phnom Penh. . . . Sophan! What is it?" Vathana lifted the baby from the older woman's frozen hands. "Sophan!"

"I . . . I don't know." The spasm passed, leaving her limp. Along the street, at the upriver levees and piers, from the market stands with their geese and fish and vegetables, a hush, then a cackle, a hush, then a building commotion.

Vathana saw people surging toward the first pier. She heard unintelligible shrieks. She clasped Sophan's thick right hand with her delicate left as she hugged the infant. Squawking birds thick as swarming gnats swirled toward them as the grayblack clog floated closer. Youngsters sprinted down the pier to get the best view as the mass approached. Behind them, young adults then younger children and middle-aged women, and behind them like a final wave the old men, mostly refugee peasants, and the old women, a thousand in all pushing onto the pier, those in back surging, forcing those in front to the very edge, against the tops of the pilings driven into the river muck supporting the old wooden pier.

"Please!" Vathana repeated. She had handed her baby back to Sophan and was now trying to protect both from the mind-less wall of flesh. "Go in front! Let us out!" Vathana's voice was firm, authoritative, yet it was lost in the mass of tittering, jostling people.

The last of the sun was upon the water and the clog. Vathana's mouth slackened. A hush fell over the front of the mob though those behind continued their noisy positioning. Below her, bumping the piling at the water surface, out across the main channel and still coming from upriver like a single fetid swollen blob, eight hundred bodies, the mob-executed Viet Namese men of Chrui Changwar, hands tied behind their backs, heads with faces, sides or backs blown off, floating lashed together like a raft of meat logs. Vathana tried to close her eyes. Yet her face drained of energy. She stared. Bodies bloated with decomposition gasses hissed at her, at all the gawkers, as they slowly spun in the current. Open-eyed corpses stared at her with gray fogged orbs glistening as riverwater lapped the faces then trickled like tears back into the Mekong. Naked bodies, bellies so swollen that genitals disappeared as if swallowed by giant expanding balloons, sickened her. Gaping jaws frozen in death fears flashed broken-toothed fiendish smiles at her. A body's leg snagged the piling against which the two women were pressed. For a moment it seemed as if the entire jam would stop. Then the pressure of the other bodies in the current overcame the snag. The legs stretched apart until the body ripped at the hip and anus and the regatta from hell, reviewed unwillingly by young mother and old wet-nurse, floated on.

"Blessed One"—Vathana squeezed the Buddha statuette on the chain about her neck—"be compassionate." The mob pressure ceased as those at the back scurried toward downriver piers to view that which they ever after would wish they'd never seen. "Compassionate One," Vathana whispered as she removed the necklace, "bless us. Enchanted One"—she placed the amulet about her son's neck—"what is to happen?"

"I can't fucking believe it," Sullivan said. "One more fucker fuckin em in one more fuckin way." He had gotten drunk after hearing the tape and reading the stories and the operations and intelligence reports and reducing them to his own analysis.

Eight hours earlier he'd been elated.

"Gawd damn!" Ron Huntley had bellowed. "You shittin me?!"

"Nope," Conklin had said. "I'll tell you the whole thing when the L-T gets in. I recorded it off AFVN."

"He goina be here in zero-five," Huntley said. "Better crack us some beers."

Sergeant Ron Huntley had just come in with Sullivan from an uneventful three-day ambush patrol. They had not heard the news. "It'll take this piece a junk zero-five just to rewind the tape," Conklin said.

"Whoa! Whoa! Whoa! Whoa!" John Sullivan burst into the teamhouse. "Did you . . ."

"Old hat, L-T," Huntley said. His feet were up on the field table, his beer was half gone. The recorder clicked as the tape finished rewinding.

"Man!" Sullivan threw a right-fisted hook into the air. "Man! They're goina do it. They're doing it!"

Ian Conklin pressed the play button and for Sullivan and Huntley it was 9 p.m. Eastern Standard Time, 30 April 1970. "It is not our power but our will and character that are being tested tonight. . . ." The voice was Richard Nixon's. He was addressing America, announcing to his country the incursion of U.S. ground troops into Cambodia. Sullivan pulled hard on his beer. Huntley playfully splashed some of his on Conklin.

". . . We take this action not for the purpose of expanding the war into Cambodia," Nixon said, "but for the purpose of ending the war in Viet Nam and *winning* the just peace we all desire—"

Sullivan pushed the stop button. "Where's Major Travis?" he asked Conklin.

"Went up to province HQ," Conklin said. "Ever since this shit came down, we've been swamped with info. He's trying to make heads or tails of it with Colonel Trinh."

"Play some more," Huntley said. He pushed the button.

". . . If, when the chips are down . . . America acts like a pitiful, helpless giant, the forces of totalitarianism and anarchy will threaten free nations and free institutions throughout the world. . . ."

"Yeah," Huntley agreed quietly. The three advisors listened to the President's speech in its entirety. A general feeling of euphoria held them. Sergeant Quay came to them when he heard that Sullivan and Huntley were back in from ambush. Jovially and profusely he congratulated them. It was a wonderful time, a wonderful maneuver. Re came too. And Lieutenant Hoa came with Major Travis.

Conklin rewound the tape and Sullivan replayed it. Something bothered him. He went into the sleeping quarters and rewound and replayed it again, now sentence by sentence. Something. He asked Huntley to listen to parts with him and the two listened and drank more beers. "Something isn't right," Sullivan said.

"Sounds more right to me than anything I heard in a fuck of a long time," Huntley shot back.

"But look," Sullivan said. He leaned forward. "Look what he's done. He's laid upon this one battle's success the success of the entire war itself."

"So?" Huntley didn't want anything to spoil his pleasure in knowing that American forces were, right at that minute, driving into Cambodia, battling NVA troops that had eluded them for years, that had struck at them and then pulled back into the unauthorized zone. Major Travis had brought back updated reports of movements, engagements and results. To Huntley it could not have been more positive.

"Damn it, Ron! Since when does an army's commander-in-chief, on the eve of a surprise assault, announce to the enemy the time, scope and goals of his raid?" Sullivan banged his hand onto his cot. "That's inconceivable arrogance. That's stupidity. It's a goddamned war crime. Imagine if, on 28 January 1968, Ho Chi Minh had announced the Tet Offensive, its scope, targets and units."

"Oh, come on, man!" Huntley said, and Sullivan got up and left and went to the operations room and got Major Travis's reports and studied them.

Years later John Sullivan would conclude that "the speech, even more than the action, ignited dozens of fuses, setting off eruptions around the world. Its immediate effect," he would write, "was numbing shock, a state in which the information distributors ignored the realities of the Cambodian nation (exactly as the highest U.S. authority had ignored many of those same realities). The biggest tactical-strategic blunder in American military history was Richard Nixon's handling of that announcement. Had America's highest leadership not been compromised by that bungling, ensuing events certainly would have turned out differently. Had the announcement come at the Saigon 'five o'clock follies,' from a junior-grade officer—after the ascent of the Lon Nol government—something to the effect of '. . . also, in agreement with, and at the request of, the Cambodian national government, American and South Viet Namese forces will begin joint operations with FANK units in the border region in an attempt to clear the NVA resupply and staging areas in the Parrot's Beak and west of Binh Long Province' . . . *period*, the explosion of antiwar sentiment and activity would have been much reduced. Top military advisors in the United States and Viet Nam had begged the President not to make the announcement a major event. General William Westmoreland had attempted to enlighten the commander-in-chief about the realities of the sanctuary area—forest camps from which the NVA could easily withdraw until the heat passed, which then they could easily reoccupy. The President's blunder, beyond all others, represented the essence of the failure of American leadership. America's body politic became like a person gone mad:

the heart and all other organs continued to function, but the seed of futility had been planted, and the spirit needed to continue the war began its slow, torturous death.

"Some historians," Sullivan would conclude, "have placed the turning point of American spirit at Tet 1968. Others attributed the bankruptcy of spirit to the transgression of the secret Menu bombings. These views ignore both American public opinion polls and the successes and expanding peace in South Viet Nam. The 30 April speech became the critical fulcrum of American will, became the instigator of actions and reactions, which accelerated exponentially. Four days later the single most decisive battle of the Viet Nam War ensued, a battle with four KIAs. That battle occurred approximately twelve thousand miles east-northeast of Saigon, at Kent State University in Ohio. But before that battle tens of thousands of Americans and South Viet Namese were committed to the new Cambodian front."

Sullivan read the first report. "On 30 April four task forces crossed the border. ARVN troops (preceded by eight B-52 sorties) rolled unhindered through Prasaut and into Chipou. Early monsoon rains have abated. The land is in a dry-season state. This has aided armored and airborne operations and favored the Allies in the border region. Guerrilla units, also moving easily, have generally fled before the ARVN and US task forces.

"A second task force, code named Operation Shoemaker," the report went on, "launched into the 'Fishhook' area on 1 May. 8,000 US plus 2,000 ARVN soldiers, led by B-52 strikes and heavy artillery shellings, the column of armor [Sheridan recon vehicles, M-48 Patton tanks and M-113 armored personnel carriers from the US 11th Armored Cav, and the US 25th Infantry Division's 34th Armor], and infantry [the US 9th Infantry Division's 2d of the 47th, and the ARVN's 1st Armored Cav and 3d Brigade], and airmobile infantry [the US 1st Cav and the ARVN 1st Airborne Division], have met little resistance. They have, however, uncovered and destroyed tons of enemy supplies including numerous large military trucks.

"As of 1900 hours 2 May 1970, no evidence of Hanoi's 'key control center, its headquarters for the entire Communist military operation in South Vietnam,' as outlined by the commander-in-chief, has been found.

"In Phnom Penh, government spokesmen have issued the following statement: 'We are a neutral country. [We do] not approve of this type of intervention by foreign forces.' American diplomatic gestures of the two-week period, 16 to 30 April, have been perceived by Phnom Penh as a repeated disregard of Lon

Nol's pleas for full support and massive aid. 'The Nixon administration,' the Khmer spokesman pointed out, 'instead of grant-
ing Cambodia's request for massive arms aid, has said the
United States would only join other nations in providing small
arms and other equipment to help Cambodia defend its neutrality without becoming an active belligerent.' "

The report also stated that Lon Nol felt that his honor had
been completely disregarded by the American President, who
had neither consulted with nor confirmed the raids with Phnom
Penh. Nor had the Khmer government been allowed to make at
least a joint announcement with Washington.

From *Stars and Stripes,* Sullivan learned that in Washington,
D.C., the Senate Foreign Relations Committee had charged the
Nixon administration with attempting to usurp the powers of
Congress. It had then approved a bill to repeal the Gulf of Tonkin
resolution. President Nixon and his chief architect of foreign
policy, Henry Kissinger, were, according to the article, in seclu-
sion in the White House, avoiding communications with the
media and Congress.

That night and all the following day John Sullivan drank
heavily. He was livid. To Quay, Re and Lieutenant Hoa his
behavior was disgraceful. To Major Travis, it was barely acceptable. Huntley thought he was celebrating and drank with him.
Conklin sat back and chuckled, "Twenty and a wake-up. Then
I'm skyin for the land of the big PX."

In Washington, General Alexander Haig sent a request to the
FBI to wiretap, amongst other journalists, William Beecher, the
New York Times reporter who'd first disclosed the secret Menu
bombings. On 3 May, Communist troops seized Neak Luong,
effectively cutting the Saigon–Phnom Penh river and highway
link.

They arrived at the rate of almost a thousand a day, arrived
with almost nothing, some not even fully clothed. By the second
of May, their number had reached twenty thousand—twenty
thousand unassimilated refugees packing the eastern swamp,
the edge of Boeng Khsach Sa at the low-lying rear area of Neak
Luong, packing together, instantaneously creating a squalid
slum, a jumble of lean-tos erected by those fortunate enough to
have been given a square of thin blue plastic tarp.

"There's no salt," a heavy, seated woman told a pleading
young mother carrying two infants. "The oil is out but we hope
to have more tonight." The mother looked helplessly at the
heavy woman. One infant grabbed her mouth. As she turned
and left the large tent she kissed the baby's hand.

Beside the heavy woman sat another young mother, shoeless, haggard though lovely even in her weariness. Her eyes were large, melancholy, shrouded by mental pain—eyes like those of a wounded fawn in the forest. Behind her in a small makeshift hammock slept her six-month-old son. The younger woman did not speak except when interviewing and registering new arrivals. She had vowed to keep a sixty-day precept of silence and fasting, speaking only when she was serving the work of the Enlightened One, eating only once daily, late each night.

"Your village?" Vathana spoke softly to a new arrival.

"Phum Chey Kompok," a young man with one eye answered. Without pausing for breath he added, "Will they bomb here?"

"I don't know," Vathana answered, recording the man's village in a large ledger.

"The bombing is terrible." His speech was quick, nervous. "The earth shook like a giant was walking in the paddies."

Vathana looked at the man. She had been hearing the same story for three days . . . the bombings, the bombings, the terrible bombings. She continued her list of questions then motioned for the man to move to Sophan for temporary identification and ration cards. As the next new refugee approached, Vathana bowed her head and thought a prayer. Ever since she had witnessed the corpses jamming the Mekong she had prayed to the Blessed One for help in strengthening her personal discipline and in being one with those who suffered, with the war victims, the refugees, the Viet Namese civilians and all the soldiers.

As the crisis had worsened during the last days of April Vathana had mobilized all her organizational abilities, had called on all those whom she had helped previously and had beseeched every well-to-do Khmer, pleading with them to earn merit by extending the greatest possible compassion to the refugees who streamed into Neak Luong. Thirty thousand came from Svay Rieng Province, flowing like a river, passing through, heading for Phnom Penh, though like a river current swirling at the bank, many stopped in the backwater eddy of Neak Luong's northeast swamp. From her father-in-law Vathana secured nearly fifty tons of rice—enough to feed the camp for a week. At the main pagoda she had arranged a special shelter for young children who had been either separated from their families or orphaned. Her original programs were expanded but in days were overwhelmed. Each day she begged local officials to establish control, each day she pressed FANK commanders for supplies and assistance, each day she telegraphed Phnom Penh pleading with Madame Pech to use her influence with upper-echelon Cambodian functionaries. And each day she received only a fraction of Neak Luong's needs. "Dear Sister, the government just doesn't have those quantities of supplies." "Dear Sister, no one ever prepared the army for such a crisis." "Dear Sister, there is only so much one can do. Perhaps we will receive aid from the IRC, or maybe the Americans."

"Sophan, we must have a medical clinic for the camp."

"Yes Angel, we must. But we have no supplies, no personnel."

"Major Fernandez has captured a large tent from somewhere. He'll allow us to use it in exchange for the barge. With the river cut it's of no use. And the premier will confiscate it if we refuse its surrender."

Sophan laid the back of her hand on Vathana's cheek. "Angel," the wet-nurse said sadly, "you're getting too thin. You can't help everyone if you waste away. Tonight, just tonight, you must go home and sleep."

"Tonight, Sophan"—Vathana's eyes flashed with the energy of total commitment—"tonight we'll erect the tent. Tomorrow we'll find a khrou and perhaps a doctor and from them"—she indicated the mass of waiting, milling refugees—"we'll gain nurses."

3 May 1970—Suddenly, in the streets of Neak Luong, short staccato bursts of automatic weapons fire. Three dead, nineteen wounded in the first enfilade. Simultaneously, at every FANK outpost—across the river where a FANK company had secured the ferry landing and roadhead of Highway 1 leading to Phnom Penh; south of the city where a FANK garrison protected Highway 1 leading to Svay Rieng, the border and Saigon; and north on Highway 15 past the villa of Pech Lim Song where national troops lined the roadway leading toward Prey Veng—huge explosions.

"They're bombing! They're bombing here!" Clouds of mosquitos rose from the muck of swamp and paddy as hundreds of panic-stricken refugees bolted from lean-tos, crashed through rice-mat walls, attempting to disperse, to flee from the unseen attackers.

"Tell the men to tighten the ropes," Vathana ordered. She stood inside the half-erected forty-man canvas structure, stood calmly by one of the thick center poles. About her, watching her, those helping fidgeted yet continued pulling at ropes leading to the canvas roof.

From outside came shouts. "Bombings! The bombs . . ."

"All the more reason," Vathana said flatly. "We'll need the clinic to treat the wounded. *Now pull that side tight!*"

More firing. In the hot musty air inside the tent the rifle bursts sounded like corn popping in a thick pan and the large explosions seemed like beats on a giant muffled drum. In the camp the firing was sharp cracking and not only were the explosions heard and the fireflash and smoke seen, but the winds of concussion felt. With each eruption more people ran into the swamp, yet most hugged the ground or simply sat or squatted where they were, many praying, most silently suffering the hopelessness of fleeing.

"Where is she?"

"Who?"

"Cahuom Vathana."

"I don't know her."

"The one they call the Angel."

"Oh. She's at the medical tent."

"What? Where?"

"Up there."

Pech Chieu Teck charged from the edge of the camp toward the large tent. He had never before entered the refugee area. The swamps, the shanties, the filthy unwashed bodies revolted him as had the street urchins and the orphanage his wife had set up so much earlier. Teck's tight polished-cotton shirt sweat-stuck to his back and shoulders as he raced in. Twenty military cots were crammed, touching, along one wall. Forty more were jammed in five rows along the back. At the front, one table served as an administrative office, a second as an examining room, a third as a small dispensary. The setup had been efficient, quick. Within two hours the cots had been occupied and two dozen aides had volunteered to assist the afflicted. Only a doctor and a khrou were missing, and even a single box of bandages or bottle of aspirin.

Teck made no pretext of compassion. He stood on one man's cot and quickly scanned the room for his wife. Spying her he walked over the wounded and ill, stepping on a woman's arm where there was no room for his feet, standing on a boy's ankle to leap across another cot to an aisle.

"Come with me." He grabbed Vathana by the pit of her arm and lifted her from the cot of an elderly woman who complained her heart was having problems. "Come on. We're going."

"Going?" Vathana shook herself from his grasp.

"Phnom Penh," Teck said angrily.

For a moment Vathana looked into her husband's eyes. She had vowed not to speak unless it served the compassionate duty of Buddha; thus, working or nurturing she was confident in her speech, but this, this served no duty, no reason, no principle. She shook her head and bowed it down.

"Now!" Teck shouted angrily. Again he grasped her. "The damn town's about to fall."

About the standing couple everyone had become silent; most had dropped their gaze in respect for the Angel. "To whom?" an old man called.

"To whom?! Does it matter?"

"Who's bombing? Is it the unseen planes?"

"It's the Viet Cong," Teck snapped. "They've overrun the ferry garrison. They're shelling the others." He turned his bitter attention back to his wife, bitter as though her aid to these wretched creatures had caused the attack. "Come with me! Now! Where's my son?"

Again Vathana said nothing. She stood limply before him, passive to the hands shaking her, rag-doll calm until the child-man flung her down over cots to the packed earth and fled as he'd arrived, stepping on whoever was in his way, screaming jumbled curses. Abandoning her, she thought. Again, she thought. When I need you the most.

By dusk, Neak Luong had fallen to the NVA. Falling did not mean North Viet Namese troops occupied the town or the camp. Indeed, though various elements of attached Khmer Viet Minh with a few Viet Namese escorts did enter the town on 3 May, generally the troops hit and overran only FANK's three garrisons and the scattered outposts, the Northern troops being under orders to maintain as low a profile as possible with the Khmer civilian community. Not until 5 May would NVA propaganda and assassination squads enter Neak Luong.

Madame Pech had fled with the first rumors that Neak Luong was the next Communist target. Teck and most of the servants fled with the first shots. All fled to the nation's capital. Pech Lim Song remained, at ease in his newly completed villa, remained, abandoned by all except his first servant, Sambath, an old genteel butler who in his youth had served as a houseboy to the French governor, then as chauffeur or butler to various embassies and foreign businessmen. He'd been in the employ of Mister Pech for seventeen years, ever since national independence.

"Perhaps, sir," Sambath addressed Mister Pech in French, "perhaps I should bring the automobile about. My third cousin's son has a ferry on the Tonle Toch. We can avoid the main roads that way, sir."

"What's the situation now?" Mister Pech turned the volume dial counterclockwise, leaned back in the old mahogany swivel chair he'd used since he'd first entered business.

"Both southern garrisons have been occupied," Sambath reported without emotion. "The northside one is negotiating its surrender. At Banam, sir, the yuon devils have routed our troops."

"And the Highway 15 outposts?"

"The far one evacuated yesterday, sir. The near one's . . . well, sir, we can't know for sure. Have you heard anything on the military channel?"

"Not since morning. That'll be the final cut. Have there been shots?"

"Only a few, sir. My nephew's third son sold the soldiers ice at noon. He felt the yellows were only awaiting orders. He saw a tank in the Khsach Sa swamp."

Mister Pech said nothing. He closed his eyes, put his hands atop his head and tilted the chair back to its stop. In the weak light of the small desk lamp the film of perspiration on Pech Lim Song's forehead shone a satin redbrown, identical in color and brilliance to the redbrown of the oiled mahogany.

"The automobile, sir?" Sambath said quietly.

"I suppose that would be prudent," Mister Pech whispered without opening his eyes. "Only . . ." He paused. A country in a bowl, he thought. And only one outlet. What a position and now it's cut. "Only"—his voice sounded exhausted—"only if my daughter-in-law can be persuaded to accompany me."

"She's in the camp, sir."

"Still?"

"Yes."

"You've spoken with her."

"Her precept, sir."

"Still?"

"She vowed for sixty days."

"And my grandson?"

"With her, sir."

"She's not coming?"

"She's a very stubborn one, sir. She's eaten so little I fear she'll fall to an epidemic in all that filth. She insists upon staying."

"Then, Sambath, we too shall remain."

Pech Lim Song leaned forward, rolled his chair until his chest hit the edge of the desk. He twisted the volume dial of the Japanese transistor radio on his left until the sound was just audible. Viet Cong radio was rebroadcasting the news of Peking's diplomatic break with Phnom Penh. The military radio before him dwarfed the am-fm. Slowly Mister Pech twisted the frequency tuners, pausing with each click, listening momentarily to each channel, hoping to intercept the military plans of the Viet Minh, as he called the NVA/VC, or of FANK or the Americans.

"Sir . . ." Sambath had waited to be dismissed.

"Certainly . . ." Mister Pech answered distractedly. Then his face tightened. "Sambath," he said loudly, "fill the generator tanks. Turn the lights on. All of them." For the first time in a week Mister Pech seemed back in control. "If the Viet Namese come," he commanded, "invite them in and serve them. The same if it be Khmer Rouge."

With the mass death and destruction of Khmer people and Khmer property came the accelerated decline of tradition. Fewer women wore the white blouse and black skirt of mourning. Fewer men wore the black arm bands of grief. Fewer heads were shaved for the killed fathers or mothers or older siblings. It was not a matter of callousness created by the enormity of the terror which had descended upon the Southeast but more a matter of the overwhelming speed with which villages and families were changing.

From great suffering comes great insight, Vathana thought. She sat on the edge of an army cot at the deepest corner of the tent. Great insight and great compassion. On the cot two women and a young boy lay listless—all with fevers, with thick nasal discharges going unheeded, with persistent black flies feeding from small scratches as if invited. From great insight and great compassion comes a peaceful heart. Vathana felt nauseous. Her thoughts calmed only a single compartment of her honeycomb mind. Carefully she swabbed the boy's face with a tiny square of cloth she'd dipped into her bucket of soapy water. The flies swarmed about her hand then relit on the boy's face; the water seemed to sizzle and evaporate on his skin like drops on a hot skillet. Vathana dropped the cloth in a second bucket, peeled another square from her bundle and then dipped it and washed the face of the younger of the two women. She rose, her bare feet swishing through uncleared rotting garbage and vomit on the mud beneath the cot. Again her abdomen tightened as if to expel its nonexistent contents. Vathana settled at the other side to clean the face of the older woman. Mother, she thought as the woman shivered beneath her touch, if you wake from your ordeal all your passion, all your desires will have vanished and you will have inner peace. The nausea had been constant for two days yet in her vow of silence and fasting she'd pressed on with her mission to relieve the suffering of these homeless wretches, to excise her own desires by becoming one with the sufferers. She rose. Her soap bucket was nearly empty, the used-clothes bucket nearly overflowing. Vathana closed her eyes. The blackness turned slowly, increasing the squeamishness of her stomach. Her left knee began to buckle. She opened her eyes. Righted her head. Stared at the lantern over the table where Sophan held her son as she processed another in the endless line of the uprooted.

Vathana reached the table, squatted behind the wet-nurse, dumped the dirty clothes into a large basket then held on to Sophan's chair with all her remaining strength. "Angel! Angel, are you . . . ? You look worse than the bedridden. Angel?"

Vathana looked up. Her face was blank. Her large eyes were sunk in their sockets. Sophan caressed her cheek. "Come," the stocky woman said. She turned to the refugee and indicated he'd have to wait to register. "Come. Let me take you from here." She wrapped Vathana in one arm like a young child, carried Samnang in the other, whispering to both a stream of prayers interspersed with curses. "No medicine. No clean water. Fourteen thousand people living on top of one another. Shit in the paddies. Bathe in the paddies. Drink from the paddies. Of course they're all sick."

In Sophan's arms Vathana trembled. The nausea and vertigo ignited in her fears far worse than the shellings. Sophan led her slowly from the camp toward the river and then toward the apartment. The queasiness of her stomach erupted in a renting spasm. "You must eat and rest," Sophan ordered softly.

"Sophan." Vathana broke her vow. "My bleeding is late."

The lieutenant's face was dark, grim, like the ash from the funeral pyre. All night he'd stared at the well-lighted villa on the rise, stared as he directed the burial squad in the proper manner of burning the bodies of their comrades in arms, his Khmer brothers who'd been killed by the surprisingly fierce resistance of the FANK outpost on Highway 15. All night he'd prayed for their souls—haunted by the image of three who'd died with their eyes wide open, died before they'd been ready to leave this earth. All night he'd prayed that when his time came his eyes would be shut. All night he'd cursed the mocking lights of Mister Pech Lim Song's villa and the arrogant capitalist dog who had dared him, taunted him, openly defied him, defied the Khmer Viet Minh and their North Viet Namese sponsors.

At seven forty-five on the morning of 6 May, Sambath swung the doors open, bowed, his hands raised high in respectful greeting, and invited in a KVM and an NVA captain and their contingents. "Mister Pech," Sambath said in French, "had hoped you'd join him last night for dinner, sir. We'd turned the lights on as an invitation."

"The house is surrounded," the NVA captain said as if reporting a business statistic. "Bring everyone here. Now."

"Of course, sir," Sambath answered. "There's only Mister Pech and I." Subtly Sambath took note of each of the officers and scanned the villa porch. Politely he apologized for the lack of servants to feed the accompanying soldiers. "If the men won't mind, sir," the old servant said calmly, "I'll serve the officers first."

The captains made no comment. Behind them a Viet Namese sergeant forced his boot heel hard against the foyer floor tiles as if mesmerized by their quality. Beside them the KVM lieutenant from the burial detail ground his teeth.

Mister Pech appeared briefly behind the upper rosewood balustrade. In Viet Namese he called, *"Chao Bac."* Hello Uncle. "At last you've come to liberate us!" He disappeared, reappeared a moment later on the stairs. A reinforced squad of soldiers entered the house through various doors. "Please"— Mister Pech smiled broadly—"make this building your command center. We've room for many. And—the best radios. I've arranged with Colonel Le Minh Lam for your units to . . ."

"Mister Pech," the Khmer captain stopped the older man. "From your mouth comes buffalo dung."

"Captain!" Mister Pech barked. He straightened, hardened like a general about to reprimand a subordinate. "Four American divisions are eating ground in this direction. Colonel Le has prepared"—the captain snapped his head to the Khmer Viet Minh lieutenant—"detailed defense plans"—then pointed to Sambath. Immediately the lieutenant raised his carbine. A shot exploded. The old servant stood motionless then began to collapse to one side, his left leg folding neatly three inches above the knee as his body crashed upon the tiles.

"You . . ." Mister Pech roared. "Colonel L—" From behind, two soldiers grabbed the magnate at his throat choking off the words, pinning his arms. Sambath whimpered.

"The first phase in the destruction of the government"—the Khmer captain spoke as if instructing the lieutenant—"is the destruction of the regime's local authority. Do this and the central government will be isolated, unable to raise an army, rendered ineffective." The lieutenant nodded stiffly. "He's yours," the Khmer captain said, and he and the NVA captain and their entourages saluted and marched out.

The lieutenant's face was grim. He closed the exterior foyer doors and then the interior doors to the dining room, the ballroom and the hallway to the rear of the house. He walked to each slowly, moved deliberately, closing off the room with almost grand gestures. As he moved his mind cleared of thought, of feeling. He became pure duty.

"*Chao Bac,*" the lieutenant mocked Pech Lim Song. He walked to Sambath, whose legs were floating in a pool of blood. The lieutenant stepped over the sticky fluid, kicked the servant's hip to flatten him on the floor, then stood on the old man so as to raise himself higher than Mister Pech. Sambath coughed. The toes of his left foot lay lifeless beneath his right arm, pointing at the ceiling. "Uncle . . ." the lieutenant said grimly, darkly, not mocking, not hateful, indifferent. He opened a folder handed him by an aide. "*La sale guerre*, Mister Pech?"

The two soldiers still held the landlord by the neck and arms. He twisted defiantly attempting to free his head but their strength was greater than his.

"You have blasphemed against Samdech Sihanouk, eh? These are your words: 'His love for power keeps him corrupt.' " The lieutenant paused.

Mister Pech's mind flashed, terrified. "Why? Why are you with these Viet Namese? They attack a neutral country. Lon Nol has declared a path of neutrality."

"Humph! Neutral! The Politburo has declared Cambodia an active participant in the war. Thus it is a legal and justifiable target."

The lieutenant pulled a second sheet from the folder. Mister Pech cringed, silent, settling his thoughts on an exterior bitterness—Why is America dragging its feet? They profess to ally themselves with all who resist tyranny. . . .

" 'Sihanouk refuses to carry out land reforms,' " the lieutenant read. "Isn't that a strange contradiction—the land baron damning the Prince? 'The Viet Namese are two-headed snakes set upon ruling all Kampuchea. What we must fear is their hegemony.' Your words!" Again the lieutenant raised his carbine. The two soldiers released their hold.

"Wait . . ."

The lieutenant fired a single round, the bullet smashing Mister Pech's left knee.

"Hang them outside by the good leg." The lieutenant's voice was flat, emotionless. "*La sale guerre*, eh, Mister Pech?"

CHAPTER NINE

As the war for Cambodia continued its rapid, perverted, escalating transformation, so too did Met Nang's role change, pervert, rise. Nang did not remain with the recruits he'd led into the forest northwest of Kompong Cham. They were turned over to other Krahom cadre for induction, indoctrination and training at the new schools. No longer were recruits sent to Pong Pay Mountain. The cloaked animosity between the Communist allies, and the now total NVA domination of the Northeast provinces, caused the Krahom leadership to close the School of the Cruel and to open smaller, dispersed, less politically oriented schools in the southwest Cardamom Mountains.

The war became more conventional and Nang became a more conventional soldier—a soldier in a small army which continued to shadow its mentor force like a little brother might follow a big even after the two have fought.

For days, as fighting between NVA and ARVN/US units flared along much of the border and between NVA and FANK forces across the southern coast and deep into the interior, Nang marched southwest, halfway across the nation. There he picked up a platoon of twenty-six newly trained boys, yotheas, and two older, teenage officers. Then Nang, as platoon sergeant, political cadreman and tactician, marched the soldiers north at a murderous pace. He did not make friends, hardly made acquaintances. His friend was the Movement, the organization, the cause. Let the platoon leader and XO make friends, he thought. He'd made friends before. He'd had family before. What had happened to them—to them all? Nang would lead the platoon, could lead them too, because they too were products of Angkar Leou. They marched around Phnom Penh, through the NVA units besieging Kompong Chhnang, led by Met Nang as

Met Sar had directed, to the outskirts of Kompong Thom where they rendezvoused with other Krahom elements, where they waited as Nang slipped from them, spied on them and on others, waited to be turned over to the 91st Division of the North Viet Namese Army for whom Nang and his boy-soldiers would serve as runners, insurgents and porters.

Before being placed under the operational control of the NVA's 91st, Nang's platoon was chosen to serve as honor guard at a one-day summit meeting of Khmer Krahom, Khmer Viet Minh and NVA officers northeast of Kompong Thom.

Dawn broke. The yotheas, only six of twenty-nine carrying firearms, entered the concealed jungle-swamp headquarters of NVA Colonel Le Duc Tu. Escorting them were four armed, strack, spit-shined and polished North Viet Namese soldiers. With few words the yotheas took up positions around the exterior of the large thatch-roofed hut. Unseen, felt, in camouflaged fighting positions and bunkers on every side, NVA troops stood vigilant, prepared less for battle than for inspection. Nang stood erect though deflated, proud yet sly. Instinctively he sensed every hostile presence as if thoughts produced odors and his nose had been sensitized to the smell.

Le Duc Tu and his entourage arrived at 0800. Met Sar arrived at nine. With him were three men Nang had never seen, yet to whom Met Sar seemingly paid homage. Ten minutes later Hen Samon, regional committee chairman of the Khmer Viet Minh, arrived with a squad-sized escort and four functionaries. The Viet Namese greeted all, embracing the Khmers as if they were hosting the meeting in their own country. An NVA staff photographer snapped a dozen pictures. Then the Viet Namese led the Khmers into the hootch, the meeting hut.

Before entering, Met Sar approached Nang. He did not speak to him, nor did he look at the black-clad boy's cold eyes, but simply stood near him as if he, Sar, were taking a last deep breath of outside air before entering the building. Without motion Nang uttered lowly, "East—twelve APCs with full contingent of troops. Seventy-nine trucks. South—two to four battalions with two AA batteries attached. West—two batteries of rocket artillery. Eleven trucks. Infantry unknown. North—no report."

For three hours the Krahom guards stood motionless, silent, taking pride in their endurance and vigilance. For three hours not a voice escaped the hut. Dark thunderhead clouds rolled in transforming the clear morning to dull oppressive noon. Colonel Le's interpreter emerged. Quietly he directed three Viet

Namese soldiers to bring food and tea. Politely Nang insisted he be allowed to serve his commanders.

The hut was dim. Four small oil lanterns cast flickering light upon the dozen men seated at two field tables, seated in collapsible chairs, speaking over pinned maps which attempted to recurl. Nang could smell the latent hostility. He poured tea at a small side table, tasted it, served the Krahom personnel.

"The Chinese have sent us sixteen thousand rifles," the man to Met Sar's left said. He paused for the Krahom interpreter to translate. "Sixteen thousand," he repeated. "We've received three thousand."

"Are you certain?" a Viet Namese major asked.

"We must have arms," the Krahom leader said. "We know there can be difficulties in transit, but we've traced the shipments through Laos. We know they reached Prey Angkoal below the Kong Falls. As you have seen, many of our soldiers are armed only with clubs. This is not right."

"No. No, it isn't right. But perhaps, Brother"—Hen Samon addressed the Krahom leader without waiting for the interpreters to translate for the Viet Namese—"your yotheas are selling their weapons to the new lackey troops."

"Bah!" Met Sar cleaned his lips. "You accuse them of what you fear?"

"Please," Colonel Le said. He held up his hands. "Let's break to eat."

"Our information network is the best in Kampuchea," the man next to Met Sar said. "Our soldiers are dedicated. We have thirteen thousand awaiting weapons. We must have them."

"You shall," Colonel Le answered after the interpreter finished.

"When?"

"After lunch." The colonel smiled. "We will discuss it after lunch."

The meeting broke. Nang, tiny, deflated, stayed, stood in the dim hootch, in the darkest corner, listening to the men chatter, their disparaging words couched in consoling tones and lavish insincere praise. Like a well-trained butler he stepped forward only when his commander's cup or dish needed replenishment. Then he melted back against the thatch wall. For two hours the men ate, bantered, spoke of the siege of Kompong Chhnang, the plans for Kompong Thom, the ramifications of the ARVN-American cross-border assaults. Sated, Met Sar belched contentedly. He looked upon Major Huu with admiration. In his soft voice Sar said to the NVA officer, "We should be good friends."

"Yes," the major answered.

"I think Lon Nol's agents try to keep us apart."

"Most assuredly," the major said. He smiled as if to himself he were saying, You fat brown fool, you think they want us united?

"Again the regime's functionaries have approached us," Met Sar continued, "but, of course, you know that."

"Yes, we know." Major Huu smiled.

Sar belched again. "An excellent meal," he said benignly. Then added, "They've offered us amnesty."

"What good is amnesty from a government that loses one percent of its country every day?"

"Ah, well, that's true, Major. That's very true." Sar smiled softly. He turned very slightly and motioned to Nang for more tea. "The agents certainly can't be trusted. They carry wood for all sides. They tell us Lon Nol offers us a position in the government in exchange for our support."

"You're intrigued, eh?"

"No. No, Major. They are losing very rapidly, though with American support they may hold out a bit longer."

Into the Viet Namese officer's voice crept an edge of harshness. "We'll control Phnom Penh by August," he said.

Sar swirled the liquid in his handleless cup. He turned, nodded to Nang as if approving the tea he'd been served. Nang inflated as he stepped forward, bulked up as he stood motionless behind Met Sar. "It's such a shame," the Krahom general said softly, "to have fine soldiers like Comrade Ky here and not to be able to arm them. President Lon's agents have offered ten thousand machine guns and have said we'd be allowed to keep our units intact under FANK's overall control."

"You are talking to a two-headed snake." Major Huu smirked.

During the afternoon session the meeting concentrated on specific ways the three Communist factions could cooperate with one another. Every delegate bent to extremes of false cordiality, each playing for time, committing as little as possible, attempting to garner concessions and commitments from the others, ostensibly carving the region into three zones.

Moments before they dispersed Met Sar stuttered, "Ah . . . as . . . as to the rifles . . ."

"Yes, the rifles . . ." Colonel Le nodded. "We shall send you word about the delay."

"Quickly," Met Sar whispered to Nang. Again they were on the march. The meeting had dissolved as it had begun, with photographs snapped of diplomatic embraces as the North Viet Namese sealed off their perimeter and the Khmer factions withdrew in opposite directions. Accompanied by his old teacher, Nang marched his platoon southeast, toward the heart of the city they would soon attack. As they scurried along secret jungle-swamp trails led by a local Krahom guide, Met Sar quietly vented his spleen.

"Now the people will hear us." He spoke softly in his convictions, rationally in his pious arguments, ruthlessly in his righteousness. "You are my brother in the Brotherhood of the Pure, Met Nang. You have been purified in fire. This battle will require you to swallow your pride and endure utter privation. But if you are pure you will carry us through. Tell the platoon Angkar Leou wishes all to construct themselves in the pure and proper mold. We are the sole legitimate leaders of the Khmer people. All others trespass against us. All trespassers are aliens. All aliens are enemies. If we are pure all enemies will fall to our sword, and their remains will be the compost from which a thousand-year dynasty will blossom!

"For the good of Kampuchea, Nang, we must struggle to excise that which is infected, to destroy the regime and liberate Kampuchea from the imperialists, the yuons and all the puppets who draw nourishment from them like ignorant calves from the teats of a golden cow. Americans storm the border, bomb every square meter. The ARVN loots, pillages and rapes. Expect them. Expect their bombs." Met Sar paused in speech though continued his quick pace. He glanced from the corner of his eye at his trusted yothea, measured him, measured the impact of his words. Then he thought, Let the yuon soldiers topple Phnom Penh. Be one pace behind. In the moments between the military collapse and the shift of political power, step in, eliminate the yuon lackeys, substitute Krahom officers. It was a good scenario, a long shot, but one that could be played with minimum risk and run concurrently with other, more staid strategies.

"This invasion brings me sorrow and it brings me hope," Sar said. "Presidents Nixon and Thieu have given their armies permission to occupy Khmer lands, to kill our children. Every Khmer is horrified. Every intellectual, every young person, every citizen who takes any pride in the nation is nauseated by this odious invasion.

"Yet more terrifying is the speed with which the yuon thrust topples the country. It must be halted. Fight beside them, behind them, but fight like a wounded soldier. Make them carry you. Let the Americans bomb their camps and convoys. If two spears are thrown at you, one behind the other, you must sidestep the first before you can deflect the second. It is *kaul chomhor*, a guiding principle, of Angkar Leou. Rebuild and replenish our forces with the arms and the yotheas we take from our enemies."

Sullivan was hung over. His eyes would barely focus. Still he stared at the reports, at the newspapers strewn about his cot in the sleeping bunker of the teamhouse. He stared and he knew, thought he knew, the reality behind the words, the reality he projected behind the wall of present time.

By 4 May the US/ARVN incursion into the Fishhook area of Cambodia was paying off. As NVA supply units withdrew in chaos, U.S. forces advanced along Highway 13 to the outskirts of Snuol in Kratie Province—an area long controlled by the NVA, the city itself having recently fallen to total, undisguised Communist control. North Viet Namese gunners, the after-action report said, had opened up on U.S. 11th Cavalry troops as they neared the town's airstrip. Almost immediately additional enemy fire—mortars, small arms, automatic rifle and rockets— had come from the town. For two days U.S. bombers and artillery pounded the town, reducing it to rubble. When American troops finally entered the devastated area they found no wounded or dead. The military commander concluded that all had been carried away—instead of postulating, Sullivan thought, that all had escaped via deep subterranean passages. Free world press reports labeled the seizure of the town an atrocity, reporting the story as if the town were a civilian bastion surrounded by enemy troops in turn surrounded by Allied troops. It did not help when the American commander said, "We had to destroy it in order to save it."

". . . in order to save it," Sullivan muttered. "Real goddamned horror of Snuol is when the NVA seized the town in March, the goddamned two thousand civilians—who worked for em without choice, for the goddamned NVA, were pressed into deeper service or driven from the border area. Why don't they report that? They were part of the wave of refugees that inundated us. Damned papers have a memory about eighteen hours long. They coulda asked me. Atrocity! Goddamned Allied atrocity of Snuol was our *complete* acceptance, *complete* dependence upon artillery and bombing as the means of subduing an enemy force in a town. That's the atrocity. Even if there wasn't a fuckin livin soul in the place."

Sullivan shoved the report away, picked up the newspaper. On the campus of Kent State University, in Ohio, National Guardsmen, confronted by a jeering mass of students, had fired into the crowd killing four and wounding eleven. "Augh," Sullivan moaned. He studied the accompanying picture, the girl's face in the photo, her pain. He projected an ambiguous image into time beyond the present. "This sucker," he whispered, "this is the decisive battle."

President Nixon had infuriated antiwar people around the country by issuing a statement that included the line "When dissent turns to violence it invites tragedy." This line was quoted four times in the article Sullivan was reading and related articles.

"Can't win," Sullivan grumbled. "Can't win by winning."

He turned back to his stack of reports. On 5 May, U.S. forces had rolled into Snuol. Other border towns—Mimot, Sre Khtum—were surrounded. In Washington the President had announced that U.S. troops would be limited to a range of twenty-one miles from the border and by a time frame of three to seven weeks. From Saigon President Thieu countered, saying the ARVN would remain if required. At Angtassom (Sullivan searched the team's new map of Cambodia—he was not familiar with that country's interior), FANK forces had faltered under heavy NVA assault. By the sixth, fifty thousand U.S. and ARVN troops had crossed the border from the Parrot's Beak north to By Dop, near Phuoc Binh. Communist supplies were being found and captured so fast and in such quantities, the Allies could not evacuate all of it.

Again Sullivan studied the map of Cambodia. In the interior, 150 miles from the closest border point, 130 miles from the nearest American or South Viet Namese troops, NVA units had attacked Kompong Chhnang. They had then opened a second battle front at Kompong Som, 120 miles from the border. And due south of Phnom Penh, national troops were reported to have retaken Koki Thom.

Sullivan punched his left hand with his right. He spread the map of Cambodia over his pillow. He crushed his empty beer can. Then he tapped a finger on Phnom Penh. "Screw Travis," he said to himself. "I'm going to be there. Within thirty days, I'm going to be there."

8 May 1970—Alone Vathana stood at the window of her fourth-floor apartment, stood by the desk at which she'd learned the rudiments of commerce from her father-in-law. The desk was cluttered with shipping ledgers, crewmen's pay slips and unfilled orders. On the floor behind the desk, leaning, facing the wall, was the framed photo of Norodom Sihanouk.

She put her hand on the sill to steady herself. Outside, the world seemed deserted, abandoned, gray, gray as she felt her skin to be, gray as she felt the future. Not a soul was to be seen. Communist soldiers, after again shelling the refugee camp with a few mortar rounds, enough to cause mass chaos, had withdrawn. In the two hours which followed not a refugee, not a merchant, not a construction worker had ventured out from their hovels, homes or apartments. Not a farmer rolled his oxcart toward the piers, not a single boatman or ferryman could be seen along the river. Even the riverwaters seemed still, reflecting the gray morning sky.

The view, the emptiness, made Vathana queasy in both stomach and mind. She placed a hand over her abdomen and rubbed gently, whispering a prayer as her hand circled. Then tears flooded her eyes. "What kind of future?" she whispered to that which she imagined might be growing in her. She thought to go to the kitchenette to make tea but she felt riveted to the spot by the window, felt as though not a single gram of strength remained in her thighs or knees or ankles, nothing there to propel her. She wished the radio were on but again the inertia of standing at the window froze her.

Vathana stood for another hour, barely moving, barely thinking, hoping to catch sight of Sophan returning. A fleeting thought of her mother and father sped through her mind so quickly that after it had left she wondered what she'd thought. An image of her father-in-law in his new villa lasted longer, but the image was still, like a snapshot. Then a bitter resentment arose in her and she thought of her husband abandoning her, thought how un-Khmer was the man who had no loyalty to his wife, his family, his home. The bitterness strengthened her, cleared her eyes and ears. She stared through the window at that whose approach she'd not sensed. A low rhythmic shudder pulsed through the glass, an eerie beating concussion reached through, shaking her to the core. Then in the sky downriver she saw them looking like locusts, eyes bulging. Below them, steaming by the ferry crossing, was the lead riverine craft of an entire flotilla. More helicopters, flank security, appeared, darting over nearside piers and beyond the far bank over the swamps. The air jolted with their rotor beats. Flags flapped on the naval craft—the yellow with three red stripes of the Saigon regime and the starred red white and blue of the Americans.

Vathana watched, motionless, as the flotilla steamed in, the South Viet Namese vessels continuing past, the American docking or mooring just out of the channel. Upon the closest vessel she saw three soldiers, one half hidden, two plainly—a large white man with an enormous protruding nose and a man blacker than she imagined skin could be. As she watched, enthralled, a streak of sun broke through the overcast. Vathana subdued a chuckle. People flooded the streets. Americans, she thought. For

Americans the monsoons delay. "Ah," she sighed, and turned
into the apartment to concentrate, "ah . . . but the monsoons
always come."

Before the battle of Kompong Thom commenced on 3 June 1970
invading armies captured or traded Cambodian territory without thought or respect for indigenous populations. Three weeks
earlier, South Viet Namese President Thieu had issued a statement declaring he and Lon Nol had arrived at an "agreement in
principle" for the continued use of ARVN forces in Cambodia.

In the United States the storm of protest had become a full-
fledged hurricane. Hundreds of universities had closed. On 11
May the Senate Foreign Relations Committee approved the
Cooper-Church amendment to the Military Sales Act, outlawing
the use of U.S. troops in Cambodia after 30 June 1970. This
amendment also forbid American advisors to work with Cambodian forces and prohibited direct U.S. air support to FANK.

Through May battle actions had flared. The South Viet Namese
navy blockaded Cambodia's Gulf of Thailand coast to curtail the
influx of supplies as U.S. units evacuated or destroyed thousands of tons of supplies from areas nicknamed "Rock Island
East" and "The City" and from fighting, training and supply
complexes too numerous to nickname. Major battles had flashed
in the interiors of both South Viet Nam and Cambodia. On the
seventeenth a ten-thousand-soldier ARVN task force with two
hundred U.S. advisors had reached the large southeastern city
of Takeo where 211 NVA troops were killed. On the nineteenth,
attempting to relieve the pressure against the sanctuaries, and
in honor of Ho Chi Minh's birthdate, VC/NVA units shelled sixty
Allied posts within South Viet Nam. The next day 2,500 ARVN
soldiers retaliated with an unsuccessful raid against the mountain base at Bu Ntoll. North of Takeo ARVN and FANK forces
linked up, driving a reported four hundred NVA soldiers into a
killing field.

On the twenty-third, ARVN forces answering the direct request
of Lon Nol made their deepest Cambodian plunge to date with
10,000 regulars plus 1,500 Khmer Krahom attacking NVA positions
in the giant Chup Rubber Plantation south of Kompong Cham.
Much of the seventy-square-mile plantation was ruined by initial "softening up" air strikes. In standard operating procedure
the NVA withdrew, avoiding decisive battle with the strong
ARVN force. ARVN units rolled into Chup and looted and pillaged the plantation they'd come to free. The units then turned
north, driving off Communist forces who had laid siege to
Kompong Cham a month earlier.

In Hanoi, Norodom Sihanouk broadcast a lengthy appeal to all Khmers to fight the foreign interventionists. On the twenty-seventh, Cambodia and South Viet Nam established formal diplomatic relations.

The immense loss of materiel, as seen by the Hanoi Politburo, was appalling. Indeed, the Communist leaders estimated that their war effort had been set back at least a year. The Politburo sent orders to the NVA command center for the north third of South Viet Nam (this headquarters was separate from COSVN) to launch as many diversionary attacks as possible against local targets—anything to take the heat off the sanctuaries. Some of the heaviest fighting of the war in the I Corps region of South Viet Nam ensued. Even this fighting went poorly for the Communists. The gloom in Hanoi was lightened by two items—Hanoi's America watchers reported that U.S. domestic turmoil would probably set back Allied war efforts at least a year, and on 3 June, President Nixon delivered his second televised "Cambodia" speech.

The President, claiming the operation the "most successful of this long and difficult war," affirmed the resumption of U.S. troop withdrawals from Southeast Asia and reaffirmed the 30 June limit on America's Cambodian incursion, including "all American air support" for Allied ground units.

On that same day, NVA units laid siege to the northwestern city of Siem Reap (more than two hundred air miles from the nearest border point) and heavily shelled the major crossroads and market city of north-central Cambodia, Kompong Thom.

The battlefield was prepared. It was time for the nationalist Communists to make their move. Nang squatted, rooted like a tree. The land to the south was intermittent forested swamps. Rice paddies stretched north and west in the Sen Valley and southwest to the Chinit. To the east, in a jungled plain, the main body of the NVA 91st Division and attached Khmer Viet Minh and Khmer Krahom units massed preparing to attack.

At twelve minutes past midnight an ear-splitting roar, freight trains rushing in the night sky, signaled Communist units—move! Sixteen 122mm rockets slammed into FANK garrison positions. Defenders scattered, regrouped.

"It's time," Met Taun, the Krahom platoon leader, whispered to Met Nang. Nang did not respond. "It's time." Taun leaned forward in his squat, ready to stand.

A second fusillade of rocket artillery ripped the night sky, erupting at the two FANK garrisons straddling Highway 6, one north and one south of the city. A Viet Namese trail guide found

Met Taun in his squat. Without words the soldier signaled the Khmer unit commander that he should follow.

"In a short while," Nang interrupted. He pulled the guide into the thicket.

The jungle to the east came alive with the muffled sounds of trucks and troops moving south. The main force was moving, circling south from where it would drive north, headlong into the FANK defenders. Again the shriek of rockets, the flashes, the explosions. Now not at garrisons but in the city's heart.

"It's time." The guide's voice was low, forceful. Nang held Taun's arm tightly but said nothing. "Get up!" The guide stood, grabbed Nang and tugged. "Get up!" He grabbed Taun. Both sat, passive as sacks of rice. "Do you understand?" The guide became hysterical trying to lift Taun. In the blackness Nang squeezed Taun's arm more tightly. "These browns are insane!" The guide snapped his head up as if he were explaining to his own superior the exasperating futility of directing Khmers. Then he fled.

Fools, Nang thought. Troop footfalls beat quick cadence on the jungle roads about him. He felt calm, centered. There is nothing in this plan, he thought. The yuons have numerical superiority and they waste it. They will not waste us.

"Met Nang," Taun whispered very quietly. "Why do we sit?"

"Do you wish to be the first to die?"

"Our place is at the front," Taun said. He had turned, still in his squat, and seized Nang's shoulder.

"What end will it serve to commit your yotheas to the yuon attack?" Nang sat as passive under Taun's pressure as he had under the trail guide's.

"Without fire one cannot blossom into a soldier," Taun retorted with a slogan from his leadership class.

Nang grunted. "This is not a battle. This is two villainous lizards crashing against each other, gouging each other's eyes as they fight for carrion."

"I have heard much of the great Met Nang," Taun began flatly. Along the trail spur the yotheas fidgeted in tiny concealments, waiting for the signal, itching to escape into the flow. "I have heard tales of courage, stories of strength. . . ."

"Stories of patience, Met Taun?"

"To me, the great Nang appears to shirk from battle."

The Great Nang, Nang thought, and smiled inwardly. Do they call me that? The thought pleased him. Stories of the Great Nang . . .

Taun clicked his flashlight, three quick, one slow. Noiselessly the boys rose—two with old SKS rifles, two with M-2 carbines,

Met Soth, the platoon executive officer, with an American army .45 caliber pistol, the remainder armed with hardwood clubs and curved-blade rice knives. A new Viet Namese guide approached, announced himself. FANK answering artillery exploded in rice fields to their west. The whistled signals of NVA sergeants ricocheted in the woods. "Patience," Nang whispered to Taun. "Swallow your pride."

All night the NVA and FANK exchanged rocket and cannon fire. All night the infantry and armor moved to the final staging point, all night Nang slowed Met Taun, the platoon and thus the assault.

"What is it now?" a Viet Namese captain demanded of Met Taun.

"One of my units has broken contact ... ah ... somewhere, sir."

"Leave them. Your high command wishes the glory of the first penetration to be yours ... for your people."

"Order Met Nang here at once," Taun snapped to Met Soth. "What's his excuse this time?" he muttered beneath his breath. "Sir"—Taun saluted the NVA officer—"I will take care of this. We will not delay."

An entire primary thrust coiled in the hedgerows and treelines between the paddies just south of Kompong Thom. "Kill him on sight," Taun snarled to Soth. Both officers searched the passage to their rear praying that Nang and the boys he'd misdirected would suddenly appear, join them and advance through the crouched NVA troops to the vanguard.

False dawn showed clear sky. Taun clenched his teeth. The ground remained dark. Heavy small arms fire erupted from other attack points. AKs barked, NVA soldiers shrieked, mortar rounds exploded. From an attack point on the west side of the highway a wave of firing soldiers sprinted toward the garrison's berm. Rocket-propelled grenades fired from shoulder tubes flashed across open ground as another wave broke from the treeline.

Behind Met Taun, a wild scream. "Yaaaaah!" A figure flew. Taun twisted. A shrieking jabbing madman kicked his rifle away. Then, bounding, he punched Soth with the force of every cell in his body aligned, cursing madly. "Where have you been?!" It was Nang. He seized the XO's pistol, cocked it, aimed at Met Taun's head. "We've waited at the front for an hour. This is disgrace." Behind Nang one Krahom squad stood poised with their clubs. Behind Soth and the prone Taun the second milled in stunned disarray. Farther back a dozen NVA soldiers watched.

"The attack falters on one weak link," Nang shouted. Suddenly, overhead, the rumbling blast of three unmuffled T-28

274   *John M. Del Vecchio*

fighters shook the ground. Then strafing runs began, began
beyond Nang, the Cambodian National Air Force pilots sweeping
in at such low level no ground troops saw or heard them until
the planes were overhead. The first fighter swooped up, left, to
set up a second run. From the forest swamp antiaircraft fire like
giant jackhammer punches made the ground tremble under a
graying sky dotted with black flak clouds. A tremendous cacophony of blasts and counterfire hid the single shot of Nang
blowing Taun's head apart.

For an hour the platoon retreated, confiscating first three automatic rifles, then another pistol, then an entire case of American grenades which had found its way into the NVA stores after
being purchased a year earlier from a disgruntled troop of the
ARVN 18th Division.

The early morning barrage and assault gave way to an uneasy
daylight lull. Attackers dispersed to preestablished holding sites
while defenders restocked their perimeter lines and prayed their
air force T-28s would sniff out and destroy the enemy. In the
almost impenetrable swamp to the south Nang lied to an NVA
major about the predawn screwup, lied shrewdly, criticizing
himself for allowing platoon leader Taun's nervous fear of battle to split his platoon. Then, like moles, the yotheas on Nang's
order dug individually into the swamp floor and buried themselves. Only three remained above ground, Nang, Soth and a
large, heavy-featured child named Horl.

"You know Met Sar?" Nang whispered to Soth as he led the
two along a low-roofed animal corridor in the vegetation. Soth
indicated he'd once seen the older man. "This battle is not our
battle," Nang whispered as if he were talking for Met Sar.
"Swallow your pride." He did not comment further.

Nang led his short file deeper and deeper into the swamp. At
a break, as he scouted forward and disappeared, Horl asked
Soth, afraid to ask Nang, "Where are we going?"

"I don't know," Soth whispered.

"Is it true, Comrade Nang killed Taun?"

"Taun wasn't pure."

A sudden slap stung Horl's ear. Both boys cringed. Nang was
inches from their backs, embedded in a tangle of vines and
briers as if he'd grown there. Without words, with rapid flicks
of his hand, Nang signaled: Silence! Troops to the east. Stay
put! Quiet! Then he disappeared. Soth froze. Horl, sensing danger, breathed shallow. His breath seemed to suffocate him. He
shivered, afraid to gulp more air. Noise came from fifteen me-

ters forward. Then a tug on his pant leg. He startled, whipped his face left into Nang's beaming grin only an inch away.

"bury these," Nang whispered. Again he disappeared. Horl looked at the weapons leaning against his knee. He turned to Soth, gestured, How-did-he-do-that? then chuckled, silent, relieved. Minutes later Nang again arrived unheard, unseen. He handed the boys a satchel with two claymore mines, blasting caps, wire, a ChiCom gas mask and a tin of AK ammo.

For three hours Nang crept silently from Soth and Horl's growing cache site to a location the boys could not see. At times the trip took only eight or ten minutes, at times half an hour. With each trip Nang produced another weapon or field gear or food. On his last trip he brought an entire field hospital medical kit. "bury it. camouflage it. remember the site."

The second assault on Kompong Thom began at 0200 on 4 June. Again Nang delayed his platoon's advance until after the first Viet Namese soldiers had been shot. Now he directed the Krahom boys to help evacuate the wounded and dead and to furnish themselves with the one best weapon they found. By the dawn withdrawal the platoon was fully armed.

On 5 June the Communist attack commenced exactly as it had on the third and fourth. Again the defenders held, though the fighting was bitter and all the homes and buildings in the outlying areas were destroyed. Peasants either had fled into the city days earlier or were captured or killed. By dawn the small adjacent hamlet of Am Leang was in NVA control. Again the attackers withdrew and dispersed. Again the defenders reinforced the city's perimeter turning Kompong Thom into a walled fortress. On the evening of the sixth, the day on which South Viet Namese Vice-Premier Nguyen Cao Ky declared before the Cambodian National Assembly that ARVN forces would assist FANK whenever and wherever requested, the NVA struck in the familiar pattern. Again the defenders countered with tremendous enfilades from the southern berm. Again NVA rocket and mortar rounds exploded along Highway 6 and across the defenders' line. Within the city, ammunition reserves reached a critical level. Troops, weapons, ammunition were transferred from north barricades to south. At 0300 on the seventh, the 91st, using their APCs for the first time in the battle, struck the north wall. Other elements hit the northwest, damaging the hospital, the west and the east. By 0400 the APCs, with a thousand soldiers in support, had broken through and flooded the north quadrant. By five the west attackers had overrun FANK positions, scattering defenders amongst the homes and alleyways of the city. At six, troops at the south gate blasted through, crossed the Sen River and swarmed in. By dawn Kompong Thom had fallen to the NVA.

Met Nang entered Kompong Thom not as a liberator or as a conquering soldier, but as a spy, an agent, a nationalist, a yothea of Angkar Leou. At first he hugged the shadows between narrow back street shops. Then, increasingly confident, he directed his armed band to rip down and burn the large posters of Lon Nol that adorned various public and private buildings. Sporadic fire could be heard throughout the city as pockets of FANK resisters were ferreted out by the Viet Namese.

"Soth"—Nang flicked the barrel of his new rifle—"tell them to watch over the Khmers. This . . ." Nang stopped, held up his hand for silence and stillness. From the far end of the street a reinforced squad of NVA soldiers appeared, advancing cautiously in well-spaced pairs. Nang studied the faces of the two pointmen. They were empty—no fear, no hate, no elation—only automaton vigilance.

This, Nang thought, this is it. This is the fight, the main battle. This is what Met Sar meant. Hadn't he warned Nang? Hadn't he told Nang that this battle, this victory and the resulting alignment of forces would change Kampuchea for the next thousand years. Yes, Nang thought. Every action is justified. Every death is an investment in the future of Khmer civilization.

Nang pointed to several yotheas, indicated they should retreat, circle the building south. To others he indicated north. To Soth he whispered, "take two through the tailor's shop, four into the gristmill."

The North Viet Namese soldiers proceeded slowly, perhaps too slowly, perhaps because their leader was far more used to fighting amongst trees and peasant huts than amid city buildings. About them the block seemed lifeless, inert. The day had dawned clear. High above Kompong Thom an American OV-1 Mohawk reconnaissance plane photographed the area. Speeding up Highway 6 from Baray a combined FANK and ARVN armored column closed in on Kompong Thom. In the streets everything remained silent. Then, as if the buildings themselves were armed, a single automatic weapon, then twenty-eight, erupted, killing eleven NVA conquerors, sending the rest into retreat.

"Cache their weapons," Nang ordered as his yotheas fell upon the corpses, stripping the soldiers of anything of potential value, slicing their abdomens, then vanishing into back alleys to the silent cheers of Khmer townsmen astonished by the speed and cunning of these small, black-clad boys. From hidden, makeshift alleyway bunkers Khmer men and women emerged, the older ones bowing, their hands clasped before them in grateful *leis*, hands held high signaling the utmost respect; the younger, less formal, asking, "Where are you from? Who are you?"

"Yotheas of Angkar Leou," the boys whispered as they scurried toward the next ambush site.

"Join us." Nang clutched at every youth that approached. "Join the Movement. Join Angkar Leou. We are the soul of Kampuchea."

Ten blocks east the band repeated their ambush, then six blocks north, then in the southwest quadrant. Then the ARVN shelling began and Nang ordered his platoon, now thirty-seven strong, to retreat to the forest.

Kompong Thom fell to the NVA on 7 June. On the eighth, FANK forces with uncoordinated "fifth column" assistance ousted the Viets.

Along the border, Communist forces regrouped and counter-attacked U.S. forces near Mimot; in South Viet Nam, VC terrorists punished the Allies by murdering 114 civilians at Thanh My, 17 miles southeast of Da Nang.

A battle pitting four thousand ARVN and two thousand FANK soldiers against fourteen hundred NVA and Khmer Viet Minh troops at Kompong Speu saw that south central city fall to Hanoi's forces on 13 June, only to be retaken and looted by the Allies on the sixteenth.

By 20 June, Phnom Penh was both inundated with refugees and nearly completely cut off from the Cambodian countryside: in the north the battle for Kompong Thom reflared; rail lines to the west (Battambang and Sisophon) were severed; huge stores of rice at Krang Lovea were seized by the NVA; Highway 1 just north of Neak Luong was again cut; and several bridges of Highway 4 (over which all of the interior's fuel oil traveled) were blown up. The popular crusade against the North Viet Namese, which had attracted more than eighty thousand volunteers to FANK in three months disintegrated as morale fell because of minimal superpower support and military realities. Only the late arrival of drenching monsoon rains bogged down the armies.

American aid to Cambodia, which had totaled about eight million dollars since March, dried up. Though 34,000 ARVN soldiers remained in Cambodia, the Americans were gone. Again Richard Nixon spoke to the American people. He ruled out any future use of U.S. forces in Cambodia. He further said the United States would not assist the ARVN with air support.

The one card he continued to hold was the option of bombing the enemy, but any such bombing was, by law, to be uncoordinated with ground troop activity.

Chhuon lay on his back. It was dark. The rain was very heavy and the noise of the drops pounding on the roof, splatting in the mud of the orchard, dinging off a pot at the kitchen, increased the tension in his chest and abdomen. Sok rubbed his forehead. The light pressure of his wife's fingers hurt but he neither moved nor spoke. On the other side of the plaited palm-frond partition Hang Tung shuffled papers, preparing for the regional chairman's visit. The rustling of the pages irritated Chhuon. Sok placed a tiny candle in a holder the size of a bottle cap, lit the wick and placed the light on Chhuon's forehead. He lay very still, closed his eyes, falling into himself, attempting to see the demon. Sok covered the candle with a glass cup. The flame immediately dimmed and Chhuon felt the sucking. The light flickered lowly. Sok muttered a prayer then fell silent. The suction became stronger. Chhuon concentrated on the demon, working his mind, pushing the demon from the back corners of his skull, from down by his throat, from his inner ears, prying the demon into the open area behind his eyes, pushing, pushing. The flame died. A small ember glowed below a thin wisp of smoke. Then that too disappeared. The suction lifted the skin of Chhuon's forehead but the demon floating behind his eyes remained anchored with lines to his ears. Chhuon went to work. The cable to his right ear needed cutting. He conjured up a hacksaw and set to, rhythmically, all but imperceptibly, rocking his jaw as the saw blade chiseled tooth by tooth into the cable. Then he shuddered. The demon, like a living amoebic ghost, rolled, shot a protoplasmic finger to the top of his skull. Chhuon tried to close the bone but the goo oozed into minute cracks and became embedded. In the dark Sok lit a second candle, placed it on Chhuon's forehead and covered it with a cup. The first suction had been strong enough only to lure the demon into the open; the second, stronger, forced it to counterattack. All inside his mind faint fingers grew like crystal trees branching, spreading, grew expanding and netting and taking over. Chhuon trembled. His body became rigid. Sok, sure it was a reaction to the departing evil, whispered a silent prayer of thanksgiving. Still the fingers flowed, penetrating easily now into tissues they'd never before attempted to control. How easily they moved. Chhuon wept, inside, watching the movement, temporarily exhausted, unable to fight the spread. Sok replaced the first cup with a third as Chhuon had instructed before he

lay down for the *choup* rite. Now the demon twitched like a
spiderweb tapped, plucked like a violin string, twitched confused abandoning fingers deep in virgin tissues, consolidating
and reinforcing the gains about the larynx, thickening the lines
to the skull anchors, rebuilding the cable to the ear. Chhuon's
breathing stopped. From deep, deep in his abdomen, a star, a
tiny sun, rose, light rays blasting into a fog-shrouded darkness,
stabbing, then suddenly shifting, the glow moving no longer in
him but a hand's width above his stomach, swirling, illuminating the entire exterior. Still Chhuon did not breathe. From the
far side came Hang Tung's complaining mumbles. The sun
blipped, disappeared. The demon turned invisible. Chhuon lay
very still, breathing slow shallow breaths. He lay confused,
uncertain if at the last moment the demon had been exorcised,
sucked into the bottle and suffocated, or had it simply rehid?
Had the sun vanished, or had it returned to his center trium-
phant? He lay, not certain, not certain.

"Uncle, come here! I need you."

Chhuon did not respond, as if in ignorance the summons
could be avoided. How hard the past months had been on him,
on his family, on the village. Ever since Kpa's visit in July he
had felt the demon, known of its existence, wished to exorcise
it, yet had not had the will or the strength. With each order
obeyed he'd grown weaker, grown sadder. After the Americans
invaded in the East, invaded only to be disgraced and beaten
into withdrawal—according to Hang Tung and the Khmer
program on Radio Hanoi played over the village's new public
address system over the village's one radio—Chhuon's hopes
had died and in the despair the demon had thrived.

Kpa had appeared at that time, appeared before dawn, dressed
in black, armed, wanting Chhuon to gather his family and to
flee. "I can rid the village of Committee Member Hang," Kpa
had whispered with incongruous formality.

"If Hang is killed," Chhuon whispered back, "twenty will be
executed. It is so written."

"They are already dead," Kpa had said.

"I can protect them," Chhuon answered.

"No!" Kpa shook his head. He left before Hang woke, promising to return, but he'd not been seen again.

For weeks Chhuon whispered with Sok whenever Hang left.
"We might escape to Phnom Penh. My sister Voen will help us."
"Yes. Voen and Chan. He's a rich man now." "We'll stop in
Stung Treng. Cheam must flee too." "How I would like that.
Kim always makes my heart light." "We'll stop first in Neak
Luong. Mister Pech will help us, too." With that mention, Chhuon

would be silent. He found he could not speak of his eldest daughter who immediately came to mind when he mentioned Mister Pech—as if to speak of her would damn her to suffering as he'd damned his favorite son and youngest daughter to violent death. Chhuon knew he was more afraid of the flood held behind that dam than he was of Hang Tung and the yuons. And, too, there was uncertainty over reports of Samay's having left the monastery, having fled, having joined the maquis. To leave might be to abandon him. Yet to stay meant Peou, Sakhon, would be educated in the new school, and that too worried Chhuon. The terrifying ferocity of the bombings deep in the forest which shook the village were not as horrible as the well of horrors behind the floodgate in his mind.

More weeks followed. Each day's talk became shorter. The pipedream, the fantasy of escape, barely smoldered.

"Uncle? Did you hear me? I need you."

Sok lay a hand on Chhuon's wrist. Quietly she rose and padded to the front room. "My husband is deep in sleep," she said politely. "May I—"

"Then wake him." Hang's features sharpened as he glared at the weathered woman, old at forty.

"Uncle." Hang smiled broadly. "The commissar wishes to know what our maximum contribution can be. The army is short of rice."

Chhuon wiped a fake wooziness from his face to stall for time. "The village is beyond its maximum," he said.

"No. No. I'm certain we can find more generosity in the villagers."

"Many of the families have no rice," Chhuon answered.

"Then let those join the People's Liberation forces. They'll be well fed."

"They are the old and the children."

"Ah, the others are holding rice, eh? Assemble the chairmen of the interfamily groups. You will tell them . . . um . . . each group will contribute ten sacks of rice."

"Five hundred . . ."

"*No!* Hundred-kilo sacks. Each group will contribute a thousand kilos of rice. That's what I will have for the commissar. Today!" Hang paused. He smiled. Then his smile vanished. Lowly he said, "Any group refusing to cooperate will be dealt with severely."

Chhuon did not look at Hang Tung but over his head. To disagree with the committee member, Chhuon knew, was useless. "I will . . ."—Chhuon muffled a belch, turned—". . . tell . . ." He fell to one knee, gasped, hunched, grabbed his stomach.

"Uncle?!"

"It's . . . it's this damned . . . heat . . ." Chhuon sputtered. He regained control of his breath and straightened. "Goddamn," he growled.

"It's painful? Yes. That I can see."

"Yes. Damn. It hits me like that. Without warning. I must lie down."

"It would be better to stay upright, Uncle. Walk. That's the best thing. I've asked the doctor for you."

The heat subsided as Chhuon walked, the repressed bitterness did not. The first chairman's reaction had been passive acceptance of the impossibility—the reaction Chhuon had expected—yet in the reaction he found great sadness. In the sadness he found bitterness. In the bitterness he found a spark of hope.

From the northeast quadrant Chhuon slogged over the mud-thick path toward Ny Non Chan's. He walked shoeless. The army had requested a contribution of footwear. No one in Phum Sath Din was allowed shoes other than flimsy Japanese clogs of aerated rubber which stuck in the mud. As he paced toward the village vice-chairman's home the earth trembled. His knees seemed to rattle with the quaking. Chhuon froze. At first there was no noise. His head snapped up, eyes searching the dense overcast. He felt a slight concussive wind, then he heard the blasts. To the north, he thought. Perhaps six, eight kilometers. He squatted. The trembling continued for a full minute then ceased. Then farther north another bombing. Then quiet stillness.

Chhuon remained in his squat. Again he looked up. The village paths were empty. Though he suspected exaggeration in most of Pen Sovan's reports over Radio Hanoi he believed the broadcasts he'd heard about American B-52s raining death upon the land. He'd heard firsthand reports from soldiers, and he'd trembled inwardly time and again when Hang Tung had shouted bitterly about the United States waging its unprovoked colonial war against Cambodia. He knew, too, that the North Viet Namese were moving in more and more units in the wake of the American withdrawals, that it was these units which were without rice, and that the units close by never remained long in one place for fear of detection by the high-altitude bombers.

What he did not know was that the North Viet Namese had begun large-scale expansion of the Ho Chi Minh Trail in Laos and Cambodia to ensure the invulnerability of the route. Approximately fifteen thousand trucks were now working the trail. New lines were being run to Stung Treng City and to Rovieng, a town fifty miles north of Kompong Thom.

For a week rumors had crisscrossed the village of a new NVA

armored unit encamped in the jungle to the north. Then Heng and Khieng had come in on pass, had strutted about flashing their new rifles at the younger boys and bragging about the tank crews whom they supported. The crews were all young women from North Viet Nam, they said. Women trained at the Soviet armor school in Odessa on the north shore of the Black Sea. With them, though not loggered together, were two batteries of 130mm self-propelled long-range artillery guns. An image flickered behind Chhuon's eyes, a fantasy of the bombs destroying the tanks. The thought scared him. Anything which could so shake the ground, which could so quake mother earth as the bombers, had to be evil.

Chhuon whispered a prayer, then quietly he vowed, "I will become enlightened for the sake of all living things." Then he beseeched the Blessed One, "What has happened to my country? What will happen to my people?"

At Ny Non Chan's, before Chhuon was able to utter the new contribution order, Chan blurted, "We have great trouble."

"We always have great trouble." Chhuon attempted to avoid the embarrassment of not knowing.

"New trouble. Aiee!" Chan pulled Chhuon close. He bowed his head, shook in empathy. "A Viet Namese soldier," he blurted. "He's been caught consorting with . . . by force."

"Who?"

"Their guards have him. There's talk of denouncing him."

"Who did he pluck?"

"She's a good woman. I'm certain it was by force."

"Who?" Chhuon pushed Chan's hands from his own.

"I cannot believe she would bed them for rice. She cannot be that desperate."

"Brother"—Chhuon grabbed Chan firmly—"tell me who you are speaking of."

Chan avoided Chhuon's eyes. Then he mumbled, "Ry. Your cousin's wife."

For a long moment Chhuon said nothing. Then, quietly, firmly, he passed on the contribution order. "That," Chhuon added, "is great trouble."

"The village can't last until harvest. If . . . if we contribute . . . a thousand kilos . . . more than a week's food for everyone . . ."

Suddenly a shot cracked. Chhuon whipped around, stared, then spat, "Come!"

The two men ran from the house, down the alley between the old homes of the Ny family, across the village center toward the wat. Before them a crowd of forty or fifty had formed about a North Viet Namese jeep. Up and down, the village street was lined with foreign soldiers. Chhuon squirmed into the mob, to the front. "Serves him right," he heard several men say as he passed. Before him, lifeless, facedown in the mud, lay an NVA soldier. The shot had evidently been fired into his skull from behind as he'd knelt with his hands tied behind his back. Chhuon raised his eyes to the officer standing in the vehicle. The Khmer crowd increased to a hundred.

"We have told you," the soldier said in perfect Khmer, "that under Prince Sihanouk there is no threat of rape or looting. Your village is protected. Our soldiers must set an example of perfect order and discipline. The Alliance of Khmer and Viet Namese shall break old barriers and build new trust."

"Did he really rape her?" Chhuon heard a villager ask.

"It makes no difference, eh?" a second responded. "It's only important to show how we are protected."

"Ah, Uncle." Hang Tung's voice came softly over Chhuon's shoulder. "You see how they honor us by punishing one of their own who transgresses." Chhuon turned toward Hang. Behind him Ny Non Chan's face distorted in an eerie smile. Chhuon shut his eyes. He attempted to repeat the vow—I will become enlightened . . . but the demon flared, exploding in his mind, and Chan's eerie smile repeated on Chhuon's face. Then Hang Tung's voice penetrated his ears and sped through the cables. "You've arranged for the rice?"

Two weeks passed. In the fields, in the depleted market, at the wat, wherever citizens of Phum Sath Din met publicly, talk was about the NVA having killed one of their own to protect the village. No one spoke of Ry. No one spoke of the rice contribution, knowing a complaint, overheard, could mean punishment. In private they worried about the food stores. The harvest would be late because of the delayed start of the monsoons, and most stores had been confiscated. "A thousand kilos is not much." Hang Tung smiled for Chhuon. "In a village this large, why, a thousand is nothing."

"That was not the first thousand," Chhuon had answered, smiling, acting, keeping it light. "Nor the second or the third," he added, almost laughing.

"You know these peasants," Hang Tung said. "They have rice hidden everywhere. The family bunkers are full."

"I think you overestimate, Nephew. Only the old families had extra and they shared it with the new people. And the army. Some people have taken to eating morning-glory greens."

"They're very good. Very good for you. People should eat more greens."

"They need rice, too," Chhuon said flatly, dropping the pretext of amiability.

"The army needs rice," Hang Tung snapped. "If COKA says one thousand kilos or ten thousand kilos or one hundred thousand kilos, the village will pay. In the meantime, tell them to plant more. You're the agronomist. How late can late-season be planted?"

"There's no paddy space left. The yuons . . ." Chhuon halted. He glanced at Hang Tung. The boy smirked. "Our brothers from across the border have, rightly so, cordoned off all the far paddies. Those close by are . . ."

"And maize?"

"The roadways are all . . ."

"And vegetables?"

"Yes. Every family has a . . ."

"You see. There's enough. Morning-glory greens. Indeed! Perhaps the orchards should be cut to make room . . ."

"The orchards! Never!"

"Uncle!"

Pressure from outside elements continued to be paramount in Cambodia. By midsummer U.S. domestic and political reaction to its own incursion had assured the North Viet Namese of their secure position throughout Indochina. In the outskirts of Kratie, at the new COSVN headquarters, the North Viet Namese began a slow, systematic emasculation of the Provisional Revolutionary Government of the National Liberation Front. The process was subtle, combining mild criticism sessions with reeducation— yet, ironically, because of the successes of the Allied incursion, the Southern rebel leadership was essentially imprisoned deep in Cambodia by the Northerners, and at a substantial distance from the war in the South. This allowed the North Viet Namese to substitute their own cadremen for Southerners who resisted reeducation. New-thought was to supplant old; socialist nationalism gave way to strict Northern Marxism; the petit bourgeois was purged; the proletariat served. To Hanoi, America's withdrawal meant the superfluous baggage of the South's fragmented political opposition was no longer necessary. The last element of civil war, not in Cambodia but in South Viet Nam, was removed, replaced by North Viet Nam's frontal and terrorist invasions in its bid for regional hegemony. In conjunction with the removal of the Southern rebel leaders, the NVA in Cambodia began a second-phase program of massive training of the essentially apolitical, headless Khmer Rumdoah—the peasant farmers and urban youth who had rallied under the name and to the call of North Viet Nam's new marionette, Norodom Sihanouk.

And yet all was not necessarily lost for the Allies. For all the bungling, the unheeded advice, and the unread analyses, the incursion into the NVA sanctuaries, albeit coincidental to the administration's announced and failed objectives, did stop the NVA from immediately toppling Phnom Penh.

Also, for the first time in the war substantial numbers of Northern soldiers had defected; twelve thousand NVA had been killed; eighteen thousand weapons had been captured along with 6.5 million antiaircraft rounds, a million rifle rounds, thousands of 122mm rockets, hundreds of military trucks, and six Mercedes-Benz autos. A quarter million rations of rice, enough to feed four divisions for three months, had been destroyed; an entire rear service group (the 86th) had been wiped out and the main communications liaison system, responsible for training, equipping and assigning replacement soldiers, was ruined.

North Viet Nam's decision was difficult and hotly debated. In the end those calling for rebuilding the sanctuaries won over those who desired to plunge headlong into the now certain military conquest of Cambodia. Yet the decision to temporarily withdraw from the secondary objective (Cambodia), and to pull manpower and materiel back to rebuild the border base complexes to assist the primary objective of capturing South Viet Nam, pivoted not so much on their tactical losses as on two other factors: first, in the wake of the American domestic storm there was no possibility of a second incursion, thus new sanctuaries would be forever secure; and second, there was the fear in Hanoi that Phnom Penh's fall would reinvigorate American hawks before they had been rendered politically impotent.

In early September, after the news of the "liberation" of Stung Treng City reached Phum Sath Din, new orders and new horrors descended like the seven plagues. The Viet Namese Communist Party Central Committee's (the Hanoi Politburo's) Central Commission for Kampuchean Affairs, headed by Le Duc Tho and assisted by Vo Chi Cong (who had engineered the Khmer Viet Minh repatriation of 1969 and 1970), ordered COKA (the Central Office for Kampuchean Affairs), headed by Le Duc Anh, to reorganize the "liberated" Khmers. Directives were routed through the A-40 subdivision at Siem Reap where COKA's headquarters were adjacent to those of the NVA.

"There is no rice left." Ry wept. "They've taken everything. Even the maize, salt and oil."

"I know, Sister," Sok tried to comfort her. It was early evening. The farmers had just returned from the fields to find the new orders posted on gates, at the wat, along the deserted market row. In their homes they found enough food for three days. "They left me only one rice pot," Sok said sadly.

"And the boys. Where is Mister Committee Member? I should scratch out his eyes."

"Ssshh! Ry, you must not be heard."

"Where are they?"

"My husband has argued with him all day. All day he has begged. Chhuon's at the pagoda. Tung's with the red-eyed devils."

"They've taken all the food. All the boys. Most of the girls."

"Only those over fourteen. Only for training. They'll come back to serve in the militia. Maybe they'll have more to eat."

"The sixteen-year-olds are being conscripted. But us . . . without food . . ."

"They said it will remain in the village. There are so many with nothing, some with hoards. Now it'll be distributed equally. It will be rationed so we do not all starve."

"Sok! Sok! Listen to yourself. You sound like them."

"Dear Sister, what can we do. My husband knows best. We must . . ."

"escape." Ry uttered the word very low. She studied Sok's face for shock, for disbelief. "into the forest."

Sok remained calm. After a moment she responded quietly, "There are patrols." Now Ry did not respond. "And the bombings. And it's against the rules."

"tonight," Chhuon whispered to Sok.

"tonight," Sok signaled Ry when they met for ration distribution.

"tonight," Ry signaled Ny Nimol, Ny Non Chan's wife. Quietly throughout the village, the old people, members of the original four families, signaled one another and went home.

"Uncle"—Hang Tung smiled at Chhuon after he'd eaten heartily, devouring a dinner of four or five rations—"in a little while you'll accompany me."

"Tonight?" Chhuon asked. He blinked his eyes, fighting for an image. Then he tried to remain as empty of emotion as a rock, tried to see himself an undistinguished small stone.

"Yes. Were you going somewhere?"

"Only to bed," Chhuon answered. "The rain's heavy and my knees are swollen. I hoped to sleep."

"Sleep later. Tonight we'll have fun. Major Nui has invited me to play cards. You must come."

"Oh Nephew, I'm so tired . . ."

"You *must* come. We'll leave at 2100 hours. Rest now."

The card game took place at Ny Non Chan's house. Chhuon, Chan, Major Nui, Cadreman Trinh and Hang Tung sat at a low rectangular table, Major Nui at one end, the other end open. At the center of the table there was a charcoal heater. Above it, boiled a pot of oil. The men had finished snacking on thin slices of crayfish flash fried in the oil. Nimol removed the pot, leaving the embers exposed. Chhuon felt mesmerized by the glow. He stared at one particular coal glowing brightly on two edges, cracked and dark through the middle.

"They're very hot, eh, Uncle?" Hang chuckled pleasantly.

"Yes," Chhuon said self-consciously.

"You seem preoccupied tonight, Chairman Cahuom," the cadreman said.

"It's the crayfish," Chhuon said. "I used to catch them in the river with my boys. I haven't tried it in years."

"Some of the soldiers caught these." The cadreman smiled. "They're camped by the bridge tonight. Perhaps we'll have more tomorrow. They shine a light into the river and it attracts them. That's how they do it."

"Oh." Chan tried to look amused. "I've always caught them during daylight."

"Ah," the cadreman chuckled. "But the big ones emerge only at night."

Nimol returned with a bowl of watermelon seeds. She removed the heater. The seeds were a gift from Major Nui. As the major shuffled the cards Chhuon, feeling guilty, ravenously yet delicately picked at the seeds.

"Do these come out at night, too?" Chhuon tried to joke but the humor fell flat. Hang checked his watch. It was nearly midnight.

In the far distance, perhaps ten kilometers, a faint rumbling could be felt. "Those bastards," Major Nui said. "Every night, every day. Why do they bomb? *Troi oi!* Almost never do they connect. They keep me awake."

"Come, deal the cards." Hang Tung laughed.

Chhuon raised his first card but he did not recognize it. He was thinking about the river, about tonight. Why tonight? Though it was not the first night he'd played cards with the Viet Namese, it was the first time the game had been called on such short notice and for such a late hour.

"The major tells me," Hang Tung began, his smile wide, "that we'll be seeing new rules tomorrow."

Chhuon did not take the bait. He still had not recognized his card but thought it was not a card at all but a faint moving growing sheath, growing like a crystal, like his demon. His eyes darted up to Chan then dropped to the card. He wondered if the others could see his card pulsate. He cautioned himself, tried to be the rock.

"What new rules?" Chan asked, picking up his second card.

"New passes," the major said. "With all this bombing we can't let anyone travel without a complete itinerary."

Chhuon lifted his second card. As it touched the first the demon's filaments spread and concealed its face. The emotions of a rock, Chhuon thought.

"No one travels now," Chan was saying. He reached for some seeds.

"Any unauthorized travel will be dealt with most severely," Hang said.

"That's as it's been. What are the new rules?"

Hang put his cards down. "It's strictly a matter of paperwork," he said. "New request forms. New passes. And enforcement."

At that, rifle fire was heard erupting by the river. Then screams. Chhuon jolted upright. Chan slumped imperceptibly. The major paid no attention. Cadreman Trinh and Hang Tung smiled.

"*Troi oi!*" The major dropped his hand. "Let's see if they've got more crayfish."

The riverbank was lit with torches and lanterns. On downriver trails flashlight beams flickered between tree trunks. A dozen Viet Namese soldiers and a dozen young Khmer militiamen cursed, prattled, strutted. Four bodies lay by the water's edge—two children, two women. The soldiers laughed, congratulated one another on the fine kills. A radio rasped. The two men who'd fled downriver had been caught.

Chhuon watched, empty, the rock, yet worried, agitated deep within. The soldiers soaked rags in gasoline and jammed them into the men's mouths. Their ankles were tied, their elbows wired together behind their backs. The soldiers toyed with a torch, bringing it close, then withdrawing it, then again bringing it near to the rags. Chhuon knew both men. One was Chhimmy Chamreum, second son of the head of the Chhimmy family, the second-oldest family in Phum Sath Din. The other was Chan's brother, Ny Hy San. Chan, very much in control, very cool, stepped toward his brother. "You idiot!" he denounced San. "What were you doing out here?" Chan reached to grasp the rag from San's mouth but Hang grabbed Chan's arm. "Let go of me. I'll deal with him. He's my brother. This is a family matter."

There was commotion on the ill-lighted riverbank as soldiers subdued Chan. Still Chhuon watched. He did not move. Did not speak. Horrified, yet numbed, Chhuon, the rock, the undistinguished small stone which no one will notice, did not even gulp air.

San and Chamreum tried to vomit the rags from their mouths. The fumes alone made them nauseous—the taste, the fear intensified. Soldiers made bets. San tried to push the rag from his mouth with his tongue, tried to work his jaw, tried to call to his older brother and to Chairman Cahuom, but the rag had been jammed in, packed in, and his gagging could not dislodge it.

"The new orders . . ."—Major Nui broke into Chhuon's numbness—"the new orders, you'll post them tomorrow, eh? Anyone caught attempting unauthorized travel will be dealt with severely. Anyone unaccounted for will cause three others to be punished."

Chamreum's rag flared. He could not scream. San shuddered, unable to watch, unable to look away. Chamreum jumped horribly as his skin burned. Unable to hold his breath he inhaled through his nostrils. Hot flaming gases were sucked into his nose, yet still his diaphragm dropped, dropped uncontrollably, dropped sucking the flame into his lungs. His face burned, the stench was disgusting. San leaped back from a soldier approaching with a torch. Chhuon recognized the troop. He was not NVA but a local militiaman, a boy, his own son's tormentor, Khieng. Chhuon bowed his head. San dodged back, jerked left, right. The soldiers laughed at the comical man with the gasoline-wet rag hanging from his mouth. Chamreum collapsed to his knees, dying from suffocation, not burns, dying as the fire consumed the oxygen about his face, dying because his seared lung linings could not have absorbed oxygen had there been any in the air to inhale.

Chan could not watch, could not save his brother, because soldiers still held him. He turned his head to Chhuon. The rock, the stone. Somehow, Chhuon, under Chan's eyes, saw himself at fault. Somehow they read him, read his mind, learned of the escape plan. How many attempted? How many others were caught, will be caught? Did any succeed? The village will hold Chhuon responsible. Hadn't he picked the night? How many villagers saw him with the major tonight? There was no other way. The rock, the stone. Without emotion Chhuon watched as Khieng lunged at San, watched as the rag ignited, as San fell back, down the bank into the current. The flame died. There was thrashing as San tried to right himself in the rushing waters of the Srepok. More thrashing then nothing. The current grabbed him, washed him away.

CHAPTER TEN

The news of Pech Lim Song's execution had reached Vathana the day the first American craft docked in Neak Luong. For months afterward, she felt she would always associate Americans with sunshine and death. Through the tedious summer-month monsoons and into the fall she caught herself at odd times quoting Mister Pech to dockworkers, rivermen or refugees. Then she'd find tears welling in her eyes as his image and that of old Sambath came to her. And she would feel as though someone had ripped out her soul, as if her insides had been scraped clean leaving an empty cavity. And always the image mixed with clouds breaking in late afternoon, with sun rays beaming upon Americans and their war boats. Long after U.S. forces were withdrawn, after the Mekong from Saigon to Phnom Penh became, if contested, a South Viet Namese military highway, Vathana found herself searching the piers at dusk for the hairy long-nosed men who when they spoke flailed their arms like barbarians, whose crudeness and uncontrolled body movements both disgusted and amused her. Not until late September, after a force of two hundred South Viet Namese riverine vessels with fifteen hundred marines swept through the swamplands across from Neak Luong, between the Mekong and Bassac rivers, clearing out a major NVA/VC base area, did Vathana see another man from the United States.

The morning sky was gray as Vathana walked from the pagoda. Early every morning since she'd discovered she was again pregnant she had gone to the city's main temple to pray for strength and the health of her baby. In her prayers she attempted to be selfless, feeling she could not ask for more than what the refugees in the swamp-camp received. Yet, for the developing new life, she asked for more, much more. A Westerner might say Vathana was under the care of Doctor Sarin Sam Ol. In the old style, he monitored her pregnancy, observed her habits. There were no sonograms in Neak Luong. If there had been, Vathana would not have been inclined to allow the test. Repeatedly she refused Madame Pech's persistent offers to have her see a Western specialist in Phnom Penh.

As Vathana walked from the pagoda through the market the overcast broke up and the sun shot through the gaps. For two days she hadn't felt the baby move. Now she feared it was dead. She fought the urge to see Doctor Sarin. It is too early, she thought. He's busy. Perhaps, she told herself, the baby only sleeps. Perhaps it is only that I've been preoccupied and haven't noticed.

The market stalls were full of goods—sweets, housewares, dried and fresh fish, chickens, pigs, vegetables. There were new items—military items—ponchos and thin camouflaged nylon quilts, canteens, a jeep radiator and truck mirrors, wiring harnesses, a few artillery shell casings, uniform shirts, American boots, a dozen rucksacks.

At her apartment Vathana lay down. She lay on the floor, her feet on a pillow. "Angel?" Sophan knelt beside her. "Are you okay?"

"Yes." Vathana's answer was calm. "I just wish to have my feet up a moment." Why she did not tell Sophan her fear she didn't know. Immediately she wished she had.

"Angel, guess what?" Sophan's face shone.

"What?" Vathana said. She hid the trembling of her lower jaw.

"Samnang—this morning—he crawled. A meter. At least a meter. He's asleep but you'll . . ."

Vathana barely smiled, barely heard. She placed a hand on her abdomen, felt its tight, hard bulge. Standing in her long full black skirt and loose white blouse she didn't look pregnant, not nearly six months, but lying on her back with the cloth falling to her sides, she looked very far along. She closed her eyes. Sophan padded softly to the kitchenette. Move baby, Vathana thought. Please. Just a little wiggle. The thought of the baby wiggling brought a warmth to her heart but immediately the smile was overridden by fear.

Vathana tried to supplant fear with other thoughts. There's much to do today. The week's food distribution plan for the camp must be recorded, copied and issued. There are still ten thousand refugees. Many have moved to Phnom Penh, yet more arrive. Vaguely she thought of the situation along the Mekong. The ARVN had taken over every riverside village in order to guarantee the security of the country's aorta. Inhabitants had been forced to retreat away from the river's edge, many into hamlets which the Communists controlled. In the Southeast the NVA and Viet Cong had instituted a deliberate program of expelling civilians and forcing them into national government areas—thus increasing the refugee burden while freeing themselves from responsibility for "nonproductive elements." American bombings, too, were worse than in the spring. How, Vathana thought, do they say it?—because few hamlet relocations have been plotted for the pilots!

A flutter. Vathana's eyes brightened. She rose, went to the desk. Then she thought perhaps she had willed the flutter and the fear crept back. To simplify the food distribution she had organized the camp into ten-family units, each unit having one appointed leader responsible for the rice, salt and oil ration. After an hour, Vathana closed the camp books and lifted the shipping ledgers. Her barge, Teck's barge, had been "leased" by the government and was no longer under their control, yet she continued to maintain accurate logs for maintenance, as Mister Pech had taught her, and semiaccurate lading manifests of what and how much was shipped, where it was shipped, what the captain and crew reported about each trip. No longer were foodstuffs exported. Another hour passed. Vathana moved on to new business. At the camp this day there would be a foreign visitor, a Swedish doctor, who was coming to revamp the sanitation system.

Suddenly there were two knocks, two raps, almost simultaneously, one at the door, one from the inside of her womb. Vathana sat back, her entire face lit with joy and relief. Inside her the fetus rolled. "What are you doing in there?" she whispered. "Are you building a house?"

"Hello." Vathana heard Sophan's greeting. She could tell by the wet-nurse's voice that the visitor was a stranger.

"Scuse me, ma'am," an immense Caucasian said in English. Vathana went to the door. Sophan stepped back. *Chow bah,"* the American said in bastardized Viet Namese. "Ah, shit!" The soldier rolled his head, neck and shoulders in what would have been, from a Khmer, a rude display of one's body out of control. "Ah cain't tahk ta these here little folk." Vathana giggled. The huge American seemed more like a circus bear than a human. "La-ten-ent!" The soldier turned, called down the corridor. "Scuse me, ma'am," the soldier said, shaking a hand with thumb pointing, "but he'll be here in a minute." To himself the soldier said, "God a'mighty, why's that J. L. go tell me ta knock if he weren't goina be here? Him en that dragon lady aide from the Foreign Ministry."

"*Monsieur*"—Vathana raised her hands in a graceful *lei*—"*parlez-vous français?*"

"Augh, shit," the soldier mumbled. He glanced furtively down the corridor. "There they go again with them hands." Loudly he yelled, "La-ten-ent! There's som-bodday home."

From the hall came the voice of Madame Pech. "Dear," she called in French. "Vathana, dear." As she entered the room she smiled a broad fake smile, not the ubiquitous smile of old Cambodia, which was a show of friendship and goodwill, but the fake smile of a Parisian debutante imagining herself before cameras. "Well, look at you," she said quickly. "You look lovely. Are you taking care of our new grandchild?" Then Madame Pech turned to Sophan. She nodded, a gesture which was almost a nonacknowledgment, then back to Vathana. "How is Samnang?"

"Mother," Vathana said pleasantly in Khmer, "who are these men?"

"This is Sergeant Huntley of the Military Equipment Delivery Team." Madame Pech indicated the large man who'd knocked on the door. "And this"—indicating the man emerging from behind the sergeant—"is Lieutenant Sullivan. You know, like the American boxer." Madame Pech raised her two tiny fists and circled them about like an old-time pugilist. "Lieutenant John L. Sullivan."

"No relation," the American officer said sheepishly.

To the officer Madame Pech said in English, "This daughter mine. She Angel Neak Luong."

Vathana bowed again. The second American was smaller than the first, not much larger than a Khmer man. His hair was coppery and his face was covered with a thousand freckles. In simple Western civilian dress he did not appear to be a soldier. "*Pardonez-moi.*" Sullivan bowed, returning Vathana's greeting with a clumsy *lei*. "Please excuse my friend and me," he said in perfect French. "We're sorry but we've not yet learned Khmer."

Vathana's eyes twinkled. In her womb the fetus flipped as if it were somersaulting. "French is fine," Vathana said. She backed into the apartment, leading the visitors into the living room. "May I help you? You're American?"

"*Oui,*" Sullivan said softly.

"How da ya like this!" Huntley blurted. "It's a dang real live livin room. With a TV!"

"Ron!" Sullivan looked up at the big sergeant and squeezed the word out between his teeth.

"Oh, ah, sorry, J. L."

"Mrs. Pech." Sullivan turned his attention to Vathana. "I need to find the man in charge of the refugee center. Your mother . . ."

"Oh," Madame Pech interrupted. She spoke quickly in Khmer. "Vathana, straighten this young man out. I've just come to tell you to have Teck's clothes packed. I'll send a servant for them. He's going to remain in Phnom Penh where he can assist the war effort most effectively." At that Madame Pech bid her daughter-in-law and the Americans adieu.

Sullivan began again. "Mrs. Pech . . . ," he said tentatively.

Vathana smiled. "Cahuom Vathana," she said. "In Cambodia a wife does not take her husband's name."

"Chum Vatana," he repeated, trying to catch all the syllables and the inflection. "You are the woman they call 'the Angel'?"

"Only Sophan does that." Vathana opened her hand toward the stout older woman. Sullivan was lost for words. Vathana's movement was at once simple, elegant and graceful.

"J. L.," Sergeant Huntley whispered, "look at this here." He had flipped open the photo album of Vathana's wedding. "Look at this dude in the gold loincloth. Wow!"

Sullivan did not answer Huntley. He had not taken his eyes from Vathana's face. Her skin was perfectly clear, smooth, the loveliest bronze he'd ever seen. Her lips were full. Ripe, he thought. But most of all he noticed her eyes. They twinkled. They sparkled. They held an irrepressible glow so steeped in love not even the war could tarnish the luster.

"Your mother—" Sullivan began after a pause.

"Madame Pech?" Vathana said. She did not look into Sullivan's face but slightly down and to the side. "Madame Pech is my mother-in-law. Her son was my husband."

"Oh," Sullivan said, taking the "was" to mean her husband had been killed. "I'm sorry."

Vathana realized immediately the American's misunderstanding but she did not correct it. She found she was enjoying speaking French to this man, found she was enjoying his exotic appearance, found herself liking his polite manner of standing serenely. What she did not like was how she felt she looked to him, her face and lips puffed in pregnancy, her walk a waddle of wide hips.

"You are looking . . ."

"Oh! Yes. For the man in charge of the camp."

"I'm the man in charge," Vathana said. She raised her shoulders and giggled slightly.

Sullivan giggled too in what appeared to Ron Huntley as the

weirdest behavior he'd yet seen from the officer, though he, Huntley, did not understand the language being spoken.

For an hour Vathana and Sullivan talked, at first very politely in the living room then rapidly over papers and charts, some of which had been brought by the officer and others of which Vathana had produced from her files. As they talked Sullivan struggled with himself, struggled to keep his eyes on the charts, yet he watched her at the periphery of his vision. He at once felt giddy and intimidated. When she placed her hand on a page and pointed to a figure, he could not keep his eyes off her hand, off the long slender fingers. He forced himself to be more businesslike than he normally would have been. Finally they finished.

"Damn it," Sullivan whispered to Huntley who was sitting on the sofa, sipping tea and watching Khmer TV, mesmerized by the black-and-white tube though he understood not a word spoken.

"What's up?" Huntley rose slowly, still watching the TV as if he didn't want to miss an important part of a dramatic plot.

"For one, they only received a hundred sheets," Sullivan said. He turned and bowed to Sophan and Vathana.

"That cor-roo-gate-tad plastic shit?" Huntley said when they were back in the corridor.

"Yup. We sent a thousand. The camp received a hundred. Same with everything. The shipping orders match but somebody's changed the numbers."

"Think she sold it?"

"No. No way."

"Why not? Cause she's knocked up?"

"Huh?"

"Wouldn't a minded a piece a that myself a few months back. What about you? I see you lookin at them swelled tits."

"Fuck you!"

"Hey, J. L., I was just askin."

"Come on. Mrs. Cahuom said we can go to the camp."

Within moments after the Americans left the apartment building, there was a harsh series of raps on the door. Sophan opened it. A young, thickset Khmer pushed his way in, slammed the door. Both women startled. From the bedroom the infant Samnang screamed.

"Cahuom Vathana! I have a message," The man spoke in rural dialect. Vathana stepped forward. "Only for you," the man snapped.

"See to the baby," Vathana said quietly to Sophan.

"How many children have you?" The messenger smiled a snarling eerie smile as he said the idiom which might be interpreted as a simple greeting between old friends who had not seen each other for a long time, yet from his lips it came as a piercing threat. He did not let the young mother respond. "Your brother, Sakhon"—the man's words were hard—"he should be with you."

"Peou! Is he here? Who . . ."

"It is your father's wish."

"My father? Where is he? Did he send you? Is my mo—"

The messenger spoke quickly, stopping Vathana's questions. "He's home. He's okay. He wishes Sakhon to live with you."

"Yes. Yes. Of course."

"For Angkar Leou to bring your brother you must help."

"Certainly. For who? Help who!?"

"If you repeat a word of what I tell, you'll not again see your father, mother or brother. You'll be told what need be done. Befriend the American."

Nang sat in the open field east of Baray, sat in the posture of perfect attention. He had matured in five months, had become bulkier with the arms and legs of a man instead of the spindles of a boy. Though he could still contract to look like a child he could no longer pull off the feat with certainty. His mind, too, had changed. A bitterness, a deeper distrust, had gripped its core. After June's successful rear attacks on the NVA at Kompong Thom, after the ARVN recaptured the city from the Northerners, Nang had been recalled to Mount Aural. There he'd endured his first real *kosang*. At first Nang and Soth had bragged of their exploits to a group of new conscripts, to an operations officer, to three political commissars. They had spoken in generalities, relaying sketchy details, then, with greater and greater élan, Soth had boasted to the commissars how easily the mighty NVA soldiers fell.

"Comrades"—Soth had beamed—"you should have been there." The commissar said nothing. "They are not gods," Soth had shouted exactly as he'd heard Met Sar shout about the Americans. "They are not gods. Me, this backward hillbilly with a minimum of arms and men . . . we inflicted great loss upon them. Great loss. More casualties than FANK with its fighter-bombers. Haw ha! They never expected it. It was Nang. Met Nang. He is to be congratulated on ordering us. He is to be honored for his courage."

Then, after accusation, led by Met Soth, a score of boys from their unit had condemned Nang, their platoon leader. For hours, senior officials berated him until he, Nang, yothea of the Brotherhood of the Pure, confessed, broke, cried, withered like a tree plucked from the earth, like a little boy whose pants had been stolen from him at school.

Met Sar had badgered him for his arrogance and stupidity. "What have you done?!" Sar had screamed. "Do you realize the ramifications? The revolution struggles to attain victory over such contemptible personal pride."

For more hours he had endured their screams. What had he done?! North Viet Namese reaction to the "fifth column" assault had been to covertly relegate the Krahom army to shadow status. No longer were battle plans, or attacks, shared. No longer were the nationalist Communists informed of NVA movements. No longer were the Khmer Krahom and the Khmer Viet Minh running parallel revolutions. The NVA/KVM-KK break was partial, informal. To the outside world, all Communist forces in Cambodia still appeared to be united under Norodom Sihanouk.

Nang's fingers tightened. His teeth ground. One hour more, he thought. One day more. After all these months, it is nothing. Before him Met Sar prepared to address the troops assembled east of Baray. To one side were units in black uniforms from the Northern Zone, to the other were troops in gray from the East. Cadre and yotheas sat, chatted amongst themselves. A few men rose, left, returned. A cool drizzle fell. Cadremen lay their kramas over their heads for protection; yotheas opened theirs like small tents or in pairs or threes sat beneath huge banana leaves. Nang did not move. He sat with his krama wrapped like a turban about his head, with his pants rolled up to his knees. He visualized himself a cat, ready to pounce, waiting, patient, waiting for battle, or for Met Soth.

After the *kosang* he had been thrown into a small bamboo cage for three days. On the second evening Met Sar arrived, dismissed the guards, sat on the earth beside his caged protégé. "It's okay," Met Sar had whispered. "Be patient." Nang had stared the stare of a captured beast. The older man had smiled and left. Hours later he'd returned. "They argue over your fate," he'd said pleasantly. "Remember, I told you you'd have to swallow your pride." The older man had rocked back on his round bottom and giggled. "Oh how they argued!" He'd turned to the cage, grabbed the bamboo with his soft pudgy hands. He rolled to his knees staring into the cage more wildly than Nang stared out. "Meditate on this." The words had slid from Sar's mouth like oil. "You have damaged the enemy. Your imprisonment has drawn out true attitudes. I am but an officer of the general staff, but I report to the one who must always remain masked. He knows of you. Of your work. When it is time, contradictory elements will be eliminated."

For minutes the two had stared, frozen, locked in an evil aura passing between their eyes. Then Met Sar had grinned, rolled back onto his plump ass, and asked, "Tell me, Met Nang, did you kill them because they killed your father?"

" 'Soldiers,' " Met Sar began the address with a passage from another conqueror's speech to his troops, " 'you have, in fifteen days, gained six victories, taken twenty-one stand of colors, fifty pieces of cannon, several fortified places, made fifteen hundred prisoners, and killed or wounded over ten thousand men.' " Met Sar stopped reading. He looked at the boy before him. "Do you think," he asked harshly, "it was because of their superior numbers? Because of their materiel?" Met Sar smiled contemptuously, dropped his head.

To the Krahom, to Met Sar, to Nang, just as to Lon Nol and all Cambodians except the Khmer Viet Minh, the new siege of Kompong Thom was unacceptable. After Nang's release from the cage, Sar had told him, "Go back, my eyes, back to Kompong Thom. I need you, my ears, now more than ever." And Nang had gleefully reinfiltrated the Northern Corridor. For months he'd slipped into unliberated villages acting the scared, disoriented orphan whose village had been bombed, who had nowhere to go, nothing to eat. On most attempts he'd been accepted, fed, treated for cuts and bruises—self-inflicted to corroborate his muttered explanations. In most villages he'd contacted or established a Khmer Krahom agent. The work was enjoyable, rewarding. He was a salesman selling his country to its people, to people he liked and wanted to help, to people he wanted to teach his just beliefs. He gathered what information he could, passed along plans and propaganda.

"Be patient," Nang had told them. "Be resourceful. Extend the network. The liberation of Kampuchea is the responsibility of every Khmer. You and I are their sole authentic representatives."

A hundred Krahom agents had moved into Kompong Thom and the surrounding villages during the late summer of 1970. By fall the Center had directed the zone armies to release all the yotheas they could for the coming battle. Scores of temporarily transferred Krahom platoons had secreted themselves in outlying jungles and swamps. Now the transferred elements were grouped east of Baray. Nang sat between groups, rigid, letting his urge for revenge fester.

Sar continued his address with the 174-year-old quote. " 'Destitute of everything, you have supplied yourselves with everything. You have won battles without cannon, crossed rivers

without bridges, made forced marches without shoes, bivouacked without spirituous liquor, and often without bread.

" '. . . Thanks to you, soldiers! your country has a right to
expect of you great things. You have still battles to fight, cities
to take, rivers to pass. Is there one among you whose courage
flags? One who would prefer returning to the sterile summits of
the Apennines and the Alps, to undergo patiently the insults of
that slavish soldiery? No, there is not one such among the
victors of . . .' of Kirirom, of Pich Nil, of Kompong Speu, of Ty
Po."

Inside, Nang sneered. Of that stinging red ant who infiltrated
our ranks, he thought. What great pleasure to kill, to weed out
the bad seed and destroy it. *Kamtech khmang*, the enemy must
be utterly destroyed. For the good of Kampuchea.

" 'Friends,' " Met Sar said. Now he altered Napoleon's words,
" 'I promise you that glorious conquest . . . be the liberators of
peoples." Met Sar omitted the end of the line: " 'be not their
scourges!' "

Met Sar spoke on and on. As the revolution progressed and
small gains were consolidated, the speeches of Krahom officials
lengthened. Had not Khmers come to expect effusive babble
from their leadership? Norodom Sihanouk and Lon Nol delivered radio harangues lasting four, five, six hours. If Krahom
leaders spoke for less, wouldn't their leadership appear to be
less?

"Ay, comrade." A thin man of perhaps twenty, dressed in the
uniform of the Gray Vultures of the East, squatted by Nang. He
spoke quietly, casually, as if commenting on the weather. "A
man's mind can build a world, ay comrade?"

Nang looked at the soldier. He'd come from the side of the
cadremen, from among an eastern zone group of which Nang
had not before seen a single man. Nang played dumb. "What? A
world?"

"You are Met Nang, are you not?"

Nang studied the man's movements. "There are many comrades called Nang."

"Ha. That's very good." The man did not look at him but
faced Met Sar. The old man was reveling in his description of
how, with the advent of the foreign invasion, the Americans and
the ARVN had inadvertently assisted them, had plucked victory
from the hands of the NVA. "Nang of Bokor. I saw you there.
Rang of Stung Treng. I was there too. What I wish to tell you,
Met Nang is"—he paused, glanced suspiciously to each side,
then went on—"is that that world may be disconnected from

reality. Under great pressure, one can build a system of justification so tight, warped thought seems straight."

Both paused. Met Sar's voice droned over them. ". . . pluck victory because the NVA are too mechanized. They are a regular army in a war which will be won by the guerrilla. Soon the battle will recommence. . . ."

"Why do you talk to me?" Nang did not look at the man, yet he sensed and memorized his every feature.

"You are a great soldier," the man said. "I admire you."

"And you? Why don't I know you?"

"You will. I'm called Rin."

"Rin of Svay Rieng?"

"Yes."

"Then I admire you also."

"I must move on," Rin said. "I wanted to meet you. Remember, warped thought can justify any action; any plan can be condoned, ay, not only condoned, embraced." As Rin stood Nang's eyes focused on the seated troops beyond. Soth was pointing to Rin and Nang, talking to a political officer. Nang returned to his rigid posture.

"Sir, I request permission to inspect the FANK task force."

"Denied." The conversation was not new. The lieutenant colonel was somewhere between irritated and apathetic.

"Sir," Lieutenant Sullivan persisted, "then allow me to go with the ARVN."

"Lieutenant"—the colonel stuck out his jaw, pursed his lips, fingered his chin—"you're not an advisor anymore. We've no authorization . . ."

"Damn it, sir!" Sullivan rapped the colonel's desk with a closed fist making the small triangular MILITARY EQUIPMENT DELIVERY TEAM sign jump. "The House of Representatives rejected that Cooper-Church amendment four months ago. . . ."

"But the President announced his offer for a cease-fire-in-place! Remember?"

"That's for South Viet Nam."

"We can't move."

"Sir, Nixon and Kissinger are forcing this fully equipped main-force concept on FANK. That's got to be authorization enough."

"Look John," the colonel said, "just between you and me . . ."

"Just between you and me, what, sir?"

"This is what I've heard." The colonel raised his left hand, fingers extended, and with his right index finger checked off each point. "There are forces in Congress so strong, it looks as if they might just legislate us into forfeiture. I'm told to keep as low a profile as possible." The colonel stood. He turned his back to Sullivan, continued. "All we need is for one U.S. troop to be killed," he said, "and with the mood of Congress, this country, just like that"—he waved an arm through the air—"can be written off."

"Sir, without us—" Sullivan began.

The colonel turned back, interrupted, his tone changed indicating the topic was no longer up for discussion. "Have you been able to get some supplies to that lady's camp in Neak Luong?"

"Some."

"Good. You know we've no authorization to do that."

"Yes sir. But the task force . . . Damn it. Don't blackmail me with that."

"That's the end of it, John. If Huntley can scavenge anything else for Neak Luong, well . . . I didn't hear about it."

Outside the office Huntley was waiting for Sullivan. Immediately the two walked from the embassy building, out through the compound gates and into the streets of Phnom Penh. "What'd the ol' man say, J. L.?" Huntley asked.

"He said, 'Don't get caught.' "

"Why are all these hoodlums on the road?" Teck's voice was nasty, accusing.

"They are on the road because they have no homes," Vathana answered. "Surely you have homeless in Phnom Penh."

Teck just scoffed. He had cornered his wife at the pagoda preaching hall, had forced her back toward the apartment so he could reprimand her in private. On the way they were verbally accosted by a group of young teens. Teck, in his new, spotless uniform and reflective sunglasses, snapped at them. In turn they increased their taunts. "Hey, she's a good fuck, huh?"

"She's my wife." Teck was indignant.

"Last night she was my wife," one boy yelled. "Without the uniform, she's much cheaper." Teck rushed into their midst. The boys parted about him. He returned to Vathana, grabbed her arm, pushed her onward.

Vathana had not seen him since the day the NVA had shelled Neak Luong. He had remained in the capital, sending word now and again. "I am a military adjutant." "I must remain in Phnom Penh." "I am with the finance branch." "Someday, I will build a villa for us."

Suddenly he had shown up. "You are my wife," Teck said. It

was a prepared speech. "Soon you will have our second child. You should be with me. You are my wife."

Vathana looked at her husband. In his uniform, erect, directed, he appeared so different than he had in his dancehall clothes slumped in opium stupor. To her he was handsome. He'd changed, almost, she imagined, as if he'd taken on the countenance of his father when Mister Pech was young. "You are very different," Vathana said softly. To herself she said, You are my husband but twice you abandoned me. Aloud she said, "What has changed you?"

"It is the army," Teck said enthusiastically. "Our army has grown to a hundred thousand. The Republic is so strong . . ."

"But the Communists still hold the North. . . ."

"A matter of time. My troops," he said proudly, "they will liberate the North, then the Northeast. Everything is possible now. Lon Nol has promised . . ."

"He has promised many things," Vathana said. She did not look into Teck's eyes but she sensed an agitation beneath his enthusiasm, an agitation which went far beyond the street hoodlums. Still she thought, Twice . . . you should have stayed . . . here, with your son . . . with me. "What will he do for my camp?" she asked quietly.

"He will win the war so the people can go home." As Teck spoke he clapped his hands as if applauding his own statement.

"In the meantime, how are the refugees to live? And you—how do you live?"

"With the best men I have ever known," Teck said smartly. "We will win and we will be rich."

"We were rich," Vathana said quietly. "Your father . . ."

"I don't mean like my father," Teck said. "He was rich for a Khmer. I mean rich like the Americans."

"Wealth," Vathana quoted an old proverb, "like poverty, doesn't last."

"Dollars last," Teck countered. "Now, come with me. An officer must have his wife with him. Besides . . ." Teck hesitated. The control fell from his features, abandoned his voice. "Besides"—he turned slightly from her—"my father would have wanted me to do the right thing."

"Yes." Vathana pondered his words, his countenance, as she spoke. "I will come. But"—she paused, formulating her thoughts—"first you must help me stock the camp. I will come when there are rations for three months."

"Three months?!" Again Teck's face became rigid. "Why should those people get so much? They do nothing."

"Three months," Vathana said firmly. "Then I will come to you."

In their small forested hideout Nang nudged his old friend Eng. They laughed hard. Beside them Soth laughed too. By November new battlelines were drawn about Kompong Thom and the Northern Corridor. As the city tottered under the North Viet Namese siege, five armed forces—FANK, the ARVN, the NVA, the Khmer Krahom and the U.S. Air Force—converged. FANK's task force, which had formed up on Highway 6 at Tang Kouk, thirty-three miles south of Kompong Thom, was a mishmash of ill-equipped infantry units with their stable of dependents, a few armored units which had allowed themselves to be mired in monsoon mud, and several artillery batteries which would fire support only if the request came between dawn and two p.m., and then only if it were accompanied by a *bonjour*. The task force had stalled at Tang Kouk for two months while smaller FANK battle groups supported (or stood by and watched) the ARVN at dozens of sites in the South, Southeast, East and near the capital.

On 27 November the FANK units rolled north. Nang guffawed from his observation point seven kilometers south of Santuk as he watched the slow parade roll, roll unhindered, being lured into a killing zone by lack of resistance, inviting an ambush because they had neither flank security nor point scouts; inviting disaster because they had neither spacing nor withdrawal routes. Nang laughed at FANK as the troops and dependents scattered with the NVA's first shots. He joked to Met Eng, "What a rush they're in," as the North Viet Namese broadsided the procession with rifle and RPG fire and followed up with mortars—never actually engaging the column in battle, simply shooting ducks in a gallery. For two days NVA gunners chewed up the mired FANK task force as it attempted to turn, to withdraw. For two days Nang and other Krahom yotheas chuckled at the lopsided event.

Then at dawn on the twenty-ninth came a counterattack that NVA/KVM intelligence had misestimated. Between Sdau and Santuk, twelve kilometers south of Kompong Thom, two kilometers north of Nang's position, an ARVN armored column crashed ferociously into the arena, smashed in from secondary roads, split, blitzkrieged north and south on Highway 6. Unlike FANK, the South Viet Namese columns, at the first sign of enemy, spread out and swept forward along broad lines, with M-48A3 Patton tanks at the points like the head of a hawk leading the wings—M-113 APCs—as all tracked through paddies, probing by fire, as unconcerned about native hamlets as the NVA, firing and advancing, meeting pressure head-on, Patton tanks forward and aft blasting their 90mm shells at a battery of NVA 130mm field guns set up only five hundred meters from the road. APCs swept forward, half mounted with 20mm Vulcan Gatling guns, half with a combination of shielded heavy and light machine guns.

Nang's platoon ran, dazed, ran to escape the collision of titanic forces. They had been told to observe, to pick at the victor, to guarantee there would be no victor—but this battle was not shaping up like the June battle for Kompong Thom. Their orders, their expectations, did not cover such immense firepower. And they ran.

As Nang's boys fled, NVA infantry gunners attempted to halt the ARVN armor, but their RPD light machine guns and AK-47s were no match for the ARVN fusillade. Two 130mm guns were destroyed after scrambling only a few salvos. Infantrymen were sacrificed to slow the ARVN advance while their armor, eleven kilometers northeast, maneuvered into secondary ambush positions.

"Come. This way!" Nang headed deep into the swamp. The ARVN column halted, withdrew a hundred meters to regroup and await air cover. "This way. No. Here." All about them Krahom elements crossed and recrossed on camouflaged jungle paths. Soth snickered quietly at Nang's confusion. It caught Nang's eye, infuriated him. The badger, he thought. He waits. He waits to pick my bones. Be patient. An OV-1 Mohawk photo reconnaissance plane came on station. It circled high over the battle area relaying immediate visual sightings to the ground group commander. Later more targets would be ascertained by film analysis. The day became hot, still. The Mohawk's twin engines droned. Peasants huddled in thatched huts as rice awaited cutting in the paddies.

Nang ran, kept running, west then north to where stagnant swamp water was thick with leeches. Behind him, his yotheas sloshed through. Clumps of grass and nets of vines slowed them but Nang refused to let them stop. They left the swamp, entered an area of intermittent forest. Soth called for a halt. The Mohawk circled lower, down to three thousand feet. Nang refused to halt. Then half a mile south of the city's southern defense Nang abruptly stopped. He knew the spot well, had fled with Soth from Kompong Thom in June over the same trail. Where, he thought, where I was betrayed. From east of the highway he heard 12.7mm DShK antiaircraft guns pound like jackhammers chipping a concrete heaven. "Cockshit," he muttered. "Eng," he called.

"Here."

"We must find a way into the city. The split-tail will bring the unseen bombers." Eng said nothing, thinking, pondering the problem. He did not feel, did not understand, Nang's urgency. "We can cache our weapons," Nang whispered. "Change shirts, separate and enter . . ."

"Comrade," Eng interrupted. "Why hide in the carrion? Why not ride the back of the tiger?"

Now Nang did not speak. Soth smirked, snickered again. Like the NVA, Nang had been caught off guard. To disengage? Nang thought. To pursue? Where would the NVA move? The ARVN, he knew, wanted the road, wanted to travel its length and enter the city. They wanted to battle the NVA but they wanted more to open the road. They would consider that a victory, even if in reality they would be like a hand passing through water. Nang also knew, had been told, the NVA command desired this battle. Like the Americans away from home, the South Viet Namese, the Communists believed, would tire and succumb to public pressure if their sons died on foreign soil—a nearly nonexistent concern for Northern leaders. Yes, the NVA would engage, Nang was sure, and from his position he would not be able to maneuver.

"Okay," he said to Eng. "We'll follow the tail, but not pat the tiger's ass."

The platoon began a slow backtracking. They entered the swamp. Hard growling broke from the sky. A squadron of T-28s, flying low level, roared over. From the east came the burp-bursting noise of grenade-cannon strafing. Then quiet. The sound had erupted suddenly, ceased suddenly.

Nang halted the platoon, backed them into the forest. Sporadic small arms fire snapped to the south. Cannons fired, not with the rapidity of intense battle, but casually. T-28s, their pilots conserving courage, swung in circles with ten-mile radii, setting up their low-level runs well to the rear of the ARVN column, skimming treetops for miles before making second, off-target bombing runs. The day wore on. Nang sat, angry, lost in self-renunciation at not being in a position to do anything, angry that no messenger had come with detailed orders.

The sun descended. From the swamp and the forest floor mosquitos rose. Battle noises moved far to the east. Half the platoon relaxed in net hammocks. The cautious and the scared had scratched narrow trenches beneath their positions. Others were dispersed, on guard. Light hung in the sky, darkness seized the ground. Artillery rounds from the FANK garrison sailed over the platoon's position, rising, heading southwest toward empty swamp. Nang could not fathom why, how anyone could so waste ammunition. Farther to the southeast ARVN artillery launched shells; the muffled explosions seemed to burst around the village of Cheam, northeast of the city.

"Met Eng," Nang said softly. He cupped a hand over his new cadreman's shoulder. "I would make mistakes without you."

"No," Eng said. "There will always be someone to keep you from failing. It is the wish of Angka."

The platoon moved again, south, through the swamp again. They moved slowly. For a time Nang led, then Eng, then a yothea with an M-2 carbine, Met Horl, then Met Soth. With Soth before him, Nang could barely control his desire to punish, to even the score. Now. Not now, he thought. Later. Someday I will get him. At the hamlet of Puk Yuk they crossed the road. Huts smoldered. Nothing remained standing. The devastation seemed enormous, seemed impossible given the size of the duel. Quietly the yotheas picked through the ashes searching for food, weapons, anything of value. They moved east, very cautious now. Enemy units were near.

At first light, 30 November, without warning, the earth trembled like Krakatoa erupting, trembled, shockwaves blowing the forest down, deep thudding, then tearing, imploding eardrums, typhoon-pressure blasting instantaneous, then stillness. Nang lifted himself from the earth. About him the forest had been splintered. A second wave erupted, rolling-thunder concussions, closer, lifting, throwing him like a rag, like litter in a storm, then stillness. Again he lifted himself. His shirt had been blown off. Blood dripped from his nose, trickled from his left ear, ran from cuts on his chest and legs. He stumbled forward, backward, grabbed a shattered tree trunk for support. "Eng," he hissed. "Met Eng." He dropped to his knees. A kilometer north the heavy footfalls of the monster again caused the earth to tremble. Again Nang raised up. He touched his chest, hips, legs. A smile spread across his lips but his lower lip was cut and the smile hurt. He felt his nose, wiped the blood away. He heard nothing, smelled nothing. The lightening sky had darkened with smoke. Then he heard the tanks, but he could not fix their direction. He stared, searching for their approach, expecting to see Pattons. His sense of smell returned as if someone had flipped a switch. Burning flesh registered amid the stench of chemicals and grease. He checked himself again. Something caught his ankle. He stumbled, righted himself, snapped his eyes to the ground. A hand gripped his foot. He pulled, twisted.

The hand hung on. What was happening did not register in his mind. He saw only a hand.

"Get down, damn you!" The hand twisted his ankle and he fell into the broken brush. "Nang!" Eng grabbed his face. "How did you get way over here? Ha. Ssshh. The bombers have stirred the tanks."

Nang squeezed his jaw, his eyes, shut, trying to reorient himself. His ears rang from the concussion and from the pressure with which he clamped his teeth. He gazed blankly at Met Eng. The cadreman was covering his cuts with mud which caked and stopped the bleeding. "eng?"

"yes."

"platoon?"

"back where we camped."

"uh."

"you were scouting. ssshh. the T-54s." Eng placed a strong hand over Nang's mouth to silence him. They were concealed by a pile of splintered wood and twisted vines. The tanks rolled west to east fifty meters away. Eng spontaneously counted them. He relaxed the pressure on Nang's mouth but did not remove his hand. Behind the tanks were trucks, sixteen six-bys, two scout vehicles. The scene hardly impacted on Nang. After the B-52s the tanks seemed less frightening. It was as if he were a prehistoric creature just escaped from *Tyrannosaurus rex* to face *Diplosaurus*. He felt as if he could walk up to the T-54s and knock them out with his bare fists. That the closest bomb dropped a third of a kilometer from him meant nothing. Somehow, his mind told him, they'll never be closer.

Eng led the platoon east, leery of encountering NVA rear guard, then more quickly south; then, completing a semicircle, headed west to the back of the North Viet Namese. Krahom runners were now scurrying like mice throughout the battle area. Their radios were few though well placed and concealed in informer hamlet huts and deep in forested thickets down animal trails the NVA, a conventional force in Cambodia, would never follow. The platoon now had orders, direction. They moved to a prepared ambush site along a camouflaged Viet Namese escape route. Other Krahom units waited in similar positions, waited for the disengagement and retreat.

It was midday when firing renewed, not slowly but a well-coordinated fusillade. NVA T-54s ambushed a column of ARVN Pattons and APCs. The Communists, attempting to inflict heavy casualties on the ARVN infantrymen who followed the tracks, dropped 81mm mortar rounds to the immediate rear of the armored line. NVA 130mm cannons blasted both the road be-

hind the column and the villages along that section. They hit
the civilian areas with just enough shells to kill a few in each
hamlet. With the first cessation of artillery villagers poured
onto the road, the ox-drawn carts, bicycles and pedestrians
jamming the highway north and south of the battle—north
toward the fortified walls of Kompong Thom, south toward
Baray.

Counterfire was immediate and prolonged. Nang's vision
cleared but his thoughts remained blurry. He had not dressed,
not armed himself. The NVA launched a second coordinated
volley. To Nang the sound of firing was distinct from one direction, muffled from others. He could not ascertain the location.
In the first minutes there were heavy casualties on both Viet
Namese sides. To the south the fight was a standoff. ARVN
maneuvering elements bogged down on the flanks. NVA troops
sprinted down concealed trenches to fire at ARVN soldiers attempting to regroup behind circled APCs. Communist troop
trucks withdrew. The 130s, deeply bermed in heavily vegetated
pockets to the northeast and southwest, closed their camouflage
covers and lay silent. Four undamaged T-54s raced for hidden
bunkers. The sky filled with the roar of South Viet Namese A-37
attack jets.

For four hours along a six-kilometer stretch of Highway 6 the
foreign Communists battled the foreign non-Communists, each
side bringing to the battle tremendous firepower yet neither
side bringing the will to overrun the other. The ARVN particularly showed no motivation to dislodge the NVA but settled
back to await more tactical air and artillery support, hoping
the bombardments would do the job only ground forces could
accomplish. The armies stood like two flat-footed boxers with
mile-long arms throwing stinging jabs but not stepping up with
knockout punches. After the first few minutes, casualties dropped
to a few direct hits. Helicopters zinged in low to evacuate South
Viet Namese. Other birds circled high to radio enemy sightings
to supporting artillery. More A-37s came on station. The NVA
relocated, hid. There were few definite targets. Pilots released
their ordnance—rockets and napalm canisters—against proba-
ble sites, treelines, high paddy dikes, anywhere troops or machines might be hidden. They restricted their target area to
three or four kilometers to each side of the highway even though
the NVA field guns had ranges ten times that. The countryside
was not their concern.

In the bush away from the battle Nang's senses returned. It
was five hours since the battle had begun, eleven since the B-52
strike. Nang thought to clean up, to dress, to arm himself, but

decided against cleaning and dressing. Only sporadic fire came from the highway. The ARVN column advanced. Helicopters were at point and flanks. Over the relatively flat land Nang could see two east flank gunships. They did not dart, did not skim low level, but hovered above the ground elements, one at perhaps eight hundred feet, the second a thousand feet higher and to the rear. The machines seemed strange. Nang had seen them in Cambodia only half a dozen times—many of the newer yotheas had never seen one at all.

"She's trying to draw fire," Nang told a young troop. He felt in control again. "Let me see your rifle." The boy looked about, unsure, hoping Met Eng would overhear Nang and tell the boy what to do. "I'm not going to fire at it," Nang said. The lack of confidence irritated him. "We aren't in range. I only want to teach you how to lead it." Nang grabbed the AK-47 and drew a bead on the distant ship. "Pow!" The word burst from his mouth. Suddenly the ship burst into flames. A moment later the sound of a twin-barreled 23mm AA gun reached them, then the noise of the exploding chopper, the bang-swish of rockets from the chase bird and additional explosions in the hedgerows between the paddies to their immediate west. The ship, incongruous to the sound, seemed to stall in air as if the heat of the flames were lifting a burning ash from a fire; then it began a slow twirling descent, then fell like a stone. The yothea stared at Nang, back-stepped, ran.

"Ssshh!" Nang whispered to the boy's cellmates. "Don't tell anyone."

Signals passed along the Krahom line. Patience. Patience. Below them the concealed trail filled with a string of tired Northern troops—men carrying their rifles, holding the barrels, the stocks over their shoulders, knowing they'd entered a secure zone.

Eng squeezed a firing device. Instantly nine Chinese Communist claymores exploded and yotheas fired into the kill zone, fired on the dying and dead, fired, reloaded, fired, perfect timing, perfect concentration of force. Inaccurate counterfire barked from unseen locations far to the rear of the kill zone. The yotheas fled. The platoon separated as Eng had determined, two teams heading east, Viet Namese in pursuit.

Nang did not react. The explosions had rekindled the pain in his ears and brain. He fell, grasped his head, his hands at the back of his neck, his forearms squeezing, covering his ears. He tightened every muscle, whipped his knees to his shoulders, curled in a tiny ball in a small hole above the path. He heard firing to the east, a quick skirmish, the noise locking his muscles. Below on the path there was groaning, a chorus of morose moans. Nang shook uncontrollably, squeezed his arms tighter and tighter over his ears. The moans became louder, punctuated with inhuman screeches. Down the line, more small arms fire, muffled. Then sharp cracks close by, then more distant explosions. Nang could not think. His body reacted, rolled, leaped straight up, ran crashing down the slope into the wall of guttural cries. On the path, frantic, his eyes viewed but his mind did not absorb. He should have been elated at the mutilation of the enemy but he barely saw them. He tripped over a body, splatted facedown onto the torn bloody torso of a second, rose, sprinted thrashing, crashing through low crossing branches, sprinted west through forest without thought, toward the battlefield, the highway.

As he ran, more branches ripped his trousers, his flesh. He ran not with a sense of forward direction but with an ambiguous sense of something fearful at his back, ran without stopping until he was out of the forest, without slowing until he was through the marshland and into a treeline between paddies. He slowed. He did not stop. About him trees and brush burned. Before him the village of Sdau smoldered. He jogged on. There was no village. About him the dead lay decomposing. Shells, bombs, canisters, rockets—for three days the village had been killed and rekilled, buried and unearthed. The stench of burning flesh and hair was so thick in the air it stuck to Nang's tongue like tar. Humans had been shredded, pulverized, reduced to mush, to charred fragments. There, Nang saw Number Two Oxcart, his agent, his KK contact, his friend, without legs. There, his son's head. They are, were, Khmer—not worthless FANK lackeys, not imperialist Sino pigs—but simple Khmer rice farmers for whom the revolution must be won.

Nang stumbled on, senseless. At the last burning hut he dropped to his knees. Globs of jellied petroleum burned on the sides of a stone hearth. He reached out. Grabbed a handful. Immediately his fingers blistered. He stared at the pain, angered, infuriated, not at the searing of his hand, but at the searing of his land. For two seconds he stared at the napalm then slapped his face to endure more, to purify himself, to strengthen himself for the fight ahead.

On the highway Nang saw the ARVN column. In it, scattered, were peasant carts. His right hand was blistered as was the entire right side of his face. He pulled himself up to full height, walked toward the invaders. He did not hesitate. If it is time to die, he thought, it is time.

*   *   *

"Lieutenant Tran," an ARVN private said in Viet Namese, "here's another one."

"Any papers?" Nang understood the words but was mute.

"Are you kidding! This kid's got nothing."

"What's on his face? And hand?"

"It's sand. He's got sand inside the cloth. Looks like a folk treatment for burns. His face must of gotten spattered and he tried to rip it off."

"I know him. Bring him here. I've seen you before." In Khmer Tran Van Le said, "Your name?"

Nang remained mute. "Augh, Lieutenant, all these brown bastards look alike."

"No! No, I've seen this kid before. I'm sure I have." Tran turned to Nang. "Name?" he repeated.

Nang's face screamed with pain as he moved his jaw to form his response.

"Name?" Tran Van Le repeated. "Understand? Name and village?"

"Kampuchea," Nang stuttered in Khmer. Kampuchea, he thought. Kampuchea, Lieutenant Tran. Kampuchea, Mister Truong Cao Kiet. "Kampuchea," Nang said again. "It is your fate."

CHAPTER ELEVEN

A drop of sweat splatted on the page. Rita Donaldson wiped it away with her little finger, pulled her head from over the papers and continued reading, making notes in the margin. Slowly she leaned forward, attempting to keep her back in the shade of the large umbrella, attempting to avoid Phnom Penh's parching January sun. It was only her third day in Southeast Asia, her first full day in Cambodia. Another drop of sweat splatted on the report. She straightened her back, angry, frustrated, rolled her head back, up, until she was looking into the segmented underside of the umbrella which covered the cafe table. Then she thought, smiled inwardly at the thought, that she was like Alice sitting beneath a massive mushroom.

For two years Rita Donaldson had worked a rewrite desk in the foreign affairs section of the *Washington News-Times*. Since the coup in March 1970 she had concentrated on Cambodia, had kept her own file on the country. Her knowledge was deep yet her feeling for the country was shallow. She pulled a hankie from her new jungle blouse, wiped her forehead. Then she rested an elbow on the table and momentarily cupped her chin in her hand. The sweat of her face on her hand, and of her hand on her face, felt disgusting. Again she wiped her face. She felt self-conscious, almost as if she were taking a bath in public. One week of this'll . . . she thought. Ten days, tops. She looked back at the report, a briefing she'd compiled for *News-Times* correspondent Tom Jasson who, at the last, had decided not to go. Again perspiration dripped from her face onto the page.

SIGNIFICANT ACTIVITIES: During the second half of 1970 SA included: combined Communist force attacks on (1) Kirirom and (2) the Pich Nil Pass on Highway 4, and (3) a series of battles, commando raids and terrorist rocket attacks around the country. By the end of September the NVA held four of Cambodia's nineteen provincial capitals and threatened twelve of the remaining fifteen. Pocheantong Airport at Phnom Penh was sporadically closed by rocket raids which temporarily destroyed runways. The capital's petroleum storage tanks at Kilometer 6 were burned; the oil refinery at Kompong Som was damaged; several strategic bridges over the Tonle Sap River were dropped. Evidence indicates these latter acts were carried out by North Viet Namese *dac cong* (sappers). The heaviest fighting of the period took place along the Mekong and Bassac rivers below Neak Luong, where a 200-vessel ARVN task force continued to hunt the NVA/VC. The Communists kept continuous pressure on the waterways, often closing them to freighters. Additional large battles were fought about Svay Rieng. In the Takeo area, the ARVN 495th Infantry Battalion rampaged through the countryside during and after operations designed to ferret out major NVA/VC supply units. The rampaging hurt the Allied cause and Lon Nol publicly protested their behavior. . . .

"How long are you here for?"

Rita Donaldson looked up. The light skin of her face was flushed, pink, covered with rivulets of sweat. Her hands and arms were so wet the hand she placed over the page she'd been reading stuck to the paper. She wiped the side of her hands on her jungle blouse. "Excuse me?"

"How long you here for?" the man repeated.

"A week," she answered. She did not know him but his being American made the approach acceptable.

"Mind if I join you?" He sat without her responding. "Jim White," he said. *"The Sun."* He motioned to a waiter. "You're the new gal from the Washington paper." She began to answer but he interrupted. "What can you learn in a week?"

"Two weeks," Rita Donaldson said. "If there's a real story."

"There's plenty of story," White said. To the waiter he said, "Two cold orange juice. *Bic?*" Then back to Rita, "You better drink more."

"How do you know? About the story, I mean."

"Just a feeling," White said. "Just a . . ." He leaned forward and grasped the report she had before her. "What do ya got here?"

"What?!" Rita was astounded. She pulled the report back.

"That's not goina be the way to get along here," White snapped.

"Who the hell are you?" Rita shot back.

"Screw it, bitch. You'll learn." White stood, yelled a jumble of pidgin Khmer, Viet Namese and English at the waiter, then stomped off. Westerners and the few Cambodians in the cafe stared at her. She swallowed, ducked her head, went back to the report.

The anniversary of Ho Chi Minh's death (9/3) was marked in Cambodia by twenty-one ARVN battalions plus support personnel— about 12,000 soldiers. In Paris, NVA General Xuan Thuy issued a "very flexible and generous" proposal for a coalition government in South Viet Nam. For peace and coalition, the negotiator said, the necessary ingredient is American renunciation of Saigon and the withdrawal of all support.

On 7 October, President Nixon, in a televised speech, offered the Communists a "cease-fire in place." The next day the Communists denounced the proposal as "a maneuver to deceive world opinion." They reiterated their demand for unconditional US withdrawal and the toppling of the Saigon government. In this atmosphere, in South Viet Nam, Nguyen Van Thieu manipulated the South Viet Namese October presidential election by eliminating all alternative candidates. The balloting, unlike the Senate voting in August, was a one-candidate charade. Even at that it might have served as a poll of Thieu's support, but irregularities negated that potential. . . .

Rita gritted her teeth. What *The Sun*? she thought. There's nine hundred *The Sun*s in the world. I should have slapped that son of a bitch, she thought. She had been angry since returning to reading, had not concentrated on the words, could barely remember what she'd read. She looked back over the last few pages, underlined "American bombing," "Ho Chi Minh's death," and "televised speech." She thought about the trip, about her air-conditioned Washington office. She had been given the assignment after Jasson's abrupt cancellation, given it as if it were a present, a job bennie, a perk, something to put on her résumé. One week in Southeast Asia because she'd been a loyal employee, a good little girl. Indeed, she had told herself, it *was* an excellent opportunity for advancement. Not unlike a military officer, a journalist needs to have her ticket punched. But Jim White had set something off in her. So too did her body's reaction to the heat. She was fair skinned, fair haired, and had a soft Nordic countenance which was finding the tropical climate of the Cambodian dry season unbearable. I can do this, Rita Donaldson told herself. I can do it and do it right.

The American military posture in South Viet Nam has become one of protective enclave defense. (Only the 1st Cavalry and the 101st Airborne still ran, though curtailed, offensive operations.)

In the US, the Army opened its case, with heavy media coverage, against William Calley. President Nixon has requested an additional $155 million for small arms and ammunition for Cambodia.

Between 29 November and 2 December, NVA units launched one hundred attacks—raids or shellings—in South Viet Nam, with the reported objective of relieving ARVN pressure against their Cambodian bases. . . .

Rita rocked back slightly. She raised her eyes, glanced up to see if people were still staring at her. Her report, she felt, and the story she'd received during her first embassy briefing, and what she'd obtained from the *News-Times*'s Cambodian stringer, didn't jibe. But she didn't know how or why. She pulled a steno pad from her bag, flipped it open, thumbed back several pages. The embassy aide had unofficially told her that in Hanoi General Vo Nguyen Giap had begun organizing for the next major phase of the war. The aide had said that ARVN/NVA engagements in Cambodia to this point had primarily been search and destroy for the ARVN, ambush and withdraw for the NVA. But with Americans banned from Cambodia, with increasing U.S. domestic pressure for U.S. withdrawal from South Viet Nam, the NVA general allegedly saw opportunity. The clashes between Viet Namese elements on Khmer soil were, to him, practice and preparation for a large-scale offensive invasion of South Viet Nam once U.S. forces were out.

On 22 December, the US Congress passed an amended bill forbidding any use of American ground troops *or advisors* in Laos or Cambodia. The Force Armée Nationale Kampuchea (FANK), swollen in one year to eightfold its precoup combat strength, was, according to US military spokesmen, incapable, without advisors, of assimilating, training, even equipping most of this new manpower. Congress has also banned the use of US airpower in direct support of Allied troops.

On the last day of 1970 the Provisional Revolutionary Government (PRG) announced it had assassinated in the preceding 364 days "at least 6,000 South Viet Namese" civilians for the heinous crime of serving, at any level, in their nation's government.

The story, Rita thought. What is it? Who, what, when, where, why, how. She paged through her notes. American bombing? FANK training? Some supposed NVA-ARVN future engagement? She turned the report over and wrote on the back: "(1) Find FANK training facility. (2) Determine U.S. role. (3) To hell with *The Sun*."

                         *   *   *

From the front seat of the jeep Sullivan saw her stop. She was
returning from morning prayers at the *sala*. He watched from a
distance as she looked up, straight up into the cloudless morning sky. To Vathana the air felt soft, compassionate on the skin
of her face, neck and arms. She closed her eyes momentarily,
inhaled deeply. The temperature was mild, the humidity early-
morning low. Vathana opened her eyes, stared into the endless
deep blue, stared whispering a prayer of thanks to the Enlightened One for seeing her through the birth, for the beautiful
healthy girl, and for the slowing of the war. And she prayed for
her country, for Premier Lon Nol who had suffered a paralyzing
stroke in early February and for Deputy Prime Minister Sisowath
Sirik Matak who now, in reality, led the nation. As she prayed
and gave thanks she thought about the depths of the sky, about
the penetration by the astronauts of *Apollo 14,* men on the
moon, again, about their journey which was barely a pinprick
into the depth of the blue that she felt both a part of and a
traveler through. As she prayed, her body felt light, weightless.
The caressing blue depths called her. It was not light traveling
infinite distances to her eyes but her spirit blossoming into the
universe, being a part of what she knew she was a part.

From two hundred meters south Sullivan studied her. He had
not seen her since their first encounter five months earlier yet
he held her in his mind as if the first impression had stuck,
lodged in some gap between brain convolutions, refused to melt
and flow, to spread thin, to be assimilated or to evaporate.
What the hell's she doing? he thought. Her slow approach and
her idle standing at the edge of the road, standing staring
straight up, irritated him. His irritation at it made him seethe.
Of all the stupid fucking things I've done, he thought, this . . .
He did not finish the thought.

Sullivan's tour with the 5th Special Forces Group had been
scheduled to end in October, yet he'd extended. The group was
now standing down, returning to the United States. The teams
had broken up, the remaining Phoenix Program personnel had
been transferred, on paper, to a different command. Nearly half
the Special Forces advisors who were ready to leave the country
had volunteered to remain in Viet Nam, to form special units to
train—in Viet Nam because advisors weren't permitted in
Cambodia—FANK personnel in raid and reconnaissance tactics,
in communications and in the most fundamental tactics of
patrolling and base security. Even concepts like flank security
had to be introduced—not taught, as in "how to," but introduced, as in "I've *no* idea what you're talking about."

In the few moments that Vathana had spent concentrating on the sky the temperature rise had begun, had taken hold of the day. It was not yet uncomfortable but the hint of heat was there and it pleased her. Vathana walked barefoot, at the road's edge, careful not to step in the debris of the past several months, debris brought to her city by the clashing armies which had surrounded it. She walked lightly, feeling renewed freedom in her body. She paused briefly at a market stall to check the freshness of the eels the vendor hawked, though she had no intention of making a purchase. She walked on, wishing to run, to skip like a schoolgirl, though she was restrained by the thought of someone seeing her, the Angel of Neak Luong, not bearing the burden of her city's suffering. Today she did not feel like suffering. Today she felt like living. Where the river and roadway squeezed the levee she again stopped, gazed out over the yellow-brown water, gazed across to the ferry landing being rebuilt for the fourth time in four months, gazed at the barges and piers and at an ocean freighter with riverine escort disappearing to the east. Sun reflections off the cockled water tickled her. For a brief moment she thought of her womb, which had nourished and nurtured her little girl and was now mostly contracted, and she sent a special small love signal from her mind and her whole body to this organ which had brought forth such lovely fruit.

The death of Pech Lim Song and Vathana's conditions to Teck for joining him in Phnom Penh had left her vulnerable to the whims and wraths of her mother-in-law, Madame Pech, who, since her husband's assassination, demanded she be called by her own name, Sisowath Thich Soen. In November the woman had descended upon Vathana amid the refugees, verbally berating her. *"Bonjour!* One hundred thousand riels?! To whom? While these people live like . . . like . . . this!" Vathana had not answered but stood absorbing the abuse, thinking, Abuse given, like love, does not lessen that held by the giver but increases it, and with abuse it becomes self-damaging. *"Bonjour?* Perhaps, silly stupid girl, perhaps some to your own pocket? Three months, indeed!" Two months later, as Vathana, eight and a half months pregnant, prayed for a safe delivery, Soen again violated her, bursting in upon her in the Neak Luong flat. "From today," Sisowath Thich Soen had said, "the barges will be controlled from Phnom Penh. And you"—she had glared at her daughter-in-law, daring her to take the offer—"you belong with your husband. Tomorrow everything will be removed from this apartment. Come to Phnom Penh or live with the filth in that camp."

From the jeep Sullivan continued to watch her, to track her

progress. He watched through the raised windshield as if he were spying. He attempted not to smile as she neared but found his heart racing, his muscles setting like a tom turkey's about to strut, his face breaking into a silly grin. At seventy-five feet she still had not noticed him. The main road had become busy with morning activity, civilian and military. He watched her face, oval with strong cheekbones and large dark eyes. Serene eyes, he thought, knowing mysterious eyes. Eyes that have witnessed a thousand years, that can see the next thousand.

At fifty feet he turned his head, watched the Mekong. He had been raised by the Mississippi on Iowa's eastern boundary and he'd always loved rivers, any river, and any river city which was still small enough to be affected by the current. "Not like New York," he'd once told Huntley. "You get a huge metropolis and people go months, years, without even knowing they're in a river city."

His mind stopped. Vathana stood only feet from him, a radiant smile, sparkling eyes greeting him. "Hello, Mister Lieutenant J. L. Sullivan," she said in English.

"Mrs. Pech," Sullivan stuttered. His tongue tripped. Sounds barely emerged. "How many children have you?" He blurted the Khmer idiom, which was a simple greeting, not knowing its literal translation.

"Two," she answered in Khmer, thinking he actually was asking the question.

He did not understand the answer and could not think of anything to say. Looking at her he smiled, then raised a hand to his face, covered his eyes, turned his head away, forced the ridiculous smile from his face, turned back and before he could speak broke into silly laughter.

Vathana also smiled. She raised her fists playfully. In French she said, "*En garde, Monsieur Sullivan*. What brings you to Neak Luong? The camp or the army?"

He grasped the steering wheel tightly. "Your camp, madame," he said professionally. "I must inspect your camp again." The smile fell from his face. There was nothing he needed to inspect. He'd come to see her but he couldn't tell her and in lying he broke the fragile bubble of joy which had surrounded them. Glumly he said, "Will you ride with me?"

The camp had shrunk from ten thousand to nine thousand. Major improvements had been made in housing, in food and potable water distribution. Waste removal was still abominable, and though the ground was dry, mosquitos and flies still swarmed. The stink of people unable to wash or clean their shelters mixed with dry-season dust.

They circled the camp, walked its main aisles between flimsy huts, chatted softly, analytically, in French. The happiness of seeing each other turned sour. Sullivan's reappearance stirred Vathana's memory of the messenger she'd not seen or heard from since the first encounter. "Befriend the American!" She had had no idea what he'd meant. She thought, too, of her father and brother, of all her family, and she grew sad. She thought of sunshine and Americans and of Pech Lim Song hung by a leg, shot, slowly bleeding to death with no one to save or comfort him. Then it occurred to her that Mister Sullivan had not come to see the camp. He took no notes, seemed uninterested in the workings of the camp or in supplies, though, oddly, he seemed to have compassion for the refugees. Odd, she thought, for an American. So unlike the few Western "contractors" she'd met.

"We never received the remainder of the roofing," Vathana said in the main camp tent where she'd brought him to a sectioned-off corner and introduced him to Sophan, Samnang, and her new daughter.

"I know," Sullivan answered.

He thinks I sold it to the Khmer Rouge, she thought. He thinks I'm a Communist agent. Perhaps he works for Soen.

As they'd walked Sullivan had become filled with doubt. Perhaps she's aiding the NVA, he'd thought. Perhaps . . . but he would not permit himself to think the thought.

"She's beautiful," Sullivan said, gently picking up the tiny swaddled infant. "Oh, look." He beamed, pulling the thin blanket back from her face. He tapped the tip of her nose. "Very pretty," he whispered.

"You have children?" Vathana asked.

"No. No, I'm not married."

Sophan braced herself, stoic, silent, watching the large *phalang* cooing over the infant, disrupting her spirit, inviting the jealousy of the spirit of the baby's last mother. The infant gave a minute cry. Immediately Sophan grasped for her. "*Oh . . . ah . . . Okay. There,*" Sullivan said. He looked at Vathana. Guiltily he whispered, "Did I do something wrong?"

"We should go. I work at the hospital, too. Have you more questions?"

"No. No. I'm sorry. Let me give you a ride to the hospital."

Away from the camp the sullen mood dissipated. In the sunshine by the river Sullivan stopped the jeep. "I'm afraid of this," he said to her without looking at her. "Your country petrifies me."

"But why?" Vathana asked, surprised by both the words

and the change of tone. "You are American. You are a soldier. The shellings in Phnom Penh have been bad?"

"No. It's not that. It's the way you think. The way your people think. You're . . . they're so beautiful. So peaceful. I could gobble you up . . ." Vathana smiled. "Oh, I don't mean me, you," Sullivan said self-consciously. "I mean a good army could conquer this country like . . . like . . . like the Germans rolled over Poland. Does that make sense to you, Mrs. Cahuom?" He didn't look at her, nor did he give her a chance to respond. "No," he said. "No, it's more than that. It's . . . it's like there's a monster outside and half the country's inviting it in and the other half is pretending it doesn't exist. I'm afraid for you."

"And for yourself?" Vathana's words were soft.

"Me? Hum? I guess," he said. He said it but he did not mean it. He did not feel fear for himself. The admission of vulnerability made him feel he was sharing something of himself with her, yet he knew it was not true. "It's a good thing we arrived," he said. "You people were about to be slaughtered." Vathana smiled a wry smile but did not speak. "Doesn't anybody understand?" Suddenly he threw his arms straight up. "The goddamned North Viet Namese have seventy-five thousand troops in here. Damn it. They'd butcher every Khmer if they could."

"You believe that and you're angry?"

"Damn it, yes. Those murdering bastards . . ." He stopped. "I'm sorry, Mrs. Cahuom. I . . . I . . . I didn't mean to use that language."

"The anger warrants that language, the language excuses the anger."

"God! That's the kind of thing a Khmer would say."

"I am Khmer," Vathana said. "Khmers are concerned."

"But nobody does anything!"

"My father-in-law used to ask, 'What will happen if we do nothing?' You sound like him."

"It's a damned good question. Giap, the NVA general . . ." Sullivan paused to see if she recognized the name. "Vo Nguyen Giap, he uses the phrase 'aggression through internal war.' Those Communist . . . pigs . . . are conscripting and brainwashing thousands of Khmers in the seized territories. I see the documents. They're trying to make it look like civil war."

Vathana smiled. "I don't think anyone takes the Khmer Rouge seriously," she said. "There are some but they're so poor. That's what the radio reports."

"But that's it. They move in their agents. And it gives credibility to the Viet Namese."

"How?" Vathana's speech quickened. Suddenly both were

speaking fast, in French, talking politics as Vathana had not talked politics since conversations with her father before the trip to the mountains. "How can anything give them credibility? And to whom? Khmers know they're evil intruders. But they do support Prince Sihanouk, eh?"

"To the international community," Sullivan said, his words overlapping hers. "Cambodia needs international help."

"Then why is it your country offers so much but delivers so little? America is very perplexing. You ask what will happen if we do nothing, but you think you do much just speaking."

"We can't bring troops in. The American Congress passed a law . . ."

"I don't understand."

"Neither do I. But, Mrs. Cahuom, that's it. That's the credibility problem . . . to . . . to the . . . Americans. Through their information sources."

"Call me Vathana."

Sullivan's mind froze. The line of thought in quick exchange disappeared like the flash from a sniper's rifle. "Vathana." He said the name slowly. To him it was the most beautiful word he'd ever uttered. "Vathana," he said smoothly, "your country still petrifies me." He reached to her and very gently grasped the small finger of her left hand. "I've seen your mother-in-law a few times. And her son. They say she's a Sisowath of the same family as the deputy prime minister."

"They're of the same family." Vathana did not move her hand. Has he come, she thought, to do Soen's bidding?

"Could you . . . I . . . Can she . . ." Sullivan stopped. He wanted to ask her to come to Phnom Penh where he might have a chance of protecting her, though he knew he had no real resources, that a month earlier downtown Phnom Penh had been rocketed by the NVA with thousands of people wounded or killed, that Phnom Penh was not safer, only closer to him.

"You are very afraid," Vathana said softly, "yet you volunteer to be here."

"Yes. I'm . . . I want to help. I want to be here. I'm mostly afraid for your country."

"Help me establish a school for the camp children."

"Certainly."

For ten minutes they spoke of school supplies, simple things, paper and pencils. "And wood for a classroom. And more roofing."

"Yes. I'll see. I'll try."

"And a slate board? In my village we had a wonderful slate board."

"I know where one is."

"You Americans can do anything." Vathana closed her eyes and her hand. "You will not be hurt," she said. "They will never hurt you." She squeezed his hand. "I see that. You will be very good for my people."

"Thank you," Sullivan said. He felt she had bestowed total confidence on him, had absolute faith in his survival and his ability to contribute.

Vathana squeezed his hand again then let go. She looked at him, smiled, laughed a very soft kind laugh. "You're welcome." She said it so innocently he could not think how to respond.

The hospital at Neak Luong had received equipment for a modern surgical room from several international aid agencies, but there were many in need and only one full-time doctor, Sarin Sam Ol, and he was not a fully trained surgeon. Vathana assisted him, primarily with patient care and paperwork, each morning after her early duties at the refugee center. An hour after Lieutenant Sullivan dropped her off, she was alone in the dank corridor leading to the new surgery room. Suddenly, from behind, a shove. She stumbled, began to rise, turn, was shoved again, grabbed. She struggled, turned. A small dark man, young yet very strong, grabbed her face, dug fingers into her cheeks below her eyes, a thumb into the soft tissue below her jaw. His other hand seized her breast. He lifted her like a rag doll. "Sakhon has been moved to Stung Treng, Sister. Your father wishes him a safe journey. Tell me all the fire-hair *phalang* tells you."

He relaxed the pressure on her face but he did not let her go. Vathana's eyes cast left, right, hoping to see someone, anyone, who might at least yell, who might scare off the assailant. The corridor was empty. She did not speak. Her mind raced to find words but the pain of his grasp frightened them from her throat. "Tell me," the man hissed. "Tell me or your baby will never taste your milk again." He tightened his fingers on her tit and twisted.

"Yes. Yes. He said nothing. Just talk. He said he was afraid."

The man smirked, then jiggled her as if to shake out more words. The hospital was crowded yet the hall remained empty. Vathana talked. She told him all she thought he wanted to hear, everything except about the school supplies.

"Listen, Sister. And obey. Be his concubine. Be his whore. You'll find it easy. Sakhon will be moved to Kratie. Khmer Patriots will protect your camp."

The khrou plastered a poultice on Nang's face, another on his left side. He gently cleansed the horn and canal of his left ear.

Nang lay quietly on the pallet in the man's home, a thatch and plastic-tarp hovel amid a thousand similar refugee abodes clumped together in the open spaces of Kompong Thom. The shaman hummed softly as he worked methodically. From his stores he poured a few drops of palm oil into a rosewood bowl. Then he ripped a cabbage leaf into squares and dropped it in. He ground the leaf into the oil until it became a green paste. To this he added bits of chopped fresh cayenne pepper and dried, powdered comfrey root. Again he mashed the mixture, adding once several drops of rice vinegar to thin it. With a finger he scooped a blob and gently pressed it into Nang's ear. "In time you'll have full hearing," the khrou said. "These foreign devils . . ."

"They shall perish," Nang interrupted.

"Yes. You've said that. You always say that yet the bombs, the artillery come closer and the siege is renewed. You heal quickly, Little Rabbit. Why did they torture you?"

"Because they are fornicating buffalo scum."

"The Northerners?"

"And the Southerners. It was the Southern yuons that burned my feet. The Northern killed my father."

"And who is Angkar?"

Nang turned to the khrou. He did not know how the man knew. He remained silent.

"You spoke of Angkar when they first brought you. You said, 'Angkar was our salvation . . . .' perhaps more like, 'Angkar will save us.' You repeated it many times."

Nang stared at the healer who continued his methodical procedure. "You are Angkar," he said. "All Khmer Patriots are Angkar."

During the final trek into Kompong Thom Nang had been corralled with a group of sullen young Khmers. The ARVN lieutenant had called them detainees, the soldiers had treated them like convicted prisoners. Most were men, most were farmers, all were interrogated by ARVN intelligence personnel at the FANK garrison in the city's southwest district.

"Khmer Rouge, where are your weapons?" the Viet Namese inquisitor had screamed at each. When it was his turn Nang had squatted on the concrete floor in the small stark cell and covered his ears. His training had gone deep but in injury, in pain, in exhaustion he could think only to remain silent, to deny everything. Then: Who am I? Think. Act. Be that part. Keep it simple so as to avoid contradictions.

"You are Khmer Rouge," the inquisitor accused. "Look at your hands. You're no farmer."

"My father, farmer." Nang's voice sputtered. "He was killed by the Communists. I bake bread."

"Yeah. Sure. You're Buddha's baker. Never touched a weapon, huh? How'd you get those scars, baker-boy?" Nang touched his face. "Not that, you shit. On your back. On your leg. Those aren't calluses from riding buffalo. What's your unit?" Nang stared at the man as if he, Nang, were an imbecile. "Hook him up," the man growled, angry that one more victim was bringing torture upon himself, justifying his actions in the anger.

Two soldiers grabbed Nang. His body was stiff, sore from the beating it had taken early that morning when the concussion from the American bomb had thrown him and broken the forest; sore too from his afternoon sprint through brambles and branches; and sore from the pokes and prods of the ARVN soldiers bulldogging the detainees into the city. Nang did not resist as they tied his elbows behind him, nor as they clamped his feet to metal cuffs on the ends of a three-foot-long wooden rod. He watched with dread as they attached wires to his toes and the soles of his feet and displayed the rheostat and switch.

"Let's try it again. What's your unit?"

"My father is farmer," Nang said in rural dialect. "I learn to be baker."

The officer flipped the switch. The tingle of a very low voltage entered his feet as if he'd squatted too long without moving and cut off the circulation. Slowly the tingle rose through his ankles, into his calves, then his knees. "Your unit?" Nang closed his eyes, concentrated on breath control. "Your *unit*?!" The tingle entered his thighs, hips, groin, buttocks, rose to his navel and became a queer indescribable pain.

"Tien!" A shouted voice came from the hall.

"Sir?" The voltage was turned to very low.

"There's two hundred more to question. Don't take forever."

"Yes sir." The interrogator walked to Nang's side. He grabbed the boy's face. "One chance. Tell me or I'll spin this to high."

Nang flicked his eyes away from the man's face, closed his eyes, whispered, "I bake." He set himself for the jolt. "Aaaacccc-houhaaaaa . . ." As the current wrenched his legs and torso he jerked in convulsive shitting, pissing spasms. Sparks flicked at his feet. Then it stopped.

"Unit?!"

"Baker," Nang whimpered.

"Make him wipe up that shit and get him out of here."

Moments after his release, ARVN first lieutenant Tran Van Le broke into the interrogation cell. He was frantic. "Tien. You had a boy here?"

"Lots of boys."

"No. A strong kid. Looks maybe thirteen, fourteen. Napalm burns on his face and right hand. Cut up all over."

"Oh. Yeah. The baker."

"Baker my ass. Where is he?"

"They sent him to release."

"Damn it. He's Hai Hoa Binh. A top VC agent. Shit, I knew I recognized him."

At Mount Aural Met Sar sat on a cushion on a bench in his personal bunker. His face was drawn tight at the corners of his mouth, drawn down into a morose mask as he lamented the fate of his units and infrastructure at Kompong Thom. The NVA 91st Division had pulled back intact, suffering, his reports said, only eight percent casualties. His own units had eight percent killed, eleven percent wounded, sixteen percent missing. Better than a third, some of his best yotheas, cadremen, village agents and informers, gone. And the government! Sar thought. What fools! That two-tongued demigod Lon Nol! His stroke proves to all Kampuchea his utter lack of merit. The siege is lifted. The NVA withdraw. The ARVN withdraw. The siege is renewed. FANK is a disgrace. Met Sar clenched his fists, spread his fingers, then clenched his fists tighter. One hundred and fifty thousand FANK soldiers and not a hundred and fifty decent leaders. A disgrace. They shame every Khmer. I should have a quarter that force. With a quarter, Sar thought, I'd make the yuons wish they'd died at Tchepone and never entered Kampuchea. Ah, fine to incapacitate the refineries, but the yuons, no, they destroy the entire facility. Without Neak Sam, FANK is a stinging centipede without a head. We must act. *Now!* Now. But do what?

Sar rose, left his bunker, strode as a fat man attempting to walk with speed, his advancing leg stretching before him, his body lagging, his rear leg seeming insufficiently powerful to propel his mass and be brought forward simultaneously. He entered the tunnel corridor to the operations bunker and map room. Two guards were there.

Sar thought of Nang. There had been no word. "Ah," he grumbled. "Nang, *he* was a yothea." Aah, Sar thought, just a soldier. Perhaps valuable but just a soldier. Has he gone to the KVM? "Echh." Sar coughed on the idea. Then he thought, Did I use him to best advantage? He pondered that thought amid scores of others.

In the cavern map room, alone, Sar did not study the maps. How? He picked up a pen from the desk, fidgeted, twiddled the pen with his left hand about his pointing right index finger. Around and around. Then he leaned forward, placed an elbow on the table, his forehead in his hand. With the pen he doodled the Khmer script symbol for "How?" Again and again: "How?" "How?" The script looked beautiful on the page and he felt pleased at the sight of his own penmanship. He pulled a sheet of paper toward him and scrawled across the top page, "It is necessary. Thanks to Angkar Leou, it is being realized."

"Realized," he said softly. He knew well how to organize, how to infiltrate. He knew when to be ruthless, when to cajole. Yet at every step the North Viet Namese gained, and he, though advancing, fell a step further behind.

How do you raise the consciousness of the masses? he asked himself. How do you change them? How do we maintain our covert posture yet swing all Kampuchea to our cause? Sar sat, pondered. They were close yet conquest was elusive. How to use other resources to his advantage? How to direct his own leaders without seeming to direct? Sar sank into depressed frustration. Can we continue to pick our battles, or should we risk all?

"In 1177," he wrote, "Angkor was invaded by Champa. In 1250, by the Sinhalese with their loathed Theravada Buddhism. In 1620 the first yuon devils penetrated Prey Nokor. Twenty years later the Khmer king was enslaved by the dogma of Islam. The French, the Thais, the Japanese, and the Viets have all invaded. Yet we endure! We shall always endure! We shall rise up and discard all alien elements! Kampuchea for Kampucheans!"

He stopped. How? he thought. How best to use the armies of Angkar? How best to use the *chrops*, the agents and spies. How best to use the Americans without falling into the trap of dependence? They are strong but they are going and will not counterbalance the weight of the yuons much longer.

Sar turned back to the paper. "First," he wrote, "commit the people. Then the army. Then Angkar Leou." Yes, he thought. That's the proper order for commitment. How? How? The people are ready to join us, to follow.

Again he thought of Met Nang. For every highly trained yothea there were a hundred with no training, a hundred poorly armed boys of the rural and urban dung heaps. The new battalions of Cham hated his Khmers as much as they hated FANK and the Viets. There was no loyalty there. Only opportunism. Mountaineers were as bad: two brigades whose main motivation was to avenge their losses and liberate the highlands from Khmer and Viet. To lose Nang! he thought. Ach! His *kosang* had revealed the evil elements. What is infected must be excised. What has been tainted by any alien form must be erased.

But first, *first,* the people must be gained.

"Angkar," Nang whispered to the soldiers of the ambush team.

"Hello Number Two Rabbit," a private whispered back. "How did you find us?"

"I asked my brother the hare."

"Ha ha. That's good. Rabbit's brother . . ."

"Ssshh. Mister Private, you must not speak so loud."

"What have you brought?" The team leader crept close. Nang unhooked a length of black cloth from about his waist and dropped it. It thudded on the earth. "Are they—"

"Use them first," Nang whispered. "They'll keep your position concealed."

"Grenades! American grenades! Rabbit, where did you get them? The garrison has none."

"My brother the scorpion showed me where they were buried."

"I don't know how you do it. . . ."

"Ssshh. Follow me. My brother the chickenhawk overheard . . ."

Nang led the FANK ambush patrol of the northwest quadrant garrison deeper into the jungle. The national soldiers had balked the first time he'd appeared at night at their listening post only fifty meters from their wire, but on subsequent nights he'd arrived with various gifts, from boots to trip flares. Always he'd come upon them from the rear, emerged within their circle. Each time he'd attempted to tell them or show them a better way to operate and slowly the scarred boy had gained their trust and respect. To the teams of one post he became known as Number Two Rabbit, to those of another Little Rabbit, and to a third Night Rabbit. No one saw him during daylight and the soldiers kept him secret from their commanders. Through the late dry season and into the early months of the 1971 monsoons Nang urged, prodded, led the teams deeper and deeper into the jungle, deeper into the swamps or farther out along hedgerows and treelines between paddies. "The chief method of learning warfare," he told them, "is through warfare."

"Where did you learn, Little Rabbit?"

"Who taught you, Number Two Rabbit?"

"Night Rabbit, for one so young, when did you learn?"

"In the conquered zones," Nang explained patiently. He used the term "conquered" instead of "liberated." It distinguished him from the Khmer Viet Minh agents who were also attempting to infiltrate FANK. "My father led the resistance in my village. He was very good but a traitorous snake bit him with its tail."

"Where do you get the weapons?"

"When you are destitute, you must supply yourself from the enemy's stores."

Slowly Nang proselytized, denouncing first the Viets and their Khmer Viet Minh lackeys. The FANK underlings agreed fully. The NVA and the KVM, whom they sometimes called Khmer Rouge, were the most serious threat to Kompong Thom. Nang then denounced Norodom Sihanouk for what he'd become. Again there was major agreement, for the ex-Prince had become the figurehead and legitimizer of the Viet Namese Communists. Nang carried it further. He denounced Samdech Euv's role, policies and actions when he had been head of state, denounced all the things Sihanouk had not done to protect Kampuchea. In every unit Nang's words convinced at least one soldier. He moved on to criticizing Lon Nol, the Americans and the barbaric South Viet Namese whom Lon Nol had brought to Cambodia, and then on to condemning the war crimes of all aliens.

By May he had nearly 150 FANK soldiers in fifteen units under his spell. He taught them to use "Angkar" as a password. They kept it secret. During daylight, in the city, Nang organized whoever would follow. From the pallet bed at the *khrou*'s hut he scurried through the camp alleyways and the city's narrow back streets, searching, recruiting children, training.

For months he worked using the remnant of the Krahom agent organization already in place, the remnant left after the NVA had wiped out at least half in the November 1970 ambushes and assassinations and the ARVN had killed or captured and turned over to FANK another quarter. Nang recruited, organized, indoctrinated and trained. He worked with an energy even he did not know he possessed, as if the painful energies of the B-52 concussions and the electroshock torture had been absorbed by him. Nang found the terrorized, besieged people of Kompong Thom willing, eager, to listen. To them, no one seemed destined to win. Battles could go on forever until all were trampled. No one presented a desirable alternative. Certainly not the Viet Namese Communists.

Nang talked of people's war but he dropped the weight of Marx, Lenin and Mao. He talked of the Americans, told government troops they were not the solution. "First," he said, "they are tied to a policy of saving their own skins. They throw away South Viet Nam because they fear the NVA. They'll never assist Kampuchea with troops. They won't even follow up their bombings." Angrily, Nang added, "The targets may be NVA but the bombs destroy *our* irrigation systems. The yuons hug villages or set up their field guns in the lee of dams thinking the Americans won't bomb. Still they are bombed." Peasants agreed with him. The colossal power of the bombs terrorized them. To those who said, "If only the Americans would . . ." Nang replied, "Khmers, only Khmers, can be responsible for the salvation of Kampuchea. If we are organized we can save ourselves."

"We don't need the ARVN," Nang told them, and the radio confirmed it. In August the Cambodian Foreign Ministry made public a 15 July report which detailed ARVN atrocities against Khmer civilians. Lon Nol's high command immediately demanded the complete withdrawal of all South Viet Namese forces and the closing to them of the naval facility at Neak Luong. Public outcry reverberated throughout Republic-controlled areas. The fact that an ARVN column had relieved the siege of Kompong Thom nine months earlier was lost in the confusion, diminished by the cost to Khmers. "The cost," Nang mused as he squatted with peasants in market stalls, "is very high, eh? We cannot rely on a crocodile who weeps over our pain as he devours us."

Of the Republic and its army, Nang told his growing number of followers, "They oppose so much that we oppose we should be very close. But that Lon Nol, that Sirik Matak, that General Fernandez—it is they who have invited the B-52s. They who brought in the Southern crocodile. The Republicans have walked the same trail as the old regime. Bureaucratic functionaries so jam the government nothing works." To soldiers he said, "When was the last time you were paid? Was it enough to feed your families? Do you have to buy your rations from your commander? How can you afford to be soldiers? Even in the army there is a Khmer Patriot's movement. Once the yuons are eliminated, we'll turn our guns on Phnom Penh. In the liberated zone the smartest Khmers are planning for the day when Khmers will be self-governing and self-sufficient."

In late summer the "Patriotic Intellectuals" distributed a document entitled "Declaration to the Khmer People from the Liberated Zone." Unknown to Nang, to the peasants, the document had originated at Mount Aural. "You see," Nang said, "there is the Movement, the resistance for which my father died. There is a man I once met, he is fat and full of merit, who can lead us into a new era, a new beginning."

"Yes," answered the simpleminded.

"Yes, yes," answered the intelligent and the patriotic.

As his network increased so too did the risks and thus the insecurity of Little Rabbit. About him he maintained a core of hardened bodyguards, agents, FANK deserters, the strongest and quickest of the new recruits. No longer did Nang reside with the *khrou* who had restored his hearing and healed his wounds but now in random and scattered "safe houses" throughout the city, in remote hamlet huts, in secret forest hideaways. In every corner he had eyes, in every wall ears. Not a comment escaped him, not a propagandist's line was missed—for exactly as Nang was attempting to organize Kompong Thom, so too were the Khmer Viet Minh proselytizers.

Unlike the Viet Cong in South Viet Nam where, because of intense military and political pressure (often by district and provincial militias using patient, proven police investigation techniques), the indigenous rebel infrastructure was methodically being dismantled, the Khmer Krahom and Khmer Viet Minh political and military organs throughout Cambodia were expanding almost unchecked. The war thrust upon the Khmer power vacuum by the Communist factions had caught Cambodia as unprepared as South Viet Nam had been a decade earlier—yet the Khmer rebellion matured far more quickly. Outside the capital heartland and the Battambang rice basket region, chaos ruled. With FANK, ARVN, and U.S. actions concentrated on countering Communist raids and main force offensives, the local proselytizers and organizers needed to be concerned only with provincial or local militias and local police—all of which, in many areas, were insecure in their own loyalties and thus easy targets for either terrorist action or rebel political recruitment.

To those who expressed worry and to those who seemed confused about which element to support, Nang said only, "When the time comes, as it will, death will come to those who oppose us."

"May I see your pass?"

"Khieng!" Chhuon looked quizzically at the young militiaman. Khieng's eyes were cold, his manner polite. Chhuon's voice filled with exasperation. "We're only three hundred meters from the village."

"Your pass, Mister Chairman!" Khieng stood stiffly behind his rifle. "Those are my orders."

"Of me! Yes. I'm sure you're right." Chhuon pulled a clear plastic bag from his pocket. He unwound the tie, reached in carefully and arranged the paper so it lay flat inside. Then he held it out. The lettering, Khmer in script and Viet Namese in block, faced him. "I'm to inspect the fields the soldiers will help plant tomorrow," Chhuon said.

Khieng grasped the edge of the plastic, pulled it to an angle at which raindrops rolled off into his palm. He studied the upside-down form then muttered, "Okay. But return by the precise time printed."

Chhuon proceeded down the dike. On the night nine months earlier when San and Chamreum had been killed by fire and water, the demon had taken full control of Chhuon's mind and Chhuon had not even struggled. That fact alone caused him immeasurable anxiety. Four families had escaped that night, thirteen people in all. True to his word, the next morning Major Nui had had thirty-nine villagers executed before the pagoda. None of the murdered were from the extended Cahuom family and in Chhuon's mind the strings which bound him to the Viet Namese became cords, the cords ropes. He became sag-mouthed, hopeless, apathetic. Though he still fantasized of escape, he put no stock in the idea. Instead he immersed himself in the meditation: I am a small rock, an indistinguishable stone. With me or without me, what has happened would have happened. I am at most a paving stone keeping Major Nui's feet from touching mud.

Yet, inside, his entire being was irritated, a rash rubbed raw as if he'd ingested a steel rasp which rampaged within his body at the whim of the demon. The irritation bubbled bile from his stomach burning his throat, had for nine months bubbled fire and agitation so un-Khmer, so un-Buddhist, his mother and wife no longer tolerated his presence and he sought solace more and more amongst the Viet Namese and Khmer Viet Minh cadremen. Through the harvest season Chhuon had not entered a paddy. Through the dry season no one consulted him. He assisted no one with seed or plow repair, advice or encouragement. At times he'd felt it would be so simple to slave in the paddies and purify his spirit through toil and self-denial as he had after Samnang's death. But he was afraid his own family would attack him, murder him. The fear prompted his absence which in turn proved to the villagers he'd become one with the new apparatus.

"How easily the chairman tells us, 'We're better off today than before liberation,' " they told one another. "How easily he says, 'We must work together as a single production brigade for our community to prosper.' What has he lost, eh?"

East of Phum Sath Din above the Srepok River, rice paddies stepped gradually up the hillside like a rock garden of slate slabs where the slate is paddy and the cracks between, dikes, hedgerows or treelines. Chhuon slogged barefoot in the rain. The lower fields were replanted and glowed with the iridescent green of new sprouts. In the middle paddies villagers, very young and very old, labored bent-back, scooping holes and sticking in seedlings. Some sang old planting songs but most, unlike in the past when all the teens and single men and women flirted, were silent. The upper paddies which bordered on the forest remained untended. As Chhuon climbed rain collected in his hair and ran down in rivulets across his face and forehead, into his eyes, into his partially opened mouth. Thoughts formed. They're so clever, he thought. Three armies. Three separate armies. The main force battles the enemy, the area forces control the people, the district militia defends us and now it helps plant the rice. So clever. Separate. The butchers don't taint the defenders even though all take orders from the same command. Eh! What could I possibly do? What is one pebble in an avalanche?

Chhuon reached the highest paddy, knelt, scooped a handful of mud. It would be best, he thought, to plant different seed here. He worked the soil in his fingers as he'd not done in a year. He grabbed a second handful and squished the red-brown muck feeling a grittiness the lower paddies did not possess. Without fertilizer, he thought, without organic compost, these paddies . . . He stopped, hesitated, closed his eyes. . . . Still, he thought. In the muck he could feel a life force. Yes. It's weak but it's there. Chhuon opened his eyes. The paddy was empty. The next level up had been deforested for another tier but the work had stopped in order to plant the existing fields. Chhuon walked to the edge. No dikes had been built between the deforested land and the upper paddy. Orange streams cut gullies into the stripped land then dumped into the upper paddy and fanned clay silt into a dozen small deltas. Let the soldiers build— His thought began, then abruptly shifted. I could walk up there. I'm authorized. I could go to the edge of the last cut. He crossed a delta and climbed into a rising gully. The field had a peculiar feel to it as if its own tormented spirit still wandered above the land. Chhuon walked on. He walked to the center of the stripped terrace and squatted. The ground had not been plowed and much of it was still covered with years of jungle-floor decay. He spread the surface leaves and twigs. An inch down they were dry even though it had been raining for weeks. He dug farther. The old cover was not as thick as he'd imagined. A hand's width in, tough roots wove a padded net. He ripped farther. Only two more inches and he exposed a mulch-clay mixture. Another two inches, homogeneous clay. If this washes out . . . Again his thoughts were interrupted. He looked up. In superstition he half expected to see the tortured spirit of the land, half expected to find a vengeful ghost about to thrash him. The sky was dull gray and close. The lower paddies and village were hidden in the mist. Only the spire of the pagoda gave away the presence of a village. Chhuon turned to the forest. It was too close, too inviting. They'd shoot my last son, he thought. From his squat he saw a flicker of movement in the mist between the trees. He swallowed hard. To run. To freeze. He shifted slowly. Militia, he told himself. Maybe the forest spirit. Resisters. I'll run and alert Khieng. Tell Hang Tung. Spies. Hang's or Major Nui's. I'll continue my inspection. A steel sliver of pain stabbed his right knee. He cursed quietly. A sudden overwhelming feeling of loss and isolation cloaked him as if he'd been covered by a tarp, snared, enwrapped. He bowed his head. "Kill me," he wept. "Kill me!" He tore at his hair, ripping out tufts. "Shoot me!" He wailed.

"Uncle!" The voice sounded as if it came from the clouds.

Chhuon turned his head a few degrees. His neck muscles trembled. He cast his eyes to the heavens. "You sent me word," Chhuon forced a meek pained voice from his throat. "You told me if our bodies toil for them our bodies are enslaved. You told me I am not my body. If my hands, eyes, process their papers, if my mouth passes their orders, my parts are their tools, but I am not my parts. I heard you tell me this. If our hearts embrace their ideology, then we have been enslaved."

"Uncle!" The voice came clearer, came from the forest.

"Hang Tung?" Chhuon called quietly, tentatively. There was no answer. Chhuon rose slowly. He turned to the forest and thought how terrible it was that the village no longer had incense sticks to light in honor of the spirits. Then an ambiguous smile crept onto his face, a smile half fear, half love. For three years the only traditional act he'd practiced consistently was the feeding of Samnang's spirit at the family altar. "Kdeb?!" He called the nickname reverently. "Kdeb? Has your spirit found its way home? It's me, Cahuom Chhuon. Not your uncle. I pray for you every day. I have wanted to tell you of my dream the night before they took you. I want to tell you of the crocodile, the tiger, the water. I'm alone without you. Never should we have gone." As he spoke he stumbled toward the treeline, his eyes blurry from the fog of emotion. "Kdeb, if it is not the fate of a person to remain alive, we must accept this. Come home to rest."

"Uncle, here."

"Who's there?"

"Kpa."

"Kpa?!"

"Quiet! Stay there. Pretend to study the soil."

"Yes." Chhuon knelt. His mind swirled.

"Listen. Keep your head down. Don't look for me."

Chhuon dug a hand into the old leaves and thin humus. "It's been very long," he whispered.

"Mister Cahuom. We need your help."

"You're not hungry tonight?" Hang Tung eyed the village chairman with disgust. Loathsome, he thought. He's perfect.

"The heat from my stomach . . ." Chhuon apologized.

"Perhaps the rations are too generous, Uncle." Chhuon did not answer. "You measured the fields?"

"Yes."

"And you've reported the needs to Cadreman Trinh."

"To the assistant. Trinh Le."

"Tomorrow the soldiers will join the people. They'll set an example of order and discipline."

"Nephew—" Chhuon hesitated. Hang Tung had become increasingly difficult. "Don't tax the village for those fields at the same rate . . ."

"You think I set the rate?!" Hang's voice was sharp with accusation.

Chhuon rushed on. "Those fields won't produce as the lower paddies. The soil's thin. There's not the same nutrients. When we plow the chaff and stalks . . ."

"Don't talk to me of that," Hang Tung snapped. "I'm not a peasant." His tone changed. "We have some new procedures."

"Yes?"

"Listen! Memorize! Everyone is needed in the fields. The pagoda is closed until all fields, gardens, orchards and roadways are planted. It's only temporary. We must do it in order to avoid famine."

"November's crop was abundant. Where's all the . . ."

"I don't control the storage of food! Damn you! Why do you accuse me?! Perhaps the rations *are* too generous. Perhaps if they had less, they'd waste less. Or are they giving it to the resisters?"

"What? The people barely . . ."

"Another thing. From now on this Khmer greeting with the hands, *lei*, humph . . . It's banned."

Chhuon's mouth fell. Away from the table Sok, Peou and Chhuon's mother licked the last morsels from their rice bowls. They pretended not to hear. "It's only a . . ."

"It will be punished by a cut to half rations."

"Nephew!"

"There's more." Hang Tung's voice was forced yet forceful

like an exhausted parent with a toddler, ready to spank the child at the slightest objection. "Henceforth the army shall be referred to as the Khmer Liberation Movement."

"The militia or the Viet Na . . ."

"They are one and the same."

"May I post these."

"Of course. Sign the bottom. No. Tell everyone. Tonight."

"It's so . . ."

"More. The Chhimmy families' homes . . ."

"New people have moved in . . ."

"Move them out. The homes will be lent to the families of our heroic People's Liberation Army officers. And the house of Ny Hy San. Have it whitewashed. Major Nui's family will occupy that one. Tomorrow we'll see the major at his headquarters. You'll have a good report."

"it's all i could get away with," Chhuon whispered.

"we're very grateful, uncle."

"kpa . . . sam, ry's mother, are they with you?"

"he's liberated. they took her to the old people's hospital."

"what of . . ."

"i must go. the village is surrounded."

"kpa . . . be careful."

The night was very dark and the rain was heavy. Chhuon's lantern had been confiscated months earlier. He bumped along slowly, smiled inwardly. He'd done it. He'd given a resister aid. God help me, he thought, if Kpa's a plant. Ah, yet he'd crossed the line. Just as an individual's resistance crumbles if he goes against his principles, one's fear crumbles if he stands by them. It's easy, Chhuon thought. What had Kpa said, "All one need do is match their flow and live in the spaces between."

Chhuon knocked on Ny Non Chan's door. Nimol let him in but she did not greet him. Nor did Chan. Since the night of his brother's death he had only passed along Chhuon's orders, never engaging his old friend in either conversation or argument. Chhuon imparted the new orders exactly as he'd been told. Chan snarled, muttered to himself but showed no outward emotion. Look at the pleasure, Chan thought, the son of . . . no, he's no son. His father's spirit must cry in pain to see him.

"Shall I whitewash my brother's home in the rain?" Chan asked without emotion.

"I was told only to have it whitewashed," Chhuon answered.

"And the major's wife, will she arrive soon?"

"I was not told."

"And if I don't."

"*Chiet!*"

"*Chiet?!*"

"That's what I've been told."

"You don't use the Khmer word any longer, Mister Chairman? Now you speak in Viet Namese?"

Chhuon hesitated. The accusation weighed heavily, its weight seeming to fall on the skin below his eyes, pulling, pushing his features into a mask of sorrow. "Dear Brother"—Chhuon bowed to the vice-chairman, bowed with his hands high and together—"what I do, I do to protect our village. I do to protect the people. Please, I beg you, I beseech you, appease the"—Chhuon dropped his voice, quickly looked about—"appease the yuon crocodiles. We have no way to . . ."

"Yes, Mr. Chairman. You've demonstrated your capacity to kiss the hole from which they pass gas. It was what my brother saw before *chiet!*"

The jungle tunnel came upon them suddenly. Chhuon didn't see the entrance until the front of the vehicle crashed against the curtain of living vines. "It's time you understood, Uncle." Hang Tung chuckled strangely, a laugh Chhuon had never heard from him.

"Why does the major want me?" Chhuon asked nervously.

The concealed road was smooth, well maintained. After the rough twelve-kilometer stretch of Highway 19, it seemed to Chhuon as if he'd entered a different world. Before Hang answered Chhuon asked, "Has Phum Nako been evacuated? Are the craters from American bombs? Why do we tear down the forest to make paddies while all these lie fallow? What kind of gun is that in the trees? Is that a hospital? Are you sure . . ."

"Uncle. You sound like a little boy on his first trip to the big city." '

"Oh. I . . . I haven't been out of the village since . . ."

"I know. It's time you became a productive element. The major, he likes you. He likes you very much. Now that he's the province chief for village administration he wants you to move up with him."

"Last night I'm like meat dripping blood thrown to the tigers with these new directives. They made a feeding frenzy of me. Today, you want me to move up! Oh, what's that?"

"Those are surface-to-air missiles. Come. We're late."

Hang Tung sped past bunkers with overhead camouflage, past idle tanks and trucks parked in earthbound revetments, past hundreds of troops without weapons. Here the North Viet

Namese were unopposed. Neither FANK to the southwest nor the ARVN/US forces to the east pressured "liberated" territory to this depth. The only concern was American high-level interdiction bombing. The vast majority of that was targeted in the Mekong–Bassac River corridor from the border to Phnom Penh. Second-priority targets were those within a few kilometers of the border; third, those at the advancing tips of NVA drives; finally, the identified supply and reinforcement columns. Even had the headquarters base been discovered, its priority on the target lists would have remained low.

"Ah, Chairman Cahuom, it is a pleasure to have you here."

"Major Nui . . ." Chhuon began bringing his hands together, then jerkily halted.

"Lieutenant colonel," Hang Tung corrected Chhuon. Hang Tung had led Chhuon to a large structure cut into a hillside at the middle of the camp. The north wall was solid mountain, the south, a meter of earth then a meter of window facing downhill. The front portion of the roof was thatch with wide overhangs giving the structure the appearance of a mountain lodge. The rear portion was four feet of earth supported by heavy timbers. Above it grew vines, bushes—near-perfect camouflage.

"Lieutenant colonel!" Chhuon corrected himself. "Congratulations."

"Thank you," Nui said amiably. "Come, I wish you to meet someone."

Hang Tung followed Chhuon and Lieutenant Colonel Nui between offices separated by woven-palm walls to a large central rear room. On two walls were maps, on the third large framed pictures of Norodom Sihanouk and Ho Chi Minh, and on the fourth small black-and-white photographs. In the center there was a low, flat sand table with a detailed model of Stung Treng City. Immediately a wave of fear flashed through Chhuon—the terror of having entered a forbidden sanctum. The model city seemed to leap from the table and seize him. His brother's warehouse, his home, pulsating like alarm lights, details so specific Chhuon felt he could be reduced and live in the model, visit Cheam, load a toy truck with experimental seed.

Chhuon swayed. He looked up to catch his balance. Black-and-white photos of his village caught his eye. There, his wife and Nimol at food distribution. There, the head of the Hem family and his cousin's wife, Ry, at Ry's front door. Another of Ry with a Viet Namese soldier. Another with two young militiamen. Chhuon looked to the maps. Lieutenant Colonel Nui prattled, asking of his health, of his family's. Chhuon responded without hearing his own words. One wall had separate maps of eleven

villages and a map of the entire Northeast. The other had maps
of all Cambodia.

" . . . you see," Nui continued, "we wish to integrate the community, not take it over."

"I've never seen anything like that." The sentence seeped
from Chhuon, detached.

"The sand table?" Nui beamed with pride.

"Yes . . ."

"I was showing the colonel how we . . . he stepped out. I want
you to meet him. He's a fascinating man. And I want him to
meet you. I want to show you off. Ha! You're important to him.
To all of us, you know. He stepped out for a moment. Where
was I? Yes . . . for centuries our peoples have foolishly hated
each other, Chairman Cahuom. We can't deny the past yet our
present struggles are interdependent. If we're to save ourselves
from the mire of imperialism and reach the shining road of the
proletarian revolution, we must join arms. By integrating we
can break the vicious cycle of prejudice."

"By integrating?" Chhuon did not understand.

Hang Tung interrupted. "Uncle Chhuon is a master of *khon
thi chet, dai cung chet, biet moi song*, eh, Colonel?"

Nui smiled. Chhuon still looked confused. " 'One too clever
dies, one too stupid dies; to survive one must know when to be
clever, when foolish!' Ha! Let's face it"—Nui rubbed his face—
"Khmers and Viets are both members of the international community. We both struggle. It's foolish to hate. It depletes our
energy. You agree?" Nui did not wait for Chhuon to respond.
"That's why my wife will live in your village. My son will go to
school with your son. As Prince Sihanouk wishes, a dozen Viet
Namese families will be so integrated. We'll have a model
village, eh? Not unlike this?" He gestured to the table. "An
experiment," he said. "Once we've achieved our inevitable victory over the imperialists there'll be no borders. In every school
children will learn to speak one tongue. We'll make a new
Indochinese man. And you, Chairman Cahuom Chhuon, shall
see the beginning."

As Nui spoke Chhuon turned a few degrees from him and
looked at the map of the northeast quarter of the nation. At first
he noted the water features were in two shades of blue, monsoon-
season water in light, year-round dark. Then he noticed the
unusual road pattern, noticed the multiple routes descending
from a hundred points along the Laotian border, merging into
eight distinct clusters with three merging at the campsite where
they stood. Various units were labeled in grease pencil on the
acetate cover. As Chhuon's eyes absorbed details the secret

supply roads came to life. He could almost feel the thrust of descending armies, concentrating, then flowing southwest, south of Stung Treng City, west through the low forest and into the swamps and rice fields of the Sen and Chinit rivers about Kompong Thom, could almost hear the clatter of tanks and self-propelled field guns of the NVA 5th and 7th divisions as they headed for rendezvous with the clearly marked 91st. From there, he thought, where? The map ended and to face the next one would put him at such an angle to his host as to be disrespectful.

"Your wife will need many things," Chhuon said.

"Committee Member Hang has a list." The colonel beamed. He had expected sighs, perhaps objections presented as potential problems with other inhabitants, but Chhuon had shown not only complete acquiescence but an apparent interest and desire to cooperate. "Ah"—the Viet Namese officer raised his hand as if giving an invocation—"here is another most honored guest." Chhuon turned to see a towering Caucasian. "Let me introduce Colonel Hans Mitterschmidt of the Democratic Republic of Germany. Colonel"—Nui changed tongue to French—"this is Chairman Cahuom Chhuon of Village 517. He is in total agreement with your integration plan."

Sullivan rode in at dusk. The sky was soft. Between breaks in the fast-moving clouds the evening's first stars glowed. He rode slowly through Neak Luong. The used BSA Lightning motorcycle purchased from a departing British embassy employee purred steadily. He had not found much time to ride since the purchase, nor the momentum to bring him to Neak Luong, until this early July night when he no longer could stand the pressure and needed to see her. Huntley had delivered a truckload of school supplies in March—more in April and in June—school supplies, roofing, and a blackboard he'd appropriated from the Military Equipment Delivery Team (MEDT) briefing room. On the last trip he'd brought a message: "Augh, Mrs. Cahuom," he'd drawled in English though Vathana understood little English and of his dialect not a word. "J. L. caint come rig-aht naa. God a'mighty, some reporter caught him teachin a FANK cap'n how ta use a prick-25 . . . radio, ya know. God a'mighty, ma'am. He's in a world a cow dung rig-aht up ta his ears. Gotta lie low."

As Sullivan rode in, for a quick moment he pictured himself a cowboy in a western, but the image did not hold off other thoughts. He blipped the hand throttle, the front wheel unweighted, the bike hopped, settled back. The town looked different. The anti-Sihanouk posters plastered to sidewalls of concrete apartment buildings had faded and shredded, and the inhabitants walking head down under the words took no notice of the slogans. The spirit which had spawned the Republic, which had brought Sullivan to Cambodia, was no longer apparent. In five months traffic in the city had become more motorized though the number of civilian cars and trucks had declined. Small motorcycles were everywhere. Old-timers clung close to building walls, seemingly trying to escape the raspy whine. The traditional buffalo-drawn farm carts had all but disappeared from the main road, though now idle they cluttered side alleyways. Military trucks, FANK and ARVN, lumbered more, as if the troops were "cruising the strip" rather than heading somewhere specific. And the people seemed different. The inflow of refugees had been nearly constant at about four hundred per month. The outflow almost matched, with around three hundred a month leaving for Phnom Penh. But the new refugees were more destitute than the old, more terrified, less likely to remain in the camp. At first they simply wandered away from their swamp hovels during daylight, but as the rainy season increasingly turned the camp into a horrid quagmire in which the sanitation system had broken down completely and malnutrition and stomach disorders, despite Vathana's efforts, became widespread, many refugees built makeshift huts against the sides of in-town buildings from material begged or stolen. A second wave of ARVN soldiers had come to man the South Viet Namese river and road bases—many who had not taken part in the earlier battles—foreign soldiers with money who saw Neak Luong as their home base much as U.S. soldiers came to think of areas of South Viet Nam as "theirs." With their wealth came higher inflation, thirty percent in the first six months of 1971; and with inflation came additional corruption and prostitution. "Whores earn more than doctors," Doctor Sarin had complained to Vathana. "Little boys who sell Coca-Cola to the Saigon troops earn more than commanders of Republic garrisons." Long-time residents of the city began to feel encircled, cramped, their early gracious generosity taxed beyond their ability to give. They closed their doors, hoarded the little they still retained, praying it would be sufficient to feed and clothe their own children. And although Sweden's foreign minister, Torsten Nilsson, had announced his country would deliver a half million dollars in medical supplies to the Khmer Republic (plus an equal amount to the Viet Namese Communists), medicine was in critical shortage. (The Nixon administration, despite MEDT requests, refused to include drugs in the Commodity Import

Program aid package and further blocked requests from Cambodia's health minister to the International Red Cross for medicine and bandages—assuming either that these supplies would be stolen by the VC/NVA or that the giving would somehow contradict the administration's "low profile" policy.)

Neak Luong's new countenance had three contrasting faces: one military, one the new rich, and one the new hungry and diseased masses, with the growing adjunct of roving child gangs, hustling young pimps, and younger prostitutes.

To Sullivan, as he continued north on the main road, the scene was familiar. Why, he thought, had I thought it would be different here? Because of her? If anything it's worse. More ARVNs. More poor Khmers. He rode past the pagoda with its high central spire and refugee huts clustered in every square meter about it. More huts, he thought. He flicked the throttle and headed to the camp.

Vathana rocked the infant girl in a net hammock as stolid Sophan crawled on the tent's dirt floor with the twenty-one-month-old Samnang. The boy's hands had loosened, though when he crawled his fingers remained closed and he supported his weight on the backs of his wrists. "Come!" Sophan called playfully. "That's it." She held a toy wagon made from a sardine can. "How do you think your mother feels when you don't crawl?" she whispered lovingly to the child.

"What should I do?" Vathana asked. She sat on the edge of the cot she shared with the wet-nurse and her son.

"What can you do?" Sophan answered not changing her tone.

"She has told all their family—" Vathana began.

"If she told the whole world and it weren't true, how could it hurt you?"

"My father's sister thought I was dead." Vathana's voice was full of anguish. "She'd heard I'd run to the forest to join the Communists. What if my father heard? What if my mother believed her lies?"

"You must renounce your marriage, Angel. What does Teck say?"

"He says nothing. No word at all. I only hear from his mother."

"What about the children? Doesn't she want to see them? She could take them to the capital, to her villa."

Tears came to Vathana's eyes. The sadness wrenching outward from her abdomen twisted her features. "To her, the Wheel of Life is nonexistent. They are not part of her."

"Angel," a young woman called quietly from beyond the partition. "Mister new-Captain John Sullivan is at the registration desk."

Sullivan bowed formally when Vathana appeared. At first he tried to repress his smile, to show shock at her loss of weight, to show empathy for her living situation, but he could not. A boyish smile brightened his face. It either reflected from her or caused her to relinquish her suffering, for she too beamed. He reached out and covered her clasped hands with his. A flood of words came from his throat before he knew he'd opened his mouth. "Yes. Yes." She smiled up at him—he at five-ten, she barely five feet, her black eyes gazing into his blue.

"The Dhammapada says, 'Do not speak harshly to anyone,' " Vathana quoted. " 'Those who are spoken to will answer thee in the same way. Angry speech is painful; blows for blows will touch thee.' "

"Americans say the same thing." Sullivan heard his voice for the first time and wondered what they were talking about. " 'What goes around, comes around.' The Marines add another line. 'Payback's a . . .' Ah . . . well, it's kind of similar." He paused, aware suddenly that at least a hundred infirm, cot-ridden refugees were staring at them. "The rain's stopped," he said, stepping back, pulling gently. "It was a beautiful rain this afternoon."

"My father used to worship the rain," Vathana murmured. "Because it renews the land. Here it only makes mud."

"Is there someplace we can go. I . . . I . . . want to talk. It's kind of American of me, I know, but I'd prefer to talk alone."

Vathana smiled, assented. Then her face tightened. An image of a dark assaulter ripping her, clutching her, flashed in her mind. Sullivan was sunshine in darkness, winking, momentary, soon to withdraw and leave eternal night. "There's a place by the river," she whispered. "Let me tell Sophan."

Vathana had been ordered, for the protection of her brother and the camp, to become the American's consort. This was terrible. She was the mother of two children. To lie with a long-nose, a fire-haired *phalang* . . . Society in Cambodia, in the camp, was closed. This was scandalous. She was ashamed. But, too, there existed a pang, a need, a growing attraction and infatuation beyond what was forced upon her.

For an hour they sat, talking quietly, fishing in the dark Mekong with hand lines and hooks baited with *parhok*, small pieces of pickled fish.

"I don't know what's happening." Sullivan's voice was thick

with concern. "My country's lost its, ah . . . I don't know. Does it make any sense to you if I say it's lost its masculinity?" Vathana sat very close to him. She leaned, pressed her shoulder against his. "Between men, when there's friendship, each man gives the friendship his best. It doesn't make any difference if one can give a lot and the other only a little. It's as though what's given is multiplied."

Again Vathana swayed into him. "Yes," she said. "That's like all friendship."

"Maybe. But . . ." He paused. "Masculine-feminine friendship is different." Sullivan jerked on the fishing line then let it fall again. He wasn't sure he wanted to go on. He didn't want to build a wall between them. "I'm talking countries here," he said. "Masculine and feminine traits in nations. If one gives in a feminine way to one in a masculine stance its like adding pluses and minuses. The given isn't multiplied. It's neutralized. When my country gives in a masculine way the given is multiplied. When it gives in a feminine way it negates what the receiver puts up. It's apron-string giving. I'll give you one hundred APCs if you'll love me. I'm at the tail end of it. I'm the guy who says, 'Colonel, you told my country you'd do this and this if we put ten thousand rifles in your hands. Now I know you got the rifles so let's see you show your love for me.' Somebody in Washington defines the 'this and this.' Maybe 'masculine' and 'feminine' aren't the right words."

"John, why is it you choose to work with Khmers? To fight beside Khmers?"

"Why? Vathana, I wish you could see it. There are some good troops here. Some good leaders. Some of these guys can fight. I know the American press is full of stories about FANK corruption, FANK incompetence, but . . . I wish I could show you. The garrison at Takhmau was hit by the NVA 12th Regiment and they waxed the Commies' asses. . . . I mean. . . ."

"It's okay."

"There's this one guy up in Baray, Lieutenant Bousa. He's really good. There's a major at Chamkar Luong on Highway 4. When his troops aren't fighting, and they're the best in the South, they're in the paddies his uncles and father had. They've got a truck farm there that feeds the whole battalion and their families."

"A farm of trucks!?"

Sullivan laughed. "I guess that doesn't translate, eh? A big vegetable farm. They have paddies and fishing boats. Some commanders charge their troops for rations. They get terrible soldiers. Major Preap's are great. I'd fight with them anytime."

Vathana leaned into Sullivan again. He put his right arm around her. Very lightly he hugged her. Visually, in the darkness, she was but a silhouette against the Mekong. He squeezed her gently. She turned her face up to his. Suddenly it hit him. He didn't know if traditional Khmers kissed. He wanted to kiss her. Instead he repeated with concern, "I don't know what's happening. My country's . . . They think"—he slipped the fishing spool under his left leg—"they can bomb without complete intelligence, without follow-up by skillful infantry maneuvers . . ." Vathana placed her left arm around his back and snuggled against him. "You can't drop an arc-light on a village because there's a T-54 parked on the green." She leaned against him and he lay back. Sullivan watched a mosquito alight on her hair. He reached up and gently pushed it into flight. About them the earth's surface lay black and still. Slowly, quietly, they hugged, kissed, embraced more and more passionately. Across the river, deep in the swamp, a firefight erupted then faded.

Afterward they talked again.

"You have only one sister?" Vathana lay with her head on his chest.

"Um-hum. Your family's large?"

"We're scattered," Vathana said. "Most of my family is in Communist areas."

"By the border?"

"In the North. Do you know Stung Treng?"

"Only from maps. It fell before I got here."

"There are many small villages in the hills and along the rivers. My father's village is Phum Sath Din. On the Srepok." Vathana hesitated. " 'They,' " she purposefully left it indefinite, inviting inquiry, "have told me my brother, Sakhon, at my father's request, has been moved to Kratie."

"That's held too," Sullivan said. She felt wonderful on him. "Your father must be a strong man to be able to let his son go."

"He used to be very traditional, very religious. Always he read the scriptures."

"My father used to make us, my sister and me, read the Bible before dinner," Sullivan said. "One passage every night."

"He too must have been very religious," Vathana whispered back. She kissed his ear.

"It wasn't so much that." Sullivan ran his hand over the smooth skin of her hip. "It was his way to teach us to think. We'd read the passage, then all through dinner we'd talk about it. What did it mean to us? What did the nuns say it meant? I remember one passage."

"Just one," Vathana kidded him, and snuggled in closer.

"Oh, lots," he responded seriously. "But I was thinking of one. It's from Matthew. Jesus said to his disciples, they'd asked him why he spoke to the people in parables, and he said, 'Because it has been given to you to know the mysteries of the kingdom of heaven, but to them it has not been given. Seeing they do not see, hearing they do not hear, nor do they understand.' "

"Are you certain, Mister Sullivan, you are not Buddhist?" Vathana giggled then turned mock-serious. "You sound Buddhist. It's written in the Dhammapada, 'If a fool be associated with a wise man even all his life, he will perceive the truth as little as a spoon perceives the taste of soup. If an intelligent man be associated for one minute only with a wise man, he will soon perceive the truth, as the tongue perceives the taste of soup.' "

"You know, I used to think Buddhism was all this mystical stuff and Christianity more down-to-earth. Never mind that. It's me. I feel like I've been given to know, not the mysteries of heaven, but the mysteries of hell."

"Perhaps it's because you are an intelligent man."

"But they're intelligent too."

"Who?"

"Why is it they see but don't see? Why don't they understand?"

"You mean your people?"

"Vathana, it's as plain to me as the freckles on my nose."

She rubbed her nose against his. "They're very plain." She giggled.

"Saint Paul said, 'Always learning, they are never able to come to the knowledge of the truth . . . they will not progress . . . their folly will be manifest to all. . . .' They study. They write. They've *no* idea what's happening. When will their folly be manifest? Is it going to take a bloodbath for them to wake up?"

"John L.," Vathana whispered in his ear. "Love me again. You cannot enlighten a fool."

After they loved again and Sullivan lay on his back with his head in the gentle fog pillow of postejaculation, Vathana massaged his forehead. "You are too young," she said softly, "to have such furrows." He opened his eyes. She looked down into his face. "How did you say it? 'I could gobble you up.' " She opened her mouth wide, placed her teeth on his forehead, gently raked the skin, half eating him, half trying to dislodge the pain and worry. "What would happen if we did nothing?" Vathana said in altered tone. "Really. What would happen if there were no you, no me? If John L. Sullivan and Cahuom Vathana did not exist? If we left Cambodia and moved to . . . to Paris?"

"Well," Sullivan said, wrapping his arms around her, twisting her down and nipping her nose, "well, first off, they'd come get me and toss my young ass in jail for being—how can I say it?— absent without leave."

"Truly, John," Vathana said.

"Truly," he whispered back. He ran kisses lightly down from her ear, down her neck to her shoulder. He felt the chain which she wore, ran a finger under it as if it blocked him from feeling all of her. Vathana lifted the statuette and rubbed it on the back of his hand. "What's that?" Sullivan whispered.

"A charm," she whispered proudly. "From my grandfather's tooth. My father gave it to me when I married."

Sullivan fought a sudden twinge of revulsion, an urge to retract his hand. For a quick moment he felt repulsed as if she'd said the Buddha was fresh feces from a hepatitis-ward latrine. He repressed the urge and gently grasped the carved figurine. As he held it, rubbed its smoothness between his fingers, a feeling of the tie to the ancient Wheel of Life rose in him, spread through him, finally reaching expressible thought. "It's very beautiful," he said.

"Truly?" Vathana giggled. "Would it be beautiful to you in Paris? Would they really throw you in jail?"

"You mean"—Sullivan flopped back onto his elbows and looked into the night sky—"in Paris. Not here. Hum . . . I think it would still be beautiful. Paris. Would your camp run without you? Could this stinking city survive without its Angel? Would any more or any fewer weapons be stolen or misused if I told Mataxis I wanted out? God, at least that damned *Sun* reporter'd be off my ass. I was with a FANK unit . . . I flew up to Kompong Thom last month. The place . . . the whole city is fortified but there's something crazy going on. I was thinking after . . . I was with the unit at Kilometer 19 near Vat Bakheng."

"Oh, John. You mustn't . . ."

"God. Those devils rose up outa the swamp. A full regiment against, I don't know, maybe five hundred FANKs. I called in the air strikes and this son of a bitch sees me do it. Did he see fifteen hundred NVA a dozen miles from the capital? Did he see them wipe out the first line? Nope. All he sees is me on the hook with a map. I thought Mataxis would shit. If *The New York Times* hadn't started publishing that Pentagon document I'd probably have been court-martialed for advising. Vathana, they see but they don't see."

"John, you take this very hard, yes?"

Sullivan rolled away from her. He propped himself up on his elbows and held his chin. "The guy paints me. He paints a picture of me and the whole team with his words. I'm working to keep these people from being slaughtered and he labels me a 'hard liner.' He thinks he's some sort of antiwar idealist and I'm a warmonger. I'm some hawk psychopath. What would happen if we moved to Paris? Who knows? But if they pull all the American lunatic hawks like me out of here, it's not going to stop the fighting."

"Truly?"

"Yeah. Truly."

Rita Donaldson let the heel of her pump fall loose from her foot. She and Tom Jasson were in the veranda dining room of Washington's Chez Pasquier, sitting, reading the latest installment of the Pentagon Papers as it appeared, exclusively, in *The Times,* sitting, sipping vodka martinis, amused and simultaneously angered and frustrated by the revelations and by the *Times*'s coup.

Rita's shoe fell to the carpet. She turned the page. The photo of a large man dressed in jungle utilities, his back to the camera, caught her eye. Tom Jasson moved his leg deeper under the table.

"Another American advisor in Cambodia . . ." she said. The words were unconnected with previous utterances.

"Um," Jasson said. Her toes found his shin, slid to the side of his leg, caressed—suddenly withdrew. Jasson looked up.

"Who the hell . . . ?" Rita said. Her foot fidgeted with the lost pump as she leaned forward, stared into the newspaper-quality photograph.

"What—" Jasson began.

"Arnold White," she said. "Arnold . . . The cutline credit is to . . . Do you remember when I got back . . . ?"

"Sure."

"Remember that obnoxious son of a bitch I told you about?"

"Yeah. Harvey called Chicago and, ah, what was it, San Jose?"

"He called all over. He even checked with the State Department. That bastard said his name was Jim White. Nobody had ever heard of him. Look at this." Jasson leaned over the table. "Arnold White!?" she said.

"Ah, maybe that's your man."

"May . . . I don't think so. Harvey checked for anyone named White. There weren't any in January."

"You're really upset about this, aren't you? So one guy was rude to you—so what?"

"He wasn't a correspondent. He was CIA, I bet. Trying to set me up."

"Rita? Rita, it doesn't make . . . Well, you tell me. You said nothing came of it, didn't you?"

Rita Donaldson sighed, thought, You jerk, glared at Tom Jasson. "I don't know."

"Look. It couldn't have worked out better for you. You spent a lousy ten days in that hell and you got a promotion. Now you get to see Paris and cover the talks. I would have gone but my dad's illness . . ."

"Yeah, I know. But you know what . . ."

"It should have been me," Jasson said. "You didn't even turn in a decent story. Who was going to read a feature on Cambodian military training? Really!"

"A lot of people read it!"

"Yeah, uh-huh."

"You envious twit! God!" She finished her martini. "You know what? I'm going to go back." She tapped the photo of the American "advisor." "I'm going to go back and nail these bastards. Goddamn gall of the government and these hooligans raping that country!"

CHAPTER TWELVE

A changed Nang stood amid his fighters. He had not uttered a
word or moved a muscle for nearly thirty minutes and the
fighters struggled to match his perfection. He did not make his
mind blank, did not meditate attempting to achieve some higher
awareness, but simply stood in perfect awareness of the here
and now. "He who breaks first," Nang had told the group, "will
face this scarred face in full sparring, just as he who breaks first
is first heard and engaged by the enemy." The boys and young
men concentrated on their breathing, concentrated on remaining relaxed. Every day they practiced being still and quiet, each
day for a longer period. Never had Number Two Rabbit challenged them, never had the stakes been so high. By his countenance they knew the situation had changed, evolved. At thirty-five
minutes one boy wavered. Eyes locked on him, then flicked to
Nang. The teacher, leader, master did not move. As the sides
had drawn tighter about Kompong Thom and American high-
level harassment bombing had increased, Nang used the sanc-
tity of the inner city more and more to train new yotheas and
chrops and his youth corps, to train them in techniques as
diverse as spying and sparring, fading into a crowd and facing
enemy tanks.

In the heart of Kompong Thom, Nang followed the developing
situation throughout the Northern Corridor, followed it as closely
as any full bird colonel followed enemy movements in his brigade's area of operation. Come on, he had thought. Come. Come
both of you. Come and fight and kill each other. Come, wound
each other. Then face the Rabbit's wrath. Nang fantasized a
thousand scenarios. In the swamps he saw himself spring from
a spiderhole, disembowel an NVA trail guide. In the city he saw
himself enter the FANK garrison in the southwest, saw himself

toying with the rheostat and electrodes that had burned his feet, saw the Republican governor weeping, lying in a pile of shit, begging Nang's pardon as Nang cranked the rheostat, no, ten rheostats, ten hanging imperialist lackeys losing control and defecating on themselves, saw himself with a long-handled knife slit the stomach of an NVA general tied neck to neck with a Republican, slit the flesh, scoop out the entrails, then fill the cavity with wet human dung. He fantasized an ambush for Met Sar, an execution for Met Sar, tortures for Met Sar. "This is the man who burned my feet," he saw himself say to his leader. "Watch as I have his feet burned off." As he thought he had touched his own feet and felt the scars. He had touched his chest and felt the thick lump where his ribs were mending, touched his face and felt the pebbled skin where the napalm had seared him. He stretched his hand open. So many months and still the hand was stiff, the fingers painful. Pain. He could bear it, bear it well, but that did not mean it wasn't there. Oh, come. Let the battle rage. Let them bear this pain.

After an hour a large young man coughed. He attempted to stifle it, to muffle it, but from between his lips came a burst of air from spasmatic lungs.

"Strugglers!" Nang screamed. *"Attack!"*

Immediately the closest five, two from the young man's own cell, plus three from an adjacent cell, spun, kicked, punched, jabbed.

"Halt!"

The room froze. "You have done very well today," Nang said calmly. "Very well. Fighters, when is the enemy most vulnerable?" As he spoke he walked, glided, through the class toward the young man who had coughed.

"When the enemy is close to his own position he is self-confident and careless," the young man said.

Nang stood before him at two leg lengths. "When else?"

"When two echelons meet on a path of march."

"The enemy is most vulnerable when . . ." Nang rebegan the answer. The young man repeated the phrase and his answer.

"When else, Met Han?"

"The enemy is most vulnerable when returning to basecamp."

"You have learned well. When else?"

"When his point element moves by us without detecting us because of our concealment, the rear elements are careless."

"Excellent. But if we cough we will not remain concealed."

"I . . . I couldn't stop it."

"Met Han, I cannot stop your cough. Only you can. You can. You must control yourself. Today you will be my partner."

Nang turned to the class, indicated that they should pair for sparring, three pairs on the floor at a time. Then he returned to Met Han. The young man stood a full hand higher than Nang yet he stood in awe of the Rabbit's speed, proficiency and power. He had seen the instructor pull his punches to some, smash the ribs or jaw of others, depending on the value he, the instructor, placed on the trainee. Han gulped. He was not certain if he was viewed as a potential yothea or as an exemplary target.

"Begin." Behind him two pairs descended into full-tilt, no-equipment bouts. Immediately one boy was thrown, pinned and choked, carotid artery blocked so he experienced the wooziness of preunconsciousness. Nang stood light on his feet, one hand relaxed, the other beckoning, wanting Han to throw the first kick or punch. Han shuffled forward, then quickly back. Then forward, feigned a left front punch, skipped back. To him Nang seemed almost asleep. He shuffled forward, raised his rear knee, spun and kicked to Nang's solar plexus. Nang sidestepped, letting the kick snap into empty air. Immediately Han regrouped, backed off, rushed forward. Behind them the second pair had ceased after each boy had landed painful blows. All eyes were on the instructor. Han snapped a right punch straight out, kicked Nang's shoulder, then a left punch to Nang's jaw. He bounced back out of counterpunch range. His entire body was tense. He breathed heavily. To the class, Nang, as he glided in and out of Han's kick range, said, "It is not enough to learn *how* to strike. You must learn to have the will to strike, to break the enemy." Han lunged in, threw a weak front left punch followed by a fast roundhouse right kick. Nang, in one motion, parried the kick spinning Han to face away, then lifting and uncoiling a rigid foot side-kicked into Han's ass, propelling Han across the room into a circle of fighters where he tripped, splatted face first, to the laughter of all the boys until Nang snarled, "Isn't there even one amongst you who can fight for his life?"

From the door came a new voice. "Yes, Met Nang," answered a small dark figure. "I can, eh? There will always be someone to keep you from erring. It is the wish of Angkar."

"There isn't a damn sonofabitch among em who can fight to save his ass."

"I don't know about that, sir," Sullivan said to the major.

"I do."

"Seems to me, sir," Sullivan said in his most diplomatic voice, "some of the field reports show improvement." The two men, along with Sergeant Huntley and a middle-aged Cambodian driver were on Highway 5 thirty kilometers north of Phnom Penh. The early morning was warm, pleasantly humid. The jeep had passed through the inner and outer defensive rings surrounding the capital and was now bumping along on the rough blacktop which paralleled the west bank of the Tonle Sap River to Kompong Luong where the road split, Highway 5 heading west, Highway 6 junctioning via the ferry crossing and running northeast to Skoun then north through Phum Pa Kham, Rumlong, Baray, Phum Khley and on to Kompong Thom. "FANK waxed ass yesterday at Prey Kry," Sullivan said.

"That's not your job, Captain," the major countered. They rode without speaking for several minutes. The major fidgeted in his seat, twisting, turning, grabbing his M-16 from the snap clip attached to the windshield support, twisting his helmet, searching for an elusive comfortable set. As they approached the southern outskirts of Kompong Luong he threw his right hand into the air. "Christ! Look at that!"

"At what, sir?" Ron Huntley asked snappily.

"Isn't that supposed to be a perimeter?"

"Where?"

"That!"

"You'd be amazed, sir," Sullivan said, "at how quickly the families disappear at the first sign of trouble."

The major let out a loud humph. The driver slowed the vehicle. A dozen young children played amid the FANK troops. To the major the scene was incongruous. The population of Phnom Penh had topped two million—including 1.3 million refugees—and here thirty-five kilometers north in a village which had been the recent point of attack of two NVA battalions, life seemed to be overly normal, overly casual. The major turned hard eyes on three saffron-clad monks standing beneath oiled paper parasols. The monks stared back, smiled, as the jeep passed. The major nudged the Khmer driver. "These good people, hey, Sambo?" The driver turned his head to the major, smiled broadly. As he turned, his hands followed and the jeep veered to the right. Someone shrieked. Quickly the driver corrected. The major heard angry women cackling. The driver's smile broadened. "God!" grunted the major.

"He doesn't speak English, sir." Sullivan leaned forward and in French said, "Monsieur, my officer compliments you and your people on their goodness." The driver nodded acknowledgment.

The jeep passed through the central marketplace and turned toward the river crossing. Huddled at the intersection was a pride of FANK APCs and scout cars. Each vehicle's front, sides and rear were decorated with large, bright Black Cobra insignias. Children with buckets of riverwater were washing, polishing, as soldiers flashed toothy smiles at young girls.

"Look at that shit," the major moaned. "They've got more patches than there're places to put em."

"This your first trip out of Phnom Penh, sir?"

"Look at those bastards. Little Tigers! They sure as hell aren't like the 'Bodes in the Delta. Be lucky to keep the Viets out another three months. Hell, throw the Commies some Khmers. That'll keep em off the ARVN's ass."

"First trip inta the count-try, ay, sir?" Huntley followed Sullivan's lead.

"First and last. I'm telling Mataxis to send me back to Nha Trang. At least the indigenous there have some military posture. I'm unvolunteering."

"Well sir"—Huntley nudged Sullivan behind the major's back—"there's a ARVN riverine craft at the dock. They'd be headin back ta double-P. Ya doan have ta be heah. Captain knows the procedure."

After the ferry crossing they traveled east then northeast along Highway 6. They passed through thriving villages and through ghost villages where battles had left only heaps of uninhabitable rubble. Every kilometer of roadway was dotted with FANK troops, some in defensive posture, some looking more like boy scouts at a hot-afternoon jamboree without planned activities. The inconsistency appalled Sullivan though he said nothing. Not only were the FANK units uneven in attitude, but even in passing he could see their military issue differed drastically.

The major had left. The degree of his discomfiture with the Khmer countryside puzzled both Huntley and Sullivan who were among the few Americans of the MEDT who consistently ventured away from the capital. "Two tours in Nam Bo"—Huntley laughed after the senior officer had boarded the ARVN craft—"you'd think he'd be used ta this."

"Ah, his wasn't two tours in Nam. His was two tours in an air-conditioned American box. Could of been in a Holiday Inn for all he knew."

"Yup!"

"Shit! Give him some credit. He came this far. Besides, he's good with requisitions. Should of stayed a supply sergeant. He knows materiel."

"He's still a dork."

Without the major, Sullivan relaxed and the trip, like the day, became enjoyable. The driver spoke sparingly, his French seemingly adequate for nothing deeper than directions and idle

chitchat. At two in the afternoon they entered the small, seemingly deserted market town of Skoun, which lay at the southwest corner of a strategic traffic island formed by the junction
of Highways 6 and 7, a three-sided island with sides of twenty
kilometers. At the north corner was Phum Pa Kham and the
road leading to Kompong Thom. In the east corner was the tiny
village of Preas and the main road to Kompong Cham. Within
the delta, scattered hamlets dotted the level plain of rice paddies. To the northeast lay two hundred square miles of some of
Cambodia's densest and richest plantations and to the northwest, all the way to Kompong Thom, lay a low country of
intermittent lakes, swamps and swamp-forests with stretches
of reclaimed rice fields. Skoun, in the southwest, sat like a
cap on the base of a funnel formed by the Tonle Sap and
Mekong rivers, sat like a protective cap shielding the northern
approach to Phnom Penh. In the crotch of Highway 6's dogleg
from east to north was the headquarters of FANK's First
Brigade Group.

The American MEDT had been authorized on 8 January 1971.
Of sixty men, sixteen were allowed to billet in Cambodia. The
MEDT's first chief was Brigadier General Theodore Mataxis. On
17 April 1971 an additional fifteen U.S. officers were authorized, though the team was not immediately brought up to
strength. In June, General Mataxis requested an expansion to
two thousand men. Two weeks later the authorization came
through channels for fifty men in Cambodia and sixty-three to
remain in South Viet Nam. The team's primary mission was to
ascertain FANK's equipment needs, to judge if equipment requested was needed, if the requesting unit had personnel trained
in its operation and if the equipment would help FANK pursue
its military goals "in conformity with U.S. policy."

Sullivan checked his map. He directed the driver to the turnoff for the FANK garrison. "No go there," the Khmer said in
English.

"Ah'll be dipped in shit," Huntley blurted. "Mister Kon, you
speak mah language."

"No speak. No go. Bad man."

"Who's a bad man?" Sullivan said in French.

"Lieutenant colonel," Kon said in English.

"You with us," Huntley said in English. "No trouble you."

"Monsieur Kon—" Sullivan began, but before he could say
another word the driver stopped the vehicle and jumped to the
road. "Monsieur, we will take you . . ."

Kon, his hands together high, bowed. "*Merci. Merci.* I walk.
Wife's brother in Skoun."

"Geez," Huntley said. He climbed from the rear seat and settled behind the wheel. "That gives me the creeps."

A moment later, speeding toward them from the garrison came a red, yellow and black jeep mounted with a 106mm recoilless rifle, the tube painted like a purple and green dragon. In the jeep Sullivan could see six or seven soldiers, two bare chested, one, driving, in a formal white and green uniform. The jeep headed toward them. Huntley slowed, pulled to the edge of the built-up dike road. The jeep aimed square at them. Huntley moved farther, dropping the right wheels over the slanting edge. "God a'mighty . . ." he screamed at a hundred feet. "Fuck em." Huntley jerked the wheel left, gunned the gas. The Khmer driver flicked the wheel hard right, left. Huntley's wheels were stuck over the edge. The Khmers' jeep veered, skidded, corrected, whisked past, soldiers shouting, laughing, racing out of sight toward town.

"Tonight, Captain"—a tall Khmer lieutenant colonel smiled broadly—"tonight we will eat and drink. Tomorrow you will come with my battalion to Tum Nop."

Sullivan bowed his head to the map spread before them. Lieutenant Colonel Chhan Samkai pointed to a village about eight kilometers to the northwest. Between the garrison and the village the map indicated almost nothing but swamp forest. Chhan was amiable, his French fluid and elegant. About him his advisors were impeccably dressed, the central room of the headquarters immaculate.

"I would like that very much," Sullivan said. "Do you suspect resistance in the area?"

"Tum Nop is an evil village." The colonel retained his smile. "You see, we have had two reliable informers."

"Are there NVA units?"

"No. No." Samkai's mouth was so stretched in smile that Sullivan was sure it hurt. He wanted to tell him it was okay not to smile so, but there was no tactful way to broach the topic. "The people are Rumdoah. Good Khmers but"—the colonel tapped his forehead with a finger—"they do not possess right thought."

For several hours the Cambodian officer entertained Sullivan and Huntley with tales of derring-do, hardships and deprivations.

"*Pourquoi, monsieur?*" Samkai lamented. He gazed through the open door. The late afternoon rains had subsided to a drizzle. "To the army in Viet Nam, American aid is without limit, but to Cambodia every gram is weighed. *Pourquoi?*"

*   *   *

At half light, 9 August 1971, Sullivan heard the slow vibration of a military vehicle convoy. "Come on, Ron. We better saddle up."

"Yeah."

As they emerged from the guest sleeping room they were immediately engaged by Colonel Chhan. Sullivan glanced about for APCs, jeeps or trucks. He listened. He could feel the low rumble but couldn't locate the convoy. A barefoot FANK soldier in a tattered uniform without rank was intercepted by one of Chhan's aides. Khmer words flew harshly back and forth. The men stopped, bowed. The soldier froze in an insolent posture as the aide approached the colonel. Again words flew. Then the aide returned to the soldier.

"Something about petroleum?" Sullivan smiled to Chhan.

"You have learned Khmer, eh?"

"I'm very sorry, only a word or two. But petroleum . . ."

"Yes. It's a French word, eh?"

"Oui," Sullivan said. Then he asked, "Do you receive enough petroleum for your vehicles?"

"As I told you last night," Chhan said, "it's always a problem."

"There's enough to go to Tum Nop, no?"

"He's a poor soldier." Chhan indicated the barefoot man. "If he were good, he would buy petrol. Perhaps he drains the tank and sells it. Now he wants more."

Upon entering the small compound the previous day, Sullivan and Huntley had scanned the perimeter. The section facing town was impressively fortified with three rows of tightly anchored concertina and tanglefoot, with a punji-stake moat between the outer and second rings. Now, as Huntley maneuvered his jeep behind Chhan's and they passed out the rear gate, Sullivan shuddered. The back of the compound facing the heavy vegetation of the swamp forest had not even a single strand of wire. He turned to Huntley, their eyes met. Huntley's did a quick 90 to heaven. Neither spoke.

Below the headquarters compound and separated from it by a wooded field and four hundred meters of paddy lay a second compound, a fetid ramshackle quagmire looking more like a concentration camp than a friendly military complex. Inside its gate two old, filthy olive-drab Isuzu buses jammed with infantry troops billowed blue smoke. Behind them was a single three-quarter-ton truck with an M-60 machine gun mounted on the cab roof.

Sullivan stretched his back, rose up in the seat to look deeper into the compound. Hundreds of starved-looking civilians—women, children, elders—stood clumped, watching, waiting for the men to leave for the daily patrol. "That's not it," Sullivan mumbled.

"Not what? That looks worse en that Neak Luong camp."

"Where's the armor? They're supposed to have five APCs. There's gotta be . . . Feel em? I can feel the vibration."

"Yeah. Why don't we stop that Chhan mothafucker? How come he or one a them aides can't ride with us?"

"Then we'd be advisors."

"Augh, shee-it! Kiss it. I just wanta know where ta go."

"Yeah, well . . ."

"Well fuck. I'm gettin somebody." With that Huntley revved the jeep, slipped the clutch. It engaged with a lurch. They pulled up beside Colonel Chhan's vehicle. "Hey." Huntley stood, yelled. Sullivan grabbed his shirt, tugged him back into his seat. "Hey, sir!" Huntley jabbed a pointing finger at the buses then to the empty backseat of his jeep. "Hey, Colonel . . ." (lowly) "jerk-off . . ." (then loudly again) "I need *uno* aide. Need me talk-talk."

Sullivan lowered his head, covered his eyes. "Cool it, Ron. Cool it."

"Get somebody we ken talk ta," Huntley demanded.

"Whoa." Sullivan stopped Huntley cold. "Let me handle it."

"Shit . . . ," Huntley mumbled. He slapped his leg to feel for his .45, then reached beside the seat to make sure his ammo box of grenades was secure.

The lead bus belched and backfired. Two young boys pushed open the flimsy wire-mesh gate. The bus rolled forward straining to climb from the compound up the slight incline to the raised graveled road. The second bus, its mufflers or exhaust manifolds shot, roared slowly into position behind the first, the noise masking the colonel's words to Sullivan. The colonel's jeep pulled in behind the truck. "Let you handle it." Huntley groaned. "Fuck!"

"There's still gotta be five . . ." A quarter kilometer farther down the road, five clean, camouflage-painted M-113 APCs clattered softly from a third compound. Whatever noise their engines and tracks made was lost in the roar of the unmuffled bus. "Yeah. See! I knew I could feel em."

"Where in hell they come from?" The buses rolled forward, stopped, let the APCs lead. A sixth armored vehicle remained on the side road leading to the third compound. "Look down there," Huntley said, pointing with his chin, his back to Sullivan. The Americans stared into the third camp, a neat fortress with, as best as they could see, well-developed defense berms. "How ya figure, J. L."—Huntley turned to Sullivan—"that one place ain't fit for grandma's pigs, one place is some sorta piece a furniture, en one place is for real?"

Sullivan cocked his head, winked, hooked a tight fist in the air. "Training," he said. The appearance of the APCs made him feel secure, not because of their power but because of what he knew of the unit. "This group's got one battalion trained at Nha Trang. Look at it. That compound's a replica of a Special Forces site. I shit you not."

"You shit me not, ah-right. Now, let's get some dinky-dau fucker that can tell us what's goin on."

The FANK 1st Brigade Group convoy took up final staging positions a half kilometer east of the hamlet of Tum Nop 3. Five APCs moved to equidistant points. Behind them bus-borne infantry troops dispersed, spread out on line. West of the hamlet lay the main village.

"I'm sorry, Sir Colonel Chhan . . ." Sullivan said apologetically. He, Huntley and Chhan Samkai stood atop the sixth APC watching the action develop. Midmorning sun seared their backs. ". . . But it seems some of your soldiers have forgotten to follow your orders."

Chhan Samkai pretended to busy himself with a map, then with a set of field glasses. The APCs clattered forward closing the deserted kilometer-wide semicircle about the hamlet. Behind them soldiers clumped into lines. Chhan Samkai coughed.

"I'm learning so much from your able command presence," Sullivan said in fluid French, "but they must have forgotten your orders about dispersing and sweeping. And, Sir Colonel . . . well, my eyes aren't as good as they should be . . . I can't see the anvil force."

Chhan Samkai pretended to be totally immersed in the operation. He coughed again, then asked an aide for the radio handset. In Khmer he growled harsh orders into the transmitter. In the field before them one vehicle stopped. Behind it a file of troops stood still. Four columns continued to move in.

"Captain Military Equipment Team," one of Chhan's aides called to Sullivan in English, "you must leave now. When the yuons attack you must not be hurt."

In April 1970 the U.S. 5th Special Forces had opened three sites in Viet Nam to train Lon Nol's soldiers. By August 1971 twenty-four battalions had been through the training cycle. Headquartered in Nha Trang, the FANK Training Command was charged with the task of transforming the Khmer army— one battalion at a time. On 1 March 1971 the unit was redesignated the U.S. Army Individual Training Group. Chhan Samkai, like some FANK brigade-level officers, felt the schooling was beneath his station. His armored unit, men and command, had been trained in June.

The APCs stopped just short of the hamlet. Huntley watched closely. The village appeared to be without life. A cluster of foot soldiers, then a second pack, sprinted forward firing wildly. Almost immediately a home burst into flames.

"Thank you for your concern for our personal safety." Sullivan's speech was slow, metered. As he spoke he and Huntley scanned the battlefield. The remaining soldiers swarmed toward the hamlet. Villagers were pulled from their houses, wrangled to a makeshift pen about the central well. "I would prefer to remain." Even from a distance it was obvious Chhan Samkai's infantry troops were looting homes, carrying out baskets of rice, rolls of cloth, anything transportable of value. "If I'm to be able to inform General Mataxis of your needs . . ."

Suddenly a skirmish broke out between an APC and a squad of infantry. Across the paddies Sullivan could hear the armor commander screaming at the ground troops. Some scattered. Some dropped their booty and marched toward the track. Other tracks began backing away from the hamlet and the infantry soldiers. Bursts of automatic weapons fire cracked hot over the ragged ground force.

"Captain," the aide ordered, "you and your driver must come right now. If you are killed by yuons it will be a diplomatic crisis. You cannot die here. Maybe go to Baray."

It was after midnight. Met Sar turned on the lamp. His paranoia was great. Although the Movement maintained its central headquarters on Mount Aural, Sar no longer spent consecutive nights there, no longer consecutive nights anywhere. The encampment east of Baray was dark, the hidden bunker was musty, cool. Sar shivered. The morning had been extraordinarily hot and the afternoon rain had barely moderated the temperature. By contrast the night was cold. Sar removed the batch of papers from his case, set the case at one end of the small collapsible table. He stared at the words he'd written. Yet on his mind was Nang. Word had come: he was alive, he was organizing Kompong Thom. Sar hunched, bit down hard.

. . . since we took charge of the revolution, despite great hardships, the Movement's progressive philosophy has never caused a setback. Our decision of 1967 to launch armed revolution put us in the most advantageous position when Norodom Sihanouk was ousted in March 1970. Even though that decision was berated and spurned by both the North Viet Namese political leadership and our Chinese allies, it proved to be an enlightened move.

Sar paused. He pulled his heavy shirt up about his shoulders, pulled the collar up about his neck. A chill skittered across his broad back. It's not yet time, he thought. Met Nang, he thought. We must maintain the appearance of a united front. He scratched through the last sentence then dog-earred the page and flipped to the beginning. For months he had scribbled notes, sketched pages, recorded his thoughts. What lay before him lay before Kampuchea. The sheet before him was no longer loose notes but the rough draft of the Khmer Communist Party history. In its final form it would not be a compilation of dates, anecdotes and personalities but a master plan for the future based on the Party's view of the past, complete with strategy on how to obtain defined ideals and the righteous justification for those plans and goals. It would be a manifesto, a religious scripture, the pure word. Politically, the Krahom had matured. For years Sar and the Kampuchean Movement had developed in the shadow of Viet Namese communism, in the shadow of its unsavory ideology of a fraternal Indochinese union masking Hanoi's desire for regional hegemony. The time had come to firmly cast that idea, and with it the Chinese Maoist thought which had so badly bungled that nation's socialist construction, to monsoon gales. It was time, too, to shun the Russian model which to Sar was a Western ideology clothed in internationalist jargon, an Occidental fascism bent on neo-imperial expansion. It is time, thought Sar. Met Nang, he thought, it is time for us to have a document of Khmer purity—of Khmer independence, national sovereignty, self-reliance and revolutionary violence.

Sar flipped through the pages of the first section, paused to read, to check his thoughts. He scanned the twelve commandments—rules based on the teachings he'd developed for the Pong Pay Mountain school—now refined, honed, designed to create, in this period of turmoil and unprecedented opportunity, instantaneous loyalty to the Movement.

(1) Thou shalt love, honor, and serve the people of laborers and peasants.
(2) Thou shalt serve the people wherever thou goest, with all thy heart and with all thy mind. . . .
(6) Thou shalt do nothing improper respecting women. . . .
(10) Thou shalt behave with great meekness toward the laboring people and peasants, and the entire population. Toward the enemy, however, thou shalt feed thy hatred with force and vigilance.

Sar paused. After the word "however" in the tenth command-
ment he inserted a caret and between lines penned, "the American imperialists and their lackeys."

(12) Against any foe and against every obstacle thou shalt struggle
. . . ready to make every sacrifice including thy life for the people
. . . for the revolution and for the Movement, without hesitation
and without respite.

Again Sar paused. The Khmer word for "movement" did not
please him. For a year Krahom cadremen had been using the
Khmer word for "organization." He reflected upon it, weighed
it. "Organization" pleased him. It sounded less Viet Namese.
Sar scratched through the word "movement" and over it in
bold letters wrote *Angkar*. From henceforth, we are *Angkar*.
He sat back. The pleasure of changing the word was fleeting.
He breathed heavily, the dampness in his lungs clinging like
glutinous rice to the sides of a cooking pot. He coughed. Coughed
again. Then a series of spasmatic hacks which broke loose slimy
green grain-sized clots that flew to his throat and mouth, one
onto the papers. He turned, hawkered on the dirt floor. Turned
back and with a cocked finger snapped at the clot on the paper.
The slime, instead of flying off the page, stuck to his fingernail
and smeared against the sheet. Sar turned. Spit again on the
floor. Wiped his finger on the far corner of the table. Then he
sat there, puzzled. He looked about. With what could he clean
the page? The bunker was bare except for the table, chair and
lamp. He clenched his teeth, snarled, banged his fist, yet he did
not call out. He banged his fist again. How could he possibly
shame himself by calling his bodyguard, yet how could he clean
the page? His suit was spotless—not the black cloth of the
yotheas or even the green fatigues of the cadre, but a civilized
light gray of the Gray Vulture of the eastern zone.
Sar slid the sheet with the offensive clot to his right, to the
edge of the table. Then he broke down the remaining stack into
four sections. His eyes fell to a top page: To defeat the American
imperialists and their lackey, Lon Nol, we must achieve *absolute*
internal unity. . . . Cadre are cautioned against regurgitating
"empty theories which will not achieve success in Kampuchea."
They are cautioned to accept only true and pure assistance from
foreigners. In past transactions counterproductive results have
ensued. . . . Foreign advice has "hindered and even . . . destroyed the revolutionary movement and progress. . . ." Until we
took charge of the Movement our organization was in peril
because of two-headed lackeys who betrayed certain cells.

Sar cleared his throat loudly, cautiously, lest he again foul a page. He lowered the lamp flame then called his bodyguard. Immediately a strack soldier entered. "Met Reth," Sar said politely, "please get me some oil. The lamp is low." The man left and Sar smiled. Again he scanned a top page:

With proper education everyone can develop the true proletarian attitude as long as the party has pure and correct leadership.

Cadre must be aware of the middle class and the intellectuals who retain the nature of their origin.

Cadre shall study the rice peasants in order to be like them, not so that they lead the cadre but so that they are comfortable in following.

Met Reth returned with a can of oil. "Here. Don't spill it," Sar said. "Sit there." He indicated the edge of the table. Met Reth hesitated but Sar, seemingly distracted and anxious to return to his work, pointed. Sar turned slightly to the left as the guard eased down toward the small table. Quickly Sar turned back, grabbed the paper stack beneath the descending thigh. "Oops!" He lifted the stack against the man's leg. "Not on these," he sputtered. "Oh, shit! Don't spill it! Do it outside!"

After his paper was cleaned, Met Sar again set to work, now on plans, not history. In a memo to members of the Center he penned, "It is time to bring renegade and independent elements under tighter control." He thought of Nang in Kompong Thom, bit his lip, thought, What is he doing up there? Sar's task, as he saw it, was to consolidate the control of the Center over the zones while keeping the zones isolated from each other. He wrote, "For too long each zone has been a separate whip flailing against the country-stealing puppets; each end has flailed but inflicted only shallow wounds. If we tie the whips like a cat-o'-nine-tails the power of the armies will multiply tenfold. Everyone is against us, yet our modest countenance adds purity to our cause."

Sar paused again. Again he thought of Met Nang in Kompong Thom. Why had he not escaped? What was he doing there? The details had been sketchy. Sar covered his eyes with his pudgy hands. The greater cause, he thought. When a seed goes bad it must be eliminated. His own army!

Sar called for Reth. He handed the bodyguard the memo he'd composed and directed him to have a runner bring the memo to Met Meas, Sar's scrivener, and to have Meas make copies for Center distribution.

Plans, Sar thought. Betrayals by allies. First in 1954 when the yuons gained half their country, leaving the Khmer Reds with nothing. Then in 1964, in the wake of American buildups, Hanoi supported Sihanouk at Krahom expense. Again in 1970, the North Viet Namese sided with Sihanouk's government in exile.

Sar threw his pen, grasped his hair and pulled. Out loud, frustrated, angry, to no one but himself he seethed, "When I was a member of the IPC only treacherous yuons led. I carried their dung to the vegetable gardens." Back to paper he wrote, "Kampuchea has been betrayed. Kampuchea has been victimized. Kampuchea has been humiliated. Either we strike with all our powers or the Viets and Americans will roast us and the Khmer race will vanish. . . .

"From henceforth Angkar will have a presence in every village. The people must be gained. Republic functionaries must be eliminated. Absolute secrecy must be ensured. Party membership must be expanded. The army must be increased. Every effort must be made to train and equip the front line. We must struggle to gain mastery over command, control and coordination. We shall be modern in communications." Sar ceased. He closed his eyes. The light of the lamp shone dimly through his eyelids but in the soft glow he saw a hundred answers and his enthusiasm exploded. "For Kampuchea, international communism is a lie. It serves only yuons. We shall mobilize the people to revolutionary battle. We must proselytize until they are committed. The Khmer Viet Minh must be usurped. Then we shall commit the army. Then, in victory, the Party shall emerge. The November battle at Kompong Thom was a heinous crime in which we lost six Krahom platoons for yuon gains. Never again. *Never!*

"The army is built of platoons, organized to companies. Now is the time to develop battalions. Viets can storm Khmer cities from the outside. We can win the people from within. *Do not let the NVA take any major towns.*

"Learn from what happened in 1968 at the New Year's offensive. Learn from the American withdrawal from the eastern sanctuaries. Learn from that drive to cut the trail in Laos. The NVA is committed first to gaining the South. Each offensive pulls their troops from Kampuchea. Each setback means they must first rebuild. *Wait! Be patient! Wait for the yuons to drain from our land. Then seize the offensive. Let the cities explode.*"

He thought of his father. It was the third anniversary of the hundredth-day rite. To Chhuon his father was calmness, peace, right thought, right action. He was everything Chhuon no longer found in himself in his new role in the new land under the foreign administrators. He knelt before the family altar, bowed his head to the floor. Quietly he uttered a chant in Pali. In most of the homes in Phum Sath Din, the family altars had been dismantled at Hang Tung's insistence—dismantled, scattered, secreted, not destroyed. In the home of Cahuom Chhuon an odd twist had taken place. With every additional order placed upon the people, Chhuon had added to his family altar. To each restriction on worship at the wat, Chhuon responded by first adding more family pictures, then pictures of the more distant relatives in Phum Sath Din and of those who had moved to neighboring villages or to a city. Soon he added a large painting of the Enlightened One and several statuettes, then another table and more flower vases and baskets and photos of other village families. Each addition made Hang Tung shudder, yet he'd borne the first in silence and acquiesced to what followed. He rationalized his laxity by telling himself that because he allowed this one quirk, Chhuon had fallen completely in line and was now a valuable member of the village's new, fraternal Khmer-Viet administration. Indeed, cooperation between the old villagers, the refugees, the new settlers and the new government had never seemed better. Colonel Nui and Cadreman Trinh escorted administrators from other villages through the Phum Sath Din model village with such regularity the peasants no longer stopped to take note but simply continued their work and basked in the cognizance that they had accomplished a peaceful, if not desired, transformation.

"Come, Uncle," Hang Tung called.

Chhuon did not answer. He took his time finishing his prayers, then arranging various articles and finally checking the rice bowl for Samnang in which there now was a constant small portion of uncooked rice topped by three delicate shrimp which Chhuon had carved from rosewood.

"Uncle, in four days the deputy commissar for political affairs from the A40 Office will visit. We must ensure that the new work is completed."

"Eh?" Chhuon looked to Tung as if he, Chhuon, had been unaware of the young man's presence. Then, "Oh. Yes. Yes. From the Central Office for Kampuchean Affairs? Ah well, another bigwig, eh?"

Hang Tung laughed. Perhaps, he thought, Uncle Chhuon is going senile.

As the two men walked, Chhuon hummed various traditional tunes. He spoke only when spoken to. In June the rice ration for the village had been increased without explanation. The rumor had spread, until it was universally believed, that Cahuom

Chhuon had somehow, quietly, persuaded the Viet Namese. Some villagers believed Chhuon had traded the Chhimmy family homes for rice, had guaranteed to the Viets that the newest settlers, Viet army dependents, would be treated kindly if not truly welcomed. Some seethed at the chairman's sellout. Some Khmers indeed welcomed the Viets. They were, after all, people. They could not help it if they had been fated to be born Viet Namese. Most neither welcomed the aliens nor scorned Cahuom Chhuon but simply accepted that the North Viet Namese power over them was absolute and they were no longer starving.

Through the village streets and out to the paddies, as Chhuon and Hang Tung headed to the new work site, children and rice farmers bowed or nodded or whispered a few words to Chhuon, showing him the respect of a traditional elder.

"You see, Uncle," Tung said easily. "The revolution develops according to scientific law, yet there is not just one formula for advancing it. We must be pragmatic, flexible."

"I am seeing that," Chhuon said.

"The revolution cannot be pushed to meet subjective wishes. It succeeds only when the people's sentiment has been raised to embrace it."

"Yes, Tung. Yes. And as they embrace it more, my stomach burns less."

Tung smiled. Before them men, women and girls of the village's northwest quadrant production team, along with two squads of village militia boys and an entire platoon of Viet Namese regional force troops, labored, digging, carrying dirt, deepening trenches and building bunkers and fighting positions.

"Hello there, Uncle Chairman," Khieng called. He leaned upon his shovel as two small girls lifted the basket he'd filled. The girls carried the basket on a pole between them, struggled to climb out of the deepening trench, then headed off to the growing fighting-point bunker.

Chhuon acknowledged Khieng with a smile. To Tung he said, "The progress is great. With this section the entire perimeter . . ."

". . . will be complete," Tung finished the sentence.

"And that . . . ?" Chhuon indicated a second point, a circular mound which had risen, complete with vegetation, since he'd last inspected the section.

Hang Tung smiled, pleased that Chhuon had asked, that he didn't know.

"What kind of barrel?" Chhuon had spied a tube with a large flash suppressor poking from the branches.

"Those are our AA guns."

"Our what? No one bombs the village."

"Colonel Nui wanted them to protect his family."

"Better to have none," Chhuon rejoined. "Better to keep the army far away and not give them an excuse to bomb, eh? What's that?"

"A KS-19. One hundred millimeters. It shoots over 13,000 meters high. We can shoot B-52s."

"Tung! This is crazy. That will bring the bombers."

"Good. Then we'll kill them, eh? The guns are radar controlled."

"No! Tung, move them back!"

Early that evening Hang Tung left the Cahuom home to arrange a meeting at Colonel Nui's home. In his absence Chhuon felt an emptiness. His mother was now very feeble and, though aware of every change, aloof. His wife was embittered. His only child still remaining under his roof was, even at six-and-one-half years, distant.

"They have made me join the Women's Liberation Association," Sok whispered.

"It's a good group," Chhuon answered aloud.

"Have you turned from me?" Sok said very sadly, very quietly. "The walls have ears and you . . ."

"We have nothing to hide," Chhuon said.

"We have nothing left," Sok retorted. "Today Peou came home from school singing revolutionary songs." She stopped. Then in a muffled, heart-rending wail cried, "How did they corrupt you?"

"I've nothing everyone else doesn't have. I look out for the people. Our people."

"Better to dig their trenches than carry their words." Tears moistened her eyes. "Quit. Tell them! Please tell them! You can no longer be their chairman. Let someone else . . ."

"Who?"

"Anyone."

"If I leave who will succeed me?" Now Chhuon spoke in a whisper. "Who will watch out for the people?"

"How horrible you've become," Sok cried. Tears dripped from her eyes. "The demon has you. My Chhuon would never support them. You've become one of them. Half the villagers say you're yuon. Is it for me? To get more rice? To have the altar? Samnang's spirit will find its way without the altar."

"It is"—Chhuon's voice rose—"dear wife, because the revolution *has* come. We still have the land. Still the rice grows. Still people need food. And people no longer suffer a *trung tian bao ta*. No more . . ."

"A what?"

"The middlemen. The riffraff agents who bled the peasants for the landlords or the governors."

"You even use the yuon language as if . . . Ea-hump!" Sok squeezed her fists before her sagging breasts. More tears fell from her eyes but she made not a sound, not a movement.

"I must go."

In the chair before the altar, Chhuon's mother cleared her throat. A raspy voice emerged. "If one is to be corrupt, it is better to be corrupt for one's own purse than for another's spirit."

The night sky was soft, laden with moisture. Chhuon walked the familiar path toward Colonel Nui's. Tonight, he thought, but he did not complete the thought. He passed into the northeast quadrant and entered the long alley which led to the old Chhimmy Chamreum home which was now occupied by the Nuis. Three doors from the colonel's house Chhuon stopped. In the alley the night was darker than along the village street. Chhuon listened. He bent as if to remove a stone from his sandal. Slowly he turned to check behind him. From below anyone walking would be silhouetted against the opening to the sky. Chhuon waited. Then he knocked quietly on the courtyard door. Two raps, a pause, two raps, a pause, one rap. Noiselessly the door opened. Chhuon rose, stepped in. The door closed. Inside, the courtyard seemed empty. Then Chhuon's eyes discerned movement, as if the clay had come to life. He hugged the wall, paced the perimeter, edged to the dark of the kitchen lean-to. Arms grabbed him. He hugged the unseen man. "kpa," Chhuon whispered. "without your spirit i would die."

"without your help, uncle, all would perish."

"just below the new bunker, there's a shovel."

"yes. we need shovels."

From under his loose shirt and about his waist Chhuon removed his krama. Rolled in it were four kilos of rice. Quickly he unraveled the cloth and carefully poured the precious grain into Kpa's sack. "in four days there will be a visitor."

"who?"

"a deputy commissar from the A40 office."

"we'll eliminate him."

"no. let him come."

"yes?"

"yes." Chhuon's words were quick, excited, hushed. "the more they bring to integrate, the more they sow the seeds of their own downfall. the people will not resist until their sentiment is raised to embrace the resistance. let them come. they are the army's weakness."

Behind Kpa, in the shadows, three boys huddled. One shivered. Chhuon could hear his teeth chatter.

"we need medicine," Kpa said.

"there's very little. they count every aspirin. every capsule is dispensed as if gold."

"sakhon has the fever. we can't treat him. capture him. let them treat him."

"no. take him back. the only kindness they'll show him is a quick trip to the ancestors. find a way. you must learn to be self-sufficient. find the khrou. he'll tell you which leaves or bark to boil. the deputy commissar. track him. allow him to come and go. big movements are coming."

"we see the buildup. many trucks from laos. many large stockpiles. many soldiers."

"kpa, i know. i know this. they've new orders. they'll move soon."

"where?"

"west. south. baray. the 32d and 33d regiments have joined the 7th division. they're to cut the north from phnom penh."

"major nui told you?"

"i saw his map. my brother had a friend. a republican. colonel chlay. get him word."

"we can send word to baray. to kompong thom . . ."

"send it. i must go. kpa . . ."

"yes uncle?"

"knock out the AA radar."

Chhuon tilted his head back. "Vo! Vo! Vo! Vo!" Colonel Nui, Hang Tung, Cadreman Trinh, Trinh Le and Colonel Hans Mitterschmidt chanted loudly in a rhythmic beat. "Vo! Vo! Vo! Vo!" The whiskey burned in Chhuon's mouth. He let bubbles gurgle upward through the dark liquid as the others watched delightedly. "Vo! Vo! Vo!" Blup blup blup. Whiskey burned his throat though he kept most of it in his mouth, his jowls expanding like a water balloon. Hang Tung burst into laughter, clapped wildly. Others rolled forward, their laughter uninhibited, loosened by the whiskey, truly joyful. Chhuon lowered the bottle, spitting as much liquor back into it as he could unnoticed. He swallowed hard. The fumes in his mouth filled his nose, made his eyes water. Even his ears felt hot. Trinh Le accepted the bottle, tilted it up, voraciously sucked down whiskey and spittle to new chanting until all applauded and laughed and the bottle passed to the East German. Colonel Mitterschmidt held the bottle at arm's length. To his comrades he was a huge man and he'd demonstrated with the first bottle a wonderful capacity to drink. "Vo! Vo! Vo! Vo!"

"To win," Mitterschmidt said in his own tongue and Colonel Nui translated into Viet Namese, "you need not be perfect; only better than the enemy." He drank to a quieter chant, chugging the remainder as Colonel Nui translated happily.

Before Nui finished the line, laughter burst from him. "Ha! . . . only better . . . Ha! We're better than Germans." He laughed.

Mitterschmidt reached over to Nui, put a strong arm about the smaller colonel and squeezed him like a little brother. "You fight hard." His sincere admiration was tinged with melancholy. "You'll win. Never has an army, except perhaps the Germans in Russia, faced such hardship with such commitment. Hardship means nothing to you. So committed! Your enemy is criminal, yet you fight. Americans have the most ferocious weapons, yet you fight. They are the cruelest nation on earth. Still you fight. And win!"

Nui gestured across the table to Chhuon who had not understood the German. "For this man," Nui said first in Viet Namese and then in German. He smiled broadly. "Viet Namese blood and Viet Namese bones will build solidarity in a sovereign Indochina."

"You face a strong ARVN, a growing FANK, the South Koreans and the Americans— Still!" Mitterschmidt was drunk. He had not heard a word Nui had said.

"Respected Colonel." Cadreman Trinh chuckled after Nui translated. "There is no strength without the Americans. ARVN, FANK, they are balloons. When America withdraws, the lackeys will go pa-fa-fa-fa-fa like a child's untied balloon."

Nui translated again, then rose. As he did Mitterschmidt pulled from his breast pocket a small plastic-coated photograph of two younblond boys. He handed it to Cadreman Trinh. "This"—he pointed to the older boy—"is Hans. Like me. This is Dieter. Next year I'll show them your picture. Ha!"

Nui unbuttoned his blouse and pulled it open, exposing a yellow, red, green and black tattoo, a snarling S-shaped dragon in the shape of the combined Viet Nams. Over Nui's heart was a column of characters. He tapped them. "Born in the North to die in the South." Nui laughed. Chhuon laughed and clapped and beamed his actor's mask. Another bottle emerged and Hang Tung drank to "Vo! Vo! Vo! Vo!" Chhuon drank to a new chant, a slogan, "Free our enslaved comrades in Kampuchea and in the South." Trinh drank to "Liberation! Our solemn mission!"

The bottle made a full round and a second, and on the third Mitterschmidt killed it.

"I have seen the pictures," Nui said to Mitterschmidt. "The Americans are like the old Gestapo before Germany was liberated. Their MPs beat people. Always! Everyone! The poor people of Saigon are *bui doi*—how to say it? They are dust. Orphans. The Americans stick the girls then throw them on the street and run them down with their trucks. When we bring the communal state, they will have the most beautiful lives. Americans, humph! They treat their dogs better than their wives. Ech! Ha! But in Laos, ha! they ran like beaten dogs with their tails stuck in their asses. What a disgrace. They should not be called soldiers. I am a soldier. We fight them. *Danh cho den cuoi!* Fight to the finish! They are . . . sadists. Yes? Sadists. Beat women! Torture children! Ah, but the glorious victories of the People's Liberation Army makes them withdraw. That, Colonel, is why we fight. It is *chinh nghia*. You say it. *Chinh nghia!*"

"*Chin na!* Ha! Ha! What do I say?"

"It is a just cause. 'Just Cause!' You will see when you observe at Baray."

Chhuon stumbled toward home, drunk. He had not been able to spit all the liquor back, had drunk enough to make him intoxicated. He fell as he reached the main village street, pulled himself to his hands and knees, then collapsed. Lying there he thought, I didn't ask Kpa if there was word of Cheam. Poor Cheam. I didn't tell Kpa of mother. Better. Better not for him to worry for her health. What's happening to my country? To my blood! Kampuchea, you bleed like a butchered pig. And I lie in the mud. Blood for Kampuchea. Nui! Humph! Viet blood and Viet bones build . . . Chhuon belched. Heat from his stomach billowed like a fanned forge fire. He worked his knees back under him. Lifted his torso. His head seemed to swirl. He vomited. Blood for blood, he thought. Blood for blood. Aloud he muttered, "I shall become enlightened for the sake of all living things. I shall become . . ."

"You knew we watched you," Eng said.

"I knew." Nang smiled. "But with my new face you didn't know who I was."

"Sar thought you'd been killed. He was pissed."

"It gave me more room to maneuver," Nang said. He spoke almost apologetically, sheepishly, though there was no apology or humbleness in him.

They squatted in the shade of a lemon tree in the tiny courtyard of a Kompong Thom peasant home. The sun beat down upon the land with a wilting intensity achieved only during the little dry season, the midsummer break in the wet weather, beat down vaporizing all surface moisture and filling the air with oppressive humidity. Nang flipped to the last page of the document Eng had given him. Through Eng, he had reestablished contact with Angkar, the Center, Met Sar. " 'To be master of the country and master of the revolution,' " Nang read, " 'is to be engaged in a determined struggle for self-sufficiency and to show a spirit of creativity . . ." In his mind Nang was once again under the older man's guidance, though in reality he was now but a midlevel cadreman subordinate to the leaders of the northern zone. " '. . . it is to endure all hardships, to be conscientious, thrifty and upright. This also means to show respect for freely accepted discipline. . . .' "

"I was sure it was you all along," Eng interrupted. "Night Rabbit, Little Rabbit. You've got a thing for rabbits. Ha!"

"Did he send you to spy on me?"

"No. He sent me with orders, guidelines. We must maintain absolute internal unity. You cannot operate alone. Soth and Horl from the old platoon will join you. Angkar is to have a presence in every village. In every way we are to gain the people. And the yuon drive must falter in open country."

Nang laughed, did not answer, but continued reading to the end of the document. " '. . . to love, defend, and respect the people. Finally, it means turning humbly to the people to learn, and sacrificing all to the interest of the nation and the revolution.' "

"We need a real base," Eng said. By mid-August 1971, Krahom intelligence had disseminated, along with the new documents, tactical information about the advancing North Viet Namese divisions. Krahom double agents had also informed FANK intelligence; FANK agents had confirmed the direction and size of the thrust via ARVN and American aerial reconnaissance. "It's Met Sar's orders," Eng said.

"The NVA 91st is moving south," Nang said. "You know that, eh?" His eyes hardened. Soth, eh? he thought.

"The 5th, 7th and 91st. Who tells you? What do you know?"

"A ghost in the wind tells me." Nang's eyes twinkled. "Lon Nol has announced the launching of his operation, Chenla II, a 'sweep' north to secure the corridor to Kompong Thom, to expel all foreigners and Communists. A real base, eh?"

"Yes."

"Then we should take Phum Voa Yeav. I have friends there."

"I don't know it," Eng said.

"It's eight kilometers north. It'll be perfect and it's well pre-pared. What is this Chenla II?"

"Like last year." Eng shook his head thinking of FANK's miserable effort. "They've formed a column north of Phnom Penh near Skoun. But, like last year, they move like snails."

"This is a great opportunity," Nang said. "We'll fight for our lives as only you and I can, Eng." Nang stood. Though the heat was debilitating, he felt strong. He felt as if he'd been toying with weak opponents, as if he'd been sitting back, waiting for an opening, waiting until now. "Gather the class," he said. "It's time."

North Viet Namese and Khmer Viet Minh control over Phum Voa Yeav was minimal. The four small hamlets harbored Khmer Viet Minh agents and militia squads but because of the proxim-ity to Kompong Thom there had not been a complete break from Republic control. Like many South Viet Namese villages five years earlier, the Communist infrastructure, backed by main force units in outlying areas, was a nocturnal government. The national government's presence took the form of infrequent daytime troop patrols, daylight administration.

"The hamlet is well prepared," Met Han told Nang and Eng the next day. The two cadremen had joined the young fighter and his small band in a hut in a treeline between paddies just east of Voa Yeav 3. "Eighty percent of the people support our movement."

Eng smiled. He turned to Nang. "How many camps do you have like this?"

"Many." Nang avoided Eng's question. "Most have moved away from the corrupting influences of the city. Every hamlet has been assigned a squad."

"And eighty percent of the people are with you?!"

"Understand, Eng," Nang said quietly, "eight in ten are with every faction. Rice farmers are pragmatic, eh? If we win, they're with us, eh, Met Han?"

"They really are with us, Met Nang. It's been exactly as you've said. When we first came we told them we were the Movement and we'd come to help. They didn't believe. We helped them repair broken dikes and they began to listen. We told them we were against all aliens. We planted rice with them and they listened more. We told them, as you've told us, it is our obligation as Khmers to protect Khmers."

Nang smiled. "Don't believe too easily," he said. "Lon Nol's henchmen say eight in ten are with him. Comrade Ote Samrin who is KVM, who has the NVA 91st behind him, reports eight in ten are Rumdoah and wish the yuons to win and return Sihanouk."

"Met Nang," Han said sincerely, "we've worked very hard with the farmers. We've served them and treated them with respect. They'll stand with us."

"Today"—Nang's voice was filled with doubt—"perhaps."

"Truly," Han retorted.

"Truly?" Nang raised his brow.

"Yes."

"Will they, in return, assist us?"

"Of course. Haven't they kept track of the yuon 91st as we asked? Weren't they the first to note the shift south? They'll help us."

"Good." Nang became very still, very calm. His head was bowed. Then he raised it and looked directly into Han's eyes. "In one hour they'll set up a diversion."

Two hours later Nang stood with Han and a hamlet elder at the gate to Voa Yeav 3. Han had introduced Nang as his teacher and the old man was both much amused by the idea of one so young being a teacher and much shocked by the terrible disfigurement of Nang's face. The rains had begun again, not the deluge which would come in a week but a clinging drizzle. Han held a large banana leaf over the old man as Nang spoke of the need for national sovereignty. Again the old man was amused. He invited the boys to his home for rice, but Nang insisted they remain on the road by the village gate.

"The village chief comes now, eh?" Nang spoke in perfect rural northern dialect.

"If he's not drunk." The old man laughed.

"And with him the province tax collector?" Nang said.

"Snakes bed together, eh, Rabbit?" The old man chuckled. "You are very young to want to see them."

"Anyone who harms you, who harms your crops, your people or your belongings, he is your enemy." As Nang said the words an odd feeling descended upon him, coated him as the drizzle coated his skin.

"You are very wise for one so young." The man smiled broadly.

"This chief," Nang said, "he serves the Viet Namese and the governor, eh? And he drinks alcohol? He is very evil, eh?"

"He is always drunk." The elder laughed.

"My father, who is now with Lord Buddha, used to say of drunks, 'The way they act is to renounce their humanity.' You will help Han change this man, eh?"

"I'm a poor man." The elder giggled. "I must support my family."

"We'll change that," Nang said. "All Khmers should share in the country's wealth. We'll change the village chief, too, eh? You help me, eh?"

The elder became more formal. "For many years the peasants want to change this man. Ote Samrin wants him to change, too. If you change him, how will Ote Samrin look? How will I look to my people?"

"Ote Samrin is humiliated because he has no effect. You shall be honored because you are with us. Look there." Nang pointed into the gray drizzle where two vehicles were emerging. "For all eternity—" Nang began. Suddenly the lead vehicle blasted its horn. Three water buffalo had climbed, had been driven, from one paddy up the dike to the raised gravel road. The lead vehicle's horn blared in repeated bursts. Two small boys whipped the buffalos with marsh reed switches. Nang laughed and Han and the old man joined in. The horns of both cars honked. The lead driver hung his head out the window, screamed at the urchins to clear their beasts from his path. The two boys ran into the paddy. "For all eternity . . ." Nang laughed loudly. Behind them on the hamlet street a dozen women had converged to witness the commotion and in the paddies the peasants straightened their backs. Suddenly a massive fireball tossed the rear vehicle into the air, then the noise and concussion slammed the viewers. Doors of the lead vehicle sprang open. Five armed men emerged running, clutching their weapons, running, collapsing to a fusillade unheard at the hamlet gate. Then the distant report of small arms fire reached the elder. Nang completed his sentence in an embittered tone, ". . . our blood will call for revenge."

The old man no longer smiled. A large mob had grown in the hamlet street. Han stood shocked. His boys had delivered a diversion but neither they nor he had known for what. Nang turned to the mob. He grasped the trembling hand of the old man beside him, lifted it, held it high, then yelled as loudly and as enthusiastically as his voice would stretch, "From henceforth and for all eternity Phum Voa Yeav shall be protected by the Organization. By Angkar. Never again shall you pay taxes to the henchmen of Lon Nol or the lackeys of the yuons."

From the fields about the wreckage of the cars two squads emerged; emerged like wraiths from a fog, emerged, walked, fourteen armed black-clad boys in single file, down the dike road toward Phum Voa Yeav.

The preparation for the takeover of Phum Voa Yeav had

been complete enough that, in the absence of NVA support, before night had fallen twice all four hamlets and the village center had been subjugated by Krahom soldiers. Immediately the fence sitters acquiesced to the slogan, "Independence, national sovereignty, self-reliance and revolutionary violence." Within another day Phum Voa Yeav had fallen under the spell of Wise Little Rabbit, and the village provided Nang and the Krahom with a platoon of strugglers and porters. Phase one, eliminate government control, was complete. Now Nang would implement the next phase, for which he'd prepared for almost a year.

Nang approached the FANK LP, the listening post, on the southeast flank of the column's night logger. There was no moon and the ground was blanketed with a layer of mist, a fog which started just above his head and was perhaps three meters thick. Above the mist the night was crystal clear, yet below, the world was close and black.

He could hear the FANK troops moving, restless, afraid but not disciplined, most not even trained to be silent and still. They talked loudly, as if by giving away their position they would make any enemy closing on Kompong Thom circumvent the LP and target a main garrison. Nang pulled, pushed, prodded his three-boy team. Twenty meters from the FANK LP they settled, rested, waited, listening until the nationals were silent, asleep. At two in the morning Nang advanced, emerged within the LP's perimeter as he had done so often, emerged to wake the sergeant in charge.

"ssst!"

"Huh! Huh! Who's there?"

"ssshh. sakhon, it's me, number two rabbit."

"Oh! You did it again. Ha! What do you have for me? It's been a long time."

"tonight, the best present of all."

"You brought a girl?!" The sergeant laughed out loud and several others awoke.

"tonight i bring liberation. tonight i bring angkar. come with me. i'll show you."

"Should I wake the others?"

"yes. ask them if they wish to come. all can come but only if they do so of their own free will."

Without fear of making noise the sergeant passed amongst his small perimeter waking the tired, underfed and unpaid FANK soldiers. "Rise up. We're moving."

"Augh, Sergeant Brother—" one began, but Sakhon silenced him with, "Number Two Rabbit wants us to follow."

The soldiers packed up and followed Nang into the blackness, each troop holding the man to his front, none knowing their small column included three armed yotheas of Angkar. Nang led them circuitously toward their garrison subpost, closer and closer, led them down animal paths and along raised treelines and finally through flooded paddies where the water had risen to waist high.

"sakhon, you and i shall go inside. the others must wait."

"Rabbit, I can't go in before dawn."

"we'll be quiet. we won't wake the officer. i want to talk to brother yu and uncle neth. i've so much to give."

Quietly Nang and Sakhon approached the perimeter. In a minute they stood with the sentries, two who recognized Number Two Rabbit. A minute later Nang, Sakhon and four sentries, the only other men awake in the subpost, were chattering quietly and opening the main gate.

In the paddies Eng slithered to the last concealment opposite the gate. Behind him Soth, Horl and eighteen men and boys, yotheas, porters and vassals, lay in the wet awaiting the signal. A softening of the misty shroud, first light, spread across the sky. Still no signal. The shroud grayed. At the gate two sentries emerged, unarmed, smoking cigarettes. They sat on their heels and stared across the lower black earth. Eng crept forth. In line with him came six armed yotheas creeping like one long segmented animal until they were a stone's throw from the FANK gate and the sentries. Nang appeared at the garrison gate, squatted between the sentries. He pointed quietly, grunted, finally lifted one guard's hand and pointed it toward Eng's position. On that signal, Eng rose, walked forward, bowed to the FANK soldiers and said, "Follow me." The two sentries left their post.

In the paddies the six yotheas stood, came to Nang, followed him into the garrison. As they entered, a group of five FANK soldiers, armed and with full gear, followed Met Soth out the gate. Then a second group of five followed Met Rong. In the billet area Sakhon and the two sentries woke soldiers one by one and told them to gather their entire issue. One by one the FANK troops obeyed until sixty soldiers had been woken, dressed, armed, and led off in groups of five, led first to Eng's waiting squad where they were given rice balls, then away, north, with their weapons, meeting up with the troops from the LP, whispering phrases of purity, sovereignty and independence.

By dawn the garrison soldiers were six kilometers from their base, six kilometers and a light-year, surrounded by welcoming peasant-soldiers armed to the hilt.

"Many of you know me as Rabbit." Nang spoke clearly. "I am Met Nang. You are welcome to join our Organization. Today I will ask you to give us your hearts and arms and we shall lead you to our forest home. I ask you to give me two days. If then you do not wish to join us, you may return to your Kompong Thom fortress."

In a temporary treeline reindoctrination camp west of Phum Voa Yeav, the sixty-four FANK "volunteers" were treated as if they were lost sheep, as if they were brothers returned. Nang did all he could to impress them.

"How many of you have M-16 rifles?" Nang smiled. He knew only half a dozen could raise their hands. "With Angkar each shall have this." He held up a Soviet Kalashnikov assault rifle. A yothea plant applauded and the FANK troops joined in. "Look at this," Nang sneered. He lifted a 1916 Berthier 8mm rifle. "What poor rascal was forced to carry this antique? He had thirty-one cartridges. How would he get more?"

For three hours Nang spoke. "Angkar's goal is a pure and classless society," he told them. "Our soldiers are instruments of the Organization. They are heros of Kampuchean nationalism. It is their patriotic endeavor to roll with the Wheel of History." Each word he spoke, each phrase Eng added, each act of encouragement the yotheas gave out was full of enthusiasm. The yotheas and cadre of Angkar ate with the volunteers, slept with them, led them on patrols. After two days the city militiamen were asked to choose: remain with Angkar for Kampuchean independence or return to the lackey puppet forces of the imperialist warmongers; vow poverty, chastity, obedience and hard work in the service of the people, the nation and Angkar or return to the graft, patronage, lust and sloth of Kompong Thom; usher in a millennium of happiness or sell the country into bondage.

Two thirds chose to take the vow, "I am desire not contrary to duty. I will do whatever Angkar asks. I will die for Angkar if it is so deemed."

A third turned back to Kompong Thom, unharmed and unarmed. Before they reached the garrison, a second and third subpost were emptied. By the second week of September 1971, the Krahom army of the North could boast of new summer recruitment or conscription of nearly three thousand FANK militiamen, village men, boys and girls. Phase two, expand the army, was well under way.

*   *   *

A pull on his arm. Nang jerked fiercely. Again the tug. In the blackness of their hiding place Nang cocked his arm, ready to bludgeon the small boy. Nang's chest tightened as he coiled. Then he relaxed. Slowly he moved his hand forward, his index finger extended, stiff as a teak twig. His fingertip touched hair; he slid it down to, into, the little boy's ear. Slowly he pushed. The boy's head rolled with the pressure. Nang continued pushing. The boy's body shifted. Soundlessly Nang bore down, pushing, pushing, the boy fell to his side on wet earth yet uttered not even the faintest whimper. Like a ballet couple, Nang flowed with him, pressing harder and harder, his fingertip jamming into the little boy's ear canal. The boy's head shuddered beneath the pressure, his body shook, he kicked his feet, clamped his teeth.

The commotion brought Eng. Almost imperceptibly he whispered, "stop!"

Nang halted. His finger was buried to the first joint in the flesh of the ear. Slowly he eased the force, withdrew the shaft and returned to his position.

Krahom recruitment success had created, in Nang's mind, unwieldy problems that came close to outweighing the gain. First and foremost in his thoughts were the crybabies. "Just let us do the job," he'd told Met Nim, a runner from Met Sar. "Half these runts need their mothers."

"Train them, Met Nang. We must increase the army. Keep the young ones separate. Let them serve you in the most desperate situations."

"Indeed!" Nang had uttered the one word. He understood. On line to his right, now, were four of these small children, tiny boys and girls trained by sugar and stick to mindless obedience. Nang thought bitterly about Nim's directive. Further expand the army! he thought. Weaken it! Dilute it! Nang hated it. Feared it. It would destroy him. To him Kampuchea needed but a small, well-disciplined elite.

The second problem concerned the liberated hamlets north of Kompong Thom City. The NVA had shifted south and left their Khmer Viet Minh village cadre behind to control the people. When the Krahom moved into old NVA positions, the Khmer Viet Minh were caught between nationalist and internationalist Communist ideologies. Met Nim had simply given Nang the order: "Clean the Brotherhood of the Pure. Once our enemies are engaged we must have no inner contradictions sapping our energy or blocking its flow. Eliminate contradictions."

Now, before him, them, sitting on stilts high above the ground, was the house of Ote Samrin. Nang lifted the boy he'd staked to the ground. "Now," he said. "For Kampuchea. You will be known as a national hero."

Down the line Eng told a six-year-old girl, "Soon you will see Buddha. He will dress you in white and you will eat the finest rice."

To Nang the little boy cried, "I'm afraid."

"Afraid! Afraid of what?"

Nang expected the boy to say, "Afraid of dying," or "Afraid it will hurt."

"I'm afraid of ghosts," the boy said. "If I go will I get a ghost-face like you?"

"Angkar"—Nang's voice was hard—"is greater than all ghosts. Angkar protects you."

The little boy and little girl stood. Between them two toddlers rose. They grasped hands, sidled forth toward the base of the ladder leading to Ote Samrin's house. The boy trailed a cord. The six-year-old girl began to climb but immediately Mister Ote's bodyguard heard them and shone a flashlight down. "Halt! Who are you?"

"Mother's ill, Uncle. We've come to get Grandpa."

"Don't move." There was bustling on the platform but nothing to be seen. The little girl led her "brothers" up a few more rungs. "Halt, damn you." The flashlight flicked on again. "Mister Ote lives here. Who's your grandfather?" The toddlers began to whine. "Oh, come up. In this blackness it's a wonder you found any house at all."

As the girl topped the ladder she called loudly, "Grandpa?"

Nang began to count. "twenty. nineteen. eighteen. . . ."

"Come here, child," the bodyguard said.

". . . thirteen. the toddlers should be up. nine. eight . . ."

"What are you carrying?"

"A basket for Grandpa."

"I'm not your grandpa," Ote Samrin said, coming onto the porch with a lantern. "I'm . . ."

". . . two. one . . ." The boy was up. "zero." Nang smacked the clacker. The boy exploded. The fireball and concussion detonated the other children and as their bodies were being thrown by the first blast they too exploded, blowing up with them the entire house, the bodyguard, Ote Samrin, his family and the KVM presence from Phum Voa Yeav. Phase three, eliminate contradictory elements, was complete.

"You've lost a lot of weight," Pech Chieu Teck said to his wife.

"And you've gained it." Vathana laughed politely.

"The children are too thin," Teck said, his voice edged with involuntary harshness.

"We manage." Vathana smiled. She lifted the eight-month-old Samol to her lap and gave her a small squeeze. The infant's eyes shone as she gurgled and cooed and grabbed at her mother's thumb.

Teck moved closer. He poked a finger into his daughter's belly and laughed, quietly pleased as the baby giggled and churned her arms, her whole body wobbling with the motion. He looked beyond the baby to the mother. Though thin and shabbily clothed Vathana was still very beautiful. As he watched her face, the winds outside shifted and blew the scent of the camp and the odor of the hospital tent into the sectioned-off corner where Vathana, Sophan and the two infants had made their home. The smell went immediately to Teck's stomach. His abdominal muscles tightened, his breathing stopped. He stood, backed away from the baby as if she might dirty his spotless uniform, then, first dusting Sophan's bamboo slat cot with his hand, sat. "Where's that *phnong* you let suckle the children?"

"Sophan? She's not a Mountaineer."

"She's as black as one."

"She's Khmer. She's at the river with your son. They went to bathe and get some fish."

"The economy's getting worse, isn't it?"

"You didn't come to see your children, did you?"

Teck dropped his head. At once he felt shame and pride, loathing for this creature who lived in filth, superiority and self-justification. "I . . . I've come to . . ." Teck stopped. "I'll get to that in a minute."

"If you haven't come to see the children . . ." Vathana began. Teck's uneasiness robbed her of her own harmony.

"There's a fable circulating I want to tell you."

"The one," Vathana broke in, "of the tiger and the dragon. I've heard it. Ever since the Foreign Ministry revealed the ARVN atrocities and those men left, I've heard it. Every day they talk of it. When the ARVN closed the river base, there was a great celebration and an *aacha* told everyone of the tiger and the dragon."

"No," Teck said. He had not heard that fable and wished to, but he could not admit to his wife that she knew something he didn't. "No. This is the fable of a cobra and an eagle and a crab. You haven't heard it because I'm the first one to bring it to Neak Luong." Teck paused. He crossed his legs beneath him as he spoke—spoke not in the manner of the traditional storyteller but spoke quickly, jerkily, at times pausing, seeming to have forgotten the tale.

"One day," he began, "there was a lovely black cobra sunning itself upon a barren rock. The snake was very long and from its head looked down at its stretching, curving body glistening in the sun, and she decided she was too beautiful for any other creature. Yet, to win her love many creatures came and piled riches about her which she accepted. A rat came with diamonds laid in a gold ring which he slipped over the end of her tail. She smiled, slithered a bit off then coiled and sprang and ate the rat, leaving only its feet. Still more animals came, until the cobra had great treasures, yet still no one pleased her. Then came a crab and an eagle. The eagle soared high, looped and rode the winds above the snake and the cobra sang out saying, 'If you will hold me and let me fly and show me all the world, I'll be your bride.'

" 'Don't go,' whispered the crab.

"The snake turned, for in the pile of gems she had not seen the crab. 'You're ugly,' the cobra hissed.

"Just then the eagle lifted the snake and showed her all the world and then lit in a grassy field where he fucked her very well. Later the cobra returned to her rock and found it barren once more. The crab had even eaten the feet of the rat."

Teck stopped. Vathana said nothing. She didn't know if there was a point to the fable, Khmer fables often being without moral. For a moment she fidgeted with Samol's small shirt. "You know," Teck began again. "We must take care of the people while keeping the boat level in the river."

"Teck," Vathana said, as she mustered her courage, "you've come for some reason. Does it suit you to divorce me?"

"No, it doesn't. You're my wife. Now let me finish."

"I'm not certain you've begun."

"I have," Teck said sharply. "Listen. Half the rubber plantations have been burned, bombed or occupied by foreigners. If the Americans weren't forcing this war on us, there'd be no war in Cambodia. We're not strong enough for a military confrontation, so for our preservation we must offer multiple support. I'm sorry if you've gotten mixed up in all this, but you have."

"Teck? What— Two months ago you said FANK . . ."

"We're all Khmer Patriots," Teck interrupted her. His voice lowered. "You must maintain absolute secrecy."

"Absol—?!"

"ssshh." He continued in a whisper. "i can offer your camp protection."

Vathana let out a short burst of laughter, but seeing Teck's serious face, her laughter ceased. "protection?" she whispered mockingly. "you?"

"I have been authorized by the Association of Khmer Patriots to say this. Also to bring you word of Peou."

"Peou! Who sent . . . ?" Confusion seized her. Words, thoughts stopped. She tensed.

"Because of American bombing about Kratie, he's been returned to Stung Treng."

"How . . . how do you know this?" Vathana's voice was thin.

"From the Khmer Patriots," Teck said. "We are Khmer Patriots."

Vathana shook her head in disbelief. "Who . . . ?" This man-boy, this flimsy failure who had barely mourned his father's death, who'd spent all their lives together in dancehalls or opium dens, who only months earlier had embraced Lon Nol's holy crusade, was now telling her he was a Khmer "patriot," using not the word form meaning a person who loves his country but, just as her dark assailant had earlier, a form designating an organization. The incongruity shook Vathana to the core. She shifted. "Do you know what you say? Do you have word of my mother and father?"

"Perhaps." A smile creased Teck's cheeks. "Perhaps," he repeated. "For the sake of your camp, Angel . . ." Inside, Teck was melancholy, disturbed, destroyed, yet he would not show it, not an inkling. Harshly he pushed on. ". . . And for your parents and your brother . . ."

"What? Do what?"

"As my father would say, 'What will happen if we do nothing?' Well, Angel, keep your American. Fuck him well. We all have responsibilities during our country's most difficult time."

"My Am . . . What do you know?!" Vathana lashed out. "What is it to you?! To your own wife you . . ."

"Don't be afraid." Teck seemed indifferent. "Others will come but no one will hurt you. I'm told that a mistake was made. Aah! Someday, Angel, we'll live in a great villa."

When Sophan returned with the two-year-old Samnang she found Vathana under a blanket on her cot clutching Samol like a child in the dark clutches a doll for security. Sophan touched Vathana's head to check for fever. Vathana shook off the hand. "Angel," Sophan said softly, "are you ill?"

"No, Sophan. Not ill. Only tired."

"Doctor Sarin is here for rounds and there's an American supply truck with mosquito netting, a thousand cans of milk and a thousand bottles of soda."

"Sophan?"

"Yes Angel?"

"What do you think of Captain Sullivan?"

"What do I think?" Sophan laughed gently.

"Um-hum."

"He's good to you?"

"He loves me as if I were a porcelain doll."

"You're . . . Angel?"

"Do you like him, Sophan?"

Sophan turned from Vathana. "He can't help it if he's American," she said.

"If he were Khmer . . ." Vathana probed.

"Even if he's American"—Sophan turned again to Vathana and smiled—"he's very nice. Much better than a husband who abandons his children."

Late that evening Sullivan pulled his BSA Lightning with a new metallic-red gas tank into the refugee camp at Neak Luong. It was raining hard. Wind buffeted the big canvas tents and the ground was slick deep mud. Sullivan revved the engine, alternately slipping and disengaging the clutch. The rear wheel spun and shot to one side then the other. He kept both feet off the pegs, legs out, catching and righting the machine as it tried to splat itself into the mire. Each time the bike tipped the headlight jarred to the side, and in the grass or in the gutters between tents, Sullivan saw rats, some scurrying, others bold enough to stand fast, their eyes reflecting like ruby beads.

Since July Sullivan had come to Neak Luong as frequently as his duties, travel restrictions and the war would allow. Each time the city had been surrounded by more barbed wire, and each time, seemingly, the outposts and perimeter had shrunk back toward the enclave. With the closing of the ARVN river base in August, the ferry crossings had come under ever-increasing pressure and night crossings were prohibited. Still he'd come. For the right price, no matter the time, it was always possible to find an independent riverman with a boat large enough to carry the BSA.

Throughout the summer it never occurred to Sullivan that Cahuom Vathana might have an ulterior motive for maintaining their relationship. To him everything was too right, too pure for there to be an evil element driving them together. He spoke freely about FANK personnel, who was good, who loathsome. He hid little about equipment delivered or about operations, though he revealed little for he believed Vathana wasn't interested in details. These things made up but a fraction of their talk.

For her part, beyond the politics and pressure which she did not fully comprehend, Vathana had accepted the relationship as she had her marriage—as if it were a professional contract. In Cambodia, marriage was a sacred conjugation with ramifications rolling into the future as the Samsara rolling through time.

Teck's visit had confused and embarrassed her. All day and all evening she'd worked cleaning the sick, feeding the disabled, scouring communal facilities and organizing rice and milk distribution. The camp had shrunk. With the announced closing of the ARVN base, thousands of able-bodied refugees had packed their belongings and headed upriver to Phnom Penh. Within a month the population, which had peaked at fourteen thousand and stabilized at nine thousand, fell to slightly under six thousand. Those left were the most disadvantaged and the sleaziest hustlers.

The bike revved one last time then died. Before Sullivan dismounted a dozen children surrounded him. In broken Khmer, pidgin English and basic French they welcomed him and he hugged them and lifted them onto the BSA's tank, consciously hefting each marsamic child, thinking each was thinner or lighter this time than last. Then from his pocket he pulled two hundred-riel notes. "You take care for me," he said to the oldest boy while tapping the motorcycle. "Understand?" he added in Khmer. "You help." Sullivan pointed to a shy girl of perhaps eight. With a bill in each hand he said, "For you—and brothers and sisters. Buy food. No candy."

"Cigarette?" a boy said.

"No cigarette. Rice."

As he talked with the children he felt restless, almost frantic. It had been three weeks since he'd seen her, since he'd touched her dark skin, run his fingers in her thick hair. "Ouch!" The children giggled. The boy who'd asked for cigarettes had ventured to pull the bushy red hair on the back of his hand.

"Hello, J. L." Vathana stood demurely by the tent flap. In the single light above, rain droplets glittered like descending sparks from the tail of a skyrocket. She stepped forward. "Where have you been?" Her French was the most beautiful sound he'd heard in what seemed like years. He stepped toward her. She burst into laughter. "You're all mud."

"You've two days to help me clean up."

"We obtained for you an office. With so many gone you can have your own house."

"Can you show me?" He blushed through his smile and through the mud that caked his face, and she felt the blush.

"Where have you been?" Vathana said later that night. "I've been so worried for you." She cuddled onto his chest and brushed a hand in the swirls of hair.

"There's so much," Sullivan said. "The Northern Corridor's as active as the border. My God, Vathana, they're driving a wedge right down to the heart and those bastards, all of them, they're like puppets, like caricatures, playing roles, reading lines without paying the least bit of attention to what the hell's happening about them."

"You've been up north again?"

"Oh, to Kompong Luong, Skoun, Phum Pa Kham and Baray. I took a helicopter to Kompong Thom. One of the nights I was there an entire FANK garrison just disappeared. No signs of a fight. Nobody knows what happened. I choppered back to Oudong and then back to headquarters."

"That's where . . . in the North, where General Lon says the *thmils* are massing, yes?"

"*Thmils?*"

"The foreign pagans."

"Is that what that means?"

"Um-hum."

"All along the corridor I heard that word but no one would tell me what it meant."

"It's a very sad word," Vathana said. She laid her head on his chest. His heartbeat was strong, slow, rhythmic, and with each beat their bamboo cot shivered. "A long time ago the prophets forecast a dark age which would be heralded by foreign atheists who would conquer the people of faith."

"Umm. *Thmils.*" Sullivan had difficulty with the idea of prophets and forecasts but he knew many Khmers strongly believed in them.

"General Lon Nol says the Viet Namese are the *thmils* and if the Communists win a dark age will descend upon Kampuchea."

"I brought you something to keep that from happening." Vathana lifted her head, put both hands on him and rested her chin on her hands. "It's a TT-33."

"And what is a TT-33?"

"It's a pistol. I'm going to teach you how to use it."

"Teach the FANK soldiers. They'll protect me."

"With what I've seen you may need to protect yourself and the children . . . from them." Vathana was about to say something but he put his hand to her lips. "Don't. I'm serious. It's an NVA pistol I got in Baray. There's four hundred rounds." Again Vathana tried to speak and again he hushed her.

"This is how it happens," he said. "It's always the same

pattern, always the same cause. The bastards don't pay their soldiers. The soldiers are as poor as the refugees. Poorer. They're ordered into a village to chase out a Viet Minh agent and they sack the place. Steal everything. Maybe rape a few women. Then that village hates FANK and they welcome the Khmer Communists and hide them. Again and again and again."

"Do they welcome the Viet Namese?"

"No."

"The ARVN?"

"No. No. They're, how do you say it? *thmils*, just like the NVA."

"And is FANK so bad?"

"That's just it. For every corrupt son-of-a-bitch commander there's a decent unit with an honest commander." Sullivan huffed. His anger rose and as it rose he could almost see Colonel Chhan Samkai at Tum Nop. "Even when they're paid," he began again, "they can't feed their families. Guys like this guy Chhan charge them for rations, for ammunition, for petrol for their vehicles." Sullivan huffed again. "I hate it. I hate seeing it. You've got some wonderful soldiers. Some who are so Buddhist they shoot the ground to make certain they don't hit anybody . . . but that's okay. That's really not the problem. There's such a command failure . . . and my embassy's part of it."

"This Chenla II of Lon Nol's," Vathana whispered, "that will drive out the Communists, yes?"

Sullivan just growled.

"No?"

"Vathana, to defend terrain for a long period, one must have an offensive thrust which can keep the enemy at bay. Otherwise the enemy sits just out of reach and picks you apart."

"But what of the bombers . . . they're an offensive punch, no?"

"You can't rely on them alone. They're one tool . . . effective up to a point . . . against troop concentrations, but when the enemy's dispersed or once they get in tight, you've got to have good basic infantry. Colby had the right idea."

"Colby?"

"The CIA guy. He wanted to arm the population, get the people involved. The idea was to build a broad political base so each community would defend itself. Then some jerk forced divisional organization on FANK and the government disarmed the people. That concentrated the political base in a few hands and most of them were old corrupt hands Sihanouk left behind."

"So why do you stay here!" Vathana sat up. She did not like to hear Sihanouk criticized by anyone, especially an American.

Sullivan was so disturbed by the thought that the war would go badly, he barely noticed her irritation and he ignored her words. "They do it like actors," he repeated the idea. "As if they don't see the enemy at all. The enemy schemes every waking moment; at first light with their first sip of tea they discuss plans and plot how to topple the next town. Every day a new scheme. Every day they initiate new terrorist acts or recruit new people. The best the government does is react after the fact. They've got to meet major offensive thrusts with counter-offensives and small scattered attacks with police action.

"Three NVA divisions are closing on the Northern Corridor and elements of the NVA 479th are infiltrating from Siem Reap. Vathana, I don't know what's going to happen. In Viet Nam the most ardent anti-Communists were the ex-Communists. The second most ardent were the Northern refugees who'd escaped their rule. It's got to tell us something. Those among us most against them are the ones who know them best. The ones who know their lies."

"John L. Sullivan. Why do you talk so much?"

"Oh, sorry. . . . I . . . I got carried away. I keep thinking about what might happen."

"So why do you stay?"

Sullivan paused. How to answer? "There's a motto I believe in," he said. He slid his hand up her bare back and softly caressed her shoulders. "*De Oppresso Libre.* It's the Special Forces slogan. 'To Free From Oppression.' "

"You are a very strange man, my Mister Sullivan. You tell me the Republicans oppress the people yet you stay to keep them from succumbing to the Communists."

"FANK's full of fools. It's inefficient. It's corrupt. But it's not ruthless. Not in the Communist sense. If the NVA win there'll be a dark age worse than anything Lon Nol predicts. If the people don't learn, if they don't understand ruthlessness and terror and absolute control, they'll never be able to counter those pathological fanatics. That's why I'm here. I'll be back in Phum Pa Kham and Baray next week. I'm here to help them change, to help them learn about the efficient and righteous use of power."

"Oh, John, doesn't every side think it uses power righteously?"

Chhuon's knees throbbed. Hot fluid burned from his stomach to the back of his throat. The taste in his mouth was foul, stale, vile. Near him, on her own sleeping mat, Sok shivered. Beyond her Peou and Grandma huddled for warmth. For a week the rains had been hard and there had been no food distribution, no lamp oil, no medicine, no clothing to replace that taken for the militias. Hang Tung flipped pages on the other side of the plaited wall, reading by the only light in the Khmer sector. Chhuon breathed deeply. His head ached. He wanted to claw his eyes from their sockets. Nimol and Chan were gone and in every village hut the people cowered in fear.

A week earlier Colonel Nui had had the bodies of the radar crew brought before the pagoda. The faces of all four men had been burnt. Nui had ordered the carriers to bring them exactly as they'd been found, rags and ash stuffed in their mouths, their faces obliterated not by gasoline but by white phosphorus or by C-4 plastique, holes burnt four fingers wide and four fingers deep right through their skulls. And all had been disemboweled. They lay agitated, without peace, all day and all night as the villagers passed, sneaked glimpses and fled. Then the village had been assembled. In the rain Nui and Hang Tung passed through the rows, asking every soul, "Did you do this? Who did it?" A thousand times from Khmer mouths, *"Da, khong biet,"* *"Da, khong biet."* A thousand times in Viet Namese, "I don't know, sir."

That night a B-52 sortie released 120 five-hundred-pound-high-explosive and fragmentation bombs less than a mile north of Phum Sath Din, hitting a convoy of about forty trucks heading for the Northern Corridor. The bomb box was well clear of the village, yet two peripheral hits (bombs don't always drop as expected; these were probably at the outer limit of what is termed "circular error probability") exploded just beyond the village perimeter. Shrapnel and fireball pierced and ignited two homes. Three people were killed, seven more wounded. Still Colonel Nui demanded that the radar men be left unburied.

A day later the stinking corpses were removed and replaced by two headless, limbless torsos who were identified by their clothing. "First," Hang Tung told the reassembled village, "resisters murdered four men of our heroic defense force. Now they have mutilated the vice-chairman and his wife. Only last week Ny Non Chan intervened on your behalf and requested the pagoda hours be liberalized, and Colonel Nui, who is a devout Buddhist, agreed."

Chhuon rolled to his side. He had been asked to say a few words and he had offered a prayer but he had not listened to his own words. It was not he who spoke but the demon, which reemerged about his larynx. Now the order had gone out that all twelve- to fourteen-year-olds would be recruited and trained for village protection, and even Peou had been approached by Hang Tung. "Little Nephew, look at this. That's it. Come here.

Would you someday like to fire my rifle? Tomorrow I'll let you shoot. Someday you'll shoot an American, eh?''

Chhuon lay back. Dear Lord Buddha, he thought, take this fake authority from me. Take this responsibility. Let them catch me. Allow me to shed this horrible duplicity.

On the other side of the plaited wall, Hang Tung checked his notes, his scratch sheets and his time charts. He smiled to himself, pleased with himself. Every hour of every day for the past month was in a vertical column at the side of the page. Beside each line was a note on Chhuon's whereabouts and activity. Here and there were blanks, and the blanks were beginning to form a pattern. Hang Tung closed his hands, squeezed his arms to his body. Uncle, he thought, a stick whittled at both ends soon collapses the tree.

CHAPTER THIRTEEN

Slowly the deep gray silhouette of Pa Kham appeared in the mist. The heavy rains of September and the first week of October, along with the equalization of the hydrostatic pressure between the surrounding highlands and the central Cambodian basin, and the final deluge of Himalayan snowmelt reaching the lower Mekong, had caused the waters to rise. Sullivan's eyes stabbed west, north, east. Everywhere he saw huge inundated tracts. Then the image reversed. He was not on land but in the ocean in an area of low atolls and before and behind him snaked not an infantry column but a ship convoy, odd ships, shaped like buses and jeeps and trucks. Far to the front were the forward guns and towed artillery pieces. But just as the berms of Pa Kham lay submerged beneath ground mist, the gun carriages were hidden and the tubes seemed to float on a choppy sea of unseen raised roadbed.

The North Viet Namese squeeze on the heartland and about the enclaved cities had become a siege of the entire country. Lon Nol's reaction had been to order Operation Chenla II. Throughout the summer skirmishes and battles had erupted, usually resulting in a decrease in the government's area of control and an increase in the number of refugees. The population in government enclaves increased, condensed, concentrated, until their simple closeness became a factor in their attitudes, their frustrations.

Far behind, the column had left the saffron-robed monks standing beneath their parasols chanting blessings, praying for the defenders of Buddhism, beseeching the Holy One, wishing the soldiers great victory in the holy war against the dark invaders. Between the buses, amongst the APCs, even clutching many of the troop trucks, families of soldiers followed their men. Each night the column halted, loggered on the road, and the unit families came to the unit soldiers and cooked the evening meal over fires they somehow started from the wet wood they'd gathered in the low forest to the west. Each morning the dependants broke camp, packed up and fell in behind their husband's or father's transport. From Phnom Penh, from Skoun, they marched, the entire column moving at the pace of the smallest child, except for the crack vanguard APCs.

In July, in a three-way contest pitting NVA against Khmer Krahom against FANK, Takeo, the largest city in south-central Cambodia, fell to the NVA. The exposure of ARVN atrocities (especially the pillaging of the village of Chebal Moun near Kompong Speu) and the subsequent ARVN withdrawal had left FANK alone to face the NVA and the fast-growing Khmer Krahom. Though there had been major accomplishments in a year and a half, FANK still lacked mobility, equipment and combat experience and knowledge. It remained fragmented, and the old feudal system, which had existed from ancient times through the Sihanouk era, continued to render the military incompetent and corrupt. After eighteen months, there still was no system for delivering rations to troops, and thus the army remained road bound, tied to village markets for the purchase of daily sustenance; and where the men were unpaid, goods were simply taken. Some units were manned by ghosts, phantom names that padded the payroll and thus the unit commander's pocket. At this time, six to eight percent of FANK— 22,000 men—existed only on paper.

Sullivan stared east. There was no flank security. It disgusted him but again he'd been warned about advising, and to be fair, the roadside fields didn't need infantry flank units but shallow-draft swamp boats or amphibious ducks—navy, not infantry—the land being so flooded. Perhaps scout birds, helicopters, he thought. But the weather was nasty and in the absence of actual battle it seemed wise to conserve that limited resource.

"Driver!" Sullivan's junior lieutenant escort said to the civilian behind the wheel. "Stop here!" He turned to Sullivan who was standing, draped in a poncho, in the back of the topless car. "Monsieur," the escort officer said, "let's urinate on this foul land."

Sullivan's face broke into a smile. "Go ahead. I'm fine." The man got out, walked to the east shoulder and peed into the paddy. Sullivan fixed his eyes on the low swampland to the west. Were they to be attacked from either side there'd be no place to go. But an attack up from the swamp or through the paddies would be suicide for the attackers. No, he thought, we're not open to attack here. To snipers, yes. To mortars, artillery, yes. But to troops . . .

The driver switched on the radio. Since the column had set off, Lon Nol had delivered daily harangues over Radio Phnom Penh. Sullivan recognized the voice but not the words. He looked back north toward Pa Kham. The silhouette seemed to advance before them.

"Has there been any word from the reconnaissance teams?" Sullivan asked his escort in French.

The man shook his head. "Too much rain today for reconnaissance teams, no?"

"Photo reconnaissance?" Sullivan prodded.

The escort officer smiled. He pointed to the radio. "He says there is a great victory in the making. The column has reached Puk Yuk, eh!" Sullivan did not recognize the name as pronounced in Khmer. "Puk Yuk. Puk Yuk." The escort produced his map and stabbed his fingernail just south of Kompong Thom. "We must have a great celebration." He clapped his hands. "Already to Puk Yuk, eh!" He clapped a hand on the driver's shoulder. Then to Sullivan he said, "Listen to him." He turned the volume up.

"What does he say?" Sullivan asked. He damned himself for not having picked up enough Khmer to understand the quick radio speech.

"He says he has a dream." The small officer smiled from ear to ear. "He says, 'I see armed Viet Namese. I see their tanks. I see them fall and burst into flame before Buddha. I see Colonel Um Savuth, commander of the Chenla II task force . . . I see him entering all northern cities carrying a statue of the seated Buddha. Behind Colonel Um I see fallen *thmils*. Soldiers of FANK, cut your skin, allow Lord Buddha to enter and strengthen you. If the foreign atheists are victorious they will usher in the last dark days when all that is evil will reign. Fight hard, holy warriors. I see great victory for you in this glorious battle. Fight for the very survival of Buddhism!' "

The escort officer beamed. Sullivan politely returned the smile. He looked up. Pa Kham floated in the mist and drizzle to the north of the stalled column. I see, he thought, I see twenty thousand soldiers and forty thousand dependants stretched from Skoun to Puk Yuk. I see an open front seventy kilometers long and two lanes wide.

Nang had led his new unit south from Phum Voa Yeav, east around Kompong Thom then southwest parallel to the highway, skipping from hamlet to forest camp to hamlet. No longer was he independent but in trade for that freedom he now commanded a company of eighty armed yotheas, the 2d Company of the KT 104th Battalion of the Army of the North.

The Krahom had made great gains in areas that the NVA had shifted away from, yet, to the Center, it was not enough to pick up scattered spoils. The radical nationalist Communists were determined to halt any further Viet Namese Communist victories. Thus did the Krahom set a course to deny the Viet Namese (in the exact terms Americans also used) the population resource. To do so the Krahom leadership had ordered an abrupt and rash reorganization, changing their light infantry army from company-sized elements (which it hadn't yet totally achieved) to battalion-sized units capable of engaging similar enemy elements.

The Krahom companies traveled in secret—covering five, ten, twelve kilometers each day or night. Nang waded his yotheas through paddies chest deep in water, pausing to rest, unseen, on scattered islands between the congested highway where FANK plodded and the higher land farther east where the NVA struggled to unmire its T-54 tanks and its long line of two-and-a-half-ton trucks which had bogged down where B-52s had found and blasted the camouflaged dike roads, swamping the countryside. One-day's march ahead of the 2d of the 104th was their sister company, the 3d of the 104th, commanded by Nang's protégé, Met Horl. Behind them were two more light infantry companies plus the battalion command post led by Met Mita, an older man in his early thirties. With Mita was Eng, Nang's politically pure friend. Attached, too, to the battalion command post, or CP, was an independent platoon of *neary* led by the legendary and ruthless Met Nu. Met Soth, who had denounced Nang so long ago, now commanded a platoon in the 2d Company of the KT 108th.

To Nang the travel, the new situation were unsettling. As they circled Baray and headed toward Pa Kham his mind lapsed from thoughts of battle to thoughts of his new chains and new powers, and of the organization he'd built and left in the North. He thought of the hamlet chief at Voa Yeav 3 and of the statements he, Nang, Nang of Angkar, had made to the pathetic man. "Anyone who harms you . . ." It was not an approved statement of proselytizing propaganda, not a tested scientific slogan designed to make the hearer respond to his Communism, but words which harkened back further—earlier than his training in China, earlier than Pong Pay Mountain, earlier than, than what? His mind wished to stop with his rebirth into the Krahom yet there was something before, something gnawing at his mind, trying to resurface, to reassert itself. How? How could something so dead rekindle?

Nang laughed to himself. They had reached a preestablished station. About him in the treeline camp his yotheas picked leeches from each other's skin. What wonderful propaganda lines, he thought as the idea continued to roll in him. At the moment he'd have liked to thank Sar, or whoever had given it to him. How the elders ate it up. ". . . who harms your crops, your people . . ." What more did they have? It was almost all he had had to do to convince some. How badly they wanted to believe. And why not? Everyone harmed them in the name of some self-righteous cow dung. The lying scum, Nang thought. Worst of all are the Americans. No, worst were the Viet Namese. Or maybe Lon Nol and his clique were the worst. Only Angkar could protect the people against the scourges of the cruel and ruthless aliens. ". . . or your belongings, is your enemy. Blood for blood." American, Chinese, Viet Namese, all had acted to denounce their humanity. "For all eternity . . . revenge. For Chhuon. Blood for blood." Nang stopped. For Chhuon? he thought. He paused, puzzled. Then, standing abruptly, he screamed, "Fucking buffalo! On your feet. Angkar wishes you to move quickly. Do not stop to think. Angkar will think for you."

"Comrade Nang," Met Hon, who had been Sergeant Sakhon of FANK's listening post, stopped the commanding officer.

"Met Hon."

"There's a runner from Met Mita."

"Has he the new map?"

"I don't . . ."

"Forget it. Bring him here."

Quickly the runner and the company commander conversed. Words flew. Fast advance, fast attack, fast withdrawal, fast dispersal. Nang pulled his hair. Four fast but none slow. How can we do this without preparation? How? "Hon!"

"Yes, Met Nang."

"Find someone who knows this village." Nang pointed to his map.

In the miles of rice fields southeast of Baray between Highway 6 and the plantations, there were hundreds of tiny hamlets connected, at best, either to Highway 6 by narrow raised dikes wide enough only for a single oxcart or, via dike roads, to the better plantation road network and then to Highway 21. During the heaviest rains many of the communities were totally cut off. Even during the dry season few peasants ventured from their village or fields—to them a trip to the next village was a major undertaking.

Hon returned. "We've no one from this area."

"Tomorrow we'll liberate this settlement." Nang pointed to an unnamed hamlet near the village of Phum Chamkar.

"Yes," Met Hon said. "Met Nang," he added, "there is new word on the radio."

"What new word?"

"There is great celebration in Phnom Penh. Colonel Um's column head has reached Kompong Thom."

"Ah," Nang sighed. "What great fortune."

"Great fortune?!"

"Yes, Hon. You'll see."

By nightfall Nang's company had surrounded the unnamed hamlet, itself surrounded by a sea of flooded paddies. The young soldiers wrapped themselves in their mosquito nets. Tired, sore, pushed to the limit by the forced march, by a lack of decent rations and by the harshness of the untamed tropical environment, they slept. "Tomorrow," Nang said as he moved amongst them, "tomorrow you'll understand. We have two enemies. Tomorrow will begin the new life. Don't complain. You've been fated for glory."

Before cockcrow they moved, silently, some along the radial dikes which converged on the hamlet like spokes on the hub of a wheel, some through paddy water that threatened to float the youngest and shortest away. They moved to the edge of the waking hamlet, then, on signal, they marched in, silent, somber, afraid yet showing no fear. Amid the wood and thatch homes the tiny marketplace was deserted. The yotheas advanced. Their black shirts and pants were soaked, filthy. Each boy wore a red-checked krama as a belt to keep his shirt bottom closed, to keep leeches from inching up onto their torsos. They turned outward and waited.

The first peasants greeted them with surprise. "Who are you? Where are you from?"

"Met Hon." "Met Rath." "Met Bun." They answered. "Met Ouk from Kompong Thom."

"Kompong Thom! So far away."

"Yes."

"And you?"

"Met Nang of Angkar."

"Angkar? Where is that?"

"Angkar. We are the resistance. We are the nationals who have come to protect you from the advancing hordes."

"Who advances?"

"*Thmils*. They're in the plantations to the east and on the roads in the west."

"Yes. We've heard on the radio. But I don't know you."

"Where is your village head?" Nang looked about. "We have gifts for him."

More villagers appeared. Seeing the yotheas chatting amiably with their kinsmen and neighbors they came without fear and greeted the boys with food and drink.

"When every day we bend our backs in the fields," Nang heard an old farmer tell a yothea, "it's difficult to pay attention to national news. Still, we are Khmer, like you."

"And like us, Grandfather," Nang interrupted, "like all Khmers, you want independence and sovereignty."

"Oh yes. We are Khmers."

"Lon Nol has sold the country to the Americans . . ." Nang began the familiar lines but before he could continue, a commotion to his back halted him. He did not turn but watched the old farmer's face and the eyes of his own fighters. There were two men or two groups approaching. Nang took a deep breath. Exhaled a small. Contracted.

"Welcome," one voice called. "Who is your commander?" Nang turned slowly. A middle-aged man faced him. With the man were two younger men. All three were dark, obviously farmers. Off to one side was another pair, also young, yet their skin was much lighter. They whispered between themselves. "We are a farm village," the middle-aged man said, now following the eyes of the silent yotheas to Nang. "There's no need here for an army."

"Papa," one of the men with him said quietly, "he said he had gifts."

The man approached Nang. They exchanged greetings. Nang kept his face turned, hiding the scarred side. He smiled his impish smile, laughed his infectious laugh. "For you, Uncle. For the protection of your village." Nang signaled and quickly Met Ouk came forward with two AK-47 assault rifles. "There are armies very close by," Nang continued. "It is Angkar's wish that we serve you." With that Nang handed the headman the two weapons. All about, villagers breathed easier. Had these boys meant them harm certainly they would not have armed the headman.

Nang hid behind an enigmatic smile as his eyes darted here, there, into the marketplace, down along the row of houses. The second pair of young men had left.

"You shall eat . . ." The man's eyes fell on the right side of

Nang's face. He stuttered, coughed, cleared his throat. ". . . with us. Share our homes. When the danger has passed, you shall leave."

"While the danger is present, then"—Nang's eyes beamed—"you will help us mobilize the people for national defense."

"Of course. It's just as Mister Ea Eang has said."

"Ea Eang?"

"Yes," the elder answered. "And Taun Than. They have organized us, too. You know them, eh?" He turned looking for the pair of light-skinned men. "You too struggle to bring back Samdech Euv, no?"

"The Prince"—Nang smiled broadly—"is behind us."

That day the rains fell in sheets and that night the wind blew with great force. Again the morning came with torrential downpours and again an evening with gusting winds. On the morning of the twelfth of October a runner from Met Mita crossed a radial dike and entered the hamlet. Met Rath and Met Von followed his approach, looking down the barrels of their rifles. They intercepted him and Von lead him to Nang who had slept in a stall in the tiny central market. Quickly they spoke. Then the runner fled, retreating along a different route.

At midday Nang squatted amongst half a dozen women at one end of the thatched open-sided structure. Yotheas had repaired the wind-damaged roof and now all were clearly seen amongst the laborers in the fields. For two hours Nang had entertained the marketers with stories of his travels. Then he told them, "My father was killed in the bombings." His voice was mournful as he described for the ladies his father's mutilated body and saddened face just before death.

A cackle arose at the far side. Then several women ran from the market and a wave of silence rolled from that corner. More women, towing toddlers or clutching babies, ran. Nang smiled. Softly he continued. "The yuons butchered the others. They toasted my smallest sister and ate her."

"There he is."

"That's him. With the face. He's the Rabbit."

On each side two armed men locked their eyes on Nang. "Some yuons wear Khmer bodies." Nang's voice came measured. "Some have been tricked into supporting the Northern Viets even though they eat children. . . ." He did not move. His listeners no longer heard his words. At first they simply looked out from the circle. Then one leaned out, slid back on her butt, rolled to her knees and ran. Others were frozen in terror.

"Move away from the women," one man ordered. Nang didn't

budge. Another lady, then a third, bolted. "Put your hands on top of your head."

Very softly Nang muttered to the closest woman, "Is that Ea Eang?"

Her voice too came soft. "No. Taun Than." She began to back away but Nang's hand held her sarong skirt fast to the ground where she sat. The fourth and fifth women fled.

"He's the yuon agent," Nang whispered. The woman didn't respond.

Taun Than aimed at Nang one of the AKs Nang had given to the village chief. Nang turned toward the closest house. Ea Eang shouted from the side. "Get up. Let the auntie go." The two Khmers who had been with the Khmer Viet Minh agents stepped away.

Nang rose, still holding tightly to the woman's skirt. "Perhaps," he said loudly, "it is time." Immediately from behind stall partitions rose three neary. Nang faced his assassins. They were not without backup.

"Now is Rabbit's turn," Than called. About the marketplace a dozen Khmer Viet Minh militiamen stepped from doorways, from the rice silo, from behind the village well. Than snickered. "Now, Rabbit, come out. Tell those girls to drop their rifles." Eang laughed heartily.

Nang laughed too. "Your boys are unarmed," Nang said.

The eyes of the agents jumped to their militia, back to Nang, to their troops, to the neary who aimed at their hearts. Than lowered his rifle. His face paled. His militiamen stepped forward, their hands on their heads. Behind each was a black-clad girl. Some held pistols, most had only knives or clubs.

Now the woman beside Nang spoke, "Drop your rifle, Than." Than lowered his. Eang dropped his. Then Than let his fall. "Take them to the paddies," the woman told the *neary*. She turned to Nang. "Now you must let go of my ass." She laughed and from Met Nang escaped a sly titter. "Met Nang . . ."

"Yes, Comrade Nu."

"Someday . . ."

"Yes." Nang's eyes jumped.

Nu's face became hard. "Today, you tell these people how to think of this."

"Yes, comrade."

Again Nu laughed. "It is as Angkar wishes."

"When it's this wet," the new escort officer translated, "we need more fuel."

Sullivan made a note in the pad he carried. In six days he had only reached one kilometer north of Phum Pa Kham. His driver, escort and vehicle had changed. The new men smelled from living cramped in the sedan, and Sullivan found he too had begun to stink.

And now this. Sullivan looked with disgust at the carnage. Colonel Chhan Samkai, too, was disgusted though the carnage delighted him.

The command post had headed three hundred meters north-west along a small road which led to an unmarked hamlet in the low forest. "First they all cheer," Colonel Chhan ranted to Sullivan in French. " 'Bravo! Bravo! The army has saved Kompong Thom!' Now they riot."

"Isn't that directed at the chief of state?" Sullivan said. A FANK soldier with a beaming smile walked by. Seeing the commander and the American his smile broadened further and he lifted and displayed the two human heads he carried by their hair. Sullivan flashed a satirical grin, then a morose look of disapproval.

"He's commander-in-chief. If he suspends the Assembly he is right to do so." On 16 October 1971 Premier Lon Nol suspended the Cambodian National Assembly and announced in nation-wide broadcasts that he had assumed full power and would rule by executive decree. Democracy, he declared, hampers the fight against communism.

"Perhaps more democracy not less—" Sullivan began but Chhan Samkai was already beyond him inspecting the hamlet. Another soldier passed. In each hand, suspended by the threads of their hair, were two heads.

The hamlet was vacant, lifeless. Sullivan looked into the huts. All personal belongings had been removed. The firefight had had no direct impact on civilians. Still Sullivan felt his skin crawling with ghosts. Not the ghosts of soldiers. Three dead FANK. Nine dead NVA. Somehow, odd, he thought, but the FANK squad had caught them napping. Perhaps, he thought, overconfident. He walked to the next home. All about were FANK rear-echelon personnel. They'd come from along the column, come after Colonel Chhan had ordered a company from his one decent battalion to secure "the front," come to see the FANK battle victory.

Where, Sullivan thought, have the villagers gone? Are they refugees in one of the villages? Perhaps Pa Kham or Rumlong. Or had they fled, en masse, to Phnom Penh? Or perhaps to the other side?

At the entrance to the village a huge flame leaped, fuel oil or kerosene burning, billowing black smoke, then catching the pyre's branches and straw, and the smoke changing, becoming thick white clouds, then turning dark again as the bodies of the FANK soldiers incinerated. At the base of the funeral pyre three women wailed and a cluster of young children cried. Sullivan too cried, cried inside for them. Without their men who would support them? Cambodia had no soldiers' insurance, no aid to orphans or widows. Let them return, walk back, to the capital. Relief agencies might feed them. Vathana would care for them were they in her sector but they'd never get that far.

The decapitated torsos of the NVA squad had been dragged to the village center. FANK troops propped one headless body up by a concrete cistern—a bowl not unlike a large birdbath used to catch rainwater for drinking. From the back the soldier appeared to be drinking but from the front fluids dripped the other way and amid the olive drab uniforms and under the mist-gray sky the only color Sullivan saw was the red of the cistern.

"It's good luck," a voice said in English.

Sullivan turned slowly. He barely realized the words were in his native tongue. "Hum?"

"They think it's good luck," an American woman said. "Ritual decapitation. It's supposed to ensure success."

Sullivan stared harshly, uncomprehending.

"Oh come on, Captain!" the woman said briskly. "You've seen it before. They were shot and killed with rifles you gave these hoodlums."

"Who the hell are you?"

"Rita Donaldson. *Washington News-Times.*"

Hans Mitterschmidt waited for the Khmer Viet Minh cadreman to complete his introduction. In the camp hall were a dozen North Viet Namese guards, half as many KVM guards, numerous dignitaries and two score elite Khmer sappers and masked agents.

"Colonel Mitterschmidt," the cadreman concluded, "is both a demolitions expert and an expert on racial harmony." The East German and his interpreter came forward.

"This," the German said in French, and his Viet Namese interpreter translated into Khmer, "is our new and most sophisticated underwater mine. It can sink any vessel, any riverine craft or freighter that sails the Mekong."

As he waited for the interpreter to catch up he laid his hands on the large metal ovoid. A dozen probe or sensor sockets awaiting their attachments peered from the top and sides like pineapple eyes. The Khmer soldiers stretched their necks to see the weapon which they'd heard would bottle up shipping for good. "Come closer," Mitterschmidt said, and motioned to the small dark boys as if they were pets. "These men," the colonel said, indicating the boys and turning to his Viet Namese escort, "they've all been trained in land mines?"

"Yes," the escort answered. "All are said to be expert sappers."

Mitterschmidt took a deep breath and somberly began his lecture. Amongst the Khmers both factions were represented. In the far back, hair cut, oiled, combed up and back, with heavy glasses, a nose expanded by having bamboo tubes jammed into the nostrils, and a face covered with a bandana, was Ly Bellon, a.k.a. Cahuom Samnang, Little Rabbit, Met Nang and other names. He had been spirited from his company, in accordance with orders directly from Met Sar via Met Mita, disguised and sent to the mine-training class.

His ability to change and to be accepted had always been one of Nang's greatest talents, but to have slipped into this group was his greatest such feat. Only two days before, five days after Met Nu had helped him take control of the unnamed hamlet, the order had reached him. Relations between the Khmer Krahom and the NVA were, on the surface, being repaired. The class represented to the high commands the reconciliation neither believed in but to which both paid lip service. The Viet Namese had offered to train forty Khmers, twenty chosen from their long-established supporters, twenty to be recommended by Met Sar. The class would be a one-day seminar on new underwater mines and on a new shoulder-fired, heat-seeking missile. Both weapons could be used by the armies attacking the FANK offensive.

On 18 October Nang and his comrades shuffled into the small compound hidden in a plantation east of Baray. The entire forest had seemed alive with troops and machinery of the NVA 7th Division and all day Nang heard more trucks arriving. In the far distance the land shivered as B-52s searched for the advancing army.

"Combatant Ly, disassemble it again," Mitterschmidt said to Nang. "Yes, like that. No, you dunderhead! Each time you make the same mistake. You'll blow yourself from here to kingdom come."

Nang bowed. "*Oui.* I will try harder, Colonel."

Mitterschmidt stared at the masked boy with the scarred, stiff hand. "You don't want two hands like that, do you?"

"No sir. I've got it now."

"*Das ist gut!* Hum. Now"—he walked to a side table where he had a motion picture camera—"I wish to take a film of all my students working. In Germany they'll want to see how well you learn. Maybe how well you fight." To the escort officer the foreign colonel said, "Soon, eh? Soon you'll let me film a battle."

Met Sar's lips pulled into a thin smile. Then his eyes squinted and his smile broadened into a toothy grin. With his staff about him in the temporary command bunker hidden below a refugee shack in Baray he studied the new reports, weighed their impact. Met Nang's had provided immense detail on the NVA 7th Division. In the four days since Krahom sappers had received the new training, forces had converged. Sar's smile dropped away. He puckered his lips, puffed out his cheeks. Snarled.

By mid-October most elements were in staging areas, ready for the great battle for the Northern Corridor. Though always a dangerous road, Highway 6 to Kompong Thom was officially passable for all but four days during the third quarter of 1971. This is notable. Operation Chenla II was launched to relieve the five-month-old siege of Kompong Thom which was being supplied by air, yet the roadway, if not the surrounding countryside, remained free. Where the NVA had attacked trained FANK units they had not advanced—not because of air power, though U.S., ARVN, FANK and even Thai fighter-bombers certainly hampered Communist advances—but because those FANK infantry and artillery units had learned to concentrate their firepower effectively.

Now FANK's column, directed by a frantic Lon Nol, held the highway from Skoun through Baray to Kompong Thom. The NVA 5th and 7th divisions (with forward headquarters at Chup) were ready to pounce from rubber plantations to the east; the 91st, which had kept Kompong Thom terrified since April, had shifted south and west. Major NVA supply routes from the Northeast had been extensively expanded with new all-weather road networks sweeping across the high plain of Stung Treng, Preah Vihear and Kompong Thom provinces. And American and RVNAF bombing sorties had increased, first hitting NVA supply lines and then suspected troop massings. (Official U.S. bombing policy in Cambodia had changed. On 16 January 1971 the Department of Defense had announced the "potential" employment of any or all of its air assets anywhere over Khmer territory. Department of Defense officials added the qualifier [justification], "if the enemy units might ultimately threaten Americans in South Viet Nam".) By October 1971 one hundred planes a day, approximately forty B-52s and sixty fighter-bombers, were attempting to interdict and destroy the advancing North Viet Namese.

Sar cupped his chin in one hand. The NVA, he thought, are hard to judge. Why had they shifted, vastly increasing the delivery of supplies to the Khmer Krahom, offered yotheas the most advanced training, offering again, essentially, reconciliation? Those bastards, Sar thought. For them it's 1968 again. That's why. That's it. They never act without design. We're the sacrifice, eh? Like the VC at Tet, eh? Ah, but Khmers can see the fangs of the stinging red ants who wear the smiles of brothers.

"Sar," Met Phan interrupted his thoughts.

"Yes?"

"The latest meteorological reports have arrived."

"And . . ."

"The winds have begun the shift to bring the seasonal change."

"And the waters?"

"They've peaked. Last week every day they rose a centimeter. This week, no rise at all."

"When will they recede enough for the tanks?"

"Another month, maybe." Met Phan returned to his plotting of FANK and NVA units on a large acetate-covered map of the entire North.

Met Dy approached. "Sar."

"Yes?"

"The arrival of four battalions from Kompong Chhnang brings our troop strength about the corridor to 5,440."

"Forty-four companies?"

"Forty-eight . . . formed into sixteen battalions."

"Have we been able to get radios to them all?"

"Two of Met Mita's companies are still without, but porters are bringing them the ones captured with the Kompong Thom garrison."

"Mita's companies came from Kompong Thom. Why didn't they receive them before?"

"Captured materiel is brought to the Center for equitable redistribution."

"Uh." Sar paused. He was angry but he did not want his anger to show. "Do you have the overlay of their locations?"

"Yes."

"Command and control"—Sar shook his hand at Met Dy's face—"is predicated upon effective communications, isn't it?"

"I understand," Dy said defensively.

"Phan! Let's . . ." Sar stood. The men arranged the overlay on Phan's plotted map and quietly studied the patterns. Clearly, in blue, along the line of Highway 6, the FANK units looked like a dashed serpent winding from Skoun to Kompong Thom. Surrounding the serpent in the paddies and low forest were evenly scattered black dots, Krahom companies, like ants searching for food. Then clustered in three groups, NVA units made up an outer pattern which looked like phantom arrowheads: one in the west aiming just south of Santuk; two in the east, one pointed at Baray, one pointed south, possibly an attempt to skirt the battle and head toward Phnom Penh. Sar stuck a pudgy index finger on the map, traced the arrowheads and their possible trajectories. The men spoke with controlled passion, suggesting moves to each other. FANK was so predictable that their discussion of the national army's movement lasted less than a minute. It was the NVA that concerned them. How could the Krahom appear to help them and simultaneously ensure their defeat? How could Angkar escape the fate of the Viet Cong, which lost half its troops and all its political clout at Tet 1968 and was usurped by the very same devils who now asked for reconciliation and joint operations in this attack to destroy FANK forever? Yes, they, the Krahom, could help their fellow internationalists, but it was supposed to be the other way around. The NVA, in Sar's mind, was supposed to help *him!*

"Reth!"

"Yes sir." Sar's bodyguard came from the adjoining bunker room.

"Send Nim here."

"Yes sir."

Met Nim carried another overlay. Here plotted were the bombing raids of the last six weeks as compiled by Krahom sources across the northern sector. The four men studied the composite picture. Again a pattern emerged—both in color and concentration. The shift of NVA units was clearly matched, if somewhat lagged, by the bombing runs. In the past week the area about Krek, the area of heaviest concentration of the two previous weeks, had received only a smattering of purple splotches. But back roads from Stung Treng across the Siambok River to Rovieng and Kompong Trabek were solid lines, and the plantation areas east of Kratie and north of Kompong Cham were under a growing purple mist. The corridor along Highway 6 was all but untouched and neither Krahom nor NVA encampments had been hit.

"Have KCh-110 move to the Chinit River, here." Sar indicated an area on the map to Met Phan. "And have the 104th come south toward Rumlong. Here."

"Why not leave the 104th where it is? They'll be able to . . ."

"I don't want them to," Sar snapped.

Alone again, Sar sat back. He planted his elbows on the field table, grasped his hair, and hung his head from his hands. A flaw, he thought. He closed his eyes trying to see the flaw. They make tremendous advances but in them there are flaws. It is only a matter of exploiting them. Oh to see them drop. To see them drop their guard, to see . . .

Met Meas broke into Sar's thoughts. "Sar. There's news from Phnom Penh."

"Yes! What?"

"Lon Nol has declared a state of emergency and abolished the constitution!"

"He's done what?!"

"Abolished the . . ."

Before Meas could repeat the news, Sar broke into a loud guffaw. "Ha! Ha! Haw! Oh what a wonderful buffoon," he shrieked. "He's such a fool. Such a fool. . . . Such a fool." Sar gasped for breath. Staff men laughed with him, at him. "From him," Sar boomed, "it's like plucking candy from a baby. Ha! Now, get back to work! We're closer to victory then ever." Sar's smile wrinkled his whole face. "Meas," he said quietly. He motioned him over. "Make a copy of Met Phan's plottings of the yuons. Be sure it reaches the right people."

Again Sar leaned forward and hung his head from his hands. This time he did not close his eyes. To see their concentration break, he thought. To see Angkar annihilate them, annihilate their *thralls* and drive the yuon army from Kampuchea. Then Angkar will inherit the revolution and all powers will pass to Khmer Patriots who will be led by the Brotherhood of the Pure.

"You know how your transistor works, yes?"

"Yes."

"This is the same," Nang said. "Met Duch, you must struggle to overcome your fear of learning."

"It's so heavy."

"Ah, but you are a proven fighter and very strong. I wouldn't entrust the radio to just anyone." Duch glanced up at Nang. His face showed suspicion and dread. "Also," Nang added, "because you'll be doing extra work, your ration shall be doubled. Two rice tubes each day." Immediately Nang saw Duch's reluctance fade.

"You know the American radio?" Duch said matter-of-factly, hiding his easy acquiescence.

"When I was trained in the far north we learned all radios." Nang was delighted. For an hour he and Duch practiced calling Met Mita's command post, practiced coordinating the squeeze-to-transmit, release-to-receive lever. "You learn so fast," Nang encouraged the boy. "When I first tried, it took me days."

"Perhaps," Duch answered his commander, "I have a better teacher."

Nang put his hand on Duch's back and rubbed. "Angkar is very proud of you."

Before dawn, 25 October 1971, Nang's Krahom infantry company 2/KT 104 received its first radio order. They were to send, immediately, a runner to the battalion command post for orders. The mechanics of communication were easier to assimilate than the principles and practice of passing commands over the air.

The farmers were slow that day leaving the hamlet for the paddies. Their work was far ahead of schedule with the assistance of the black-clad boys. The women, too, seemed to drag out the morning chores. Everyone had learned of the radio. Now they wished to hear the news the runner would bring.

The rains had abated but not stopped and the morning broke gray, as it had for weeks. Children sprinted from peasant house doorways to the village edge where the land fell away into the paddies. They stood there, watching, shrieking, jumping about, happy. Then they ran back home, wet, excited. During the night the earth to the east had quaked and the elders had grumbled and repeated slogan-thoughts taught by Nang and other yotheas, repeated fears and hates about bombs they'd never experienced. The quaking had been far off. Some had not felt it at all and these grumbled about the platoon of *neary* who'd come, caught the other outsiders, assassinated them and their two village assistants, then left, vanished, leaving only the unburied bodies in the near paddy.

Yotheas joined the children, enjoying the morning leisure, enjoying the company of the villagers as if they were family they had not seen in an age, and enjoying the company of one another, free, for the moment, of struggle. The congealing of an infantry unit is strange chemistry and the 2d of the KT 104th was, as a unit, new. Less than a month earlier they had been six separate squads whose only common bond was a loose or strong tie to Met Nang. In short order they'd been increased, filled out so each squad had four three-man cells, then formed, been formed, into three platoons: Tiger, Monkey and Rabbit. The platoons were given leaders, joined to form the company. The idea of each yothea being responsible to a battalion called the 104th was awkward in their minds. Responsibility to Angkar was easier, for Angkar was, to them, Kampuchea—was Kampucheans for Kampuchea, was the very soul of the revolution. But the bonding to middle echelons of organization was weak. And the bonding to one another, in the absence of combat, also was pale. At times they fought not for one another, that would come later, but for an ideology built on slogans and catchphrases and a mixture of love, respect and fear of Met Nang.

"He's coming!"

"Where?"

"I saw a flash in the trees."

"You can't see that far!"

"Says who . . ."

"He is coming!"

The runner loped from the concealment of the trees to the exposure of the dike. At first he looked small, looked as if he were barely approaching, as if he were stationary bouncing up and down afar on the long dike. Slowly there was more paddy behind him than in front. His speed seemed to quicken and he became a man, no longer a toy.

"Nang! Met Nang!" the runner screamed as the distance fell to fifty meters. "Nang! Get me to him!"

"What message are you carrying?" yotheas asked.

"They're coming," he panted. "Get me . . . to . . . Nang!"

"Who?" yotheas shouted, trotting with the runner.

In minutes Met Hon emerged from the house into which the runner had disappeared. "Met Nang wants the platoon leaders and one man from each cell. Now."

Farmers who had reached the close paddies returned. Women who had set to work braiding palm mats or preparing the day's meals put the tasks aside. The unnamed hamlet had never experienced such suspense, never, until the 2d of the 104th moved in with its violence.

The cell and two of the three platoon leaders exited the house of Hem Teng where Met Nang had been invited to set up his CP. To the boy they were somber, cold. Not one deviated from a direct line to his cellmates. Not one answered a question from the villagers. Not one let even the slightest grin or warmth betray his face. Immediately they armed themselves, packed their rucksacks and formed. At first the villagers were amused, then a pall crept over them and permeated their damp souls. Slowly they meandered to the village center, toward the end where Nang, Hon, Rath and Duch remained sequestered with the hamlet chief, his wife and his two sons.

Met Bun, leader of Rabbit Platoon, burst through the growing crowd. He'd been fishing in a nearby creek swollen with flood-water yet full of hundreds of silvery fish with red bellies. "There are new orders?" He blurted the words as he entered the house.

"Yes," Nang answered loudly. "The Americans will bomb here in thirty minutes."

"Then we must evacuate."

"Yes. We're giving the fighters a few minutes to collect their gear and tell their hosts. In a moment we'll tell those outside. The evacuation has been organized."

In the hamlet the yotheas circulated, not to tell their hosts but to disarm the militia boys. In the few peasants who witnessed these actions a wariness of the yotheas spiked. Unseen by most, the black-clad company abused their Khmer hospitality, rifled the homes at which they'd been welcomed, taking food, money, knives, machetes, any items they desired.

"The Americans are going to bomb!" Nang shouted. "Everyone must go. Everyone."

"Wait, let me tell them." Hem Teng grabbed Nang's sleeve. Nang whipped his arm away.

"The bombers are coming," yotheas shouted. "Go home. Grab a blanket. Follow us. Run to the treeline."

"You said . . ." Hem Teng was at a loss. In his house Nang had been adamant about reducing panic but now he and every yothea promoted it.

"Run. Run. Run. Let me help you. We must rush." "No. Leave that." "Don't take anything. One blanket." "The bombers killed a village last night. Now they're coming here." "Follow us."

The first families poured onto the dike down which the runner had come. Before them, two cells urged them to quicken the pace. Yotheas dropped back to help the youngest children and the very old while those in front demanded that the quick clear the dike road as soon as possible. "When they come they'll strafe the dike," yotheas told the peasants, told one another. "They shoot everyone. Get to the treeline. We'll bring the children."

More families poured onto the muddy dike. Peasants fell in the slick slime only to be jerked up by yotheas. "Don't stop! Don't stop! Run."

In the hamlet many lingered—some refusing outright to leave, others packing belongings. "Don't take that. You'll be back tonight. One day at the most."

Rush! Rush! Rush! The pace was frenetic and in less than ten minutes all but the stubborn had reached the dike conduit to the sanctuary of the treeline. Even Hem Teng, his wife and eldest son had left.

"There are no bombers." Hem Daravong laughed cynically when Nang reentered the village chief's home. Nang smiled but did not answer. "What will you do to them?"

"They'll be protected," Nang said softly. "The bombers did kill a village last night."

"What village?" Daravong's nares flared. This ugly boy was repugnant, his ideas repulsive, his organization loathsome.

"To the east," Nang said.

From the dike there were shots. The first people were reaching the trees. "Don't stop," yotheas ordered. "Follow that trail. It leads to our last camp in the grove to the north. Not you, Grandma. You go this way. It'll be best if the old and very young take shelter amongst the column on the highway. The Americans won't bomb there. We'll be sure you're brought back together. Head for the road. Head for the highway."

"Would you like to join us?" Nang asked Daravong. "You know we are the only true representatives of the Khmer people."

"So you say."

"Come with me."

"If I don't? Are you going to kill me?"

"No. I won't kill you. If you wish to kill yourself that's up to you. Now"—Nang's voice became stern—"go to the dike."

"No."

"I'm under orders to deny you to the Viet Namese."

"To what?"

"If you don't come with us, you'll be captured and conscripted by the yuons. You'll be used against your own people."

Reluctantly, bitterly, Daravong acquiesced, moved. "We won't return, will we?"

"There is a more beautiful village in the North," Nang answered. Again his voice was soft.

On the dike the two boys turned. Black-clad figures were scurrying from house to house. Smoke rose from beyond the closest row, then from every structure. Flames leaped from the smoke. From the paddies about the hamlet air was sucked into a swirling rising firestorm. In minutes the settlement ceased to exist.

A tremendous thunderclap jerked Sullivan from his bent-back sleep. He sprang up, awake, alert yet disoriented. In the dark his left hand searched for Vathana, his right grabbed the M-16 he'd commandeered a week earlier. Another thunderclap jolted him, jolted the sky, and the rain shook loose and crashed hard on the sedan roof. He shook his head. Amid the sky's cacophony he heard other rumbles. He squeezed his eyes. Opened them. His night fantasies vanished as if he'd never dreamt.

For ten days Captain Sullivan had visited various FANK units, visited, observed, was pleased, was horrified. Rita Donaldson had dogged him at first but her mission was to grab a story and scoot back to the capital to file it before another reporter filed the same observation, thought or impression which they called news. Still he, Sullivan, found himself looking over his shoulder each time he approached a FANK unit.

Two weeks had passed since the vanguard of Colonel Um Savath's task force had reached Kompong Thom and the column had settled, stalled. On the raised roadway twenty thousand troops plus dependants bivouacked. From Skoun to Pa Kham and up through Tang Kouk, Rumlong, Baray, Tang Krasang, Puk Yuk and on into the provincial capital, FANK had camped without spreading out, staying high if not dry, in the lanes of Highway 6 above the flooded land. Officially the road was open, but the congestion of the column made it, for cargo trucking, all but impassable. Sullivan had been able to move up as far as the Chinit River bridge north of Baray only by bribing his Khmer escort and driver and they in turn bribing various unit control personnel. There he unobtrusively counted the men of one battalion carried as 450 strong. He'd found forty guarding the bridge, seventy-five to eighty living with their families in the dependant camp. In his mind he'd shaken his head. It was the worst unit he'd found. The degree of deceit appalled him. Ten percent was one thing, seventy-five another. These bastards, he'd lamented in his mind to Vathana, this elite scum. Immediately "elite" brought to mind Madame Pech, or Sisowath as she now called herself, and the "elite" who were milking the American cow while honest commanders had to beg for supplies, while troops of the most vile had to pay for rations, medical supplies and ammunition.

The return trip had presented more difficulty. On the twenty-second a trickle of peasants had mixed with the dependants. At first he'd thought it was farmers and hamlet women come to sell their produce and wares but the people had had nothing with them, had not stopped, had not set up shop. By the twenty-third it seemed clear that only the old and very young were coming to the highway. "Has someone talked to these people?" he'd asked his escort. "Of course," the liaison had answered, indignant. Immediately he'd known he'd blown an opportunity, had placed the man on the defensive. The next day the highway had been clogged not only by the column but with hundreds of pushcarts, with thousands upon thousands of children and thousands more of enfeebled elders shuffling along north or south, or simply sitting on any open bit of blacktop—all without provisions, without pots to cook in, without tarps for shelter. They begged for food. Surrounded by six hundred square kilometers of ripening rice they begged because they had no way to harvest, to thresh, to winnow or to cook.

By the afternoon of the twenty-fifth, as the sedan crept at a speed slower than a child's walk, Sullivan had not been able to stand it any longer. Rumors of forced hamlet evacuations and impending bombings were rampant. Some elders wailed with unrestrained grief while children sobbed or shrieked. He had reached the town of Tang Kouk, the section of roadway which ran tangentially west of the town, when he requested the escort and driver to let him out to stretch and urinate. From there he'd meandered amongst the people.

A kilometer south he'd seen the road rising to the bridge over the main drainage canal between Tang Kouk and Pa Kham. Sullivan had walked toward that point, weaved his way between soldiers and dependants, APCs and oxcarts, terror-stricken peasants and a few hotshot junior officers with souped-up jeeps. "Do you speak French?" he called to various peasant groups. "*Français? Français?*"

An old man. "*Oui.*"

At last. "Why have all the people come to the highway?"

"We were told to come."

"Who told you?"

"Does it matter?"

"Certainly."

"Then why doesn't the government ask us? Why not the army big shots?"

"I will tell them to do so."

"Now the government comes back." The old peasant shrugged his shoulders. "Now the yuons come back. Now the Patriots. Who cares?"

"Then why do you leave your land?"

"I plow. I plant. I weed. I harvest. The government tells us to get out, the Communists are coming. We hear that on the radio. The Communists tell us to get out, the government is coming. We see them on the road. Then the Patriots tell us to flee, the planes are coming. Good, let the planes come. They can destroy all the soldiers. Good, eh? They will destroy my fields and my dikes. Not good, eh! Not good for me. The Patriots burned the village so no one will capture it. Not good for me, eh! The planes come and blow up my son. Go away! You go away."

Another thunderclap jarred the sedan. Sullivan gritted his teeth. The first bombing raid in the western part of Caoutchouco Plantation east of Phum Chamkar was flown a few minutes past midnight on 24 October. Acting on ground-sighting reports, a single B-52 released eighty-four 500-pound bombs in a target area said to house an NVA regiment. Over the next two days the bombing increased significantly.

Then, close by to the south, a huge fire cloud leaped from the earth. Then came the explosion, then the concussion sweeping the bivouac like an angry wind. Blackness returned and the rain beat hard on the roof. Sullivan flung the door open. Already the escort officer had leaped from the car, from the roadway, and was off somewhere in the dark murk of the paddies. Sullivan stood tall, looked about. In the distance he could feel the unmistakable rumbling quake of high-level sorties pummeling the plantations to the east. About him people dashed in aimless frenzy or rolled back to sleep or simply sat, frozen, unable to think of a direction to go. Just north, at the intersection to Tang Kouk, several FANK APCs turned on their headlights, aimed themselves toward the deluged fields, silhouetted themselves by their own lights. To the south there was more commotion. Sullivan reached into the sedan, grabbed his ammo bandoleers, his steel pot, his weapon. He slammed the door. The distant rumble came again, lasted less than a minute, then stopped. He marched south, toward the bridge, the commotion. Where the road began its rise over the canal, a Patton tank fired its machine guns, red tracers looping into the downpour for 300 meters then vanishing as if extinguished or blocked from view. Candles, flashlights and straw torches illuminated the road. Soldiers ran from their units to the dependant camps to make sure their families were safe, and from the dependant camps soldiers ran to their unit loggers to receive orders and prepare for an attack.

Sullivan walked. He cursed himself for not understanding the language, for not having taken the PRC-25 radio from the sedan even if he couldn't understand the transmissions. He walked determinedly, cursing himself and his country for the half-assed effort, for the Nixon administration's seeming approval of Lon Nol's latest political blunder, for not having seen the attack coming and for not having advised—yes, damn it, Rita Donaldson or not—advised, found a way to subtly convince Colonel Chhan of the intelligence importance of the road refugees. He stopped. He had to have the radio. Now he ran, frantic, anguished by the thought that someone might have stolen it. The distance was short. He was there in minutes and indeed four young boys were pillaging the vehicle.

"No way, jack!" He growled, snarled, barked in English, grabbed one child and threw him off the road. Then he rammed his face into the backseat, felt the floor. "Oh thank god!" He strapped the radio on and jogged toward the bridge, his helmet banging even though he held it, the light web gear barely keeping the PRC-25 from smashing his lumbar vertebrae.

Sullivan glanced at his watch. The luminescence was dull. He moved toward a large straw torch. 0310. To the elders and children clustered below the fire he shouted in French, thinking, Damn em if they don't understand, "You make yourselves targets with that light. Target! Understand? If there are—" in his anger he almost said "gooks," then caught himself—"Viet gunners, they'll see you. Understand?" No recognition. No response. A hard long quaking vibrated the road. In the distance—how far?—southeast where the plantation land jutted into the paddies and approached Highway 6—how far?—six, eight, ten kilometers, flashes, faint, not even certain. "Target! Understand?" Wet faces in the torchlight hardened, with fear, with hatred. Backs turned. Go away. You go away.

Sullivan marched off, south. APCs and tanks had clustered near the bridge approach. Spotlights and mortar flares illuminated the twisted steel beams stabbing the blackness at eerie angles.

"Monsieur! Monsieur Captain!" It was Captain Sisowath Suong, Colonel Chhan Samkai's aide who had ordered Sullivan to leave Tum Nop when the skirmish between FANK APCs and infantry had broken out. "The bridges are out."

"I can see that," Sullivan answered, angry, sarcastic.

"No. No, monsieur. Not just here but over the Chinit north of Baray and near Phum Chamkar. All the main bridges. We are trapped."

At the edge of the plantation forests Colonel Hans Mitterschmidt filmed bright bursting flashes against the black night curtain. The B-52 devastation three kilometers south jiggled the saturated earth beneath him as if it were Jell-O. Uncomfortably his NVA escorts held oiled parasols over him and over the camera.

"Sir, we're much too exposed," Lieutenant Nam Thay cautioned him in French.

"Not so," the colonel responded. "I want to move forward."

"It's not safe, sir."

"I didn't come here to be safe. What are they doing over there?"

"That's the 209th Regiment. They're preparing the battlefield, sir."

"Excellent. But so noisy?"

"There's no one to hear. The lackey army doesn't send patrols."

Colonel Mitterschmidt dropped to one knee and hunched over his camera, a modified Bolex H-16 EBM motion picture camera with a specially designed 8mm to 90mm zoom lens set on a gunstock mount. As Lieutenant Thay held a flashlight, Mitterschmidt removed exposed film and inserted new. Then he placed the exposed film in a plastic bag and put that in the waterproof ammo can his porter carried attached to his rucksack. For several days the East German had filmed the NVA 7th Division in high-gear motion, closing in on their chosen battlefield. With the 7th came the 40th Artillery Regiment: antiaircraft and 130mm field gun batteries, 122mm rocket teams, and 120mm mortar squads. Quickly the infantry had shifted southwest, seemingly jumping from one forested area to the next, always moving, attempting to avoid aerial detection and subsequent bombing. Behind them came the artillery and, interspersed, the armor. The weather had been advantageous, a continual heavy mask of clouds rendering normal visual aerial detection ineffective. The more sophisticated electronic, radar, infrared and laser target detection systems had picked up the general movement but without cross validation most targets had been denied at embassy level. Behind the attack force had come long, heavily laden truck convoys—the concentration of heat-producing engines giving the bombers their only targets.

With each kilometer covered, Mitterschmidt had grown more and more anxious, exhausted. To him each sight was new and he viewed it all as if framed, bracketed by the edge of the film. Whenever possible he filmed the troops in their prepared environment. In the past day his travel group had seen an intermittent parade of peasants marshaled toward some rear point by black-clad Khmer soldiers. These, too, he filmed as he ogled each group, searching for his Khmer students, knowing how ludicrous was his thought that elite *dac cong* might be used this way but unable to overcome the racial stereotyping, thinking all Khmers looked alike and thus one of the boy-soldiers should be known to him. Then there had been the first glimpse, beyond the forest, broken by vegetation, shrouded by rain, yet there, unmistakably, of a land torched. By early evening a double score of fires had dotted the flat land and the smell and sight of smoke quickened, neared, as night had fallen.

"Lieutenant." A messenger came to Nam Thay. "There's good news."

Mitterschmidt watched the two men, uncomfortable in his lack of understanding of their words. In the darkness they were black silhouettes against a black backdrop. The German looked east. Before him the land fell away, the canopy disappeared. What earlier had been flatlands alive with fire now seemed to be an endless black void. By 0330 hours the rain softened and the fogmist fell to hug the earth in a layer no thicker than a man's height. Across the unseen quagmire the raised highway emerged, a line of lights—torches, flashlights, headlights, spotlights, and mortar-launched parachute flares.

A second messenger came to Thay, spoke quickly and left. "There's good word, sir." The Viet Namese escort officer beamed. "You're to be congratulated."

"The bridges?"

"Yes sir. They floated the mines downstream to them with complete success. All three have been dropped."

"Without *dac cong*?"

"The sappers floated with them to the bridge supports, then floated on."

"Is that one?" Mitterschmidt asked as a parachute flare lit a twisted sculpture in the distance.

"That's the Tang Kouk Canal bridge."

"I should like to film that when it's lighter."

From behind them in the forest the tremendous bang of two 130mm guns lobbing a salvo toward the small airfield between Tang Kouk and Rumlong made the German dive flat. His fear-leap caused Thay to respond alike. A minute later the explosion of outgoing erupted again and both men sat on the wet forest floor and laughed. Then again and again the blasts. Farther north a sister unit launched a series of 122mm rockets. Still the 130s banged out their rounds. With each salvo the ground jumped. The concussions hit Mitterschmidt's ears as hard as if he were being hit by fists. Now he did not smile. Methodically he cleaned the Bolex. Three kilometers south, almost exactly where the bombers had hit earlier, there was more firing. A forested plantation ridge protruded into the vast sea of rice fields to within a few kilometers of Phum Pa Kham. From it four 120mm mortar squads were unleashing a continual barrage. All along the twelve-kilometer stretch from Pa Kham to Tang Kouk and Rumlong shells burst, and under the shelling, under the tully fog, the regiments of the NVA 7th Division moved out, ran along prepared trails, along dikes and through paddies with shallow water cover, trotted forward in the dark following the dim red or green flashlights of guides who had moved in as the farmers had evacuated. Behind the first wave of light infantry came a second. Behind the second a third and with the third trotted Hans Mitterschmidt, his two escorts and his personal porter.

At 0330 hours 26 October 1971 the siege and shelling of Pa Kham, estimated population 9,000 began. At 0335 hours shells began to rain down on Tang Kouk, estimated population 8,000. An hour later the airfield north of Tang Kouk was probed by ground assault teams. At 0440 hours the shelling of Rumlong, estimated population 12,000, commenced. The shelling of all four sites and the connecting roadway was heavy and sustained.

"Get them off the road!" Sullivan screamed at Sergeant Seng Sovat as he recognized Colonel Chhan's enlisted aide. Sullivan grabbed Seng's shirt shoulder with his left hand. With his right he pointed furiously at a mixed group of dependants, soldiers and refugees. "Them! Them!" He gestured. "Off there!" He pointed to the dark murky waters off the west side of the road. "Shit!" he cussed himself. For an hour he had coursed up and down the roadway attempting to force organization on anarchy. "Where's the colonel?" he railed in French. "Perimeter! Here!"

The refugee farmers needed little prodding. Their section of roadway wasn't under attack but both north and south were being pulverized with thousands of rounds. Fear grabbed them. The bridge to Pa Kham, almost within spitting distance, was out. Terror grabbed them. They had nothing. Their past had been destroyed in the fires. Their future, the bridge to Phnom Penh, to reinforcements, to escape, was a twisted mass of steel with the long center span lying one end up, the other in the deep canal. The old, pulling and chasing the very young, hobbled over the edge. "Stay with Grandpa! Don't get lost." "Where's Mama!" "Gone with the Patriots. We'll find her later. Come down. Come down here. Help your grandmother."

At first the FANK infantry soldiers of the First Brigade Group just north of the bridge panicked. They, like the peasants, scattered, dove, ran, fled. But quickly half realized there was no place to go. To swim or float the canal would only place them in the mortar explosions to the south. To sprint north would risk the artillery barrage on Tang Kouk or the airstrip. East was the enemy, west the uncharted paddies and formidable swamp. With no place to go, with their families hugging the west bank of the road, half the FANK troops rose and assembled in fire teams, squads and platoons. Those with training, no matter their rank, took charge while those who'd bought their office either obeyed or fled, huddled with the civilians or shouldered rifles and slid off the east bank into the paddies, sliding down the embankment under the tully fog until their feet and legs were in the cool water and their eyes were below the tops of the stalks—trained and untrained, officers and peons, a concealed perimeter without cover, without fields of fire, without observation ability—waiting, without offensive, counteroffensive or defensive tactical plans.

By 0500 hours the sky had lightened, the clouds had thinned, the rain had ceased. Along the road the six APCs of the brigade's armor battalion had dispersed—two, with the section's only tank, near the bridge ramp to cover that flank if the NVA launched a waterborne assault from the canal, then one every half kilometer to the outskirts of Tang Kouk. Sullivan found Colonel Chhan Samkai and his command post in a troop bus, behind the first lone APC north of the southern flank. To Sullivan the CP was a criminal cluster-fuck. Chhan Samkai was in a funk, a pout which he did not, could not, hide from the American captain.

Diplomatically, the colonel's senior aide-de-camp, Captain Sisowath Suong, greeted the scowling Sullivan. "Son of a bitch," Sullivan growled. If he could have, he would have taken charge retrospectively, back three or four months, back long enough to have ensured that the men were paid, equipped and trained.

"Pardon?"

"I said"—Sullivan curbed his anger—" 'son of a bitch.' " Then he laughed. He shook his head as might one standing with beleaguered teammates. "This is the shits," he said, coughed, laughed out the words in French. "We are caught with our pants down, no?"

The aide laughed in the oppressive atmosphere of the CP inside the bus. "Yes and no," he answered. "Let them come. You talk to the forward air controllers and the bombers will kill them all."

"Have there been orders? The APCs are so far apart. Could they be moved closer to cover each other?"

"He tells us," Colonel Chhan injected, "he tells us to create an illusion."

"An illusion?" Sullivan smiled with false sympathy. "Who tells—"

"Our orders come directly from General Lon Nol. He has given the identical order to every commander. 'Create the illusion of many soldiers and frighten the enemy away.' "

Sullivan swallowed. He attempted to hide his disapproval.

"Here, Captain"—Chhan motioned to a field table with an unrolled map—"here is the situation."

Sullivan studied the map. The entire corridor was in disarray. With the three bridges down Kompong Thom was cut off. The middle column between Tang Kouk and the Chinit River was isolated; the southern section, which might expect reinforcements from Phnom Penh, was suffering the heaviest artillery barrage of the war. From Radio Phnom Penh, not military channels, Lon Nol was urging his troops to destroy the *thmils*, to fight the holy fight against Communist atheists. As they listened, as Suong translated, Sullivan removed the PRC-25 from his back. The NVA 130s shifted south to the roadway just below Tang Kouk. In the clearing dawn, clouds from the explosions could be seen rising only a kilometer north. South by the bridge ramp sniper fire dinged off an APCs shell. The gunners returned cannon and machine gun fire, spraying haphazardly. The urge to fire rolled up the FANK line—first a few, then entire sections, then an entire kilometer of troops wasting their ammunition against unseen "targets." Sullivan keyed the handset. "Birddog Oscar Victory One, this is . . ."

Fourteen kilometers north-northeast of John L. Sullivan's location, the 2d Company of the KT 104th Battalion of the Krahom Army of the North marched single file down a mud-slick dike, marched west under the trajectory of the NVA rockets blasting Rumlong, marched toward a battery of FANK 105mm howitzers that was answering the NVA shot for shot. The FANK battery, one of the few that was well trained, paid and supplied, had laid and registered its guns when the column halted a week before, and for a week they'd improved their defensive position. Using ground radar to determine the launch sites of the NVA rockets the nationals systematically fired half-battery salvos into the forest.

Quietly Nang's troops advanced. Overhead the rockets roared horrible roars, passing low, impacting and exploding fifteen hundred meters ahead, ahead where the blasting of the 105s terrified the Krahom boys. To the boy, they were frightened. It was one thing to conquer a lightly armed hamlet, one thing to run the unarmed villagers to detention centers for further evacuation, one thing to burn the land, kill the animals—it was a totally different thing to march into battle against a heavily armed enemy force backed by air support that most of them not only didn't, but couldn't, understand.

On another approach route a hundred meters north, Met Horl's Krahom company, in parallel file to Nang's, followed another NVA guide. Farther north and farther south, the 1st and 4th of the KT 104th also advanced. Bracketing them, with far greater intrinsic firepower, were elements of the NVA 141st Regiment. Behind them, in the forest, was the NVA 40th Artillery.

Nang squatted on the dike. Met Duch closed behind him, squatted. Then Hon and Rath stopped. Ahead of them the Tiger

Platoon continued, but behind, Monkey and Rabbit waited. Nang motioned for Hon. "I don't like it," he whispered.

"What?"

"There's no plan."

"The plan is to overrun Rumlong."

"I've fought with them before," Nang whispered. "This isn't the way to fight. We're too late. It's too light. This is not a plan."

"There's money in the city," Hon whispered. "There's evil there. To reform the people we must destroy it. It's as you've said."

"Yes. No. That's not what I mean. We're . . ."

Whistles blew before and behind them. A guide came back, out of breath. "Quick. Move. Fo . . . w . . . ward," he stuttered in broken Khmer. "Quick. The attack c . . . co . . . mence now."

Overhead the full assets of aerial surveillance also converged. With the thinning clouds, photo reconnaissance satellites 150 miles above the earth beamed images of trucks and tanks down to earth stations in Thailand. From 85,000 feet an SR-71 Black-bird picked up columns of humans. At 15,000 feet RF-101 Voo-doos with high-powered telescopes mounted on inertial stabilized platforms and using a variety of light and sound enhancement techniques, including infrared and radar, produced quick and accurate photo maps of troop deployment. A C-130 came on station, dropped light bombs, gigantic flashbulbs, clicked pho-tos and verified target locations. Though the targets were mov-ing the aerial reconnaissance workers had no problems keeping track as bombing missions were computer developed, ordered and loaded. On the RF-101s, exposed film was automatically processed and scanned and the images were converted to radio beams which were relayed to ground stations with high-resolution TV screens. Within minutes of overflight, technicians were iden-tifying specific targets, calculating the ordnance needed and requesting permission to destroy.

Across the rice fields from Pa Kham to Rumlong seven thou-sand Communist soldiers advanced on the FANK column and on the cities of Highway 6. Every move was timed, coordinated, efficiently meshing exactly as the planners at COKA's A-40 office had foreseen. Four fighter-bombers from Da Nang screamed in low over the plantations, across the paddies, up over the highway, up and north, east, rolling, beginning their bombing runs. The ground was dark, landmarks blurred. The enemy had frozen, doused its lights, covered its machines. East of Pa Kham a jet unleashed a pair of napalm canisters where the pilot believed target coordinates and visual observation matched.

The plane shrieked up over the land as the cans tumbled. The jet turned south, the jellied gas ignited splashing fire in two jagged cones lighting the land, exposing a gun emplacement. Again the jet dove, this time with visual contact of its target. As the pilot aimed in he relayed target data to a slow-moving, approaching OV-1 Mohawk forward air control aircraft, then released two high-explosive iron bombs. Before they exploded he was off station. No Allied observer, ground or aerial, saw the impact, the concussion eighty feet off target, the shrapnel slashing rubber trees, mostly spent before clattering against the armor plate of the field gun. East of the airfield, east of Phum Chamkar, east of Baray, similar attacks were repeated and the first wave of bombers went off station.

Nang took control of his unit. "Now! Yes! Quickly!" They were less than three hundred meters from the berm which led up out of the paddies to a small cluster of homes and the only buildings of Rumlong east of the road. "Quickly," he said to Hon. "The fog is lifting." Still in file the yotheas ran toward the berm which loomed above them like a great castle wall. Two hundred meters, one hundred. Still rockets crashed into the city. Through the ground mist a plume of smoke could be seen rising west of the road into the dawning sky. Still the FANK 105 howitzers reported, the clap at such close range jolting the boy soldiers. Behind them, north and south, two A-130s with mounted 40mm cannons strafed the flatlands, grenades bursting at, on, in the water with odd PWOCK, PWOCK, PWOCKs. Screams— paddies away. "Quick. Quick," Nang urged his fighters. "Hit the berm. Hug the enemy. Make his planes useless. Don't stop. Don't fire until you're at the top." Twenty meters. Ten meters. Three-point attack. Concentrate fire. The berm loomed like a wall. Suddenly phftp! phftp! phftptptptptp! About them, small arms bullets.

"Down there!" Screaming from FANK soldiers on the berm. Nang sprinted up, through Monkey Platoon, returning fire. He saw his enemy, fired, saw the body jerk, collapse. Tiger Platoon was being mauled. Rabbit Platoon was over the top, firing, throwing grenades. Nang crested the berm. He was directly before the battery of FANK 105s. Cannoneers were cranking the tubes down, loading beehive rounds. Rabbit yotheas were killing the ammo bearers, firing their rifles into the storage culverts trying to explode the stacked rounds, being shot by FANK troops with AK-47s or M-16s, diving, scrambling for cover. Monkey Platoon reinforced. Tiger had broken, those able splashing back into the paddies. A 105 cracked, the sound deafening, stinging Nang's damaged and redamaged ears. One round, eight thousand flechettes, and three cells of yotheas were mutilated, decapitated. Nang, lying against the sandbagged side of a gun emplacement, sensed abandonment. There were no more rockets. The ground heaved spasmodically, as if immense hammers were pounding the plantations and paddies. The sister companies of Nang's unit were being picked apart, piecemeal, by FANK riflemen, machine gunners and grenadeers. None of the NVA 141st Regiment's elements had engaged the nationals.

Nang was pissed. Down the line there was a lull. About him there was chaos. From Rabbit Platoon a rocket-propelled grenade burst against a howitzer—shrapnel zinging, dropping the cannoneers. Nang lurched up, leaped, tossed a grenade, dove. More explosions. Thick smoke. Dust, mist, acid taste hanging in air, in lungs, clinging to skin, eyes. Nang leaped again, up again. Rabbit Platoon had seized half the battery, was fighting hand to hand, gun to gun, firing outward from the defensive rings at approaching reinforcements. Behind Nang the remnant of Monkey pinched in, catching the cannoncockers in deadly crossfire. Along this sector they were the only fight. The day dawned clear, the sun turning mud to dust. From a bunker four FANK soldiers jumped, fired, readied to flee. Immediately they were shot. Nang jumped into them, bayonetting the one unscathed troop, then viciously stabbing the wounded.

"Disengage! Withdraw!" Nang signaled the order. All about him was carnage and calm. He didn't want to attract the enemy to his position. He grabbed a yothea. They cranked a howitzer around, loaded, barrel sighted. What was left of the 2d of the 104th quickly policed up usable, carryable weapons. They fled down the berm. Two cells fired constant rearguard action, pinning down the FANK troops who'd responded to the fight at the 105th battlement. An APC, machine gun firing quick sporadic bursts, rolled toward them from six hundred meters south. Behind, beside it, FANK infantry soldiers fired wildly, full magazines, into the air, the ground. Nang pulled the lanyard and the howitzer roared. Yotheas had reached the dike, sprinted a hundred meters from the berm and begun slipping into the paddies searching for concealment in the water and rice stalks, dispersing, alternately hiding and lurching farther from the roadway. There was a huge explosion as the APC burst apart, metal chunks skyrocketing, seemingly hanging in the air, then crashing toward earth.

"Quick. Withdraw."

As fast as they could run the last yotheas leaped the rampart, tore for the dike, the paddy. From concealment, a few yotheas sniped at the berm. On the berm FANK soldiers poked their heads from foxholes where they'd hidden since the fight had erupted. One drew a bead on the last fleeing Khmer Communist. He fired, semiautomatic. The first round too high. Adjust. Fire. Fire. Fire. A rifle kicked from the fleeing boy's hand but he did not stop.

Throughout the morning the sky cleared and all morning the planes came. Deep in the plantation beneath the high trees Viet Namese soldiers improved their overhead camouflage or dug bunkers, trenches or tunnels. The ground rumbled constantly. Thirty-four B-52 sorties hit suspected plantation staging areas, artillery rear bases and logistics lines. Sixty fighter-bomber sorties blasted the paddies and specific plantation targets. For a time the German "military strategist" attempted to film the attack aircraft flying low over the flatland, but with each sortie he withdrew toward the new bunker, withdrew into himself, the bravado of the night giving way to a somber and pensive mood.

A single B-52 bomb box encompasses an area of approximately two and a half square kilometers, with complete destruction by cratering occurring over roughly one percent of that surface area. One fighter-bomber strike destroys about .003 square kilometer. As the day wore on, thirty-four sorties by B-52s and sixty by fighter-bombers resulted in the complete destruction of less than one square kilometer in an area of approximately 1,400 square kilometers, or roughly .07 percent of the battlefield—a percentage so small that indiscriminate or random (vs. specifically targeted) bombing would be completely useless.

"There must be a way to make them bomb elsewhere," Mitterschmidt said to Lieutenant Thay as the two scrunched into a hole which had been dug for them.

"We've taken steps," Thay answered. He was annoyed that the German's size cramped him, and further annoyed by Mitterschmidt's implied disapproval.

"Steps?"

"Their ability to detect us under the canopy is based on engine heat," the escort officer said. "Our infantry advances along different paths than the supply trucks, armor or towed artillery. That way, even if a convoy is attacked, the loss of life is minimal. Trucks can be replaced."

"But why sacrifice even a few?"

"We've sacrificed for decades. We'll sacrifice until the last imperialist has been driven from Asia."

"But you don't sacrifice needlessly."

"No. Of course n . . ."

"If they're drawn to heat, why not build fake convoys? You build fake bridges. You set up fake lights to draw them away from more lucrative targets. Why not a row of spaced, covered fires? A few damaged truck parts to . . ."

Throughout the afternoon more sorties were flown. Every inch of the rice land was filmed and analyzed. North of the Chinit River elements of the NVA 91st Division were observed making a swing back north through the swamp forest toward Puk Yuk and Kompong Thom. The planes shifted to the new area. The NVA 5th Division, north of but on line with the 7th, split, elements heading toward Baray. Again the planes shifted. Long columns of refugees were identified, some streaming along the government-controlled corridor toward the enclaves, other columns, in the "liberated zones," trudging into the upper Chinit and Sen valleys. The rice lands between and about Highways 6, 7 and 21 looked deserted. In the past month four hundred hamlets had been abandoned and torched. Every farm animal had been killed.

Late in the afternoon of the twenty-sixth clouds again formed over the land and by evening a thick tully fog sealed the fields under an impenetrable layer of mist. Again the attacking ground forces came, came from the earth like rodents, like ants, came as if the subterranean sanctuaries were endless, held endless resources of men and materiel. Artillery batteries attached to the NVA 91st Division broke off and trailed south to within range of Rumlong. The 130s which had so shaken Mitterschmidt a night earlier raised their tubes toward Rumlong, well within their thirty-kilometer range. Mortar teams were trucked through the forest and down paddy dike roads to treelines. Rocket teams prepared hundreds of launch tubes. Mitterschmidt waited. This time he would not go forward but instead film the activity at the mobile command and control bunker now on the outskirts of Phum Bos Kanda on Highway 21, the largest city within the plantations.

The attack on Rumlong was by the book. As soon as darkness gripped the land, infantry units moved down prepared trails following the blipped lights of trail guides, moved quickly because they knew the trails were secure, because there was no need for point-slack teams scrutinizing every step or flank squads offering their protection. As they moved, the 130s launched a series of salvos aimed at the city's heart. This was not terrorist shelling but obliteration shelling. The 130s fired sixty rounds then moved along preestablished trails to preestablished, supplied positions three kilometers away and again fired at Rumlong. While the field guns changed positions to avoid bombers the 122mm rocket teams launched their devastation by delayed fuses. In the air, surveillance and reconnaissance aircraft easily pinpointed the launch sites but the launch teams were long gone when the targets were bombed. Then, from the west, new NVA artillery units, 107mm guns, lobbed their horrible projectiles into the city and along tangential highway sections. And NVA infantry closed and waited. The shelling did not cease. By midnight more than 600 rounds had landed on Rumlong, another 250 on the highway. Between explosions hysterical human shrieks stabbed into the blackness, penetrated to the ears of the NVA infantrymen creeping closer, closer. Still the shelling did not stop. B-52s box-blasted target coordinates in the plantations with iron bombs and seeded the paddies with time-delayed and external-stimuli fused CBUs (cluster bomb units—bombs comprised of grenadelike bomblets, the cluster exploding above the earth and fusing and dispersing the bomblets like some evil milkweed pod opening and spreading its seed). Still the shelling continued, still the infantry advanced. Within Rumlong three quarters of the buildings were destroyed, leveled, reduced to rubble. Of the 12,000 residents and perhaps half that number again of refugees, the death toll would never be known. Most dead were already buried in the rubble, luckily buried, buried never to be exhumed.

FANK units at Rumlong tucked their heads between their shoulders. All day they'd built flimsy shelters believing that they and the bombers had repulsed the enemy, showing by that very flimsiness their belief that Buddha would now, after their first ordeal, protect them. "No longer are there the 105s to attract enemy attention," soldiers told one another. "What would they want here? We're nothing."

The shelling shifted. The 130s, 122s and 107s stopped. Now the 120mm mortar teams set their hand-dropped projectiles to tube. Drop, launch, change elevation. Drop launch change elevation. Four hundred rounds from four tubes in twenty minutes. The FANK sector tactical operations center (TOC) lost all radio contact with its units in the first minute. By the tenth it had lost all but one receiver, which could pick up only a unit at the Tang Kouk airfield. The unit could transmit but not receive. Over and over again the TOC radio operator heard his counterpart begging for reinforcements and air or mortar support. Then there was a crackle of white noise and silence.

West of Rumlong there was new activity. FANK scouts sighted tanks. Unable to radio the visual pickup, they ran, ran like hell, ran praying, into the city to the sector TOC where they reported. Then back, running to perimeter units, attempting to rally the defenders. The shelling ceased. From the east a wave of NVA 141st infantry troops stormed the Rumlong berm under a hail of rocket-propelled grenade and recoilless rifle fire. To the shock of the NVA, thousands of FANK riflemen answered their fire with a storm of lead which broke the charge the moment it commenced and left 150 NVA dead. Now runners sprinted from the TOC to every unit and back. For the moment there was optimism even though the civilian city had died. From one perimeter came a radio and again the TOC was in contact with the outside. Immediately air support was requested and in-air diversions brought two U.S. F-4 Phantoms screaming in on strobe-light beacons. As the planes closed, long-range NVA artillery fire again exploded on the highway and in the city. Then the first two canisters of napalm exploded thirty yards off their mark and what the NVA had been unable to do, the U.S. bomber in one pass accomplished. In a perimeter section fifty meters long every FANK defender was either killed or incapacitated. More napalm wounded the enemy in the paddies, continuing to burn them even as they dove under water. From the west two NVA T-54s rolled out of the swamp-forest, rolled along undetected prepared roads to the western berm, fired point-blank at points of resistance. Behind the NVA tanks, NVA jeep-mounted 57mm recoilless rifles zeroed in on the few FANK artillery pieces, destroying or capturing them. NVA artillery continued to shell the road north and south, repressing any reinforcement action. Finally the North Viet Namese infantry assaulted again. For a minute a mad frenzied man-to-man firefight raged.

Then FANK broke. Soldiers ran to ground holes and hovels where their families hid. "Run! Run! Into the dark!" But enemy infantry cut them off, turned them like a sheepdog herds its flock, turned, turned, concentrating what they saw as subhuman cowering brown devils, then pouring in the ordnance, point-blank, firing their rifles into surrendering soldiers, into mothers with their arms hugging their children, bodies, heads exploding, chunks ripped off, smashed as if they were no stronger than ripe melons dropped from a truck onto the blacktop.

From the top of a tamarind tree in a treeline between paddies five kilometers east-southeast, Nang watched the obliteration of

Rumlong. His right hand throbbed horribly. What drove him
was difficult to pinpoint—whether training, indoctrination, fear,
unconscious fanatical desire or simple hate. Whatever it was it
drove him to struggle up the tree with three fingers shot off his
right hand as cleanly as if they'd been hacked by one blow from
a butcher's knife whacking down on a cutting board, cleaving
them between the knuckle and first joint. At first he hadn't even
felt the wound. His rifle had leaped from his hand as he'd fled,
leaped as if it were alive and itself fleeing his grasp. He hadn't
stopped to retrieve it. There were enough small arms in Cambodia that a smart yothea never need be without. Nang had
jumped from the dike into the nearest paddy, had dove under
the surface water, into the thick rising rice stalks, had then
attempted to pull himself through the reeds by grasping and
only then discovered, surprised, his right hand had but thumb
and forefinger. By day he'd hid, crawled, crab-walked in and
through the field, over the low dike and into the next paddy,
becoming as rigid as a dead tree trunk each time an aircraft
approached. At one point he ripped strips from the end of his
krama to wrap the half-inch meat and bone stubs protruding
from his hand. By late afternoon he'd rendezvoused with Duch,
Rath and half a dozen fighters from Met Horl's company. Quietly,
slowly, they made their way to the treeline. Three other yotheas
were there, dazed, confused, ready to shoot them until realization hit and then overly apologetic, ready to assist. Someone
produced a flask of gasoline, washed and disinfected Nang's
hand. Another chewed the tobacco of a cigarette into a salve
and the boys bandaged Nang's stubs with the poultice wrapped
against the wound.

"Mita's dead," one boy had said. "I saw him fall."

"What of Met Hon?" Nang had asked.

"He was cut in two," Duch had answered.

"Of Eng? Horl? Van? Ith?"

"I don't know." "Dead." "Shot in the legs and couldn't run.
They'll decapitate him while he still breathes." "His company
is lost."

During the afternoon other stragglers had arrived. "Why didn't
they fight?" "Who?" "The yuons, the stinging red ants!" "They
pulled back as soon as we attacked."

"Ssshh," Nang had hissed authoritatively. "Listen. Let this be
our lesson. We must rely only on ourselves. Allies are enemies.
Enemies are enemies. Let that bind us. Spread out. Search for
others and bring them to me. Let's teach the yuons a lesson,
too."

*　　*　　*

"That corrupt son of a bitch," Sullivan cursed under his breath. All day and all night he'd followed the military reports, talked with American forward air control and fighter pilots, heard the civilian radio, both the Khmer, translated by Captain Sisowath Suong, and the English, which he translated into French for Suong. He jammed a shovel into the road embankment, showing some dependants how to dig a foxhole for protection from artillery. "That stupid son of a bitch," he seethed.

"Which one you talk about?" Suong asked. He descended from the roadbed to be with Sullivan. Before them, in the paddies to the east, FANK soldiers were digging, establishing a forward line, setting mines, building fighting positions.

"Just once, just fucking once, I'd like to see you guys play your cards right. Play em without some idiot in Phnom Penh screaming orders without the slightest idea what's happening here."

"Ah, Captain Sullivan"—Suong laid his hand on the American's arm—"you know what they taught me at Nha Trang? They said, 'Sometimes a leader must make decisions which have a great effect on others. Must decide even if he has inadequate understanding of the situation.' "

"Yeah. But if he's got the ability to gain an understanding and he doesn't . . . Ah, Captain Suong . . ."

"I know," Suong lamented. "The colonels are afraid to give him accurate reports. He thinks more about ancient glories and Angkor kings than he does about yuon armies."

"He's ordered a counterattack on Rumlong, hasn't he?"

"Yes. I think we will soon attack."

"And Pa Kham?"

"They're being shelled like Rumlong yesterday."

"Then the enemy's shifting south and he's ordering us north."

"But Rumlong . . ."

"You can't mount a countermove on this road. All you can do is feed your men in a few hundred at a time. They'll be mowed down."

"Please, again talk to Samkai."

"On one condition." Sullivan's anger drained and he smiled mischievously.

"Yes."

"At dusk, you come with me. We'll take a recon squad out as far as we can."

By dusk on the twenty-seventh early reports were confirmed, new reports were in and already civilian analysis was being broadcast. Bombing had been heavy throughout the Northern Corridor during the day, particularly during the clearest hours about noon. As he slowly inched east along a dike under the returned tully fog and clouds, Sullivan seethed over the new reports and over his own orders to withdraw, to be extracted, individually, by American helicopter. Once again NVA artillery fire commenced.

FANK the foolish, Sullivan thought. FANK the pathetic. FANK the laughingstock army in the eyes of the world as seen through the eyes of the world press. "FANK forces broke and fled." The radio words grated in his head. Never mind, he thought. Never mind that the concentration of artillery on tiny Rumlong was greater than that on mighty Stalingrad during the winter siege of what, 1941–42, '42–43? All up and down the corridor other FANK units were reeling, were feeling betrayed by their brothers at Rumlong, betrayed by the ease, according to rumor and radio, with which the column center had given up, been cut, putting those to the north in even greater jeopardy and trapping those south of the Tang Kouk bridge to what horrible fate. In Kompong Thom, Baray, Tang Kouk, Phnom Penh and worldwide, reports of the loss were broadcast. No mention was made of the massacre of at least eight thousand civilians and dependants. Little was made of the Viet Namese artillery barrage. Over and over the reports stressed, listed, the national army's losses: four tanks, four APCs, one jeep, twenty buses, twenty-one quarter-ton trucks, two 105mm howitzers, one bulldozer, and one hundred automatic rifles. How many soldiers were killed the reports did not say, as if none were lost because none stayed to fight.

Sullivan and Suong's recon team turned south toward the main canal. Only two of the eleven Khmers had been on night patrol and Sullivan had insisted they split, one at rear drag, one at midsquad, to assist and keep the uninitiated from foolish mistakes which might get them all killed. Sullivan walked point. At Kompong Thom Colonel Um Savath's demoralized elite vanguard had begun their ordered return. Almost immediately reports reached corridor units that they'd driven head-on into the NVA 91st Division. From Pa Kham early reports indicated that the NVA had in store for that delightful town the identical treatment bestowed on Rumlong.

Night fell quickly upon Sullivan's inexperienced team. About them, unknown to them, aerial reconnaissance aircraft detected truck traffic. Sullivan moved slowly. Suong held a hand on the American's backpacked radio. Behind, soldiers attached one to the next by short braided reed ropes shuffled forward, feeling the mud and grass with their bare feet. Step, shuffle step, listen, look, smell. Sullivan's agitation at the operation fell away. That his action was against congressional decree neither concerned him nor even entered his mind. He was Special Forces, a trained, experienced and highly competent soldier establishing his own mission for the protection of others. His night patrol concentration returned as if it had been in continuous use instead of in abeyance, supplanted by the slow-growing logistical and bureaucratic bullshit he hadn't, until the patrol began, realized he hated. This was what he wished to do, wished to accomplish.

For four hours they meandered like a segmented toy snake held together by reeds. What he was searching for he knew not. How his team coalesced pleased him. There was no talk. Little noise. To their north, east and south U.S. or RVNAF bombs were exploding. To the south, across the canal, there was the distinctive sound of battle. Pa Kham was being hit hard by the NVA. Overhead, intermittently, were the sounds of helicopters, Mohawks, A-130s and T-28s. Still Sullivan's team roamed. At intervals he keyed his radio handset in preestablished patterns, breaking squelch on the radio monitored at Chhan Samkai's mobile bus TOC. Four kilometers out, along the canal leveé, they spotted the first fire. It took nearly half an hour to close on it. At first only Sullivan and Suong crept forward on their bellies. Sullivan expected a mortar or rocket station, manned by trail guides, waiting, ready, for the team to occupy the site long enough to launch their ordnance then flee. What he found was an old truck hood with a small wood and bamboo fire beneath. "To cook on?" Sullivan whispered to Suong.

"I don't know," Suong said. "Hard to cook like that."

Fifty meters east they found a second fire with half a hood. Then a third under a fender where the canal turned south. Farther, a fourth, and with this one not only a hood and fender but bed staves covered by a ruined tarp. Sullivan keyed the transmit bar of the radio. The find, he felt, was significant. Suddenly a forward air control plane fired a white phosphorus marking rocket into the levee by the first fire. "Holy Shit!" Sullivan scrambled out of the radio, dropped over it. "Birddog Oscar Victor . . ." He searched for the frequency the forward observer should have been monitoring as a second rocket exploded beyond them, bracketing them. To Suong, "Get em out a here!" Back to the transmitter, "Birddog Oscar Victor One . . . this is Juliet Sierra." Again. Again. Hastily. The rockets burned white hot.

"Juliet . . . this is . . ."

"Stop the bomb run. Friendlies. Repeat . . ." Jets shrieked in loud, low, all sound enveloped in their engine roar. Sullivan tucked, rolled to his side screaming into the handset, unable to hear his own voice, expecting napalm or strafing. Instantaneous sound abatement. No fire. No bombs.

B-52s now unloaded their ordnance sixty kilometers away, southwest of Kompong Thom against suspected and verified elements of the NVA 91st, and in a radius about Pa Kham. The latter brought the bombing within terror distance of Nam Thay and Hans Mitterschmidt, who were in position to observe the destruction of the fake convoy. They didn't understand the fighter-bomber runs without ordnance. "Because of the levee?" Mitterschmidt questioned.

"I wouldn't think so," Thay said. "The imperialists aren't concerned with such things. Not here"—he chuckled—"where no one is watching."

"No?" Mitterschmidt was somber.

"Perhaps. That would explain why they used dive-bombers instead of B-52s. But not why the bombers didn't engage the targets."

"What might explain it," the German speculated, "is another advance in through-the-clouds night target detection."

"You mean you think they could see them?"

"What else? Tomorrow night the 209th attacks Tang Kouk, yes?"

"Yes."

"Then we should follow them. We'll go along the canal. I want to see the targets."

The battle of Chenla II raged on four fronts. Despite the heavy use of aerial bombing, the outgunned, outmanned and outmaneuvered national forces were being mauled. Throughout the day of the twenty-eighth, Colonel Um Savuth's forces pushed south from Kompong Thom, advancing only a few kilometers behind a wall of nearly fifty B-52 sorties plus close-in tactical air and helicopter support. Another nearly fifty B-52 sorties struck in the plantation zone east of Pa Kham.

In Phnom Penh Lon Nol ranted and raged, condemning criticism of his personal control, urging his holy warriors to follow his *kboun*, his orders, as holy writ, and sending urgent requests to U.S. Admiral John McCain, Commander of the Pacific Fleet, for more helicopters and amphibious vehicles.

In NVA-held Rumlong the living were rooted from holes and hovels, herded, classified, arrested and prepared for evacuation.

Captured national troops were detained for "political retraining" and marched west into the swamps. Police, village officials and council members were sent northeast; civilians southeast across the paddies. Those suspected of working for the CIA were taken to the nearest treeline never to emerge.

As night closed upon the Northern Corridor on 28 October, the NVA counterattacked Colonel Um Savuth's column at Kompong Thom. Now the disillusioned and demoralized nationals did break as the NVA 91st approached. In unopposed frenzy, the *thmils*, behind four T-54 tanks, killed three hundred FANK soldiers. Again the loss was listed in the aired reports: two APCs, eight two-and-a-half-ton trucks, four Land Rovers, twenty jeeps, eight buses and a 105 howitzer. To the south, by midnight the eastern hamlets of Pa Kham were in the hands of NVA infantry. Mortars shelled the city as troops advanced behind recoilless rifle and rocket-propelled grenade fire. Then the big guns were turned on Tang Kouk and on the units trapped on the road south of that town.

At one in the morning Nang screamed the most anguished, horrible, painful cry he could produce. Then he squatted silently. All evening his regrouped unit had trotted the paths of the forest edge, had passed within meters of its NVA ally with complete impunity. Of the original 342-man KT 104th, 146 were killed or missing in action. The entire 4th Company was gone. The *neary* platoon of Met Nu had vanished. The 108th had also been tricked, pulverized. A few stragglers joined Nang's group. From the 180 boys that Nang, Duch and, finally, Eng, with a severe facial wound, had collected, they put together two companies. Nang had appointed himself, without opposition, battalion commander.

A minute after Nang's shriek, Met Puc, at 120 degrees from Nang, emitted an eerie blood-curdling laugh. Then silence. Just north of their attack routes, at the edge of the plantation lands before the paddies, the NVA 209th Infantry Regiment had set up a combined listening post–observation post, rear headquarters, transfer station. In the perimeter there was banging, clattering, the sounds of stumbling. Then Met Puc again laughed, Met Rham growled, roared, others hissed, howled, producing an evil inhuman chorus. Then all ceased. Quietly they moved clockwise two to four meters about the 209th's small rear detachment. The Viet Namese radioed for help. Monkey Platoon of the 2d Company froze, waited. Minutes later they again exploded in shouts and guttural shrieks. An NVA soldier opened fire. Then another. And another. The yotheas lay flat. The yuon rear guard, to a man, fired high, spraying AK-47 projectiles in a 360-degree arc, spraying so high that troops facing a second NVA listening post actually fired upon their brothers.

The yotheas remained still, quiet. At two in the morning, as the NVA ground attack on Tang Kouk commenced, Nang screamed like a monkey thrown to crocodiles. Immediately the LP again radioed for assistance. How easy, Nang thought. How easy it is. Puc laughed his weird laugh, Rham roared his spitting vomiting roar, Met Krom hissed his nasal hiss. Up trail a reserve squad approached the LP. Before they arrived they were beaten and knifed to death. To the far west the cacophony of battle was intense. A trickle of wounded were brought to the station.

"Did you see anything out there?"

"Anything? Like what?"

"Spirits?"

"Spirits!"

"It's terrible. I tell you they've surrounded us."

"Tag this comrade and send him to the hospital. There are more wounded. I must go. Spirits, indeed!"

The trickle ceased. A bomber dropped its ordnance close by and four yotheas entered the perimeter dragging Viet Namese bodies. Silently they met the rear guard. More yotheas pulled in bodies. Amongst the score of Viet reserves there stood thirty yotheas. Nang dropped the ankle tie of his dead NVA soldier. He looked wide-eyed crazy into the face of the receiving yuon. Then suddenly he shrieked and all burst into growls, laughs, hisses. They leaped upon the yuons, stabbing, slashing, impaling with bamboo daggers until all station personnel were dead. Nang stiffened his hatchet hand, chopped, smashed skulls until they burst, shouting madly as he hit, "For my hand. For my land. For Kampuchea." Then, "On to their rear."

The yotheas moved through, cleaning the site of every weapon and cartridge, every piece of usable clothing and gear, every radio, battery, boot, telephone wire and medical kit.

Along the canal Hans Mitterschmidt stopped. This scene had to be filmed. No one would believe it. "I must have more light."

"Do you—" Nam Thay began. He shook his head in amused disbelief. "They couldn't have dropped them from the air."

"But how else?"

"I don't know. They would have burst if the planes had dropped them."

"Then who has been here? One more torch."

"It's not safe."

"Just one more. One moment. They won't react so fast. Bamboo bombs! They bombed the convoy with fake bombs!"

Sullivan was in the most foul mood of his life. Half the buildings in Tang Kouk village had been blown apart by artillery. Three of the APCs on the highway were destroyed. One still burned, its flames licking up into the night blackness like long red-yellow snake tongues flicking at unseen morsels. The lone tank perched on the road, useless, out of fuel and ammo, its crew having expended every round for cannon and machine guns, sitting, terrified, under orders to remain to create the illusion of strength. FANK mortar men kept continual flares in the sky east and west of the highway and over the canal, ensuring their army's visibility to enemy observers. Still NVA infantry did not attack. At Chhan Samkai's command post, now on the ground behind the bus, everyone, everything, was in disarray. The lieutenant colonel himself was studying topographic maps, not for ways to counter the enemy's moves or to assist target acquisition and forward observation for FANK, American, South Viet Namese and Thai fighter-bombers, but to find a retreat route through the western swamps and to organize a rearguard action.

Sullivan was deeply conscious that his role as a military equipment need-and-use observer was ludicrous, yet he was not an advisor, did not have even the limited authority of an advisor. His jaw clenched as he watched Chhan Samkai's seemingly casual, negligent, command. His teeth ground as he waited for the commander to issue commands which never came. His fists squeezed tight at his sides as he thought of the half-assed commitment of his own country, a halfway move which simply ensured slower death, a life-support system for a brain-dead nation which for no reason he could find needed to be brain-dead, a commitment to keep it, the Cambodian body, alive for a little longer, which amounted to no commitment at all.

"Explain once more," Sisowath Suong yelled to him over the tremendous noise of incoming artillery, diving jets and exploding bombs.

"Has he opened it?" Sullivan shouted back, and Suong, an obscure smile on his face, yelled the question into the transmitter. Back and forth, back and forth, question question answer translation answer. Was that advising? Telling an infantryman on the front line in the paddies via interpreter via radio how to use—ready, aim and fire—a LAW, a light antitank weapon?

At 0300 hours on 29 October 1971, the NVA 209th launched its first attack, a point thrust, at the bridge ramp. FANK's forward line ran, from the road, two hundred meters out along the levee, then north parallel to the road, behind a paddy dike. Every fired weapon in use in Southeast Asia except .45s and flamethrowers had an effective range greater than two hundred meters. The only weapons in common use which could not reach the main body of the FANK force on the road were thrown weapons, grenades. The Viet Namese did not use this to great advantage. Their point hit head to head with emplaced cross-fired machine guns and a determined platoon of FANK riflemen. The large artillery pieces ceased firing. Communist mortar rounds now seemingly fell at random in the paddies before and behind the frontline dike, all over the road, and back into the swamp where the dependants had clustered, had set up camp, terrified yet convinced of their own foredoom, unable to dig in or to flee. Horrible cries, distressed anguished wails, rose and spread over the blackness like a blanket of abomination, spread to the road and into the paddies where the chorus rattled the very souls of the fathers, husbands, defenders.

NVA reinforcements moved up. Using small, 57mm, recoilless rifles, firing from outer dikes, the attackers engaged the machine gunners. FANK soldiers returned fire for fire. Allied jets dived, swooped in, strafed the field between facing lines, dropped cluster bombs with external-stimuli fuses essentially mining the entire area. NVA gunners countered by shelling the fields, exploding the mines and clearing paths for their infantry advances. The fields transformed from wet paddies green with filled rice to massive yellow-brown mud ponds with floating splintered straw and ash.

The Communist infantry withdrew, the heavy artillery recommenced, then again stopped and was supplanted by mortars. Again the NVA ground troops attacked. This time into Tang Kouk village, at the canal and at four points between. From behind, a unit of NVA river commandos rose from the canal, climbed the shattered bridge and with a medium, 75mm, recoilless rifle, destroyed the last FANK APC.

Government troops broke.

For Sullivan, for Suong, the command post was no longer of consequence. The commander had withdrawn into himself to prepare for his fate. Most of the staff personnel had fled to the dependant camp or into the swamp. The bus caught fire, flared, then smoldered. All radios were abandoned.

"Which way are you going?!" Suong grasped the American.

"There." Sullivan paced east. He had his PRC-25, an M-16 and all the grenades he'd been able to police up from the deserted CP.

"Wait!" Suong ran back to the bus.

"Fuck that!" Sullivan called. He leaped off the road and let gravity jerk him down the embankment.

"Sullivan!" Suong shrieked, his voice cracking. His small hands grasped an M-60 machine gun. Over his shoulder and about his waist were a dozen cartridge belts.

Sullivan turned from the dikehead. Again Suong shrieked his name. In flat mortar flare light he looked dwarfed by the weapon, looked like an evil weighted Christmas tree gleaming brass and hung with grenade balls. "Down here!" Sullivan called. A moment later, "I thought you'd split."

"I go with you wherever you go, eh!?" Again the obscure smile. "Which way we going?"

"Point of attack," Sullivan said calmly. He pointed to an area of the perimeter from which FANK-fired red tracers showered the advancing NVA 209th, at which NVA-fired green tracers impacted.

To the direct rear of the midpoint of the 209th's assault, Lieutenant Nam Thay hugged mud below clumps of dike surface grass. From four thousand feet U.S. Army helicopters were unleashing rockets at barrel flashes seen through the ground mist. The aircraft commanders, the copilots and, in the Hueys, the door gunners had the almost impossible task of identifying targets, of separating friendly from enemy troops. Without ground forward observers, they attempted to err toward the enemy rear thus leaving a wide aerial no-fire zone between the lines. "Stupid, insane, buffalo shit," Thay grumbled to himself. Beside him Hans Mitterschmidt's legs churned, moving the East German in agitated spurts as the colonel, torso atop the dike, attempted to get ever-greater camera angle on the battle.

From the FANK side, Sullivan sprinted the middle distance then low-crawled the last to the dike berm. Behind him Suong struggled with his gear. About them defenders lay twisted, broken. Some moaned. Some cried. Some jerked spasmodically with each B-40 rocket or recoilless rifle explosion near their position. The dead didn't move.

Where FANK was faltering the NVA moved to reinforce their attack points. Break through, isolate, separate, annihilate. An old tactic, tried and true.

"Are you with the relief column?" A FANK soldier hugged Suong as he lay splat on the earth.

Suong laughed. He turned to Sullivan, the obscure smile visible under a fluttering flare. "He asks 'Are we with the relief column?' "

"Ha! Tell him we are the . . ."

As Sullivan spoke a wave of Communist soldiers which had advanced through the aerial no-fire zone of paddy muck and wriggled silently like water leeches from rice stalk to rice stalk lobbed satchel charges over the dike. The NVA soldiers dropped as the charges, almost in unison, exploded along fifty meters of FANK berm. The concussion kicked Sullivan onto his back. He stared straight up. Then Viet troops leaped to the top of the dike. Sullivan pulled the trigger. Eight rounds lifted, blew one man back. Sullivan rolled. His fire drew fire. Down the line a FANK gunner sprayed continual M-60 lead a foot over the dike, chopping rising NVA at the knees then killing them as they fell. Other FANK troops fired up from the paddy where they'd been thrown. Ten meters from Sullivan, FANK and NVA soldiers smashed wildly at each other with rifle butts and bayonets, each being killed by other FANK or NVA soldiers, men firing at every unidentified disturbance in the violent flow. The FANK troops regained their berm but from the paddy and the next dike east the attack intensified. Suong struggled with the 60. Sullivan pushed him his 16, grabbed the heavier weapon. Beside them a soldier sucking an amulet caught a round in the head. He did not jerk, did not fall, as if the round had passed through his skull with such velocity as only to make its immediate minute entry hole without jarring the package. Then wet blood gushed in one immense spurt, then oozed, flowed down his face, splitting into dozens of rivulets before the soldier wobbled, then collapsed and sank beneath the paddy water.

To the FANK rear, with Chhan Samkai and his CP withdrawn, as the front berm held, FANK troops discarded their weapons, fled, sloshing into the west swamp, running, diving into the canal, attempting to swim south or float west. Some dependants and refugees joined them but most stayed put. How does a mother carry and drag her two-, three- and five-year-olds through a hostile swamp in the middle of the night? Better to sit, sit and wait, wait and weep and let fate reveal future sufferings or mercy.

Those FANK soldiers who fled, fled under conditions they had never expected. With each backstep they were met with increasing hostility by refugees and local inhabitants who no longer viewed them as an army of salvation but as the hopeless Nationals, as a detested scourge which had, by their very attempt to liberate, brought fighting which had destroyed the land, which had separated the refugees from their families, which now caused death amongst them. To them FANK had not launched an offensive against invading *thmils* from North Viet Nam but had sucked greater numbers of NVA deeper into the area.

*   *   *

"They're breaking apart," Mitterschmidt said to Nam Thay. "Let's move forward."

"Sir, there are still the aircraft. You can't be injured here."

"I won't be. We must press forward."

"Then please, along the canal levee. There, I think, the bombers have been ordered not to hit."

"You say that. My film shows otherwise. Okay. Either way we'll be there for the greatest rout of the war."

"We can't let the yuon drive succeed," Eng whispered to Nang. "Those were our orders."

"Let them rest," Nang whispered. His tone was soothing, smooth, masking great agitation. The two had pushed the battalion of yotheas to the limit of human endurance. Throughout the night they had attacked and destroyed small rear elements of their ally. The NVA 209th's rear transfer station for wounded had been first, along with a reserve security squad. Then a mortar team moving independently to a new firing site, then a supply platoon. Each time they'd moved in close, then, counting on their ally status, infiltrated a few, then more, then many amongst the Viets or, as with the supply team, Khmers supporting Viets. Each time they'd killed without shots or grenades, killed by stabbing, slashing and bashing heads. The noise was localized. Their mission remained covert.

"We must move. *Now!*" Eng was emphatic.

"*No!*" Nang was more so.

"To knock off a few yuons behind their attackers won't stop their drive."

"To rush head-on into the attack won't stop it either. Move them to the canal."

"That'll put our backs to the water. We won't be able to move."

"Exactly, Eng," Nang whispered, soothing, smooth, insane. "Exactly. On desperate ground their only hope to live will be to fight more savagely than you and I ever conceived."

The fighting was now very close. Viet Namese and Khmer riflemen exchanged shots point-blank. On the canal levee two dozen men were battling hand to hand. Still, two hundred meters north of the canal, Sullivan, Suong and a small, hardened, tired core covered their section, increasing their deliberate rifle fire, shooting only on semiautomatic to conserve their nearly exhausted ammunition. Despite constant attempts Sullivan had been unable to make radio contact with the ever-changing aircraft and he'd given up. Perhaps, he thought in a momentary lull, it's the battery.

"You are a brave man," Suong said to Sullivan as the Khmer reloaded. He smiled, too emotionally spent to hide the warmth.

"You too, my friend." Sullivan grabbed Suong's arm and squeezed, then let go and raised his head back above the dike.

"But you, Captain. You are braver. After all, this *is* my country. Only you few Americans who are here and fight for Cambodia understand. Only you care. Where's the rest of the free world?"

"Whoa! Look! Another!"

Suong poked up. The murk of the dark paddy below was broken by a dozen floating corpses. "Where?"

"South. There. We've got a hole."

"Eh!" Suong unclipped a grenade from his belt. He and Sullivan crept-sprinted below the berm. Suong pulled the pin, cocked his arm. An NVA rifleman fired a burst. Suong threw. Rounds tinked at Suong's waist. Sullivan fired at the flash. Suong dropped, collapsed beside him. The thrown grenade exploded. "You hit?" Sullivan spit the words.

"No." Then Suong jerked, grasped at his belt. His last grenade had been armed by the rifle bullet. He ripped frantically. Sullivan fired on more enemy. Suong leaped over the dike. He crashed, sloshed screaming toward the NVA. The grenade stuck on his belt blew. The cell of NVA attackers stood, stunned. Sullivan fired a long burst, swept back and forth. The last mortar flare died. There was no more fire from the FANK position.

In the first predawn lightening of sky the NVA 209th began its mop-up operation. Flash skirmishes erupted along the roadway. Hans Mitterschmidt, securely surrounded by a full squad of NVA reserves plus his porter and two escort officers, proceeded methodically toward the twisted carriage of the bridge. Behind him, emerging from the 209th's rear like dark pincers, two companies of armed black-clad boys advanced, enveloping the slower-moving Viets with their white foreign observer, advisor, strategist.

"Who are they?" Mitterschmidt demanded.

"Khmers, eh?" Lieutenant Thay shrugged.

"Didn't they attack?"

"These browns"—Nam Thay spat disgustedly—"are cowards. You saw that."

"It's on film."

Under the oil-slicked water of the last paddy before the wrecked bridge, John L. Sullivan sucked air through a reed, testing his ability to stay submerged. The water/rice surface was dark. The sky grayed from charcoal to ash. All about him he could hear the NVA mop-up, Viet Namese voices, light chatter. Soon, he thought, they'll bomb this place to hell and back and blow these cocksuckers to shit. Me too. If the bastards don't get me first.

Sullivan periscoped his head up for a look then ducked back under. The twenty-three-pound M-60 was an adequate anchor, yet again he popped up. In the several days he'd been in and out of the paddies the water had dropped six inches, to three and a half feet. How long could he hide? More voices. French! He dove, tried to raise only an ear, but it filled with water and he couldn't hear.

"Now!" The scream was hysterical, incoherent Khmer. Every yothea fired. In the midst of 400 NVA riflemen and porters the surprise fire by 180 Krahom soldiers was devastating. Each yothea had prepicked targets. Before any Viet could react, a hundred died. Then rifle fire enmeshed all, all firing at all, all ducking, diving for cover, dying, suicide attack by black-clad boys storming up from the bridgehead and canal, down from paddies two hundred meters north, killing everything in their path, being killed by NVA troops on the highway firing from old, FANK-prepared positions.

Sullivan popped up. The fighting, to him, meant FANK reinforcements, FANK counterattack. What else could it be? He tried to determine the lines but sensed he was in the middle. He ducked under, excited, sucking air through the reed. He duckwalked underwater, under cover of thin mist, shattered stalks and shadowy earth.

Nam Thay dropped to his knees. The pain in his abdomen was horrible, odd, not severe but horrible in its fearsomeness. Things had crunched, blown in, out. He dared not look. His head fell forward. His eyes saw red, saw slick whitish tubes, split, spewing shit. He looked up. There was no sound. No pain. Nam Thay saw Mitterschmidt's ankle protruding from the German's boot, but saw no more of him. Nam Thay fell to his side. His knees drew up. Five meters away Mitterschmidt knelt on the leg without a foot. He screamed unintelligible orders, then collapsed into the paddy.

Sullivan poked up. Twenty meters from him a man crashed into the water. Sullivan ducked. In his mind he shook his head. He'd seen a Caucasian with a camera. Fucking reporter, he thought. Fucking reporter. Have to stay under. He poked up. A boy dressed in a black uniform had the reporter by the hair. With a bayonet held in a bloody hand with but two fingers the boy stabbed the Caucasian's throat then ripped out. Sullivan swallowed. He sank till his eyes were half below water. Names flashed. Sean Flynn. Dana Stone. The deserter McKinley Nolan. Who? Other black-uniformed children severed the head. Then with it they ran for the canal.

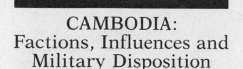

CAMBODIA:
Factions, Influences and Military Disposition

HISTORICAL SUMMATION
Part 3 (1972–1974)

Prepared for
The Washington News-Times
J. L. Sullivan

April 1985

How did the Republic of Cambodia fall? What changes, what political events and tactical decisions, brought the rise of the Khmer Krahom?

The Battle of Chenla II was the Antietam, Gettysburg and Shenandoah of the Cambodian "civil" war. It marked the end of Lon Nol's "Popular Crusade," which had seen over 80,000 Khmer youths volunteer, in just the first months, to fight the Viet Namese Communists. Never again did FANK seriously attempt to dislodge any major opposing force. Nor did FANK ever mount a sustained counteroffensive, even though intelligence reports indicated dramatic tactical changes, changes which meant the national military could have retaken vast tracts of land virtually unopposed. Still, like the Confederate States in America 109 years earlier, the Khmer Republic held on, sometimes via the most heroic military actions, for three more torturous years.

The Battle of Chenla II—the military ramification of the storm set off by Hanoi's early 1970 decision to accelerate its Campaign X to conquer Cambodia—raged until late December 1971. Then the fighting abruptly stopped, gave way to an unexpected lull, an eye in the storm, because North Viet Nam's Communist leadership suddenly shifted its short-term political aims and thus its tactical disposition. With Free World public attention concentrating on Phnom Penh as if the city were all of Cambodia, Hanoi decided to temporarily drain its military forces from the Khmer countryside. Why, when the North

Viet Namese Army was on the verge of toppling Phnom Penh, did Hanoi's Politburo order this sudden abort? What did the ensuing drain-off of NVA troops, and the subsequent NVA disaster of the Easter offensive in South Viet Nam, mean for Cambodia and the Krahom movement? What effect did the Paris peace talks and the signed agreement have on the Cambodian nation?

And what events and pressures in the United States, France, South Viet Nam and China influenced all the Khmer factions?

The behavior of the Khmer Krahom in the late months of 1971 deserves special attention. Its actions were omens foreshadowing not only the immediate future but a future beyond the second eye of the storm.

CHENLA II—BATTLEFIELD ACTIVITIES

The Battle of Chenla II raged until year's end. On 2 November FANK forces counterattacked about Phum Pa Kham lifting the siege and driving the attacking North Viet Namese back into their plantation bases. In the counterattack, 291 Viet Namese were killed.

Five days later the NVA launched a new series of attacks west of Phnom Penh. On 10 November elements of these units shelled Pochentong Airport at Phnom Penh killing 25 civilians and soldiers, wounding 30, and destroying 9 aircraft. Cambodia's main international radio transmitter west of the airport was hit by Communist sappers, leaving 19 Khmer dead and the nation radio-silent for hours.

At Rumlong on 13 November a task force of 400 FANK troops was mauled (370 killed) by advancing NVA units. A reinforcing column of 400 was slaughtered when it was fed piecemeal into the maw of Communist fire. Circumventing FANK's column, NVA units from the Northern Corridor headed for Phnom Penh. On 16 November the NVA vanguard was temporarily halted ten miles from the capital by heavy U.S. and South Viet Namese bombings. Three days later Lon Nol, reversing his order of August, issued an urgent plea to South Viet Nam for ARVN assistance. On 22 November 25,000 South Viet Namese ground troops entered Cambodia. Meanwhile, the NVA attacked and overran a FANK column and garrisons about Baray on 1 and 2 December setting off the largest stampede of Khmer national troops of the war. Parts of Baray had been lost to the NVA in 1970. FANK had recaptured Baray early during Chenla II only to lose it all to the NVA division-size force. During this attack 10,000 FANK soldiers fled unrelenting NVA artillery fire. Within a week Radio Hanoi was claiming 12,000 FANK "soldiers" killed in this battle alone.

By 7 December, North Viet Namese artillery units on the front west of Phnom Penh, dug in in an arc about the capital, began renewed shelling of the city.

From the Northern Corridor the NVA advanced seven more miles. Refugees from the entire northern region deluged the already swamped capital. For a week the battle seesawed. FANK, its back to the wall, fought hard and gained small victories. On 11 December FANK abandoned Phnom Penh's major defensive position, at Phnom Baset, only eight miles from the capital's heart.

Then, only days later, the ARVN column with FANK reinforcements rolled into the capital zone under cover of U.S. air support. They found the NVA had withdrawn. Scattered fighting continued until 20 December.

The meaning of Chenla II for Lon Nol, his government and FANK can be found in 600 years of fatalism. Throughout the campaign Lon Nol slowly transformed the national battle into a mystical Buddhist-Brahmin campaign. Like the leaders of nearly all Khmer factions, he became swept up in the concepts of Khmer purity, the Khmer patriot and fanatical racial pride. Chenla II was the high point and then the breaking point. A new pessimism grabbed the nationals and this manifested itself in FANK's never again seriously attempting to dislodge a major opposing force, in FANK's not even gathering the intelligence which would have told the national military leaders that the NVA had pulled out and that FANK could have retaken many areas nearly unopposed. FANK's force of 130,000 to 150,000 had not improved substantially since 1970. What it had gained in experience and better equipment, it had lost in morale. From the day the column at Baray broke, FANK's offensive spirit, like that of the American Confederacy after Gettysburg, was destroyed.

Pessimism became depression. Without spirit, without hope, internal chaos became rampant. Eighty percent of Cambodia's primary schools were closed. On 16 and 18 December 1971, anti–Lon Nol and antigovernment riots broke out in Phnom Penh. Though the capital was on the verge of collapse the government found the energy to ban all protests, political meetings and public demonstrations. As living conditions deteriorated, the need for external support increased, but the will of the main source of that support, the United States, continued to crumble.

Government authority existed only in scattered enclaves. In January 1971, the U.S. Defense Intelligence Agency reported that the North Viet Namese Army (in reality, all Communist factions) "controlled" 65 percent of the land and 35 percent of the people. The same report indicated that the Viet Namese had recruited 10,000 Khmers into their army and had induced an additional 35,000 to 50,000 to join their political infrastructure (the KVM) in the "liberated" areas. By mid-1971 NVA control had spread over 75 percent of the land, and the population of Phnom Penh had more than doubled to 1.5 million. By January 1972 the percentage of land and people controlled by Communist factions was at an all-time high.

And yet disclosures about FANK during Chenla II—not about its pathetic maneuverings or its corruption, but about its strength—are astounding. Had it been better led, what might have been the results for Southeast Asia? Was Chenla II the nail, for want of which the battle, the war, was lost? And what other ramifications did the lack of that nail have? Did it lead the United States to back into appeasement? Calling it a decent interval? Did that loss set up the Kampuchean genocide?

THE KRAHOM

Just before and during the multi-battle Chenla II campaign, the Krahom, for the first time on a massive scale, evacuated all the inhabitants from a region and then, in actions they labled "pure flame," scorched the earth to deny all others the "natural and population resources" of the area. From north of Kompong Thom down through Phum Chamkar to Tang Kouk, Krahom yotheas torched some 400 hamlets. By force they evacuated at least 50,000 villagers and forced a nearly equal number of elderly and very young to become refugees. Though "pure flame" had been used earlier, this policy of transferring the population as a means of control, of forcing "unproductive elements" to flee and become a burden upon the government, of annihilation of resisters, and of rendering the land barren, was elevated to a new level during Chenla II.

Some historians have said American bombing both killed hundreds of thousands of people and caused the turmoil within Cambodia that created the Krahom and the ensuing holocaust. These historians cite refugee reports and bombing maps to support their theories. The KK (and to some extent the NVA and KVM) used the threat of U.S. bombings throughout the Northern Corridor to induce the rice farmers to quit their lands. When the North Viet Namese Army advanced across this deserted and charred "pure flame" region, Americans did heavily bomb the area. To the peasants who'd been evacuated, the bombings (the NVA went unseen) confirmed to them the words of Krahom yotheas.

The often strained and mended relationship between the North Viet Namese, with its Hanoi-led Khmer Viet Minh, and the nationalist Maoist Krahom was now destroyed. With strength gained through conscription of FANK deserters and the relatively nonpolitical, Sihanouk-supporting peasants (the Khmer Rumdoah, which remained unorganized, fragmented, and under the influence or control of the KVM or KK), the Krahom attacked the rear of the NVA. Unlike June 1970, which saw a small number of skirmishes, or the heavier ambushes of November 1970, which widened the KK-NVA rift (on the surface ameliorated in May 1971), the Chenla II attacks were devastating. For the first time the Krahom attacked in battalion-sized units. They so terrorized the rear of the NVA 5th and 91st divisions that the pathetic FANK column escaped total annihilation.

Of the sixteen Krahom battalions (5,400 troops) fielded as the battle commenced, a quarter were destroyed in early suicide attacks against FANK positions when the North Viet Namese pulled back without notifying the indigenous Communist force. Another quarter never saw battle but were used for evacuee control. How many were lost to Allied bombings is unknown. Upwards of 2,000, in units from squads to battalions, attacked the NVA.

To the outside world Norodom Sihanouk remained the official head of the seemingly monolithic resistance, yet within Krahom-controlled areas, political cadre increased the frequency and severity of their denunciations of the Prince. Krahom leaders continued to maintain ghostlike public profiles while they consolidated their powers. Ieng Sary became chief emissary to Mao, often snubbing Sihanouk. Khieu Samphan, Hou Youn and Hou Nim—known as the "three ghosts" because in spite of their reported deaths three and a half years earlier their presence continued to be felt—rose to hold administrative, organizational and ideological power in the Krahom block. Rising to head the Krahom military (and covertly to hold the office of secretary-general of the Khmer Communist Party) was Saloth Sar (Pol Pot).

THE NVA DRAIN-OFF

The North Viet Namese suffered a strange fate during Chenla II. Essentially they won a great military victory. On 10 December the Associated Press reported that U.S. officials estimated Communist forces (no breakdown by factions) controlled "as much as 80 percent of Cambodia and *can do anything they want*. . . . They could take Cambodia in a week, if they cut loose everything they had."

But they didn't. Why? Was it an awakening to the desires of the Khmer people? Chenla II had set off a deeper "true" Khmer revolution than had yet occurred. Concurrent with the NVA offensive, a new concept of Khmer Patriot spread amongst all segments of society. This new sense of nationalism and racial integrity permeated all zones, whether controlled by the KVM/NVA, the KK or FANK. Though the concept held varying nuances in different regions, it helped bind the disparate zones and, by giving the people a common cause, preparing them for a single, unified takeover.

Or was it NVA political savvy—the realization that if Phnom Penh, and thus Cambodia, fell, the waning American commitment to Southeast Asia might be rekindled? Gallup polls in late 1971 showed that a majority (50 to 55 percent) of Americans approved of President Nixon's war policies. Would a toppling of Phnom Penh have been used to reverse American withdrawals? Or was the North Viet Namese leadership responding to military factors that outweighed these reasons?

Hanoi maintained its belief in the simple assumption that domestic political pressures would sooner or later force American leaders to accept the Communist terms for disengagement. "Those terms . . . amounted to unconditional surrender—unilateral withdrawal of all American troops and the replacement of the anticommunist . . . [Saigon] regime with a Lublin-model Communist front government," wrote Stewart Alsop in *Newsweek* in September 1969. That observation remained valid in 1971, especially with the new domestic political storm brewing in the United States.

On 13 June 1971, *The New York Times* began publishing excerpts of the 47-volume, 7,000-page Pentagon analysis of how, over thirty years, the United States had become committed to the defense of Indochina. Long after the controversy generated by the publication of the "sensitive" Pentagon Papers had become a footnote to the war, some scholars condemned the excerpts as "highly selective." For example, the papers contain details of the Truman administration's military aid to France in its war against the Communist Viet Minh, but omit details of the U.S. effort to convince the French to grant full independence to their colonies. This becomes important only in light of the emphasis placed on the meaning of that U.S. aid by the antiwar movement in the early 1970s and the impact of that movement on U.S. policy. Facts such as the above did not appear in *The New York Times*'s "complete and unabridged" 677-page volume. (Complete and unabridged with respect to what it had published in its own pages, not with respect to the Pentagon document—by page count *The New York Times*'s account is 9½ percent of the Pentagon study.) The tone of *The New York Times* edition was set early when it critiqued U.S. military planners. "The conflict in Indochina," Neil Sheehan wrote in the introduction, "is approached as a practical matter that will yield to the unfettered application of well-trained minds, and of the bountiful resources in men, weapons and money that a great power can command."

Hanoi's America watchers were also paying attention to the continuing My Lai uproar. Five percent of all American network television coverage of the entire war—473 of 9,447 stories aired from 1963 to 1977—dealt with this one atrocity. What happened there is abhorrent. Still, it is incredible that the American media became fixated on an event that accounted for only 3/1000 of one percent (.0003) of the deaths in Indochina during that period.

The North Viet Namese Communist leadership—secure in the belief it had a firm hold over the Cambodian revolution, seeing expanding negative U.S. domestic reaction to news from Southeast Asia, knowing that Nixon's approval rating was based on the American people's desire for a guarantee that all U.S. servicemen held captive by North Viet Nam would be fairly treated and released when all U.S. troops were withdrawn, and placing great emphasis on the increasing limitations set upon the Nixon administration by the U.S. Congress—ceased their attacks on Phnom Penh and redeployed much of that force to the east, not for any of the reasons suggested above but because Hanoi had decided to go for broke in South Viet Nam. This decision, made at the time the KK was engaging the NVA about the Northern Corridor, was a precursor to the largest military offensive to that time in Southeast Asia, North Viet Nam's Nguyen Hue, or Easter, Offensive.

Why did North Viet Nam decide to go for broke? Communist propaganda states that the NVA were attempting to shore up the remnant of the Southern rebel government, the PRG (which the NVA still held in house arrest near Kratie), and its forces, the VC (though Southern rebel units were now manned almost exclusively by Northerners, and, generally, Southern officers were being passed over for promotion and the positions given to Northerners). One must suspect that with U.S. troops mostly withdrawn (all American ground forces were disengaged from combat roles by March 1972) the new NVA strategic target became the destruction of the Republic of Viet Nam Armed Forces (RVNAF). Cambodia could wait.

North Viet Nam's generals saw Southeast Asia as a single mobile battlefield for trucks and armor, whereas the US-ARVN, FANK and Royal Lao militaries tended to see Southeast Asia as three (or, with North Viet Nam, four) separate theaters. Outside Cambodia, the NVA, in mid-November 1971, began a massive buildup at Ho Chi Minh Trail trailheads leading from North Viet Nam into Laos. Concurrently, major road construction was reported throughout the Laotian panhandle, and new and expanded surface-to-air missile sites were photographed all along the trail network. In response, the United States increased the number of B-52 sorties over Laos and thus decreased the number over Cambodia.

Though Chenla II was FANK's breaking point, the republic's death was far off. A major event, the next tsunami—caused by the NVA drain-off—was yet to occur.

STAGING

In December 1971, the NVA 5th and 7th divisions, and part of the 91st, were pulled from "international duty." This is why, when the 25,000-troop ARVN emergency relief force entered Cambodia at the beginning of December, they found very few NVA soldiers to engage. This sort of pullback was not new. In April, May and June 1970, the NVA had pulled back from the Khmer heartland, first to protect the fall-back from the border sanctuaries of other NVA units fleeing the US-ARVN incursion and then to rebuild those sanctuaries in the wake of the U.S. withdrawal. Again in February 1971, in reaction to the Laotian Incursion (Operation Lam Son 719) by ARVN units staging at Khe Sanh, South Viet Nam, and leapfrogging to cut the Ho Chi Minh Trail at Tchepone, Laos, the NVA drew combat and support units from Cambodia.

In late 1971 the NVA continued to maintain its COKA headquarters near Siem Reap. Elements of the 91st Division remained in the North and Northwest. Other units remained spread about the interior (near COSVN headquarters at Kratie and elsewhere), yet, employing more than 15,000 vehicles, the NVA shifted forces from Cambodia, Laos and North Viet Nam. This shift, given great importance by Krahom leaders, created a fundamental change in the balance of forces in Cambodia. Entire armies had been removed, and hundreds of thousands of soldiers were now massed in the border sanctuaries.

In the first two months of 1972 U.S. bombing of the Ho Chi Minh Trail in Laos and of transfer points above and below the demilitarized zone in Viet Nam intensified in an attempt to forestall the anticipated offensive in South Viet Nam. Along the Cambodian border in South Viet Nam, the ARVN generally withdrew and entrenched, letting B-52s and tactical air strikes slow the NVA buildup and advance. Indeed, throughout 1972 the bombing of Cambodia remained at low levels. The sorties flown in all 1972 equalled 40 percent of those flown in 1971, and the majority of the 1972 flights were along the border trail network in the NVA-held northeastern highlands. Significant bombing did not return to the Cambodian interior until after the January 1973 signing of the Paris peace agreement.

The Cambodian Communists saw 1972 as a year to consolidate gains, look for opportunities and stimulate internal contradictions— political struggle versus armed struggle—inside the ranks of all their enemies. Outside of the border provinces only a few major engagements occurred during the year. From 12 to 28 February, a 6,000-man FANK force attempted to unseat the 4,000 NVA holding Angkor Wat near Siem Reap. During this operation Lon Nol reinforced his troops with an additional 4,000 soldiers. Still FANK was unable, or unwilling, to dislodge the North Viet Namese from this long-established headquarters complex. For the remainder of the year FANK battalions settled into a lethargic defensive pattern of protecting enclaved cities. Their mobility, as measured by battalion-days in the field, equalled about 70 percent of that of 1971. Even this, however, is probably a padded figure. On 21 February 1972, Richard Nixon became an unwitting accomplice to Krahom goals by removing one of the main and longest-running motivations for U.S. commitment to Southeast Asia. On that date the American President was greeted in Peking by Prime Minster Zhou Enlai. Suddenly, U.S. containment policies were deemed senseless.

THE EASTER, OR NGUYEN HUE, OFFENSIVE

The NVA offensive into South Viet Nam was World War II Panzerlike action—fast, hard and with a modern twist, helicopters. Some have reduced the violence to Allied air power versus NVA tanks and surface-to-air (Sam-7) missiles. Yet a more conventional victory— crushing firepower decimating an enemy fixed in position by infantry units—has never been gained. The offensive and the victory of the counteroffensive constitute, in the United States, the least-known period of the entire war. In launching the Nguyen Hue Offensive, North Viet Nam's leaders made a fatal assumption. But the consequences of their error were mitigated by Allied political bungling and by Communist "scientific" propaganda. And though these events may seem isolated and distant from Cambodia, the results formed part of the continuum of events leading to the rise of Pol Pot's forces.

On 29 and 30 March 1972 the North Viet Namese Army came out of its enclaved, tactically defensive posture and launched the long-expected offensive against the South. Twelve divisions, 150,000 men supported by more than 500 Soviet tanks plus heavy artillery and self-propelled antiaircraft guns, surged across the demilitarized zone (DMZ), in from Cambodia and Laos, in from the sea.

The first attacks swept across the DMZ from Khe Sanh to Dong Ha, killing hundreds of troops and civilians. On day two, NVA gunners hit twelve DMZ outposts with a cumulative 5,000 rounds of artillery fire. Firebases and small posts were abandoned; and the first skirmish of the second front was fought near Tay Ninh. On 1 April the NVA 304th Division supported by attached artillery and surface-to-air missile units, about 30,000 men, swept across the DMZ, routing the thinly spread ARVN 3d Division. South of the DMZ, Highway QL 9 filled with fleeing refugees. By 4 April most of Quang Tri Province had fallen. About 40,000 refugees fled the onslaught.

Under heavy cloud cover, second-front blitzkrieg assaults rumbled out of Cambodia's Mondolkiri and Kratie provinces and crashed against the ARVN defenders of An Loc in Binh Long Province. Reports of the period are fascinating. During World War II and the Korean War the media were sympathetic to our beleagured allies, but not so in the case of South Viet Nam. Beginning on 3 April, American news coverage nearly universally criticized the ARVN for pulling back without fully engaging enemy forces. They failed, however, to mention that the enemy was numerically superior and was advancing behind superior firepower.

The RVNAF (Republic of Viet Nam Armed Forced: regular forces = ARVN, provincial forces = PF and regional forces = RF) were, with the exception of the Airborne and Marine divisions, stationed in their home provinces, where they were spread thin. When the NVA were dispersed and operating in their terrorism-and-harassment mode, the RVNAF offered maximum protection to the population. But when the Communists massed for tactical offensives, the RVNAF, spread out as they were, were unable to hold and could only blunt the initial assaults. The ARVN then had to adjust to the enemy's numerical superiority by shifting forces to the attacked area. Often, the response time was days; however, once aerial and ground forces reacted and fixed the attackers, the advantage fell to the defenders.

On 6 April the skies cleared and U.S. pilots flew 225 sorties against attackers below the DMZ, and NVA mobility slowed. In the Central Highlands the NVA captured Loc Ninh and trapped the ARVN 5th Infantry Division to the south.

The Communists opened their third major front on 8 April, assaulting east out of Ratanakiri Province, through Duc Co and Plei Ngai and across to the north-south Highway 14. There they cut Kontum from Plei Ku and potential reinforcements. To the south An Loc fell under siege, and American installations at Cam Ranh Bay and Nui Ba Den were hit by rockets. To the north, the next day, U.S. and ARVN air power fixed (prevented from maneuvering) an element of the NVA 304th Division. With their lines of communication and supply broken, the Northerners were trapped beneath a rain of bombs. One thousand men were killed and thirty tanks destroyed.

American ground forces were no longer a part of the Viet Nam War but air power was an ever-greater part. On 10 April two additional aircraft carriers were ordered to the theater, bringing the U.S. total to six. B-52s began hitting NVA lines west of Kontum and within 1½ kilometers of An Loc.

By mid-April, to keep the ARVN dispersed and reinforcements away from the main attack points, NVA rocketeers dropped dozens of 122mm shells on Saigon, Da Nang and other civilian concentrations, while small units assaulted over a hundred sites in the South, nearly all for the first time since Tet 1968.

At first, NVA generals were ecstatic. Although the bombings were taking a significant toll, their progress was awesome. The ARVN 3d, 5th and 22d divisions were at the point of collapse. Major firebases in the north and central regions had been overrun. Underestimating the resilience of the ARVN and the capabilities of regional and provincial forces, and expecting the South to fall, the NVA leaders pulled strategic reserve units from Cambodia and ignored serious reports of Khmer Krahom positioning and attacks.

Meanwhile President Nixon moved away from America's long-term policy of strategic defense—that America would not attack the source of the war, North Viet Nam—and ordered U.S. strategic bombers to hit Hanoi and Haiphong. Within a day, the first major antiwar protests of 1972 erupted on America's college campuses. Within a week, as South Viet Nam fought for its very existence, eight Ivy League college presidents issued a statement condemning U.S. bombing of the North. As NVA attacks intensified at An Loc, at Ah Khe and throughout the Central Highlands, the U.S. House of Representatives' Democratic Caucus voted (4–20) to set a termination date for American support. As the NVA opened up a minor front in the Mekong Delta, as NVA divisions nearly annihilated the ARVN 22d Division, as the number of refugees in South Viet Nam skyrocketed to over 1.5 million and as a dozen Cambodian towns in the Parrot's Beak were overrun by North Viet Namese, 90,000 Americans demonstrated against the war in New York City, San Francisco and Los Angeles.

Within a month, in addition to their gains in South Viet Nam, the NVA held all of Cambodia east of the Mekong with the exception of Neak Luong, Svay Rieng City, a few minor enclaves and the vast tracts the KK had usurped in the absence of any strong presence.

By 1 May, American B-52 and fighter-bomber sorties over North Viet Nam had risen to 350 per day. Now, as nearly 200,000 Communist soldiers attacked on three major fronts in South Viet Nam and as the South Viet Namese people, instead of joining the "popular uprising" resisted or fled ruthless and indiscriminate NVA artillery fire, sixty U.S. college presidents petitioned for the immediate and complete withdrawal of all U.S. forces from Indochina.

On 8 May President Nixon ordered the mining of Haiphong and other North Viet Namese harbors, ordered a naval blockade of North Viet Nam and ordered the rail lines from China bombed. He announced that these orders would be rescinded when all U.S. POWs were released and an internationally supervised cease-fire was signed. In exchange for those conditions, not only would he rescind these orders but he would withdraw all Americans within 120 days. Hundreds of thousands of antiwar demonstrators took to the streets of America.

FACTS AND SPECULATIONS

Although the offensive would continue for another hundred days, the NVA had lost the element of surprise. The ARVN had responded on all fronts, shifting forces to match the massed attack points of the Communists, and the offensive had been blunted. That's not to say the NVA did not continue to advance in some areas. As in their small-unit operations, once the Allies fixed them in position they attempted to withdraw, escape, regroup and reattack elsewhere. Nixon's semistrategic offensive against North Viet Nam stimulated no major reaction from either Moscow or Peking. One suspects the Soviets and Chinese were conceding the war and acquiescing to a new order, as in Korea, of a split Viet Nam. North Viet Nam had wreaked havoc on the South, yet by mid-May analysts for all superpowers knew the North would not topple South Viet Nam. Soviet and Chinese aid to the NVA decreased, not as a response to American military moves cutting supply lines, but because of political fluctuations in the face of America's show of will to stick by its fighting ally.

But Nixon's 8 May announcement, for the first time, did not demand the withdrawal of Northern troops from the South (a pivotal point later in the year). In Hanoi, political and military leaders interpreted the President's speech as acceptance of a cease-fire-in-place concurrent with U.S. withdrawal. Ex-VC Minister of Justice Truong Nhu Tang noted in his book *A Vietcong Memoir:*

> Practically the entire North Vietnamese army was now inside South Vietnam—to stay. . . . Nixon and Kissinger had decided . . . they could have no choice but to accept . . . the *fait accompli* of a full Northern military presence. . . . Their decision was of course induced by powerful factors. The American press was already screaming its rage about renewed bombing of the North. Nor was there anything subtle about the reaction in Congress, which . . . was well on its way toward legislating the United States out of the war.

At this point one sees, on the one hand, a major offensive by the NVA being crushed by the ARVN and by Allied air power; an American military shift from a strategic defensive to a semistrategic offensive posture, no significant political response by North Viet Nam's major allies, and a cutback in Communist materiel supply. On the other hand, in America, the reactions of antiwar demonstrators, the media and Congress (on 9 May the Senate resolved to cut off all war funds) had convinced the administration that it must, in Nixon's words, ". . . bring the war to a decisive military conclusion." The Nixon regime thus accepted the one element President Thieu feared most, allowing the NVA to remain on Southern territory. In Communist terms, the North Viet Namese had achieved their major goal, that of stimulating their enemies' internal contradictions—separating South Viet Nam from the United States and President Nixon from the American people.

As an example of that latter separation, an analysis of television news coverage (three major networks only) for the period 15 April to 15 May 1972 reveals that of 258 stories, 132 supported "antiwar" viewpoints, 15 presented "pro-war" perspectives and the remaining 111 were neutral. Of all the NVA shellings of civilian areas, of the leveling of entire cities, America saw only two clips. There was not a single mention of NVA weapons captured. On the surface this seems insignificant, but the capture of enemy weapons has always been a symbol of victory in battle, so the zero mention juxtaposed with mentions of ARVN losses is significant. And only one story was a battle analysis. Again, Truong Nhu Tang makes a relevant point:

> The idea that continued American intervention was immoral was gaining widespread credence in the United States. . . . These were signs that told us the offensive was a success and at this stage of the war we received them with as much satisfaction as we received news of any military victory.

ARVN counterattacks and other military successes increased through-out May. A thousand paratroopers hit the NVA behind their lines in Quang Tri Province and killed 300. B-52s inflicted immense casual-ties on NVA massed formations. Along the Ho Chi Minh Trail and in North Viet Nam, B-52s destroyed pipelines and pumping stations, reducing the amount of fuel available to the NVA's fleet of vehicles. The ARVN 23d Division counterattacked at Kontum and the 9th and 21st divisions at An Loc. In the midst of the fighting, Richard Nixon flew to Moscow for a summit meeting with Leonid Brezhnev. As the NVA reattacked Kontum (the tank-led frontal assault was shattered *in* the city by B-52s) and as they opened a fourth major front against provincial and regional forces in the Mekong Delta, politicians in Saigon and Hanoi both feared sellouts by their superpower patrons.

Although North Viet Nam committed a 200,000-troop force to the spring offensive, some commentators labeled it "Hanoi's essentially political offensive." In the long run, they were right. Hanoi's political goals were to capitalize on U.S. domestic antiwar sentiment, to discredit Saigon and Viet Namization, and to convince the United States to acquiesce to their negotiation demands. Senator George McGovern told the American people on 7 June that he would go "anywhere in the world" to negotiate an end to the war. On 3 June, Seymour Hersh had made the secret Peers Report on My Lai public. On the 17th, five men were arrested while breaking into the

Democratic National Committee headquarters at the Watergate Hotel in Washington, D.C. A month later, as the U.S. Senate voted to force the withdrawal of U.S. support within 120 days of the release of all American POWs, Ramsey Clark and Jane Fonda "visited" Hanoi. In August, as an average of 206 South Viet Namese civilians were killed or seriously wounded every day (60-day average) by attacking NVA, 3,000 antiwar protestors marched behind death masks at the Republican National Convention in Miami.

Still the fighting, the offensive and counteroffensive continued, but the NVA had been hurt by Hanoi's miscalculation of the RVNAF's abilities and by the premature assumption on the part of Hanoi's Politburo that the state of American resolve was so low there would be no significant response by U.S. air power. The NVA suffered an estimated 100,000 casualties plus the loss of 50 percent of its heavy equipment. Those figures are astonishing. A modern army unit which loses 15 to 20 percent of its fighting men is considered operationally out of commission, and with regard to the NVA, subsequent military and political activities indicate that it was so crippled. North Viet Nam's most famous general, Vo Nguyen Giap, victor of Dien Bien Phu and designer of the Khe Sanh and Tet 1968 offensives, was eased from power and replaced by Senior General Van Tien Dung.

Still the offensive did not stop, though by 1 September it was a matter of public show not territorial gain, a matter of keeping up the appearance of a major offensive though the NVA had actually reverted to the tactical defensive generally launching only battalion-sized cross-border forays. Meanwhile, the morale of the ARVN, flush with mounting victories, was riding an adrenaline high. As for television, there were no news stories about NVA defections, though they reached an estimated 20,000 during the offensive.

For the Khmer Communists, both the KK and the KVM, and thus for the battle for Cambodia, there was probably no single event more important than the NVA Easter offensive. FANK and the republic had become nearly totally dependent on foreign financial assistance. In the wake of his disastrous meddling and his mishandling of Chenla II, in March 1972 Lon Nol dissolved the National Assembly and declared himself president and supreme commander of the armed forces. Internal conflicts, corruption and ineptitude increased. American support for Lon Nol increased as his situation worsened.

The decimation of major NVA elements made the NVA unable to return to their deep Cambodian bases and protect their hold on that country's revolution. The drain-off occurred in late 1971; the offensive had been launched in March 1972 and had continued until August. The drain-off continued during the last months of the offensive because Hanoi's desire to obtain the greatest political concessions of the war required every last troop it could scrape up. In that nine-month period the KK purged much of the KVM infrastructure and conquered (not "inherited"—the most frequently used word in histories of the period) many of the old NVA "liberated" zones.

THE PARIS PEACE AGREEMENT

On 27 January 1973 "An Agreement Ending the War and Restoring Peace in Viet Nam" was signed in Paris by American, North Viet Namese, South Viet Namese and Viet Cong representatives. American and Communist officials signed one version; Saigon's agents signed another. The Saigon version stood fast by Nguyen Van Thieu's unwillingness to acknowledge or legitimize the Viet Cong's Provisional Revolutionary Government. The settlement included eleven essential points, of which the most important were a cease-fire-in-place coupled with the withdrawal of all American forces (including advisors) and the dismantling of all U.S. bases within 60 days, the release of all U.S. prisoners of war, the recognition of the NVA's right to maintain troops on Southern territory, the withdrawal of all foreign troops from and the prohibition of resupply lines through or sanctuaries in Cambodia and Laos, recognition of the temporary status of the 17th Parallel DMZ until reunification of North and South, North Viet Namese "respect" for South Viet Nam's right to self-determination, and a renunciation of the use of military force to "reunite" the country. No Khmer faction signed any version of the agreement.

American, Viet Namese and Cambodian military actions of 1973 can be understood only in light of events prior to the Paris accords: the Nguyen Hue Offensive, the Christmas bombings, Operation Enhancement Plus, land-grab tactics, and Norodom Sihanouk's and Lon Nol's offers and other actions.

Bombing allegedly had broken the ability and the will of the NVA to continue its massed blitzkrieg spring-summer offensive in South Viet Nam. After pulling seasoned forces from Laos and Cambodia and augmenting them with green troops from North Viet Nam, after suffering 100,000 combat casualties and after the destruction of 50 percent of its armor, artillery and trucks, the NVA dropped this military strategy and reverted to dispersed terrorism and small-unit engagements. In Saigon, in Washington and in Phnom Penh, as well as in Hanoi, Peking and Moscow, military planners and political leaders rediscovered the effectiveness of tactical-strategic bombing. Even though ARVN ground force counterattacks, supported by U.S. and South Viet Namese tactical air power, played a greater role than the oft-noted B-52s, some observers, including many leading civilian detractors of South Viet Nam's forces, concluded that bombing won the battle.

In the periods of the drain-off from Cambodia, of the reversion to guerrilla tactics and the rebuilding of forces, when the NVA could not sustain combat, Hanoi launched the political offensive that led to the initial "breakthrough" agreements of October 1972. Those agreements led the Nixon White House to implement Operation Enhancement Plus, a move to transfer two billion dollars in materiel from U.S. forces to the RVNAF. (The figure included the value of bases of little use to the defending forces, who had a parallel network of bases, plus used weapons valued at replacement cost. The amount of arms and munitions was still significant.)

The breakthrough agreement was seen in Hanoi as America's capitulation. In negotiations after the agreement was "reached" (Saigon's leadership never accepted it), North Viet Nam increased its demands. On 21 October Pham Van Dong announced five conditions for the cease-fire, including the realignment of Saigon's governmental structure to reflect a VC-RVN coalition and the demand for a general election within six months. On the 26th, Le Duc Tho, in an atmosphere of U.S. congressional, media and public disgust with the war, won agreement for a total U.S. withdrawal and the permanent presence of the NVA in the South.

In response President Nixon declared there would be no signing until all issues were resolved. This need for resolution, Pham Van Dong stated, *forced* the NVA to launch 142 attacks on 2 and 3 November in South Viet Nam.

Ten days later, as the United States turned over the Long Binh facilities to the ARVN, and as indigenous Southern rebel troops (VC) unsuccessfully revolted against a major purge attempt of Southerners by Northerners in the border-based units, Norodom Sihanouk, nominal head of the Khmer Communist government in exile, rejected Lon Nol's offer to join the cease-fire agreement.

The situation deteriorated further in early December. Hanoi ordered strategic reserve units throughout North Viet Nam to head south to grab as much territory as possible before any agreement was finalized. (Saigon's forces were doing the same.) Bien Hoa and Tan Son Nhut were rocketed; heavy assaults were launched in the Central Highlands and south of the DMZ. In Paris the Communists demanded that the International Supervisory Team be limited to 250 members (the United States wanted 3,000), and Saigon's representatives demanded that Southern sovereignty be recognized. In Cambodia, Khieu Samphan rejected Lon Nol's renewed request for negotiations. On 13 December U.S. jets caught and destroyed one hundred Soviet-built T-54 tanks heading south on the Ho Chi Minh Trail in Laos. All talks broke off.

Now came Operation Linebacker II, the "Christmas bombings." At 9:43 p.m. on 18 December 1972, U.S. B-52s unleashed their bomb loads on Hanoi. For seventeen of the next eighteen days (Christmas excluded), American planes dropped 40,000 tons of explosives on North Viet Nam. Fifteen B-52s and eleven escort planes were shot down during the raids, which amounted to 729 B-52 sorties and 1,000 fighter-bomber sorties.

During the period, Hanoi reported 1,623 civilians killed. Free world press reports were heavily critical of "America's immoral act." There were almost no reports of NVA attacks on civilian population centers in South Viet Nam during the period even though Northern troops attacked or shelled cities throughout the South, peaking with fifty-six attacks on 27 December. Operation Linebacker II ended on 30 December with indications from Hanoi's representatives that they'd had enough. Again, military and political planners in all the countries involved concluded that the decisive element that had returned Hanoi to the negotiations was bombing. Again, bombing allegedly had won the battle. Bombing was a decisive tool.

To many in the West the issue was confused—internal contradictions were stimulated. Martin F. Herz and Leslie Rider, in *The Prestige Press and the Christmas Bombing* (1972), revealed major discrepancies between the reports and the reality.

"The U.S. prestige press [*The New York Times*, the *Washington Post*, *Time*, *Newsweek*, and the commercial TV networks] was outraged. . . . The *Times* said that 'civilized man will be horrified at the renewed spectacle of the world's mightiest air force mercilessly pounding a small Asian nation.' " Later it called the bombing "terrorism on an unprecedented scale." The *Post* said it was "the most savage and senseless act of war ever visited, over a scant ten days, by one sovereign people upon another."

Editorial writers and columnists also uncritically accepted certain assertions. A December 28 *Post* editorial said:

> To pretend . . . that we are making "enduring peace" by carpet-bombing our way across downtown Hanoi . . . is to practice yet one more cruel deception upon an American public already cruelly deceived. It is, in brief, to compound what is perhaps the real immorality of this administration's policy—the continuing readiness to dissemble, to talk of "military targets" when what we are hitting are residential centers and hospitals and commercial airports. . . .

According to Herz and Rider; the *Post* accepted as fact Hanoi's charges that residential areas of Hanoi were "carpet-bombed"; "it accused the administration of 'cruel deception' " about why the peace talks broke down; "it was convinced . . . that the bombing would not lead to an agreement; and it rejected the Administration's statements that our bombers were *aiming* only at military targets. . . . The *Post*, like the *Times,* had for years given greater credence to enemy claims about the war than to statements issued by U.S. officials—not always without justification."

Yet eyewitness accounts of the damage to Hanoi contradict the claims of carpet-bombing. A *Times* writer reported from Hanoi after the January agreement that the damage "was grossly overstated by North Vietnamese propaganda." A *Washington Star* reporter wrote from Hanoi in late March: "Some press reports had given . . . the impression that Hanoi had suffered badly in the war—but in fact the city is hardly touched."

Herz and Rider concluded, "The editorial position of the prestige press doubtless affected their selection of news stories . . . converting news reporting to editorializing via selection and thus subverted the free formation of opinion essential to a democracy." Further, the authors found, "The relative silence of the U.S. government . . . deprived the media of some information . . ."; that there was "no evidence that the U.S. Air Force engaged in the 'carpet-bombing' of civilian centers" and that "As an incentive to resume serious negotiations, the bombing . . . appears to have been . . . effective . . . this reality has never been acknowledged by the prestige press, which did so much to obscure the issue."

All these perceptions and more, accurate and inaccurate, by planners, policy makers and the public, were brought to bear on Cambodia. The peace accords, by dealing with only one of four fronts, set the stage for the war's continuation. Now, the Krahom would begin in earnest to launch its own offensive and would simultaneously attempt to eliminate all "tainted" elements from within its own structure. And America would respond with its only "decisive tool."

Then would follow the second eye of the storm, a lull after that most violent of firestorms—a firestorm of pure flame and arc light combined.

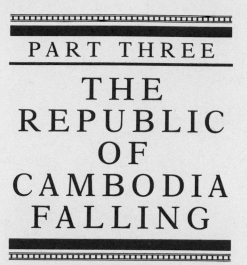

PART THREE

THE REPUBLIC OF CAMBODIA FALLING

The breaking of a nation's will to
resist is the final object in war. . . .
In international power politics, the
willingness to accept challenge
is far, far more important than
physical capacity to wage war. Here
we have failed. Currently, ally
and enemy alike regard the United
States as having lost its will to
resist Communism in all other parts
of the world with the exception of
the United States. [Though we]
have affirmed and re-affirmed our
commitment . . . our actions do
not follow our words.
                    —Ernest Cuneo,
                     syndicated columnist,
                     April 1970

CHAPTER FOURTEEN
1972

He stood in Oudong, in his filthy stinking Caucasian skin, in his rotting fatigues, in his disgust, attempting, why he didn't know, to control his exasperation and the volume of his voice. "Talk to the refugees," he said. "We still don't know what really happened. Talk to them."

"Oh yes, Captain! We know." The FANK liaison officer smiled broadly. "It is very good that you aren't killed."

"Damn it!" Sullivan could no longer control it. "There's a proper system for this. There's a way to get results. You can't continue to fall headlong into these things without knowing what you're hitting." With Sullivan were a small group of frightened civilians, as filthy and emaciated as he from their months of hiding, trudging through backwater swamps, not knowing the front had evaporated, not knowing they could have safely emerged weeks earlier.

"Here"—the liaison officer's smile pasted on his face infuriated Sullivan—"in Cambodia we have our own ways. My senior officer . . ."

"Let me talk to him."

"Of course, Captain. You must clean up; have dinner with . . ."

"Damn it," Sullivan barked. "Look!" He grabbed a map from a second rear staff officer. "Look, you've got to get to the heart of this. Your commander has a responsibility to more than the glory of command. He's got people. He's got . . ." Sullivan stopped. Ten feet to his right Rita Donaldson was snapping his photograph. "What the hell're you doing?"

"Are you advising, Captain?" She laughed mockingly. "Phew! You're a sight!"

"Only observing end use, Mrs. Donaldson." Sullivan backed a step away from the Cambodian.

"Ms."

"Hum?"

"Ms. Not Mrs., Captain. I think the photos will show you advising. You've been . . ."

"You got a real obsession with that, don't you, lady?"

"Do you mean, I'm obsessed with following the letter and spirit of American laws?"

"God! For what, a month I've . . ." He curbed his speech.

"Yes, tell me. You were missing in action. General Cleland will be happy you're back."

"Back! I . . ." Again he curbed his tongue. "Who?"

"While you've been doing what you say you haven't, MEDT had a command change. Cleland for Mataxis. Now . . . it's John, isn't it? May I call you John? Call me Rita."

Sullivan sighed. He shook his head. "I . . ."

"Yes? Where have you been?"

"I've been watchin guys, the bravest soldiers I've ever known, stop an NVA charge. One guy . . . You bitch! I've been struggling to get back. . . . Where the fuck do you think I've been? I watch this guy, Suong . . . poor fucker got greased . . . and you, Mrs. Donaldson! come up here one fucking hour after I get dragged from the fucking swamp and tell me I'm advising!"

"Photographs don't lie, Captain."

Stung Treng was symbolic. The Krahom had moved back, east, into KVM-NVA territory. The NVA had withdrawn its main force units to border sanctuaries and staging areas for duty yet farther east. The drain-off was at hand.

The Standing Committee of the Central Committee of the Kampuchean Communist Party, the Center, infiltrated the city. Riding a wave of questionable victories they met secretly, not like animals in forest hovels but as winning commanders in conquered territory behind the new front, met in a modest wood and brick home overlooking rice fields that reached west to the Mekong. Met Sar welcomed each member. With him, smiling, her political demeanor as pleasant as the best of first ladies, Sar's wife, Met Pon, also welcomed the party's "old men."

"You've lost weight." Met Yon grasped Pon's hands after passing the guards.

"A little." Pon tilted her head slightly to one side. Her smile twitched involuntarily.

"As always you're lovely," Yon said. He himself was gray haired and frail. "Did China agree with you?"

"A little yes"—Pon's eyes fixed on the planner—"a little no. What weight I've lost, the Prince has gained."

"Ha! He grows fat, yes?"

"More than ever." Pon smiled.

Inside, the intensity of Sar's, Met Phan's and Met Dy's informal talk was rising. "We've learned so much," Yon heard Sar say.

Phan agreed. "When that terrifying, murderous force broke loose, our soldiers, just children, jumped into those flames, into those explosions. I"—the tactician tapped his chest—"taught many of them at Pong Pay. Ah, many died. Still their heroism saved the revolution for millions."

Sar's eyes flicked to the others as he spoke. "Their sacrifice makes my sense of life more acute. What greatness! What courage! The willingness to die for the future of others. Angkar must, forever, record their sacrifice."

"And yet," Met Dy said with bitterness, "there was the other. There was tragedy." He turned slightly from Sar. Dy had lost a son in the Northern Corridor fighting. As the personnel chief of the Krahom, he felt as if he'd lost a thousand.

Sar seethed. "Tragedy is caused by disgraceful elements, by irresponsible allies."

The Center's January meeting was the most important meeting of the year. Security was tight. The entire Krahom leadership was assembled; the first planning session was attended only by the Center's very core—the ideologues and the high generals.

"They hold Kampuchea by fear, terror and ruthlessness." There was disgust in Met Sar's voice. "Kampuchea can be delivered only by greater terror, greater ruthlessness. Answer terror with terror, attack with attack."

Politely Met Yon interrupted the general. "Our forces," Yon said, "have taken magnificent steps, yet military advantage does not always fall to the successful. Until it does, the main thrust of our energies must be aimed at stimulating the internal contradictions of our enemies. Now it's American hearts and minds . . ."

"It's no longer a matter"—Met Phan shot the words at the frail Yon—"of anyone's hearts and minds. Words are slow. We have the force."

Met Yon rushed to change the subject. To Sar he said, "You met with the Prince, eh?"

"Meas"—Sar impatiently indicated the secretary-scribe—"has the record."

Met Meas opened what looked like a great ledger. He recounted the formal meetings with Norodom Sihanouk and Penn Nouth. "In China," Meas said, "there is the slogan 'Revolution is Endless.' Met Sar told the Prince, 'In Kampuchea, revolution has just begun.'" Meas paused, glanced at Met Sar, continued. "Chairman Mao stated long ago, 'War is the highest form of struggle for resolving contradictions.' Met Phan told the Prince, 'In Kampuchea, contradictions have just been broken into their elements. Now the dialectic process may surge forth.'" Meas closed the ledger, looked back to Sar.

"Meas"—Yon leaned forward—"I want to know more of Sihanouk. What does he do? What did he say about the battle in the Northern Corridor? About irresponsible allies?"

"We have his support," Sar answered for Meas. "We've guaranteed him ours."

"And the arms?"

"He'll press the Chinese." Sar turned to Phan.

"I told him," Phan began, "the Viet Namese steal weapons destined for our armies."

"What did he say?" Yon asked.

"He's cognizant of yuon hypocrisy," Sar said.

"All Khmers, I told him," Phan continued, "need beware of the Viet desire for hegemony. He agrees. But he's powerless. Without us."

"It makes no difference," Sar said, cutting the point short. "We have reached a critical moment. Perhaps, all our enemies can be defeated by destroying just one. That should be our focus, eh?"

"Who?" Meas said. "The Yankee aggressors? That traitorous Lon Nol–Sirik Matak clique? Those stinging red ants from North Viet Nam?"

Met Sar and Met Phan laughed. "For a year," Sar said, "we've waited for Hanoi's withdrawal. This is the greatest of opportunities. We've inherited what is justly ours."

Phan added, "To achieve national unity we shall neutralize the propaganda of our enemies, divide those of the unliberated zones one against all and all against each other until there is confusion and no ability to withstand the Will of Angkar."

Phan and Sar laughed again and, for a few moments, the meeting broke into paired talk. Then Met Dy addressed the group. "We reorganized the army," he said. "We expanded our forces even while they were engaged in combat. Last quarter we lost four battalions in the Northern Corridor yet this past year's gains have resulted in a great influx of yothea-trainees. In the northern zone alone, Met Koy notes in September he fielded five thousand fighters. Now his strength is doubled."

"Reports from other zones are similar," Phan said. "Along with FANK deserters, more and more recruits flee unliberated cities to join the Khmer Patriots."

"Our territory has doubled," Dy said. "We've expanded against Lon Nol and greatly against the yuon. Our population resource has increased sevenfold."

Phan spoke again. "We were able to completely frustrate the NVA in all except the eastern and northeastern zones, and the Americans everywhere they attempted . . ."

"How?" Sar barked. "How have we used the Americans? Dialectics! American strength is down by four hundred thousand. Those troops once brought a false economic boom to South Viet Nam that seeped across our border. Now they're going. In their wake is massive unemployment. Recession. Depression. Here too! As the economy worsens the lackey clique will be hard-pressed to satisfy its greed. Prices soar. FANK's corrupt leaders steal more and more. Victims are our most vehement supporters. Organize the urban populations to prepare the way for our military advances!

"For a year we've denied the yuons a major city," Sar continued. "Now we must deny them the ability to communicate their position to potential supporters. Stimulate yuon internal contradictions and isolate them from the people. Our military position must be strengthened. There's where to use America. Assist the imperialists in destroying the yuons and assist the Viets in evicting the imperial running dogs. Public opinion is an objective factor which must be manipulated. America is vulnerable. Nixon promised the war would end. His people scrutinize his every word. Help the yuons force concessions. Be a sliver in the foot of the giant. Be a mosquito in his ear. Distract him while the wolves tear at his throat.

"But don't publicly harm the North Viet Namese. We will beat them. Met Nang of Kompong Thom has shown all that they are not gods! But the world must witness our united front under that lackey Landless Johnny in China. Sihanouk! Bah!"

Sar stood. "Let the goal be two pronged. In prepared areas let the armies respond. In enclaves like Neak Luong and Battambang where the government still dupes the people, proceed with political offensives. As to the yuons, their flaws are our opportunities. They're tied to preparation for a new offensive in the South. Can we eliminate that painful humiliation of COKA? FANK's military weakness makes the republic vulnerable on the political front. Let our ideology control our actions. Our system is righteous and pure. Our strength grows. The Khmer people, all the world's people, have become skeptical of Lon Nol and the morality of the imperialists."

"You can go now," Sullivan said.

"Yep. I kin go now," Huntley answered. He hung his head. "You gonna be ah right, sir?"

"I'm okay, Ron."

"Goddamn fuck, J. L. . . ." Huntley lumbered over to his old team leader, grabbed him in a bear hug, squeezed him, then let go.

Sullivan returned the hug but without feeling, as if he needed to cap his emotions, as if, if he didn't, they would break, run wild, explode. "You really got them to extend you until I got back?"

"Ah, weren't nothin. I knew you'd make it. But I couldn't go till I knew you'd made it."

"Thanks, Ron."

"Jus one other thing, J. L."

"Yeah."

"Mrs. Cahuom in Neak Luong . . ." Huntley paused. A flash of pain shot onto Sullivan's face. "Naw. Nothin like that," Huntley said, reading Sullivan. "I got word she knew you was missin and was real concerned. That's all. Ya oughta take some time, go en see her."

"Yeah. When, Ron? When?"

"Soon as you kin, J. L."

"You're going to miss your flight, Ron."

"Yeah. I gotta git."

"I'd take you if they'd let me out of here."

"It'll blow over."

"Yeah."

Huntley turned to leave, then turned back: Again he embraced Sullivan. This time Sullivan squeezed back. "I love ya, J. L.," Huntley said. "Don't get yerself KIAed. This war ain't worth it. And, ah . . . J. L. . . . you don't gotta kill all the commies yerself."

"You hold, within your bodies, within Angkar, infinite powers." Sar paused. In the long center aisle of the warehouse, nearly a hundred top cadre and fighters of Angkar sat on makeshift pews of rosewood, mahogany, teak or ebony. They had come from all zones, though mostly from the north, northeast and east, a hand-picked elite subcore, representing their zonal army or party center apparatus. Some had been trained at Pong Pay, some at newer schools. Some were children, most were teenagers.

Seven were secretly, unknown even to themselves, tapped for provisional membership in the Kampuchean Communist Party.

The themes of the general meeting rehashed the conclusions from the Center's meeting: move with force against the KVM and NVA and seize their areas; move militarily against FANK to create ambiguity and doubt within government-controlled areas and within the minds of the republic's chief sponsor; covertly increase Angkar's propaganda and proselytizing in the enclaves to stimulate contradictions and weaken the people's will to resist. But the crux of the meeting was not themes. This was Met Sar's show, a moment for him to display his soft-spoken piety, his polished confidence. It was a stage to build his personal following, to solidify allegiance to Met Sar. In other meetings other elements—higher cadre, zone secretaries, zone commanders—would be the target audience. But in the Stung Treng warehouse the aim was to develop ties with those just beneath the zone leaders, to develop allegiances which could circumvent the chain of command when necessary.

For an hour Sar lambasted the traitorous Phnom Penh arch-antipeople fascists: Lon Nol, Sirik Matak, Son Ngoc Thanh, In Tam, Cheng Heng, Sosthèns Fernandez and all others whose names and titles flowed from his cunning mind to his tongue. In a sweet voice he explained the failings of Norodom Sihanouk and the gang of exiled leaders in Peking. He noted that their sins were caused not by malicious hearts but by stupidity and incompetence. He added that although this was a family matter to be kept within Kampuchea, those sins, for whatever reason, were committed and the people had suffered horribly from the commitment.

Then Sar stopped. A mangled hand caught his eye. "We shall develop into a society where the great majority of the working class is served by all," he said. His eyes jumped to a disfigured face. "As in China, we too shall give the people five guarantees: enough food, enough clothing, enough firewood, an honorable funeral, and education for the children." Nang shifted. He lay his mangled right hand on his clean black trousers. Sar's voice roughened. "For this," he said—his eyes would not leave Nang's features—"we must rely solely upon ourselves. Never again can we ally ourselves with tigers who are black on one side, white on the other. Kampuchea for Kampucheans."

Four hours later Nang stood alone with Met Sar. "You've sacrificed greatly for Angkar." Sar struggled to keep his eyes from Nang's face and hand.

"I am . . ." Nang began. Suddenly, before Sar, he felt power-less, felt as if he'd been reduced to a robot. ". . . the sacrifice."

"Angkar recognizes your sacrifice." Sar's voice was flat. "You're to receive special privileges."

"I ask nothing," Nang responded.

Sar reached forward. He grabbed the boy gently by both upper arms. "This must be kept absolutely secret," he whispered.

"Never has a secret seeped from my lips," Nang answered.

Sar raised Nang's right hand and stared at the jumbled, scarred mass. In his mind the repulsive paw reduced the yothea's worth. Nang suspected the older man's thought. He sees an invalid, Nang thought. An ugly pathetic cripple to be used and discarded.

"Struggle," Sar hissed. "Struggle hard, Nang. Nothing is im-possible. Let your will drive ten cadre. Let theirs drive ten leaders. Let the leaders' drive ten squads and the squads' drive ten cells. In that way your will multiplies and the revolution expands."

"It is the Will of Angkar?"

"Yes. Each Khmer shall kill thirty Viets before he dies. You must drive them. Some will kill less. You must kill more to make up for them."

"It is the Will of Angkar!"

"In this way we will regain our lands and liquidate our enemies. Indochina shall have no Viet Nam. Six million Khmers will rule."

"I am desire not contrary to duty," Nang answered. Inside he tensed at his own answer. As much as he loved Sar he did not like the near-magical control that Sar had over him.

"Very good. Tomorrow you shall be brought before the Center."

Nang had not had, perhaps never would have, an adolescence. He had the School of the Cruel. He had yothea training. Cadre training. Ever-growing combat experience. Beneath the hun-dred layers of barbarity still lay a small boy who had never grown up, who perhaps would never grow up, who would react to every confrontation, no matter how slight, with survival-mode behavior learned at eleven and twelve years of age, react be-cause the very core beneath the cold layers was as insecure and fearful as a child in nightmare, was, since the scalding of his face and the cleaving of his fingers, further frightened for its own biological integrity. At fifteen Nang was, as Sar fully recog-nized, a perfect candidate for provisional membership. Along with Met Rin of Svay Rieng, Met Nu, head of the quickly expanding *neary* force, and four others, Nang was tapped for membership because he was controllable, predictable, capable of great violence without visible remorse. Sar knew the awarding of provisional status would whet Nang's appetite and further cement Nang's loyalty to him. Too, it would encourage others to struggle. Giving the new status to Nang was like improving the guidance system of a sophisticated weapons system. Despite his human core, Nang had reached a new automaton level—an ideologically preprogrammed intelligence capable of learning, capable of the most complex reasoning, yet still an ideopathic robotoid. Like every weapon system, inside, at the core, lay a flaw, a vulnerability, a weakness. In Nang, it was the fear, the nightmarish insecurity of preadolescence, that made him both capable of being controlled and susceptible to losing control. As older boys were shaped for the brotherhood Nang remained aloof, alone, loyal to Met Sar's ideology, ever climbing, ever grabbing for more influence, more power, more something to sate the insatiable, to fill a void of the past that could have been filled only in the past and thus would always remain hungry and grabbing. And to it would come new confusions, new inner contradictions.

"Come Nang." They had met, as Met Nu had suggested at the end of the general meeting, at dusk at the back door of the now vacant warehouse. For half an hour, Nang had wandered the streets of Stung Treng. There were no cars, no *samlos*, few carts or trucks. Where market women once had cackled behind stalls heaped with produce, fish, tobacco and common wares, there were only the wooden skeletons of stalls. Where boys and girls had lingered before dancehalls, there was no one. Where students had wandered aimlessly listening to their transistor radios there was a jeep with a tape recorder and an amplifier blaring a recent speech by Norodom Sihanouk out to the sampan village which still clung to the south bank of the Srepok. ". . . join with all Khmer Patriots to oust . . ." Distant small-arms fire north of the confluence had interrupted Nang's concentration.

"Come Nang," Met Nu said again. She was as tall as he, as heavy as he. Only in her midtwenties, Met Nu was the commander of the *neary* force, an all–girl-woman brigade of the Krahom. Nu's skin, deep brown from years in the jungle, was lined and cracked but her vibrance made up for what she lacked in personal care, youth, natural beauty.

What's happened to the city? Nang thought but he did not speak. A slow, steady, hot dry wind was being sucked from the mountains toward the vast central plains. In it city dust swirled.

The city had fallen to the NVA/KVM without much of a fight and again to the Krahom without battle. Few of the two- and three-story structures showed signs of war. Stung Treng had not been bombed. Nothing was reduced to rubble. Still the city's countenance was one of war weariness and depletion.

"Come back into the warehouse with me." Nu smiled pleasantly. "I want to show you something." Then harshly she cursed, "Did you hear that fucking demagogue say all that crap about Khmer Patriots? Someday I'll have him under my guns."

"Oh," Nang said as they entered the darkened cavern, "the broadcast . . . I don't listen to him anymore."

Again Nu's voice was sweet. "Come Nang," she said. "Come here next to me." She stood with him close, face to face. "I like you. Do you know that?"

"I owe you my life," Nang said, thinking of the unnamed hamlet south of Phum Chamkar where, by holding her skirt, he'd pretended to use her as a hostage and thus kept the Khmer Viet Minh agents at bay. Her closeness made him uneasy.

Nu stepped closer until their breaths mingled in the stale air of the warehouse. "It's okay," she whispered sweetly. Nu placed her hands at his hips. Nang thought of countermoves, of parries, of leg sweeps. Her touch was soft even though her hands were rough and callused. "It's okay," she whispered again as she slid one hand between his legs and gently squeezed him. Nang stood perfectly still. He was afraid, confused. A yothea was pure. A yothea was righteous. A yothea was desire not contrary to duty. Nu massaged the growing erection in his pants. "You like that, don't you? I can tell." Nang's face flashed a silly smile. Nu unbuttoned his fly. Then she took his left hand and brought it to her breast. "It's okay, Nang," she said sweetly. "Squeeze me. Feel me."

Nang squeezed Nu's breast as she lightly stroked the hard rod pressing against his pants. For him the sensations were new. Her soft firmness, the nipple projecting into the center of his palm, the warmth. With his right hand he rubbed her hip, back to the hard muscular ass, down her outer thigh. She nuzzled her face into his neck and nipped him, then turned her head and gently bit his jaw, then his chin. As she did she slipped two fingers into his pants and touched, pulled at his cock. "I . . . I . . . I am of the Brotherhood of the Pure," he stammered, confused.

"And I, of the Sisterhood of the Pure," Nu purred. "That makes it okay. Two pure people can do this. It's right for us. Undo my shirt."

Nang raised his right hand to the buttons. Nu opened his pants. Immediately Nang dropped his hand. Nu grabbed both his hands and crushed them to her breasts as she thrust her groin against him. She grabbed his right hand and kissed the stubs. She licked them. She sucked them, all the time forcing his good hand under her shirt. "These"—Nu gasped, licked the stubs again—"these are a symbol of your love for our people and for Angkar." Her left hand was strong, hard. With it she held his right wrist and jammed his mutilation into her mouth. Her shirt was open. She gyrated her breasts against his arm and chest. She grabbed his erection and pressed it against her pants. Then she backed half a step away to stare at the manhood in her hand as she roughly stimulated her own left tit with his two-fingered paw.

In Nang's mind a floodgate holding back the long-inundated past creaked open, splashing his consciousness with humiliation. *Some of the girls already saw me*, a voice whimpered. *Khieng and Heng held me.*

Nu opened her pants. Nang's erection wilted. Nu mashed his two-fingered hand against her pubic bush, mashed and rammed it back and forth opening her labia. "This is your first time, isn't it?" Her mouth was wet, juicy. "I'll make it very special," she whispered. She pushed him down to his knees, circled him, removed his shirt and hers. She stood before him. Removed her pants, advanced, rubbing her thigh against his scarred face. Then Nu put a foot under his cock and balls and worked it side to side, back and forth, working her big toe to the rim of his anus. "You're such a sweet boy," she babbled. Again she held his right wrist, now working his stubs over her clitoris. As if moonstruck Nang bit her thigh, hard from thousands of miles of trail walking, bit her as she undulated against his hand and head. "Do you think, my lovely Nang," Nu mumbled, "that that bastard in China does this? He steals a hundred thousand riels every month to wine and dine Chinese whores while we fight and die for the people. Ooo!" She rubbed his stubs hard over her clit. "Smell me! Do I smell like Sihanouk's whores? Oh, my little piggy. Can you smell other men on me?" She grabbed his head and forced it between her thighs. "Smell me, Piggy. Snort me. Root your nose in me, Pig. Am I a butterfly? Ummm . . . !"

Nu backed away, panting, spent. She smirked at the mostly naked boy still kneeling before her. "Next time," she said as she pulled her clothes on, "I'll make it very special . . . for you." Then she left.

For a moment Nang remained on his knees staring down the length of the warehouse. He felt used, dirty, humiliated. He felt excited. He could not think. Then his mind cleared as if he simply erased all thoughts, as if in so doing he could protect himself, maintain his biological integrity. Then he thought, where's the forklift? There used to be a forklift truck in here.

The room was dark. On a table at one end two small candles in thick glass cups flickered red-yellow. Behind the table were four men, Met Phan, Met Yon, Met Meas and Met Dy. There were others in the room, along the side walls and behind him but in the darkness Nang couldn't see them. By his side, having led him to the room blindfolded, led him through a labyrinth of twisting corridors, was his mentor, Met Sar.

"Comrade, you bring before the Center a candidate." Phan's voice was cold.

"I do," Sar responded.

"Are you his sponsor?"

"He's his own sponsor."

"Let him stand alone," Phan directed. Sar disappeared into the blackness.

"Candidate"—in Meas's voice there was disgust—"who are you?"

"I am Met Nang," Nang answered. The two dim candles in the darkness seemed to move, rise slightly then fall. The entire room felt liquid and Nang felt off balance.

"I know of no Met Nang who qualifies for membership," Met Dy responded.

"I am Met Nang of Kompong Thom," Nang said more loudly. "I am the commander of Battalion KT-104."

"A battalion commander? That's all?" There was a pause. Then Dy added, "Who is his sponsor?" No one answered. "Take him out of here."

"Wait. Ah, I . . . I'm my own sponsor," Nang said.

The leaders talked quietly amongst themselves. What reached Nang's ears was "Only a battalion comm . . ." ". . . 104th? Lost half his strugglers, didn't he?" "Perhaps he didn't fight . . ." "I heard some ran." "Okay. Okay."

"We have but two questions for you." Phan was harsh, sneering, speaking as if Nang's presence were an irritant. "Why should we accept you as a provisional member of the Party?"

The candles tilted again and the room seemed to shift. Nang was unprepared. The first slogan that came to mind blurted from his mouth. "I believe in what Angkar has done for me, for all people and for all eternity." Nang hesitated. No one spoke. To fill the void he added, "I believe Angkar is a gift to the people. I praise and adore Angkar."

"Hump!" Dy leaned toward a candle. The light streaked eerily up his face. "What can you do to advance the Will of the Party?"

"I can fight." Nang's words were clipped. "I can struggle. I can use my will to drive others as Angkar directs. I know how to fight the Viet Namese. And the nationals."

When Nang stopped Meas asked curtly, "Is that all you have to say?"

Nang felt his answer was good. He stuttered incoherently.

"Blindfold him," Phan ordered. "Take him away. The Center will inform the candidate in a short while."

Sar led Nang to a pitch-black holding cell. "Remain here," he directed the boy. "Think only of how much you wish to be a provisional member and of how much you love Angkar. I'll be back shortly."

"Met Sar . . ."

"I'm sorry. You're not allowed to talk now. Leave the blindfold on. I'll return shortly."

An hour passed before Sar returned. His steps were heavy. At first he did not speak but only opened the cell door and sat beside Nang. A terrible foreboding swept into the cage with him. "Nang."

"Yes. What's happened?"

"I'm sorry. I've spoken for you but there are problems."

"Problems?"

"Have you ever . . . No. Never mind. I don't understand but someone has given you a dagger and not a blossom. It must be unanimous."

"Who? Huh? What?"

"I don't know. You received a dagger. All the others have been accepted. You know them. Met Rin. Met Nu. Even Ngoc Minh who was trained in Hanoi and surely is a yuon in Khmer skin."

"I haven't . . ."

"I know." Sar sighed long and low. "Would you like me to attempt to talk to them again?"

"I . . . I . . . I don't know. Would you?"

"Do you truly love Angkar? Do you truly wish to serve the Party?"

"Oh, yes. Yes!"

"Can you serve me with all your energies?"

"Met Sar, I've always served you. With all my heart."

"Then I'll try again. This has never happened before. Wait my return. If you don't receive all blossoms you'll be banished. It is so written."

Again Sar left. Nang began a long torturous wait. At first he was numbed by Sar's pronouncements. "Never before . . . only you . . . banished . . ." Why? he asked himself. Why? Because of

my face? My hand? What Nang did not know was that all of the
candidates were being treated identically, all told the same
lie—a ploy designed to deepen their commitment to Angkar
Leou. Yet in Nang the questioning and anguish swiftly shifted,
and in numbness other questions surged. A dagger? Who would
dagger me? In his mind he visualized Meas grasping a tiny
carved bamboo sword from the double basket and dropping it
into the empty side. Banished! What would I do? Why didn't
Sar sponsor me? That bastard. I've been set up. Oh . . . Oh shit!
I *have* been. Nu is accepted. She talked. I'm . . . I'm no longer
pure. Nang squatted in a corner of the cell and hung his head
between his knees. Do they know? Did she tell them? Bitch!
Smelly stinking whore! Wait. Just wait! Banished! They can
fuck dagger holes in the dead. Meas! Hump! "Who am I?" Who
did he think I was? He didn't know? Everyone's heard of Met
Nang. "I know of no Met Nang . . . !" What an idiot. Or was that
Dy? They didn't know I commanded a battalion? A *battalion*!
Morons! Prepare the battlefield. Why didn't I know it was a
battlefield? I'm part of them! They can't banish me. I can kill
them. I'll kill them all. They . . . They . . . They're the ones who
need be banished. Who need elimination! If they're the best, I
don't need them.

Nang stood but the cage roof was low and he wasn't able to
stand without stooping his head. Still he tried. Then he knelt,
held his head high, his shoulders square, but he saw in the
darkness Met Nu's nakedness, smelled her aroma, tasted her
saltiness. The vision excited him but he hated it.

Two, three, four hours passed in solitary confinement. No
word. No sound. No light. No water. Nang was thirsty. He
needed to relieve himself. As the hours passed his thoughts
vacillated but generally they moved further and further from
Angkar, from the Movement, from the Brotherhood. They had
already abandoned him. Now he mentally mourned the passing
and prepared for banishment. A robotic cold swept over him. I
don't need them, he told himself. What a waste of my struggling
. . . But *I* don't need them. He relieved himself at one corner of
the cage.

"Nang. Come, Nang." It was Sar.

"Where . . ."

"Don't talk. Let me check the blindfold." His voice was flat,
revealing nothing.

"Are they—"

"Don't talk."

Sar led the boy through the twisting maze to the darkened
room. No one spoke but all around Nang could hear people

shuffling, sniffing, breathing. Sar pushed him, guided him forward, to the side, then turned him to face away from the table. At each elbow he could feel another standing. Then, through the blindfold he could sense bright light.

"Candidates," Sar's sweet ceremonious voice bloomed in his ears, "remove your blindfolds."

Nang shoved his thumbs under the cloth and lifted. The light was blinding. All around the room men were clapping, cheering, smiling. At his right was Nu, at his left Ngoc Minh, then Rin and three men he didn't know. The applause grew louder then slowly faded as old members converged on the new patting them on the shoulders, grasping their hands, congratulating each with great sincerity. Sar grabbed Nang and hugged him and Nang raised his arms and hugged his mentor. As he hugged, his chin over Sar's shoulder, he stared at his mangled hand and thought, I don't need them. I don't need any of them.

The next morning Nang appeared before Sar and Dy. Without recognition of the previous day's event Sar said, "Your battalion will spearhead the drive east. There is a small town"—Sar pointed to a map of the Northeast—"here, called Phum Sath Din. Just beyond it there is an NVA headquarters and hospital complex. Rendezvous with the resistance. Ngoc Minh has more specifics."

"You have reached the age of reason," Chhuon said. He was sitting on the step with his youngest son, Sakhon, whom they called Peou. "From tonight, you can be my assistant." The night was clear and dark without moon or lantern light. Only a single small candle burned on the low table in the central room behind them.

"Papa," Peou said, his voice questioning, demanding, "was Grandpa an exploiter?"

"My father!" Chhuon immediately glanced back though he knew Hang Tung was not in the house.

"He rented land to farmers, yes?"

"No. The Cahuoms always worked their own land."

"But you didn't. I remember when you had a truck. You drove everywhere. We had fields so you must have rented them."

"Who tells you that?" Chhuon lightly put an arm about his son's shoulder but the boy pulled away.

"They say in school everyone who owns land but doesn't work it is an exploiter."

"My cousins worked our land," Chhuon said defensively. "I didn't exploit them. When I was young I worked in the fields.

My father insisted all his sons go to school and each of us moved from the paddies to more important responsibilities."

"My teacher says nothing is more important than growing rice."

"What about obtaining the seed?"

"That's what she says. Nothing's more important."

"Does she allow you to think about where the seed comes from? About those who develop new strains? About the men who ship rice? About those who build the boats in which rice is shipped?"

"She said, 'Nothing's more important than *growing* rice.' I think she's right."

"Growing rice is important, Peou, but . . ."

"It's the only important thing."

"Peou, you are still very young. What one sees is not independent of what one is."

"Oh, Papa!"

"It is true."

Dinner that night was rice from the new harvest, a tough dark grain with short ears cooked into a heavy paste with a few crayfish for flavoring. Chhuon barely spoke. His mother no longer ate with the others; his wife was trapped in bitterness and no longer looked at her husband. Without Hang Tung Chhuon's conversation was restricted to chatter with his youngest son.

"Do you remember the beautiful white rice from before the war?" Chhuon asked.

"No," Peou answered. "Before the revolution we didn't have very much so I don't remember it."

"Oh, we had lots. More than . . ."

"No we didn't." Peou was staunch.

"Yes," Chhuon responded. "We had wonderful rice."

"That's because you exploited your cousins."

"Damn it!" Chhuon smacked his fingertips on the low table. "I did not exploit my cousins. You've got to resist their teachings."

"You're calling my teacher a liar."

"Where do you learn these things?"

"My teacher says that exploiters will say that things were better before. That . . ." The boy became excited and tongue-tied.

Chhuon tapped his chest. "I . . . I am chairman here. The new seed is wrong. It's old. It's the wrong strain. Better suited for lowland provinces. Even the monks in the fields knew the seed was poor. I . . ."

"She said," Peou, in tears, blurted, "exploiters would call her a liar. But she's not. You're the liar." Peou jumped up jarring the table. He ran from the house.

*   *   *

Before Lieutenant Colonel Nui and Political Officer Trinh, Hang Tung made his accusations and displayed his timetable evidence.

"You're sure?" Colonel Nui asked.

"I'm sure," Tung answered. About them, in the NVA headquarters camp east of Phum Sath Din, was but a skeleton staff of logistics and personnel officers and workers. On the mountain below the main headquarters building the dispensary had been enlarged to hospital size. Operating and ward rooms had been carved into the earth and, aboveground, a set of hootches had been erected for convalescence.

Nui stood. He walked toward the wall, then back to Hang Tung then again toward the wall. In the village to the west there were now twenty Viet Namese families, almost one hundred people, or ten percent of the population of Phum Sath Din. They were dependants of cadre and officers with semipermanent stationing at the NVA headquarters, and their integration into the life of the village was nearly total. They lived in homes amid Khmer homes. Their children went to the new school with Khmer children. The wives "shopped" and received rations with Khmer wives. And all suffered the demands of the army. Even Colonel Nui's wife complained about the army's needs and the lack of quality production materials. In perfect Khmer she chatted quietly with others while waiting in line for tins of rice. "The war demands more," she would say, "and we produce less. With each new regiment coming south their needs increase." To her husband she would say in private, "These people, these poor people. Must they sacrifice so?"

Nui turned, stopped. He looked at Tung. "You're sure?" he asked again. How badly he wanted the Viet-Khmer integration to work. How badly he wanted liberty for all Indochinese under the tutelage of the obvious leaders of all Indochinese, the North Viet Namese. And how well it was working. The Americans had suffered heavy blows and were "*bo*-ing" Viet Nam, not simply withdrawing but discarding their ally.

"Colonel," Cadreman Trinh addressed Nui. "Let me call him in for interrogation. Perhaps he'll confess."

"Of all men," Nui lamented. He plopped down in the chair, exhausted.

Chhuon could not overtly disobey. It was not in his character, not in the national character. To even verbally contradict one in authority, or a friend or relative, was painful to both. For Chhuon his entire body would physically tighten, cramp, giving him painful stomachaches which would be followed by burn-

ing, and painful headaches which could cause his eyes to blur
and his teeth to throb. Thus each directive he received from
Hang Tung or Colonel Nui he followed, passed on and enforced.
He had learned to keep quiet, to show no emotion, learned this
as much to avoid the pain as to avoid ostracism or reproaches.
When Nui was feeling harassed or was in an ugly mood, Chhuon
assuaged his irritations by asking for and usually receiving
extra work or extra compliance from the villagers. They too
could not overtly disobey. When Nui was in a generous mood,
Chhuon made requests for more lenient rice taxes or administrative control, for better rations, more oil and salt, or for less
militarism in the civilian areas. And Nui, if it was possible,
complied. On the surface their relationship was good. Too good.

When village resentment increased dramatically in late 1971,
Chhuon openly sought solace amongst the KVM/NVA cadre and
soldiers. When his wife's bitterness forced him from the house
and when his alienation from the old families hit its peak,
Chhuon spent nights playing cards or listening to the radio at
Colonel Nui's. The alienation from his own home served him
well. Night after night he was found wandering the village
streets, so often that the militiamen looked forward to chatting
with him to break the monotony of guard duty. Yet though he
could not overtly disobey, he did have an outlet.

Each night he wandered in a pattern. He checked the pagoda
which now housed Hang Tung's office and that of several new
officials. He sat there with the guards and smoked a cigarette.
Then he meandered amongst the old market stalls, pausing here
and there to listen to the chirp of the crickets, walking softly,
attempting to draw as close as possible before they sensed him
and ceased their forewing songs. Then on he went, between old
homes and new huts to the edge of the berm where always he
found a militiaman in need of a smoke. Then, particularly if he
thought Sok's laments and wails had been heard by the neighbors, a most un-Khmer embarrassment, he followed the alleys
to Nui's abode, called lightly so as not to wake the children,
then entered. And often, somewhere, between the market and
the alleys, Kpa or Sakhron or his cousin Sam would appear and
an exchange would take place.

What joy! What elation it brought to his heart. Sam was
alive, well, resisting. And Chhuon too, though he could not
overtly disobey, resisted.

"what have you?" Chhuon whispered.

Without a sound Sakhron slid a cartridge trap from his black
trousers and placed it in Chhuon's hands. Chhuon did not look

at it but immediately slid it into his shirt. "maha vanatanda has dug the hole," Sakhron whispered.

"there's a new machete at bunker six," Chhuon whispered back. Both departed.

In the darkness Chhuon wandered back to the pagoda to smoke with the guard, then out to the berm where he quickly found the small hole in the path which led to the command bunker from which the Viet Namese cadre oversaw the militia. Chhuon twisted quickly, checked to ensure no one was near. From his shirt he removed the trap, a small circular board about three inches in diameter with a nail sticking straight up inside an attached bamboo tube. Chhuon dropped the trap in the hole, pushed it down until the board was on firm earth. Then he armed the trap by placing an AK rifle round in the bamboo tube. Quickly he camouflaged the hole. Only the tip of the round was exposed. Then he backed quietly away and fled into the alleys thinking, Blood for blood. Blood for the Holy One. Blood for blood!

"Hello! Hello! Colonel Nui! It's me, Chhuon. Hello!"

"Ssshh!"

"Oh! Excuse me! Hello. Is the colonel in?"

"Please, Chairman Cahuom." Nui's wife spoke in a hush. "Both little ones are asleep. You understand. They've got the fever."

"Oh. I'm sorry."

"It's okay. My husband's in camp tonight. I've just gotten the littlest one to sleep. Please, come tomorrow."

"Of course. Please accept my . . . What was that!"

"Don't wake the children!"

"I'm sorry. I heard a small explosion. Let me go investigate."

The Khmer Krahom regimental task force had crossed the Kong River just north of the ruins of Phum Sath Nan. There they set up a bivouac in a small, tight canyon about a trickling rocky creek. Four battalions strong, they packed the canyon, concentrated yet hidden, like a nest of bees.

"Our task," Ngoc Minh said, "is to prepare for the orderly transfer of administrative control." Nang nodded. He did not answer. His lethargy, his foot dragging, antagonized Ngoc Minh, the new regimental political officer. Again, as an outcome of the Stung Treng meetings, the Krahom armies had reorganized to a higher level. The battalions that first had been seen during Chenla II were now clustered under loose regimental command. The independent insurgent squads of the recent past had become main force units. Though the units did not have the rear-echelon personnel and logistics support of modern armies, they did have the intelligence and command support structures.

"Met Nang," Ngoc Minh called the youngest battalion leader. They had been together since their provisional induction into the Khmer Communist Party. "You seem preoccupied."

Nang grunted. He did not like Ngoc Minh, did not like his mixed ancestry. Yet, before the other unit commanders and the regimental staff, he did not wish to provoke Ngoc Minh's animosity. Instead he raised his half-coconut shell and sipped the sugary palm juice. Duch, Nang's radioman, nudged him. The silence about the command post was as oppressive as the humidity in the shadowy canyon.

"Nang!" Ngoc Minh snapped. "Your battalion will . . ."

"I was thinking," Nang interrupted, "of Mita and Horl. Such heroes."

"It's time you thought of this operation," Ngoc Minh said flatly.

"There's time." Nang answered as if his inner clock had run down. "Patience, Minh," he said softly.

"We must advance," Minh countered. "The path to success is through unremitting patriotic struggle."

"Ngoc Minh," Nang said. "You are strictly a political struggler. Your achievements are impressive and your revolutionary spirit is beyond question. I am but a soldier. I remember those who fell in battle when the situation was not favorable." Nang sipped from his shell. He smiled gently. His eyes were bright, shining, hiding the ice coursing in his veins, covering the schemes hatching in his mind. "My orders are first to make contact with the local resistance. Eventually we shall regain the lost people and the lost land."

Nang rose. Met Nhel, the regiment's commanding officer, rose too. Nhel was not a combat veteran and had received his position on the basis of his long membership in the Party. In 1970, he had organized the communal conversion of villages near Rovieng, seventy kilometers north of Kompong Thom, in the first district entirely controlled by the Khmer Krahom. During and after the Northern Corridor fighting, Nhel's communities received most of the evacuees, processed them and expanded. All was done away from the ground fighting though there had been sporadic, terrifying bombings. Met Nhel dreaded the new assignment.

Nhel walked behind Nang as Nang meandered to the trailhead which would take him to the 104th area. "You know this area," Nhel said. "You should be the one to make contact."

"We've no preparation. Where are the files?"

Duch joined them as they slowly walked to the creek then climbed the slippery rocks heading back into the ravine. "The Center is sending them," Nhel said. "We move faster than they, eh?"

"Then we must stop," Nang said. To Duch he added, "Go to Met Eng. Tell him Angkar needs a spy." Nang stopped in the creekbed and let Duch pass. Alone with Nhel he whispered, "Ngoc Minh, if he stays there will be no success. If he goes, we lose nothing."

For ten days the regimental task force sat, hid, cramped in the gorge with few rations, few comforts. The young yotheas became restless. Each day they cleaned their weapons and ammunition and sat. At dusk they swatted mosquitos and retreated into night darkness, into their lonesome existence. Each morning Eng ran a political education class for the 104th in which he extolled the virtues of work, order, discipline and celibacy. The soldiers drank from the trickling rill, turned rocks to find tiny clams to eat, washed their kramas and themselves and grew hungrier and wilder. Nhel attempted to ameliorate the friction between Nang and Ngoc Minh and between Ngoc Minh and Von, one of Nang's *yotheas* in the Northern Corridor fighting and now commanding officer of the 81st Battalion, but his efforts were to no avail. Each day the innuendos grew coarser and more blatant. "I've heard," Ngoc Minh said sincerely to Nhel in the presence of the battalion commanders and regimental staff, "if a soldier is wounded twice he becomes overly cautious, even cowardly." Before Nhel could answer, Nang snickered to Von, "How would he know?"

Then the runners arrived. Not one, but a squad—messengers, armed yotheas, a guide-scout and eleven porters. With them were carefully prepared maps of the area with NVA installations marked and quantified. Included were detailed orders and directions: contact the local resistance; supply them with the weapons the porters carry; organize them, use them, take control; reconnoiter the area; plan the attack; prepare the battlefield. Then wait. Do not attack until the NVA has committed itself to the new offensive in the South. At that time, your mission is to strike at the NVA, liberate the Khmer villages and return the people to the Northern Zone for protection. With the orders was a file box of dossiers on resistance, village and enemy leaders.

With Nhel, Ngoc Minh and the others, Nang reviewed the dossiers. Lieutenant Colonel Nui's file was the thickest and on the jacket there was a yellow X, marking him for elimination. Another folder described Political Officer Trinh, and a third

Deputy Political Officer Trinh Le. Both folders carried the yellow X. A thin dossier had been compiled on Committee Member Hang Tung. This one was marked with an asterisk. Files on Ny Non Chan, Maha Vanatanda, and Cahuom Chhuon were like marked. A packet of folders wrapped in red cellophane were designated by a symbol which to Nang looked like a tower of the Angkor ruins. In the packet were details on Kpa, Sakhron, Cahuom Sam and Neang Thi Sok.

Nang swallowed. He did not speak, did not allow his recognition, his shock, to show. Yet inside the names seemed to crash against the side of his brain. Chhuon! Sok! Sam!

Chhuon bowed his head before the small sun-dappled spirit house in front of his home. Within his mind he muttered, I shall become enlightened for the sake of all living things. He raised his head and straightened a tiny plaited curtain on which a picture of Buddha in the lotus position had been painted. He whispered a prayer. "Lord Buddha, Enlightened One, Blessed One, I have destroyed a man's foot. For this I am sorry. For this I am guilty. What is the right path for my life? Angel Spirit, protect my home and my family."

"Uncle." Hang Tung had approached silently from behind. It was unusual to see him during the midday rest period. His singular utterance betrayed his nervousness and irritability. With each soldier withdrawn, with each AA gun moved east, with the continuing reduction of the NVA camp, Hang Tung's nervousness had become more and more manifest. "Uncle," Tung repeated. "You must join me."

Hang Tung said no more. He motioned for Chhuon to follow him to his office in the old pagoda. Chhuon's mind raced wildly, searching for a reason for Tung's silence. Immediately he thought of his night rendezvous with Kpa. There had been no exchange. Only a message. "Do not launch an assault until the yuon army commits itself in the South."

"Kpa," Chhuon had asked, "what does this mean?"

"I can't tell you," the mountain boy had said. "Only we have new weapons. Gifts from the Kampuchean Patriots Liberation Front."

Chhuon's mind jumped track. Seed, he thought. We've gotten the new seed and Hang Tung wants to organize the first planting so the seedlings will be ready in May. Too early. Much too early. What have they discovered? Do not think. I am a stone. Do not betray yourself. "Nephew," Chhuon said as they reached the pagoda steps, "have we received new seed? We must have a better strain than last year's."

"Oh," Tung said slyly, "this has nothing to do with that. Cadreman Trinh wishes to speak with you. That's all." Hang Tung escorted Chhuon to Trinh's small office. Then he left. Trinh was not in.

For three hours Chhuon sat, waited, alone. At first he glanced about the windowless cubicle. The walls were bare except for portraits of Norodom Sihanouk and Ho Chi Minh. The small desk was full yet orderly. In each of the upper corners were two perfectly aligned stacks of papers. To the right were five ballpoint pens, parallel and squared. At the upper center edge were two eraser pencils with brushes and between, twenty paper clips evenly spaced, and forty overlapping rubber bands laid out as two flowers. Chhuon counted the pens, the clips, the rubber bands. He visually measured the stacks. Each was precisely the same height. He recounted, remeasured, relooked and renoted. Then there was nothing to do. His mind jumped to his guilts—to Kdeb and Yani whom he'd abandoned, to the soldiers his boobytrap had killed, to his inaction at the river when Chamreum and San were gas-ragged to death. He thought of Ry, of the NVA soldier she'd entertained and of his corpse which had lain only a few meters from where he now sat. Then he thought of Kpa, of Vanatanda, of Sam, of the foot he'd helped blow to pieces and of his ruse with Nui's wife and his insincere assistance with the shrieking young soldier as other Viets had loaded him into a jeep to be rushed to the headquarters hospital.

Chhuon sweated. The sweat poured from him in rivers as it might from a fat man exercising for the first time on a hot tropical day. He fidgeted. He squirmed like a seven-year-old who needs to urinate but who has been ordered to sit for punishment for a transgression he can no longer recall. Then Chhuon froze. I am a stone, he said in his mind. A pebble. An insignificant pebble.

"Chairman Cahuom." Trinh finally entered. "Do you have your papers with you? Are you all right? You look ill."

"Fine. Fine. I'm fine."

"Have you been here long?" Trinh asked pleasantly.

"For a little while," Chhuon answered.

Trinh smiled. For three hours he had watched through a peephole as Chhuon had squirmed. "There are to be new papers." Trinh smiled. "New passes. Everything will be color coded. A good idea, eh?"

"Ah . . . yes. I'm certain it is. I'm afraid I didn't bring mine. Tung startled me while I was cleaning by my home. I thought it was urgent. I didn't go back in."

"Oh, that's all right. Actually I wanted to talk to you about other matters. There are enemy agents and spies in the village."

"Here?!"

"Yes." Trinh leaned toward Chhuon. In a harsh whisper he said, "We know who they are." Then he leaned back. "What would you do with them?"

"I, ah . . . I . . . I don't know."

"Hiding an enemy is punishable by death." Trinh smiled a forced, tight smirk. "If someone knows a spy and doesn't come forward, both will be eliminated."

"Surely," Chhuon tittered nervously, "you don't suspect any of the villagers."

"Yes. That's exactly whom I suspect. There have been nine incidents of violence this year. Poor Sergeant Doan lost a foot. These are manifestations of narrow-minded nationalism."

"Let me talk to the people," Chhuon said. "Let me talk to the quadrant chairman and the association leaders. Certainly we can stop this."

"Yes. That may help. Talk tonight. Tonight we'll have a village assembly."

As the sun set villagers began congregating before the old wat. Along the village street militiamen posted kerosene torches and connected these with a long red cordon tape. On the steps Cahuom Chhuon reevaluated his opening remarks. More villagers arrived. Some straggled in, others came en masse with their quadrant group or production group or age or sex or trade association group. For a few it was a festive time, a time to rest, to talk with neighbors whom they seldom saw anymore because of the arduous work schedules, but for most it was another imposition on their limited time with their families. Most dragged themselves in without enthusiasm, expecting nothing other than perhaps a new tightening of some minor regulation—just one more thing to endure, to repress, to drive them mad.

The meeting began. Chairman Cahuom, standing before Colonel Nui, Cadreman Trinh and Hang Tung, explained about the new passes and papers. Then, for a long moment, he stood silent. He seemed to be looking for a face in the crowd. The yellow torchlight danced and trembled on the few brown faces turned up, glimmered off the few hung heads with just-washed hair, seemed almost like a cloud sinking to the rounded shoulders of the workers, settling there, one more weight. Chhuon cleared his throat, began to speak, but no sound emerged. He cleared his throat again. People stilled. "There is amongst us . . . ," Chhuon began, but again he stopped. "I am told . . ."

He abandoned that opening. "You all know me," he said. "You know that what I have done, what I do, I do for the good of the village. You know I'm a devout Buddhist." In the crowd all motion stopped as if the yellow glow from the torches had gelled and encased them in a clear acrylic block. "Today, I have been informed there are enemy agents amongst us. Spies who endanger the village and our lives by their activities. Saboteurs who plant bombs which threaten the lives of our children as well as those of our village militia and the protection forces. This situation, these activities, are very serious. Crimes of sabotage, of hiding enemy agents, will be dealt with most severely. I have asked Cadreman Trinh and Colonel Nui to establish a lenient amnesty program for any villager who has, in the past, committed a crime against the people and who, by tomorrow night, comes forward and makes a full confession."

Chhuon stopped. He took a step back, looked up into a clear night sky where stars glittered untarnished. Among the nearly one thousand people crammed into the cordon before the wat, there was little movement, though amongst the guards there were nudges, smirks, a few derisive comments.

Colonel Nui stepped forward but immediately stepped back and let Cadreman Trinh come forward and address the silent throng. "It is," Trinh said in a solemn voice, "a principle of government and of the army that one who serves must love the people. He must love all the people as if they were his own flesh. He must learn from the people and aid the people. It is only through such love that one can truly serve. Yet there are those who serve not the people, who love not the people, but who whittle the stick at both ends, who engage in the duplicity of seemingly serving two masters while they serve only themselves. Manifestations of feudalism, neocolonialism or narrowminded nationalism must be eradicated. A few years ago every Indochinese rice farmer was enslaved by indebtedness, by taxes introduced by colonialists, by the price-fixing of imperialists, by exorbitant interest rates charged by moneylenders. To exist a peasant sold pieces of his land until what remained was a plot so miserable he was barely able to feed himself. We have eliminated all indebtedness. We have increased plot size to bring back efficiency. This we have done, because of love. Phum Sath Din has become the model of the new Indochina, because of love, because of hard work—your love, your labor. Now, amongst you we find a traitor, a man who deceives all in his attempt to reestablish the power of the imperialists and moneylenders. A man who supports the Lon Nol clique which so humiliated Prince Norodom Sihanouk, which soiled his name and continues to debase and insult him in the most wicked and unjust manner."

Trinh paused. His expression was one of calculated sorrow, not anger. He continued to face the crowd. "Chairman Cahuom, you've asked for an amnesty program, yes?"

Chhuon stepped forward. His chest was tight. "Yes," he said.

"The charade goes on!" Trinh erupted at the crowd. "We know the truth! No one! No one can get away with lying! We have captured a traitor who has identified all criminal elements." Trinh stopped. The villagers startled. Eyes flicked to each side, heads remained rigid. Chhuon swallowed the rising burning bile bubbling at the back of his throat. "Traitors," Trinh shouted, pointing before him to the bottom step of the pagoda. "Stand there! *Now!* Now there is amnesty. Now you may be reeducated. In one minute there will be no amnesty. One minute and you will be treated like the criminals you are."

There was silence. No villager moved. No guard. Chhuon's teeth chattered. He clamped them shut to control his jaw. Who? he thought. Who have they captured? Who would tell? It's a ploy. Where's Vanatanda? Chhuon's eyes searched for the derobed monk. His eyes widened until they felt as if they'd pop from their sockets.

"Ten seconds!" Trinh screamed.

Still there was no sound, no motion.

Then, in the Children's Association group a small boy jumped up shouting, "I know. I know who the traitor is. It's him." Peou ran toward the wat porch. "It's him!" he yelled angrily. "He's a traitor," he shouted, pointing at his father.

"Come here," Trinh said kindly to the boy. Peou climbed the steps. "Him?" Trinh squatted by the child.

"Him," Peou cried. He stood ramrod straight with a stiff arm, hand, finger aimed at Chhuon. The mob of villagers buzzed.

"The chairman?" Trinh asked sweetly. "A traitor? What has he done?" People nudged one another with their hands or elbows, kept their heads and bodies stiff.

"He said we must resist. He said the teachers lie. He calls Viet Namese 'yuons' and says we must resist their teachings."

Behind Chhuon a man's voice boomed, "He also plants bombs which kill innocent civilians." Hang Tung smiled from ear to ear. "That fact has been established." The villagers now began to shuffle, mumble, tremble. "You can't deny it," Tung shouted.

"You don't know what you're saying." Chhuon's voice was weak.

"You are a traitor. A saboteur," Hang Tung said. He relished the public accusations. "You must apologize to the people."

"I've never done . . ." Chhuon began a stronger defense.

"Your colluder has been identified," Cadreman Trinh interrupted.

Chhuon's energies rose. "I've no colluder," he snapped. "I've done nothing. I am the chairm . . ."

"Kpa has confessed," Trinh snarled.

"Kpa?" Chhuon repeated. The revelation of the mountain boy's identity shocked him. He sucked in an erratic breath. The mob, too, stood shocked.

"Tonight"—Trinh's voice was menacing—"you'll tell me all."

Now Colonel Nui addressed the crowd. The people froze. "The evidence," he said sadly, "against Cahuom Chhuon is irrefutable. In spite of his subversive duplicity we have progressed rapidly. There will be further realignment and expansion of the fields for work by mutual-assistance groups. The May planting will be the first totally communal operation with Khmer and Viet Namese working together as brothers. Cahuom Chhuon"—Colonel Nui sighed—"I've treated you like a friend, like a brother. You've betrayed me. But worse, you've betrayed us all. On 18 March, to commemorate the vile ousting of Norodom Sihanouk by the American imperialists, you shall publicly hang until dead."

CHAPTER FIFTEEN

Vathana bent to the amputee, placed the back of her fingers on his temple. His fever had spiked again. The young man moaned quietly but did not speak. His eyes did not focus on her nor was he conscious of her hand. "Your suffering is my suffering," Vathana whispered. "Let your pain be my pain. Let me bear it for you. Let my eyes weep your tears."

She looked up to see Doctor Sam Ol watching her. "Has his fever returned?"

"Yes," Vathana said. "It's very high. My hand burns."

Sam Ol sighed. There was a critical shortage of medicine. To give the soldier anything would be to deny it to someone with a chance.

"Angel," the FANK soldier called out in delirium. He'd been wounded ten days earlier in a skirmish along the Mekong four kilometers to the south. At first he'd been high spirited, hyper even though there was nothing below his left knee. Slowly infection spread up his leg. Every morning and evening Vathana had changed the dressing and washed with boiled water the tight flap of skin Sam Ol had sewn over the bone end. For this man there were no antiseptics, no antibacterials, no antifungals. Only boiled water. On the fifth day the young man complained of the smell of his leg. On the sixth the fevers began their sine-like spike and drop pattern. No family came to visit him, to feed him, to pay for his care or to bring or buy medicine. Without that support he was relegated to Vathana's team of volunteers.

"I'm here," Vathana whispered. She felt embarrassed under Sam Ol's tired gaze—embarrassed by her inability to do more now than just hold the quivering hand, embarrassed by the malodorous stench of the leg, embarrassed for Sam Ol who died a little more each time a patient went undertreated, embarrassed for the soldier reduced in painful delirium to begging for the last kind face he'd seen.

"Angel, it hurts. It hurts me. Please."

"Give me your pain," Vathana whispered. She wished the doctor would leave so she might be alone with the dying boy, alone with him and two young volunteers and forty more wounded without means to pay for care, alone in the small windowless storeroom she'd begged them to open for at least the semblance of care, alone with all the odors of live and rotting flesh. The soldier's back arched, his stomach thrust upward, an arch suspended atilt by shoulders at one end and the good leg and stump at the other. Immediately at the stump end a red growth oozed across the bandage.

"Angel," the soldier called. His body relaxed. From his chest came an eerie rattle as if small wooden cubes were being shaken in a dried gourd.

Vathana closed her eyes, squeezed the soldier's hand in her two.

"Your American is here," Sam Ol said softly.

For six months Vathana had not seen or heard from John Sullivan. In that time she'd immersed herself ever more deeply in the swarming disease-ridden ghettos of Neak Luong's refugees and in the world of the wounded without families. Before dawn each day she walked barefoot to the pagoda to pray and bolster her spirits, then she made first rounds at the hospital or at the infirmary tent in the camp. At noon she went to the small refugee hut she'd taken as her own. Nothing bolstered her more. Each noon she was met by Samnang, now 28½ months old, and by Samol, just over a year. The boy had grown, lithe yet hard, strong and wiry—not a typical toddler. Perhaps it was his limited ability to interact with and thus be affected by his surroundings which allowed him to be so healthy and happy. With a wonderful smile and a slobbering "ba-ba-ba-ba" greeting, he would run with his distorted arms to his mother, wrap her legs in his iron hug and not let her go, thrashing his seeping nose back and forth on her thigh, singing, laughing "ba-ba-ba-ba." Samol would wait until Vathana entered the hut then totter her delicate frame toward her mother, chattering with a vocabulary of forty or fifty words. After the midday meal and rest, with the children being cared for by Sophan, Vathana spent two hours organizing, doing administrative chores for the camp, the hospital or the pagoda orphanage. Then she again would make her rounds of the sick, wounded and starving.

It was 22 February 1972, the day after Richard Nixon had

arrived in Peking, arrived and altered the geopolitical conditions which so strongly affected every life in Southeast Asia. Vathana's morning rounds were over. Two orderlies came for the corpse. In the doorway beyond Sam Ol, Vathana could see a swath of dust-speckled sunlight. "Captain Sullivan," the doctor said. "He's in the reception area."

Vathana nodded. "America," she mumbled to herself, "sunshine and death."

"Are you in good health?" Sullivan uttered the Khmer greeting idiom which had replaced the traditional "How many children have you?" or "Have you had rice today?" He stood there looking uncomfortable in civilian clothes, his hair lighter than before, red-blond, his skin darker, his eyes staring not just at her but through her and beyond, not unlike the eyes of the soldier she'd just left.

"I'm well," she answered in Khmer. "Are you in good health?" Vathana wanted him to hold her but she remained very formal and he didn't move. She wanted to say, I was afraid when you were missing, but he was here now, alive now, and the other had just died.

"I'm being crucified." Sullivan switched to French. "Or about to be." He too wanted to hold her, wanted to release six months of death and frustration, wanted to bury it with an intimacy they once shared. But all about them was more pain and imminent death.

"Crucified?!"

"Figuratively. My photo was in all the newspapers back in the World. I've been accused of advising FANK troops and that's against the law." For Vathana to understand what Sullivan was talking about required more energy than she, at that moment, could muster. She let the comment go unquestioned, unexplained. "The hospital appears to be packed full," Sullivan stammered.

"Come and see," Vathana said matter-of-factly. "My rounds are complete." She turned and walked toward the first ward, a long narrow room with windows on both sides. "We've added all the cots we could get," she said, stopping at the ward entrance. "Some patients sleep on mats on the floor and there are two in each bed. There's no medicine. Little medicine." Her voice was flippant. "Sometimes we just let them die so we can give their space to someone else. If all the relatives would go home maybe we'd be able to walk in there."

Sullivan followed her, stared into the crowded ward with its mingling of the sick, the healthy grievers, the listless children.

He glanced back to her thin face, her straggly hair. Two flies buzzed at her temples.

"We've added at least three beds for each one that was here"— Vathana's voice cracked—"but we haven't added a single nurse or another doctor." Tears ran from her eyes. "Just once I'd like it if a politician were in there. Ill. Without tetracycline and without sterile bandages. War is for politicians, isn't it? For mine and for yours who started all this!"

Sullivan did not console Vathana. He had no compassion for that viewpoint. Instead he said coldly, "I'll see that you get some. Tetracycline?"

Vathana did not look at him but gazed over the heads of the people in the ward to a picture of Buddha in repose someone had taped to the far wall. "It's good against typhus fever, lung and urinary tract infections, and . . ." She did not finish but turned and led him down the corridor to a second open ward where the scene was similar, then out a door to a small shed surrounded by wailing women and workers with their mouths and noses covered by dirty surgical masks. Amongst the crowd were three children with shaved heads.

"They come here to claim the bodies," Vathana explained. She attempted to be detached, impersonal. "But now many bodies go unclaimed because . . ." she stammered, ". . . with the land broken people die without their families."

Sullivan looked at Vathana as she looked at the morgue and kept her side or back to him. He wanted to reach out to her, say to her, I've seen thousands die with their families, wanted her to understand, but the chill kept him at bay. "That's why there are only a few shaved heads?" he asked.

"No," Vathana answered. She turned again. "With so many deaths," she said as she moved toward the storeroom, "the practice is not so much anymore."

They entered the dank stench-fouled storeroom. Immediately several broken bodies quivered and from anguished faces came the call, "Angel. Angel, touch me." "Angel, hold my hand for a moment. Just one moment." Vathana squatted by a mat here, a cot there, squeezing hands or saying prayers.

The scene disgusted Sullivan. Mutilated and ill ex-soldiers, still unwashed and in the tattered uniforms in which they'd been wounded, lying en masse amid swarming flies and filth. Sullivan grabbed Vathana's blouse at the shoulder, gently pulled her back into the sunlit corridor. "What the hell's going on in there?" A dozen flies had come out with them. Sullivan jerked his arm to get several out of his red hair.

"They've no money," Vathana said. "No families. There's no money to pay for their care."

Sullivan snapped his left arm back, setting the pesky flies abuzz. One landed on the sweat of his upper lip and scurried to his nostril. He shook his head violently, snorting like a horse, then grabbed Vathana's wrist and pulled her farther from the storeroom door. "It doesn't take money to clean the place up."

"It takes more than we can do," Vathana said, politely, cold.

"More?"

"So many casualties. We're not equipped for war. War is civilian casualties and dead young men and my country destroyed." Again several flies landed on Sullivan's left arm and burrowed beneath the red hair. Slowly he moved his arm down and before his torso. He squeezed his left hand into a fist making the arm hard and rigid. "We look to America to save us," Vathana said, not looking at Sullivan but back toward the storeroom. "In our time of need we look to America for salvation. But of course America must first protect its own soldiers in Viet Nam." Sullivan made his right hand into a rigid paddle and slowly brought it into striking position. "We suffer from this limited intervention," Vathana said. "Better all or none. Why do you hold back? If ever there was a country with a just cause, with need, it is Cambodia." The flies on Sullivan's arm were both facing toward his face. Sweeping in low-level from behind, slapping hard, he splattered two insects, the fly guts popping like pimples, leaving puslike globs smeared in the red hair. The slap snatched Vathana's attention.

She bit down, repressing an urge to retch. "Do not kill," she ordered, "the living thing."

Sullivan looked up. Her eyes were on his. "Do not kill . . ." he mocked. "You've got to be kidding. Flies?"

"If all would care about all living things"—Vathana dropped her eyes—"perhaps all these people wouldn't die."

"Five hundred men are murdered around me. Suong! Villages as far as you can see wiped out! And you care about a fly?!"

"Buddha says all living things."

"God!" Sullivan slapped a hand to his head and pulled his hair. His speech was quick. His eyes bugged. "You Buddhists are nuts. Tell me, where does it stop? A fly! You asked me for tetracycline. What do you think that does? Do you think it escorts bacteria to the bladder? Maybe carries it there to be pissed away. Waves good-bye, too. Those are living things. You want to kill them. You've got to draw the line someplace. What will you do, what will you kill, in order to save living things?"

Two hours later, after a nearly silent lunch with her children and Sophan, Vathana and Sullivan strolled beneath the shade trees at the edge of the Mekong just north of Neak Luong's center. They had not been able to reestablish the warmth they had once shared, yet both wished for, needed, the warmth.

"The land is broken," Vathana said. She placed her hand in his. "The economy is in shambles. Troops are demoralized. I don't know if the country can survive."

"It's got to," Sullivan said sadly.

"The government's weak," Vathana said. "It can't protect us. They collect taxes but abandon the people. Nothing is right anymore."

"It would be worse if the Communists won."

"I don't know. There are rumors of . . ." Vathana paused. She wasn't certain if she should continue.

". . . a coup." Sullivan finished the sentence.

"Yes. They say Son Ngoc Thanh may become the new head of state. That Sirik Matak has urged Lon Nol to relinquish total command."

"And what do you hear the Americans say?"

"What *do* they say? You must know."

"I don't. I think the embassy plays ignorant."

"Maybe they're not playing," Vathana said seriously. Sullivan took it as a pun and laughed. He moved to put his arm around her but she squeezed his hand and kept it at her side.

"The students say he no longer knows the country." Vathana repeated a phrase which had become common. "There's no longer a reason for the people to fight. *Bonjour* is everywhere. Worse than before."

Sullivan released Vathana's hand. They had reached the spot along the bank where they'd made love a year earlier. How badly he wanted her again, yet how angry he was with the morose talk of demoralization and corruption, the fatalism in her tone. He knew disagreeing would further drive the wedge between them, yet accepting the defeatism would drive a wedge between him and his own beliefs.

"He is corrupt," Sullivan said. "And he's inept. His stupid orders botched Chenla II. But still there's reason to fight. Fight the enemy and the corruption."

"We get no support," Vathana responded. "Officers build villas with paychecks from phantom troops, from sales of weapons to the Khmer Rouge. Why should our soldiers fight?"

"God damn em," Sullivan rasped. As he let his anger ooze its intensity flashed. "Damn em! Even you. They're getting to even you."

"Yes. They are getting to me."

"Those jackasses!" Sullivan blurted. "There's a blatant murdering evil out there and their fanatic corruption masks it. Damn it! Damn it! Damn it! Leaders! They derive their strength from those led, not from some sort of 'High Holy Powers'! Those bastards. They concentrate on false glory, and they forget responsibility. That's what's losing. Don't get sucked in!" Sullivan stopped as abruptly as he'd begun. His tone softened. "Vathana. Dear, dear Vathana." He almost whispered the words. "Don't get sucked in by the rhetoric. There's good reason to continue to fight."

Late that afternoon Sullivan made hospital rounds with the Angel of Neak Luong. He knelt by feverish soldiers in the storeroom and held their hands or rubbed a coin on their chest as he'd been shown. He washed wounds with boiled water and rebandaged infected tissue with stained, boiled, air-dried reused strips of cloth. He cleaned watery shit from floors, cots and mats, and he struggled to maintain some sense of cause and effect. After four hours of listening to the gasps, wheezes, painful groans, after only four hours of being shit, pus and blood covered, after only one shift of watching Vathana hold and comfort two men until death, he, American army captain John L. Sullivan, who had seen thousands die in battle, found himself wondering if capitulation to the Communists might not end the war and the suffering.

When evening came Sullivan and Vathana washed the residual filth from their bodies and clothes and left the hospital. But the residual stench clung in their nasal sinuses like creosote in a chimney and the residual images stuck in their minds as if stored on film.

"There's a film at the cinema," Vathana said. "We can go. I'll translate for you."

Heat from the road radiated up and kept them hot even though the air had cooled. They walked in bursts, quick paces interspersed with pauses. She led him first into an alley, up a set of stairs, across a long balcony and down a second alley to a small room with a few tables—a backdoor cafe. There they shared a bowl of shrimp soup cooked with lemon grass, kaffir lime leaves and hot Cambodian chili peppers. To cool their mouths they shared a Howdy Cola. At first they spoke little, only enough to keep them in motion.

"Tomorrow you return to the capital?" Vathana asked.

"I can say I missed the chopper." Sullivan smiled.

"Can you miss it a long time? There's so much to do here and so few hands."

"I'm afraid only one day. With the charges and all, I'm lucky to have escaped at all."

"I wish you could stay longer. In two nights there is a meeting of the Khmer Patriots for Peace. And the next day there's the meeting of the Rivermen for a Just Government."

"Khmer Patriots?" To Sullivan the phrase meant a Communist front organization.

"Yes. It's a very good group. Very active. The Refugee Association has become a branch. Without the KPP the camp couldn't survive. Every day the KPP attracts more members."

"Are there more groups?"

"Oh yes. I've joined the Khmer Women's Association but you can't come to that meeting. Most of the hospital volunteers are KWA."

"I wish I could come."

"To the women's meeting?" Vathana laughed.

"To the KPP, maybe."

"If you do, I'll introduce you."

"Who runs these organizations?"

"People."

"Vathana . . ."

"Yes."

"Be careful."

"Be careful?"

"Yes."

"Of what?"

"In Viet Nam the Communists would develop organizations like these. There'd be a hidden core of guerrillas. They'd infuse the whole group with their slogans, their 'revolutionary spirit.' "

"Oh John! We're not Communists! These are the *only* groups doing anything for the people. We can't wait for outside salvation. Buddha teaches us to depend on ourselves."

Again Sullivan backed off emotionally. As he did, he wondered why his love was so tied to his ideological beliefs, why there was no room in his heart for variations in thought. Vathana also cooled. She kept her face turned, not just the slight, polite amount to one side but far to the side, as if it had become painful to look at the red-haired foreigner so laden with inner contradictions.

The movie was the most popular film in Cambodia in 1972. A king of the Angkor era was the focus of an evil plot by his third wife and her secret lover, a powerful warlord with a huge army. Through black magic the monarch discovered the conspiracy and with hexes he forced the soldiers of his adversary to battle and decapitate each other. Quietly Vathana translated the Khmer to French and whispered it to Sullivan, but he seemed not to need the translation so she stopped.

When the movie was over and they were alone she told him, "Sometimes I think of you, my American, like that king."

"Do you plot against me?" Sullivan tried to joke.

"No. Of course not," Vathana said seriously.

"If you did," Sullivan said, clutching her hands, not giving her time to explain, "I would forgive you." He attempted to embrace her but she stepped back. He pulled her closer. She put her head down and gave him only her hair to kiss.

"You forgive me?" she whispered.

"Yes."

"Even though I've done nothing?" She pulled away. "Humph!" She recommenced the walk to her camp hut. "Do one thing for me."

"Anything."

"Tomorrow, when you go, take a photo album to Phnom Penh for me. To my mother-in-law. Safer there than in Neak Luong, eh? I don't wish it destroyed."

For days they had not tortured him, had not asked him a single question, had even allowed him a bucket of water in which to wash himself and his clothes. The dry season was in its last weeks and each new afternoon sky seemed to grow heavier, darker. Still it had not rained. After six weeks of beatings and rope tortures in the small ex-storeroom of the ex-pagoda, Chhuon's body was raw, bruised, as sore as if he'd been caught beneath a stampede of water buffalo or pounded by the concussion of a large bomb. As his strength had drained and his will to resist paled with each blow, his beliefs hardened. Even snared in fatalism and hopelessness his Buddhism, his nationalism and his adoration of Khmer family traditions strengthened as if the ropes and blows were concentrating his beliefs into his very core. The eighteenth of March had been preceded by threats, had arrived with the "last" interrogation, then had passed without explanation. To Chhuon's disappointment they—Hang Tung, Trinh, Trinh Le, who else he didn't know—had rescinded the order of public hanging, had bettered his treatment and had ceased the physical torture, only, he thought later, to change tortures.

At first he welcomed the break. Every day he had been dragged from the blackness of his cell, interrogated and beaten. Sometimes his wrists were tied behind his back and he was hung by his hands until just the tips of his toes touched the floor and his shoulders screamed in pain, the muscles and ligaments slowly tearing under his own weight and the good-natured slaps on the shoulders by the guard. "Names! Everyone who has helped you."

"I've done nothing."

"You are the head of the resistance. We know that."

"Someone lies."

"You are known as Cloud Forest."

"Never. They made it up."

As the ligaments stretched farther, as cartilage popped and Chhuon's feet rested more squarely on the floor, his interrogators raised the rope. "Cloud Forest. Give us all the names."

"There are no others."

"So you confess to your crimes alone."

"No crimes."

Some days the tortures lasted only a few minutes, other days he was beaten for six hours straight. Sometimes they tied him and left, then returned in five minutes and beat him again. Other times they tied him and left him alone for hours. He never knew what they would do. In the beginning, on the days he braced himself for the worst, it always seemed they were most lenient. Then he'd lapse and they'd set upon him with such vengeance he'd pray for the release of death.

"You can get away with nothing. We know everything. What we don't have are two identifications to verify each conspirator. We've picked up sixteen. Ten implicate you. They've provided us with many names. Only a few have been identified by just one. Should we incarcerate those with just one identifier? You're the leader. Tell us the names so that we don't unjustly kill a villager to avenge the whim of one of your evil lackeys."

"I know no names."

"You know code names."

"There is no one. I've done nothing."

"It's only a matter of time. Vanatanda supplied you with the plastique. The boy Sakhron brought you the cartridge trap."

"Vanatanda is a monk. I know no boy Sakhron."

Again and again and again the questions and beatings until Chhuon could barely remember what was real and what was the reality they wished him to tell. Then it stopped. His shoulders, fingers, ankles, feet, hips and back tightened, recoiled as if they were springs overly stretched. And his mind recoiled. At first his anxiety grew because of the pattern of greatest wrath following lax days. Then that gave way to a vision of himself hanging by the neck from a rope secured to the pagoda's porch roof carrying beam. And that to thoughts and conjectures about the rumors. How had he heard? He couldn't recall. All Viet

Namese officers had been withdrawn to the headquarters camp.
Why? Were the nationals gaining? Had the Americans invaded?
He had been cut off from all news except that which the guards
or interrogators passed on. Had they indeed told him of the
extractions? Certainly they had. Why else would Trinh Le have
told him it wasn't true? There was a plan to remove the Viet
Namese settlers too. Of that Chhuon was sure. Oh how he
wanted to ask for news of his family. He had had such a good
life. What merit he must have earned in the last to have been
granted the good wife, Sok. And his children—each one so
special. Vathana in Neak Luong with her husband, both under
the guidance of Mister Pech. An image of her at birth floated
pleasantly in his mind's eye. For the moment he breathed easily
and his pains evaporated. Samay would be twenty now. Perhaps he had found his sister in Neak Luong. That would be best.
There were the little ones who had died so young, at birth and
at one year, died to be spared witnessing the atrocities of what
had happened to our country and our people. And Kdeb and
Yani . . .

Chhuon's thoughts froze. Ceased. Four years had not only not
erased or eased the memory but had nurtured his shame and
guilt. Why? Why had he left them with Y Ksar? Why had he
even taken them on the trip? Life is suffering. Life is suffering.
Blood for blood. It meant nothing. It roused nothing in him
anymore. It was not the fault of the Viet Namese but his own
fault. He, Chhuon, their father, their earthly guardian, who had
left them in the path of death. The path was there, had always
been there, was as plain to see as if it were a street in Stung
Treng with a hundred large trucks barreling up and down. Only
he hadn't seen it because of the *numpai.* He had let his two
beautiful young children play in the road and they'd been obliterated by a death truck and for years he'd blamed the truck.
He'd even, he knew now, blamed his children. Lord Buddha, he
thought, when I die let my eyes close for I am ready to leave
this earth. Let my youngest son not think badly of me. If it is
your will, let me once more walk a forest trail and smell the
orchids by my Srepok River.

Nang shifted slowly. The filth of the observation site disgusted
him. His eyes darkened, sunk toward the back of his skull. In
the sweet stench and predawn stillness elements of his personal
inner contradictions battled for prominence. What had Ngoc
Minh said, "Twice wounded makes a soldier cowardly"? Humph!
But was it true? Had he lost his boyish invulnerability? No,
that wasn't it. That, he told himself, was the stamp of Ngoc

Minh's bourgeois classism shining through his thin veil of purity and brotherhood. There's a difference between being cured of seeking impossible targets and being overly cautious.

For three weeks KT 104 soldiers had silently watched, planned, prepared the battlefield. The 81st Battalion was Nang's reserve, reinforcement and ambush unit. Two other battalions of the KT task force were charged with regaining the village. Units from other zones had converged on the Northeast, readying a systematic, village-by-village liberation sweep. Nang's and Von's strugglers had been assigned the NVA headquarters camp.

Again Nang shifted. He had chosen the observation point, and since the offensive had begun across the border, the site had been deluged with tons of medical offal. Each night three strugglers slithered into the camp and rearranged the body parts so a cavern existed beneath the sheared-off legs, the amputated arms, the splintered chunks of rib cages. Then two left and one nestled down amid the waste and swill of the morbid pit behind the hospital complex.

In the predawn Nang occupied his mind alternately with a flood of thoughts and then with perfect attention to his own inner void. He listened, then fell into himself. He could barely see—occasionally a door opened and light squirted from the hospital or from the headquarters operation center up the hill. He dared not smell, feel or taste. At one point he thought about ice, huge slabs, not the blocks he'd seen as a boy in a Stung Treng warehouse but sheets covering lakes or rivers. What a wonderful horrible thing to be able to freeze all the water, to freeze a body, to have ice for blood, to have that total control to freeze or thaw one's own blood and that of all others. The air pulsed, vague, distant. Dossiers froze people, Nang thought. Cahuom Chhuon, village chairman. Eh? So now he's chairman of a yuon village! He must have abandoned the people, must have abandoned the Khmer race. Ah, what could have been . . . The thought was vague—a pang, not words. And his wife, a resister. Ha! Sok a resister! Mama a resister! That's crazy. Ha, the inner contradictions of the yuon apparatus—as disgusting as this hospital pit. And this Hang Tung. He lives in the chairman's house! Beyond doubt he rubs the chairman's wife's parts with broken bones.

The pulsing became more distinct. Nang shifted, bringing his eyes to the arranged narrow slit between a mangled thigh and a discarded arm. There was little room to move beneath the parts, enough to hide, to blend in, when the orderlies brought new loads to the pit, then to shift, to observe when the way was clear. The sky had grayed since Nang's last look. Now the pulsing became a loud whacking. Between the headquarters center and the hospital there was a flurry of activity. From a bunker men dragged several very old women toward the hospital surgical cavern. At a leveled area a dozen men pulled back the woven living canopy, opening a landing pad. Then the helicopter appeared. Nang recognized it from his training in China. Other yothea observers had reported the narrow, black, round-nosed ship but Nang had not believed them. Always the reports were from veterans of the Chenla II fight. "Helicopter fever," Nang had whispered to Eng. "They see helicopters everywhere. They feel them in their sleep." What the yotheas described, what Nang now saw, was not an American Huey or Cobra or a CH-53 but, Nang realized, a four-blade, single-rotor, grasshopper-looking Soviet Mi-4. From the pit of human sludge Nang could see soldiers, hospital porters and guards converge on the ship. The ship did not shut down, barely idled down, its tripod of tires touching the earth tentatively as if it were an insect set to jump away. High-ranking casualties, Nang thought. More vomit for my pit. They'd never bring in a soldier like that. Let them die and bury them trail-side. But the guards? He strained his eyes to ascertain the details of the picture unfolding a hundred meters away. He could see them separate the wounded, but could not tell what distinguished the groups. Then it hit him. Four were POWs.

The evening sky over Phum Sath Din was low, gray, filled with the light premonsoon haze which characterized the foothills of the Srepok Forest. From the treeline above the highest, and as yet never plowed, irrigated or planted paddy, Met Nhel and Ngoc Minh squatted amid a square of two dozen local resisters. "We all are the masters of our own destiny, eh?" Nhel said quietly to Kpa, Cahuom Sam and the others. He spoke in the idioms and accent of those with whom he sat. Cahuom Sam nodded. Sakhron grunted affirmation. Only Kpa kept his thoughts hidden.

For more than a year the local resistance had had loose contact with the Khmer Patriots via a series of small, tangential local groups. When Ngoc Minh's units arrived, Kpa's locals were desperate for food, down to the last of their weapons. "With the weapons we've given you," Ngoc Minh whispered, "your unit will be able to match the best yuon militia."

"We're grateful that the Kampuchean Patriots Liberation Front has arrived," Sam whispered back. "We've had too little fire-power to be effective."

"But you've been very effective. The Center has depended upon you for intelligence. You've never let the Center down."

Kpa flicked his little finger and tapped Sakhron. The boy, acting more the country bumpkin than he was, asked quietly, "What center?"

"It's not important," Ngoc Minh said. "What is important is the liberation of the people. How do you know about Colonel Nui's request?"

"That's not important," Kpa said quietly. "Only that he requested a return of troops and that it was denied."

"He wanted more troops about the village?"

"He reported to the next higher headquarters that an 'uprising' was possible."

"Because of your increased activity?"

"One cannot know another's mind," Kpa said respectfully.

"This man Hang Tung, he . . ."

"He has four bodyguards," Sam said. "He had one but he was killed by a trap set for his master. Now he has four. He's smart, nervous."

"Mister Kpa"—Ngoc Minh turned toward the resistance leader—"I need only one of your men for a guide. The village will be easy. But the headquarters will be difficult. Send your squads there."

"You must"—Sam cleared his throat—"rescue my cousin."

"It will be done."

"When?"

"In three days," Nhel said. "In three days the village will be liberated. Our fighters at the yuon complex will attack first."

Quietly, almost as if he were a spirit without physical substance, Kpa walked the animal path along the river toward the village. With nightfall, mist had settled amongst the trees, between the bunkers and houses, isolating the area as much as if it had been surgically pared from the earth and set afloat in the ether. Kpa did not crawl through the minefield but walked where his feet told him he'd walked a dozen times before. He did not slither over the berm but stepped slowly through the gap the militia had left, left secure in the knowledge that no one would cross the mined belt between the river and the berm. He did not sneak along the alleyways toward the home of Cahuom Chhuon but strolled the middle of the main street as he'd done dozens of times, strolled to the turnoff, walked to the small angel house before the Cahuom home, said a silent prayer for Chhuon, then relaxed, motionless, awaiting the changing of bodyguards in the courtyard.

To the east the resistance squads had rendezvoused with elements of Von's 81st Battalion and were being used to assist Von's yotheas in their preparation of attack and withdrawal routes and of ambush sites in case the NVA attempted to reinforce from the east or in case the headquarters troops attempted to break out or counterattack. Farther east, across the border, the NVA had finally opened the third front of the Nguyen Hue Offensive and was fully committed to battles at Plei Ku and Kontum.

Two hours past midnight Kpa heard the familiar commotion of Hang Tung's bodyguards. Like a cat he moved. Quickly he leaped from tree to tree within the small family orchard, then to the wall of the house where Hang Tung slept. "Get your rice-bottom up," Kpa heard a guard grumble. "You've snored enough." "Uhh. Not as much as Mister Committee Member, eh?" "I'd like one night to sleep on his mat." Kpa glided to the window. A guard would be inside on a mat below the sill. Another across the threshold. "I'd like one night to return to my wife's mat."

Kpa waited. When all was again silent, he traced the jamb with his left hand, raised his right foot to the sill, his toes just reaching, then as if a helium-filled balloon, he rose effortlessly. Immediately he separated the curtain, dropped his foot, tenderly felt for the body which he had heard breathing beneath. He felt the mat, dragged his foot to its edge, stepped in. Hang Tung slept by the plaited curtain dividing the central room. His breathing was irregular, spasmodic, as if dreams haunted him. Kpa shuffled toward his symbol of evil. Slower, he cautioned himself. Quicker, his hatred ordered. Suddenly his legs felt as if they were sacks filled tight with a rush of water. He stopped. The guard across the threshold coughed, rolled, sputtered back to sleep.

From his sleeve Kpa removed a bamboo stiletto. Its tip was needle sharp, its edges like razor blades, its entire length soaked in poison made from an extract of wild raisins. Kpa listened carefully. He could not see even an outline of Hang Tung's form. Which way were his feet? When Kpa descended upon Tung to clamp a hand over his nose and mouth, to ensure silence he needed to know whether Tung slept mouth-nose or nose-mouth from him.

Kpa slid a foot. Then another. His shin contacted the low table and he froze. Something, a jar, a lamp, wobbled. "Umph!" Hang Tung hacked, arched his neck, resettled. Kpa knew. Mouth-nose. He turned ninety degrees to the body, slowly descended, slowly passed his hand up until he felt the heat of exhausted breath. He waited. Inhale. Exhale. Inhale. Exhale. Clamp. Hang Tung tried to gasp. Before he could, Kpa's dagger found the soft tissue beneath his jaw. He drove the dagger in, down through the mouth, tongue, palate and into the brain—exactly as a butcher might kill a chicken. Hang Tung's body shuddered, first head and shoulders, then arms, hips, legs and feet. Then all movement ceased.

"One slow, four quick! One slow, four quick!" Nang chanted as the main force concentrated on the few strong points. Their attack on the NVA headquarters east of Phum Sath Din followed classic North Viet Namese tactics. The first LP/OPs were knocked out as Hang Tung shuddered and died, two days, not three, after Ngoc Minh had met with the resisters. An hour later every KVM/NVA village in the lower Srepok Valley was under siege and Lieutenant Colonel Nui's lightly defended headquarters (not a single artillery piece, AA gun or even mortar had been left back) was being prepped by Krahom 61mm mortars as KK commandos penetrated the perimeter, grenading fighting positions, hitting the internal structures with 57mm recoilless rifle fire and creating general chaos amongst the defenders, POW guards, medics and porters.

"Move! Move! Move! Attack!" Adrenaline surged through every cell of Nang's body. The rapid barking chorus of his yotheas' AKs elevated the excitement. "Without this," he shouted back at a cell of new yotheas as they huddled behind a large tree trunk, "without Angkar, all Khmers are doomed. The Khmer race prevails or vanishes tonight. Move!"

His troops moved. They ran into sporadic return fire, disciplined fire from those few soldiers who remained along the south berm. Within minutes, perimeter pockets of resistance fell back or were flanked and destroyed. The fighting moved deeper into the camp. From the north berm a huge explosion—a bomb to be transported, no Krahom soldier knew where—a fireball flashed/leaped skyward illuminating attackers, defenders, structures. Then blindness in blackness as the concussion blasted outward knocking troops of both armies flat, ripping eardrums, zinging stones, tree splinters, charred jeep shrapnel. Wounding. Killing. "Move!" In the second-long pause following the concussion Nang rallied his fighters. "Through the center," he ordered. "There, there, there." Nang pushed yotheas into the gap between the hospital and the main operations bunker. "Duch, get Thevy. Cut it in two."

"Got it." Duch radioed the Rabbit Platoon leader of the 2d Company. He monitored others. Nang was too excited to direct;

Eng also was too deeply immersed in the direct killing of NVA resistance pockets. Duch radioed orders as if Nang had told him: 3d Company take the operations center, 1st mop up the perimeter, 2d to the hospital complex. "Met Nang!" Duch grabbed the CO's shirt. "Met Nang. Hawk Platoon is out of ammo."

Nang paused, looked eerily at Duch. "Have them fall back."

"Hawk! They're the recoilless rifle team. Rifle fire can't penetrate the operations bunker. There's a company of defenders there."

"Get Von. The 81st has a recoilless platoon, eh?"

"Yes sir." Duch smiled and set about with his calls. All about them yotheas were in a destroying frenzy.

Nang ran downhill toward the hospital. Firing was sporadic. He found Rath, the company commander, talking lustily with Puc, the leader of Monkey Platoon. "They've no way out." Met Puc laughed. "First we eliminated those in the upper wards. Now our strugglers have sealed all the exits. They're working through the caves room by room."

"Bring me there," Nang said triumphantly. "Have those standing around collect all the medicine. Police up the weapons."

"Should we set up our own bivouac?"

"No! We don't want terrain. Let them have it back so we can trap them here again."

Nang scurried in through a tunnel opening, down a short corridor and into a large room. The bodies of half a dozen dead Viet Namese orderlies were strewn amid the floor clutter. That of a traumatically decapitated yothea lay on the table in the center of the room, his mangled head set upon his chest like some repugnant cancerous growth. Nang smiled broadly at the few yotheas relaxing with the corpses. From a narrow connecting passageway came the muffled sound of small arms. "Have we taken the next room?"

"Oh yes, Met Nang. The next two are ours. It's the middle one that's fortified."

"Fortified?"

"Met Nang." A small thirteen- or fourteen-year-old boy stood. "You remember me?"

"Yes," Nang said.

"Met Tam. I helped you at Baray."

"Yes. Yes, I remember."

"Met Nang, this is too much. Must we kill those who lie helpless?"

"Would you have us leave them to heal and attack us again?"

"I . . . I would . . . Could we take them prisoner? Most have been wounded by American bombs. Wounded in the same fight we fight."

"We fight the same enemy, Tam, but if they win they'll turn again on Kampuchea. A tiger doesn't change its stripes because it's been maimed by an eagle."

"I just . . . think . . ."

"Why is there fortification in the center room?"

Another yothea stepped forward. "It's their prison," he said. "That's what Thevy thinks."

"Prison! POWs!"

Nang squeezed through the passage to the second room, a large ward in which forty or fifty patients in narrow three-high bunks had been bayoneted. He squeezed through another passage into a third opening, a room with four operating stations. Again there was the litter and stench of death—doctors, nurses, their heads smashed by clubs or rifle butts—and patients, tubes and hemostats removed, allowed to drain.

Nang slowed, took his time. He sauntered about the ward ordering yotheas to confiscate various medical supplies and instruments. The underground facility was more modern than anything Nang could have imagined—better equipped than any operating room he'd ever seen. "What's this?" he asked, lifting a chromed instrument.

"I don't know," Tam said. From the back of the third room came childlike whimpering. Tam glanced up, looking for the source.

Nang grabbed the handle of the instrument he'd found and shook it. The outer chamber began to whirl about the central handhold. Nang smiled. To him the centrifuge was like a shiny toy. Into the narrow slit passage leading to the final room, two yotheas were firing short bursts. Nang turned, turned back. "What's that crying?" The distraction of the instrument had temporarily broken his drive for immediate conquest.

"There's a jail cell back there," Tam said. He had made a brief investigation and now walked past Nang, his head down as if he were about to vomit.

"Stop!" Nang ordered. With the instrument in his claw he motioned for the young yothea to lead him back. Tam covered his nose.

At the back of the surgical ward Nang, Tam and several yotheas stared into two small dungeons. Inside each were perhaps a dozen Mountaineer or Khmer elders. In one the people were dead—drained human bags—rotting in a half-resealed cave. In the other the living huddled, terrified. "Open it," Nang said to the yotheas. Immediately two ripped the bamboo-slat door apart. The elders cowered farther to the rear. Nang stepped in, squatted. He still held the chromed centrifuge. "Why are you here?" he asked quietly. No one answered. He pointed at an old woman. "I know you, Auntie," he said. "Come out." Still the old people didn't move, didn't answer. "Come," Nang said, gesturing with the instrument.

"take me," an old man said. "you take me. leave moeun."

"Moeun?" Nang said.

"take my blood," the old man said. He rolled to his knees expecting to be dragged from the dungeon. He did not comprehend what had happened in the underground surgical ward before him. In his bitterness he crawled and swore and mumbled at Nang. "bastard. yellow bastard. you don't need that instrument. i'm O. O positive. you typed my blood twice already, bastard. you keep us for blood for your wounded, then suck us dry and seal our bodies in the caves. go ahead, bastard."

Nang and his yotheas stumbled back as the barely human creature crawled from the dungeon. Then Nang said, "Get them out of there. They are Kampuchean. To be regained." Nang turned, stepped toward the slit passage where two yotheas were sporadically firing toward the central wardroom. Then Nang stopped. "Moeun," he muttered to himself. He turned to see his soldiers assisting the old people. Moeun, he thought. Aunt Ry's mother! How did she get in . . . What have those yuon bastards done to Phum Sath Din?!

Nang clamped his teeth, strode to the slit passage. A yothea was about to roll a grenade into the tunnel. Pistol cracks exploded from the far end, the unaimed rounds impacting the sides of the curved tunnel.

"Stop!" Nang barked the order.

Heads snapped. Some yotheas looked at him with who-the-hell-is-he? glances. A few leaped up. The grenadier snarled, "This'll get em."

"No. Angkar wants those POWs—alive." Nang pointed to the man with the grenade. "You. And you, Puc. Go out and come in from the other side. Order the fire ceased."

In the absence of Krahom fire from the operating ward the firing of the NVA guards in the center chamber increased. For ten minutes they fired wildly. For ten minutes Nang could hear the muffled sounds of KK fire from the other side. Then all fire stopped.

In Viet Namese, to the astonishment of the Khmer Krahom soldiers about him, Nang shouted, *"Dung ban nua! Dung co so."* Cease fire! Don't be afraid! To his astonishment the NVA firing stopped. *"Di ra day!"* Come out here.

"Who are you?" a voice shouted.

"I am Comrade Nang, commander of the KT 104 Battalion of the Khmer Liberation Army. Come. You will not be harmed." With hand signals Nang directed yotheas to move or cover up the corpses.

"Why have you attacked us? Colonel Nui will be furious. We are allies."

"Yes. A grave mistake. We have ceased our fire. Have you American prisoners?"

"A mistake!"

"Yes. Terrible." Nang stopped shouting. "Come out now. You'll see."

"What?"

"I said"—Nang raised his voice infinitesimally—"if you come here, you will see. We mean you no harm. Some agent must have penetrated our system. You're not part of the ARVN offensive, are you?"

A soldier peeked around the curve in the corridor then pulled back. He peeked again. Nang laid his rifle at his feet. The soldier stepped into view. "What offensive?"

"Haven't you heard? The ARVN has attacked all behind the lines."

"No! How?"

Nang held his arms out as if to embrace the soldier. The man edged back. Behind him a second guard peered about the earthen wall. "Two American divisions and the ARVN Airborne Division have landed to the west. They're trying to cut off your troops from the rear. We were told they'd captured this camp."

The Viet Namese guard turned and spoke quickly to the men behind him. A moment later he emerged alone. "Are we free to go above?"

"Yes." In Khmer Nang ordered free passage for the allied troops. Yotheas glanced at one another quizzically. A few, copying Nang, smiled at the NVA guard. The guard retreated into the center room then emerged leading seven men. Nang did not attempt to disarm them but let them mill a moment amid the yotheas. In Viet Namese he addressed the soldier who had emerged first. "Have you American prisoners?"

"No. Only an ARVN captain."

"Seven guards for one captain?"

"No. No. Two guards. These others fell back when your troops came."

"Are there more?"

"An orderly with the captain."

Nang smiled. In Khmer he said, "Give these men cigarettes."

None of the Viet Namese indicated understanding though all smiled tentatively and, when offered, accepted the smokes. "Give them more." Nang smiled. "Then take them to meet their brothers."

The light in the center room was faint, worse than in the wards, much worse than in the surgical cave. The air was stale, foul, smelling of infection and mildew. A single orderly, a man of sixty or more years, sat on a gray metal chair reading a recent copy of Hanoi's newspaper. In the only occupied bunk a severe-looking man lay grinding his teeth against a constant pain in his left arm and hand—pain in a limb that was no longer part of him.

"You"—Nang gestured to the orderly—"why do you sit there?"

The man slowly lifted his head from the news and looked without understanding at the filthy black-clad boy with a filthier scarf wrapped about his waist and a dust-covered assault rifle held by a two-fingered claw. Nang repeated the question in Viet Namese. "I understood the first time," the orderly said in Khmer. "Your Viet Namese is Northern."

Nang pointed the weapon at the orderly's chest. "Forget my Viet Namese. Who's that?"

"He is a wounded man," the orderly answered gently.

"Why haven't you killed him?"

"Me?!"

"Your command. Why do you let an enemy live?"

"He is a wounded man," the orderly repeated. "I could never hurt him. As for the command, they think he may be of value. Maybe to you, too, eh?"

"Who is he?" Nang demanded. The soldier grimaced at Nang's harshness but seemed to pay little attention.

"He is from somewhere. Saigon maybe? The Americans washed his brain."

Nang pushed the old man back with the flash suppressor of his rifle and approached the patient. "You were captain?"

"An intelligence officer," the orderly offered. "An intelligent intelligence officer. But I don't think he understands Kh . . ."

"Captain?" Nang repeated in Viet Namese.

"*Có. Dai úy.*" Yes. Captain.

Nang stared at the soldier, at his left arm truncated and wrapped in gauze. Nang raised his own stubbed hand and smiled a slight smile. "For you they brought in the Mi-4?"

The captain acknowledged Nang's hand with a flick of his eyes and an easing of his grimace. "*Không.* No," he said. "It was for a colonel but they let me come, too." It was a joke, the second part, and the captain tried to grin.

"Where's this colonel?"

"He's dead," the orderly interrupted. "He didn't have much blood."

"These murdering pricks killed him." The captain's words were acidic. His countenance changed. His pain-tensed features became caustic.

"I know you," Nang said. "What's your name?"

The captain didn't answer.

"Name? Unit? Tell me everything."

Still the captain didn't answer.

The old orderly stepped between Nang and the bunkside, put a hand on the prisoner's forehead, then said, "He is too hot to talk."

Nang lifted his rifle and aimed it at the orderly's head. "Name, Dai uy Tran." The captain's eyes snapped to his filthy captor. "I know you," Nang repeated.

"He is a wounded man, eh?" The orderly turned and looked down the barrel to Nang's eyes aiming in on his own. "Such a small world. You know . . ."

Nang squeezed. The AK cracked three times. Teeth, eyeballs, brains burst, splattered. The body fell. The captain, covered with wet bloody tissue chunks, startled, shivered, amazed not by what had happened, but by its suddenness.

"I know you, Lieutenant. Oh, now Captain. Tran. Tran Van Le. Or is it Mister Truong Cao Kiet?" The captain's eyes widened. He searched Nang's face for a clue to who this madman might be. "Hey, now you're *my* detainee. Ha!" Still Tran did not recognize Nang. "I bake bread. Remember?"

Tran Van Le shook his head. Then a faint memory clicked. Then flowed back. "Hai? Hai Hoa Binh?"

Nang laughed. He laughed unroariously. "Ha! You do remember!"

Tran attempted to sit up but the wounds in his abdomen shot pain throughout his body. He fell back on the bunk. "Who," Tran gasped, "are you with this time?"

"I am the Liberation Army of Kampuchea." Nang smiled, giggled.

"Then let me help you," Tran said. He did not plead. He did not show weakness but even in supplication showed his strength.

"Help me?" Nang removed his bayonet from its sheath.

"How are you called? You're not Binh."

"Call me . . . Nung. Nung Angkar."

"Lao? You are northern Khmer?"

"First Khmer," Nang said. "Very first." He walked slowly to the oil lamp and placed the bayonet in the flame.

"You wish to rid your home of Communist Viet Namese?" Tran said.

"Of all Viet Namese," Nang responded. He flipped the blade over, looked at the carbon smudge on the side which had been to the flame.

"I wish the same," Tran said. "Let me help you expel the Tonkinese."

Nang laughed. He pulled the blade from the flame, spun, grabbed Tran's left ankle and slapped the flat of the steel on the sole of his bare foot. Immediately Tran jerked. Nang pulled. Tran's abdominal sutures ripped and pain flooded him as he flopped back unable to kick, punch or pull away. The skin blistered beneath the blade, almost immediately filling with fluid, pushing the heat source away and protecting the inner tissues. The pain dulled.

Nang laughed, dropped Tran's foot. "Yes, Captain. You can help me. That's how my feet were burned. Mine were worse. Ha! That will heal. You get out of here. I'll see that you make it back to your country, Captain. Go fight the Tonkinese. But remember, Captain . . . Remember Kampuchea. It is your fate. It is the fate of all Asia."

There was but a single pin-sized hole in the wall, just below the roofline of Chhuon's cell. Chained by the ankles to the floor he could see nothing but the faint beam lighting the dusty air when the sun shone brightly or a pale glow when the moon was full. Otherwise his cell was blackness. Twice a day for a few minutes the door was opened and he was given a bowl of rancid rice. His sanitation bucket was exchanged every other day. Then, in blackness with the door rebolted, his only friend was the pencil beam of light. He had tried to keep track of the days but in trying he'd confused himself. Had a day passed while he stared at the dust floating free and lazy in the still air, passed when he blinked, blinked or slept? He could not distinguish minutes from hours from days from lightdark. They feed me off schedule, he thought at one point. Surely they do. To confuse me. It's not once a day. Not twice. Once then fifteen hours then twelve then eighteen then nine.

He slept. The sound of an immense though distant blast woke him. He sat up. Looked for the pinhole but saw nothing but black. He felt his calves and ankles. Once muscular his legs had thinned while he'd been chairman, had atrophied while he'd been shackled. He lay back. There was scurrying about the pagoda. Then silence. He listened more carefully, listened for hours. A faint glow shone above. When it had first come he did not know. He'd missed its gradual appearance. For that he chastised himself. He wouldn't have another chance until the next dawn to . . .

"Murdered," Chhuon heard someone whisper.

"How?"

"In his sleep."

"By a bodyguard?"

"Trinh Le arrested them all. Nouk says they deny it. Now there are the trucks across the bridge."

The conversation passed. Chhuon strained to hear more but there was nothing. A moment later he heard a guard rant that none of the radios worked. Then again silence. No one came with his morning ration. To Chhuon it confirmed his erratic schedule theory. He felt in the dark for his bucket. When his fingertips tapped it he withdrew his hand then laughed to himself. Things have sunk pretty low, he thought, when you feel for a bucket of shit for security. Perhaps, he thought, to laugh aloud will get them to open the door. He began to laugh loudly, laugh about his friend the bucket of shit, but the stentorian outburst was only in his mind. When the guards did not respond he thought about the noise and considered the classic paradox, if no one hears it is it still noise? Then the corollary hit him: if one person hears a noise that's not been made, is that still a sound? Ha! He chuckled delightedly, filling his entire mind with laughter and music and then with visions to accompany the sound. An entire gathering, family, friends, relatives from distant cities all milling around beside the wat and along the beautiful stretch that dropped to the river. He emerged and smiled and bowed and one by one they greeted him with graceful, respectful *leis*. In the dark he raised his hands returning the salutation. Then in graceful arcs he brought his arms to his sides. One finger, just the nail, ticked the bucket and the reverberation blasted across his mind, destroying the laughter, the music, the images. He lay back and wept.

Real noises from outside did not reach him or he did not register or record them. As Nang's 104th overran the hospital complex to the east and as Von's 81st ambushed two small squads coming to assist and a third, a transportation detail carrying dead and wounded from Plei Ku, the Krahom 71st and 24b Battalions led by Met Ung and Met Sol respectively parked three Soviet six-by-six transport trucks by the small bridge that spanned the Srepok. Chhuon's laughter upon learning the story would astonish the still-proper village elders. For all his sophistication, for all his yuon learning, Cadreman Trinh—in charge of a village whose chairman was imprisoned, whose senior

committee member had just been assassinated and whose senior officer, the province commander for political affairs, Colonel Nui, was absent—Trinh ordered the Trojan horse hauled
into his fort.

Later, when Chhuon finally heard the entire story, he would
be generous in his estimate of Trinh's abilities. With Hang Tung
dead Trinh had arrested the Khmer bodyguards. Then, fearing
Khmer reprisals, Trinh had had his small contingent of Viet
Namese soldiers quietly, sector by sector, disarm the Khmer
militia. Then the trucks, with NVA markings, had been reported
and reconnoitered. The top crates were full of arms. In the
village, all the radios had been sabotaged. Trinh did not know
about the regional fighting, about the Krahom attacks on Khmer
Viet Minh villages. When two platoons of seemingly lost black-
clad youths emerged from the trucks, Trinh was completely
confused. Then an additional force of yotheas appeared at the
village gate. With the two Krahom platoons in their midst, with
most of the village defense force disarmed, the remaining militia and the Viet Namese allowed entrance to these anti-FANK,
anti-U.S. soldiers. Phum Sath Din did not resist. It did not "fall
without a fight." It welcomed the guerrillas. Trinh accepted
them as an allied force. The people, Khmer and Viet, and the
leaders had no knowledge of Angkar's intention.

Chhuon's cell door opened. The light blast was blinding. It
was noon. "Mister Cahuom Chhuon?"

Chhuon answered but he was unable to control his voice and
the sound came garbled.

"Cahuom Chhuon, Chairman of Phum Sath Din?"

"Ay" was all Chhuon was able to squeeze out.

His eyes had not yet adjusted. He could not see the speaker.
"I am Met Nhel, Commander of the Northern Zone Task Force
of the Kampuchean Patriots Liberation Front." The voice approached. Several fuzzy figures passed through the lighted doorway. One unlocked the ankle shackles. "Come with me, please."

Chhuon clamped his eyelids shut then opened them. The man
in the doorway looked huge until two others gently lifted him,
Chhuon, to standing. Then, to Chhuon, Nhel seemed to shrink.
Nhel backed into the hall. "There is some confusion as to your
status."

Chhuon's legs seemed detached as he attempted to walk. The
muscles of his buttocks would not coordinate with the motion
of his feet. One cheek twitched in spasm, the spasm carried up,
across to his anal sphincter. Chhuon hopped and wobbled as a
person might whose legs had been injected with novocaine and
who was having a stick shoved up his ass.

"Our records," Nhel said, attempting to ignore Chhuon's grotesque motions, "do not indicate your resistance work, yet local members and your evident incarceration vouch for your patriotism."

Nhel lead Chhuon to the porch of the pagoda where he and Ngoc Minh had set up their command post. As Chhuon's eyes adjusted to the light he saw six dozen men, boys and girls—the village Khmer militia force—sitting in the sun on the dusty main road, their elbows wired together behind their backs. At one end he recognized Heng and Khieng. Both were bruised. About the prisoners were nine black-clad boys with red-checked kramas. All carried assault rifles. Closer, on the porch, the stairs, surrounding the wat, was an entire platoon; farther, in the quadrant where the Viet Namese dependants had moved into the old Chhimmy family abodes, Khmer boys were roughly extracting the foreigners, pushing the women and children up the alleys away from the village center.

"Please sit," Nhel said to Chhuon. Chhuon attempted to settle in a chair but halfway down his legs collapsed, his butt caught the seat edge and he splayed like a water drop falling on the deck. Two aides righted him and the chair and sat him respectfully. At the west end of the street another squad marched several Khmers toward the pagoda. To the north there were shots.

Nhel hefted Chhuon's file. He pursed his lips. The shooting seemed to bother him. A yothea came and reported that all the communal rice had been confiscated. Nhel rubbed his face. Chhuon, caught by a wave of vertigo, wobbled, began to fall forward out of the chair. The yothea caught him by the shoulders. "Are you ill, Grandfather?"

"Please, let me sit there." Chhuon indicated the floor.

As the soldier lowered him, Nhel said, "See that every Khmer family has enough for the journey."

"See to your brothers first," Ngoc Minh injected. "Be sure no food is left for other forces."

"This is very difficult." Nhel returned to Chhuon. "Very complex. The resistance heroine, Neang Thi Sok, she is your wife?"

"Heroine! Sok!" Chhuon's face cracked into smile, then broke and beamed in laughter.

"Perhaps you prefer the cell," Ngoc Minh said.

Chhuon tried to force the ridiculously broad smile from his face but could not totally hide it.

"Are we funny to you?" Ngoc Minh scowled.

"No! No! It is I am so delighted you are here." Chhuon took a deep breath. "Sok. Yes. She is my wife but I hid my resistance from her. She's not capable . . ."

"She's a heroine of the Khmer Patriots," Ngoc Minh snapped in his harsh, dour manner. "You, Chairman, on the other hand, have colluded with stinging red ants to sell your country. Your traitorous behavior . . ."

Chhuon bowed his head. Nhel interrupted. "Yet they charged you with being head of the resistance."

"You must"—Ngoc Minh came closer—"write out all your activities. Start with the day you sold your son to the yuons. Put him in the cell."

Across the village street a Viet Namese woman shrieked. Two children, five or six, ran from a house toward the wat. Four yotheas were in the alley. As the first child reached the street a yothea guarding the militia soldiers pounced on him, knocked him flat, then bashed in his skull with the butt of his rifle. The second child skidded to a halt. The mother shrieked wildly. Swore. A guard grabbed the second child by the neck, lifted her and threw her into a house wall. The mother ran a step toward her children and was shot in the back.

Chhuon watched, horrified. Another incident broke out in a cross alley, out of sight, identical of sound.

Chhuon heard his voice demand, "What son did I sell?"

"Samnang. Cahuom Samnang. You sold him to the yuons in August 1968. Angkar knows. Angkar saved him."

"Samnang! Sam . . ." Chhuon's voice trailed off. Then, "he's alive?" Then loudly, "Kdeb is alive! *Alive!*"

All afternoon screams and small arms fire and the smell of smoke penetrated the walls of Chhuon's cell. He was again shackled but the door was not closed. He had been given a ballpoint pen and a spiral notebook. In it, as he recorded his memories, tears of joy splashed on the pages. Again and again and again his mind shouted *alive! alive!* Oh, to see him again, Chhuon whispered inside, whispered even within his own mind for fear that the wish, the desire, the passion would damn itself, yet he was unable to control the passion. *Alive!* Oh, to touch him. He'll seek me out. I must go on. I must find him.

The next afternoon Chhuon was led back through the wat to the porch. There, hanging from the porch roof support beam, by the neck, were Trinh, Trinh Le, and fourteen others—the quadrant chairmen, the heads of the women's and the farmers' associations, and the leaders of various production teams. Beyond, half the homes of Phum Sath Din had been destroyed as if a whirlwind had ripped a swath of destruction across the village.

No one, other than a few yotheas, was to be seen. Chhuon's face collapsed, his heart wrenched. He gasped, clenched his teeth.

"Come on, Grandfather," the yothea who led him said gently.

"Where?" Chhuon's voice was weak.

"We must catch the others."

"Why have you ruined my town?"

"To keep the yuons from having it, Grandfather."

"And all the people?"

"They'll be given new homes in the liberated zone." The boy helped Chhuon down the steps. "I'm sorry for the village, Grandfather," the boy said respectfully. "The older troops, the ones who have been with Angkar, they are very enthusiastic. Most of us would never treat the people such. Most of us . . ." The boy's eyes watered. He did not attempt to hide the tears.

Chhuon's voice came hoarse. "I understand, Nephew."

"You must learn, Grandfather." The boy looked away. "Hear nothing. See nothing. Say nothing."

At the bottom of the steps Chhuon turned and looked at the hanging dead. *Alive!* he told himself. Kdeb is alive. I must be alive too to find him.

Nang stared at the small, well-kept Angel House on the post. He had not seen another standing in the Northeast, yet this one not only survived but was in impeccable condition. Beyond it the modest home had been destroyed; one wall and half the roof were caved in, the large hearth of the kitchen was dismantled and the bricks shattered and strewn. Nang stood listless.

For two days his 104th Battalion had attempted to overrun the final bunkers of the headquarters complex only to have each assault frustrated by heavy NVA return fire. Then came the first small counterattacks, then reinforcements that had evaded Von's 81st and its contingent of local resisters. "Ours is not to hold terrain," Eng had cautioned him. "Ours is to strike, to destroy as much as possible, to withdraw and preserve our forces, and to protect the people."

By 15 April 1972 most of the hill towns of the Northeast had been evacuated. Nang's 104th fell back, allowing a small contingent of NVA to emerge and chase them until they, the Viet Namese, outran their covering fire and the 104th reversed and slaughtered all but two who fled back to the command bunker and by their chaotic and frenzied reports gave the Krahom 104th and 81st time to withdraw, to sweep backwards, pillaging, looting and burning, retreating but ready to fight as rearguards but never again being hit. As the KK swept back, they left a wasted, barren, depeopled buffer zone.

On the seventeenth, at the outskirts of Phum Sath Din, soldiers of the 104th stumbled into a mass grave—a heap of unburied
bodies piled two meters high and covering an area seven meters
long. Nang was notified. He came and took great pleasure in the
sight and the touch. Two hundred bodies were piled atop one
another. He flipped the body of a young woman as if he were
flipping bags of trash looking for one in which he'd perhaps
misplaced something of value. A cheap plastic cigarette lighter
fell from her clothes. He snatched it up and jammed it into his
pocket. Then from the depths of the pile came a low moan that
slowly rose through the dead. Others searched for gold rings or
necklaces, oblivious to the sound. Nang looked into the trees.
The leaves were still. The moan grew louder. "Ahk!" He forced
a laugh and a smile. "If I know Met Nhel, not an earring hidden
in an asshole has been left."

Nang entered the village where he'd been born and raised.
About him yotheas were picking through homes, confiscating
anything moveable, destroying anything uncarryable. He did
not stop to join his strugglers in their frolicking. He marched
past the pagoda where bodies hung like sides of beef in a meat
locker and where other fighters were desecrating the statues
and scrolls. Without thought Nang walked to the southwest
quadrant, to the home of the Angel House. He stared at what he
considered a hideous and archaic icon from an unenlightened
time. Still he did not destroy it. Oddly, as if touched by déjà vu,
he glanced about for the small pickup truck that should have
been parked right where he stood. He looked for the little girl
and her brother who should have been playing in the orchard or
in the small courtyard. Nang sidestepped to better view the
home. The entry door had been ripped from its hinges and
the stairs to the threshold had been overturned. He summoned
the energy to approach. Though it took no energy it took all his
energy; though it took no courage, it was the most difficult path
he'd walked; though he sauntered forward lackadaisically, almost apathetically, his inner fight was full-scale mayhem.

He climbed to the front doorway, ducked under a broken roof
beam, looked about. The low table in the center room could
have been from any peasant home in Cambodia. Otherwise the
room seemed bare. He stepped farther in. On the floor there
was a filthy rag, an old krama tattered and stained. Nang
grabbed it, spread the folds of its center between his good and
mutilated hands and examined the cloth as if he half expected
to find a written message. Then, without desire, he raised the
cloth to his nose and sniffed. He pressed it to his face, rubbed it

against his cheeks, held it, against his overt will, tightly to his chest.

Nang raised his head, glanced back to ensure he was alone. He looked at the plaited curtain that divided the room. Beyond the edge he could see a family altar, a large table and two small, covered with photographs of family members. At the angle and in the confused light and shadows beneath the shattered roof he could not make out faces. Amid the framed pictures were a pair of boy's pants, several pens, pads and gum and a bowl of rice. Nang tried to step toward the altar but could not lift his feet. He stood there, dazed, his leg muscles flaccid, vaguely trying to move forward or back but somehow unable to send the right message from brain to legs. Then his abdomen tightened and a hot burning sensation rose from his stomach up through the center of his chest to the back of his throat.

He sniffed, snorted, shook himself. He looked at the krama in his hands, dropped it, turned to leave. Something intangible seized him. He turned again, snatched the old rag from the floor, wrapped and tied it about his waist. Then he strode to the door, hopped down, carefully collected a handful of splintered wood, piled it inside the threshold and ignited it with the lighter he'd found earlier. The flames spread quickly as if the home were entirely tinder. In minutes the flames leaped out and above the roof, reaching for the trees. Nang stood back to the far side of the parking space and watched fire backlight the little Angel House. Inside he shuddered. Good-bye, he thought. Now I have no home, he thought. Maybe I have never had one. I am the First Khmer. I have never had an ancestor. No one came before me.

By midday 19 April the column of deportees from Phum Sath Din had traversed nearly sixty kilometers of dense jungle, following a circuitous path, generally east toward the Mekong. There were nearly eight hundred refugees and they were a miserable lot. Met Sol's 24b Battalion had split the people into three groups: villagers and peasants in the lead; the militia and lower-strata phum workers, whom they guarded heavily, in the middle; and a loose group to be questioned and their status determined at the end. Among the last group was Chhuon and his mother, wife and seven-year-old son, plus Maha Vanatanda and three young men who had worked at the pagoda before Phum Sath Din had fallen to the Khmer Viet Minh and NVA, a half dozen strong young men who were feared to be KVM plants, and the heads of nearly all the oldest families of the village, along with their wives, children and grandchildren.

Krahom soldiers ordered a midday halt. Refugees settled on the hillside among tall grass and dry brush. They did not spread out. No one attempted to slither off and escape. The sun was high, hot, beating the last vestiges of strength from the elderly and infirm. From the valleys of the wild forest to either side came the fearsome whooping of gibbons and the tat-tat-tat-tat of woodpeckers hammering on standing-dead hardwoods.

"They say, Uncle Chhuon," a young pagoda worker said respectfully, "where we are going it is very beautiful."

"Yes, so I've been told." Chhuon's spindly legs and bony ulcerated knees attracted flies. He had labored beyond his body's capacity in order to reach and keep up with the column. In sitting he ached. In resting he feared he would never again be able to stand. Yet over and over he had told himself, Alive! To find him we too must be alive! It had driven him. Sok wiped Chhuon's legs with a moist cloth. On the night of the first day's march, when Chhuon and Sok had been reunited—physically for the first time since his incarceration, emotionally for the first time in four years—they exchanged only silent touches of hands and heart, not because of old cultural norms requiring decorum but because they were very afraid. Each now knew the other had done secret resistance work. Chhuon also, because he feared telling would damn the truth, said nothing of Samnang being alive. Nothing could yet be voiced aloud.

The young man continued. "They told me, Uncle, that there is a town waiting for us. All the houses are new and the granaries are full."

"First we are liberated from Lon Nol," Chhuon said. "Now we are liberated from the yuons. It's good to be liberated, eh?"

The young man did not answer but squatted in respectful silence before Chhuon—respectful not just of his age, or only because of his past status as agronomist, as village chairman, as resister, but respectful of the man for the pain and imprisonment he'd endured. In the eyes of the villagers Chhuon was more than a national hero, he was holy.

Sok prepared rice, fed her husband. A slow, steady stream of people came to check on Chhuon, to offer him encouragement, to give him small gifts. All the while he wrote in the spiral notebook. To one side of the trail Chhuon's mother lay on a mat. The trek had been very hard on her. The monk had helped her the first day, two boys the second, a young man the third. On this day they had helped less because they themselves were weary. In semidelirium she called for Peou though the boy had wandered off to talk to the yotheas who surrounded the column, to ask about Angkar and to look at their fine rifles.

An entourage of soldiers followed Ngoc Minh into the small clearing. "Cahuom Chhuon?" Ngoc Minh said.

Chhuon stared at the stiff political officer. "You know me," he said wryly.

"You will bring your family."

"Where?" Chhuon's voice was demanding.

"Your efforts for Kampuchea are to be rewarded."

Now Chhuon did not look directly at Ngoc Minh but kept the political officer at the corner of his eye. "A reward! Let me return to my town," Chhuon said. "Let me plow the paddies and ready them for planting."

"You do not know," Ngoc Minh said caustically.

"Know?"

"There is no more town."

"I saw it as I left. We could rebuild it."

"There is nothing left. We rescued you in the nick of time."

"Now what's happened?"

"What's happened! You provincials are so naive. All over Kampuchea the Americans bomb towns. Two days ago they hit yours. Had we not rescued you, all would be dead."

"Bombed! But why? Why would they . . ."

"Because they are savages."

"I don't bel . . ."

"It's all for the better. There's nothing but evil in cities and towns. There's old money that infects the spirit. From now on there will be no money. Now"—Ngoc Minh attempted to be pleasant—"come with us."

Chhuon rose. The young man who had remained with him helped him up. Then he helped Chhuon's mother. Sok began a furious search for Peou.

"Bring all your belongings," Ngoc Minh said. "You'll ride in the trucks when we reach the road."

"My little son—" Sok began.

"He's with the soldiers." Ngoc Minh suppressed a scowl. "They'll bring him."

Once they were deep in the forest, a hundred meters from the column, Ngoc Minh withdrew a piece of paper from his tunic. Sok held Peou gently by the shoulders. Chhuon supported his mother. Ngoc Minh unfolded the paper and began to read. "Cahuom Chhuon, capitalist rice merchant of Phum Sath Din, born 1923, member of rebellious forces, Angkar Leou has investigated your activities. You have . . ."

Chhuon froze. Sok hung her head. The old woman seemed oblivious, Peou without understanding.

". . . colluded with stinging red ants to sell your country . . ."

Chhuon's eyes darted. Alive! he thought. We must be alive to find him.

". . . these traitorous facts are clear and proven . . ."

Chhuon's mind raced. About them was a squad of armed soldiers. Thoughts of flight vanished. Thoughts of resistance were absurd.

". . . the security of Kampuchea. For such you are ordered to be severely pun . . ."

Chhuon pointed up the hill, behind Ngoc Minh. "Look!"

". . . ished." Ngoc Minh turned.

"What is it?" Sok whispered.

"I don't know," Chhuon said. There was a commotion back at the perimeter.

"Perhaps," came the coarse, raspy, yet lucid voice of Chhuon's mother, "perhaps they remember it is the new year."

"The new year?" Chhuon repeated. "Is it . . . already?"

"Who are those soldiers?" Met Mey, the leader of the execution squad, asked.

"Cease!" A voice boomed from the hill. Soldiers appeared from the forest below the group. Then at both sides. One boy with Ngoc Minh's armed squad swung his rifle toward those crashing closest. Three soldiers fired at him, catching him with rounds in the head, chest and abdomen. As he crumpled and fell the others dropped their arms.

"What—" Met Mey began, but immediately was cut short.

"Who's ordered this?" the loud voice came from a short distance uphill.

"Who stops us?" Ngoc Minh called. His voice trembled. A company of KK regulars had encircled his execution squad. "You," he said, recognizing one of the soldiers. "You're with Met Nang's 104th. What are you doing?"

The soldier didn't answer. Instead the voice from uphill spoke. "Tell your squad to return to the column. The job of the Liberation Front is to help the people."

"Is that you, Met Na . . ."

"Tell them to help the Cahuoms. They are to be protected."

Ngoc Minh's squad did not wait for their leader to repeat the order. Two boys stepped toward Chhuon, one to Chhuon's mother; three fled toward the path leading back to the column. One yothea bent to retrieve his weapon. A single round barked. He slumped lifeless. The others doubled their pace. Peou led Sok. A yothea virtually carried the frail old woman, another unweighted Chhuon and hauled the family's bundles. As they moved past the voice from the hill, Chhuon caught a glimpse of an ugly soldier whose face was severely scarred and whose right hand had been blown apart. He wished both to stop and thank the youth and to flee, vanish as fast as possible.

Nang stumbled to the clearing. His feet were bloody in his sandals from his forced march. He walked up to Ngoc Minh and stared the man in the eyes.

"Why do you interfere?" Ngoc Minh demanded. "The 104th's supposed to be along the river."

Nang bent and picked up the paper that had been dropped on the forest floor. He unfolded it, began to read. As he did he said, "One must develop a proper patriotic spirit, eh Brother?"

"Why have you interfered?" Ngoc Minh said again.

"A spirit of serving the people and the national revolution," Nang said menacingly.

"A spirit of proletarian nationalism and internationalism," Ngoc Minh corrected with disdain.

Nang laughed. He stared Ngoc Minh in the eyes. With his pincer hand he raised the page before him so as to be able to see it and Ngoc Minh simultaneously. "My father used to say, 'Never forget our people's legacy. Never forget the Path of the Revolution.' You seem not to know which people are our people."

"I know . . ."

"You've never fired upon the enemy. You've never been fired upon. Yet you direct us."

"I'm a politica . . ."

"*Silence!*" Nang snapped his claw in the air. Yotheas from the encircling company closed in. "Ngoc Minh," Nang paraphrased the sheet, "puppet of the Viet Namese Politburo, agent of the foreign devils, Angkar Leou has investigated your activities. You have colluded with stinging red ants and aided enemies of the Khmer nation. These traitorous facts are clear and proven. You have endangered the security of Kampuchea. Angkar orders you detained." Nang lowered the sheet slowly. His cheeks lifted, his nares expanded, his mouth curled in a bastardized smile. "You're of Viet Namese ancestry, eh?"

Ngoc Minh shook his head.

"You trained in Hanoi, eh?"

"Yes!" Ngoc Minh's voice was excited yet firm. "Yes. You know that. Met Sar knows. I . . ."

"You have a network of spies?"

"No!"

"The yuons"—Nang overpowered him—"they rape Khmer

women and girls. I've heard they rub broken bones against
women's privates until they scream."

"You're crazy."

Nang turned to Met Puc and his group. "Take him." He gestured toward Ngoc Minh. "Subject him to ultimate measures."

For two days the refugees sat, rested, regained some of the
strength and composure their immense losses and forced migration had sapped from them. As they rested the Krahom task
force leadership struggled for new direction. Met Ung of the
71st and Met Von of the 81st advised Nhel to put Nang in Ngoc
Minh's position. "A promotion," they said, "which surely the
Center would confirm." But Nang declined. "I'm but a soldier,"
he told them. A soldier he told himself. A soldier cannot be near
his origin, for if he is he will not carry forth the revolution.

To Sar, Nang wrote a long report. In it he included a criticism of Ngoc Minh's activities and said despite those activities
the task force had achieved all the Center's objectives. To
the report Nang attached a short request. Then he sought out
the young yothea, Tam, who had objected to the killing at the
hospital complex. With passes and written travel authorizations
from Nhel and Eng, who had moved into the task force's vacant
political officer's slot, Von was ordered to go directly to Angkar's
headquarters at Mount Aural. Nang's sealed message to Sar
read: "I know my future. It cannot be where I once was known—
but it is at the heart where more important functions await.
Rabbit Number Two."

Two weeks later, as Nhel, Nang and others led the various
columns of regained peoples into the new wilderness zones
between Kompong Thom and Preah Vihear near the junction of
the Cambodian, Thai and Laotian borders, little Tam returned
with additional orders and with an answer to Met Nang's request. "Rabbit Number Two will report to Central Zone headquarters for assignment. He is directed to select two cells of
yothea volunteers for hazardous duty."

CHAPTER SIXTEEN

John Sullivan sat on the edge of his cot, his elbows on his knees, his hands limp, hanging toward the floor. His head hung, too. He stared at the floor without seeing it. The report of fire-crackers—youths celebrating the Khmer New Year—jolted him internally, yet physically he masked the agitation with near catatonia. Beside him on the cot was a lottery ticket, number 797. He'd purchased it from a street vendor to use as a book-mark. The book, Faulkner's *The Unvanquished*, lay splayed on the chunky square rag pad he called a pillow.

He was not the same man. He'd made his report, then rewrit-ten it, then been forced to reconsider and rewrite it again. His lament, his constant urgent depression: the provinces are being fucked over and those embassy bastards are drinking French wine. We must do more. He'd thought the thought a hundred times. He ran his own mental review: last week the NVA shelled Saigon with 122s, crippled Phnom Penh's incoming freighter traffic, blocked the river, overran the border; and those guys in the embassy are in looney-tune land. The surface route between the capitals is all but closed and they swill cognac and suck down Camembert. Every day there're new reports of Khmer Rouge atrocities—reconfirming what I wrote—but no one cares. They don't really believe it.

Sullivan arched his back, neck, looked up without removing his elbows from his knees, thought of Sean Flynn decapitated in the paddy, of Suong, of the new major handing him the report and saying, "The whale that surfaces, Captain, is the one that gets harpooned."

Sullivan rose. He walked to the wall, laid his head against the old plaster, leaned in and closed his eyes. There was fear in his eyes, behind them—a fear as if everyone he saw, everyone he'd seen while returning to his quarters, as if he'd seen them dead. The circle of men betting on fighting crickets—soon to be dead. Amid the celebrators, the students still demonstrating against Lon Nol's disposal of Cheng Heng as chief of state—soon to be dead. The groups of boys and of FANK soldiers kicking and throwing their puppet-balls—a ritual game reaffirming friendship —all to be shot, not heroically like Suong, but ritualistically like those dead at Tum Nop and those he and his group had skirted on their slinking trek back from Tang Kouk. The wealthy rubbing shoulders with the starving, the jugglers and fortune-tellers performing for small fees, the monks being honored and casting blessings—"What's he saying to them?" Sullivan asked the *samlo* driver. "He say, 'Happy New Year.'" The driver smiled—and Sullivan smiled back and felt warm and then saw them, the monks, the blessed, the driver, soon dead too. Becoming Khmer, he thought. Accepting fate, he thought. So fucking un-American, he thought. The NVA 312th and 320th Divisions were pulverizing Kontum; the 324th and 304th Divisions, with fifteen thousand troops each plus fifteen thousand attached in support and surface-to-air missile units, were leveling Dong Ha and Quang Tri; Firebase Bastogne was under siege; and Saigon was again being shelled. Action, America, he thought, and he felt good about the thought that B-52s had begun revenge bombings of Hanoi and Haiphong.

Sullivan returned to his cot, picked up the novel, reread the page he'd been on for two days. "... this was to be the last time we would see any uniforms at all except as the walking symbols of defeated men's pride and ..." He closed the book. "... the walking symbols of defeated men's pride ..."

Fuck it, he thought. He stood, snapped up straight, rolled his shoulders. Conklin was chiding him in his memory. "I got me a fine young lady ... the most wonderful smile ... How come you aint got a gal, L-T?" "No time to commit, Conk," he'd said, or, "Haven't found the right lady." But in his mind too, Huntley reminded him, "... in Neak Luong ... she was missin ya. She was real concerned."

Sullivan breathed deeply. Everything was such a clusterfuck. His "advising" had blown over and he'd been allowed restricted roaming privileges, but then "advising" had rereared its horrible head and he'd been reconfined. He squeezed his hands into fists, flexed the fingers back as far as they'd go, stretched his arms up until the ceiling fan ticked his fingernails, bent straight-legged and palmed the floor. He moved to the desk. They could have rotated him, to Saigon, to the World, even to the new training facility being built in Thailand, but they'd kept him in

Phnom Penh writing and rewriting the same report until he was completely sick of thinking about it . . . until he was confused as to what was real, what he'd invented.

She is the right lady, he said inside. He repeated it in a nearly audible mumble, then again in a clear soft voice that sounded alien to his ears.

Sullivan sat, opened his box of thin airmail sheets, removed one and in French began, *Ma Amante Vathana . . .* He stopped. He had not thought of what to write.

> Again, as you surely know, I have been restricted. I think of you every day. I think of the war, of what I've seen, of the psychic roller-coaster we are on. It is so good to be alive—why must some spoil that for all? Life is wonderful. It *should* be fun. Unconquered obstacles bring suffering and the wonder stops but that's not necessary. It is not inevitable. Though I am not allowed to leave the capital I have been able to secure some supplies for the camp and orphanage.

Sullivan paused. He would not give her the full figures but would cut them in half. If the pilfering was less, she'd be elated with the extra.

> Food is being rationed to the refugees here but much becomes sidetracked. I have been able to secure the return of 2,500 kilos of cassava flour but for it to be replaced into the system would cause the shipper and warehouse manager great loss of face. It is yours. Also, via the mother of an embassy employee, we have obtained materials to build and equip a health station for your camp. Since Ron Huntley left, other items seem harder to scavenge.

Again Sullivan paused. He had not seen Vathana for two months, not since agreeing to take the wedding photo album to her mother-in-law. The longer he was away the more he pined, the more he fantasized, the more perfect she became. Come to Phnom Penh, he thought to write. Come live with me. Come be my wife, forever. But he did not write those words. Instead he reread his last line and then continued.

> I am again very afraid for you. There is a pattern to Communist revolution. (1) The corruption of the established regime leads to disenfranchisement of the masses which is a vacuum for insurgency— the initial blame lies with the old guard. (2) Idealists and nationalists, with good intent and reason, are attracted to insurgent agent-led associations. The revolution begins in the countryside. (3) Once victory over local or national government is achieved,

the core Communists of the associations emerge. There is then a second revolution—the Communists attack the leading idealists and nationalists. This is what occurred in North Viet Nam in 1946 when the Lao Dong Party began its liquidation of non-Communist, anti-French nationalists—about thirty groups. (4) After the second victory the Communists become more ruthless and eliminate all non-Communist rebels. (5) After the third victory they disarm and purge all elements other than their own hard-core elite. (6) Finally the hard core directs a fourth revolution against the leaderless and unarmed masses—a revolution which stands the culture on its head—the communization of all property and all patterns of life. At this stage the population is reduced to serfs or slaves depending on the benevolence or belligerence of the new regime.

Dear Vathana, enclave Cambodia is in stage two; "liberated" Cambodia, the reports we all ignore, is at stage four or even five! How can I urge you not to be seduced into the morass of sincere-sounding Communist altruism? What can I say to convince you it is only bait, a lure to bring you under their control? With what is happening across the border—ARVN intelligence has broken the NVA radio codes and the Communist army is being smashed—it is more important than ever that you remain independent. The depths of Communist deception are bottomless. I've told you before some of what I've learned. Now our embassy has picked up radio traffic of North Korean "engineers" directing Khmer Rouge units in combat against FANK. And yet the key to our victory remains simple: destroy their urban political structure while counterattacking their main-force units in the countryside. (FANK is reorganizing to divisions, which is both beyond its leadership capacity and, since Chenla II, its spirit.)

Perhaps I go on too long. But it is because I worry about you and because I [Sullivan hesitated then finished the line] love you.

J. L.

PS: I was not able to give your album to Madame Pech but left it with your brother-in-law, Teck. He was very grateful and immensely kind.

Vathana entered quietly. She padded softly behind the audience looking into the dim room for her new friend, Ney Nem. At the front of the room, on a small raised platform, was Keo Kosol, the poet. Vathana spied Nem seated on a mat to the right. Quietly she moved to her and sat. Kosol began his newest *ayay*, "Broken Land, Broken Heart." Nem squeezed Vathana's arm in greeting, said nothing, stared at Keo Kosol.

Two hours earlier the rain had stopped, the children had lain down and fallen asleep and Sophan had gone to assist in the health tent. On Vathana's sleeping mat was the unopened letter from Captain Sullivan. Vathana had had an urge to open it immediately upon its arrival but had instead denied herself the knowledge of its content, telling herself to conquer the passion and to strengthen her self-control. The letter remained un-opened for two days. She stared at it. It was fat. As a New Year's precept she'd vowed to refrain from sexual misconduct. Not seeing, not acknowledging Sullivan lessened her anxiety over their affair. The letter raised it. Perhaps, she thought, this is not self-denial.

From deep in the camp a radio began blasting Western rock 'n' roll. She tried to shut her ears. Life was more complex than ever. Every day people were murdered—by bombs, by artillery, by terrorists. The camp population was again increasing. Neak Luong was again a government island in a war-torn sea. Vathana unsealed the flap, removed the pages, read, reread, returned the letter to the envelope. ". . . destroy their urban political struc-ture . . ." she thought. ". . . idealists with good intent . . ." she thought. Sullivan's arrogance irritated her. Perhaps it was something more. Perhaps, she thought, it was that he was American and she Khmer. I should stay with Khmers, she thought vaguely.

She dropped the envelope on the mat. With her left hand she smoothed her hair. Samnang's noisy breathing in sleep mixed with the buzz of mosquitos and flies and the loud distant music. Since the New Year she had not allowed a single grain of sugar, not a single smile other than a compassionate softening of her features to a patient, to part her lips. Tonight that precept was over. When Sophan returned, Vathana kissed the sleeping chil-dren and left for the meeting.

Keo Kosol's voice was very beautiful. His *ayay,* or talking blues poetry, to Vathana was the most lyrical and meaningful she'd ever heard. And he, older than she, gaunt, intense, was the most holy *laic*—layman—she'd ever seen. When he finished the sorrowful "Broken Land, Broken Heart" Vathana's face glis-tened with tears. Nem put her arm about Vathana and whis-pered, "This next one is more frightful. I heard him last night at the Women's Association meeting. I think it's his best."

Keo Kosol's sonorous voice filled the vacant store, its deep bass resonating into every individual. "I wrote this poem," he said, "after my first night in the Khsach Sa camp. My mother had been killed only that morning. My father was paralyzed in grief. It is called 'Struggle Against Fire.' "

"He lives in the camp?!" Vathana whispered to Nem.

"Yes. Didn't you know?"

"No."

No sound but the moth's wing on the saffron-flowered hibiscus
No smell but the aroma of the blossom
   Monks' robes flutter in gentle Kampuchean zephyrs
   Thmil sky fires saffron blood roar devouring moth flower
"Mother," cries the child father brother . . .

Outside a posse of young "cowboys" ran by the storefront. Some shouted ugly words. Some screeched. Vathana reached to her neck. She unbuttoned three buttons, reached in, removed the Buddha statuette and kissed it. Kosol continued. Vathana's concentration broke. She glanced outside. For days the city had been under internal siege by groups of old residents demanding lower rice prices. Since January inflation had increased fifty percent, food prices were up twenty-four. Many stores, like the one in which the Patriotic Youth Club and the Khmer Patriots for Peace were now meeting, had closed. Owners vanished. Shops were looted, stripped.

Two jeeps sped by. Then an amphibious vehicle with large Black Cobra insignias. Vathana brought the statuette back to her lips, kissed it, whispered a prayer. Then she looked back to the stage. Kosol was staring at her fingers as they caressed the amulet between her breasts. He had finished "Struggle Against Fire." People were congratulating him. Two lanterns were lit and the room became bright.

"May I have your attention, please," someone began.

"Isn't he wonderful," Nem said to Vathana. All about them people were standing, talking, exchanging phrases of kindness and caring. Several women produced ceramic dishes with curried eel and rice and invited all to share.

The man on the platform again called for attention, then ceased trying to overcome the drone of individual conversations. Nem clasped her hands and beamed. "Mr. Keo . . ."

"Kosol," he said, not looking at her but at Vathana.

"Kosol," Nem said self-consciously. "I heard 'Struggle Against Fire' last night. And tonight. It's so sad. So moving."

"Did you like it?" Kosol addressed Vathana.

She still clutched the Buddha. His eyes flicked from her face to her breasts, then back. "Yes," she said simply. "But I think I must hear it again." For an instant she thought he looked like her father, thinner, not as old, handsome, better looking up close than onstage. "When the army went by I began thinking of . . . of the Americans. They've broken the North Viet Namese radio codes, you know. Their bombing has been devastating to the Communists."

The man on the platform stood on the chair Kosol had read

from. In smiling joyous tones he began ranting, "The citadels of U.S. imperialism shake with the sights and sounds of International Workers' Day. Everyone must be mobilized . . ."

"Then I will recite it just for you," Keo Kosol said. He reached out and gently grabbed her wrist. "Where do you hear this about radio codes?"

". . . as we stride toward the day in the future when all peoples of the earth shake off the yoke and seize power . . ."

Nem leaned slightly in, separating Kosol from Vathana. "We should listen to Mister Thun," she murmured.

"We'll be back in a minute," Keo Kosol said confidently. With that he directed Vathana toward the door. "You are the Angel of Neak Luong, aren't you? I've seen you in camp and at the hospital." He ushered her out, into the street. Several blocks down, before the Office of the Mayor, a crowd had gathered. People were chanting slogans. The fringe looked turbulent. They walked toward the storm. One chant became clear. "We want rice! We want rice!" Kosol spoke in quick sentences, urgent phrases. Vathana felt secure in his confidence, felt as if she'd known him from life in Phum Sath Din.

"Phnom Penh doesn't need to protect farms or farmers," Kosol said. "It depends on America for food. It couldn't give a damn if the entire country collapsed."

He led her into the midst of the throngs, into the heart of agitation and vulnerability. "Tell me more, Angel. Of the radio, tell me more." Vathana told him about the North Korean advisors directing Khmer Rouge units, about the coming FANK reorganization. About them people were pushing. At the fringe the most radical threw rocks breaking the windows. Police and army troops descended upon the crowd. Tear gas canisters popped and hissed. Now stampede, chaotic, not directionally away but swirling to avoid the gas and remain on the scene. "Goddamn government can't do a fucking thing right!" Kosol raged, his voice booming in her ears. Suddenly a blast exploded inside the building. The windows flared orange, glass shards shot into the masses. Again the swirling bodies, now screaming. FANK troops opened fire. A dozen people fell. Now the stampede surged over them. Vathana fell. Someone stepped on her arm, another on her ankle. Above her hundreds of bodies hurled over and around, flashing shadow arms, elbows, torsos running, more shots, mouths shrieking. Then strong arms swooped her up, away, into the quiet of an alley.

"Immoral bastards." Kosol seethed. "Do you feel it?"

"Yes," Vathana cried. She was shaken, shaking. He held her. His chest was hard, his arms strong. She lay her face against his neck, grasped his arms, the arms that had saved her, had kept her from being trampled to death. She clung to him, pulled herself into him.

"Immoral foreign fucking bastards," he snarled.

"What would you do, Louis?" Teck did not look at his friend but beyond into the restaurant's best section where Japanese and Western journalists were eating, chiding one another, drinking heavily. In the courtyard the jacaranda trees were heavy with violet clusters. The waiter came with the wine, looked disgustedly at Louis in his rumpled civilian clothes, disapprovingly at Teck in his impeccable uniform. Teck gritted his teeth. He was certain the waiter assumed he'd brought this male prostitute into the dining room to soften him before the evening's vice began. Fine, Teck projected the thoughts of the waiter. Fine for a foreigner but undignified for a Khmer.

"I cannot even begin to know," Louis said. He smeared a thick gob of butter on the warm slice of French bread and shoved half of it into his mouth.

"If she were corrupt," Teck said, "I would divorce her. Just like that! But the Communists wouldn't have anything to do with her . . . if . . . if she were corrupt. It's because she's become a symbol of Khmer honesty for the whole city that she's targeted. They'll either corrupt her or eliminate her. But if they corrupt her, then I should . . . well."

"And he himself brought the photo album?" Louis asked after swallowing. "What gall."

"Actually, he was charming," Teck said lightly. The journalists, more than usual, were acting like buffoons.

"Mister Tall-Nose?" Louis said. "Charming?"

"Sullivan," Teck said.

"Eh. The blue-eye."

"Yes."

"The Western guy? His name is Su-van?"

"Sul-li-van. He's an American advisor."

"He's corrupt?"

"I think he's just naive. I rather liked him."

"Teck!"

"Things happen in war, Louis. The whole East is cut off. Except Svay Rieng and Neak Luong. I . . ." Teck hesitated. Louis jabbed a second thick slab of bread into his mouth. Teck leaned forward, "put some in your pocket," he whispered. "for later. mother's paying a fortune for this table, we might just as well use it." Teck cleared his throat, leaned back, sipped his wine. "You spied her at the demonstration?"

"Yes." Louis plopped the remainder of the loaf into his jacket pocket. "Three people were killed. Seventeen wounded."

"By the soldiers, eh?"

"Yes. All. Others were hurt in the rush. I don't know how many."

"He wasn't there, was he?"

"No. She was alone, I think. There were people who helped her up."

"She's still my wife," Teck said, businesslike. "I miss her. Look at me. I've made something of myself. She must come here."

"She was . . . ah . . . with the American."

"You can say it. She was fucking him."

"Do you want him killed?"

"What do I care? You like her, yes?"

"Yes! Ha! She's too good for you, Teck. You want to give her to me? Ha!"

"Sure. I'll ask her to fuck you, too. You need some good ass."

"Teck. Don't be a fool."

"Eh. When the war is over, I'll . . ."

"Go see the fortune-teller, Teck. That's what I would do."

Nang studied his face in the mirror. For months he'd harbored a new hate he could not identify. It festered in him. The infection encapsulated, pressured his entire being. Still he could not identify it. He repressed it, denied it. Soon Sar would have him back to work, soon the festering would be buried beneath one more layer, but now, in the lull, in the void, it expanded, seeking a weak route to the surface, silently screaming to manifest its repressed horror.

His eyes locked on Rin. How easy it was for Rin to change clothes, change looks, enter Phnom Penh. How easy it was for him to find a girl. The thought disgusted Nang. He tightened the tucks and folds in the krama he'd wrapped about his head turban-fashion. Again he looked in the mirror. Rin left. They'd barely spoken. Reth had left hours earlier. Vong was asleep. Their basecamp on the outskirts of Phnom Penh between the railroad tracks and the Tonle Sap River was little more than a refugee shack in an area of scattered hovels. Neither police nor soldiers bothered to patrol there and they were free to move, to bring in supplies, to carry out Sar's directives.

Nang grasped the rippled scar of his cheek with his pincer, squeezed, stretched the skin, searched for changes, for repair. Instead he saw a deepening of color in the valleys, an absence of pigmentation on some ridges. The landscape of his right profile was grotesque. He turned, looked at the image of the left side. He smiled. A handsome youth smiled back. He faced straight on. Looking back were the fused halves of two different people. He raised his good hand, placed his thumb below his left eye and with the fingers extended, covered the scar on the right. The eyes, he thought. They are nice. The nose is okay . . . except right there. He adjusted his hand to cover the stabbing blade of scar tissue which curled onto the right nare. I could have a girl, he thought.

Vong, in sleep, startled. His legs twitched. Nang watched, amused. Then he sat. Other than a cooking pot, a few plates and mosquito netting, the shack looked empty. Hidden, in walls, in the floor, above the rafters, were the squad's tools. "There are places," Sar had told him when he'd reported to Mount Aural, "right in the city"—the high general sounded amazed at his own revelation—"places to do secret work. The soldiers are foolish. The police have eyes like moles in sunlight. We can move about as easily . . ."

Nang thought of Met Rin. He was pleasant. He was competent. But he and the Gray Vultures of the Eastern Zone, Nang thought, have not suffered as have the Black Watercrows of the North. Rin can smile, can laugh. He thinks nothing of patronizing the business ventures of impure women. Nang ground his teeth. His stomach churned. Outside, the evening sky rumbled and raindrops broke loose and crashed heavily on the roof.

Nang thought of Sar, thought of him as his first teacher, thought of his great influence. "Shanghai Communique or not," Sar had said. "Nixon, Zhou Enlai or not. China will not discard Viet Nam. Perhaps the imperialists will sell out, but not the Chinese." Sar had leaned closer to Nang. He had whispered conspiratorially. "This is absolutely secret. I've just returned. Sihanouk sees the military aid. He says, China grants the yuons aid on the same massive scale as the Soviets. But what of the Krahom? We brought the yuons here, we can get rid of them, eh? That spring offensive, it wanes but it determines the nature of future actions. Or of negotiations. Still our 'allies' hinder our supply delivery. Still there are Khmer Viet Minh cadre. This is where you come in, Nang. Did you know in China, hero leaders are killed? In this way potential leadership is eliminated. The revolution is protected, eh?"

Warped thought, Nang thought. Someone called Sar's words "warped thought."

Nang ran the tip of his tongue over the edge of his teeth. His thoughts jumped back to Rin. "Did she make you kneel?" he had asked quietly the first time Rin had returned from the district by the old casino.

"Kneel?" Rin had laughed out loud. "No! Of course not."

"Did she suck your fingers?" Nang had asked.

"My fingers!" Rin guffawed. "Fingers?!"

"Mine sucked my hand," Nang blurted. "Really. She did."

"You've never been with a girl, have you?" Rin's smile was bright, his words loud enough to attract Reth and Vong.

"I have," Nang insisted. "Not a prostitute, either."

"Maybe your mother?" Rin chided him without maliciousness.

"She was a sister. A sister in the Sisterhood of the Pure."

"Doesn't sound pure to me," Reth injected slyly.

Nang spun. Reth backed off. Rin chuckled, coughed out, "Fingers?!"

At the first combined meeting with Sar, Rin had whispered over Nang's shoulder, "Hello, good friend. Do you remember me?"

Nang had not needed to turn. He recognized the voice. "Met Rin of Svay Rieng," he'd said slowly.

"Ay. Now we get to work together. This is very good."

"Only twelve of you," Sar was saying. "You'll work the capital in three teams. One runner, one sniper, one agent, one sapper. This is where you each fit in."

The second time Rin returned from the old casino district he put his arm about Nang's shoulder. "You're a puppy, aren't you?" He'd laughed and winked toward Reth.

"A puppy?! What are y—"

Rin tapped the scar on Nang's face. "You're so young . . ." He slid his fingers under Nang's nose. Nang jerked his head away. Rin laughed. "You know, Puppy"—Rin laughed—"you were right. It is like she sucks your fingers. Do you like her smell?"

Nang shook Rin's arm from him, stamped to the wall of the hut. I don't need to sneak off, he told himself. I don't need that . . . that . . . disgusting odor.

After the team had settled and become accepted amid the refugees, Vong left, returned with word from the Center. "There are four names," Vong had said. His speech was standard rural.

"Use the capital dialect," Nang admonished him. "The walls may hear you."

"Tell us!" Reth sat up, delighted, their work would finally begin.

"Not everyone, Met Nang"—Vong was angry—"is as good with words as you."

"Tell us," Rin said.

"Xiao Zhongshu," Vong said. "He's a butcher but he supplies rice to FANK soldiers so they do not desert."

"I know of him," Reth said. "His shop faces an open area on Mount Penh. The shot will be easy."

"Ney Suon and Non Sarar," Vong said. "Both are Sihanoukists. Suon was KVM but he wants to defect to Angkar. He has said the NVA liberation war is only for the South. No longer Cambodia. Yet he has told some that he is afraid of Krahom bitterness."

"Better to concentrate on those overseas Chinese imperialists," Rin said. "We should leave the KVM alone."

"Ah," Reth scoffed, "you say that because you're from the East. I know them too. I can eliminate them."

"It is the wish of Angkar," Vong said. "Last is Pech Chieu Teck. He is reported to play all sides. Do you know him?"

"No," Reth answered. Rin shook his head. Nang squeezed his chin with his claw.

"His mother is a Sisowath," Vong said. "She is very corrupt. And his wife sleeps with an American. He is reported to have had contact with KVM agents, to have received documents from an American advisor."

"The name is familiar." Nang had tapped the side of his head, unable to place it. "It makes no difference. You point him out to me. I'll take care of him." I'll take care of him, Nang thought. Again he rose, looked in the mirror. I'll take care of them all.

"Having a drink, Captain?"

"Oh! Mrs. Donaldson. Ah, no! I mean . . ."

"Rita."

"Rita. Just a Coke."

"You don't drink?"

"With friends."

"Then let me join you and buy you one. I owe you that."

"You don't owe me . . ."

"You know what I wrote, I didn't mean to harm you . . . personally. I've done some homework on you. You're a real Boy Scout." Sullivan swallowed hard. "I mean that as a compliment."

"Thanks, I guess."

"I'd like to get to know you better."

Sullivan looked into her face. Her blue eyes were clear, hard yet pretty. He turned away. "I'd like that, too," he said.

Two hours earlier John Sullivan had been wracking his brain over the new reports and his half-finished letter to Vathana. In South Viet Nam President Thieu had declared martial law and lowered the draft age to seventeen. Saigon's students were in an uproar. Many who were three, four, even five years older held

seventeen-year-old IDs to avoid the eighteen-year-old draft. In
Washington, antiwar Congressmen and demonstrators were
saying they would allow full capitulation in exchange for peace.
Peace? Sullivan had thought. The fighting in the South had
deadlocked around An Loc with high casualties on both sides.
And a new U.S. Senate delegation report on Cambodia had just
been released. The report concluded:

> The government of the Khmer Republic, and especially the Khmer
> military, has taken advantage of United States assistance over a
> sustained period of time, substantially subverting the intended
> purpose of that assistance. The situation which the delegation
> found is wholly unacceptable.

"Good God!" Sullivan had fumed. "Those jackasses. Of course it
is. The Cambodians don't have any idea what the hell they're
doing and they've got no one to teach them. No one, because
you jackasses have made it illegal."

Sullivan had banged his fists on the desk, stood, paced. He
tried to sit but couldn't. His stomach was knotted so tight he
could barely breathe. He had written twice more to Vathana.
Both letters had been trivial, light and, he hoped, attractive.
But he had not heard from her. Again there was talk of Neak
Luong falling but with the siege and relief of An Loc, fighting
about the lower Mekong had tapered off. Still, Sullivan felt he
could read the writing on the wall. The Senate report was so
damaging. What was the alternative to fighting? he'd thought.
Accepting the indiscriminate abuse of power by those totalitarian humanoids passing themselves off as . . . as what? Nationalists? What could he do to save her? Yes, he thought, he would
marry her. He ripped up the letter he'd begun . . . started again.

> Vathana,
>   Just a few words from the Faulkner book I told you about. I'm
> sure you'll like these quotes. ". . . victory without God is mockery
> and delusion, but . . . defeat with God is not defeat." Also, ". . . one
> child saved from hunger and cold is better in heaven's sight than
> a thousand slain enemies."
>   He is one of America's greatest writers, yet to me, now, he
> sounds very Cambodian.

Sullivan paused. He asked himself if he should send those quotes.
Was he encouraging her to accept the Khmer Rouge? That was
not his intention. How could he attract her? How? How? How?
The same corruption which had caused Sihanouk's downfall
was present in the new regime, and after the combat deaths of

so many, dissatisfaction with the government had become disgust. And he, John L. Sullivan, represented that government! He returned to the letter, wrote a bit about Lon Nol, his *kbuon* (holy writ), his racism, his rantings over the history of the glories of Chenla the Rich. He changed subjects, wrote about the success in South Viet Nam of dragnet operations against the VC—how his and many other teams had worked into ever-higher echelons of the Communist infrastructure, how they had been able to protect most of the population, how the Viet Cong had been on the verge of collapse and how the present offensive had been partially conceived to reestablish VC strength. But none of it was the letter he wished to send. Such an ache wrenched his gut he could no longer concentrate. I must be with her, he thought. She must come and be with me.

"Another cognac, John," Rita Donaldson said.

He smiled. She wore thin tropical pants which came to her ankles, but with her legs crossed her ankles showed and the skin radiated a delicious glow. "Sure. Let me get this one."

"The paper'll pay for it."

"Oh. You sure?"

"You really did give it your best shot," Rita said. "You shouldn't feel so down. Really. They all took their best shot."

"Best!"

"Yes. You've been very professional."

"So fucking what?" His voice rose. Immediately he reined it in. "That don't mean . . . shit." He was feeling the alcohol. "What's important is victory."

"Victory? John! All that means is another ribbon on your unit flag."

"It means not defeat." Sullivan seethed. "Defeat is failure. Failure means . . ."

"Is that what you're afraid of? Failing? Your male pride! The 'can-do' spiri . . ."

"Failure means slaughter and enslavement. There's no grade for effort."

"Maybe it means an end to the killing."

"You want to stop the killing? Then, damn it, let us win the war."

Ferns brushed his legs soaking the tattered cloth of his trousers. Rotten limbs snapped dully beneath his barefoot steps. Vines caught him, held him. Branches slapped his face, covering him with their accumulated raindrops and with ants, aphids and small ticks. He, they, had walked for months. Each time they had settled they were told the land was taken and they'd been forced back to the roads, to the forest, finally forced north into the undulating foothills of the Dangrek Mountains—the new wilderness zone.

"Phum 117," the cadreman announced.

Chhuon looked at the land. Two days earlier he had buried his mother. Before him, before the living vestige of Phum Sath Din, was a broad slope covered with low brush and high bamboo stands. Surrounding the slope was intermittent forest. The land appeared virgin, as if not a single being had ever traversed it. It was not inviting.

"It is a beautiful town, eh?" The cadreman beamed. Behind him his skeleton crew of armed yotheas silently nodded approval. Behind them the bulk of the unarmed militia, the Rumdoahs, quietly acquiesced. Behind them villagers shot furtive glances at one another.

"They said there was a town waiting," Chhuon said. His voice was clear. The months of walking, settling, waiting, walking again, which had worn down many had been a time of recovery for Chhuon. The Krahom had provided minimal rations for the regained people. There had been no starvation. The Rumdoahs, responsible for direct food distribution and care of the people, were basically honest, basically sincere, basically traditional Khmer. Chhuon's status as elder, as anti-yuon resister, as one who had endured torture, elevated him to a protected position. On daily marches when rations had not caught up to the column, small gifts of meat—a bird's breast, a rodent's leg—or vegetable matter—bamboo shoots, morning glory greens—appeared in Sok's cooking pot without her seeing the contributor. " 'New houses,' they said." Chhuon's words carried back into the column. " 'Full granaries,' they said. Comrade Soth, where are these things?"

"Chairman Cahuom," Met Soth said softly, "if you open your eyes very wide, you can see the granaries, the houses." Soth moved closer to Chhuon, spoke even more softly. "don't be like mister hem or mister ny. for the good of the people. remember, had we left you where you were, everyone would be dead from american bombs."

As quietly as Soth, Chhuon said, "i remember my mother."

The old woman had succumbed slowly to the hardships of the march. Over and over she had lamented beneath her breath, "Our ancestors, lost. Our home, lost. Our friends, lost." For her it had become a marching cadence. "Lost. Lost. Lost." No hardship is as difficult to bear as the loss of one's country and for the Khmers of Phum Sath Din the forced relocation was essentially that. "lost. lost. lost." Every step represented greater distance between her and her cultural roots. "lost. lost. lost." The evacuation from her homeland added depression and loneliness to the depression and loneliness of old age. For days she did not eat. Each ounce Chhuon gained his mother lost. Just as his legs became strong enough to negotiate the roads and trails without crutches or cane, her legs deserted her. For several days young men of the column helped her, but each already had a heavy burden and there were but a few who had not been conscripted. "Peou," Chhuon's mother called. "Let me hold the little one for a moment."

"He's with the children's group," Sok told her.

"Just for a little while," the old woman pleaded feebly. Her face did not contort, her heart did not break, when Chhuon, after beseeching Soth, told her Peou could not come. He was in lessons. "Just for a little," she mumbled sadly. "Like I used to hold him." Then she lay down on her side and curled about her youngest grandchild who was not there. The column was at rest. Men gathered firewood, women prepared the rice. Chhuon's mother stroked Peou's hair, then snored softly, then ceased. When Chhuon went to wake her she had returned to the corner where the ancestors sit.

"See! There!" Soth pointed toward a bamboo thicket. "There are houses there, eh?"

"Houses?"

"Yes, Mister Chairman. And there. Granaries, eh?"

Chhuon did not answer. Met Nhel stepped to his other side. "I see paddies, there. And there, a *boray* to catch and hold rain and runoff. Those paddies will give two, maybe three crops a year with such efficient irrigation."

"Now you see it, Mister Chairman, eh?" Soth laid a hand on Chhuon's arm. His face beamed. "It is a very beautiful town, eh?"

"The soil is poor," Chhuon said. "It's mostly clay."

"You see the village?" Soth demanded.

"A very beautiful town," Chhuon replied with scorn.

"Now," Soth ordered. "Build what you see."

The new Khmer Krahom structure of government which now controlled the regained people of the Northeast, along with the people evacuated from the Northern Corridor, varied little from the KVM structure of the Viet Namese Communists. Names changed. "Provinces" became "areas"; Khet Kampot became Dumbon 35. District names were dropped for numbers; Kompong Trach became District 77. The term for "village" remained *phum,* and *phums* retained their original names unless relocated, whereupon they too received numbers. Other levels were added: the *krom* or family group, 10 to 15 families, up to 90 people; above the village came the *khum* or canton, a cluster of villages; above that was the *srok* or sector, which in some areas was equal to a small district. Chhuon's new "town" became Phum 117 of Khum 4, Srok 16, Dumbon 11. And Chhuon officially became 11-16-4-117-1. On paper everything had achieved perfect order.

For weeks the regained people of Phum 117 cleared the land without tools. Hands bled, arms ached. Almost as quickly as they cleared, the underbrush grew back. A single saw blade was secured and the first mutual assistance group, a *krom pravasday*, was established and directed to cut bamboo poles and distribute them directly to the heads of each interfamily unit. "You are the main force driving the revolution," Soth told the workers. "Follow the Movement and you will master the countryside and own the land."

Shovels were requisitioned from *srok* level. Fields were laid out, the *boray* was cordoned off with scraps of bamboo driven into the saturated earth like defeated sentinels slumping at irregular intervals. "Build a new mentality," Soth encouraged the shovelers. "Build a spirit of combative struggle. This is your land, eh, Mister Chairman? Anyone who harms you, who harms your belongings, who harms your phum, he is evil. He is your enemy."

". . . he is my enemy," Chhuon repeated. He jabbed his spade into the clay, pulled back on the handle. The earth parted, making a long sucking *tthhhth-muk*. Anyone . . . Chhuon thought. He looked down the line of the lengthening irrigation ditch. It's past planting time, he thought. There are no seedlings. There will be no harvest. Above them on the slope were a line of family dwellings—simple huts. Anyone who harms you . . . He lifted the shovel and dropped the contents into an old winnowing basket for the two young girls to take to the dike. Again he jabbed the earth. Amid the dwellings was a small, low, curved hut built on a platform and lashed to four vertical corner poles. It was little more than a woven pup tent, a two-person cocoon. "We've no children," Chhuon had said to Sok. "Peou is with the Liberation Youth Class. Samay . . ." He shook his head. "We've no belongings. All we need is a roof to keep the rain off while we sleep."

. . . who harms your belongings . . . Chhuon thought. I know those words. As he continued to dig he thought of Vathana and Teck and their infant son, Samnang. The thought made the work lighter. Certainly, he thought, Mister Pech has straightened out that young man. From proper seed comes proper behavior. Chhuon thought of his sisters, Voen in Phnom Penh and Moeun in Battambang, of his brother Cheam and Cheam's wife. Had their mother's ghost visited them? He had not been able to give her a proper cremation but he felt her soul was neither disoriented nor bewildered. For four years she had been ready to join her husband. He was certain the new state, death, was welcomed. Her soul would adjust easily. She might visit her children, but she'd not frighten them. Not harm them. Still, Chhuon wished he had a white cotton string to wear about his neck for protection.

. . . who harms your phum . . . Chhuon thought. I've said that myself. On the sixth day of the march Sakhron, the resister who'd fought with Sam and Kpa, had turned himself in to Nhel, Soth and the then still large unit of soldiers. Chhuon had seen him briefly, before a squad heading to the forest. Then never again. Of the others, there had been no word. When they settled and the long column closed up, Chhuon realized that the heads of most of the families had disappeared along with all the quadrant and production team leaders. Only the militia boys seemed intact—though they were isolated from the phum and seldom seen.

. . . he is evil. He is your enemy. Those are my words, Chhuon thought. I said them to Y Ksar, his boy and Kdeb. Kdeb! Alive! He must be alive!

"Kosol." Vathana looked back over her shoulder. "Not here," she said. "Not now." He had put his hands on her waist and had tried to turn her, to pull her toward him.

"Not now?" the poet said in his deep sad voice. "Always you say, 'Not now.' Always I say, 'When?' "

Vathana turned. Kosol backed to the door of the small storeroom. His eyes rested on her bosom, his face drooped in woeful unfulfillment. "Maybe . . ." She tried to smile sweetly but her face too was pleading—desiring understanding and patience. "Maybe when my shift is over."

"Tonight! Tonight I speak to the Rivermen's association."

"After. Maybe."

"You love this hospital. You love those who decay."

"Kosol!"

"You do. And you love that infested puke pit of pitiable people."

"Kosol! Why . . ."

"*Why!* Because I love you. You are an angel. I want you to be my angel."

"I owe you my life. If you hadn't lifted . . ."

"Oh, shut up! You don't owe me. Be with me because I am a man! Because I am me! Me. You like me."

"Yes. But . . ."

"But! But Teck, eh? Ah! Some papa, eh?! When was the last time he saw the children? Let me be their papa."

Vathana dropped her eyes from Kosol's face. "He comes today," she said.

Teck was nauseous. The noise of the jet engine above his head, the heat, the overcrowding, the stink of cramped people mixing with the stink and feel of machine oil, the sway of the banking CH-47, of the nylon-webbed seat as the cargo helicopter followed the twisting path down the Mekong toward Neak Luong was, to him, torturous. It seemed there were more than a hundred people on board. Uniformed government soldiers en route to the Neak Luong perimeter, government functionaries making their mandatory inspection trips, whole families—who would they be? who would be authorized to be on the flight?—a few Western aid agency workers, a few Western contractors, two Japanese reporters and that Western guy from the Military Equipment Delivery Team. Ha! Teck thought. The guy would try to see her in the camp. He could fuck her there. He was so predictable. I'll see her first. At the hospital. Yes, at the hospital, tell her what the khrou said, what our fortune will be. Teck leaned back in the seat, pushed his head back against the nylon strap, cranked his neck so he was looking up at the support structure for the rear turbines. He swallowed hard, tightened his stomach muscles, told himself he must not vomit, must not draw attention to himself, or the long-nose might see him, recognize him. Better, Teck thought, to be just another "Bode." Bode! Ha! I know. I know what you Americans call us. You see us all as Bodes. That tall-nosed wife humper, too.

Again Teck swallowed hard. The helicopter felt as if it were disintegrating. Vibrations coming through his feet made his legs rubbery. He shifted his ass but was afraid to make a major adjustment in his position. The window gunner, in his thick flight suit and visored helmet looking like a cyclopean grasshopper perched on the black branch of his aviation machine gun, seemed nonchalant, but other passengers looked nervous. Teck swallowed again. Thick phlegm clogged his throat. Their nervousness elevated his own. The helicopter lurched in a thermal. Teck gritted his teeth. No, he told himself. It won't happen. Not today. The fortune-teller said this is a lucky day.

Three days earlier Teck, with Louis, had visited a long-haired, middle-aged man with a tattered fortune-teller's book. The man's mortar-and-wood house near the new market in Phnom Penh had been light, airy, with a back room opening onto a small courtyard and formal garden. The men exchanged greetings and Teck slipped an envelope beneath the edge of the ancient book. "Your friend," the man asked kindly, "he is not to join us, eh?"

"Who? Him? Louis?" Teck stuttered nervously. "No. He'll wait out there."

"Then tell me, what do you wish to know?"

"It's a long story," Teck began. Once his words began to flow they did not stop. He told the fortune-teller of his marriage, of the refugee camp and Vathana's work, of his mother and father, his own escape from Neak Luong and the separation from his wife.

The man listened politely, asked Teck a few questions, asked him his birthday. Then he opened his large book and read an ancient legend about a virtuous man who, thinking his wife unfaithful, ordered her kidnapped and killed by marauders. The bandits beat her, raped her, but they did not kill her. Instead they took her to a remote forested region and released her. From there, the wife overcame many obstacles in her struggle to return. The virtuous man, thinking his wife dead, had himself beheaded. When the good woman reached home and found his tomb, she, in anguish, thinking he had killed himself over her loss, poisoned herself. Before she died her sister found her and told her her own husband had been responsible for the kidnapping.

The khrou stopped. Teck looked at him, completely befuddled. The man flicked his head tossing his long hair back over his shoulder and away from the pages. He turned more pages, read a few lines to himself, then said, "Today is a bad day. Tomorrow also. On the third day go see her. Join in association with her and all things will come to pass."

As Teck and Louis left through the rear garden gate an ugly man on an ugly *samlo* pulled up before the khrou's house. "What did he say?" Louis asked Teck. "Did he say eliminate the blue-eye?" The driver wedged the back of the bicycle cart against the front door of the house then fled on foot.

"He said, 'In three days join her association,' " Teck said.

"What association?" Louis asked.

"I don't know. She must have a new one. She always has a new one. 'Today,' he said, 'is a bad day.' In three . . ."

A sharp explosive BAAM! blasted behind them. It came so quickly, lasted but a bare instant and ceased, neither Teck nor

Louis reacted by more than snapping around. As they did they saw the roof of the khrou's house collapse, disappear below the courtyard wall. Louis looked up. Teck's mouth fell open. He looked around. There was nothing unusual. From the new market dozens of people were converging on the sudden destruction.

"A . . . a rocket?" Louis asked, disbelieving.

"No." Teck was dazed. "No. We would have heard it. I think."

"Should we see . . ."

"No. What if another one comes in?"

At the front of the helicopter cargo bay Sullivan stood with the forward gunner looking out the porthole at the saturated land beyond the south bank of the Mekong. He was thinking of Vathana, trying not to think of her. From the air the land looked like a map yet without the neat lines—this side, ours and that side, yours—the embassy people drew. The new overlay of government-controlled territory had looked to Sullivan like a six-legged octopus with its Phnom Penh beak-head consuming everything dropped into it, and its legs of various sizes reaching out amorphously to Takeo, Kompong Som, Battambang, Kompong Thom, Kompong Cham and Neak Luong. In some places the legs were thin, broken or bent. The Neak Luong leg was a forty-kilometer stub protruding from the heartland. Still, he thought, the overlay isn't indicative of the perils of travel down any leg . . . nor out beyond the legs. Damn, she's got to see it. The defensive perimeter about Neak Luong has never been smaller. Thank God Rita agreed. I've got to get her out. Got to! Got to!

The hospital was very busy. Attacks along the lower Mekong had been heavy all month and many of the military wounded had been sloughed off on the civilian and volunteer staff. Medical supply delivery was sporadic. At times Neak Luong was inundated with tetracycline, ARALEN hydrochloride and diphenoxylate hydrochloride with atropine sulfate—stop the bugs, stop the chills, stop the shits—but between deliveries there was drought.

"Go home," Dr. Sarin Sam Ol said gently. "Let the others take over."

Vathana looked at the kind man. "What time is it?" Her voice was full of surprise as if she'd expected to stop much earlier but had worked longer than she knew.

"It's not too late," the doctor said. "Only six."

"The rain stopped early," Vathana said.

"A little break." Sam Ol smiled. "Are you going to the rivermen's meeting?"

"Y . . . yes. You've joined, eh?"

"No. No, not me. But I spoke with that man who heads it up. What's his name? You know. Anyway, he's given us some guidelines. We should have an association, the 'Patriotic Hospital Workers,' eh?"

"Can we!?"

"Yes. Why not? You think it would be good?"

"Oh, it would be my dream."

"Good. I want you to help me organize. You're very good that way."

A short "ssst!" interrupted them.

"Eh?" Dr. Sarin said.

Again the "ssst!"

"Oh. Someone for you. I've more rounds. Tomorrow, Angel."

"Teck!" Vathana's tone indicated shock yet her voice was small.

"Have you smiled today?" Teck greeted her. He'd spied on her while she'd been speaking with Dr. Sarin.

"Have I . . ."

"They ask that now—in the capital."

"Oh."

"I am so happy to see you," he said formally.

"I thought you would be with the children."

"In a while. I wanted to see you, alone." Teck grasped Vathana's hand and very meekly tugged her toward an exit. "You can come, yes?"

"I'm finished. You should see the children. Samnang is getting so strong. And Samol, you'll want to eat her up."

"Vathana . . ." Teck said her name very slowly. They left the hospital and walked into the dense humidity of late afternoon. "You know . . ." Teck appeared to search for his words though he knew exactly what he would say. "I am a FANK officer and a Khmer Patriot."

"I know."

"I have a very good house in Phnom Penh."

"Yes."

"I miss the children. I miss you. Terribly!"

"What is it you're saying, Teck?"

"There is a coup coming. I can feel it. The Patriots' group in the capital . . . it's not . . . cohesive. It needs someone who can take charge. Mother runs some things but she's a . . . well, you know . . . not like my father was. Come back to Phnom Penh with me. Help me there."

At first Vathana did not answer. When Teck had surprised her she had been thinking how exciting it would be to tell Kosol about the "Patriotic Hospital Workers." "A coup?" Vathana's eyebrows raised with her voice. "Teck," she said, "there won't be a coup. The Americans won't allow it. They wouldn't even allow In Tam to run for election."

"Oh ..." Teck mused. "Yes ... I forgot. You know how Americans think."

"Everyone knows."

"Not like my wife," Teck said. He controlled his tone to ensure it was not an accusation.

"I thought you approved," Vathana snapped back sharply.

"Don't get me wrong, wife. What has been has been. I am not the same, nor are you. But this dirty war, it will not go away. What we have left is our families, and they are being shredded. I want us to reconcile. I could be a good husband."

"Show me! Damn you!" Vathana stopped, stamped her foot. "Why"—she stabbed a pointing finger at him—"why has it taken you so long? No! No, no, no. Damn it!"

Teck clasped his hands before his face. "I beg you to forgive me. I heard. I heard the doctor. I want to join in association with you. But in the capital. A hospital association in ..."

"You show me. Here." Vathana's voice was cold, angry. "If you can be a father and a husband, here, then ... maybe."

"But I'm assigned there."

"Get assigned here."

"There's a middle path. We can live here and there. The khrou, he said it will come to pass."

Teck left Vathana before they had walked halfway through town toward the Khsach Sa camp. He did not tell her he knew Sullivan was waiting but told her he would go straight to the Neak Luong garrison commander and request dual posting. Instead he went to see his old friends Sakun and Kim, went to smoke a pipe.

Vathana was furious. She did not know why. To have her children's father return would be proper. Everything in her traditional rearing reminded her this was right behavior, right thought. Yet she did not trust him. She thought of Kosol.

Quickly she walked the main road. She passed the apartment building where she'd been married, where she'd learned the river barge business. The lower story had been sandbagged to the top of the windows, the entrance to the central courtyard had been blocked with fifty-five-gallon drums filled with dirt. Only a narrow slit remained. At the inner entrance to the slit

was an armed guard. How, she thought as she entered the alley
which led to the trail to the camp, had Captain Sullivan
explained it? "The criminal element" was what he'd called it.
"The criminal element goes wild because there is no effective
police, no social order." Starving people rioting for food are not
criminals, she thought. That's what I should have written back.
Kosol would have said it. "No structure in the society is capable of responding to the internal violence," Sullivan had written. "Every crime goes unpunished . . . domestic tranquility
cannot be guaranteed." What of Lon Nol's crimes? What of the
corruption? America . . . what does it do? A coup? Ha! We'd be
more successful trying to oust Mr. Nixon!

"Hello, John Sullivan," Vathana said, entering the administration and clinic tent of the camp. "I was just thinking of you."

Sullivan looked up. From his seat behind the reception table
he beamed a boyish smile. He did not rise. Samol cuddled in his
lap watching her feet as he gently tapped them on the table
edge like drumsticks in time to a rock 'n' roll tune coming from
Sophan's new tape player. Samnang clung to his back like
Quasimodo's hump. A dozen children were bouncing, jerking,
flailing their arms, imitating Sullivan's earlier dance show.
Even Sophan was shaking her round bottom, lifting her arms
alternately in backwards arcs.

"Angel." Sophan giggled as Vathana had never seen the obsti-
nate wet-nurse giggle. "Come!" She waddled over. "Do the
Mon-kiii," she said in English. "*Svaa*," she repeated in Khmer.

Vathana shook her head in mock disbelief. She could not help
but laugh. Two score of the infirm had dragged mats to the
reception area and were sitting in a semicircle about the music.
"Mon-kiii!" an old woman called. "Oh my!" Vathana laughed.
She clasped her hands on top her head and looked at the tent
roof. "*Svaa Amerik*," the old woman called.

"Now you are a dance teacher," Vathana called to Sullivan as
Sophan pulled her to dance.

"Better to dance," Sullivan called back as he double-beat
Samol's feet, "than read the news."

"What news?" Vathana called. The song tailed off. Her voice
sounded very loud. "I mean . . ." she said more quietly. "News!"

"Would you like to make news?" Sullivan rose. Sophan was
rewinding the tape. Samnang dropped from his back and dashed
to the recorder to push the buttons. Samol squirmed in his
hands. He bent over and put her down. She too ignored Vathana
and pushed into the crowd of toddlers around Sophan's new
machine.

"Someone I'd very much like you to meet," Sullivan said,

going to Vathana. He stopped before her, raised and clasped his hands. "I think . . ." His voice bubbled with enthusiasm. ". . . this . . . more than anything . . . It could be the most important thing I do in Cambodia. For Cambodia."

"What news? What do you do?"

"Can we go out . . . to, ah . . .?"

"To walk . . ."

"Okay."

"Things have changed . . . for me."

"I'm not surprised. Things change everywhere."

"No, John, that's not what I mean." They reached the camp path which led to Vathana's small hut. She directed him away, toward town and the river.

"The handwriting is on the wall," Sullivan said. Vathana looked at the side of the nearest building. "No, I mean . . ." Sullivan laughed, continued. "What is about to happen is pretty clear. Congress, the U.S. Senate, they passed an amendment to the military aid bill this week."

"What does that mean?" Vathana could not follow Sullivan's thoughts.

"It's a clause in the document which authorizes my government to spend money on the military effort here. They put a condition on the spending. It says all Americans will be withdrawn from Indochina within four months of the time North Viet Nam releases our prisoners."

"You're going home?"

"No. Nixon will veto the bill but sooner or later it'll pass. Vathana . . ." Sullivan stopped, forced her to stop, turned to her. He looked at her face, held his hands out palms up. She turned, looked at him, clenched her fists by her side, then slowly raised one hand to touch his. "Those bastards in Washington don't understand," Sullivan said. The shine of her hair, the glow of her skin, the sparkle of her eyes excited him. "Their concern is only that Lon Nol fight the NVA. That FANK tie them up on this front. Then they can cut and run."

"That's news, John?" Vathana kept her eyes averted from his face. With him there with her, all the attraction she'd felt for him came rushing back. She fought it.

"No, not that." Sullivan's voice dropped to a whisper. "But what we can do about it is . . ." He smiled his beautiful boyish smile. She smiled back, locked eyes with him. "There's a very influential American reporter"—Sullivan now squeezed both her hands—"in Phnom Penh. The one who's gotten me in so much trouble."

"The lady one?"

"Um-hum. Donaldson."

"I thought you disliked her."

"I . . . that's not important. She needs a new interpreter. If she could see Cambodia through your eyes . . . Don't you see? Her reporting would be so much more accurate. Americans might come to a better understanding of Cambodia. American policy might change . . . for the better. It could save thousands of lives."

Vathana's brow furled. "She wants me?! We've . . . I don't know anything about news."

"I told her about you. She was very impressed. She'll hire you. You could . . . I . . . I could . . . We . . ."

Vathana laughed.

Sullivan's silly grin covered his face. He turned slightly to the side. "Come live with me. We can get a house. I . . . I can't be without you any longer."

"John." Vathana hugged him, sweetly, not passionately. "I can't leave right now. Maybe . . ."

"For Cambodia, Vathana," Sullivan whispered. "For your country. And for us. If . . . if . . . You could stay with that dragon lady if you don't want to . . ."

"John, it's not you. I have my work here. The associations. Oh my . . . the meeting. I've a meeting right now! I must go."

"I'll come."

"No. It's . . . it's the Women's Association. Go home and I'll send word soon. Okay?" She stretched up and kissed his lips, turned, then ran back to the camp.

"What do you mean?!" Vathana's speech was quick, urgent. The entire hospital was abuzz. "No one stopped them?! You." She pointed to an orderly. "You know where the rivermen meet? Good. Run there. Get Keo Kosol. Tell him." The orderly left immediately. Vathana had stopped in at the hospital on her way to the association meeting—just to check, to see that all was running smoothly. The soldiers had just left. "Tell me again." She pounded on the wall with her small fist.

"They just barged in," a volunteer said. "Maybe two dozen."

"Are you certain they were FANK soldiers?"

"Oh yes. The new security unit. I know the commander. He was our neighbor before the war."

"And who else did they take?"

"No one."

"Just Doctor Sarin?!"

"They said he was a Communist. They accused him of being a Communist. They tied him and dragged him off."

"Where?" No one answered. "Where?!" Vathana shouted, exasperated, angry.

"Where else?" an amputee said from the back of the crowd. People stepped aside so he could speak directly. "Where they take anyone accused of that crime, eh?"

An hour later Vathana was walking the back alleys with Keo Kosol. He held her tightly to his side with a strong wiry arm. "From great suffering comes great insight." Vathana whispered the prayer. Her eyes were sore, foggy from tears and rubbing.

"From great insight comes great compassion," Kosol said. "It's a very good prayer. Thank you for teaching me."

Vathana slumped against him. "When will this end?" she whimpered. "When will the war end?"

"When all the foreign devils leave," Kosol said. "When the superpowers withdraw and let Khmer talk to Khmer and let us solve our own problems."

"From great compassion comes a peaceful heart," Vathana said. Her head was against his chest and she could hear his heartbeat. She raised her head to look at Kosol's lean, drawn features. I am Khmer, she thought. I must be with Khmers. She put a hand on his chest and whispered, "Tonight, Kosol. Tonight."

"Nothing is more honorable than growing rice, together, eh, comrade?"

The cadreman did not look at Chhuon. "You have grown rice all your life, is this so?"

"Ay." With his returning health had come a cluster of old emotions and suspicions.

"In your dwelling, you have a sleeping mat, mosquito net and rice tube, eh?"

"Two, comrade. One for me, one for my wife. Except only one mosquito net."

"And clothes?"

"What was issued, no more." He struggled with himself, forced himself to say as little as possible.

"If you hide material possessions you will be severely punished, eh?"

"We don't need more, comrade. The Movement sees to all our needs."

"Good. You have a cooking pot and utensils?"

"Yes. In the cooking area, not in the dwelling."

"Okay. When Met Nhel is ready for you, go to him. Next."

Chhuon exited the small administration gazebo and squatted by the door of a hut with several other men. The heaviest rains of the year had not yet begun but each day the sky became darker, the clouds grayer, the air thicker with moisture. Many changes had taken place in the few months since they'd cleared the land. Met Soth had moved up to *khum* level along with most of the Krahom soldiers and cadre who had not returned to fighting units. Rumdoah soldiers, *mekongs* (low-level cadre), ran the new camps and cooperatives. Life was spartan, collective behavior was tightly controlled, yet the Rumdoahs were benevolent within the range of the new policies, policies which essentially imprisoned the people within a military encampment, within a sealed perimeter surrounded by a half-kilometer-wide mine belt—a continuously patrolled barrier out of sight if not out of mind.

Paddy and reservoir building had gone slowly. A few fields had been planted and the irrigation system was more a crosshatch of ditches than an efficient holder and distributor of water. A backyard furnace had been constructed and the camp's first hoes and rice knives had been forged and fitted with handles in the adjacent workshop. Life was not easy—nor was it torturous. It was primitive. All the time new people were added, either directly to the phum or by establishing adjacent phums, part of the same khum. Srok 16 now held more than ten thousand people. Why Met Nhel had come down from srok level to conduct Phum 117 interviews Chhuon did not know.

From inside came the laugh of an older man. Nhel laughed too. Then Chhuon heard the man say, "Lomphat, it was leveled, oh, two years ago. Burnt to the ground . . . I don't know. Some said by yuon artillery, some said by the ARVN. For all I know it was those renegade Mountaineers. They've burned all their villages so the yuon Communists couldn't take them . . ."

The man spoke freely and Chhuon wondered who he was, if he knew the fate of Keng Sambath. "There's an empty village, maybe four, maybe five kilometers from here," the man said. "Why don't you people let us move there? I saw the well. Good water . . . No, fields . . . sweet potatoes, I'd say . . ."

Then Met Nhel's voice came hard, cool, without anger. "Angkar Leou," Nhel said, "wishes you to construct a new village . . . occupation of the existing units will be severely punished . . ."

Everyone was being interviewed. Family histories, work records, education levels, were recorded. For no apparent reason. Chhuon thought of his first interview six weeks earlier. A young Rumdoah had conducted it. "I'm an agronomist," Chhuon had said.

"Huh?" The boy had stared blankly at him.

"I know rice," Chhuon said. "What kind to plant. Where to put it. All the new and all the old strains."

"You plant rice, eh?"

"Yes. For more than twenty years."

The boy had made an entry into the ledger. Chhuon's second interview had been similar. "I am an agronomist," he told a woman with a dark peasant face.

"A what? It says here for twenty years you plant rice."

"Yes. That's true. But I know how. I know where. I know what kinds. Eight hundred kinds grow in Cambodia . . ."

"Comrade," the woman had said, "everyone knows how to plant rice."

"Next," Nhel called. Chhuon rose. I am an agronomist, he said to himself. I should tell him that. Let them punish me if they must. "I am but an ignorant peasant, comrade," Chhuon said to Nhel. "I don't know why I was made village chairman."

"But you resisted," Nhel said. "That's why you are of such value to the cooperative. Now you'll be responsible for all the families in your group. If one person defects, two families will be held responsible."

I am a stone, Chhuon told himself. An indistinguishable pebble . . . "I understand," Chhuon said. He'd been through it all before. "Comrade Nhel, I must ask you something . . , I . . . I have a son. Maybe about . . . well, younger than you. Met Soth, about his age. I think he is with the Khmer Liberation Army. Samnang. Small. He was always very small, very thin. Do you know him?"

"No," Nhel said. "I don't know your son. If he is in the army . . . well . . . it gets larger every day."

"I'm sure . . ." Chhuon said quietly, ". . . certain he's alive. I think he seeks me out. I think he must find me. Could you ask Met Soth?"

"Soth is busy with the land reform," Nhel said. "Perhaps when the war is over. Then you will find him. Work hard and the war will end sooner."

"Met Bella, she thought . . ."

"She thinks nothing."

"Yesterday I spoke with her at the *boray*. She . . ."

"She has been disappeared. She was tainted."

"Was tainted?"

"Yes. Her mother's mother was Viet Namese."

They were not at the work site but in their small cocoon, lying, in their exhaustion, side by side. The cloudburst beat on the woven roof only three feet above their heads. For a week the rains had beaten the earth. The *boray*, built without a spillway, had overflowed at the center; a rill had cut a small channel in the loosely packed dirt, releasing the caught water behind which had gushed through the gap cutting a chasm to the base of the dam. The deluge had flooded the few paddies, had washed away the dikes and the crop. Over the noise of the rain Chhuon said, "When the war is over we'll go back home. We'll rebuild our village."

"Yes," Sok said warmly, yet too fatigued to add enthusiasm. "Bella is gone, eh?"

"Yes. Van and Mey and Heng, too."

"But why?"

"I don't know. Can you get the notebook?"

"You're still going to write it?"

"Of course." Chhuon's tone was very slightly defensive.

"Because . . ."

"Yes," he said. "You know my dream the night before Plei Srepok . . ."

"If they find them . . ."

"We'll keep them in the wall."

Sok parted a plaited section of the woven cocoon wall and removed a plastic bag with Chhuon's current work. He had filled up three and was halfway through the fourth. "Mey was a compassionate leader," Sok said. They spoke sporadically while Chhuon made his notes.

"The compassionate ones are disappearing," Chhuon said. "Nhel considers them weak. Anyone who had any tie to the *reach* is tainted. They no longer even allow the word. Now everything is *kana*."

"Bella? She couldn't have been tied to the royalty. She was a peasant."

"Maybe her father . . ." Chhuon shook his ballpoint pen. The paper was damp and the pen skipped. He was afraid of running out of ink. "When the rain slows," he said after a pause, "I'll cut your hair. You must wear it straight."

"Like them?"

"Yes."

"How strong do they have to be?" Sok asked, referring back to the Rumdoahs who had disappeared. She thought the criteria of the new leaders were trivial, inane.

"I don't know," Chhuon answered. "I don't think that's it. It's a leadership struggle, eh? Angkar Leou can't share leadership with the others."

"Nhel said that?"

"No. No, he said we must struggle to strengthen the revolution. We must fight to launch the land reform. He said people can be reformed but not places. That's why there are more and more new people. A whole column today from near Kratie. You know what he told me? He said, man is born from rice and by his labor and sweat he learns what is of value, what is worthless."

"He's sweated, eh?"

"I once thought like him, Sok. I once plowed and planted to search for understanding. To search for the right way of life."

"But while you labored you *did* search, eh?" Sok put a gristly callused hand on Chhuon's forehead and rubbed the furrows until they relaxed. "You did search," she repeated. "They pretend."

"You know the other thing he says?" Chhuon closed the notebook, rolled to his side, handed the book to Sok. "Nhel says new villages are being bombed. We're going to have to dig bunkers. He picked me as chief of interfamily bunkers."

Sullivan sat on his cot. After his return from Neak Luong his travel restrictions had been lifted and he'd accompanied Rita Donaldson and a few other correspondents down Highway 4 as far as Kompong Speu. Rita had wanted to know if "this Cahuom Vathana" was going to work for her. "I don't know, yet," Sullivan had said. "She has to make arrangements."

"Well, when are you going to tell me? I can't wait forever."

Embarrassed to be without an answer Sullivan had slipped away from her, made a few quick stops and returned to the capital. For two months he'd lamented the disastrous trip to Neak Luong. Every day, every hour, he thought of her. He visited units, checked equipment usage and delivery. His concentration was splintered. Night after night he lay awake thinking of her, wishing she'd write, show up, send word. He thought of Suong, of many of the Khmer troops he'd gotten to know, learned to respect. They had come to rely on him, to trust him to make small corrections in their unit behavior. Now, he was certain, he was failing them. Vathana had become tied up in his ability to question, to analyze. Atrocity reports were getting worse. The Khmer Rouge were spreading, and FANK's overall lack of discipline under the increasing stress was leading toward disaster. Neither the Lon Nol government nor the American embassy wanted either story released. They said they were afraid of panic. Really, Sullivan thought, they're afraid of exposing their own failings. Cover yer ass.

Sullivan rose. He sat. He picked up the copy of *The New York Times* he'd gotten from the colonel. There was a long article on Saigon's "Land to the Tiller" land-reform program. ". . . probably the most imaginative and progressive non-communist land reform of the twentieth century," the *Times* said. Two-point-five million acres taken from absentee landlords and given to landless peasants in two years. Sullivan translated the pertinent passages into French. It told of the joy of the people receiving deeds to the fields they'd worked all their lives for others. He'd seen it himself. It was quite a story. Sullivan added his own description and placed it into the letter he was compiling for Vathana.

Twice since seeing her he had been in Neak Luong on official business. Once he'd stopped at the hospital. She hadn't been there and he hadn't had the time to search the camp. The other time he'd arrived at the garrison during the late afternoon. New demonstrations were wracking the downtown area. The Khmer colonel in charge had blocked his every attempt to leave the compound until he had helicoptered out the next morning. From the bird he'd thought he'd spotted her walking from the spired pagoda, walking with another man.

How many times had he written? He had not kept track. He wasn't certain any of his letters ever reached her. "Have you received the materials for the clinic?" He'd written that knowing she should have, knowing that it was a neutral question, a question without pressure, a question to which the response could in no way commit her. Still there had not been an answer. He wrote about the new anti–Viet Namese rioting in Kompong Cham, about lawlessness and about neutralizing the intelligence and proselytizing cadre who were upstanding but misguided citizens. He spoke about changing their minds, enlisting them into the national cause. It came from his training as an advisor—he'd seen it work in South Viet Nam. It could work in Cambodia. Again he cautioned her: "Terror must be introduced and all opposition leaders liquidated during the first days of occupation." They were the words of Vladimir Ilyich Lenin. They fit the reports from the "liberated" zones. Finally he wrote to her about the results of the still-sputtering Nguyen Hue Offensive, the impact of the U.S. presidential election, the cease-fire talks, the stand-down and withdrawal of the last U.S. ground combat unit in Viet Nam and the renewed buildup of NVA materiel in the border regions even as the Northerners dispersed and licked their wounds.

Sullivan was out of things to say. He could think of nothing more except the words "Marry me." And those he was afraid to put on paper.

*   *   *

Quietly, one by one, they slipped from their hovel between the tracks and the river, slipped into the crisp blackness of the night. The winds had shifted, the rains had ceased. Evening stars dotted the sky. Vong had been killed. No one but Nang knew how. He had been replaced by two seventeen-year-old girls, *neary*. Their comings and goings roused less suspicion than Vong's but Nang did not like them. Itha was very pretty. She aroused impure feelings. Rin was always trying to get her to his mat. Sithan was very ugly, repulsive.

Nang carried a newspaper bag over his shoulder as he walked, strolled, toward Phnom Penh's Old Chinese Market. He did not appear to rush, seemed to be without direction, yet his progress through the fringe of the refugee area toward his target was steady. The closer he came to the old market the finer became the homes. Trees lined the clean streets and lights from small shops spilled into the dark. The sights sickened him. It was not so much the rich exploiters themselves as it was the old Khmers and the refugees. Old residents avoided the Chinese section because of language and cultural differences, avoided the Old Market out of habit, a simple capitulation of the very best of Cambodia. More loathsome were the refugees. How can they live like this? Nang asked himself. In the jungle with so much less, with nothing, we lived so much better. Someday, we will teach them pride and the right way to live.

Nang reached into the bag, withdrew a white painter's cap and stretched it over his turban-covered head. He adjusted the bag, headed away from the market and back toward the railroad station, circled several blocks, emerged at the neighborhood's south entrance. Here were a series of small banks, apothecaries, jade and camera shops and the city's best restaurants. Nang smiled to himself. Outside one eatery Itha was propositioning two Chinese men. Both were obviously drunk. Nang cast a quick glance back to see if Rin was in view. He saw only a scattering of the rich. Two more men joined Itha. One pinched her ass, one tried to kiss her. To act, Nang thought, the way they act . . . He spotted Reth four buildings beyond the revelry, across the street by a tree. Where was Rin? Where was the signal?

Nang continued his approach. He pulled his hat lower. From the bag he pulled a newspaper and shoved it under the door of a closed apothecary. At the next shop he repeated his delivery. He could feel the approach of police. His breath became shallow. A fifth gentleman joined the four with Itha. Nang was now less than thirty feet away. He knelt, removed a cardboard box from the news bag and plopped it down by the corner of the restaurant facade. Then he looked up as if searching for a sign. One man had a hand under Itha's blouse.

"Hey, you!" Nang yelled like a fresh kid. "Hey, chalk-face. Where's Cherry Blossom Garden?" The men ignored his Khmer shout. "Hey, Chink," Nang yelled. "You, white-face! Where's . . ."

"Who's the brat?" one man said angrily.

"I'll tell him," Itha said. "I'll get rid of him." She strutted away from the men, her firm behind drawing their leers. "The Cherry Blossom . . ."

A shot cracked. One man fell. Screamed. Another shot from up the street. Nang bolted. A third, fourth, fifth. Four men were hit. Itha sprinted after Nang. Almost immediately a siren wailed. Nang turned a corner, shed the hat, pulled a skirt and other clothes from the sack. People began congregating by the restaurant. A FANK MP vehicle raced into the Old Market. Blocks away, Nang and Itha, he without head covering, she in a long sarong skirt and shawl, strolled arm in arm, her head leaning against the scarred side of his face. The box blew. "The way they act," Nang whispered in Itha's ear as if they were lovers, "is to denounce their humanity."

Sixteen people—four FANK soldiers, one policeman, the rest Chinese civilians—were killed. Within minutes Rita Donaldson and two cameramen arrived. Shortly the entire area was lit by American network TV camera lights. The devastation was picturesque. Rin crowded against the police barricade, meandered amid the crowd. "They're saying it was government hoodlums," he murmured, repeated every few meters. "I don't believe it, but that's what I heard that MP say. No matter, eh? This government offers us no protection. What do you think?"

"We must love the Party, adore it, and serve it sincerely without reservation or condition . . ." Sar paused to see the reactions of Phan, Dy, Yon, Meas and Sen, to get their first impression of the concluding statement of the final draft of the Party's history—the manifesto. None showed emotion. ". . . to repay the effort with which the Party has educated us, to be unreserved revolutionaries and Communists . . ."

Met Reth, Sar's bodyguard, tapped on the jamb of the open door. Sar finished the paragraph before acknowledging him. "Nothing is more precious and honorable than to belong to the Party's ranks, and nothing is better than to be a Communist." He looked at Reth. "What is it?"

"Met Nang of Team SA-3 has arrived."

"Shortly. I'll see him shortly," Sar said.

"It's very powerful," Meas said. "Yet do we wish to make public our Communist . . ."

"*No!* Of course not!" Sar scowled at the scribe as if Meas were an idiot. "This is strictly for internal use. Only for the Center."

"Then I think we all concur," Phan answered for the group. "Yes. It is very good."

An hour later Nang was allowed to enter the inner sanctum of the Center's mobile command post. They were only four miles south of the confluence of the Tonle Sap and Mekong, between Takhmau and the heart of the capital. Sar sat at the table. Before him were Khmer, French and Chinese newspapers—each telling the story of the breakthrough at the Paris negotiations. "An Agreement in Principle," the French paper declared. "A sellout," Sar muttered. "Cease-fire-in-place Accepted by Kissinger," the Khmer daily said. Sar spit on the floor.

"Met Sar." Nang immediately sensed Sar's mood. He addressed the senior general formally. "It is very good of you to grant me this audience."

"It's good of you to come, Nang." Sar rose. He stepped to within inches of Nang, making the boy think the man was about to embrace him. Nang slid one foot back but Sar stopped him by gently hooking his right hand about Nang's head. Sar leaned forward inspecting the scarred face. Nang was not sure what to do. He stood very still. "Has it faded?" Sar asked abruptly.

"I . . . ah . . ." Nang was immediately off balance.

"It doesn't matter," Sar said. "One looks at a man from the inside, not the out, eh?"

"Yes . . ."

"You've received good coverage in the Yankee newspapers," Sar said. Nang nodded. "Our first enemy is Lon Nol's rodent-infested army, eh?" Sar did not wait for a response. "Without the imperialists, FANK will collapse. Your work is very important. Keep it up."

"It is why I've come." Sar glanced at Nang as the boy attempted to regain his purpose. "I wish to discuss with you my future."

"When we are victorious," Sar said, "you will be remembered and rewarded."

"I think I can do more. Now. To speed victory."

"If I had a thousand . . . what? . . . seventeen . . ."

"In a month I'll be sixteen."

". . . sixteen-year-olds like you, Met Nang, we'd finish the war in a week."

"It is exactly what I wish to request."

"What is?"

"I want to change assignments. I want to teach . . . teach new yotheas." Nang now stepped slightly forward. He shifted his weight to the balls of his feet. Sar rocked back on his heels. "I could be a master teacher," Nang said. "I know the land, the people. I know what to say to make them respond. I know the enemy, his tactics, how to use his power against him. The bomb which hit the FANK line at Stong . . ."

Sar interrupted. "Where the South Viet Namese pilot . . ." Sar chuckled. "Where he accidentally hit FANK troops . . ."

"It was not an accident."

"What was? The ARVN, they were punishing . . ."

"No. I called in the A-37. I was on their radio. I called in the fictitious fight and described the enemy position."

"You!?" Sar began to chuckle.

"Yes. If I could teach a thousand others, the victory will be ours that much more quickly. Let me direct a youth training camp. Let me tell what I can do . . ."

Sar sat. He stared at Nang as the boy, in his enthusiasm, rattled off his plan to expand the new training school program to include more technical material like what he'd received in China, plus more physical drill like that which had been dropped with the closure of Pong Pay Mountain. ". . . it's too short," Nang was saying. "The new yotheas don't know a fraction of what the old ones were taught. They don't have the drive."

Now Sar leaned forward, placed his palms flat on the desk, his elbows locked. "We can," he said, his face smiling though his entire bearing radiated anger, "indoctrinate a boy, especially if he's been prepared for monastic training, if he's ready to renounce his family and all worldly things, we can break him in three weeks, convert him in three weeks into a disciple of Angkar Leou."

"Certainly," Nang agreed, attempting to regain command of the conversation. "But is an untrained disciple, no matter how devoted, as valuable as a yothea trained in supply, in underwater mines, in proselytizing, in recruitment?"

Sar rose. He glanced at the papers on the table. "We have a core of trained soldiers," he said amicably. "You're one. This is a rice war. First we deny Lon Nol rice. Rice we trade to the yuons for American dollars. Ha! They get so much from China and North Korea. With dollars we can buy anything. We buy from FANK. We don't need to rely on supply. Now we stockpile for when the imperialists leave. It will be soon. Then we strike. You want to teach yotheas how to strike, eh? It is more important to teach them to have the will to strike and *to break* the enemy." Sar paused. "We already have the force to break FANK. By the way ..." Sar added cynically, "Pech Chieu Teck, he's still alive, eh?"

"Alive?" Nang's eyes snapped to Sar's lips as if he might see the words. Had he failed?

Sar rose. Again stepped to Nang. He grasped the boy by the shoulders, smiled insincerely and said like a loving father, "Met Nang, go back to your team. Keep doing your job. You've a good mind, strong ambitions. I like that. Someday ..." He winked at Nang. "You'll be contacted."

When Nang left, Sar called in Met Sen, the new chief of security. "That boy," Sar said. "He's very smart, very ambitious. Make sure he's kept where he can't gain his own following."

Throughout the remainder of October and through all of November 1972, Nang brooded in his hovel between the tracks and the river. B-52s, released from flights over North and South Viet Nam by the paperwork in Paris, were redirected to Cambodia and Laos. (The level of bombing from the Easter offensive carried over to these countries despite the lack of massed forces or confirmed targets. This was to ensure that the appropriated money was used, not returned to the Treasury, thus indicating to Congress a lack of need for such funds. Some bombing missions at this time were purposely targeted—by target-control personnel, navigators and pilots—against such "enemy" installations as the center of the Tonle Sap, specifically picked to avoid areas of human occupation.)

Each time Nang heard the rumbling of the bombs his body tensed. He did not connect the feeling to the times he'd been in the bomb boxes but instead became more and more depressed about having exposed himself, having trusted Sar with his ambitions, his plans for his future. That they had not been accepted, Nang knew, was disgraceful, dangerous.

In November he and his team, with the help of North Viet Namese sappers also released from the eastern front by continued progress in the Paris talks, neatly dropped a span of bridge over the Tonle Sap River only two miles from the heart of Phnom Penh. A firefight ensued. Thirty-six Cambodian national soldiers were killed along with twenty-eight Viet Namese. Nang's team fled intact. Still Nang brooded. Every success increased the distrust which now surrounded him. Somehow, he thought, he would have to lie low. Somehow, he would have to shift the blame.

Doctor Sarin Sam Ol's house had been burned. His two eldest sons had been conscripted. Sovanna, his seventeen-year-old, had moved, with Sarin's wife, to Phnom Penh to live with his mother's brother and family. Two months after Doctor Sarin's incarceration, Sovanna fled the capital, his destination unknown. In reprisal Doctor Sarin's private office was sacked. It was now the tenth day of November 1972—one hundred days from the time of his arrest. The sun broke from the eastern horizon; its rays splashed on the spire of the wat's *vihear* and glistened off the bells and ornaments of the *sala*.

Vathana stood on the upper steps of the preaching hall. She had been praying for the doctor for three hours. Nem had joined her just before dawn. Sophan and a few nurses and aides had arrived moments later.

"Kosol will come," Nem said from the step below her friend.

"I know," Vathana answered.

"Truly. He said he would."

"Yes. So he said."

"It's not too late. Do you really think they'll release the doctor?"

"Sann said they would. He said he'd heard from his brother . . ."

"Little Sann, the orderly?"

"Yes. His brother's a guard at the detention center." Vathana turned, looked toward the camp. "Where is he?" she said quietly.

"One hundred days." Nem pursed her lips. "Is that normal for 'Communist sympathy'? I mean, he . . . oh . . ."—Nem noticed the direction of Vathana's gaze—". . . poets are like that, eh?"

Vathana looked down at Nem, then looked back north, up the highway toward the FANK facility. Others joined the vigil. A lay priest came, questioned them, left. In a short while he, several monks, a number of nuns and orphans, and teachers and students from the *sala rien* joined the congregation.

An hour passed. A monk led a group of refugees in prayer. A teacher gave her class a lesson in arithmetic. Street urchins hustled about the fringe attempting to sell small cakes of ice. Others raced the half mile up the roadway to within a stone's throw of the prison gate, then raced back to the pagoda and back again toward the FANK post. By eleven most of the children—orphans, urchins, students—had wandered away seeking more interesting adventures or simply a place in the shade.

"There he is!" a hospital worker shouted. "He's coming."

"That's not him. That's an old man," shouted a second.

"That's him. I know him well," the first yelled.

"Don't crowd him. Just two go. Only two. Angel," a third worker called, "you go. You're his favorite."

"Let's cheer him," the second worker yelled.

"No," the third snapped. "Give him room. We'll have time to cheer later. You don't know what . . ."

Vathana and a man she did not know were nudged to the front of the crowd. Quickly they stepped toward the small approaching figure. Even at a hundred meters Vathana was not certain . . . the eye patch, the uncertain walk. A minute later the doctor wrapped an arm over the man's shoulder then collapsed. Vathana lifted his other arm, placed it about her neck, and the two helped Sam Ol walk the quarter mile to the pagoda. There they seated him on a monk's pillow and brought him citrus water with honey and ice. At first Sam Ol did not speak. All about him people tried to get a good look, to catch his attention. Many called quiet, subdued wishes and encouragements. Some vowed to help him seek retribution. Vathana knelt by him, washed his face. This, she thought, this is destroying the infrastructure! She gently lifted the eye patch. The doctor lifted his hand to stop her. "Don't." His voice was sad, hoarse.

"Did they . . ." Vathana began.

"I can still see with the other," Sam Ol said. Then he leaned forward and sobbed.

"Let's take him to the hospital," the man who'd carried him said.

Vathana nodded but the very mention sent a spasm of torment through the broken man. His sobs came louder. In the crowd people embarrassed for him shuffled back, wandered quietly away. Others embarrassed by their own inability to deal with his anguished cries put up various fronts—bitter, hostile, profane. They too left, but with angry oaths dripping from their tongues.

"Home," Sarin Sam Ol pleaded.

Vathana looked to the man who had helped. He glanced back, then whispered, "to my home."

Later Vathana snapped at Keo Kosol, "How can you write that?!"

"It's an *ayay*. It's good. Listen. I will call it 'Doctor Ol.' "

"You didn't come." Vathana's lips were pulled thin. "You never came. You didn't see."

"But you saw," Kosol said. "And you described it to me. Especially the eye. He was disgusting, eh? Ha! I'll read it at the Women's Association tonight. Those sluts will love it."

"What!?" Vathana spun in place. She had no outlet for her anger. For months she'd loved this old poet who had steadily become more of a burden to her. Now he looked to her too old, too pretentious. "Sluts?" She hissed the word. "Sluts?!" Never, not even in her mind, had she used the word.

"Oh come now," Keo Kosol said. He stood, dropped his pen on the writing sheet. "That doesn't offend you. I know the women who join. They sleep with everyone."

"Is that what you think of me?"

"No. Not you. You only sleep with me and your foreign guy but I understand that . . ."

"You . . . you . . ." Vathana shook with rage. " 'Struggle Against Fire,' " she lashed out at him, ". . . your mother, was she . . ."

"She lives in Sisophon with my father. They have a big farm. They own lots of peasants. Ha! They . . ."

"Get out of here!" Vathana regained control. "I let you come into my hut and you . . ."

"And I what?" Kosol snarled sarcastically. "What, eh? You think you are some angel, eh? You're like all women. You want catastrophe so you can play angel. Eech." Kosol raised a hand, scolded her. "You listen. The Americans are pulling out. All our sacrifices, all our actions, are vindicated. Soon we'll run . . ."

"They haven't *all* gone." Vathana bit the inside of her lower lip. "Mister Nixon's been reelected. I don't . . ." She couldn't complete the sentence. Why was Kosol saying this? Who was he? What did American withdrawal have to do with his not coming to see Doctor Sarin? With his faking his personal experiences in the *ayay*?

Before Vathana's questions could coagulate in her mind Kosol laughed maliciously. "It makes no difference. We believe, with or without Nixon, the American Congress will continue exactly as they have. Amendment after amendment. Cut off funds for their insidious military adventurism. It's a matter of time. A short time."

"Who?" Vathana did not know this man at all. "Who is this 'we'?"

"You don't need to know," Kosol said. "Just continue doing what you do and you'll be protected. Stay away from that disgusting doctor. You look at me, not him."

Vathana could barely believe what she'd heard. She stood very still. Then slowly, anger and frustration drained from her face. Slowly, disbelieving, she shook her head. "Poets," she said quietly, "are supposed to be driven by love and truth . . ." In her mind exploded the word *infrastructure.* ". . . not by hate."

"Viskii," the waiter said to Sullivan. They were in a backdoor restaurant in a southern section of Neak Luong.

In Khmer Sullivan said, "No. Not whiskey. Beer. A bottle of Singha if you have it."

"Yes. I have Singha." The waiter smiled at the foreigner's decent Khmer. "A bottle for Angel, too, eh?"

"Maybe she'll have the viskii," Sullivan joked, and the waiter thought it was very funny.

"A cola for me," Vathana said. "John." She looked at his face. "You really have learned a lot. You're very good."

"I'm trying," he continued in Khmer. "I still flip-flop the nouns and adjectives."

"You're better than any American, any Frenchman, I've ever heard. I'm so happy you came again. You'll stay awhile?"

"Two days. I have to be back on the twenty-sixth."

"For Thanksgiving dinner, I bet."

He laughed. Her eyes sparkled in the candlelight. Her teeth glistened. So close, she was driving him wild. "No. For the colonel. What do you know about Thanksgiving?"

"I'm trying, too." She smiled. "Maybe too late?"

"Too late?"

"The cease-fire. The American withdrawal. You'll go now?"

"No. Not yet. I'm . . . I can be carried on the embassy list."

"Your job is done though." Vathana sighed. Sullivan could not keep his eyes off her. To him, everything about her was exciting, perfect. Even this seemingly sad sigh. Did it mean she would miss him?

They had been together much of the afternoon, at the hospital tending to the helpless and the hopeless. They'd spoken little except about patient care, yet they worked well as a team and knowing that made them both comfortable. After cleaning up they'd walked by the river talking sporadically, becoming reacquainted. As always they spoke about the situation of the nation as much as, if not more than, about their own circumstances. Sullivan asked what he could tell Rita Donaldson. "If the war ends," Vathana had said, "she won't need me."

"It won't end," he'd said.

"The fighting here is down."

"Just a lull. Not even that. Everyone in South Viet Nam is scrambling to grab as much territory as possible before the cease-fire goes into effect. The NVA have shifted to that front. And Sihanouk has . . ."

"I know." Vathana had stopped walking and they'd turned to each other. She put her hands flat against his upper arms, not pulling him in, not pushing him away, touching him lightly. To her he was, in some ways, such a boy. In other ways he was such a strong man. "I know," she'd repeated. "But I don't understand. Why would Prince Sihanouk reject Lon Nol's offer of a cease-fire?"

"It's a game," Sullivan had said. "I saw a copy of a captured NVA document at the embassy. Signed by Le Duan of Hanoi's politburo. It spelled it right out. '. . . take as much territory as possible before the cease-fire . . . then, for political reasons, our forces must scrupulously observe any cease-fire for the first sixty days. In that time the Thieu regime will undoubtedly violate the accord by attempting to retake lost land. After formal protests we will be justified to commence renewed military struggle.' That's exactly what it said. That's the plan."

"Then it's a hoax!" Vathana held her hands as if praying, praying it would not be so.

"Yes. It's a way of getting America out of the picture."

"I hate this, John. I hate this all. This breaking the infrastructure! What it is doing to my people! When I told Mister Keo about the Americans breaking the NVA radio codes . . ."

"What? You told who?"

"Oh. A . . . an old poet friend. I haven't seen him in weeks now . . ."

"Shit! Those things weren't to be . . . ah, I guess it makes no difference."

"It's all inevitable now, isn't it."

"Nothing's inevitable."

"The Khmer Rouge, they move at will, they own the countryside. They can strike within the cities at will."

"No. That's not true. Believing it makes it worse. We've trained eighty-three FANK battalions in two years. There's a core of good troops here. It's the goddamned leaders . . ."

"They're all fascists, aren't they? Lon Nol, the Khmer Communists, Sihanouk. All of them. Extremist nationalists. Autocrats. Racists. How . . ."

"Do you remember when I wrote about the stages of Communist victory?"

"Of course. I shared it with the others."

"President Thieu said a few days ago, 'Coalition with the Communists means death.' He's right. Here or there."

From the river they had gone to the Khsach Sa camp where old Sophan had greeted Sullivan with such an impassioned hug he'd reeled in shock for five minutes. How he had won her heart he didn't know but he did catch amid the words she shot at Vathana, "This one, Angel, is better. The other is bad for you." For an hour John Sullivan had played with camp children while Vathana conducted camp business. Then they'd gone to eat.

Amid the small talk they again talked politics and war. Every moment they spent together, Sullivan felt he was being drawn to his destiny. They did not argue but agreed on most points, lamented some, felt bonded by the sadness which engulfed Cambodia. "There should be an alternative to Sihanouk and the Communists versus Lon Nol and the military," Vathana said.

"If only we could have influenced the FANK command more," Sullivan began.

"Doctor Sarin"—Vathana shook her head—"he says, 'The roof leaks from the top down.' He blames those at the very top."

"He should. Lon Nol and his astrologers . . ."

"And Mister Nixon, too."

"Definitely," Sullivan agreed. For a long while they did not speak of politics or of war but ate and looked at each other, smiled, fed each other particularly tasty morsels from their plates.

When they returned to the camp the hut was vacant. Sophan, Sullivan realized, had taken the children so they could have privacy. Quietly they undressed each other. Slowly, for a long time, they made love. When they were temporarily sated Sullivan, still entwined in Vathana's legs, whispered, "When I go, I want you to come with me."

"To Phnom Penh?" Vathana cooed in his ear. A pang of guilt hit her for she sensed the possibility of escaping the responsibility of the camp and her growing fear of whomever Keo Kosol represented.

"Come to America with me," Sullivan said. "Come with me. You and the children. And Sophan. Let me take you from this horrible place."

Vathana pushed up on his shoulders. He raised so they were nose to nose. He began to nibble at her chin but she stopped him. "This horrible place," Vathana said, a cool tone entering her voice, "this is my country."

"Vathana." Sullivan kissed her. "Marry me. I love you so much. Marry me. Be my wife."

"But"—now she pushed him higher off her—"I'm already married."

"Mar . . ." Sullivan stopped. It took a moment for the words to sink in. "I thought your husband was killed in action."

"No." Vathana held his shoulders, caressed them yet held him a foot above her. "Pech Chieu Teck, he's my husband."

"Teck? He's your brother-in-law!"

"No. We don't live together because he's too . . . Our marriage, it is only a legal contract, but I am married. Teck, too, wants me to join him. In Phnom Penh. But I . . ."

"Wha—" Sullivan could not grasp what he was being told. "Married?!" He rolled sideways releasing himself from her legs, rolled farther, sat, next to her, alone. "Married? Is it perma-

nent? I mean . . . are you, did you leave him? That's not what I
. . . whoa!" He rolled to his knees. Vathana put her blouse on. "I
love you," Sullivan said. He said it as much to himself as he did
to her, said it as he'd said it a thousand times when he was in
his room, on his cot, alone, talking to her. "I've wanted to
marry you since . . ."

"Isn't it enough to love me?" Vathana said. "I do lo—"

"No!"

Sullivan lay head bent, in her arms, her small breasts with
their hard nipples under his cheek and neck. His eyes were
open. He could see his left leg, her right, her pubic bush. She
was very lovely. Very kind. Only it was, for him, all very unsat-
isfying and it increased the turmoil.

"Are you okay?" Rita said softly.

"Yes," he answered. "Did you come?"

"Yes. You're a bit bigger than I imagined."

"Oh. Am I hurting you?" He raised his head, began to move
off her.

"No," she said, hugging him. "I mean your dick. I haven't
been with anyone in quite a while . . ." She paused as if to
think, then added, "We could do this again."

"I'd like that," Sullivan said. He felt sad. "Only . . ."

"Only?"

". . . I'm leaving. I've requested reassignment. I've decided to
get out . . ."

"John!"

". . . of the army."

CHAPTER SEVENTEEN
1973

The land is arid, barren. Before him rises a cliff. Rock outcroppings project to the sides. There is a shack of wide, crude-cut boards. In the harsh sunlight it looks old, weathered. He stands before it, barefoot, bare chested. There is no door. The shack is built into the rockface, the opening arch is very dark. He approaches. He attempts to peer into the blackness. About him there is not a single tree, not a blade of grass. The opening is an adit, a mine shaft entrance. The sound of digging comes from in deep. He moves into the shadow of the shack but does not pass beneath the timber frame. He thinks to call but he has no voice. He thinks to call but he has no voice. He thinks to call but he has no voice.

For a time he stands still. The cliff shadow lengthens then melts into night. Now all is dark. No longer can he look into the darkness, into what is before him, into what is behind. Still the sounds. Groans. Digging. Laughter. The night becomes cold. The wind carries minute ice crystals, then thick snow, driven, drifting up against the shack, sealing the adit, encasing the groans, the digging. He is so cold his teeth chatter. The laughter comes from there, and there, from behind, to the side, over there. He wraps his arms about his chest, shoulders. His fingers sting near frostbite. He squats, tucks his head, hugs his legs to his chest tucking his hands between his calves. There is a crack, a snapping, a rap. He can't . . .

"John! John! Come on. Open up." Sullivan rolls to his back, straightens his legs into the sleeping bag. "John, are you in there?"

"Ah, yeah, one second." His voice is sleep-hoarse. He shuts his eyes, pulls his legs back up, attempting to recall the vision, the thought.

"Come on. It's freezing out here."

It has taken the last days of December and the entire month of January for him to begin reacclimation to the cold winds of an Iowa winter, has taken every minute of that time to begin to defrost his emotional numbness, his intellectual stupor. At the end of his first tour of duty in Viet Nam his folks had thrown him a large welcome-home party. Then he'd gone back. On his second homecoming he was greeted at the airport by his parents and sister and her boyfriend. He'd gone back again. At his third return only his father met him and at home only his mother was there.

"You aren't going back again, are you?" his mom pleaded.

"No. No more," he'd said without looking at her.

"You've done enough," his father said. "Let somebody else go."

"Yeah, I guess so. I'm out for good."

"I can always use you here." His father put his hand on John's forearm. "Gus could use you, too."

"Henry, that poor boy just walked in and already you've got him rushing off to work." Mrs. Sullivan wiped her hands on her apron then smoothed it down against her dress. "Tomorrow night we'll have ham with pineapple slices. And baked beans. I'll start em soaking right now."

"That's nice," J. L. said. "But . . . ah, I think I'd like to go out to Uncle Gus's."

Two days later he'd moved into the heated tack room of his uncle's old barn. Then for a month he'd walked the frozen snow-covered fields, walked them at sunrise and at sunset, alone. For a month he'd slept in the tack room, not talking, not listening to a soul.

"Come on." Margie banged on the door. "I brought you the paper. The war's over."

He moved deliberately, pulled on a pair of dungarees, let his sister in, pulled a quilted wool shirt over his tee shirt and long-johns top.

Margie held up the newspaper. "They've signed the peace accords in Paris." Her smile was broad. She was happy, thrilled, not by the agreement but for her brother.

J. L. looked quizzically at her. He smiled his boyish smile and said, "That's nice." It was the same "that's nice" he'd said to his mother about the beans, the same "that's nice" a parent, not really listening, might say to a child who's just reported that her imaginary friend has been run over by a bus and is now lying splattered against the walls of her mind.

"John"—Margie dropped the paper on his sleeping bag—"why don't you come and live at home?"

"Yeah, I will," J. L. said. "In a little bit. I just want to resettle a bit first."

"It's been five weeks."

"That's not so long."

"They signed the peace agreement."

"Yeah. That's nice."

"Please come back. Mom's sick with worry about you."

"There's nothing to worry about, Kiddo. I'll be back in a bit. Right now I'd just like to rest."

What nonsense, Vathana thought. Dear Holy and Enlightened One, what can it mean? She blinked. She dared not leave her eyes shut should the apparition return. Tigers, she thought. Of all things. Chased by tigers, as if I didn't have enough complications. In the darkness of the hut she turned to the soft sounds of Samol and the synchronous snoring of Samnang and Sophan. Papa, she thought, he'd say it means someone is in love with me. Oh sweet Papa, sweet Mama, how I long to kiss you again. What is your life in our beautiful little town? The best of Cambodia, eh Papa? The best. Have they left you alone to grow rice? Surely they tax you horribly. It's not as bad as some say, eh? Do you remember the time Samnang got stuck in the tree in the orchard and I went up to get him and the branch broke. Oh Papa, I thought you'd die laughing. Tigers! Of all things. They almost caught me.

For hours she lay with her eyes open, talking to herself, to Sophan who'd become so much a part of her, to her parents and children, talking to rivermen and peasants, talking happily to hundreds of people in her mind—trying, trying so hard, to hide her fears. Through cracks in the blue plastic tarp she could see the sky graying. She thought to rise, to visit the pagoda before the children woke, but as she rolled forward her abdomen tightened spasmodically and she fought back an urge to vomit. She lay back. Where is my energy? she thought. I feel so ill. So weak. Always tired. She tried to think why but she was afraid to pursue the thought. Instead she thought of the camp. It had never been anything but poor huts with poor sanitation and poor people but now it seemed shabbier than ever. The sun had corroded the blue plastic of the tarps and many were cracked, some shredded. What would they do when the rains came? What would they do if the FANK security teams came? Overtly it was not a crime to belong to an association but there were new, unwritten rules. Even to have a friend in the associations could label one an infiltrator. From the Khmer Rouge came irregular nocturnal conscription raids. No one was safe. Association activity had become covert, more radical. The city, like the nation, continued to move outward along the dim lines of political polarization.

A few days before, Teck had visited her in the camp. His constantly shifting beliefs confused her. "There are rumors," Vathana had whispered.

"I know," he quieted her.

"They say they are very cruel. They kill every soldier they capture. And they kill the families, too. They take all the other people out to the forest."

Teck chuckled at her fears. "It's only a transitory step, eh? It's a necessity of war."

"Are government troops equally cruel?" she asked.

"How would I know?" Teck said. His tone was light, amiable. "With the Americans gone from the South, well, one can see the future, eh?"

"They say," Vathana said, "the Khmer Rouge have launched new attacks against Kompong Thom. Here FANK cracks down on . . ."

"FANK is much better," Teck had retorted. "Our battalion-days in the field are back up to the best months of 1971."

"And you say the cruelty of the KR, it is empty rumor, eh?"

"Some of it. Khmer are Khmer, yes? We share certain values. Some KRs might be terrible, but not all. Those madmen and atrocity stories, they're exaggerated. You know what I believe . . ."

"Teck, we should speak more quietly . . ."

". . . I think it is the government propagandists that start the rumors. If the KR win, they won't be any worse than Lon Nol. Ha! They won't be so corrupt like that Sihanouk."

"They say . . ."

"If you are so afraid, move to Phnom Penh with me. Aah, why do I ask?"

". . . some people"—Vathana avoided his remark—"have escaped. They say the KR soldiers rip children apart with their hands. That they line up all the pregnant women and stab their bellies with long bamboo needles . . ."

Teck broke into full-blown laughter. "I can't believe I'm hearing this from an intelligent woman. You'd believe anything. Ha! Besides, you've got a flat belly, eh?"

"Then you, you a FANK officer, you think we've nothing to fear from them?"

"No. You can be afraid. Be afraid of war. But I think the war will stop. I think maybe a few more battles. Lon Nol, he's asked for a cease-fire. Kissinger worked a cease-fire for Viet Nam. Now, maybe, for us."

"Cease-fire!" Vathana shook her head woefully. "They still fight—like Captain Sullivan said they would. What did we have, a four-day lull?"

"What would he know! Four days now. Then a few battles. Then maybe forty days. Then maybe four hundred."

"So, the attacks in the North, you think . . ."

"I think it is time my wife and children came to live with me."

"You were going to come here."

"My orders, you know . . . Anyway, you are for peace, eh?"

"Of course."

"Then I think it's time we settle with the Khmer Rouge. What do they want, eh? An end to corruption? Me too. You believe just like me. Soon we'll stop this war."

Again Vathana thought to rise but again she felt nauseous. She sat up. Teck's visit had been short. A perfunctory gift to each child. Then he'd gone—where, she didn't know. Probably to gamble or to see his friend Kim, she'd thought. Or maybe to find Louis. Louis had been drafted and was assigned to the southern Neak Luong garrison. She stood. She felt dizzy. For a moment she stood with a hand touching the wall, her eyes closed. When she opened them she felt better. "Sophan," she called quietly.

"Yes Angel?"

"I'll be at the clinic tent. When the children wake, maybe they would like to wash in the river."

Vathana worked with the patients for an hour before Keo Kosol appeared. He had not spent a night with her since Doctor Sarin's release. He arrived and departed on no schedule. Vathana had not learned any more about him, his true identity, his reasons for coming, what he wanted. At times he laid his eyes on her with such longing it made her think of a heartsick puppy, yet because of her rejection he stubbornly refused to recognize or give in to his desires. She had not and would not chase him away. She could not report him to the authorities. How could she subject him to the possibility of the same torment as Doctor Sarin?

"Hey Angel"—Kosol's loud and beautiful voice made her face snap up from the woman she'd been tending—"you know what I hear?"

"You don't even say hello?"

"Aah! Who needs it?" Vathana stood, stepped toward him so their voices would not be so public. Kosol boomed for the entire infirmary, "If we want to see Samdech Euv, we must give him our support."

"Kosol." Vathana shut her eyes, put a hand to her forehead.

"No. It's okay to say so. I heard he's in Preah Vihear. Or maybe Stung Treng. All we need do, if we want him to return, is offer him our support."

The words set the infirmary abuzz. Norodom Sihanouk might return! He might bring peace! Return us to the peace we once knew! Even within Vathana, though she struggled to keep it hidden, the idea sent a flutter through her bosom. Or perhaps the flutter was caused by feelings she still harbored for this poet. Simultaneously she felt embarrassed by his loud, obnoxious behavior.

"Hey Angel, you know what else?" He opened a Khmer newspaper. "This is straight from an American. Listen to what she says. 'I would think that if you understood what Communism was, you would hope and pray on your knees that we would someday become Communists.' Ha! She's very famous. Jane Fon-da. Very famous, very smart, eh? She visits Hanoi. Here's what else she says. 'I loudly condemn the crimes that have been committed by the U.S. government in the name of the American people.' Here, you read it. Have everyone read, eh? She knows. She knows they are immoral fucking foreigners." Vathana froze at his last words. Perhaps the war led to rough language, but not in her infirmary. Again she was embarrassed. Worse. She was terror stricken. What if they came and took her away, took her like they'd taken Sarin Sam Ol. "Immoral fucking foreigners," Kosol boomed in his beautiful sonorous voice. "I've got to go, Angel. See you later." He stopped at the tent flaps. "Just think," he shouted back, "our choice: Samdech Euv or the fucking *phalang*."

Vathana could not keep her mind on work. Still for two hours she projected a confident, content facade. But when she left, tears welled to her eyes. She returned to the hut where Samnang and Samol both greeted her with leg hugs. "Up," Samol sang. "Pick me up." "Ba-ba. Ba-ba," Samnang said. His face sparkled with an earwide grin. Vathana lifted Samol. "Ba-ba-ba."

"Yes, you too," she said, and Samnang climbed to her arms as a monkey climbs a tree. "Oh," Vathana sighed as Sophan came and lifted both children, "oh, you're both getting so big."

When they were in, out of the sun, with the children off on an adventure, Vathana moaned, "Sophan."

"Angel, you look very sad."

"I'm so tired," Vathana said. "And . . ."—she thought to tell her about Kosol but instead said—". . . there's so much to do."

"*Saye*, Angel. Tomorrow. Tomorrow things will be better."

"Sophan." Vathana's chin furrowed, her mouth quivered. "I'm so afraid." Again her eyes filled with tears.

"Afraid?"

"I'm going to die. In childbirth. The soldiers are going to kill the children."

"What soldiers? What birth?"

"No soldiers," Vathana blubbered now, and Sophan held her. "It's a feeling. I can't shake it. What will happen to them if I die? They'll be orphans. Teck . . . he'll never . . . what if Samnang becomes a soldier?"

"There, there." Sophan squeezed Vathana to her. "He's a long time to go before . . ."

"And . . . I think I'm . . . again . . . pregnant."

"You're . . ."

"Oh Sophan! I don't even know by whom. Maybe Kosol. Maybe Captain Sullivan. Oh God, what will I do?"

"You'll love the baby, Angel, eh?"

"Of . . . Yes. Of course."

"So! It makes no difference by whom, eh? If the father were a prince or a peasant, by now the war would take him and you'd raise your child yourself. Ah, Angel, but with me, too."

"Sophan, you must think I'm a very terrible girl."

"No Angel. I don't think that."

"A very stupid girl."

"No Angel. No."

"Last year three men wanted me. Wanted to marry me. Or with Teck, wanted to remarry me. Now none. No one. No one. No one would think to have me. . . ."

5 February 1973—Sithan had brought the orders. Team SA-3 was to disband. They had terrorized the capital city for an entire year; now larger game, the orders did not indicate whom, was being sought.

"You'll go back east," Nang said. One by one the team members had left. By midnight only Nang and Rin remained.

"Yes. You'll go north, eh?"

"Yes. I think. Only I'm to rendezvous near Oudong. That's all it said."

Rin studied Nang's eyes in the dim light of the single candle. "They've renewed attacks in the North. Be careful."

"Ha!" Nang scoffed. "What can get Met Nang, eh?"

Rin smiled. "I don't think of FANK rifles," he said. "I think of warped thought."

"Warped . . ." Nang straightened his back, increasing the distance between himself and Rin.

"You know"—Rin changed his tone—"we never did get that spoiled brat Pech Chieu Teck."

Nang scratched his forehead, looked down at the candle flame. "He was afraid to leave his mother's house, eh? How could we get him?"

"Ah, someday, my friend. Someday we will, eh? Sar thinks you failed."

They sat in silence. Nang thought briefly about being a great teacher, then about the liquidation of the hooligans, the new Khmer Viet Minh cadre sent to Kampuchea by Hanoi, the Khmer who'd sold their bodies and souls to the yuons. He did not ponder any particular thoughts but simply allowed them to come and go. His mind fell on warped thought—not analyzing it but tasting its sour taste in his mouth. Other tastes, bitter tastes, produced shallow thoughts yet deep emotions. He thought of the *thmils* who'd shot off his fingers, of the imperialists who'd dropped the napalm which he'd used to purify himself but which had disfigured him, made half his face ugly; he thought of Soth who'd betrayed him, of the boys—what were their names?—who'd humiliated him in his youth by stripping him. He thought of revenge. It was not enough to knock off a few evil ones here and there. Someday, he thought, someday Rin—he addressed his teammate in his mind—we will carry the fight to the yuons and, maybe, to America. We'll disfigure them. We'll disfigure their land.

At sixteen Nang was a full yothea, a cadreman of the Krahom, a provisional member of the Kampuchean Communist Party. He'd been trained, indoctrinated, baptized in battle. He'd proven resourceful in the most adverse conditions, he'd led troops against superior forces, he'd spied, informed, instigated riots and organized an entire city's fifth column. And he'd terrorized the capital. Yet he did not feel fulfilled, sated, even competent. In him, as there had been for years, yet now growing even wider, was a void, an abyss which demanded filling yet was unfillable. He wanted revenge—fulfilling revenge even though at some level he knew revenge would never be fulfilling.

"You must go now," Rin said. Nang looked at him but did not rise. "All this talk," Rin warned, "these speeches against our allies, take them with a grain of salt, eh?"

"You think it's warped thought, eh?" To Nang, his own voice sounded different, eerie, challenging.

"They've a system for justifying any thought," Rin said as if the voice from Nang had been normal. "That's why I say to you, be careful. You know who the enemy is, who he's not. Don't let them infect your thinking."

"The yuons," Nang whispered harshly, "you know they killed my father. The Sihanoukists too. KVM! Rumdoah! *Thmils!* All are evil."

"No, Nang." Rin also whispered yet his muted words were condescending. "Viet Namese are not evil. Chinese are evil. Americans are evil. I was trained in Viet Nam. You didn't know that, did you?"

"Then you've gone to them. In your mind. Only your body is Khmer."

"No." Rin's conviction was strong. "I'm as Khmer as you. Too much self-righteousness, Nang, leads to fanaticism. Too much rigidity without principles, it too leads to fanaticism. Don't be someone's fool. They'll use you and throw you away."

"If they use me as I wish to be used . . ."

"Someday, my friend," Rin injected, "someday you'll need me. Someday I'll be useful to you and you'll come to me. You ugly Watercrow, when you understand that, you come and I'll help you."

Two days later, near Oudong, Nang rendezvoused with the escort team taking Met Sar's mobile headquarters nearer the new battle zone. Afternoon light was dying in clouds of dust stirred from the dry earth by lethargic winds. Yotheas sat idly, only their eyes piercing from the red-checked kramas bandana-wrapped over faces, hair, ears. Without words, without greeting, Nang joined the armed, dust-covered elite protecting Sar's bunker; without words, thinking that he, Nang, should have been the director of the camp where this inert rabble had been trained.

Sar was in a panicked and foul ranting mood, subjecting members of the Center to sprayed spittle, to spattered sweat each time he slapped his forehead. "Betrayed," he swore. "They have left us open to this!" He stamped to the wall. "Just like Geneva 1954. They've sold out the Kampuchean revolution. They've . . ." In his anger his lips sputtered. "And that fornicating curly-haired dog—who the fuck does he think he is telling the world the cease-fire extends to Kampuchea! De facto! Kissinger! Ha! Seven days! Seven days they did not bomb! If we stop fighting! Get the yuons to quit Kampuchea and we'll explore a cease-fire."

"Met Sar . . ." Met Yon rose from the field table where they sat. His wispy voice and frail countenance belied his persuasive powers. Sar turned a calculated sneer upon the gray-haired old man, yet Yon, meeting the high general's stare with the porosity of a sieve, was unintimidated. "This cease-fire, it calls for the withdrawal of all foreign troops from Kampuchea, eh?" Sar gritted his teeth, snorted. "It prohibits foreign armies from moving through Kampuchea, eh?" Yon, of all the members of the gathered headquarters, was calm, efficient, well prepared for the meeting. Only Sar ranted.

"So," Met Dy asked without conviction, "you say it is nothing more than an attempt to have us lay down our arms and rob us of total victory, eh?"

"Damn it, yes." Sar steamed back to the table. "The yuons have cut off all supplies. They say join the cease-fire. Shit! We sent them a request to dismantle their bases and clear out."

"This should be a time of joy," Met Meas, the scribe, said. "At last, the Americans will leave. What is FANK without American support?"

"*You*"—Sar's face widened immensely in caustic fury—"*stupid*"—he raised both arms—"*fucking*"—slammed both fists down on the table—"*idiots!* Don't you understand! We can't agree to a cease-fire. If we did the yuons would overrun Kampuchea within a year. American disengagement! That's the damned *sellout*. If we don't agree to the cease-fire, the Americans will concentrate on Kampuchea! It's yuon criminal egoism. We've been set up for annihilation! Either way! Attack. We must *attack!* We must achieve quick victory or the stinging red ants will take it from us."

Sar sat. He breathed a heavy sigh as if this venting had purged his pent spleen. His body seemed to settle, to spread over his chair. In a most rational and patient manner he said, "Met Sen, you have a detailed report, eh?"

"Yes," answered the new security chief.

Sar looked about the table. "Let Lon Nol take the blame when the cease-fire collapses. The people already . . . rightfully . . . hate him. Or let Sihanouk. We have a tape of his speech, eh?"

Sar's aide, Nim, sheepishly raised his arm. "Here." He hesitated. "Should I play . . ."

"Just tell them."

Nim ran a finger down the transcript to the proper point. Sar's rancor had unnerved him. " 'Never, never will I enter into negotiations with the treacherous Lon Nol clique,' " he read. " 'Our future shall be determined by the resistance operation in the interior.' "

"How does the interior resistance now stand?" Sar asked.

Met Sen answered. "All factions combined control seventy

to eighty percent of the land, perhaps forty percent of the population."

"Do we have the maps?"

"Here," Nim answered.

As he unrolled them Sar looked to Met Dy. "Within sixty kilometers of the capital," the personnel chief said, "we've seventy dispersed battalions—nearly twenty-five thousand armed strugglers. We have an additional one hundred battalions spread from Battambang to Takeo to Stung Treng. With six more battalions in training, our forces, because of excellent utilization and economy, have reached nearly sixty thousand. That does not include the militias of Rumdoah and *mekong*."

"And then how many?"

"One can only estimate. The figure changes rapidly. Perhaps two hundred thousand."

"A quarter million, eh?" Sar smiled. Met Phan, the tactician and strategic planner, plunked an elbow on the table, dropped his head into his hand and scanned the map. "Then we have the ability to achieve victory," Sar said. "All we need is the will."

Phan cleared his throat. Eyes turned to him. "A comparison of our forces"—he smoothed down the curling map and overlay before him—"with those of Lon Nol's over the entire area does not show any areas of numerical superiority. In order to obtain proper advantage we will need to abandon the Northwest, pull troops from the South and Southwest. We dare not pull troops from the East or Northeast."

"Why not?" Dy asked. He pointed to heavy concentrations of symbols in Kratie and Svay Rieng Provinces. "We've more troops there than . . ."

Phan cut him short. "We can't attack. Not yet. Not a major offensive."

"Why?" Sar sat forward, his body condensing.

"When an army launches a frontal attack on a civilian population"—Met Phan spoke with the tone of a university professor—"it tends to strengthen the society. Lon Nol's support will increase. The people's determination will increase. The way we are spread, the way we must remain spread . . . we cannot guarantee victory. It would be better to continue the political offensive, to increase terrorism. We should use every conceivable backdoor maneuver. The people's will withers and we are victorious without all-out assaults."

"FANK is rotten to the core." Sar snarled. "If we do not launch the offensive the NVA . . ."

"A city at a time," Phan injected. "Gauge the American response. If Kompong Thom falls within a week, if the United States remains . . ."

"If we do not attack, the yuons will grasp control."

"We need them." Phan was adamant. He did not want Sar to railroad them into a decision. "We still rely on NVA artillery. Their tanks and artillery will be a decisive element in any offensive."

Sar banged his fist on the table. "We will rely on no one." He turned to Nim. "That landless johnny is in Preah Vihear, eh?"

"That's as reported," Nim said.

"Have we reached him? Have our messengers told him we've been abandoned by Hanoi?"

"There's been no word."

"That NVA-KVM puppet," Sar seethed. "Just as Lon Nol's a valet of American imperialism, Sihanouk's an agent of Viet Namese expansionism." Sar pushed back from the table. He pointed at Meas, then at Dy, at Yon, at Phan. "The will to attack, the will to break the enemy . . . Each of us must harbor a burning rage toward the enemy. Sihanouk awaits word from Hanoi. They wish him to keep the war going for their benefit. He publicly rejects negotiation and tries to draw the people from us." Sar turned to Nim. "Tell them. Tell them what has happened in the East. Tell them the true situation."

Nim shuffled the reports. " 'The NVA,' " he read, " 'at least in the second military region of the South, is exhausted. They cannot attack east or west. The South Viet Namese are spread thin and have no reserves. Their Airborne and Marine Divisions are mired in the North. They also cannot attack. From Bu Ntoll up past Duc Co and up to the triborder we have a secure flank. For the moment.

" 'What is disturbing,' " Nim continued, " 'is the amount of men and materiel on the Ho Chi Minh Trail. They have never been so well organized. The NVA 559th Transportation Group now has fifty to eighty thousand workers and combatants. There are two pipelines being extended from Mu Gia all the way past An Loc with lines into A Shau, to Duc Co and to Tay Ninh—one, a twelve-inch gasoline line; the other, a four-inch oil line. Also, they've begun a massive road-paving operation throughout the Laotian panhandle.' "

"Road paving?!" Meas was astounded. "How many trucks . . ."

"Sixteen, eighteen thousand," Nim reported.

"Now," Sar snapped smartly, "do you understand?! If we do not win quickly, the yuons will return in force! But, right now, they are occupied with rebuilding. For the moment all Sihanoukists are vulnerable. Now, we can attack. I have ordered a doubling of the assault on Kompong Thom. Now, come up with a plan to take the capital!"

Sar smiled. His long white teeth glistened in the sun. He mopped his high forehead with a handkerchief. Then he clapped a hand on Nang's shoulder. "Your new assignment . . ." he began. His smile was so wide his upper gums showed a quarter inch. He did not look at Nang but past him, did not focus on the scarred face but on his own hand on the boy's shoulder. Sar laughed amicably. "Just as you wanted, eh? You must teach them very quickly. Met Paak will tell you. Ah, it is so good for me to be able to give you what you desire. Go now. Be desire not. It is the will of Angkar Leou."

All that happened next happened quickly. Nang was sped north, rushed with a thousand toward Kompong Thom, split from them as they fragmented to reman the units of attack. On 7 February 1973 Sihanouk's informal announcement was made public—the battle for Cambodia would continue. On the 8th, word reached Krahom cadre that Henry Kissinger was in Thailand to coordinate a new bombing war against Communists in Cambodia. On the 9th, U.S. bombing hit the Cambodian interior in full force.

"Ay, Met Nang. It is so good to see you. Have you quit whoring in the capital and returned to soldiering again?"

"Met Eng!" The words, the idea that Eng thought he, Nang, might have been with women, embarrassed him. But to soldier again, that was the reward. Nang embraced his old friend. They were just east of the sieging forces. "I'm to have a regiment for the new offensive," Nang said proudly.

"New! Ha! Ah, a regiment like me, eh? You will be very proud."

"You've a regiment?!"

"Mostly. We've been at the front knocking off lackey dogs. You know, the *old* offensive." Eng chuckled. "Today we refit. Tomorrow we attack again. Can you join us? I'll teach you how to hug the cur's neck so tightly their damned bombers and helicopters are neutralized. Ha! It's good to have seen you. I've got to get my fighters prepared."

So quickly people came, went, Nang barely heard, saw or understood what was happening. It was as if a fine veil had been draped over everything before him and though he indeed did see, did hear, he saw and heard muted sights and sounds. Still it made him itch to fight, to direct yotheas against the despicable oppressors, to hear the sounds of battle, feel the power of the guns, smell the odor of cordite and blood.

Northeast of Kompong Thom, Nang was transferred to a squad of neary. The girls were young, serious, nearly mute. For a day he walked forest trails forcing himself to keep up. By nightfall they had melded with a company, by midnight with a battalion, by morning with a reinforced regiment.

"Met Nang." Met Nu found him eating alone amid clustered cells of neary. "You've become soft in the city, eh?"

"Soft, comrade?" Nang fought to keep a grin from his face.

"You've no fighters?!" she said.

"I'm to have a regiment." Nang stood, puffed out his chest.

"I've two," Nu said. Her voice was cool. "All *neary*. Three thousand strong."

"Three thousand girls! What can they do, eh?"

"Neary! Young women! They fight with the utmost resolve." Nu snickered. "They burned Bailaing College and recruited all the students."

"Bailaing? In Kompong Thom?"

"Yes." Now Nu smiled. "You are still only a little piggy, aren't you?"

Again Nang moved north, first to Rovieng then northeast to the intermittent grasslands and jungle east of Kompong Pranak. With each step he beat his fists against his stomach or against his thighs or into his shoulders or chest. Soft, he thought. His chest burned. Only a piggy, he thought. Whoring, he thought. His vision blurred. New offensive! He heard Eng's laugh rattle in his mind. The jungle was dry, water holes were tepid and greasy with decomposing vegetable and animal matter. He stumbled on, squeezing his left fist and right pincer into sledgehammers. What they have done, he thought, to my father, he thought, they have done to me. Plei Srepok! Sraang! Yani! Names without faces bombarded him. Burned the college! "Without the people," he thought, "we shall have no information, we shall be able neither to preserve secrecy nor carry out rapid movements." They were General Giap's words. Yuon scum, but they were good words. "The people . . . hide us, protect our activities, feed us, tend our wounded." No more! Nang thought. No more. He punched his face. The blow jarred his head and hurt the muscles at the back of his neck. Soft no more.

At eight o'clock Vathana excused herself from the refugee processing table and walked back, behind the blue tarp curtain, deeper into the clinic tent toward where she, her children and Sophan had again taken up residence on a single cot in a far corner. She was exhausted. The camp was again being assaulted by waves of new arrivals. Quietly Vathana stepped between the

rows of people, over the pitiful belongings of the listless and ill.
Here a woman beseeched her quietly, cautiously, asking for a
blessing, perhaps a smile. There an old man hunched, arms
akimbo, one leg splayed to the side, three grandchildren tucked
into the arches and aches of his pathetic body. Vathana's eyes
skimmed from his cot to the next, to the next, to the next. So
many people, she thought. They are impossible to count much
less help. Here one lay dehydrated, there one feverish, there one
broken from a beating or a fall while fleeing. Blessed One, she
thought, as she crossed beneath the huge, sagging ridgepole
hung with a hundred bundles of food or clothes or whatever the
inhabitants believed valuable. Blessed One, give me the strength
to help as long as I may be of help. She thought of the new
arrivals, of those animated with terror chattering continuously
and of those shocked into painful withdrawn silence. Which do
I prefer? she thought against conscious desire to think. Why
must I prefer one to the other? But I do. The terror-stricken
talkers scare me to death with their tales of children being
nailed to trees by Khmer Rouge soldiers, yet they are easier—oh,
is that the word, the feeling, easier?—easier to register than the
ones in stupor. Those . . . they act as if they are afraid of me!
   "Da-da deet-ta, deet-ta dcet-ta, da-da . . ." Sophan had a
bucket and wash towel and was methodically removing the
dust, the camp filth, the vile stench of their clinic-tent home
from Samnang. ". . . deet-ta, deet-ta deet-ta . . ."
   Vathana paused, watched from a dozen paces. Samol lay on
her side watching the stolid woman scrub her brother. The
little girl's cheeks were hollow. Her eyes watered from airborne
dust and perhaps low-grade fever. Seeing her daughter so, all
the hates and all the fears of the new order inundated Vathana's
mind. "Truth and patience," Vathana thought. They were
Sophan's words. Truth and patience and a gratitude for what
we do have, Angel. But what we have, she thought, are new
attacks, new bombings, more refugees than ever before and
fewer ways to help.
   Vathana raised her hands, clapped them to her nose and
mouth. Her innards trembled. She fought back tears. What had
Kosol said? We've a new radio grid. A direct link to the North.
She'd thought it meant Ratanakiri or Stung Treng and had
thought she'd be able to talk with her mother and father, and
had said so to a frightened, registering young man but he, a
deserter, had said no, it means Hanoi. A radio link to Hanoi?!
But why? I don't know, the deserter had said, and she'd processed him as a refugee, as an orphan, using the name Keo
Samnang. All the fears. In February FANK's 1st Shock Battal-

ion had driven into Phnom Penh and staged a sit-down strike at the presidential palace. How can they protect us? Root out the infrastructure! Torture innocent civilians. It is only a matter of time, eh? She had confessed that feeling to Sophan and Sophan had looked at her as if she'd gone mad. Don't think it, Angel. It's not good for the baby and it's not good for you. But the associations, Vathana had replied. I've been so active. And if it was because of Captain Sullivan that we enjoyed protection . . . he's not here any longer. Vathana's mind leaped to new fears. The old wet-nurse was subjecting Samol to the same torturous body-scrub which Samnang had endured, had—such a strong boy, the Ba-Ba Boy—enjoyed. What if she died? Poor frail Samol. Or the new baby? Or Vathana in childbirth? Had she heard the owl hoot? A chatterer had, and her child had been stillborn. With so many sounds, how could she know if she'd heard the owl hoot? Why had they been abandoned? Any day, any day the Khmer Rouge might enter the city. It was only a matter of time. Of waiting. They might be hit tonight. Takeo had fallen. That's what the deserter said. And Svay Rieng and Prey Veng and dozens of villages closer to Phnom Penh. Everywhere, people said, there were battles. Would FANK abandon them? Would the Khmer Rouge pass Neak Luong by? Why had America abandoned them? Why had John Sullivan gone? So abruptly! So abrupt. Oh, Vathana thought, I cannot feel this. I have never felt this. I wish all Viet Namese would perish. Dear Beautiful Enlightened One, do not let me feel so. Do not let me hate. How does John say? . . . Discipline one's mind. Form a habit of patient investigation . . . like Sophan. If it would just . . . just . . . just could end. Right now. Right now. I cannot go another step. How can I be trapped here, trapped in this pregnancy, in this camp? Teck would take me . . . Not another step . . .

A young couple with two children and a crippled uncle occupied the cot to Vathana's left. For some time they'd waited for her to move from their space. Her standing there just was not proper. The young woman reached up and nudged Vathana. Vathana startled. "Every step a prayer, Sister, eh?" the woman said. "Every step a prayer."

Before she could move a boy from the registration desk called softly into the dim, crowded corner. "Angel, there's a Western lady here to see you."

It pained Vathana to depart, to leave the children even before she'd reached them, hugged them. The idea of returning the short distance to the reception area seemed to her like a major task, a trek of light-years. Still, she turned, obeyed, raised her head and set off on the return voyage. She hesitated, thought, "A

Western lady?" Who can it be? What does she want? Why don't they all go away? She approached the table without her usual confidence.

Rita Donaldson's eyes followed Vathana from the moment she emerged from the blue tarp. Immediately she saw the trepidation, the fragility, the delicacy of the brown woman, saw the brown woman's thin face and arms and shrunken breasts, saw in her the lost resilience of Cambodia, the lost elasticity and strength of a people whose diet has been reduced every year, on whom emotional strain had compounded physical hardship, people in dire need of a solution before they succumbed.

For a moment the two women stood facing each other from opposite sides of the reception table. Gradually, simultaneously, both smiled. Rita's light blue eyes twinkled as if she'd just discovered she had a younger sister; Vathana's eyes sparkled, too, feeling, oddly, that this woman knew her as well as any person had ever known her. Very quickly they were talking, in French with scattered common Khmer phrases, getting to know each other, chattering not as interviewer and interviewee but as colleagues.

". . . the Khmer Rouge," Rita was saying, "their growth has been phenomenal."

"Not so phenomenal," Vathana explained. "They grow because FANK is so stupid, so corrupt and ruthless. Captain Sullivan would say that. You agree, eh?"

"With John Sullivan? Yes. He was one of the few who actually cared. Actually took the time to know what it was all about."

"He cared very much, eh?"

"Yes. I think so."

"Do other Americans? The bombs get closer . . ."

"Hmm. Most of the bombings, at least in the reports, are said to be against the NVA buildup in the border sanctuaries. Are they coming into the interior after the Khmer Rouge?"

"Oh yes. I think. I think it's good America hasn't abandoned us completely, but then I think they will as they did South Viet Nam. Ten years then, poof! they're all gone."

"Real poof!" Rita chuckled. "Real Nixon hocus-pocus. There are still fifty-four thousand American troops in Thailand and another sixty thousand on 7th Fleet ships off the coast."

"So many!?"

"Um-hum." Rita reached out and touched Vathana's hand. "I need someone in this area to help me get my stories. A stringer." Vathana nodded understanding of the term. "It doesn't pay much. A pittance. But when people come and tell you about the bombings, then you tell me . . ."

"Captain Sullivan told me how important this is," Vathana said. "So America can know Cambodia and then behave better toward her. That would be much more than a pittance."

"Yes," Rita said professionally. She added, "Do you have enough rice for yourself and your family? With inflation running, what was the last report, 257 percent . . . I have a few black market connections . . ."

"These," Met Paak said, "are yours." Nang and the commander of the Northern Zone Army stood on the edge of a long narrow platform overlooking Nang's new command. "There are sixteen hundred," Met Paak said. "Teach them. Train them." Nang looked out across the opening and into the brush to the west where a mass of young boys were sitting or standing, milling about in clusters. "Met Sar tells me you can do it more quickly than any commander," Paak said. "Good. I am entrusting you with creating a new regiment."

"And cadre?" Nang asked. He gritted his teeth, swallowed. Them! he thought. They're nothing. Children.

"Of course." Paak chuckled. "You've a *core* of trained yotheas— all who've served with you before. Duch, your old radioman from the battles in Ratanakiri—he heard you were coming and he's gathered them. Von, Ung and Sol, eh? You remember. Make them your battalion commanders. Some others. Met Nang, you are the 91st Armed Infantry Regiment of the Kampuchean Liberation Army. Train quickly. We must attain victory before the yuons or they will use the South as a base to consume Kampuchea. In three weeks you will move south."

Nang stood alone on the platform. He could not see all the boys but what he saw was disheartening. Children. Little brown boys with thin arms and skinny necks. Eng, Nang thought, has a real regiment. Nu has more than two. But me, I get a handful of untrained, frightened children.

On 9 March 1973, before Met Nang had even met with his cadre, other Krahom yotheas toppled the towns of Chambak and Samrong only twenty and twenty-four miles, respectively, south of Phnom Penh, and shelled Takhmau, only six miles south of the capital. Ten days later FANK's elite 7th Brigade counterattacked and retook the two towns, but the Communists disengaged and seemed to slide sideways like a matador behind a smokescreen cape, then attacked at the nearby town of Phrasath Neang Khmaru. Additional KK units assaulted at Angtassom at the junction of Highways 3 and 25, at Roka Kong and Mouk Kampoul on the Mekong northeast of the capital and at Romeas on Highway 5 to the northwest.

Nang followed the reports with glee and with envy. Quickly he organized his command. Along with Duch, Von, Ung and Sol he was given Met Rath, Met Thevy and Met Puc whom he ordered, respectively, to establish new transportation, weapons, and supply-propaganda companies that would support the battalions and the regiment. In a day Nang had grasped the orderly format; in three he'd filled the command slots; in five his regiments—each unit commander having the power of life and death over the conscripts and volunteers—had achieved orderliness. It was still a mess.

On the third anniversary of the ousting of Norodom Sihanouk, Cambodian national troops abandoned Oudong after KK mortars ignited a FANK ammo dump near the Tep Pranam pagoda. Nearly four thousand FANK troops and civilians fled the rebels charging Oudong, and at least two hundred people were captured and herded away toward "liberated" zones. East of Oudong FANK's best unit, the 80th Infantry Brigade, after eleven days of battle, withdrew to a new defensive ring at Chekei Themei. Before the month was over FANK suffered additional setbacks at dozens of sites along the Bassac River, and in the marshes lining the Mekong across from Neak Luong.

Amid these FANK disasters a disaffected FANK pilot bombed Lon Nol's presidential palace, throwing the national leader into a rage which in turn precipitated his declaring a state of siege, closing the print media, banning mass meetings, and imposing a nine p.m. curfew. In response, teachers, students and proselytizers staged a general strike closing the little industry still operating in republic territory. Protest demonstrations increased as peasants and workers joined to demand an end to corruption and soaring inflation. Nang laughed at the reported follies and passed the stories on to his training yotheas. "Lon Nol has ordered nationwide conscription," Nang told his troops. "And Nixon has announced the United States will bomb us until our offensive halts."

They did not move south at the end of three weeks. The unit was not ready, could not possibly have been ready. Nang attempted to motivate the boys with more stories, more information. "We are on our own," he told them on 29 March. "Hanoi has released its last American POW and the United States has withdrawn its last soldier from South Viet Nam. Now they are both free to come here. Now we are on our own."

*   *   *

The 91st Armed Infantry Regiment trained day and night. It was Pong Pay Mountain accelerated. What luck, Nang thought at the end of the fourth week when Puc brought him a student who'd stolen a bottle of whiskey and become drunk. The regimental commander grabbed the boy by the shoulders, almost hugged him for the great opportunity he presented, led him to the drill field where Met Von's and Met No's battalions were practicing hand-to-hand combat. "Let them kill him," Nang told Puc. "Have every struggler kill him. One learns to kill by killing, eh?"

Each day the little boys changed, changed as every yothea had, as every soldier must, transforming from innocent to executioner, from individual to expendable. Each day new word had come from the front. Each day rumors and stories of the bombings spread. Each day new recruits came and filled out the battalions until the 340-fighter units exceeded 400, until the regiment of 1,500 with support and staff topped 1,950. Each day reports came of the NVA buildup. Rush, came the word. Faster, came the word. We must win, now! The people have been mobilized. The army is committed. Faster. Faster. Move south.

In early April Nang again stood at the edge of the long narrow platform overlooking his troops. "Strugglers," he shouted. The troops froze in the posture of perfect attention. "Strugglers. You are my brothers. You are my family." Met Puc clapped his hands. Eyes skittered toward the noise. Then the boys saw it was the propaganda company leader. A few clapped, then more. "It is time to go to the front . . ." A few cheered. "It is time to knock off some lackeys of the running dogs . . ." Yotheas hooted, howled. "It is time to bring Kampuchea a humane and modern government."

The ugly regimental commander's voice boomed and the yotheas went into a frenzy of anticipation of battle, of victory. As they cheered, Nang seemed to grow. "Seventy battalions of our brothers attack Lon Nol's heart. Should we sit here?"

"No."

"Should we let them strive to liberate Kampuchea without us?"

"No!"

"Should we attack? Should we kill?"

"*Yes! Yes!*"

Nang's eyes beamed, his evil smile was infectious. "You have within you the blood of warlords from Angkor, from Funan. For centuries Kampuchea has been victimized." Nang crouched, swept his hands out from before him to his sides as if he were erasing everything in the past. A hush fell over the regiment. "If we lose, not a single Khmer will remain. Kampuchea will cease to exist. *But* . . . it is within you, through the Will of Angkar, to be victorious."

"*Yes! Yes! Yes!*"

Again Nang paused. These boys had been well trained by their unit leaders. How flexible they were, how susceptible to his oration, how easily he plucked the strings of their fears, their insecurities, their xenophobia, their memories of their families' discontent before they were ripped away and pressed into the new family of their cell, their platoon, their company, battalion, regiment and Angkar Leou.

"You are dead." The words splatted from Nang's mouth. "Only the moment of your death has yet to be determined. But if you are dead, you cannot be killed. You are invincible." The little brown boys, still thin yet harder than before, stood, shouted, raised their weapons, assault rifles amid clubs, rocket-propelled grenade launchers amid hoes, mattocks and bush knives, raised them, shook them, pounded their chests with their free hands until Nang held his pincer high. "In rain . . ." Nang boomed.

"In rain . . ." came nearly two thousand voices.

"In wind," they chanted together, "in health or wounded, day or night, I will obey . . ." Looking upon them from the platform Nang was seized with a commander's love for his troops, with a tyrant's adoration for power. "I am the offering."

In April they'd begun the march south, yet even as they marched into the maelstrom of Allied firepower, their indoctrination and purification continued.

"Sihanouk, he eats well in Peking, eh?"

"How should I know?"

"Damn, I'd like to have just one meal like his. I hear he's become yuon."

"That can't happen. If you're born Khmer, you're Khmer."

"You must be right. Go see Met Puc. He'll show you how."

While Krahom units counterattacked the FANK Task Force attempting to retake Oudong, Met Puc systematically weeded out the Sihanoukists. By the time Krahom units forced FANK defenders to flee from the outposts between the Bassac and Mekong across from Neak Luong, the 91st Armed Infantry Regiment had lost nearly a hundred troops to the internal cleaning. The purge in the midst of battle was Krahom-wide. Even as KK units confiscated five 105mm howitzers with forty truckloads of ammunition from units of FANK's 7th Division that they'd ambushed near Takeo City, the anti-Sihanouk, anti-monarchy, anti–Viet Namese campaign of the ultranationalists exploded. By May Krahom propaganda teams were infiltrating villages and cities throughout the liberated areas, were rendezvousing with association leaders and overtly denouncing Sihanouk and his ties to Hanoi and proclaiming the supremacy of Angkar Leou. In Svay Rieng the Gray Vultures and the people reeled. The backlash halted the progress of the KK offensive. Quickly the Center responded, backtracked while moving forward, announced, there in the East about Svay Rieng only, that the KK was pro-Sihanouk. The monarch, the Center proclaimed, had confessed to errors, had apologized and had been reinstated as head of the government-in-exile. Norodom Sihanouk, the statement said, wished to return not as a prince but as a private citizen.

When a hardened yet still inexperienced 91st reached the northern front in mid-May, the KK in the East was again advancing on Phnom Penh. "Which army?" Nang asked Met Duch and Met Von.

"Southern Zone Army," Von said.

"I think the Eastern Zone," Duch countered.

"Met Paak won't tell, eh?" Nang was angry. He'd worked very hard for this battle, this fight. It was the eve of the 91st's first assault! The reports said Krahom mortar rounds had crashed into the southern half of Phnom Penh.

"Does it matter which army?" Duch said.

"What's a mortar's range?" Nang shot back.

"Ask Thevy," Von said. "He's head of weapons—"

"You should know," Nang snapped. "Sixty-ones, two thousand meters; eighty-twos, thirty-six hundred meters. That's how close they are." Nang squeezed his right pincer. His hand, his arm, his entire torso shuddered in anger and envy. "We must be the victors," he stammered. Hot acids billowed from his stomach to his throat and into his mouth. "No one can beat us to Phnom Penh. Is this battlefield prepared?"

That dawn Nang's 91st had its baptism by fire. They attacked the village of Prek Yan. There had been no battlefield preparation other than the nocturnal massing of the regiment before FANK's defensive perimeter. There was little artillery preparation. The 91st had but two 61mm mortars and a pair of 107mm recoilless rifles. Sister units in the 4th Brigade and in the 7th and 54th Regiments had circumvented Prek Yan and were set to attack farther south. From the flanks the 107s banged, the rockets flew, a poorly aimed one sailed high over the berm, a low one skittered along the earth, lodged and exploded in a clump of reeds. The wave, fifteen hundred strong, shouting, only a few firing, swarmed toward the defenders. Mortar rounds popping from tubes behind them exploded in the village. Then the government troops awoke, reacted, returned fire, spraying M-60 machine gun rounds across the horde as if spraying water hoses on a grass fire. Almost immediately the 91st broke, yotheas scattered, dispersed into the thinly treed forest about Prek Yan.

All that day Nang reinvigorated his troops. "Now you know. Now you understand. Tomorrow—kill everything. Burn everything. Destroy everything." In the dirt of their forest command post, Nang snarled and chided his leaders. "Rath, how many casualties? Aah. Who cares? How many attackers for the morning?"

"Twelve hundred. We've a hundred wounded to carry."

"If they can't attack," Nang said coolly, "leave them." With a stick he drew the village, marked the machine gun emplacements, pinpointed the weak points. "Yon," he said, "tomorrow . . ."

Before the next dawn his infantry moved into position; before dawn his 107s hammered bunkers and gun emplacements; before dawn his mortars set the village afire and backlit the FANK berm. Then the troops attacked, now sprinting and firing, concentrating column spearheads against the weak points while spread teams sprayed suppressive fire. By dawn the 91st had broken through and in violent resentful frenzy they chopped, killed, destroyed. In an hour only the FANK soldiers who'd hidden successfully or who'd fled Prek Yan were alive. Only the conscriptable and usable elements of the civilian population, and those who'd escaped, still breathed. Quickly Nang ordered his fighters to police up and withdraw. As they departed Met Puc's team erected a handmade poster by the village well: BEING FORCIBLY GRASPED BY THE EVIL HAND OF IMPE-RIALISM, YOU HAVE LIVED YOUR PRECIOUS LIVES IN VAIN. TO CONSOLE YOUR SOULS WE HAVE PREPARED A GRAVE FOR YOU. REST IN PEACE. Into the well the propaganda team dumped the heads of ninety-one victims.

The 91st moved south. FANK reinforcements moved north. American fighter-bombers "walked point" for the government column—F-105s screaming in low then sweeping up as they lobbed their ordnance at unseen targets before them. Now the bombers came in twos, now in fours. The 91st retreated through Prek Yan. The bombers hit the village, reducing its charred ruins to rubble and killing those who'd escaped Nang's brutality by hiding. Government troops reoccupied the village. They found it pocked with craters, the orchards broken and shattered, the ground littered with broken and twisted cooking pots and human parts. All day bombers and artillery blasted the surrounding forest, not attempting to ferret out the KK but hoping with random explosions to kill anyone in the wild. Then

FANK withdrew. Nothing remained in Prek Yan worth defending. As they pulled back the 91st followed.

For more than two months, mid-May to mid-July 1973, the 91st Armed Infantry Regiment with its sister units of the Army of the North continued to attack down Highway 5 toward Phnom Penh. With every battle they became more experienced. With every battle their tactics improved. With every battle they added new recruits or new conscripts to replace those killed. "Forward" became their motto. Go forward at all cost. We must win, *now!* Even when the Congress of the United States voted on 30 June 1973 to force a complete cessation of American bombing in forty-five days, the Krahom did not pause. Instead they moved constantly, moved to avoid detection by VATLS, the American Visual Airborne Target Locator System, of which they knew nothing but its uncanny ability to bring the bombers to wherever they rested, if they rested for more than a few hours.

Mid-June 1973—Chhuon's head was down in subjugation but his eyes were up, locked on the new canton deputy chief, Met Soth's counterpart, the *kana khum.*

Until the bombings began life had been improving. Now everyone was terror stricken. More heads would roll.

Dry-season projects had progressed well. Unlike the earlier earthworks the peasants had been given control over the layout of small dams, dikes and canals within the much larger scheme. "Finally," Chhuon had told Sok, "finally a woman like Than." "You like her, eh?" Sok's tone had been light, humorous. "She even works with us," Chhuon had said. "And if one asks her, she will listen to reason. Ha! She knows water doesn't roll uphill. More than Soth, eh?" "ssshh." Sok had patted her husband's shoulder as they'd lain in the two-person cocoon. "ssshh. knock on wood. don't let anyone hear your voice." "Ah, Sok, it's not Phum Sath Din, but with Than there's no corruption, no gambling. Everyone eats the same, dresses the same, works the same. As much as I dislike them, she is very fair. The bunkers are well prepared, the paddy dikes are straight, the feeder canals are level. There's talk of being allowed a cooperative store. I think they mean a market. You know how they change the language."

In the months after the rains ceased, Phum 117 of Khum 4, Srok 16, had become a strategic cooperative. Beneath each family hut of Chhuon's interfamily group a digging team had burrowed into the earth, forming an S-shaped tunnel leading to a small cubicle. Around each set of *krom* huts an interior defensive perimeter had been built. About the phum as well as about the entire khum, fences and the belt of minefields and boobytraps had been widened and improved. Everything was in perfect order. Seen from above the fortifications were symmetrical.

The *kana khum*, Met Ravana, did not speak. Before him sat every inhabitant of Phum 117. Every head was bowed. Maturing in the liberated zone was a system of checks without balances that ensured that every boy and girl, every man and woman, was constantly under surveillance, continuously watched by every other person about him or her. Anyone could report on anyone else. Anyone could claim that so-and-so had anti-Movement or antirevolutionary thoughts or said anti-yothea words, or behaved in an anti-*phum* manner. Without being able to face the accuser, the accused was automatically guilty, could be automatically punished. The result was a total breakdown of the normal fabric of Khmer society. In the name of "liberation," in the name of "the people," guilt was impressed on every psyche. Sanctimonious double-talk combined with totalitarian rule destroyed traditional social networks. The organized and "scientifically" planned transformation of the culture destroyed, as did other factors in government zones, Khmer resilience.

Throughout March and April 1973 the Krahom offensive against the heartland intensified. From the hinterlands Angkar had called as many yotheas as possible. They'd vacated the liberated lands in waves, leaving the liberated peoples in the hands of Rumdoah troops overseen by but an aroma of hardened yotheas. As the offensive blasted huge holes in FANK's capital defenses, Allied bombers reached out to crush supply lines and rear bases. Convoys and fortifications were targeted.

Three weeks before this meeting of Phum 117, Sok had been quietly preparing the evening rice when without a half second's notice the growling roar of three government T-28s shook the village. *Lap kats (slap kats,* or sawed-off wings) swept in fast, so low that had she had a long-handled rice knife she'd have been able to split the plane's belly. Then instantly they were gone and napalm fires roared and consumed the family-group huts beside theirs. Chhuon, on his spindly bowed legs, had run to her and pulled her. She'd frozen like Lot's wife. Flames sucking for air, heat rising, forming small tornados, had whipped the earth about them into a dust storm. Still Sok had stood agape. Then, later, huddled in their tiny bunker room, she'd collapsed sobbing, calling the names of her mother and father and of the seven children she'd borne—four dead, three lost. Hopelessness had engulfed her like black billowing napalm smoke.

"We are lost," she'd cried. "Lost. We are no one. We are nothing. We are without family. We cannot even use our family names!"

"Someday," Chhuon had tried to console her, "someday, when the war is over, when we're truly liberated . . ."

A week later Khum 4 had again been bombed. This time a nighttime arc-light drop had unleashed its violent pent-up hate at the edge of the canton, the high explosives blowing iron shrapnel out hundreds of meters, ripping through huts and humans, punishing the land and any inhabitants who dared be on it. The next day a third punitive strike, American F-105s, had hit the commune, killing, destroying the dikes, a *boray*, some just-plowed fields which would have grown rice to support Angkar's troops, fields Chhuon saw as his fields, his future food. Chhuon's will had weakened. Then came the quiet days when the bombers moved south onto the points of attack or east against supply trails laden with trucks. Still he, Sok, so many, slept nights in their airless bunkers or slept in fields as far from their huts as the defensive rings about the commune would allow.

"Sihanouk is near." Met Than, the straight-haired *mekong*, had whispered one evening to Chhuon and a group replowing and reflattening a paddy for the May planting.

"Who says?" a survivor of a devastated phum had asked.

"Everyone," Than whispered. She too was depressed by the bombings, by the *phum*'s, *khum*'s, *srok*'s, by every level's inability to retaliate. "A *mekong* from 116 told me."

"Who needs him?" the survivor had snapped.

"But . . ." a third man said, his voice trembling, ". . . he is our . . . savior."

Chhuon had bitten down hard, had pushed harder on the three-man bamboo bar from which the ropes trailed to the plow. The survivor had snorted. "Sihanouk's been infected with yuon disease."

Each day Chhuon had withdrawn more. The terror of the bombings, different from any terror he'd ever known, so remote, so unreachable, frightened him to his core in a way physical torture had never been able. He understood torture. He understood pain. He understood pain's infliction. But the bombings. Those he did not understand. Their sudden onslaught, intense violence, sudden cessation. All from such a distance it might as well have been the moon exploding. One night he'd written in his notebook: "They say Samdech Euv is near, but the bombings keep him from returning. Perhaps Kdeb is with him."

Now, to call the meeting to order, Met Ravana clapped his hands. Near Sok a woman's bowels shuddered in terrified spasms and the smell of shit wafted across the cowering people. "All *krom* leaders," Ravana shouted, *"stand!"* Chhuon and three others shot up. "You are charged with the responsibility of the order. Sit." Chhuon dropped, thudded onto the dusty ground. Slowly the words crept from Ravana's mouth, then gradually accelerated: "You will dig in. All movement will be by orders. Only. All aliens are subject to ultimate measures. Anyone not from Khum 4 is an alien. You will work for the Revolution. All material things belong to the Revolution. You may not talk, you may not pray, you may not smile. Your energy belongs to the Revolution. Talking, praying, smiling sap energy. Every infraction will be reported."

The smell of shit reached Ravana. His face contorted. Then his eyes glinted. A flat smirk broadened his jowl. "You have heard that Norodom Sihanouk is near, eh?" He felt repulsed by the continuing smell. "If yes, stand." A few stirred but no one stood. *"Stand! Everyone!"* The nearly four hundred people rose. Ravana walked into their midst. He walked between the silent rows, pacing, disgusted, following his nose. Then, "Are you ill, comrade?"

"N . . . n . . . n . . ."

"Don't be afraid," he said calmly. "Go with those yotheas. They will escort you. In case of a bombing."

The woman who'd soiled herself left. Ravana strode back to the small one-step-high stage. *"Sit!"*

His eyes shifted. Still the smell lingered. "Turn yourselves over to Angkar to be rebuilt. Trust in Angkar, in the Movement, in the Revolution. Sihanouk was corrupt. Sihanouk was despicable. Sihanouk was oppressive." Ravana paused. Chhuon's eyes were locked on his. "You will launch an offensive to gain great victories of rice production to sustain the army and to defend our independence against imperialists and monarchists." Chhuon thought of Met Than and her whispered news of Samdech Euv. This denunciation, this level of denunciation, was new to the "liberated and regained peoples." It marked the transition from physical relocation to political reeducation. Why? Chhuon tried to think. Ravana ranted on. "Our goal is pure and classless humanity unencumbered by the dogma and doctrine of false gods and false civilizations." The bombing, Chhuon thought as the *kana khum* raged, it has dislodged their fears. They are weak. They are vulnerable. ". . . in cities civilization is born, grows. In cities civilization differentiates between people, and that begets classes. Cities must be destroyed . . ." What stops something from reaching in and annihilating them? Chhuon thought. They are afraid! The thought amazed him. They are more afraid even than I am. They don't believe their own words. It's fear that induces in them this fanaticism—fear of revenge against them, fear of . . .

Again Met Ravana was ranting against Norodom Sihanouk. ". . . to speak that name, henceforth, will be punishable by death . . ." No, Chhuon thought, I must not have heard correctly. Without moving his head he attempted to force his eyes far enough sideways to seek Sok's reaction. He could not see her.

So afraid, his thoughts began again. Then he saw Met Than, saw her short straight hair neatly combed, saw the even bangs lapping at her eyebrows, saw her clouded eyes. It did not register. It could not be. Than was one of them. She was there, before him, a head on a board, there without her body. Met Ravana slapped the head and it flew from the board into the midst of shrieking women. Chhuon swallowed. He thought, awkwardly, How, how, how did I do that?! And then he knew, was certain, without thought, that he, like Sok, like them all, was unalterably trapped in a commune of his own making.

In June there had been six nocturnal meetings in Phum 117; in early July, none. As B-52s were unleashing their ordnance about Phnom Penh and Neak Luong, the liberated commune in the far North was slowly recovering. The hopelessness and depression of April, the feeling of being incompetent in the new ways, had ebbed. The tension of May, the continual fear of being a bomb target, abated. And the horror of June's night sessions faded in the constant forced labor. Even Sok, though daily she still muttered "We are lost," seemed to have finally acclimated to the order of Angkar.

"A little more, eh?" Chhuon's voice resounded in the pelting grayness of an early July rain. "Raise it higher," he shouted. The water in the seedbed rose steadily until it was a finger's width from the tips of the rice seedlings. "Ah. Close it," Chhuon yelled up to his helpers. "Let's move on to the next." In the larger fields below the seedbeds men dragged logs over the furrowed mud, flattening the earth in preparation for planting the seedlings. "That's it," Chhuon called. "Open it for this feeder." Water from the small *boray* gushed into the trench which led to the seedbed where Chhuon now stood. The operation was efficient, the water moved swiftly. Chhuon smiled, then remembering it was criminal to smile, cleared his face. Still he felt happy, pleased that the new agricultural layout was working, pleased at how perfectly the rain had fallen, at how beautifully the seedlings were growing, at how straight were the dikes and how level were the feeder ditches and at how well the water-control teams and the log teams worked. Only the memory of Than, the *mekong* who'd let him build a proper system but who'd been beheaded for speaking the old monarch's name, only that thought dampened his spirit this wonderfully rainy morning.

Since the rain had begun in earnest, there had been no bombings. At first Chhuon had thought the planes couldn't fly in the heavy rain, but he knew that wasn't the case. Then he'd thought that the aerial detection men must have finally realized that Phum 117, Khum 4, was not a fortification or a training camp but only a peasant commune trying to raise enough rice on which to subsist. He knew nothing of the great bombings about Phnom Penh and the lesser bombings at Kompong Cham, Neak Luong and to the west at Siem Reap. Things were looking up. Even the local cadre had eased off. As long as the work progressed steadily, as long as everyone labored hard, they were being left alone.

"Let's go," Chhuon called to the two men who'd opened and redammed the spillways to the various seedling paddies. "Well done, Sichau." Chhuon's voice was clear. "Well done, Moeung."

Quietly Moeung said, "You'd best call us 'Met,' Chairman Chhuon. There may be ears in the paddies."

Chhuon did not pause or acknowledge the warning. "Let us spell Team Four. They've pulled the log all day. Let's show them what three old men can do, eh?"

Chhuon's enthusiasm infected Sichau but the fever, like all enthusiasm in Phum 117, was low grade. Soon, as the three skinny men—Chhuon now fifty, the other two in their mid forties—on their six spindly legs with the six bulbous knees well displayed beneath their rolled-up trousers—pulled the log, they were puffing and panting and only occasionally talking.

"Chhuon . . ." Moeung blew words out one per breath, "I . . . heard . . . Soth . . . he's . . . replaced . . . by . . . Ravana."

"Eh?" Chhuon puffed back.

"My wife . . ." Sichau spoke more smoothly than the others, ". . . she says . . . she heard from the *mekong* . . . we are to raise . . . to the next level . . . of community."

"What . . ." Chhuon did not turn but continued pushing on the bamboo pole—". . . does that . . . mean?"

"Eh . . ." Sichau said. ". . . tonight we'll hear."

Chhuon, Sichau, Moeung, all the new and old peasants of Phum 117, didn't know what event triggered that night's reeducation session and the new harsh reprisals. But some cadre knew; some were held accountable. Fifty kilometers south-southwest in the direction of Kompong Thom, in the absence of a strong force because so many Khmer Krahom yotheas had been sent to the front, forty thousand "liberated" peasants had escaped to government lines.

"It is the most severe crime . . ." Ravana addressed the men workers of Phum 117. They had not been permitted to return to their huts; they had not eaten. Torches had been brought to the field Chhuon had been dragging at dusk. ". . . in the eyes of Angkar. Anyone attempting to escape will be arrested, tried and taken away. Why should anyone wish to leave? Angkar provides for everything. Angkar cares for all. Angkar is good.

"Are you curious? What's next door? There"—Ravana pointed north into the night—"there is a commune of monks. There they learn to become productive members of the community; they are taught to earn their own way." He ranted for an hour then was quiet for some time, then he left. He did not dismiss them. All night they sat in the field. One by one the torches burned out. The rain came at times hard, at times gently. When the rain was softest the omnipresent metronome of crickets lulled the men toward sleep. Yet all feared sleeping, for sleeping during a meeting might be a crime. Sichau's head drooped onto Chhuon's shoulder. He snapped it up. Another torch burned out. He laid his head against Chhuon and fell asleep. On the other side Moeung did the same, turning slightly so the back of his shoulder was to Chhuon's back. Chhuon moved slightly so the three formed a tripod. At first he could not sleep. He pondered one line Ravana had repeated several times: ". . . though our rice farmers were greatly oppressed and are now free, they must still learn a proper agricultural worker's nature. They must be instilled, via socialist ideals, with a working-class spirit. . . ."

The next day they worked the field without having seen their huts, without having eaten. Chhuon pondered . . . to mold all members of our society into productive elements . . . To him, the phrases seemed overly simplistic, but in his weariness and hunger he wished only to use them to sidetrack his mind. For a while he repeated to himself . . . reeducation through work . . . reeducation through work . . . He thought of his notebooks and thought what he would write. By dusk he was feeling very weak and fantasized about the bowl of rice Sok would have waiting for him. Still they worked. . . . productive elements . . . he thought. Why not productive people? Productive families? Ravana's shrill voice had lambasted them about families. Families were for producing productive elements—some such non-sense. When families could no longer produce new elements they should be dissolved. Chhuon almost chuckled to himself at that thought. Dissolved! We're not lumps of sugar. Once you are a father, a mother, a son, a daughter, he thought, you are always that. It is not something that can be dissolved.

Again that night the men were grouped in a field. The rain had stopped and the ground came alive with thousands of large brown moths. A new kitchen staff came to the field and served the men rice soup and bananas. They were not released and again slept in their back-to-back tripods. Again they labored without sustenance. Chhuon forgot about Ravana, and all day he fantasized about Sok and the meal she would prepare. That night when the men returned to their huts there were no women. They had been moved to a new women's barracks built a forbidden half kilometer to the east.

As the assaults on the capital heart area continued, as other government enclaves were attacked, Vathana sat, sat by the first of the small mud huts, sat in the rain staring into the dying embers of the night's cooking fire, letting the rain soak her long thick black hair and run down her cheeks like tears though she was not sad, not crying. Around her the few soldiers and the many association women huddled in the dark, eating, picking the last grains from their plates, barely moving, yet to her they whizzed by, passed so quickly their speed blurred their images. Time accelerated, yet each moment stretched out for all eternity.

Keo Kosol had tried to talk her out of it. He had grabbed her shoulders, touched her as he hadn't in months, she so passive in his hands he'd dropped them to his sides in disgust. "You want to believe the rumors," he'd said, "then go ahead. But then you'd believe anything, eh?" Still she'd remained inert. "The reason"—Kosol's voice rose—"they were so harsh in the border area was because the Americans and the Viet Namese were there."

"And in the North?" she'd whispered without moving.

"Everyone knows those people . . . those province people are lazy. They don't work hard like our peasants. But we're hard workers. We'll produce for them and we'll gain the paradise they promise." He had yelled at her many more things. "Look at this." He'd waved an old newspaper before her. "The American actress, Fonda, remember what she says. '. . . if you understood what Communism was, you would hope and pray on your knees that we would someday become Communists.' She knows! Americans know, eh?! Now you must stop this craziness."

Still Vathana had not responded. Kosol ranted on. "They'll kill you with their bombs. You want that, eh? Look here!" He'd waved that day's paper. "'Eighty B-52 sorties. Sixty-four hundred bombs! Each day!' Americans ... they don't care about Khmer people. Only about their bomb-making industry. Two million dollars ... every day ... yet children in your camp starve. What aid comes to the refugees? Not even half a million for a million refugees in three years! They've removed the middle path! They must go!"

Then Vathana had wept. Then tears had slid down her cheeks. More gently Keo Kosol had said, "The Khmer Rouge are Cambodian. Do we need Dr. Kissinger's approval for Khmer to talk to Khmer? When the war is over, the cruelty will cease. We shall walk the middle path again."

Still she had gone forward, led how many she did not know, did not count. It didn't matter to her whether they were organized or not, whether they brought a kilo of provisions or ten thousand. Only that she go. That she was followed by forty from the Soldiers' Mothers Association she did not know. That members of the Liberation Youth, the Rivermen for a Just Government, the Refugee Association, and the Khmer Patriots for Peace all joined her, did not gratify her. The rain came harder.

Earlier, even before Kosol's harangue, she'd sat looking at her babies, at Samnang, at Samol. How the war overshadowed their lives, she'd been thinking. How will it be on this one? she'd thought, passing her hands over her bulbous abdomen. Will the schools reopen? Will they ever know their father? She'd felt so tired, so numb. Rumors were being passed that cigarettes, gasoline and even electricity were being rationed in Phnom Penh. She'd heard and she'd thought, Good! Perhaps they will understand what life is like for us.

She'd wanted to stop thinking about the children so she'd left the tent only to see hundreds, thousands more—idle children beneath the growing number of cardboard or thatch or scrap truck fender shanties disintegrating in the rain. Why? she'd thought, and the pain sat heavy on her shoulders and in her bowels and in her tired legs. Why hasn't the rain stopped the Khmer Rouge? Still they attack the capital. Will it fall? Today? Or Kompong Cham? She could feel the shaking earth as she watched the children, then she could hear the not-so-distant sound of explosions, and she'd thought, Are they invincible? Where is Norodom Sihanouk? He would never allow things to be so bad. He must not know. Where is Teck? Where is Papa? Her lower jaw trembled and she tried to chase those thoughts away. Some people say the Khmer Rouge have engaged an evil spirit. In exchange for invincibility they have traded their souls. If only . . .

Windswept raindrops flew beneath the poncho roof over the fire and sizzled in the embers. The front was very close. Indeed, she was now at the back of the front. In the rainbound dark a wide circle of fires of FANK's defenders flickered sporadically. Neak Luong, the southern citadel on the Mekong, defender of the southern approach to the heartland, was again an isle in the Communist-conquered sea.

Sarin Sam Ol had heard of her plan and had come to the camp to talk. "It is very dangerous," he cautioned her half-heartedly.

"Yes," she'd said, not agreeing but confirming that she'd heard, that she knew the words though they no longer had meaning in Neak Luong, that she respected the doctor's thought.

"I won't come to help," he'd said.

"I understand," she'd answered.

"Then I will say good-bye. I have received a visa for France. There is an eye doctor . . ."

"Then see him."

He reached out, grasped her hands as if passing a blessing. "You understand. I can do nothing. Nothing."

After Doctor Sarin had left, Vathana had written a sketch of his anguished ordeal and sent it via messenger to Rita Donaldson. It was her twentieth such letter. For each she received the equivalent of two dollars, enough to buy eighteen pounds of rice on the black market—at just above starvation levels, enough to feed her, Sophan and the children for one week.

"You understand," she had ended the account, "I can do nothing. Nothing."

But *I* can do something, she'd thought. She'd talked to Rita— when, she couldn't remember. Time had become so warped she was unsure if it were this life or the last. "This is Louis"—she'd introduced the young man who'd been her husband's friend. Rita had glared at the disheveled, angry soldier.

In Khmer Louis, glaring back at the blue-eyed Western woman, snapped at Vathana, "Does she know you carry a kid that's not your husband's?"

"You came to me," Vathana shot back. "This is what I can do."

"What does he say?" Rita did not hide her dislike for him.

"He says," Vathana spoke alternately in Khmer and in French as if Louis did not understand French, "he needs help. He says he will desert unless he has food and is paid."

"When was the last time he ate?" Rita asked.

Vathana translated then listened and translated back. "Two days," she said. "But he says they have had only small rations for two months. Had he not been caught in the general conscription he would never serve this government." Louis sprayed out another angry burst. "He says, those with families here eat because the families bring them food but those without families are starving."

They had talked for an hour when Louis said he had to go or they'd come for him. Alone the women spoke amiably and Rita Donaldson pulled from her shoulder satchel a plastic bottle of protein tablets. She kissed Vathana and whispered, "For your baby. So it will be strong." Then again she pulled a book from her bag and said, "Translate this for me, dear. Now I must go. Your stories are very good."

Vathana had held the book, staring at the sad cover for some minutes. She opened the bottle and took two tablets then looked back at *Regrets for the Khmer Soul* by Ith Sarin. The cover was a heart-shaped map of Cambodia torn in two by the Mekong River. Before she could open it Louis had returned, had scowled, spat. "Teck has joined my unit," he'd said. "Give your pussy to others, but give your husband some food."

A mile, perhaps two, into the blackness, lights popped hazy through the rain, burst in a row in the amorphous dark. Then came the quaking and the thunder. The ash of the cooking fire tumbled exposing the last hot coals. A mud hut collapsed. Three soldiers cussed and stamped and shook the clods from their heads and bodies.

Vathana and three association women rose. There is something we can do, she had told them without emotion, without ardor. "We can help the wounded. We can feed the unfortunate. We can show compassion for those who seek only to defend their own homes and their own families, for those demoralized, for those who fight without hope of victory."

16 July 1973, 0430 hours: What was that! He jerked but did not rise. His eyes, red, angry, obsessed, flicked, searched. Behind them the village still smoldered. Before them FANK troops were moving—maybe withdrawing. In two hours it would be light, in two hours the Krahom 91st Regiment would again attack. Nang pushed his torso up off the earth, swept his eyes back and forth across the battlefield. The B-52s had hit them—hit them again, hit them at dusk, two three-plane flights, six sorties, 324,000 pounds of bombs. The eleventh straight day of being hit, still they attacked, the thirty-fourth day in two months, yet they continued forward, always forward, nearly six hundred

million pounds of iron-encased high explosives expended against him, against Nang and his 91st Armed Infantry Regiment of the 4th Brigade of the Army of the North, against some forty to fifty thousand armed Krahom yotheas—expended in the heaviest bombing of the Southeast Asian war, expended against the most ruthless "Pure Flame" land assault in history. Attack! Nang ground his teeth. We must attain victory before the yuons rebuild and devour us. The Party line—it was his faith, his need to believe to press on. Again the noise. He startled. What was that!

By July, the 91st's mission and tactics had been perfected. "It is better to maim than to kill," Nang told his fighters. "When useless elements are killed they are soon forgotten, but if they are maimed they are always in the sight of those who oppose us. The maimed drain the enemy's resources. Their suffering demoralizes the lackey troops who must watch them whimper and die like pathetic dogs. Maiming is good. Better even than having bombers."

Each battle varied, each was the same. Increasingly FANK withdrew in the face of the KK assault, withdrew and condensed into refugee-clogged enclaves. The yotheas grew confident, overzealous, exposing themselves to aerial reconnaissance and thus bombing. The yotheas wavered and FANK pulled back without cause. Nang directed his mortars, now mounted in ox carts, to target fleeing villagers, thus blockading FANK's withdrawal. "If they escape," he screamed at his battalion commanders, "the officer responsible will be executed. Now attack! Attack! *Attack!*"

What was that! Slowly Nang rolled to his knees, then rocked back on his heels into a squat. The earth was soft, mulched, pulverized. The rains had become heavy, had combined with the earth, not so much making mud as making warm red-brown slush. "duch," Nang call-whispered. The 91st was dispersed and concealed amid cratered forest, mashed fields and the rubble of a previous battle. "duch."

"met nang." Duch had two radiomen, each with two small radios, and a man with a field phone set. Messages were relayed point to point to point.

Nang stared into the grayblackness. Clouds were machine-gunning billions of slow projectiles of rain onto the earth, dousing the fires behind them. "duch." Nang could not hear his commo chief because he'd re-ruptured his ears during the campaign. "duch."

"Met Nang, here." Duch squatted beside him, slapped his arm.

"What was that?" Nang said.

"What?"

"I heard something. A minute ago. Very odd. Loud."

"I didn't hear anything. How could you, eh?"

"I did."

"Aah! You didn't hear. You can't hear."

"I can't hear bombs," Nang said. "That's good, eh? If you couldn't they wouldn't frighten you so. But I hear death walking."

"You get more mystical—"

"No. Listen. Does the enemy move out? Tell the battalions to move in, now. Now. Tell them to move up to the berm and dig in. Dig in with FANK. Don't let them escape. Now."

"Yes, Met Nang." Duch thought to ignore the order.

"Duch," Nang said.

"Yes."

"Have them jam the fighter-bomber frequency with Radio Peking."

Suddenly, amid the rain Duch heard the drone of a spotter plane's engine.

Quickly orders passed. Quickly the yotheas sneaked forward—not fierce human-wave assaults but owl-quiet approaches—a wave in midocean closing on an atoll. They were now south of Ponheapon, ten miles north of Phnom Penh's heart. The earth burst.

In Phnom Penh, the evening of 15 July 1973, Rita Donaldson was at the typewriter in her small office. "Western sources," she wrote, "have estimated one hundred civilians are killed every day by American bombs. This figure is believed, by many observers, to be conservative." Rita Donaldson looked at the sentence and shook her head. Reducing the atrocity to words lessened its impact upon her and that somehow made her feel guilty, as if even though her writing might expose the atrocity to world view, it could never catch the horror, the crime, the pain she'd witnessed. She reached up, adjusted the goose-necked lamp to reduce the glare on the page and continued. "Embassy sources, who have asked not to be identified, have confirmed the existence of a secret communications center in the embassy which gathers bombing requests from the Cambodian General Staff then forwards them to U.S. 7th Air Force headquarters in Thailand. These same sources state that civilian property damage and death are being kept within 'acceptable limits.' "

"Goddamn," Rita growled. She checked her notes to ensure she'd quoted the phrase properly. "Acceptable?" What's acceptable? she'd wanted to ask on the page, to put into the story, to ask her source, but her source had insisted on no questions. She didn't need to ask. She knew the answer already. Acceptable limits were defined as the number killed. If it were one hundred per day then one hundred per day was acceptable. If five hundred per day . . . She lit a cigarette, inhaled, put the cigarette on the ashtray lip, blew the smoke aside, wetted her lips with her tongue. Why? she thought. Why didn't he say something? The light flickered, paled, then came back.

"Last year," she typed the words quickly, "American B-52s dropped nearly 37,000 tons of bombs on this devastated land. In March alone the Stratofortresses released 24,000 tons. The payload reportedly increased to 35,000 tons in April and 36,000 tons in May. The source, deemed reliable, said the June figures had yet not been tabulated. Those numbers do not include fighter-bomber releases, which last year totaled 16,500 tons and which have allegedly reached that amount each of the three months of this spring bombing campaign."

Again Rita stopped. The cigarette had fallen from the ashtray and burned a fat line in the desktop. He could have told me, she thought. Again she went back to the story. "The Nixon administration has repeatedly stated America has no formal responsibility to uphold the Lon Nol government. According to Secretary of State William Rogers, 'U.S. air strikes . . . do not represent a commitment to the defense of Cambodia itself but instead represent a meaningful interim action to bring about compliance with this critical provision of the Vietnam agreement.' "

She stopped, lifted a ballpoint from the desk, tapped her forehead, stuck the pen between her teeth, then, without consulting her notes, typed, "The volume of bombs dropped has become the embassy's yardstick to measure the 'effective response' of the bombings on the Khmer Rouge. The volume measures nothing of the sort. This bombing has gotten totally out of hand. It is as if a surgeon attacked a multitude of metastasized pockets of cancer with an ice cream scoop." (She smiled at that line, knowing it would never be printed.) "Perhaps the degree of accuracy is what embassy officials claim but its effect on the reported 25,000 to 30,000 Communist troops attacking this city seems minimal. Every day Communist units push government soldiers back. The true effect seems to be that the bombing has driven the people off the land and into the government enclaves. Village agricultural systems, the very basis of Khmer life, have been destroyed. And the Khmer Rouge, a force nearly nonexistent two years ago, has exploded in size and might.

"Though, allegedly, the accuracy and effectiveness of the bombings have kept the massed Communist battalions from sweeping into Phnom Penh, in adjacent and distant areas it seems to have become a game played by American military planners. Which group can fly the most sorties? Who can drop the most ordnance? Who can destroy the most 'targets'? Whose aircraft utilization ratio is highest?"

Rita chomped on the pen in her mouth. The words were coming fast. "The bombing cost, in U.S. dollars to U.S. taxpayers, in civilian casualties and ecological ruin, as well as in the stiffening resolve of the enemy, is not part of their equation. Tactical close-in air support remains effective. Where the Khmer Rouge have massed troops, perhaps high-level sorties are effective in the defense of Phnom Penh. But rear-area bombing is out of control."

Rita spit out the pen, lit another cigarette. She looked at the papers and reports scattered on her desk and on the floor. "WATERGATE" was in every headline. She hit the return bar several times to add disconnected notes.

"Communist regular force development, despite the bombings, continues to evolve. Where only a year ago the Khmer Rouge could operate at best at company level they have reportedly grown in organization to battalion, regimental and even division-size operations. Air power, without effective infantry, cannot hold this enemy at bay. The all-out Khmer Rouge assault on Phnom Penh . . ."

She stopped. It was a bit like writing one's own obituary. She made a note to go back to the front, now only a few miles north. Then she stood. Then sat back down. "Air power is the last American military involvement in Southeast Asia . . ." Watergate, she thought. Again she stood. She packed the small bag she carried when on assignment. Those sneaky bastards, she thought. What more can we uncover? Again the light flickered. She sat, typed quickly, picking up where she'd stopped, ". . . and in forty days it will come to a legislated halt." Sneaky, she thought. He could have told me she was so damned pretty. Damn that Sullivan. Damn him. The light dimmed. Then it went out. Phnom Penh's electricity was gone.

The earth burst. The earth gushed fire. Shrapnel slashed the forest, the cratered and mulched paddies. High explosives churned the debris and ruin of yesterday's fight. Clods of dirt rained into the vacated positions of Nang's Krahom 91st Regiment. A mist of seared sand coated them as they huddled in against FANK's berm, hid directly under FANK's protruding gun barrels, froze in the flashes of bombs and the flat light of parachute flares. In minutes the bombers, drained of their potency, departed. The night closed down. FANK's defenders relaxed. Nang nudged Duch. They're so predictable, eh? he conveyed without words. So predictable.

"should we attack now?"

"wait until the wives come with the food." Nang was jubilant.

Jubilant too were Met Sar and Met Sen. Jubilant in their roles as victims, as martyrs, as targets one pace ahead of their assassins. Twenty kilometers north of the 91st, thirty-five kilometers from the capital, Met Sar and Met Sen fed each other's self-righteous hate. "He has confessed," Sen sneered. "Confessed."

"And . . . ?"

"And he has been dealt with."

"To kill me!" Sar said.

"To wipe out the Center," Sen corrected.

"And he was yuon."

"He was Viet Namese, all right," Sen said. "He doesn't know, but we have other security reports. Hanoi is on the move."

"How dare they! How dare they!" Sar banged his fat fist on the table. In his most pious voice he repeated, "How dare they!" Then he opened Met Nim's report. He skimmed one page, another. "More men," he growled. "More tanks. More trucks. More guns. More of everything than ever before. Why the fuck do the Americans bomb us? The yuons are the real threat. Look at this."

Sen leaned over. He already knew the contents. A month earlier North Viet Nam's 7th Division with the 297th Tank Battalion and the 40th Artillery Regiment (130mm) had destroyed Polie Krong just west of Kontum in South Viet Nam. It was the first major assault since the peace accords, and America had not responded. "And some"—Met Sen snorted—". . . want us to stop. Some say stop until the legislated bombing halt."

"The Americans won't stop bombing." Sar chortled. "Push them. We must be victorious. Now! That traitorous snake in Phnom Penh, that imperialist lackey . . . I want his head. Ceasefire!? Negotiate!? It's the most despicable conjurer's trick; it's designed to manipulate international opinion. *Make*—the offensive—go forward!" Sar elatedly banged his fist. "Forward. Rid the land of this evil. Let the armies be purified in the rain of flame! Forward!"

Twenty kilometers south Nang whispered to Duch, "have them move forward."

On the other side of the berm, inside the FANK position, Rita

Donaldson watched a government sergeant erase the enemy
91st Armed Infantry Regiment from the map area surrounding
them. "How can he do that?" she asked her interpreter.

"Do what?"

"Say they've been destroyed without going to see."

"Go where?!"

"Where that unit was."

"But what if they're still there?"

"Then how can you erase them?"

"They've been bombed."

Rita left the command bunker. It hit her that she—how could
she think this?—that she would make a good sergeant. First light
grayed the sky of 16 July. Many of the troops who were, or were
supposed to have been, on guard had left their posts and were
milling about a small squad about to go fishing. The ground
about their post was still cloaked in darkness. Light rain fell.
From the southwest came the distant *thawap-thawap* of helicopter rotors on the cool morning air. This is stupid, Rita thought.
She moved toward the chopper pad. In a semicircle at bermside
were a few hastily erected mud and poncho fighting positions.
No one had cleared fields of fire. Beyond the berm a black
shroud cloaked the rice fields. Within the perimeter FANK had
allowed a dozen pieces of heavy equipment—three howitzers,
trucks, a small bulldozer, several jeeps—to anchor the unit to
passable roads.

"More resupply ammunition, eh," the interpreter said. It was
a statement and a question.

Rita could now see the headlight of the lead American Huey;
then six lights—an entire flight. Government troops slowly con-
gregated within a fifty-meter radius of the landing zone—close
enough to watch, far enough to avoid being pressed into the
unloading detail. No pay, Rita thought, no work. She'd heard it
from numerous soldiers. No pay, no food, no work. The helicopter bodies took form in the sky. The noise grew louder. Women
and children began to emerge from the dependants' camp (Rita
thought it would be appropriate to reverse terms) carrying
baskets of food, jugs of water, even boxes of ammunition, on
their heads—bringing the true resupply to the FANK soldiers.
Very low the first helicopter shot in over the people's heads.

"Now," Nang said. Duch signaled his radiomen. To four points
the message passed. Almost simultaneously, from four points,
rocket flames streaked, then came the bang-wooosshh of the
SAM-7s, shoulder-fired surface-to-air missiles, then the jackhammer pounding of two 12.7mm antiaircraft guns. The helicopter flight split—first bird still racing low across the compound,

second bird up left dropping its hung load of 105 rounds, third bird up right, doorgunners popping flares to distract the heat-seeking missiles. Behind, the fourth bird, despite its exhaust deflection cowling blowing the hot jet gases into the rotor-wash for dissipation, despite flares, exploded, a bright ball of flame and fragments blackening, descending, crashing into tarp lean-tos.

"Attack!" Nang screamed.

"Attack!" Von, Ung, Sol, No.

"Attack. Kill everything!" The Krahom platoon leaders, squad leaders.

"Burn everything!" The cell leaders.

A thousand rifles, two KK 12.7s, seven, ten mortars, firing. Firing.

"If the attack fails," Nang shouted, "the company command-ers will be executed."

For a second Rita stood dumbfounded. The odor of burning hair engulfed her. A cloud of blood-mist blinded her. Her interpreter—she'd never learned his name—lay dismembered at her feet. The first helicopter had kicked out crates, tilted, zipped campward and was gone. Then it was back, miniguns illegally hosing the berm. Another bird was grenading tangentially to the camp. Others were over the fields strafing. Screams hit her ears. Not pain. Commands. FANK troops sprinted to positions. Survival. More smell of hair fire. Hers.

Nang did not direct the assault but was part of it. Here he sat, exposed, an AK-47 to his shoulder, one foot under his ass, one knee up, aiming, aiming up, waiting for the strafing run to descend upon him. How he hated them, hated the helicopters, hated the Americans, hated them with his whole heart and his whole soul. The chopper approached closer, closer, firing front minigun and side-mounted 40mm cannons, a stream of tracer fire spewing from the nose punctuated with grenade-launched thudding, the ground explosions lost in the cacophony of the battle. Nang aiming, waiting, locking in on the forward stream, firing up the stream as the bird scorched over, firing into the nose, the belly. The bird did not crash but he knew he'd hit, knew he'd forced it away. About him there were dead. About him there were wounded, moaning. His ears ached yet he could hear the moaning. "Go forward," Nang shouted. "Forward at all cost. Leave the wounded."

The perimeter had been breached. FANK soldiers fell back, firing, firing like deer hunters in a blind, into the crazed charge, killing exposed Krahom yotheas yet the yotheas kept coming, coming as if once killed they self-healed, resurrected, recharged;

as if invincible. Two F-4 Phantom jets roared in from the east, roared in with the rising sun to their backs. They passed over. Without regard for his losses, their losses, Nang, the 91st, the entire Army of the North, surged against the crumbling yet firing FANK line. The fighter-bombers passed again and again without delivering their ordnance. FANK fell back through the dependant camp. Krahom mortars shelled the road, the fleeing. KK infantry moved in from roadside flanks. Rita, three thousand dependants, trapped. Then the F-4s bombed the road, ". . . forced," Rita would write, but never be able to telex, "to destroy the civilian entourage in order to save the army and in turn those civilian survivors of our own bombs, including myself."

Still the fighting raged. New Krahom units, replacement personnel, were massed at the front's fringe. All day the 91st attacked, the Northern Army attacked. To the east, the south and the northwest more Krahom armies were committed. Behind them the earth was charred, pulverized. Now came the B-52s. The circle about Phnom Penh became the epicenter of the most intense bombing in the history of warfare. "Stay close," Nang ordered. "Hug them." He forced Duch to pass the word—messengers, not radios. "Pick up the dud bombs. We'll mine their escape route." To his damaged ears the bomb-box explosions were dull thuds but to his body the quaking was violent and his hate surged higher. Again, maniacally, he pushed the fighters, himself, to the limits of human endurance. In the afternoon the Krahom pushed Phnom Penh's defenders through a small hamlet, then the yotheas fell back into the village and regrouped amid the rubble—a temporary safe zone—a target area not yet cleared.

Rita Donaldson broke through the FANK-civilian traffic jam and headed for her office in the capital, now only eleven kilometers away. Now 122mm rockets launched from the morning's battlefield, from the now continuous B-52 target area, were crashing into city center. She was afoot. The velo-cabs had disappeared. Some streets were vacant as if the inhabitants believed their flimsy houses could protect them from the rockets. Other streets, particularly in refugee-dense quarters, were packed with bodies bumping aimlessly into one another. There was no refuge, nowhere else to go.

By dusk new KK units and replacements had ventured into the no-man's-land—many, perhaps most, successfully crossing to the front line. The attack recommenced its suicidal fury. Bombers received clearance to release death closer. Bomb boxes overlapped, sorties doubled, tripled on single targets, dumping more than three hundred bombs within a square mile; doubled again, saturating identified massed-unit zones—650 five-hundred-pound bombs in under one minute. On the ground there were no options left except savage fanatical assault. *"The Americans are not gods,"* Nang screamed again and again. He'd been jarred to the core—numbed to the core—reduced to bashed painless-ness, to zombodial shocked let-them-expend-themselves-on-me-because-I-can-endure-ness. Attack. Attack the hated imperialist lackeys, hate their war tools, hate the FANK pawns. The more he was pounded the more energy was absorbed by his hate, by his angry appalled detesting abhorring hate. Hate driving re-venge. Hate demanding vengeance. Every step now, every order now driven by the need, the need to destroy that enemy, the need to destroy everything associated with it, the need to slaugh-ter, murder, liquidate, the need to ravage that fungal distant nation which had sent its robotic war machines to pulverize Kampuchea. For five days the attack continued. For five days firing raged, the Krahom advancing in spurts, FANK digging in here, there, falling back, returning, both armies near total ex-haustion, both armies devastated.

On the fifth day, 21 July, a bomb's eruptive force blew out from its earth crater a windwave, out, up, expanding, throwing shrapnel from casing and crater in a billowing sphere, expand-ing concussive shock-sound-heat then collapsing in upon itself. Nang grabbed his face. Beside him Duch tried to speak, was speaking, pointing at Nang, but Nang couldn't hear. Blood flooded Nang's left eye. He couldn't see. Yet he saw the image of horror on Duch's face, Duch screaming though the side of his own head had been blown off.

"22 July 1973—Phnom Penh:" Rita typed. "Though the Com-munist offensive against the southern and eastern fronts of this city continues, the line of last resort has held. Field and aerial reconnaissance reports indicate the northern defensive ring has halted the Khmer Rouge advance and has broken that attacking force."

It marked the end of sympathy, the end of charity, the end of compassion. It marked the end of life and the beginning of life, the end of love and its rebirth. 6 August 1973—yetdark.

Vathana sat cross-legged at the head of the cot in the far corner of the infirmary tent. Above her, rain patted the canvas; to her left side, water trickled off the base of the flap into the flooded drainage ditch. On the cot to her right she had a sheath of handwritten pages, the first half of the translation of *Regrets for the Khmer Soul*, for Rita Donaldson. Resting facedown against her eight-and-a-half-month-pregnant belly was Ith Sarin's

book. Passages of the book were reassuring; others were terrifying. Angkar this, Angkar that. Angkar, the Organization, a dehu-
manized entity demanding complete, yet at times benevolent,
control; a near-mystical omnipotence combined with assistance
to farmers and an absence of corruption. Plus battles between
Khmer and Viet Namese rebels! Could Ith Sarin be believed?
Certainly John Sullivan would have believed him. Plus, the
book reported, Norodom Sihanouk was but a dupe, a powerless
figurehead!

Vathana had turned the pages against her belly, closed her
eyes, and was thinking of these strange revelations when she
felt the earth tremble, opened her eyes and saw the flame jump
off the candle then burn down the smoke and reignite. So many
bombs had fallen about Neak Luong that their devastating
rumble outside the city barely brought conscious concern. But
beneath, amongst all the other tensions of war-torn Cambodia,
amid the continuing and renewed offensive along the Mekong,
the quaking was one more repressed horror. Only one cannot,
Vathana thought, give in. One must keep going, keep doing
what is necessary. Then she thought of the book on her abdomen, the descriptions of ruthlessness on her fetus, and she
immediately jerked the book up and tossed it away like a hot
coal.

Southeast of the city, Teck sat with Louis in a new Auto-Defense
Militia prepared fighting position. Teck had given up his FANK
commission to return to this city. The Auto-Defense Militia was
a home district defense force similar to South Viet Nam's regional and popular forces. In six months, while growing to a
strength of 57,000, it had become the Republic's first line of
defense for the enclaves. Once the Khmer Rouge drive on Phnom
Penh began to falter, to deteriorate with amazing speed, the
militias blossomed. Still the Communists had not stopped, but
now they assaulted neither daily nor in such force as they had
only two weeks earlier. Neak Luong's defensive ring was now
the front.

"It's not a Monet," Louis joked, shining his flashlight onto
Teck's chest.

"Not bad, eh?" Teck had pulled his shirtfront up to his
shoulders. "Really, pretty good, eh?"

"When did they do it?"

"Four months ago. Maybe five. At a parlor in Phnom Penh."

"You think it'll stop bullets?"

Teck laughed. "No, my good friend." He let his shirt fall
down over the tattoo. "It was a lark, you know?"

"You can have a lark, eh?" Louis said. "You smile so much now. More than ever. Me, I wish we could go back like before the war."

"You know why I'm happy?" Teck said. "You know, eh? Every day Vathana brings me food. Every day I pat my hand on her belly and I say I am a lucky man."

"With a bastard!?"

"With a wonderful wife. Ahh! So I've shared her? So what? I watch her with all these men. I see her direct all those women who come to help. I see she really is an angel and I think I am a very lucky man."

"You sound like a dumb peasant!"

"Maybe. Maybe by choice, eh?"

"You've told her these things, eh?"

"No. How could I?"

"If you're so lucky," Louis said—in his dejection he could not smile again—"wish that the Khmer Rouge go away. Maybe . . . if only the Americans would bring in a few battalions, eh? Then they could be out here in this filth listening to those damned bombs explode."

Vathana opened her eyes. The sound of a Cambodian air force unmuffled T-28 came from over the river. It's early, Vathana thought, for them to be up. Who could pay so much *bonjour* to have them up this early? She closed her eyes. The sound and the thought passed. Her fetus moved. Just a small kick. Pretty soon, baby, she thought. Her mind descended into her abdomen, into the fetus. The baby was in good position. Vathana was certain, was certain the baby told her this. No complications, eh, my sweetlove, her mind sent the message and again she was certain the infant answered: Yes, Mother, nothing to fear. Vathana felt a rush of joy, an overwhelming flood of contentment, but the fetus did not release her mind. Instead it directed it and she sailed out her back to Phum Sath Din to a time when Norodom Sihanouk held power and her father talked of an emerging Buddhist-socialist state. Vathana looked up. Her mother was laughing and humming and busying herself cleaning the house. Vathana rushed to her with the wild flowers she'd picked and she hugged her leg and smelled her mother's fragrance—sweeter than any flower, sweeter than ripe bananas, sweeter than sugarcane. She looked into her mother's face so wrinkled from her wonderful smile and Vathana felt the simple and quiet tie of love from generation to generation which . . . she spiraled back, snapped back like a rubber band stretched to breaking . . . the devastating rumble outside the city—immediately her subconscious alerted her it was off pattern . . . a part of her lingered in Phum Sath Din, but time released, sped, and Vathana saw the wrinkles in her mother's face deepen to the day Samnang and Mayana were lost . . . snapping back through her back, through the fetus, her eyes wide open.

Miles above, a B-52 had locked on a navigation beacon located improperly at the mayor's in-town villa-office. Miles before the bomber was over Neak Luong the navigator—had he been reading about the upcoming National Football League season on the long flight from Guam?—"forgot" to flip the offset switch which would order the plane's flight-direction computer to make the minute adjustment away from the beacon toward the targeted coordinates. The bomb bay doors were spread. "Hack," said the pilot. "Hack," answered the bombardier. For thirty seconds the load spilled from the mother ship's abdomen. The plane banked for its return flight before the first five-hundred-pounder, following an unturned trajectory, burst behind Teck and Louis and Neak Luong's 1st Auto-Defense Battalion.

In the infirmary tent, in the camp, in town, the constant subconscious terror which keeps war-zone inhabitants alert in sleep exploded tens of thousands awake. In ten seconds thirty bombs, fifteen thousand pounds of iron and explosive, erupted down Highway 1, down Main Street, hitting the hospital, the old stilt houses, Doctor Sarin's looted office, piers, the concrete apartment building, the fish market and pagoda and orphanage and on up into the old Chinese section and FANK's north-city garrison, then farther, the remainder of the load blowing in the few secure paddies and vegetable fields still enclaved.

Vathana leaped, leaped like a gazelle with a ball and chain, up from the cot leaving her abdomen fractionally behind, crashing into the lurching Sophan, Vathana's belly pulling her back down, Sophan's body smacking her as the stolid old peasant woman smothered Samnang and Samol beneath her protective muscle and fat and bone. Vathana, sprawled flat on her back, rolled to her knees and plopped atop Sophan, protecting too the precious future of Kampuchea, yet the danger had already passed, the last bomb's concussive force was spent.

Neak Luong, which had been purposely shelled and reshelled by the NVA, which had been intentionally mortared and rocketed by the KK, which had been callously looted by its own child gangs and maliciously abused by FANK and foreign Allied soldiers, which had come to look more and more like a war zone, like an old battlefield, now smoldered and reeled from this most terrible, accidental bombardment.

"Dear Sweet Buddha," Teck mumbled, shocked at the instantaneous devastation behind him. He rose.

"What the fuck . . ." Louis rose with him. Teck took a slow numbed step toward town. "Where are you going?"

"Where would she be? It's almost dawn. She'll be praying at the wat."

"Wait!"

"No. I've got to"—along the front hundreds of Auto-Defense men were up, appalled yet numbed into momentary disbelief—"find her. Oh Dear Sweet Buddha."

"I'll go too," Louis said. He grabbed his and Teck's M-16s. Now others were running, now they too ran.

"Halt!" an officer commanded.

"My wife!" Teck shrieked.

"Get back!" the officer boomed. "What if the Communists attack?"

Thousands swarmed in from every side of the city. "I must go," Teck cried.

In the tent many people were crying. Some were packing their worn clothing, leaving. The entire camp was up. Sophan was quietly hugging the children, not fully aware of Vathana's weak moans. Vathana blew out her breath, then panted. She was on her knees holding the edge of the cot. Her uterus had clamped down like a giant's fist trying to squeeze a pea from its pod. Past pain is impossible to remember but in pain it is easy to recall, to anticipate, to fear along with all the fears and concerns of birthing. Again she blew out her breath, panted. She wanted to grab Sophan's arm but she could not. She wanted to ask someone, anyone, for help, but she could not. She gritted her teeth. The contraction passed and another came. She would hold on a moment longer, she told herself. She would cross the great ocean alone like all mothers must. Sweat beads broke on her brow. The kneeling position was not uncomfortable and she did not have the energy or the willpower to waste on moving. Again a contraction grabbed her and she thought of the pain, of the struggle, or the suffering and she saw them as a gift to this child and as a repayment to her own fragrant mother.

"Oh good, you're all right." The voice was deep, mournful.

Sophan released the children who'd not once squirmed to escape as if they'd known how great their being hugged consoled their old "aunt." "And you," Sophan said politely.

"Immoral fucking foreigners." Keo Kosol's voice was loud. He wanted everyone in the tent to hear it, to know how he felt.

"Why pray?" he snapped at Vathana who had not turned to him. "There are thousands who need your . . ."

"Angel!" Sophan blurted.

Rita Donaldson jumped gingerly from the press helicopter. The day was partially overcast yet behind the clouds the sun stood high in the sky. Newer reporters, younger cameramen, jostled for position but she barely moved. Her left leg was wrapped tightly with elastic bandages because of knee ligaments she'd torn on the rush from the northern front two weeks earlier. She thought to excuse herself to her colleagues saying she couldn't run after them but that was not the case. She simply could see, without moving, the destruction. "You"—she gestured for a teenage boy. *"Parlez-vous français?"* No response. She held out two stacks of riels. In Khmer she said, "Mrs. Cahuom Vathana. Angel of Neak Luong." She gave the boy one stack, waved the other. "Here bring," she said.

"Sending the kid for Cokes?" a reporter from Boston asked Rita Donaldson.

"Um," she answered. She did not wish to have the young man follow her.

"Did you get the part from the briefing officer about the payments?" he asked.

"Hundred dollars per death," she said, not looking at him.

"Yeah," he scoffed self-righteously. "Thirteen thousand seven hundred dollars. It cost more to deliver one bomb!"

"Yeah," Rita said.

"Did your paper send you that *Air War* report by the Cornell group?"

"I've read it."

"You remember the part about the mismatch in power in the confrontation between a major industrial power and a predominantly rural, underdeveloped country?"

"Quentin"—Rita turned on him—"how long have you been here now?"

"Ten days, Rita."

"Ms. Donaldson." She glared at him.

"Ah, yeah. Anyway, what do you think? The report said in the absence of reciprocity, they can't bomb us, right? The battle raises moral issues beyond military factors. I'm going to use that in my lead."

"Um-hum."

"The military keeps denying the inaccuracy of the bombings," he went on, "but look at this place."

"They also deny that Cambodia is in crisis situation," she

said. She thought to continue but decided against it. The entire press corps chatted constantly about their stories and what finally came through was a homogeneous puree of reduced and preedited facts. Rita bit the inside of her cheek. What, she thought, would have happened on the northern front, without aerial support? Absence of reciprocity? Do you want to be bombed?

Vathana was now on the cot. Her knees were spread, her heels were under her buttocks. Keo had been overly attentive, holding her shoulders, supporting her, talking in his most beautiful voice into her ears. At first it had bolstered her waning confidence but quickly it became bothersome. All about the tent people were talking about Vathana's labor and about the air raid. Many were still weeping. The number of dead and wounded crept up—50 and 150, 100 and 200, 120 and 250. Many people were stoic, spartan, denying, repressing, internalizing the grief. Vathana too was bitter. Three years, she thought. Three years for naught. These people are no better off today than the day this tent was raised. Another contraction hit.

"That's it, Angel. Give in to it. Surrender to it. Let it flow. Let me see the baby."

The contraction passed. Shyly Samnang came close for a hug and Vathana held him and kissed his hair and he blubbered, "ba-ba-ba-ba," and ran off to see what else was happening.

Again Vathana's uterus squeezed down. Again she lost herself in thoughts of what could be done. The country has never been worse off. And she answered herself, Nothing. Nothing. Despair grabbed hold of her heart.

Then, "Yes. Yes," Sophan sung, cheered.

"Eh?" Kosol's face was brilliant. His chest puffed out.

The contraction's force was immense. Vathana's buttocks tightened, her thighs quivered, as she exhaled her cheeks flapped. She pushed. She pushed. She stopped. Her chest heaved regaining air. She shifted to the cot's edge and Sophan squatted before her. Then her whole body bore down. "Very good," she heard Sophan's words. "Let it be very hard. Give me that baby." Now came the top of a hairy, wrinkled, waxy head. "Oh come, baby," Sophan cried. "Come, little darling." Waters covered Sophan's hands. Vathana grunted. More head comes, ears and eyes. Sophan lifts Vathana's hand from her quaking thighs and places Vathana's fingers on the infant's head. Vathana feels the nose, the mouth. The baby's mouth seems to kiss her fingers. Vathana's entire body is recharged. Again she pushes and the head is in Sophan's hands, turning as if searching upward for mom, then shoulders, an arm, now quickly the torso. Sophan wipes the infant's face, its head. She pulls and clears its nose. Catches it. "A *girl!*" She squeals. She hands the baby to Vathana, who is being lowered to the cot by Kosol.

"*Immoral fucking* phalang!" Kosol's voice explodes. Everyone in the tent, half the camp, hears. "Red-haired *fucking* bitch." He throws a towel he'd had on his shoulder on the baby. Immediately Vathana's hands, arms swing to protect her. Kosol barges by Sophan, shoves Samnang to the ground, storms from the tent.

"Ms. Donaldson," Quentin, the reporter from Boston, said. Rita looked at him. He was pale from witnessing the festering and filth of the wounded, ill from the volume of dead. She herself, though hardened, was queasy. More than queasy. Angry. The boy she'd paid to find Vathana had returned with a French-speaking friend who'd told her Mrs. Cahuom had just given birth to a baby girl and could not come. Stupid girl, Rita had thought. What kind of person would bring a kid into this world?!

Quentin smiled. He needed reassurance, yet he tried to keep it light, to not irritate the veteran correspondent. "Hey," he said. "Did you hear about the miracle?"

"Hum?" Rita would not allow herself to be friendly.

"Did you hear about the lady here who gave birth to a blue-eyed, red-haired baby when the bomb fell. Some of these local yokels think it's a miracle. Ha! An angel, they say."

Rita's look stopped him cold. He huffed, half turned away. "Shit," he stammered. "You don't have to be so sensitive. I'm not writing the story." His smile was gone and he too was angry. Then with his head cocked, he said, "Oh, I get it. 'Yokels.' Look, none of these people understand English."

In the tent Teck knelt beside Vathana's cot. He held her hand. Samnang hung from his back. Samol sat on Sophan's lap on the cot's end, and Louis stood behind Teck. "Step by step," Teck whispered. His heart was bursting with love for his exhausted wife. "You've taught so many the prayer. I looked at the pagoda. I was so afraid. Every step a prayer. Every step a prayer for a miracle." His face was radiant.

Vathana looked at him. Her eyes closed, opened halfway, closed. The swaddled baby lay in the crook of her arm.

"My father is dead," Teck whispered to her. "We don't know where your father is, when we will see him again. Should we ask my mother to name her?"

Vathana smiled weakly but did not open her eyes. Then she whispered, "no. she is named."

"Eh?" Teck whispered, not hearing her.

"Pech," Vathana said. "pech. pech su livanh." She fell asleep.

There was no option. No words could assuage the feelings, the anger, the hate. Even later when Met Sen said, "Come with me," he could not release it. The clean and pure victory against U.S. imperialism was empty in the absence of a final victory over FANK and Lon Nol. Not simply a victory. Revenge.

Nang ran his pincer index finger down the scab and scar. For two weeks they had carried him north in a hammock hung from shoulder poles. He wouldn't have done that for any of his wounded yotheas but they were doing it for him. The shame, the disgust, further fueled his inner rage, yet there had been no options. He'd walked as soon as he was allowed. The rains came heavy. A porter had guided him by pulling him with a rope. Each day had been a cleansing struggle purifying his hate and vengeance. They stopped north of Skoun where FANK commanders had abandoned their troops on 2 August and the troops had broken and fled and Angkar had had a great victory devouring and evacuating the enclave. Nang touched the scar where it parted his hair above the left eye. He picked the edge of the scab. The rain had softened it and it smeared beneath his fingernails. His left hand fingers followed the scar to his eyebrow. The skin was a glass-smooth lump. Why the shrapnel had not totally blinded him he didn't know. His eye had been damaged yet he was sure it was healing. He closed his right eye to test the left. Yotheas and porters were rising from their rest. Through Nang's left eye they were but blurry green or black oblongs. He closed both eyes, thought he heard the drone of T-28s, shivered. Even with both eyes open he could see Duch's head, see Duch's face staring horrified at Nang's, not because of his, Duch's, own wound, but because of Nang's.

Nang rose. His fingers followed the scar below his eye where it split into two main branches and a dozen interlacing twigs. Puc, Von, Thevy, Ung, Duch were all dead. Rath, Sol and No had control of the remnant of the 91st. Nang didn't know where he was going. Nor why. All he'd been told was "Trust Angkar." The Americans had been legislated out of action yet the offensive had not rolled forward. Indeed, it had sputtered worse than under the bombings. Nang did not know, was never to know, that air strikes had killed perhaps half, perhaps more than half, of the attacking KK yotheas, their conscripted porters and their militia aides. The cessation of bombing had coincided with the destruction of the Northern Zone Army and the crippling of those of the South and Southwestern Zones. Only the Gray Vultures of the Eastern Zone were able to pursue the battle, and they were now smashing FANK's defensive ring about Kompong Cham.

They walked north for another week. Each day new reports reached the column. The yuons had attempted to assassinate the high generals of the Center, not once, not twice, but three times. Each time loyal yotheas had sacrificed their lives protecting the leadership of the Kampuchean revolution. The battle for Kompong Cham soured. Lon Nol had decided, with the relief of Phnom Penh, to commit totally to the salvation of that Mekong River city. On 18 August FANK reinforcements from the heartland reached Kompong Cham. Then FANK's 80th and 50th Brigades caught a poorly commanded, poorly controlled Krahom force in a hammer-and-anvil operation, annihilating most of the yotheas, the stragglers fleeing to take refuge in the university and monastery of Angkor Wat—structures which the Cambodian air force would not bomb. More reinforcements arrived—twenty naval convoys—and Kompong Cham was recaptured by FANK. Seventy percent of the city was in ruins. Still the Center claimed partial victory. The civilian administration had been wiped out and the Khmer Krahom had evacuated twenty to thirty thousand regained people.

North of Kompong Thom, Nang's column crossed paths with the transportation and security companies escorting the Center. The next two hours changed the direction of Nang's life.

"Eh?" Met Reth said quizzically, looking at the line of wounded. "That one you say?" Met Sar's bodyguard had been sent for Nang, sent to bring him to Sar for debriefing and reinspiration. "I don't see him."

"The one with the pink scar through his left eye, there," the porter said.

Met Sar smiled very wide when Nang arrived but after the first moment, Sar did not look at him. "We," Sar lamented, "have suffered greater than any revolutionary army ever! Look at you." Nang shuffled uncomfortably. A moment before he'd arrived he'd imagined Sar would hug him, would hold him and praise him for his hard work. "Two hundred days of bombings," Sar went on. "Two hundred nights without interruption. No other nation has suffered so under the thumb of American imperialism. Only we. And only our superhuman will has enabled us to survive. Aah, look at you. You're still alive, eh? A symbol of defeat! Go. Go away. Perhaps Met Sen has something for you. I won't look at you again."

The sense of abandonment was immediate. Reth led Nang out. Total confusion flooded the boy's mind. Yet immediately he was before Met Sen and Met Sen was hugging him and comforting him.

"You never had a chance," Sen said in his wispy voice, "to loot that capital. Ah, too bad," he said. "Never a chance to play city folk. You will yet. I promise you, Met Nang." Sen looked deeply into Nang's destroyed face. "There are special privileges for a man of your record," he said. "So come with me. Work in security with me, Met Nang of Kampuchea. We are far from finished. So Sar broods about Kompong Cham? So what? He'll get over it and the imperialists and the lackeys will always neak-luong themselves. If you help me, I'll take care of you. Come with me into the secret zone. Security—this is where the true power is."

The next eighteen months for Nang, for Chhuon, for Vathana were extensions of the descending spiral which was dropping Cambodia into the worst horrors of human history.

Throughout the American spring and summer of 1973 revelations by Watergate investigators had accumulated and multiplied. Wiretaps, ordered to plug the leaks which had spilled the news about the secret 1969 Cambodia bombings, were exposed, as were the "plumbers' " break-ins. Each new report spurred bigger headlines and deeper searches. The Nixon administration shelved its dubious policies and plans for Southeast Asia and entrenched for the coming domestic battle.

The Krahom also entrenched, jerking along in sporadic fits of minor offensives, terrorist acts and withdrawals. By the time of the legislated halt of American bombing (15 August 1973), half the Khmer Rouge attacking force had been killed. The Krahom, and FANK too, recoiled from the long campaign. The Krahom Army of the North lay low and licked its wounds much as the NVA had after the 1972 Easter offensive in South Viet Nam. For the rest of the year the Krahom rebuilt and reequipped their battalions, and they stockpiled materiel for the final battle. In addition to their military losses, the Krahom suffered significant political setbacks, both with the population under their control and with their "allies." American intelligence reports concluded:

The most significant development during the past quarter was the increasing disaffection of large segments of the population with KC [Khmer Communist] control. Reports from the countryside in all six KC regions reveal a rather widespread failure of the Communists to enlist the support of the villages under their control, as well as a general inability to recruit desirable persons into their organization. The openness with which the population has voiced its displeasure varies widely including several areas where dissenters have begun to band together and demonstrate publicly, despite a relatively strong KC presence. [*The Situation in Cambodia*, October 1973 (CIA report number 7881/73)]

For the Krahom the situation further deteriorated in November 1973. On the 6th, Communist rank and file troops in Kampong Trach District openly revolted against the local Krahom leadership; in the ensuing firefight Rumdoah soldiers succeeded in stopping Krahom yotheas from forcing the evacuation and relocation of the "liberated" population. Two weeks later in Kampot Province peasants and Rumdoah troops, armed with scythes, machetes and rice knives, drove off a KK force that had come to collectivize and confiscate the local harvest. The villagers were doubly incensed by yothea denunciations of Norodom Sihanouk.

Along the Viet Nam border the NVA continued its massive, unopposed buildup. Hanoi, viewing the exhaustion of the Cambodian factions, both KK and FANK, judged it had gained at least a year along its western front. In secret negotiations with Krahom leaders, the Hanoi Politburo thus agreed to keep its forces out of the Cambodian interior in exchange for a Krahom promise to end the purge against Khmer Viet Minh and Rumdoah cadre. In the enclaves of the interior, Ith Sarin's *Regrets for the Khmer Soul* peaked in popularity. Its descriptions, along with those of a growing number of escapees from the "liberated" zones, of Krahom evacuations, "pure flame" policies, ruthlessness, and even growing Rumdoah totalitarianism, foretold virtually all the horrors that were to come. The Lon Nol regime, believing the book was Communist propaganda, dismissed the revelations. The Krahom leadership, however, was incensed. Security in the liberated areas was tightened. Krahom security chief Met Sen, along with zonal security officers, set out to establish high-level reeducation facilities in the "secret zones" for "students" requiring extensive and long-term classes on how to live in a pure society.

As Nang's face healed, as his hearing partially returned, he was set to work on this expanded security concept. By November Nang had gathered a small core of subordinates; by February 1974 he had his first class, not of soldiers but of security agents. His dream of being a teacher was again fulfilled yet again he found the fulfillment penultimate. By mid-1974 he was itching to be back in battle.

For Chhuon the twentieth anniversary of Cambodian independence from France, 9 November 1973, was a moment of great sadness. Angkar bestowed its blessing upon Phum 117 and all of Khum 4 by forcing the settlement to abandon its nearly harvestable rice and to again relocate on uncleared ground—a mere six miles west. Communization at the new site was raised to a new level—a new alien mentality to the Krahom inverted pyramid of Khmer culture. Angkar Leou, the High Organization, the Party, now was institutionalized not only to yothea trainees but also to the peasantry as the highest abstraction of love and devotion.

In December Neang Thi Sok died of cholera . . . died of Krahom policies which forced unsanitary and starvation conditions upon the population, forced them to renounce their pasts, forcibly removed them from their cultural roots, forced them to exist without modern or even semimodern means to protect themselves from hazards in their environment. In January Chhuon was allowed to return to the old settlement, to dismantle his two-man cocoon, carry it to the new site and rebuild it as a one-man hut. *Chrops*, internal spies, multiplied. Chhuon barely trusted his simplest thoughts to his closest friends, Sichau and Moeung.

In 1973 North Viet Nam added 200,000 replacements to its forces in South Viet Nam and along the Cambodian border. Soviet and Chinese military equipment deliveries reached record levels and continued to increase in 1974.

In Neak Luong Vathana withdrew more and more deeply into herself and her family. The refugees, many who had lived in the camp for three years, who had suffered intermittent harassment or terror at the hands of NVA, VC, FANK and ARVN units, who had been horrified by the errant American bombs that had killed 137 and wounded 268, now had a new fear. Local youth gangs rampaged out of control—uncontrollable because FANK had taken all their fathers and uncles, the traditional authority in the culture, and because the nation's leadership, while ineffective, set an example of corruption and brutality. The refugees came to be afraid of remaining in the camp at night—some even during the day, except to stand in line for rations.

With three children, including the Amerasian Su Livanh, Vathana spent virtually no time with the associations, only a little at the hospital and orphanage. Sophan took over many of her routine duties in the Khsach Sa camp. Kosol, Nem, Doctor Sarin were no longer a part of Vathana's life. Often she dreamed of Phum Sath Din and of the wonderful years of her childhood. Teck came infrequently, his duties with the Auto-Defense forces, the constant improvement of the "last-resort line," keeping him at the front. Daily Vathana trekked to the southern berm to bring him provisions, supporting not just him but also Louis. In all the hardship Teck found himself happier than ever before. He was now a man with a cause, a man with a family to protect.

At the beginning of the dry season in 1974 Madame Pech again offered to have Vathana and the children live with her in Phnom Penh. Constantly Vathana thought of the offer, telling herself, At least we'll be near Aunt Voen, at least we'll be away from the gangs, at least I will not spend every night clutching Captain Sullivan's pistol. Without the weapon Vathana too would have dispersed nightly with the refugees into the swamp. Captain Sullivan's pistol . . . she often thought. Captain Sullivan, not a single word from him since he left Cambodia. Still, Vathana could not bring herself to leave Teck in his need, to move to the city that had been John Sullivan's home.

In January 1974 the Krahom temporarily regained momentum. From dispersed patrols and small unit ambushes they moved to heavy artillery raids. Their main targets were the densely packed refugee camps of Phnom Penh. By March they had killed over a thousand dependants and destroyed more than ten thousand homes and huts. In March FANK rallied and drove the KK from the rocket-launch belt, and for seven months, until the end of the next monsoon season, the capital breathed easier.

The United States continued to assist the Lon Nol government and to supply FANK units. In May Kampot, Oudong and Lovek were recaptured or relieved of siege by American-supported FANK units. Arms and ammunition were delivered by U.S. C-130 cargo planes to Phnom Penh airport and carried forward by armed U.S. helicopter teams. The C-130s were escorted by fighter-bombers that engaged enemy troops under the terms of protective reaction. In addition America continued to send in "special teams" on temporary duty. Senator Alan Cranston, Democrat of California, helped to shape the American public's mood by denouncing this involvement on 15 March 1974. As the head of the Senate Armed Services Committee, he said this ". . . covert and illegal war cannot be condoned by Congress." Southeast Asia has been a "breeding ground . . . of lies, deception and illegal practices long enough."

By June, the spectre of the impeachment of Richard Nixon, for keeping, or ordering to be kept, secret the "Menu" bombings of Cambodia on and since 17 March 1969, had paralyzed U.S. commitments to Southeast Asia. On 16 May the village of Dak

Pek, north of Kontum in South Viet Nam, fell after being battered by seven thousand rounds of NVA artillery. Eleven days
later Tuy Atar fell to the NVA after a thousand-round barrage.
The United States did not respond.

Monitoring the American scene, the high command of the
Krahom met in June 1974 to plan "the final offensive to liberate
all Kampuchea." At this meeting the complete evacuation of
Phnom Penh was formally discussed for the first time. Also
analyzed was the new NVA offensive in South Viet Nam. Encouraged by the stimulation of American internal contradictions and motivated by fears of an NVA victory over Saigon
which would release troops to attack Cambodia, the Center
decided to launch the final battle with the upcoming dry season.

On 9 August 1974 Richard Nixon resigned the presidency.
Nixon's early Cambodian policies and his paranoid attempts to
keep them secret were at the root of the Watergate scandal.
Despite the tremendous progress of Viet Namization, despite
the first signs of the maturing of Cambodia's Auto-Defense Force
and the crippling of the Khmer Krahom, Watergate caused the
final collapse of American will to defend anyone in Southeast
Asia.

At the end of 1974 the U.S. Senate—as North Viet Nam's 7th
and 3B Divisions attacked Phuoc Binh, capital of Phuoc Long
Province, 60 miles north of Saigon; as Krahom armies again
besieged Phnom Penh—voted to reduce military and economic
aid to Cambodia by 47 percent. (Aid to South Viet Nam, which
had been reduced from $2.8 billion in 1973 to $700 million in
1974, was cut to $300 million in 1975.) Hanoi, the Krahom
Center, Moscow and Peking concentrated their attention on
Phuoc Long Province. The ARVN, they all saw, no longer had
the mobility or power of main force units to stage large-scale,
flanking counterattacks to halt or recapture strategic sites. Perhaps more importantly, America's intention had now become
clear. Phuoc Binh, a major provincial capital, fell 6 January
1975. Still the United States did not respond. In Saigon, in
Phnom Penh, in Neak Luong, the mood was one of abandonment, betrayal, hopelessness and gloom.

By the end of January 1975 the NVA had increased its forces
in the Central Highlands of South Viet Nam to five divisions.
This was the staging for the battle of Ban Me Thuot. Throughout Southeast Asia there were scattered spots of panic. At Neak
Luong 350 FANK soldiers deserted (not to the Khmer Krahom
but to back-alley hideouts), placing the onus of defense more
heavily upon the local militia. By mid-February FANK losses
for 1975 stood at 4,260 dead, 10,000 wounded and 1,000 missing.

In addition more than 12,000 dependants had been killed. The Mekong was again cut near Neak Luong and all FANK garrisons downriver were destroyed.

On 10 March at 0200 hours the NVA launched the main attack of its final drive—a mechanized assault led by T-55 tanks and BTR-60 armored personnel carriers—against Ban Me Thuot.

For the Krahom, for Nang, for Vathana, for Chhuon, for all Cambodia, the race for salvation seemed to be a race to win or hold out until after the Communist victory in the neighboring land.

CHAPTER EIGHTEEN
31 March 1975

The shelling stopped. All was quiet. Then an odd noise came out of the mist and smoke and dark. He cocked his head trying to stretch his ear, his hearing. The noise was clear, familiar, yet Teck could not identify it. He pivoted his head, back, forth, back-forth, looking without seeing, searching the line, wondering if others had heard, had identified the source. He placed it in the shroud of yetdark a hundred meters out, a hundred to his right. Perhaps a thousand, perhaps fifty—chir-rick-chrik ... chir-rick-chrik. Not moving, he thought, yet because of the shroud he wasn't sure. Then it stopped.

Behind him Louis slept in quiet agitation as if churning thoughts drove his bodily twitches but his body knew to muffle its sleep noise. A howitzer far behind the line fired. For three months the sounds of war had been constantly upon them; the quiet made him tense. His mind raced. He checked his M-16, his bandoleers of magazines, his gas mask. In January the Communists had started using incapacitating gas fired from B-40 rocket launchers. Equipment delivery had responded. The entire Auto-Defense force, along with FANK's main force units defending Neak Luong, had been inundated with masks, U.S. jungle fatigues and small arms ammunition. Food remained scarce.

Again the howitzer report—seemingly random sporadic outgoing. Beyond Louis was a small lean-to, Teck's squad's headquarters. No one slept there—superstition, unlucky, a magnet attracting artillery. Up and down the last-resort line Krahom mortars, 107mm rockets and rounds from captured 105mm cannons had blasted defender lean-tos to shreds. Radios with drained batteries slept there. On the civilian transistor they'd heard reports of rumors that Lon Nol was willing to abdicate if the Communists assured the government that peace talks would follow.

Teck looked over his shoulder. The low lean-to stood in vague silhouette. Beyond, almost in town, a huge, hazy orange-pink semisphere glowed in the blackness—the continuous military pyre, the unending obsequies of cremation. In three months more than twenty thousand government soldiers had been killed. Teck turned forward. The first graying of night's mantle revealed the shattered tops of two tall palms which marked the bank of the Mekong. The sounds, he thought, had come from there. The sky grayed. A thin white vapor rising from the river spilled over the embankment, crept onto the dry paddies, thinned further and vanished. Teck looked out over the floodplain, down the sentinel line of broken palm trees protecting the riverbank. In the still air not a frond ticked, not a leaf rasped its brother like the rear legs of a cricket. Louis stirred.

In January the Khmer Krahom committed five thousand troops to closing the Mekong below Neak Luong. Using sophisticated Chinese Communist antiship mines, the 1st Eastern Brigade sank twelve freighters. By month's end the Krahom, equipped by Peking—the results of a new agreement with Hanoi—with more arms and ammunition than ever before, controlled both banks of the river along with all major midriver islands. In February FANK's 1st Division received a new commanding general and the previously mauled and demoralized unit regained its lost pride. FANK's 1st took the fight to the Communists. Gradually they enlarged the southern enclave and pushed the front downriver. Throughout the country the Krahom sacrificed the lives of ten thousand yotheas stemming the counterattacks. KK desertions ran higher than ever, and again the Center had to scramble to stave off tactical defeat. FANK's February successes spurred the Auto-Defense militia to greater aggressiveness. For several weeks these soldiers, too, counterassaulted with the newly coordinated armor, infantry and artillery. It was FANK's finest hour, its period of highest leadership. By 31 March, though the defenders had fought hard, the closing of the river and the ensuing unlifted siege ran them dry. Food and certain military supplies, particularly batteries, needed to be scrounged. Communications with Phnom Penh and between units all but ceased. Inside the Neak Luong perimeter, sixty to seventy thousand artillery-battered civilians languished, half starved—the rice airlift to Phnom Penh did not extend to the southern citadel.

"You're still up, eh?" Louis joined Teck on the berm.

"You slept well?" Teck asked, looking at his close friend.

Louis grunted. "Like water splashed in hot oil," he said. "I'm so tired but I don't sleep. Are there provisions?"

"I haven't gone to see," Teck answered. "Maybe there's lemon grass fish with hot chili rice, eh?"

Louis scoffed. "The only hot chili here is between your legs. Look, Brother, I've saved this all year but you must give it to her."

"Eh?"

Louis pulled from his pant-leg pocket a wad of cloth. Slowly he unwrapped it. In the gray air a thin ring shone gold. "When she comes, give it to her. Tell her to get us some better food. I have to have more to eat. All night I dreamed of food."

Louis dropped the ring in Teck's palm. Teck rubbed it with his thumb, feeling its smoothness. He did not speak but only looked at his friend. Louis did not look back but kept his head down. Down the line other defenders were moving. Behind them the pyre glow dissipated into the dawn. Louis mumbled, bitched lowly as he took up his position. Finally Teck said, "You still don't like her, do you?"

"Aa . . . ," Louis sneered.

"Vathana. You're still angry with her."

"Without her I'd have starved."

"No," Teck said quietly. "I mean over the red-haired *phalang*."

"She's your wife. Not mine. I only think of you."

"I know," Teck said. "It's good to have you watch over me. But, Brother, I'm not angry. For me, don't be angry with her." Louis cleared his throat, spit the night's phlegm into the dry dust, did not speak. "Do you know what my littlest imp did yesterday? Or two days ago?"

"What?"

"She saw her brother—"

"Naw. Don't tell me. Not yet. I forgot to tell you. Last night the civilian radio had Khieu Samphan's speech. He said the regime of the seven supertraitors is 'withering in death throes.' He said the Khmer Rouge are only interested in bringing 'that flesh-eating clique' to justice. Everyone else will be pardoned."

"You believe him, eh?"

"I don't care anymore. Again we are losing, eh? Let them win. So what? I just want peace. I want to live in peace."

"You fight well for someone who's losing. Tell *them* to stop attacking. Then we'll have peace."

"They aren't attacking!" Louis looked up. Not a round had fallen since predawn. He looked at Teck. A smile cracked his grouchiness. "Do . . ." he began. It was hard to say because to say it might hex it. Still he could not keep from blurting, "Do you think it's over?"

"Get the radio," Teck said. "Maybe . . ."

"It's dead," Louis interrupted.

"Hey, you're back in," the shopkeep said pleasantly.

"For mail and provisions," John Sullivan answered. He had been living in a rented cabin along Owl Creek in the Badlands of western South Dakota for nearly two years.

"Mrs. Em's got those books you ordered," the man said. "Been there awhile."

Sullivan looked at the round-faced man. "Hum?" he grunted.

"Something about physics, Em said. I think that's what she said." Sullivan's reserve made the man uncomfortable. "Quantum mechanics, right? And organic chemistry."

"Good," John Sullivan said. The flow of his thoughts masked the shopkeep's inquiry. Since the spring of 1973 he had secluded himself; solitarily hunting, fishing, hiking the streams and hills into eastern Wyoming. In the fall of 1973 he'd shot, cleaned and butchered a deer but it had made him queasy, the meat and bones without hide looked too much like human flesh he'd seen without skin. He had not hunted since. In the winter he holed up in the cabin, read the Bible and began studying an advanced mathematics text someone had left behind. He had no radio, no television, no stereo, no phone. He received no mail, no newspapers or magazines. Early in 1974 he had ordered a set of textbooks on chemistry and microbiology and set out to learn, for his own pleasure, what they had to offer. Then came the physics and philosophy of science texts. How beautifully, he saw, each revelation dovetailed with all the others. And where they didn't, he saw, it was not the material but the presenter who erred. All year he fished and trapped and read and tried to formulate for himself, for his own satisfaction, a theory of existence which could encompass all life, all energy, all the absurdities and hurt and all the wonderment and love.

"Well," the shopkeep said, "that's all you ordered. Might take a paper, too. Don't hurt none to know what's goin on in the world."

"Thanks," John Sullivan said. He lugged the cardboard boxes out to his jeep and drove to Mrs. Em's Last Chapter book and gift shop—a store stuffed with Indian moccasins and turquoise bracelets and one case of books for bored travelers passing through in their motorized travel homes. As he parked he glanced at the newspaper in the box on the passenger seat. As if there were no other words on the page a byline jumped at him: Rita Donaldson. Quickly he opened the door. His head jerked back to the box but he did not read the headline. He slammed the canvas wire-frame door. It popped back at him. He closed it more deliberately. He'd been thinking of something he'd read about particle physics, about how everything is on a cyclic continuum of creation, transformation, destruction. Over and over. Had been speculating on the ramifications of the cycle—if one observed the smallest elements, creation and destruction or annihilation did not exist—only transformation, a continual recombination into different patterns. Then Rita Donaldson had stopped him.

Sullivan stood by the side of the jeep. The morning was clear, crisp. After the winter it felt warm. He cupped a hand about his face, drew it down over his beard, down his chin and neck. Then he wiped it on the side of his dungarees. He had not read a newspaper in fifteen months, since he'd visited his folks at Christmas in 1973. At that time he'd said to his Uncle Gus and his sister, Margie, and her new husband, Bob, "All the evidence pointed to this incredible buildup by the North Viet Namese. There was some hard proof but no one wanted to exploit it. Instead, it seemed the whole world was beaming in on Thieu and Lon Nol, and because they had access to it they exploited every bit of corruption and ineptitude they saw."

"Oh cut the bullshit, John," Bob had said forcefully. "We've been reading *The New York Times* while you've been hiding in that cabin. We know you guys bombed those places so bad there's hardly a civilian left. We know what impact the war and America have had on those poor people. How our country's turned Cambodia, especially Cambodia, into a goddamned moonscape!"

"What?!" John had looked at his uncle expecting some support from the World War Two veteran but Gus had his head hung and his eyes on the floor.

"Okay, now." His father had come into the room. "There'll be no more talk of this. It's Christmas. This is no time for politics."

Sullivan walked into Mrs. Em's, purchased his ordered books and left without speaking more than two sentences. In the jeep he glanced at the paper. Then he looked at the window of the Last Chapter. Mrs. Em was peeking at him. Thinks I'm out of it, he thought. He looked back to the paper. He had not even known the date: Monday, 31 March 1975. Sullivan started the jeep, let it idle. The front page was full of stories of battles raging in South Viet Nam and Cambodia. His eyes wouldn't focus. He couldn't read Rita's article. Instead he began one with

a *New York Times* credit: "Western diplomats," the article began, "say that the Lon Nol regime has treated its people so
poorly, it has forfeited the right to govern." Sullivan huffed. He
did not read on. In the middle, just below the fold, there was a
map of Cambodia with five arrows ending in exploding stars.
One star engulfed Neak Luong. Sullivan gritted his teeth, thought,
Boy, did she make a fool of me. She was probably part of the
KR's people's intelligence network. External reconnaissance!
What a jerk I was.

He looked back at Rita Donaldson's article, jumped to the
middle. "When the end comes . . ." His eyes jumped to another
paragraph: ". . . the hatred here runs so deep," she'd written,
"victory and peace may be more brutal than the brutality of
this war." The theory of relativity, he thought, allows one to
experience time and space, life and death, as abstractions.

He put the paper into the grocery box. He would save it, but
he would not, could not, yet, read it.

With her right hand Vathana balanced the small bundle atop
her head. She walked the worn path gingerly, watching for
sharp objects. Quickly she was to the alley and then to the
street which led through Neak Luong. As she walked she tried
not to look, tried to protect herself from a cityscape which
could have been plague-ravaged Europe during the bleakest
period of the Dark Ages, tried not to witness the pleading eyes
of fatalistic beggars, the dull faces of children resigned to lives
of poverty, starvation and war. A maimed soldier sitting splay-
legged in a pocked doorway called to her. Her scant energy
drained. She attempted to not see him, not hear him. Still the
drain. Each shattered building, each burned-out ruin, each tattered lean-to of plastic sucked life from her exhausted body. The
urge to sit, to lean into a doorway, to sleep, to join the thousands of homeless, listless, grabbed her. She fought it, attempted
to shed it.

Earlier, as she and Sophan had set about their separate tasks,
she'd been snared by a spurt of timid eagerness—by hope. "It's
so quiet out there," she'd said to Sophan.

"Yes," Sophan whispered back. "Why have the shells stopped?
What do you think's happening?"

"I don't . . ." Vathana paused. Then her eyes widened. "Clean
the children," she declared. "Dress them in their best clothes."

"Do you think . . ." Sophan's entire face lit. "Oh Sweet Blessed
One, is it over?" Sophan had put a hand to her lips to hide the
words but she could not hide the anticipation which had infected all Neak Luong. "What will they look like?"

Vathana hunched, lowered her voice. "Like us, eh?"

"Yes. Yes, of course. They're Khmer, after all."

"Today," Vathana asked rhetorically, "you're at the hospital? Maybe their radio is working."

Vathana had stepped to the tent corner where all three of her children were playing. She bent, kissed each. A melancholy smile spread across her face. "I must bring your father his clean shirt." She smiled. "Sophan will clean you up. Today you must listen carefully. And"—she tapped a finger into her left palm— "stay clean."

"Ba-ba," Samnang said happily.

Sophan had clutched the five-and-a-half-year-old boy. "He knows, Angel," she'd said. "He's sensitive to things we can't feel. I told you he'd be perfect, eh? In his way." Vathana had smiled a euphoric fearful smile and hugged the three children and Sophan. Then she'd added the shirt to the bundle for Teck and Louis.

Vathana walked around a shell crater. Inside, at the center, she could see a half-buried rocket canister. She picked her way over the debris only to enter the debris ring of the next crater, then the next. By one crater people were picking at the mashed remains of a dog. She turned away, detoured around a pockmarked house. Behind the house she saw a young woman holding a small girl. The infant looked peaceful, angelic, except for one eye slightly opened and her left leg and foot neatly missing.

Vathana stalled. She had to decide to stay, to help, to mourn, or to go on. "Arrange for a funeral," she ordered the dazed young mother. She walked on. It was a snap decision and it haunted her even as she told herself, First I must tend to my husband and to the living.

"There are no KR in sight," Teck told Vathana a few minutes later. He had withdrawn to their rendezvous point, a vacant shack near the crematory.

"Doesn't anyone know?" Vathana said. She'd opened the bundle and given Teck the clean shirt.

"What else do you have?" He unbuttoned his filthy fatigue blouse to remove it.

"These." Vathana removed two bread rolls. "Once," she said, "I would pay four riels. Now, they cost eight hundred. And . . ." She brought out two rice balls wrapped in pages removed from Ith Sarin's book. "Also"—she smiled at Teck—"these." From a shirt pocket she delicately pulled two cigarettes.

"I have something for you, too," Teck said.

"What?" Vathana asked.

From a pant pocket he pulled Louis's cloth. Carefully he

began unwrapping. "Remember when we were married?" he said mischievously. Her eyes flashed at his words. "Remember?" He teased her.

"I remember," she answered.

"It's . . ." He stopped. "This is from Louis for food," he said seriously, "but maybe . . . for a minute"—he held up the thin gold ring—"I could put it on your finger and pretend, like the wedding song, you are still jealous of my hot green chili, because . . . because you love me."

"I am jealous"—Vathana touched his thin chest—"because, like the song, I love you. I shall be jealous of you every day."

"If the nation is to fall," the stocky doctor said to an orderly, "the new nation will need doctors, eh?"

Sophan looked at their backs, looked beyond them into the ward. The hospital had been rebuilt after the 1973 American bomb had hit it, but it was much too small for a city of sixty thousand plus defense force troops during active battle. Each bed was cramped with five, seven, ten patients. Rivers of diarrhea flowed from cots of those so ill they couldn't rise. Clouds of flies swarmed amid aisles packed with family members.

"Then you think it's over, Doctor?" the orderly asked.

"I wouldn't have returned if I didn't think that traitor was about to lose his head," Doctor Sarin Sam Ol answered.

"But surely, now," the orderly retorted, "President Ford will send in troops. As a matter of honor."

"Honor?" Doctor Sarin scoffed bitterly. "In Neak Luong? All the world knows America's shame. My sons . . ." The doctor stopped, turned, stared at Sophan with his good eye.

"Is it over?" she asked weakly. "We've no radio . . ."

"Ha! It was over years ago," Sarin Sam Ol snapped. "My eldest son is dead. By my second son's words, FANK is ready to surrender. My *peou*, in the maquis, now he can come home."

To the Krahom, Preah Vihear was a *svayat* or autonomous region. In the "secret zone" south of that city Nang had prepared his team for the final victory. He was bitter. "A high-level reeducation facility," Met Sen had told him, "to instruct 'students' how to live in a pure society." Banished, he'd thought. Shunted aside just as victory is within our grasp. "Angkar Leou wishes for you to go forward and establish Site 169," he'd been ordered. Expelled, he'd thought. Kept from the rewards of conquest. His bitterness imbued each of his *a-ksae teos*, his "telephone wires," his new soldiers who would use the wire to bind students' hands behind their backs.

Nang stood at the edge of a small clearing. He burped and hot acid seared his throat. In February there had been a secret high-level meeting of the Kampuchean United Revolutionary Front—the Center plus zonal secretaries and delegates from the *dumbon* and *phumpheak* levels and from the *svayats*. Nang had not been invited. He touched his face and the bitterness sizzled in him. He'd received but a verbal briefing. All the sacrifices, he thought. The years in the swamps, the months below the bombs. My face. Every *a-ksae teo* knew. Every one of them had been betrayed with him, abandoned with him, isolated with him. Hate coagulated them into a demonic band.

"We'll need a hundred peasants," Nang said to his aide.

"Yes Met Nang." The young boy's answer snapped.

"This is much too small. Clear it so when I stand here, I can see the Dang Rek cliff without looking through trees."

"Yes Met Nang."

"Have it done in ten days," Nang said. He did not look at the boy-soldier. Met Sar's words, from the messenger, were simple. "Immediately upon victory, all cities will be emptied. Prepare for many new people. Annihilation of class enemies is the highest form of class struggle."

Nang taught the *a-ksae teos* the last line. Met Sen had sent a separate message which Nang did not pass on. "Extermination," he'd said, "is more productive than war. In your facility, you are God."

It was twenty minutes past noon, 1 April 1975. The battle lulls of the previous day had been broken by tremendous artillery barrages during the night. Rita Donaldson crouched with her back to a sandbagged revetment. On her knees was a steno pad. She scribbled furiously. She looked up. The Air Cambodge jet had vanished into the hot dry air. Before her stretched Phnom Penh's Pochentong Airport. The runway was cratered from thousands of rounds of 81mm mortars and 107mm rockets which had impacted in the past two months. At one end was the skeletal wreckage of a DC-8; close by the charred remains of a C-130. Rita lowered her head. The roar and rumble of a departing airlift plane vibrated the pen in her hand. Then that craft too was gone.

"President Lon Nol has left," she wrote. "The head of state and marshal of the army, with his weeping wife and an entourage of 29, has left this war-torn nation en route to Thailand and Indonesia. Assisting the president's wife was Madame Sisowath Thich Soen, an elegant woman who some say acted as the go-between for U.S. embassy officials and the Republic's government—"

Rita stopped to collect her thoughts. She would later rewrite the notes into a cohesive article. Now it was imperative to record her observations. "The president, wearing a dark gray business suit and looking somber, slowly limped from where he had been assisted from the helicopter which had brought him from the Chamcar Mon Palace to this point, to the waiting white jet. Twice he raised his cane, necessary since a stroke partially paralyzed him in 1970, to salute those troops who have been loyal to him for five years."

A C-130 cargo plane, a rice and ammo flight, dove in steep approach and landed. Very quickly a team of Khmer soldiers, directed by U.S. Air Force officers, unloaded the craft. Immediately it roared off.

"For the past 30 days," she wrote, "this city's perimeter defenses have been continuously battered and progressively pushed back. In this atmosphere and at the urging of both American ambassador John Gunther Dean and Lon Nol's own party and general staff, the president has stepped down. According to sources close to Prime Minister Long Boret, this will remove a critical stumbling block to opening negotiations between the Republican regime and the Communist Liberation Front. An aide to Acting President Saukham Khoy believes the new chief executive and his cabinet are acceptable, for talks, to Khmer Rouge officials. Prime Minister Long Boret had, as recently as two days ago, stated that American diplomats here 'are not working for our surrender,' but that the 'provisional departure' of Lon Nol will assist the U.S. embassy here both in convincing Congress to appropriate additional aid and in giving them 'a margin of maneuverability' in their attempts to negotiate a peace settlement between the warring parties. A dissenting opinion, it is rumored, will be forthcoming from ex-prime minister Prince Sisowath Sirik Matak. Further bitterness was expressed by a head government financier who asked not to be identified but who alleges that Lon Nol was given half a million dollars as an incentive to flee."

Another plane approached. The airport rocket warning siren erupted, its penetrating wail sending cargo crews scrambling for cover. "One . . . two . . ." Rita pressed her back harder to the revetment, pulled her knees in tighter. ". . . six, seven . . ." she counted. She forced herself not to look up, put her hands and the steno pad atop her head. By fifteen, she knew, the round would explode, somewhere, on the kilometer-long facility. Concentrating on counting was the only way to avoid terror. Then, beyond the DC-8 carcass, an explosion.

Rita looked up. Filled her lungs with the acrid air. Exhaled.

Wrote. "Statements from the Communist side have been contradictory. In February Khieu Samphan announced that every Cambodian would have an important role in the new nation 'no matter what his past held.' Norodom Sihanouk, later that month, stated in Peking, 'The Khmer people have nothing to fear from a Khmer Rouge victory. There will be no bloodbath. Cambodia will be governed not even by a Communist state but by a Swedish-style kingdom.' " After this note Rita added a parenthesis, "(check exact wording.)" She continued, "However, the Communist hit list of supertraitors has been expanded, according to Khmer Rouge radio, from the original seven to a present figure of twenty-eight. All on the original list, now labeled the "arch-traitors," according to KR radio, will be executed. The added twenty-one, KR radio said, will be dealt with by a people's tribunal after victory. All other 'imperialists, lackeys, stooges, puppets and traitors' will be granted general amnesty 'if they cooperate with the new regime.' Still there is here the fear of harsh reprisals. U.S. embassy officials privately seem miffed at Secretary of State Kissinger's warning of 'serious consequences to American credibility,' without at least equal caution and concern expressed about serious consequences for the Cambodian people."

Again Rita paused. She looked out beyond the airstrip, over the paddies to the forested fields in the west. Because of all the close writing she'd done, her eyes focused slowly and the distant trees remained blurry. It made her feel as if she were aging too quickly and that, along with her fears and prayers for the many Khmers she'd come to respect, made her feel tired. Again she returned to the pad.

"America has had many good people stationed here," she wrote. "Perhaps its best team, including Ambassador Dean and General William Palmer, are here now. (Or is it me?)," she wrote. "(Have I changed? Maybe matured or become wiser or hardened from my years here? Once I had a simple desire to see peace return to this gentle land. Now I suspect peace will be as violent as war. At once I feel there is a moral obligation to push for surrender and let the killings cease . . . and I fear they won't. When I arrived here earlier today I spoke with an airport guard. I asked him how he felt about the president's abandonment. He would not answer. I said, 'There is so much hate now. If the war stops, can the hate be forgotten?' He looked straight at me like I was crazy. 'Western Lady,' he said, 'hate, you know, it lasts thirty generations.')"

Rita clasped her hands over the pad. In the heat she shivered. "America," she wrote, "has had good people in Cambodia, has had decent advisors with the best intentions. Why were all their best plans and policies blocked by Richard Nixon and Henry Kissinger?"

Chhuon could just barely hear the words, and not all of them. They had been given the afternoon off—the first break from the *kara than*, the official worksite, in thirty days. Quietly he weaved palm leaves into the deteriorating fabric of his sleeping cocoon. His knuckles ached as he laced the strands delicately into the pattern, yet he worked steadily. One's body, he'd been thinking, deteriorates exactly like old leaves in the sun. Then he'd seen the three men approaching.

"You are responsible for your own safety." Chhuon overheard the shortest one say. The others did not answer. They drew closer. Chhuon ducked behind his cocoon. He recognized the speaker, Met Soth, chief of Khum 4, and with him Met Vong, enforcer of Phum 117. The third, too, looked familiar. "You understand," Soth said. "Vong and I have secured for you a chance to redeem yourself."

"I will serve and honor Angkar Leou," the third man responded. Chhuon squatted behind his hut. He knew this young man.

"If ever it is reported," Soth warned him, "you have been with a neary, without Angkar's approval . . ."

Chhuon pretended to concentrate on the lashings which held the platform of the cocoon to the corner posts about a meter above the earth. That, Chhuon thought, that is Khieng. At first he, Chhuon, felt a surge of joy at recognizing the boy from his home village. But quickly the joy died. That, he thought, that is Khieng who stripped my Kdeb. That is Khieng who was a yuon militiaman and who humiliated me, my family, the entire village. That hen shit, he thought, brought the yuons, brought the Khmer Rouge, uprooted us. Ha, Chhuon thought. He crept to the other side of the cocoon, stood and watched the yotheas' backs as they strode between the line of huts. Ha, once again we encounter each other, *Met* Khieng. Now it is my turn to prevail.

Teck crouched in his foxhole. The shelling had begun, not along the southern perimeter but to the north along Highway 15, which led to Prey Veng. All night shells had landed at the far garrisons. They'd thought little of the explosions except perhaps that they meant a new assault would begin or—thank the Lord Buddha—that it's up there this time and not on us again.

During the night Louis had chided him, "A clean shirt! For

what? She thinks the war is over? Or are you going to celebrate the New Year before the city falls?"

"Just eat your roll," Teck had answered lightly. "Tomorrow she'll sell the ring and we'll celebrate whatever comes."

"Next is the Hare, eh? I've had enough of the Year of the Tiger."

"It's not been all bad," Teck said. "No matter what they say in the papers, we've fought well, eh?"

"Ha! Tigers fight, Hares flee. I'm going to run away."

Teck laughed. "Maybe so, Louis. But not for another twelve days, eh?"

The shelling of the northern berm and garrisons increased. By morning the rumbling of explosions rolling across the city was nearly continuous. Before them, beyond the FANK outposts, there was no sign of life. Teck had eaten his rice ball but not his roll. Now he gnawed the hard crust, rasping a hole into its side, savoring each crumb, forcing the roll, the fragrance and taste, to last as long as possible. There were new sounds, explosions to the northwest. An attack was coming down the river road from Banam. Rumors spread beneath the second barrage. Still the southern front was quiet.

Louis was restless. "How can you eat that fucking thing so slow?"

"Like this," Teck teased. He continued his gnawing. Out to his right he heard a faint chir-rick-chirk. He jerked his head. There was nothing to be seen. He closed his eyes and he saw an image of his eldest son and he thought how beautiful the little boy had become. He decided he would work with him until he could say "mama" and "papa." When Teck opened his eyes he was smiling. He'd slept for hours. The sun was high. He still clutched his roll. Then, on the southern berm, down the line, a round exploded. Then again and again. He dropped. Louis leaped from the lean-to, slammed down atop him. Artillery rounds burst only meters away. The air filled with smoke, dust. Gravel rained on them. The storm swirled violently above their heads then moved up the line. There were long screams. Loud cries. Soft pleas.

Teck coughed. Rubbed his eyes. Pushed Louis off him. Blood trickled down his face. He touched it. There was no pain. He raised higher and saw the swarm approaching.

"Ooouw," Louis cried. Teck's head snapped to him. His pant hip was bloodsoaked, a ragged flap of flesh opened as he righted himself.

"Here they come!" a sergeant yelled.

They had never been so plain, so open, so clear. FANK rifles cracked. Teck focused on three black-clad soldiers sprinting toward him. He was aware of hundreds beside and behind them. He set his left arm firmly on the berm, lowered his head to the M-16 stock, aimed, fired. A soldier collapsed. Teck adjusted, aimed, fired. A second boy dropped. A third disintegrated in a volley by Teck, Louis and Sahn in the position next to them. Hundreds of bodies lay crumpled. The charge disappeared. The artillery barrages to the north could again be heard.

Teck checked his face. He looked at his shirt. It was blood splattered. Again he felt his face. "Cock shit," Louis growled. "It's mine you idiot."

"What's yours?"

"That blood on you. Look at my hip. Patch me up. I quit."

Teck pushed Louis down flat at the edge of the foxhole. The earth was better than table height but Teck remained in the hole as he scrutinized the wound. Then he laughed. "It isn't so bad. Ha! Now I'll call you Half-Ass."

"You wouldn't laugh if it were you, Brother!" Methodically Teck surface-cleaned and bandaged the wound. "They fight well, too," Louis snarled. "Damn them."

"How are they so accurate with those shells?" Teck said. "Right down the line. They plan, they prepare and they execute. But they are stupid, too. Had they shelled us a little longer . . ." Teck paused. He looked down the line. A dozen teams were carrying bodies toward the crematory; a score were evacuating wounded. Up the line the numbers were higher. ". . . we'd never have been . . ."

Again there was that sound. Now the second bombardment began. Both men huddled at the hole bottom. Shells roared over, burst behind them—without roars burst before them. The earth heaved. Black clods smashed them. Teck watched as Louis rose. He seized his pant leg to pull him down. The air was thick with smoke and dust and sand. Smoke burns Teck's eyes. Louis shakes his leg, pulls fiercely. He is gone. The barrage does not let up. There are screams to the front. Teck inches up. There are thousands of attackers. No defenders are firing. Rounds land behind them. Teck takes his position, aims, fires. A person drops, dies. He fires on semiautomatic, one round per . . . per . . . the shrill screams are not boys, men. They fire on him. Rifle rounds kick in the dirt by his face. He fires. A girl dies. Girls, women, neary continue to charge, to die to his bullets. They have no cover, no concealment. Teck's arms twitch yet his aim is accurate. His chest is tight. Before him there is a leg, an entire leg with a boot, tossed by artillery. The shelling is farther back, now. Corpses are strewn before beside behind him. Rockets roar over on their trajectory to Neak Luong's heart. Immediately Teck knows the enemy artillery has moved up, in for the kill.

The Krahom has committed two entire divisions plus a separate brigade, over ten thousand troops, plus three thousand of Met Nu's ten thousand neary, to the annihilation of Neak Luong's defenses.

"Fall back! Fall back!" Sergeants and officers are manic yet orderly. "Back to the last trenches! Keep firing!"

Teck reloads. He does not move from the foxhole. Twenty rounds, he thinks. Twenty kills. "Back to the 105 battery! We'll target the line!" Target the line, Teck thinks. Target the line. Observe the line. In the maelstrom he pauses to look to his right, down the pickets of palm trees. Chir-rick-chirk, he thinks. Observers . . .

From behind and to his left there is an incredible bang. FANK cannoncockers have lowered the tubes for point-blank fire. Teck slithers out of the hole, scampers like a rat. He steps on a chunk of flesh and falls. He rises, runs on.

Beyond the howitzers Louis has stripped off his uniform and thrown it away. He is sprint-hobbling for town, for a hovel in which to hide.

The assaulting force increases. The southern line is breached. Half of Teck's unit has clumped together, has banded into a smooth withdrawal force, firing and backpedaling. Half of FANK's troops are standing fast at the trench line before the artillery batteries. Everywhere there are soldiers retreating in panic. Teck, Sahn and others fall back to the crematory and take up positions behind an ash heap. The full brunt of the Krahom force is sweeping in upon them. Fear and terror are anticipatory emotions and Teck no longer sees his own existence beyond the exact moment in which he is. He fights without hate, without fear. He is a technician with his M-16, trusting his fate not so much to others or to his God but to ignorance, to a calm present-only mind-set.

In the infirmary tent in the Khsach Sa refugee camp Vathana's mind was running wild and scattered. A few soldiers in nothing but underwear had run in looking for peasant clothes. "It's over," people were saying. "FANK has lost. It's over."

Vathana grabbed a white towel. She cut two nicks in the side then ripped it into three swaths. Where is Teck? she thought. She tied a swath to Samnang's right wrist. Will I ever see Neak Luong again? She tied one to Samol and the third to Su Livanh. There are rumors they make everyone go back to their home village. How will I get there? Oh my beautiful Phum Sath Din with Mama and Papa. Where is Teck? What's happened to our wedding album? Sweet Lord Buddha, what's happening? Why are they still fighting?

"Angel," an old man called to her. "I have just heard . . . on the radio . . ." The man was crying. "Lon Nol, he has fled. He's abdicated. Praise Sweet Buddha. Samdech Euv can now return."

Phnom Penh was frantic. Rita locked her door to add several lines to her story. "Prince Norodom Sihanouk this afternoon on KR radio has called Lon Nol's successor, Saukham Khoy, 'a war criminal and an executioner.' The head of the government-in-exile further stated, 'I proclaim openly . . . that on no account, under no circumstances . . . will the Cambodian resistance agree to be reconciled with the traitors . . . [We] will always fight . . . in the spirit of no retreat or compromise . . .'

"In other developments, along the southern front there are reports that captured towns are being ravaged by Khmer Rouge 'slaves' and that everything salvageable, from rice to automobiles, is being loaded into boats with Viet Namese crews and is being shipped east."

Rita sat. The excitement of the impending collapse invigorated her professionally, yet personally she felt spent. She could no longer feel disgust at the Republican government, at FANK corruption. Now she felt pity and fear for them. Yet she could not write that. If America felt pity or fear for the new regime, President Ford might attempt a last-minute life-saving maneuver. To Rita, nothing, *nothing*, could possibly be worse.

The river was low. He could see the river, smell it, almost step in it. Teck, Sahn and dozens of others had pulled back to the southernmost neighborhoods of the city. Teck hid amid the stilts of an old house. Others were tucked into doorways or behind courtyard walls of homes and shops on the landward side of Main Street. On the levee a small battered Ami 6 Citroën lay on its side. Near it a military deuce and a half truck billowed smoke and shot flames into the tormented postnoon sky. Still they came.

Behind the withdrawing troops, artillery rounds from captured 105s were blasting chunks out of Neak Luong's already scarred facade. Teck aimed, fired, watched an invader drop, then crept back a few more meters into the dim light beneath the house. What if they come for me? he thought. I can go there, then to that post, then that hole. He shot another attacker. The din of small arms rose, fell, never ceased. Teck saw Sahn firing his M-79 grenade launcher, lobbing rounds over the burning truck. The enemy charge had been fanatical. Every inch was paved with dead and dying. Now they came more methodically, insidiously. Teck fired an entire magazine. Retreated. Up the street he could see people, city people, tearing posters of Lon Nol from the walls of the few concrete structures. FANK, the Auto-Defense force, no longer had command, control, communications, yet the soldiers fought hard, fought house to house, stilt to stilt. The Communists, FANK command or not, were their hated enemy. KK rifles were killing them. KK artillery was reducing their city to a trash heap.

Teck dashed the short distance from beneath one house to beneath the next. A wave of frustration washed through him. He could not stop them. He knelt and pressed a piling. Tears flooded his eyes. He raised his M-16, aimed but did not fire. He looked townward. Soldiers, many soldiers, were stripping, throwing away their uniforms, their weapons. Beneath a shattered cart he saw Sahn, saw him sitting, staring at him, his, Sahn's, hands on his abdomen, his, Sahn's, intestines squirming out between the fingers.

Teck turned forward. He fired. He fired again and again and again and he cried as he fired. He shot another, thinking, One more down. If I can kill one more, kill one more, we could still win. If I could kill them all, we could . . .

In town the street blossomed with white rag flags. "Lon Nol is gone!" Teck heard the shouts. "Lon Nol has fled the country!" He heard but he did not believe he could hear those voices, thus he could not have heard the words. Lon Nol fled! The thought sunk in, jarred him. He, Teck, had not fled! He raised his rifle, but except for the crackling of house fires, all about him was now still.

Emptiness engulfed him. He could not move. In the shadow of the stilt house he could see the battlefield, could feel the desolate spirits swirling, could sense the 2,000 ex-KK and the 2,600 ex-FANK, Khmer souls, weeping at the stupidity of their passions which had embroiled them and delivered them to untimely enlightenment.

Now the street was empty. Now he saw his comrades, milling, aimless, wrapped in white sheets, awaiting orders. He remained still. An urge to join them infected him. Then an urge to flee grasped him. Momentarily his leg muscles tightened. The urges dissipated. His legs lay limp. A thought of Vathana, the children, sped across his mind. He thought to lean forward, to rise, but a flash image and an aversion to seeing her, them, as he'd seen Sahn froze him. Then he heard the calls. *"Cheyo yotheas! Cheyo yotheas!"* Peace! Peace, brother soldiers! A few men from the milling undressed came forth. They waved a white sheet on a bamboo pole. "Peace!"

Teck lay his M-16 at his feet. He thought to throw it into the river but he didn't have the strength. His jaw quivered. He tried to stop it, tried to grind his teeth but he could not. He was covered with dirt, grease, filth. His good shirt was shredded. His face squeezed uncontrollably and again he cried. Then he saw them, saw not the charging black-clad horde but saw two files of silent little boys dressed in Chinese Communist green fatigues and Mao caps. They did not smile, did not speak. Before and behind each column was a black-uniformed leader but between all were little boys with assault rifles and rocket grenade launchers which looked comically too large for them. How? Teck thought. Two platoons passed softly. Then came two platoons of girls. Small, dark, resolute, perhaps frightened. Townward the boys dispersed, took up positions at intersections and alleyways. Undressed men called to them. They did not respond. Townspeople threw flowers, brought them fruit. Old women tried to give them coins. Precious hoarded hopes and belongings poured forth and showered the conquering, liberating army. More platoons passed. Teck could not understand. How? How did they beat . . . Then came the trucks, the cars, the guns, the black-uniformed troops he'd fought inch by inch all day, fought for months. His tears stopped. Now he understood. The first platoons were the expendable, the chaff, sent in to emotionally disarm the people, to physically disarm willing government soldiers who saw them and believed they had nothing to fear. In the best cars were gray-uniformed officers who directed the metastasizing of Neak Luong.

Teck's ears opened. His senses let go of his self and picked up the in-sweeping force. "Put out white flags," a lead yothea shouted. "It is peace. Peace!" He fired his carbine into the air. "Peace!" he screamed angrily. A townsman waddled from an alley. On his shoulder was a sack of rice. "Hey! Brother! What have you?" The man stopped, turned. Yotheas surrounded him. The man tried to backstep. "Please, Brother. Don't be afraid. We are patriots, eh?" The soldiers jostled the man. "This"—the one with the angry voice shouted, grabbed the sack—"Angkar Leou wishes to borrow. In a day, maybe two, you'll get it back." The yotheas laughed. The man fled. The rice sack was tossed onto the roof of a commandeered car.

Teck was now taut. He rolled to his side, crouched on hands and feet, peered out. In his vision was his rifle. Carry it or abandon it? He crept deeper into the stilt forest, without the weapon, crept upriver, townward, toward the "unliberated" neighborhood of the northwest quadrant where Communist mortars were now blasting the pagoda and FANK resisters were still killing vanguard yotheas.

Everything was chaos. There were *yotheas* in the wards. Yotheas screaming from the operating room. "I said," Doctor Sarin Sam Ol shouted, "come in! Come in! You do not have to behave such!"

"We enter Neak Luong as conquerors!" The KK officer's voice was shrill.

"No. No," the doctor yelled, not authoritatively, only loudly, trying to be heard over the massive turmoil. "You don't understand! I have just returned from France. I've come to help you."

"You are a traitor," the officer shrieked. To his bug-eyed yotheas he ordered, "Get them out! Out!"

"They can't be moved." Sophan stamped forward.

The officer shoved her. Sarin Sam Ol intervened. "Understand," he shouted emphatically, "I came back to greet you! To cheer your great victory."

Around them yotheas were screaming at patients, pushing the ambulatory, the families, out of the wards, out of the corridors, out of the hospital. Broken men limped, wives pushed hospital beds with IV drips of saline still flowing into the arms of their husbands.

The first calls had been milder. "Brothers, Sisters, Mothers, Fathers, you must leave at once. The Americans are about to bomb again. Go at once." Only a few moved. The hospital had become their home, their refuge camp built about the base of loved ones' beds. "At once! Evacuate at once! Leave everything and run!" Many had gone, but many of the patients were amputees or severely wounded or acutely ill and they and their families had not budged. Then the yotheas began shoving and clubbing and screaming more harshly than any of the patients had ever heard. "Get out or else!"

"Stop this!" Sarin Sam Ol shouted. He grabbed the officer's arm. In the nearly vacant ward yotheas grabbed decrepit bodies, ripped them from their beds, piled them like trash in a heap at floor center. "Stop it!" Doctor Sarin ordered.

"Stop it!" Sophan barged up to the officer.

"What are you doing?" Sarin's one good eye protruded menacingly. He slapped at the officer like an angry child slaps an adult. Now yotheas were clubbing the bodies in the heap, stabbing those who'd not been tossed.

From the street came the blare of a truck-mounted public

address system. The voice was soft and lyrical and melodious and its beauty engulfed the fleeing who had not seen the executions. "The Father," Norodom Sihanouk's taped voice beseeched them, "wishes you to support the liberation soldiers. They free you from the bonds of American imperialism and from Lon Nol, the dog of the Americans. You will be safe. Your Father will be back."

Khmer believed him. Khmer trusted him. He was the beloved prince, Samdech Euv. He promised the war weary peace and security.

Sophan was dumbstruck. Sarin was livid. He leaped from the officer to the executioners. They laughed as he grappled with a small lad. Then the officer pulled his pistol and shot the doctor in the back. Immediately Sophan jumped on the officer. She was not childlike. She smashed him to the floor. The pistol clattered, slid to a bed. Her attack was so unexpected the yotheas burst into giggles. With her pudgy thumbs she gouged the officer's eyes, tearing both corneas. His arms jerked up but he could not see. Sophan grasped her fists together, smashed them down on his face. Again and again. Yotheas reeled in convulsions of glee—an old lady was beating the cadreman! Then Sophan rose, turned, looking not like an old woman but like a mythological monster about to breathe fire. The yotheas chuckled nervously, backed off, formed a U, their clubs and knives ready. Sophan roared. "GET OUT!" The boys jumped. One dropped his club and fled. Then one attacked, bludgeoned her. She fell and the rest beat her to death.

"We're going to see Sihanouk," one soldier told Teck. The firefight at the pagoda had abated, the officers in charge had surrendered or been killed. Teck had been too late, thought of himself as too late and cried because he'd not been able to tell them what was happening behind the advancing facade. "They think there are some Americans hiding in the city with a bomber beacon. So right now we all have to go so they can search the city."

From the roving speaker truck came the voice of Major Rin of the Gray Vultures. "Only political criminals will be tried . . ." The loudspeaker was focused on the surrendered garrison troops who had fought so bravely about the pagoda. "Angkar," Rin continued, "will need administrators during this period of transition. All government officials and all military officers must report immediately to the Office of the Mayor of Neak Luong. Victory to the Revolution!"

"We should help them, eh, Brother?" Teck looked at the FANK

soldier who'd told him of Sihanouk and the hiding Americans. He wanted to shake his head but he was too exhausted to respond. Like most of the others, Teck had shed his uniform. Those still clothed were now told to rid themselves of the vile material. "You were an officer, eh?" the soldier asked.

"Once," Teck mumbled. "The Khsach Sa camp, it's been liberated?"

"Maybe," the soldier said. "Maybe leveled in the fighting, eh?" Teck's heart dropped lower. More announcements came from the speakers. The captured soldiers began to separate by ranks. "Officers there." The man who'd talked with Teck nudged him toward the smaller group. Down the street yotheas were pulling furniture from the apartment building and piling it against the wall. Some shot the refrigerators. Others burned cars. A few raced, crashed commandeered motorbikes. Cooking pans and transistor radios were confiscated and tied to backpacks and web gear. Anyone protesting was forced into the alleys. Fires burned in every direction.

"Parlez-vous français?" a Krahom officer asked a senior-looking underweared prisoner. *"Oui,"* the man answered. He was hustled away.

Teck glanced back at the soldier who'd nudged him. There was no place to go. Nothing else to do. He stepped slowly to a group of lieutenants. His feet dragged, his mind felt like wet muck. Rumors, opinions, flowed subtly all about him. "Siem Reap has fallen, too." "They're pulling six thousand from here. Going to use them on Phnom Penh." "Those bastards deserve it." "They've already set up street committees to monitor security. We should have surrendered months ago." "Listen to that. Listen! That *is* Samdech Euv!"

Teck's group was trotted barefoot down the main street to the government building. ". . . There will be a general amnesty . . ." Sihanouk's voice surrounded them. ". . . All government employees, leaders and soldiers, if they surrender unconditionally to the glorious liberation forces, will be granted amnesty . . ."

Inside, one by one. "You are . . ."

"Pech Chieu Teck."

The Krahom major laughed. "Pech Chieu Teck, eh?"

"Yes."

"Son of Sisowath Thich Soen?"

"Yes." A smile flicked to Teck's face. To be recognized, he thought, by a major, that's something. The smile sagged in the melancholy of his fatigue and bereavement. Cambodia was dead.

"You are a very corrupt supply officer, eh?"

"Brother." Teck bowed his head. "I . . ."

Met Rin interrupted. "When did you come from Phnom Penh?"

"That's what I must tell you," Teck said. "I am surprised you know me, but you are right. Once I was with supply, in the capital. But I was not meant to be corrupt. I was very young, you know. The corruption sickened me so I quit . . . that's maybe two years. Now I am just a corporal in the Auto-Defense."

"Just a corporal, eh?" Major Rin said pleasantly. "A bourgeois corporal, eh?"

"For that, Brother," Teck answered, "I am very sorry. You know, I admire what you have done for our country. The war is over, eh? It is a great burden lifted from our backs."

"Ha!" Rin chuckled behind closed lips. "Corporal Pech, you could turn white to black."

"Truly, Brother," Teck answered calmly. "I want only to help the nation, to join the entire population in reconstructing our country."

"You shall." Rin smiled. To the guards in the office Rin nodded. They grabbed Teck's elbows.

Teck jerked. "Now what?!" he demanded.

Rin smiled pleasantly. "Now," he said, "you will help build the country."

Teck froze. He stared Rin in the eyes and he sensed a tremendous shallowness. "You are not Khmer after all, eh?" Teck shook his head. The guards grabbed him again. Sadly Teck muttered, "You are only Communists."

Behind the mayor's office the executioners laughed. "Another one," one said, "who's spit on his own chest."

Night descended upon the Khsach Sa camp. Many people had come, run through, vanished. A hospital worker had pulled Vathana away from her children. "Your sister, Sophan, they killed her. You must flee."

Vathana had stared blankly, at once convinced and disbelieving. "I will wait for my husband."

"Go now, Angel." The worker sped on.

An old association friend had come. "Angel, you worked with the poet."

"Yes, everyone knows."

"He was Viet Minh. They're killing all the Viet Minh."

"I'm not Viet Minh."

"They'll kill you anyway. Go quickly."

"Teck will come."

All afternoon they had heard the fighting and withstood the flow of those deserting and those fleeing the forward line of the Krahom. Late in the afternoon when the sounds of battle slowed, a few Krahom advance soldiers came and told them to remain where they were until they were called. That began the refugee camp evacuation. Then came dusk and the flames leaping into the dimming sky as the pagoda and orphanage were consumed. Vathana prayed and clutched her children and prayed and collected their few belongings and rolled them into a bundle and prayed again. She prayed to Buddha, she prayed to the spirit of the sky, she prayed to Norodom Sihanouk. "You are such a gentle king." Vathana's lips moved but she made no sound. "I love you very much. Bring us peace. I miss you very much. Bring us peace."

Then came a naked soldier. He ran into the tent. He ran to her corner, blubbered, "If you cry, they shoot you." Vathana rose, grasped an old krama to give to the young man. He took no note. "Pech Chieu Teck," he reported. "I saw him. They ate his liver."

CAMBODIA:
Factions, Influences and Military Disposition

HISTORICAL SUMMATION
Part 4 (1974–1978)

Prepared for
The Washington News-Times
J. L. Sullivan

April 1985

The storm and tsunami set off five years earlier by the shifting of international plates did not end with the fall of the three Southeast Asian capitals to Communist regimes. Aftershocks of mass evacuations, concentration camps, bloodbaths, starvation, waves of forced migration and murder, and continuous attempts at cultural extermination continued to batter the peoples of Cambodia, Viet Nam and Laos. In the West, political and social repercussions rumbled through America. And the war, wars, fighting, did not end! Not only did battles continue to be fought within each nation, but almost immediately fighting erupted between Democratic Kampuchea and the Socialist Republic of Viet Nam.

Having won the spoils of war, one must ask, *why* did the new regimes pursue policies which led to more internal and external conflict and killing? Why did the Communists of both Viet Nam and Kampuchea strive to eliminate some or all cultural memory? What drove the victors?

Also, how important was, is, the end—the final collapse or final victory, depending on one's perspective? Of course it is important as a historic event, as a human tragedy or human triumph—but is the event itself important in terms of understanding the event itself?

It is not in the scope of this report to recount all the political chatter, the attempts to negotiate "controlled solutions," the verbal ruses; nor can all the battles and maneuvers that led to the fall ("liberation") of Phnom Penh, Saigon and Vientiane be detailed. Yet, to understand the impact on the Cambodian people, it is essential to reconstruct at least a skeleton of that time.

A SOURCE OF AMERICAN MISUNDERSTANDING

Conclusions about the final collapse, often based on media reports, have tended to be simplistic and shallow. To those who believed deeply that American involvement was wrong, illegal and/or immoral, Saigon and Phnom Penh fell because the U.S.-backed regimes were corrupt and had the backing of neither their people nor their armies. The falls signaled the end of a long and bitter American mistake. To staunch supporters of American efforts to stop the Communists, those Southeast Asian capitals fell because the United States, through diplomatic sleight of hand, and beneath a veil of "peace with honor," "decent interval," and "legislative mandate," quit and abandoned Viet Nam and Cambodia by drastically reducing military aid, by effectively pulling the rug from under its friends.

Generally, Western press coverage of the events of that time, and reviews and reports of those events in the ensuing years, have focused, like a coroner's conclusions, on the final outcome, on the last four months, without analyzing the events of 1973 and 1974. For example, in the 641-day period from 1 March 1973 (after the Paris peace agreement was signed) to 1 December 1974 (before the final offensives began), the three major U.S. television networks aired 785 news stories relating to Southeast Asia—an average of less than three items each per week. Of those items, 219 related to the fighting in or bombing of Cambodia. By contrast, the networks broadcast 645 news stories in the 61-day period beginning 1 March 1975 (when Saigon's and Phnom Penh's collapse seemed certain)—an average of twenty-five items each per week. Newspaper and news magazine coverage followed similar patterns. Among the numerous accounts of the falls, there are a few good ones. *The Fall of the South*, part of the Boston Publishing Company series *The Vietnam Experience*, presents a balanced assessment.

THE FALL OF PHNOM PENH AND SAIGON

On the evening of 1 April 1975 the enclave of Neak Luong, swollen to a quarter-million people by refugees and FANK soldiers, fell to Krahom yotheas. The fighting had been intense and the city smoldered for days. The fall of Neak Luong released 5,000 Communist soldiers with six newly captured 105mm howitzers to join the assault on the capital.

During the next sixteen days, the Krahom armies tightened the noose strangling Phnom Penh. Using tens of thousand of rounds of artillery, the Communists concentrated their fire both on civilian concentrations, including the sprawling refugee camps, and on FANK garrisons. American efforts to effect an orderly surrender and transfer of power were scoffed at by both government-in-exile leader Norodom Sihanouk and the chiefs of the Kampuchean Communist Party (KCP), Khieu Samphan, Ieng Sary and Pol Pot. With military victory imminent they had no reason to negotiate. Of major importance to them, however, was capturing Phnom Penh, and thus Cambodia, before North Viet Nam could capture Saigon and South Viet Nam. As we have seen, the leadership of the KCP was, and had been for many years, fearful of Hanoi's hegemony. KCP motivation in 1975 had not changed drastically from 1973 when the Krahom attempted to withstand American bombing in order to topple Phnom Penh before the ramifications of the Paris peace agreement allowed the NVA to recommence attacks on Khmer territory; it had not changed from 1971 when yotheas attacked behind NVA lines during Chenla II in an attempt to keep Hanoi from winning in Cambodia; indeed, it was the same motivation which sent Solath Sar (Pol Pot) to Peking in the early 1960s to attempt to establish an independent Khmer revolution with a separate sponsor and supply source; and it was the same impetus from 1954 when the KCP saw the Geneva Agreements as a sellout of the Khmer insurgency.

At 0500 hours, 11 April 1975 (Phnom Penh time), American Ambassador John Gunther Dean received permission from President Gerald Ford to commence Operation Eagle Pull—the evacuation of American embassy personnel and dependants from Cambodia. In slightly more than two hours the next morning, 82 Americans, 159 Khmer and 35 people of other nationalities were whisked via helicopter to U.S. ships in the Gulf of Thailand. Krahom soldiers marched into Phnom Penh five days later. America's direct involvement with Cambodian affairs had ceased.

Saigon's fall was perhaps more dramatic and more tragic, for the resistance to that fall, though bungled, was more heroic. For years we have been told Saigon fell with only limited resistance. Perhaps this impression lingers because there were TV cameras in Saigon but none west of Ban Me Thuot, outside Hue, in the Mekong Delta, or at Xuan Loc, with the actual fighting. This excerpt from *The Fall of the South* reflects the usual view:

Throughout the city [Saigon] isolated groups of government soldiers and civilians fired on the advancing [NVA tank-led] columns. Barely eliciting a response from the victorious army, these acts of resistance were largely futile. For the most part, the North Vietnamese marched easily into the city.

It was the lesser-known political and military events of 1973 and 1974 which established the conditions for the fall of Saigon and for the way in which that fall was perceived. Since the Easter Offensive of 1972, South Viet Nam's Airborne and Marine Divisions, Saigon's only strategic reserve—that is, the only divisions the ARVN command could call upon to blunt new offensives—were tied down in I Corps below the DMZ. Throughout 1973 the NVA remanned, resupplied and expanded its trail and sanctuary system unhindered by U.S. bombing. The expanded trail system included not only the old network in Laos and Cambodia but the new Truong Son Corridor crossing the DMZ and descending through the Khe Sanh plain and the A Shau Valley, past the triborder area, Duc Co, Dak To, the Ia Drang Valley, Duc Lap, Bu Prang and on south, west of Song Be City (Phuoc Binh) to Loc Ninh. Allowing the establishment of this new corridor, which enabled the NVA to have quick and extensive mobility along the western edge of government-controlled territory, would prove to be the fatal pathogen which led to the death of South Viet Nam. This corridor covered the exact physical area on which so many American-NVA battles were fought, areas which often, even as those battles were being waged, were described by American antiwar legislators as useless ground (for example, Hamburger Hill).

By June 1973 the NVA had recovered sufficiently to strike in the Central Highlands. The NVA 10th Division, led by the NVA 297th Tank Battalion and supported by the NVA 40th Artillery Regiment (130mm howitzers), assaulted at Polei Krong near Kontum. South Viet Namese counterattacks were so strong that two regiments of the NVA's 10th Division were rendered combat ineffective. Again in August and September the NVA attacked in the highlands, this time the NVA 320th Division near Plei Ku. Again the ARVN was victorious although victory took longer. In October 1973 NVA Provisional Division 95 attacked farther south. The ARVN reacted well, shifting forces to counter the thrust. By the end of the year, the South had again stopped the North.

These battles illustrate several major points. The NVA could mass forces and attain numerical superiority almost at will, but these engagements, and indeed all NVA assaults from the cease-fire to early 1974, demonstrated the growing ability of the South's Regional and Popular Forces to slow main force NVA attacks. The engagements also demonstrated the ability of, and the necessity for, mobile ARVN reaction forces to turn the tide of battle once the engagements commenced. At the same time these battles exposed serious weakness in the NVA command. As Captain Bill Betson, an instructor at the United States Military Academy, has noted, NVA "generalship does not match that of the South." He further explains, however, that these battles show the "rifle platoon superiority of the North Viet Namese Army."

At this point major changes occurred among the backers of the two sides. The U.S. 1973-74 war budget for South Viet Nam was 4 percent of its 1969 level. The 1974-75 funding was only 43 percent of what the U.S. Defense Attaché Office had requested. Adjusted for inflation, this sum equaled approximately 1 percent of the 1969 allocation. By contrast, Soviet and Chinese aid to the NVA, which had been reduced in response to the apparent Northern defeat in 1972, increased by 50 percent after the peace agreement was signed, reaching a level 10 percent higher than the previous high of 1971. In 1974, support for the NVA quadrupled, reaching 440 percent of the 1971 high.

The reduced aid to ARVN caused the retirement of 224 military aircraft, including 61 fighter-bombers, 36 of 46 Spooky gunships (C-47s or C-119s) and 50 percent of the South's C-130 air transport cargo planes. In addition, 4,000 tanks, APCs and trucks were immobilized because of a lack of spare parts. Beyond this, although the South had the manpower to create a new strategic reserve division (reaction force), under reduced U.S. aid levels, the ARVN did not have the money to equip this unit with artillery, transportation and communication equipment. All this came to mean reduced ARVN mobility (helicopter repair and maintenance was poor—during the battle of Ban Me Thuot, 13 of 14 CH-53s were grounded within three days) against a tremendously expanded NVA force with vastly increased, motorized mobility.

Before the final assault began in 1975 the NVA would have 370,000 troops in the South—200,000 seasoned combatants, 100,000 support soldiers and an additional force of seven newly deployed divisions. The NVA also had 600 to 700 Soviet tanks—a two-to-one advantage over the ARVN—400 130mm howitzers, 200 large-caliber antiaircraft guns and numerous batteries of SAM-7 surface-to-air missiles (which effectively negated RVNAF air power).

In spite of this lopsided advantage, or perhaps in ignorance of it, many commentators have viewed the effect of lowered American support as chiefly psychological—a fatalism, not unlike that of FANK, caused by ever-decreasing American commitments in the face of ever-increasing Russian and Chinese support to the NVA. Nineteen seventy-four was the bloodiest year of that long war in South Viet Nam. Still the ARVN fought well when attacked. Not until January 1975 did the NVA capture a provincial capital. On 6 January, Phuoc Binh (Song Be City) fell to the NVA. Two significant points must be noted: (1) the ARVN no longer had the reserve forces to flank or to counter NVA movement, and (2) there was no American reaction to the fall of a major South Viet Namese population center. The NVA now became certain that the United States would not, in any way, reenter the war.

In March, the ARVN in the Central Highlands, anticipating a major assault, deployed its forces around the northern highland towns of Plei Ku and Kontum. The attack, a five-division mechanized assault, hit Ban Me Thuot far to the south. The ARVN was unable to react and reinforce. Ban Me Thuot's five battalions held out against 24 NVA battalions for a week. This was followed by preposterous Saigon-ordered withdrawals and a series of other tactical and strategic blunders. By the end of March, six of South Viet Nam's thirteen divisions had been destroyed. Panic in the northern military regions multiplied these errors. Some major centers evacuated even before the NVA approached. Even had President Thieu been a tactical genius and a great leader, it is doubtful that seven ARVN divisions could have held out against 25 well-equipped NVA divisions for any great length of time. The mid-April 13-day battle of Xuan Loc, during which the ARVN 18th Division not only stalled but severely damaged three NVA divisions, was the last major heroic stand of the South Viet Namese army. Although unseen and unnoted in the West, fighting continued in numerous locations for many months. Saigon fell on 30 April 1975.

THE IMPLEMENTATION OF COMMUNISM IN DEMOCRATIC KAMPUCHEA

The Khmer Krahom victory of 17 April 1975 ushered in a new age, one the Khmer call *peal chur chat,* a sour and bitter time. One thing it did not bring was peace.

Phnom Penh's nearly three million inhabitants were herded from the capital in coerced chaos beginning only hours after Khmer Krahom soldiers entered the city. Battambang (population, 120,000) was similarly evacuated the next day. Western reporters and editors, some who had ignored or downplayed earlier reports of Communist atrocities, expressed public shock. Banner headlines, such as "REDS BEHEAD FORMER CAMBODIAN LEADERS" (from the Los Angeles *Herald Examiner*), appeared as early as 19 April. By the 23rd the victorious Khmer Communists had emptied most of Cambodia's medium-sized to small cities (Pailin, Kompong Chhnang, Pursat and others) and many of the nation's towns, villages and hamlets. Surprisingly, the southeastern region about Neak Luong, which had fallen more than three weeks earlier, was one of the last areas to be subjected to evacuation. Throughout the country evacuations were swift and *always* termed temporary. Frightened people, told that "the Americans are going to bomb" (Communist officials moved into Phnom Penh almost immediately, knowing no bombs were coming) and expecting to return home within a day or two, took few belongings. Soon, escapees later reported, many people were out of food and at the mercy of the Communists. Because they had to rely on the soldiers for basic subsistence, they obeyed orders. Of first priority to the Communists, and thus among the first orders issued to the evacuees, was the collecting of personal data on individuals and families. Each person was "requested" to write his or her autobiography, including family relations, occupation and education. The KK ruse was to tell people that the new regime needed them to help rebuild the country. Within weeks, sometimes days, this hoax was exposed. The new regime wished only to identify "enemies" of the new state.

Some reports of bloodbaths seeped across the closed border into Thailand. Within a month of Phnom Penh's fall, 7,000 refugees reached Thai soil; 300 more were shot and killed at the border by KK yotheas. In late April came unconfirmed reports of the methodical killing of FANK soldiers and families on a platform at Mongkol Borei. On 8 May the *Los Angeles Times* reported under the headline "REDS 'PURIFYING' CAMBODIA":

> The Red Khmer forces which took over the country on April 17 had long ago prepared a plan to move millions of inhabitants into liberated zones where they would be instilled with the spirit of service to the revolution.
>
> And as the revolution started from zero, so will the people of Cambodia.

The 12 May 1975 issue of *Newsweek* reported that all the officers of the old army, down to second lieutenant, were being executed. *Newsweek* said that thousands had already been killed and that the figure might reach into the tens of thousands. By June, while KK units attacked Viet Nam's Mekong Delta with the announced intent of exterminating the Viet Namese and annexing "lost" territory, there were unconfirmed reports (flatly denied by several prominent journalists) that 3.5 million city dwellers and half a million peasants had been "deported" in the forced migration; that 300,000 had died in the first month; that at least 8,000 corpses, and perhaps up to ten times that, lay along Highway 6 north of Phnom Penh; and that there, too, stood a forest of 200 heads on stakes.

In August, new evacuations and executions, "forced" by Viet Namese counterattacks following KK June and July raids into the Mekong Delta, were ordered by the Center. At the time of Phnom Penh's fall, Ieng Sary (deputy premier for foreign affairs and number-two man in the KCP) said the Krahom army had been charged with "driving out the Viet Namese who had been [in the border area] throughout the war." The NVA (now PAVN, the People's Army of Viet Nam) had, even after Saigon's fall, refused to withdraw. Battles flared from the triborder area southward through Ratanakiri, Mondolkiri and the Fish-hook to the disputed offshore islands. Krahom leaders, paranoid about the Viet Namese counterattacks, ordered all cadre of all divisions who were trained in Viet Nam (or by Viet Namese—that is, "had the wrong background") arrested and killed. In April there had been 14,000 members of the Kampuchean Communist Party (KCP) and approximately 68,000 yotheas. In May, Party membership was closed. By August the inner-Party and inner-military political purge was under way, and General Pol Pot had ordered the establishment of a wide no-man's-land along the entire length of the border. (This was why, when U.S. Marines attempted to assault the sparsely inhabited island to free the crew of the seized U.S. freighter *Mayaguez*, they were met by a large, deeply entrenched, heavily armed Krahom force. The U.S. suffered 38 killed. General Pol Pot and the Center used the *Mayaguez* raid as "proof" of U.S. designs on Kampuchea and for two years beat the drums of imperialistic adventurism. This, according to refugee reports, was used to justify the purging of additional thousands as "CIA agents.") A third (second nationwide) massive forced relocation was ordered in late October and carried out in November and December 1975.

This new wave of postvictory forced evacuations came just as the rice, which would have fed half a million Cambodians, was ripening; and these evacuations were not confined to areas near the Viet Namese border. Some commentators have bent over backwards to justify these Communist policies, as can be seen in this quote from *Cambodia: Starvation and Revolution,* by Gareth Porter and George C. Hildebrand:

. . . only the revolutionary left in Cambodia had the will and capability to resolve [the food] problem. . . . The National United Front of Kampuchea [NUFK, KR, KK or Angkar Leou] . . . with only its own resources, not only fed its own people but also the more than 3 million people living in GKR [Government of Kampuchean Republic, or Lon Nol's regime] enclaves at the close of the war. . . . By the summer of 1975 the NUFK had successfully dealt with Cambodia's postwar food problem. . . .

The stark contrast in determination to meet the most elementary human needs clearly reflects the social and political character of the NUFK and the GKR. The Lon Nol side had no commitment . . . for the prevention of famine. . . . NUFK . . . had from the beginning an ideological and political commitment to bring about the development of Cambodia's economy and

raise the living standards of Cambodia's people. Moreover, its
. . . political success clearly depended not on vast quantities of
aid from abroad but on its ability to assure a minimum diet under
the most difficult conditions. The NUFK was able to produce
sufficient food only by adopting revolutionary forms of organization, which permitted the mobilization of the Cambodian people
. . . an achievement completely beyond the capabilities of the
old society. Then, through careful management of centralized
food stocks at the village level, the NUFK was able to feed its
people, its soldiers, and the refugees.

In the aftermath of the Cambodian war, however, the U.S.
government had a significant stake in attempting to deny the
NUFK's success. . . .

Cambodia is only the latest victim of the enforcement of an
ideology that demands that social revolutions be portrayed as
negatively as possible, rather than as responses to real human
needs which the existing social and economic structure was
incapable of meeting. In Cambodia . . . the systematic process of
myth making must be seen as an attempt to justify the massive
death machine which was turned against a defenseless population in a vain effort to crush their revolution. The lessons of the
Cambodian experience, moreover, have a significance that goes
far beyond Cambodia itself. We hope that they will not be lost to
the American people in the rewriting of history that is already
taking place.

In light of the third mass relocation in which an estimated half million
people were expelled from areas they had cultivated for six months,
expelled just prior to the ripening of the crop and "deported" for no
food reason (those in the West were moved east, those in the East
moved west), to areas which not only had no surplus but which
already had shortfalls; in light of the thousands of confirmed reports of
soldiers confiscating most of the harvest for shipment to Center granaries (not in villages, and little was ever shipped back); in light of the
documented policy to break the bonds of the people with everything
past (in Pol Pot's words, "to make an additional, total and permanent
break from the old culture"), a policy which included the purposeful
denial of sufficient sustenance to the masses; in light of the systematic
and ruthless elimination of all previous authority and the total uproot-
ing of all towns—not a reprisal reaction by local cadre to the horrors
they'd endured, but exact, deliberate, long-formulated policies and
plans originating from the high command; in light of all this, it is
absurd to see these evacuations and executions as anything other than
willful, malicious mass murder in the name of cultural revolution.

In addition to the October-November deportations, there was a new wave of killings. Radio orders went out to all "exterminators" that the new regime "no longer needed" certain classes of people. *All* former government soldiers, civil servants, teachers and students, and their families, were to be "weeded out" (because many had learned to hide their backgrounds) and eliminated.

Another wave of killings reportedly began in January 1976. The methods of Angkar Leou were so inquisitorial that KK troops, many who had been primarily Sihanoukists (Rumdoah), defected en masse. The "era of happiness" promised them if they achieved victory proved to be a lie. Bloodshed and tensions remained high or increased in every area of the country. Only the Party hierarchy prospered. Defectors became prisoners of war. Local controllers received the following order: "Prisoners of war are no longer required by Angkar Leou. Local controllers will dispose of them as they see fit. These are the wishes of Angkar Leou."

Still the Center was able to further consolidate its power. A new security apparatus emerged. Total class warfare was declared. Now, according to Pol Pot, came the "Second Revolution." Murder waves swept Democratic Kampuchea as the Glorious 17th of April Independence and Victory Day was celebrated. Efforts to weed out the last vestiges of the three mountains of previous power intensified. Kampuchea lay mutilated. The Center now decreed the New and Glorious Constitution of Democratic Kampuchea. This document included the following clauses:

Article 12
Every citizen of Kampuchea is guaranteed a living. All . . . working people have the right to work. There is absolutely no unemployment in Democratic Kampuchea. [Read that to mean Kampuchea is a slave state.]

Article 20
Every citizen of Kampuchea has the right to worship according to any religion and the right not to worship according to any religion.
All reactionary religions that are detrimental to Democratic Kampuchea and the Kampuchean people are strictly forbidden. [Not a single religion, including Buddhism, escaped being called reactionary.]

Khmer reaction to this ruthlessness was increased resistance. Some documents refer to the time, for different reasons from those of Pol Pot, as a second revolution. Bou Thong, who was KK minister of defense, led Krahom Regiment 703 in an uprising in Ratanakiri Province against Pol Pot's local forces. Hun Sen and Ouk Boun Chheoum participated in another abortive revolt in Eastern Zone 203. All the above, along with Heng Samrin and many more, fled from Kampuchea to Viet Nam. In 1977 they became the core of a new KVM. In addition, Joint Voluntary Agency workers in refugee camps in Thailand in 1977 reported that a "lot" of former Khmer military men left the camps and joined resistance forces in Cambodia to fight the Khmer Rouge. Along with many old Rumdoah troops, these men became the base of the KPNLF (Khmer People's National Liberation Front) still on the border.

Still the worst was yet to come.

The main product of the second famine was the total loss of faith by "peasants" in Angkar. Angkar had promised "more work and more food" but it had delivered "more work, more food produced, less distributed." Dispirited, most people worked at just above a "to-be-disappeared" level. And there are numerous reports of entire *sangkats* escaping into the forest only to be massacred by KK ambushes. Without firearms, against those with firearms, fleeing is resistance. It is well documented that moderates within the Communist Party plotted to oust the hard core over the bloodletting.

In history there is power. Kampuchean Communists knew this. For them history was a main point of attack. That was the reasoning behind their "divide and conquer, divide again and again, and control" philosophy, the justification behind their complete atomization of society, behind their total iconoclastic assault on all remembrance.

After the first and second deportations, the sacking of libraries, the decimation of the monarchy and the Buddhist church, the leaders saw that the people still had not been broken, had not remade themselves in the image of Angkar. Ethos lives in people's minds, in repeated cultural myths. And in those myths lay the moral distinctions and moral truths of Khmer society. Communist policy decrees that if the myths and the history are destroyed, then lost in that iconoclastic debris will be the moral foundation of the society; lost will be the role models that children and adults strive to emulate. What remained was remembrance.

The famines, purges and deportations were purposeful. *Starvation was policy*. The methods adopted were designed to destroy the family structure. In the words of exiled Czech writer Milan Kundera, the totalitarian aim is "the destruction of memory." To that objective the Center of Angkar Leou employed Stalinist methods of overwork and undernutrition combined with Maoist attacks on culture and family. Children became the property of Angkar Leou. The second mass deportation was followed by a third, and the third, in some areas, by a fourth. With each move, with each abandonment of an old area, the people were coerced to restart one step further removed from old familiarities. In many areas the 1976-77 harvest was bountiful. But the people did not see the food. The preharvest famine did not abate. In some areas the crop was minimal, and even this was not shared. Exactly what happened to this rice from more paddy area than Cambodia had ever had is not known. Some speculate that the grain was secretly exported to China in exchange for arms, or for money which Pol Pot and Ieng Sary deposited in Swiss bank accounts. There is no verification of this, yet there is verification of similar detours. In 1978 the United States gave 10,000 tons of rice to Laos to avert famine there. The food was confiscated by Viet Namese overlords and kept from the Lao; much of it was sent to Hanoi.

Khieu Samphan, chairman of the State Presidium, explained it all. Questioned about a *million* deaths in his country he said, "It's incredible how concerned you Westerners are about war criminals." It could have been Joseph Stalin decades earlier expounding, "One death is a tragedy; a million deaths are a statistic."

Why? Why did those bastards do it? Why did they wish to erase the cultural memory of all Kampucheans? What drives the dictator?

Some have suggested that the war taught the Krahom to fight with skill and ferocity and to govern only by force. Some have postulated that early humiliations of Pol Pot and/or Khieu Samphan produced massive vengeance which became infectious, which was taught and spread—a form of posttraumatic stress elevated to the utmost ruthlessness. Some have said there was no cult of personality, only Angkar Leou. Why, Mister Pol Pot? Why, Mister Ieng Sary? Why, Mister Son Sen? You were devious, calculating and cruel—was that a manifestation of your "purity of purpose," your desire for pure communism in a pure Khmer land?

Columnist William Pfaff once wrote: "It is dangerous to sentimentalize about the principled revolutionary, because more often than not principles end by rationalizing crimes as acts of principled necessity."

And what crimes. In Democratic Kampuchea, "Purge followed purge but the 'enemy' [of the state] grew ever more elusive, and ever more powerful in the party's mind," wrote Elizabeth Becker, in *When the War Was Over*. Early postvictory killing periods were purges of the old order. Later purges were more specific. Prostitution was "eliminated" by killing all the prostitutes (or any woman who could have been one). The favored method was to bury the woman to her neck, then slowly insert a bayonet into her throat. At Wat Ek in Battambang Province, 2,000 imprisoned "educated impure" (teachers) were murdered. Another 1,000 were killed in a second camp to the east. Ethnic Chinese were segregated and subjected to the harshest conditions and tightest security in Cambodia at a camp named Phum Chen Yuom ("village where the Chinese cry"). There, Pol Pot's machine systematically slaughtered "many" of Cambodia's 425,000 (1970 estimate) Chinese.

In July 1976, Koy Thoun, minister of commerce, once commander of the Northern Corridor Army and secretary of the northern zone, was arrested because of economic failures. He was interrogated and tortured into confessing a nonexistent network of disloyal conspirators. All who had ever served under him became suspect. Following his elimination the northern zone political and military cadre were "purified" by eastern zone troops. In the northwest zone, crop failures were blamed on zonal leaders. The Southwest Army was brought in to disappear the controllers, chiefs, enforcers, yotheas and *mekongs*. Peasants were gathered in mass meetings and told their hardships had been the results of enemies who had now been killed. Everything would get better. Nothing changed.

Some areas experienced two, three or four purges of local cadre. An entire village in Siem Reap Province was massacred to *celebrate* the second anniversary of the KK victory (17 April 1977) because the village had been Lon Nol's birthplace. Three hundred and fifty families, about 2,000 people, were murdered because "they were of the same blood as Lon Nol." Their names were recorded and displayed at the anniversary celebrations. Widespread purges followed. For the "first" time there was open opposition to the cadre of the Center. Again the nation was in limited civil war. Soldiers battled soldiers, and peasants joined in taking advantage of the upheavals to avenge the deaths of loved ones. For months there were massive retaliatory killings. The eastern zone suffered perhaps the "bloodiest" purge (how could anything be bloodier than the murder of all cadre, as was reported?) for not defeating the People's Army of Viet Nam in the growing border war. Perhaps the deaths went deeper than cadre level. The Center reportedly feared that the Gray Vulture Army of the Eastern Zone was secretly allied with the Viet Namese. Defectors or "potential" defectors were purged. Rich peasants who had become Communist soldiers were eliminated; yotheas (no matter what their combat record) who came from "rich" backgrounds and Party members who had "improper" backgrounds were killed.

Pol Pot, the head of state, has been quoted as explaining the killings thus: "We cannot feel sorry for the million lives that have been wasted. The Party is strong because of it."

By 1978 Radio Phnom Penh broadcast: "The Party had flushed out the Khmer–Viet Namese running dogs of the aggressor, expansionist and annexationist Viet Namese enemies who have sneaked their way into the ranks of our Party. . . . Our youths have basically smashed and wiped out those agents."

Many of the politically purged were brought to Phnom Penh's Tuol Sleng Incarceration Center—the headquarters of Angkar Leou's Special Security Police. Of the 16,000 to 20,000 prisoners interrogated and tortured, four survived.

Then the killings got openly out of hand. More and more, cadre explained at education sessions the *need to kill* massive numbers of Khmer citizens. Of the 15,000 at Kok Moun Om, 10,000, it was announced, must be eliminated as enemies of the people. Within a year 6,000 had been murdered. Dare to object, dare to see, and you are next.

Still, that was not enough. Medical treatment reverted to the Dark Ages at best. Again this was purposeful. Had the leaders of Democratic Kampuchea desired, even just allowed it, medicine which could have stopped the epidemics which swept the land would have been donated by Western, Eastern, and/or third world sources. Yet all medical aid was contemptuously rejected. Only the Center's desire for a total, rapid, fundamental and violent change in the values and myths of Khmer culture kept Kampucheans suffering. Cholera, dengue fever, dysentery, lung and brain fluke infections, tuberculosis, malaria, yaws, beri-beri, smallpox, leprosy, hookworm and fungal infections, typhoid and other diseases ravaged the population, which had been rendered so susceptible by the forced labor and enforced starvation. People died by the millions; of those under Pol Pot's tyranny— between purges, starvation and disease—nearly *one half* died, were *murdered,* in less than four years. And there is no Nuremberg?! Such was the implementation of Communism in Democratic Kampuchea!

AFTERSHOCKS IN THE SOCIALIST REPUBLIC OF VIET NAM

In Viet Nam the situation, although not as serious, was still severe. The Aurora Foundation, after extensive study, concluded that 70,000 South Viet Namese had been executed within ninety days of Hanoi's victory. An additional one to two million people were either sent to "reeducation facilities" (a euphemism for "concentration camps") or sent to "new economic zones" to establish farming communes, often on unfarmable land. In the words of Truong Nhu Tang, a founder of the National Liberation Front, and the ex–minister of justice for the Viet Cong:

Unfortunately, when the war did end, North Viet Namese vindictiveness and fanaticism blossomed into a ferocious exercise of power. Hundreds of thousands of former officials and army officers of the Saigon regime were imprisoned in "reeducation" camps. Literally millions of ordinary citizens were forced to leave their homes and settle in the so-called new economic zones. A rigid authoritarianism settled down over the entire country—an authoritarianism supported by the 3d largest army in the world. Members of the former resistance are now filled with bitterness. For the first time in our history people have risked their lives to leave Viet Nam: large numbers of Viet Namese never tried to flee the country to escape French domination or the American intervention. The North Viet Namese Communists, survivors of protracted, blood-drenched campaigns against colonialism, interventionism and human repression, became in their turn colonialists, interventionists and architects of one of the world's most rigid regimes, becoming at the same time dependent clients of the Soviet Union.

DEMOCRATIC KAMPUCHEA VERSUS THE SOCIALIST REPUBLIC OF VIET NAM

Long before the fall of the respective capitals, KK and NVA troops had battled each other; with their victories and the need for consolidation, one would have expected a pause in the border conflict. Although there may have been an abatement in some areas, by mid-1975 the frequency of incidents had begun to grow. In an almost straight-line progression, those incidents increased for two years. PAVN troops outnumbered KK yotheas seven or eight to one. Hanoi used its superior numbers and firepower to roll forward and grind up vast tracts of the Srepok Forest, the Parrot's Beak and the lower Mekong and Bassac floodplains. By May 1977 the fighting was heavy all along the front, with artillery in use by both sides and with the new PAVN air force bombing and strafing Khmer targets. Khmer communes in the East and Northeast which rested along the edge of the no-man's-land were abandoned. By October 1977, 60,000 Cambodians (an unknown percentage of whom had Viet ancestry) had crossed the border and were being warehoused in camps in Viet Nam.

Historical documents indicate sophisticated Viet Namese Communist intelligence work and planning. Colonel Heng Samrin's defection and the establishment of the new Khmer Viet Minh structure allowed the Hanoi Communists to revive their old plan of installing a Viet Namese–controlled regime in Phnom Penh which would appear to be a legitimate Khmer government. In late 1977, a PAVN "meat grinder" campaign, as far as the east bank of the Mekong River, was designed and executed to demoralize the Khmer interior while the PAVN assessed the KK's strengths and weaknesses in guerrilla and large-scale conventional assault warfare. All the while, Hanoi propagandized against Pol Pot. This, in the wake of Western denial of the Kampuchean holocaust, followed by guilt over that denial, served to disguise Communist hegemony in a cloak of moral benevolence.

The Krahom did little to improve their image. In January 1977 they attacked three villages in Thailand, leaving behind piles of mutilated corpses, gruesome piles easily accessible to Western media personnel. The Viet Namese increased their reportage of Khmer Rouge atrocities—the spear rape of women, the slitting of pregnant women's abdomens and the smashing of the unborn against the faces of the dying mothers, the traumatic mastectomies of large-breasted women, and the torture and decapitation of Viet Namese males (in the documents they are always fishermen). In late 1978, as waves of political and racial purges continued to roll back and forth through the Khmer interior, as the Center continuously sought to weed out ever more "enemies of the people," the Viet Namese army massed for a new final offensive.

PART FOUR
DEMOCRATIC KAMPUCHEA

I never believed for a moment that you would
have this sentiment of abandoning a people
which has chosen liberty.
—Cambodian minister Sirik Matak in a letter to American ambassador John Gunther
Dean delivered as U.S. personnel fled
Phnom Penh, 12 April 1975

I will remain until the end on the side of the
Red Khmers, my allies whom I would never
betray.
—Norodom Sihanouk's 12 April 1975 written
response to U.S. liaison chief in Peking,
George Bush, on U.S. initiative inviting
the Prince to retake control of the Phnom
Penh government.

CHAPTER NINETEEN

Nang walked the platform. His black uniform and red-checked krama were new. Though scarred, he was spotless. Beneath an afternoon sky splotched gray, a dozen flags and banners hung listless. The upper winds had shifted, wet air was gradually supplanting dry. Mist had begun to form, to ooze from the forest floor. It hung in the low vegetation, making the jungle walls impenetrable.

For a week peasants of a new people's group had labored—crudely nailing, lashing or simply laying boards, logs and bamboo poles together—raising and extending the platform under harsh glares from scattered yotheas and urged on by enthusiastic utterances from an old people's foreman. In the middle of nowhere, the platform resembled a commuter train station without the rails, without the stationhouse. Simply a raised platform eighty meters long by three meters wide with stairs at each end, a simple platform erected on an exact north-south axis.

Nang stopped below a banner: EQUALITY—JUSTICE—DEMOCRACY. He faced the empty clearing, raised his arms, both fists clenched so as not to expose his claw. "Soon," he shouted to imaginary multitudes, "all will see Norodom Sihanouk." He brought his arms down, chuckled, "Yes, tell them that."

During early construction, he had not walked the length of the platform but had only climbed the south stairs and peered down, grabbed the foreman if he, Nang, saw a board out of line, and politely requested that the offensive protuberance be aligned. As completion neared, Nang examined the structure centimeter by centimeter, cajoling the workers to make repairs, demanding reinforcements, visualizing the platform in operation.

He walked back to the south stairs, stared down the empty

length, laughed inwardly. The jungle along the western edge
had been cleared. On the east it was close, high, thick, blocking
his view toward Preah Vihear. To the north, rising above the
treetops, he could see the rocky cliffs of the Dang Rek mountain
escarpment less than four kilometers away. He paused. All around
him he sensed wilderness, virgin forest awaiting his order and
creation. He looked down, off the platform edge. The drop, he
thought, is not so great to make them afraid yet great enough to
make them hesitate. He barely heard the radio his site assistant
had brought, ". . . the Revolution seeks to achieve an independent, unified, peaceful nation . . . a democratic state enjoying
territorial integrity, a national society infused with genuine
happiness, equality, justice and democracy, without rich or
poor, without exploiters or exploited . . ."

Nang stared north over the trees, envisioned the entire site—
not the platform, not just the few camps already established
but a sprawling complex, a seemingly liberal, highly advanced
state agricultural commune with the best housing, the best
provisions, the best equipment, the most productive paddies.
They'll flock to me, he thought. Willingly. Glad to be sent up.
He fantasized dozens of separate communes dispersed in his
wilderness like leaves dropped in a pond—independent, isolated,
yet all in the same water. He saw, amid the best communes, his
prisons, his confession centers, his platform designed to protect
the revolution and guarantee internal security.

". . . a society in which all live harmoniously . . ."—Nang
flicked his face toward the radio—". . . in great national solidarity . . ."—the voice of Democratic Kampuchea, soon to be
Radio Phnom Penh—". . . to do manual work together and increase production for the construction and defense of the country . . ." Shunned, Nang thought, by weak-stomached, two-headed
snakes at the Center. A quick titter escaped from his throat.

From a jungle trail at the southwestern edge of the clearing a
column of people emerged. "Welcome," Met Nang shouted from
atop the long platform. They walked timidly, a line of seventy
captured FANK officers and NCOs surrounded by their families,
four hundred people in all. As they approached the platform
and clumped before Nang, who'd moved back to center stage,
their fears dissipated. Amongst them were but a few armed
yotheas.

"They will come," Nang had told his underlings weeks earlier,
"and they will see the platform, the clearing for five thousand,
and they will believe. Tell them"—he had smiled—"they may
bring nothing to the Prince's reception. Say, 'You understand,
Brothers. Security.' Have them place their belongings neatly on

the benches in their huts. Say, 'It will be there when you return.' Have them straighten their uniforms and clean the children's faces."

To his surprise they'd come exactly as he'd said. Now he chatted briefly, seemingly absentmindedly, with an officer, a yothea, a young mother.

"Where are you from?"

"Pa Kham." "Oudong." "Roka Kong."

"All from the Northern Corridor, eh."

"Yes."

"No one from the capital?"

"No. The capital still holds, doesn't it, sir?"

"Perhaps. But you'll see. Samdech Euv will tell you how glorious the future is. Though you're much too early."

There was an enforcer in each new phum, a chief in each *sangkat* (the term *khum* was being eliminated), a controller in each *srok;* and all were to be suppliers for Nang's high-level reeducation facility. In Dumbon 11 alone there were sixty-four commune-farms, *kasethans*, from which his site could pull "resources," sixty-four communes needing purification, sixty-four camps of potential resistance requiring the most scientific police work and surveillance. Already the Viet Namese sickness threatened Kampuchea. Spics and subversives were plotting with the CIA and/or the KGB to overthrow the new order before it was even established, and the overseas Chinese capitalists were seeking to regain their perverted exploitive businesses. He, Nang, he'd told himself, would expose the networks, purify the people. He would excel. The Center would never shun him again.

"We were told to come now if we wished to be close enough to hear," a captured major called up to him.

"Eh. Not for three hours," Nang responded. "That would still be early. Even the Prince's advanced security escort hasn't yet arrived."

"Met Nang," a yothea called up, "should we march them back?"

"Hum! Which camp are you from?"

"A-26."

"That's what, four kilometers?"

"More like five."

"They've already come so far, eh? Don't make the little ones march. Have them all come up here out of the dirt."

"Yes!" The yothea nodded. "That's good, eh, Sister?" "Better up there away from the ground snakes, eh, Little Brother?" "Let me help you to the stairs, Auntie." When the ex–government soldiers and their families were aligned along the platform, Nang shouted to a distant yothea, "We have a cameraman, eh? Have him take a photo for each family." Then to several nearby officers he said, "You'll have a photograph of the day you were with Samdech Euv, eh?"

"You are very gracious," a middle-aged ex-lieutenant said.

For an hour the soldiers and their families and the minimal escort waited. The photographer methodically worked his way down the line arranging families about the father-husband, snapping a picture, then moving a few feet to the next. The mist in the jungle grew thicker. The clouds reddened as the sun dropped. Then from the jungle trail came a reinforced company of strack, black-clad yotheas, marching neatly, two by two, shoulder arms, bayonets affixed. "They're the best, eh?" Nang said, forcing all attention on the soldiers as they entered the clearing. "The Prince, he should have the best, eh?"

The yotheas marched, eyes fixed straight, to the south stairs. Two by two they climbed. Without shouted orders, without a side glance the entire column ascended the platform and spaced themselves perfectly along the entire length.

"If the Prince is coming we should jump down," the ex-major said, loud enough for those about him to hear.

"No!" Nang snapped. "I mean, no. Not that way. This is the advance guard. There's still time."

A whistle blew and the spaced yotheas, facing north, spun, snapped their rifles into assault position, aimed their bayonets at the ex–FANK personnel.

"No one move." Nang's voice was coarse, authoritative. "All FANK soldiers, two steps forward. Kneel." Slowly a few obeyed. *"Kneel!"* Others moved more quickly. The pressure of their prostrate peers brought the few who wished to resist to their knees. Like clockwork from north to south, one yothea of each pair stepped behind the ex-soldier before him. Children clung to their fathers but were pushed away. They grabbed their mothers' legs. Women began weeping. Most were numbed by the change, disbelieving what their eyes were seeing, yet believing because they had always believed, believed since capture, that this was their true fate. Then, in gasps, entire sections pleaded, "Have mercy, Brother. Samdech Euv, he wouldn't . . ."

"Eliminate!" Nang barked the order. Seventy yotheas lunged from behind, burying their bayonets in the backs of the FANK men. Seventy lunged from the front stabbing throats, faces, hearts. Wives shrieked. Children, faces contorted in horror and agony, froze, fell. Some lurched forward, threw themselves on their fathers. A few mothers shoved children from the platform,

wanting them to run to the forest. Immediately from below, unseen yotheas leaped, impaled the boys with lances, decapitated the girls with axes. Again and again the FANK troops were stabbed, blood spurting, oozing, splashing beneath footfalls. Then from the south end the mop-up team proceeded up the line, family by family. As a man lay dying his family was forced to kneel by his body. They too were bayoneted. Airless, windless, breathless—when all were dead, when no voices and no moans could be heard, when the only sound was the trickle of blood dripping from the platform into puddles below, Nang quietly ordered old-people–drawn carts from the forest. Methodically the carnage was pushed from the stage into small wagons and tugged from the site.

"Met Ku," Nang called to his site assistant.

"Yes, Comrade High Controller," Ku responded.

"How shall we clean the platform before the next group?"

"There's the peasant workers' platoon. They draw water from . . ."

"That's too far. Look at this mess. With so many, this will never do."

"Perhaps . . . for now?"

"Yes. For now. Until . . . something more efficient . . ."

Betrayed, she thought. The street was not vacant. She had expected to be alone with her children yet scurrying in the dark from burned-out cars to building-rubble heaps like rats at the city dump avoiding cats, scores of people, shadows, blipped at the periphery of her vision. How could I have been so wrong? she thought. The street was dark. How, she thought, could I have ignored all the signs? All the warnings? Su Livanh slept in the *khan* that hung from Vathana's neck. Samol held her hand. Samnang walked at her other side. How, Vathana thought as she stepped softly, leading her children from Neak Luong, could I ever have believed anything they said? Kosol! The associations! Even Teck! My poor Teck. "They're Khmer, eh?" At the end they'd shown their true colors. At the end the Patriots had sunk all the boats along the levee. "Owned by Chinese capitalists," they'd said. The internals had set fire to all the government buildings and to the pagoda and the apartment building. Then Khmer Rouge soldiers had looted the town, had shot any civilian caught looting. For a week the crying had been continuous.

Neak Luong was not evacuated immediately. Under control of the Eastern Zone Army the population of more than 200,000 was not, on an hour's notice, forced to flee. Locally FANK was disarmed but few conquerors remained. Like a wave over a sandbar they'd swept in, over, then continued west in a military rush toward Phnom Penh. A subtler pressure crushed in upon the inhabitants. The fighting had been ferocious, the last battles block to block, then house to house, causing immense destruction. For months there had been little food, little potable water. Now there was nothing.

Day after day Vathana had crept about the camp, crept like a mole fearing light, crept uncertain, scattered, numbed. She could barely talk. She hugged her children to her for hours, slept in fits. Each time she woke she looked for Sophan, looked to say, "Sophan, watch the children. I must take Teck his ration." Then, knowing Sophan was not there, would never be there again as she had been for five years, such a part of Vathana's life, of her routine, such a part of the children's lives, not there . . . Not there. "Sophan, while I'm at the hospital, take the little ones to the river to bathe. Sophan, Sophan, Sophan . . ." To say the name meant to open her mouth and to open her mouth meant to allow the heartache to belch forth like an acrid gas, to burn in front of her. And yet she did say the name. And she called for Teck. "It could have been so much better, my husband. It could always have been like it was at the end. We did not have to lose our country to love each other. Oh Teck! How your children will miss you. How I will miss you."

Then the first Krahom cadre had returned. Then Vathana had packed their small bundle, clothing for the children, a sleeping mat, a blanket, a small cooking pot, the last of their rice. In her skirt waistband she'd rolled the gold chain necklace John Sullivan had given her. She'd placed Su Livanh in the *khan*, hung it from her neck, grabbed the two older children and escaped onto the midnight highway leading north.

For a week the wind had carried the aroma of rotting flesh. It wafted in from battle areas where corpses lay unburied, it hung in the humid night air. It coated her skin, burned her eyes. Maggots had become flies in the mutilated carcasses lying where they'd fallen. Now the night air was thick with buzzing.

She did not scurry as did others. With Su Livanh hung in the cloth and Samol, at four, and Samnang, strong at five and a half yet still a little boy, by the hands, how could she dart from concealment to concealment? Instead they walked calmly, lightly, attempting to keep to the shadows but also trying to appear normal. She spoke quietly, encouraging and reassuring the children. "In a few days," Vathana said, "you'll see your grandmother and grandfather."

"Grandpa's house!" Samol's voice was loud, enthusiastic.

"No. Not the villa. Much farther away. My father's house. You've never met him."

"Bu-ba-ba-ba."

"He loves you very much," Vathana said to Samnang. "Before you were born he came to pray for you. He is the most wonderful grandpa."

They walked for hours. The outskirts of the city were in ruin. Sophan . . . Teck . . . The ache in her heart nearly swallowed her. A hundred times Vathana repeated inwardly, Don't look back. Don't look back. Yothea presence on Highway 15 leading north was sparse, by night seemingly nonexistent. Vathana paused frequently. Will I ever see the pagoda again? she thought. Then she thought, No, it has burned. What of my first halfway house? The levees? The fish market? Don't look back, she thought, yet she turned and she knew she was near the spot by the river where she had taken John Sullivan. Where Su Livanh had been conceived. Why did you abandon me, Captain Sullivan? Don't look back. The night seemed quiet, quiet between distant explosions. The air felt peaceful, peaceful between sporadic acrid-metallic waftings, between the clouds of flies and death smell. The children tired but bravely pushed on. Don't look back. Oh, Sophan . . . Don't look back. Oh, Teck . . . Oh, my Teck . . . Don't look back. This hurts so much. Vathana's eyes filled with tears.

Somewhere in the blackness to their right stretched the dried marsh swamp and Boeng Khsach Sa. Still they walked and walked and walked. Then they could go no farther. Vathana's mouth was dry. It was difficult to speak. Samol began to whine. Only a little farther, Vathana thought, and we would see Mister Pech's villa. Does it still stand? Dare she mention it to the children? Silently she herded them off the road into the shadow of a bamboo hedge. Quietly she brushed the ground to clear it of stones, twigs or insects. Then she unrolled the mat, yawned, lay along one edge with Su Livanh cupped in the bend of her body. Samol and Samnang snuggled in. She unfurled the blanket and they slept.

The sky was crystalline yet the ground air was hazy with dust churned up by the passing of a mobile work brigade. Chhuon stood bareheaded, relaxed, waiting as ordered for the phum enforcer. His skin had darkened, his hands grown coarse, his feet callused. Before him, sitting on the ground in the shade of their hut in the line of children's huts, four small girls, no more than seven years of age, sat cross-legged obeying every command of the neary, herself but eleven. Gracefully their hands moved, as gracefully as ballet students of the old court. Back and forth to a softly hummed cadence, back and forth lightly honing the edges of the bamboo daggers.

"Now all Comrade Children have fifty." The neary's voice was severe. "By noon all will present Poh one thousand." She glanced over her shoulder at Chhuon, then turned, jerked a *punji* stake from one little girl and tested the tip and the blades. "No!" she screamed. She lunged forward, punched the girl's face. The girl fell, scrambled back to position without a sound. The neary sat back. "Angkar wishes you to work better. Or do you wish to be disappeared?"

Chhuon eyed them, a slight scowl on his face, Krahom approval. Through all the turmoil and deprivation of the past five years he had learned when to speak, when to be silent. His special knowledge of rice had made him valuable to Met Vong, the enforcer in charge of Phum 117. Vong called him Poh, a rural dialect form of *Pa*, the equivalent of "Pop," or "Pappy." At fifty-two Chhuon was an elder and Vong, for all the new speak and new order, still maintained a remnant of traditional respect. With Vong, Chhuon did not act the ignorant peasant. The time and need had passed. Under Vong, though living conditions were harsh, he, the entire commune, had entered a state of stable systematic enslavement. Poh, Chhuon, was again a boss, not the nominal chief of rice. The 1974 crop had been decent, the quota for the army had been met, no one had starved. It was something few Krahom communes could claim.

As Chhuon watched the girls, Vong approached. He halted behind Chhuon. "Soon," he said quietly, "we'll have many more mouths to feed." He issued no greeting, wasted no words. "You must make the rice grow faster." Chhuon turned. He watched the enforcer's hands. He did not look at his face. The hands jittered. "Angkar has achieved glorious victory. The oppressed of all cities have been liberated."

Chhuon tilted his head in such a way as to keep it bowed yet to glance at Vong's chin. "Comrade Enforcer, one can only be kind to rice. One cannot hurry it."

"Poh, when new people arrive, they will be hungry. Grow the rice quickly."

Chhuon's mouth opened slightly, his cheeks tightened—almost a smile, not a smile, smiling was prohibited. If Angkar's representative said it will grow quickly who was he to say otherwise? "You say new people, Met Vong?"

"In the whole world"—Vong's face beamed—"in all times, no people have ever driven out the imperialists to the last man. Only Khmer! Only Khmer revolutionaries. Only we have scored total victory. Khmers can do anything. From the very highest center the word has come, 'This is the work of God. For mere humans it is too imposing.' "

Now Chhuon did smile. It was not the ancient enigmatic smile of Cambodia but a lesser grin, an approval without happiness or ambiguity. "We must prepare for them," Vong continued. "When they are fed we shall celebrate the great Seventeenth of April Victory. Come."

Chhuon followed Vong. They walked a narrow raised path through the low forest of the wilderness zone. Hundreds of thousands of *punji* stakes lined the broad trenches below the path, aimed not outward to stop attackers but inward to keep the inhabitants from fleeing. In the heat Vong paced like a rising executive. They neared a work site where half the commune's inhabitants, about five hundred people, were expanding irrigation canals and dikes. Weeks before Vong had pointed to the old half-kilometer-long dikes and said, "The new fields must be doubled. If that dike were moved five hundred meters how much more rice would grow?"

"It can't be moved before the rains," Chhuon had answered.

"It is the wish of Angkar," Vong said coolly.

"It would be better to build a second dike and leave . . ."

"Have it moved or deal with Met Khieng."

Chhuon had forced his teeth together. He'd paused, run quick mental calculations. Five hundred more meters would achieve twenty-five hectares. In the best conditions that would yield thirty metric tons of paddy. But even if the half-kilometer dike could be moved and two 500-meter connecting dikes constructed in time, the area just wasn't suitable. It had been cratered by bombs or artillery. How was not important. What had happened to the subsoil was. Like much of the Cambodian basin the subsoil of the northern new wilderness zone was laterite, a substance that remained soft and permeable as long as it remained wet. Once dried the laterite hardened like brick. Rewetting had little effect. The bombing had drained the area of Vong's proposed expansion. Clods of hardened laterite surrounded stagnant puddles of oily water. Once again, Chhuon had thought, we're to revert to know-nothingness. "I'll do whatever Angkar Leou asks of me," Chhuon had responded. "I'm happy to serve." Then he thought of a silent, subtle retribution, a retaliation for this stupidity, a simple satisfaction to sabotage Angkar, to assuage new pain and old. "Yet . . ." Chhuon paused.

"Yet what?" Vong sneered at Chhuon's apparent challenge.

"Yet Khieng . . ." Chhuon whispered.

"Khieng what?" Vong snapped.

"Comrade," Chhuon said, "if we're to finish such a project before the rains, we'll need all the workers."

"Of course."

"Khieng . . ." Chhuon hesitated.

"Yes?" Vong was adamant.

"He . . . he takes . . . he takes all the women. Sometimes one or two, sometimes ten. Even more! He keeps them from work . . . all day."

"On the last day," Rita Donaldson wrote, "everywhere I heard the questions, 'Why has . . .' " She stopped, steadied her quivering hands. The tremor would not cease. She wrote on, a wobbly scratching on the page. " '. . . why has the United States abandoned us? Why don't the Americans do something?' " Again she paused. The trip from Phnom Penh to the Thai border had been an extension of the nightmare she'd been witnessing for months . . . an ever-worsening nightmare. Snatches of news had circulated among the expelled Westerners. In South Viet Nam the ARVN 18th Division, which, she'd read, had severely damaged the NVA 6th and 7th Divisions at Xuan Loc in March and had held off the 6th and 7th reinforced by the 341st for the first two weeks of April, was said to have been destroyed by the NVA 10th and 304th Divisions flanking them en route to Saigon. "Five to one," the rumor went. "Tremendous ARVN gallantry," many whispered, "but too little and too late." Was, Rita thought, America abandoning South Viet Nam, too? Rita bit the knuckle of her right thumb. She tried to think, to ponder the question, but the horror and fear that engulfed her blocked her inquiry. The Khmer Rouge had corralled the Westerners in the French embassy, then expelled them, overland, via bus and train, to the Thai border. Some expellees had been allowed to group together. Others were partially or totally isolated. She had not been allowed to write, had been restricted from viewing. Still she'd heard rumors, glimpsed an atrocity—a heap of bodies by a rail siding east of Pursat. Arriving in Thailand she'd been dazed, exhausted, in shock.

Slowly she jotted notes. "Many of Lon Nol's troops voluntarily relinquished their arms in order to attend assemblies with Norodom Sihanouk . . . It is rumored that Sisowath Sirik Matak, on the last day, sent a letter to President Ford in which he wrote, 'My only mistake was to have trusted the Americans.' . . . One Khmer man said to me, 'You Americans, you don't really believe there is any other world. You sent millions of boys, spent thousands of millions of dollars, but you never knew that we Khmers lived here. That this is our country, because we have always lived here. It's like you just want to have war, eh? Yet what you do, you were right to do, but you are frivolous. That's why you tire of war. You never knew us. As a nation you were never serious. That's why when—how do you say?—the fad, the fad of war, it wears off. That's why you can abandon us.' "

"Bu. Ba-ba, ba-ba. Bub-ba!" The sun had risen. Twenty meters away on the road a thin unbroken line of refugees flowed from Neak Luong. "Bub-ba!"

"What is it, Precious Heart?"

"Bub-ba! Bub-ba!" Samnang grasped his mother's wrist and pulled.

Vathana rubbed her eyes. She shook her head. Her long black hair fell from her scarf and cascaded down her shoulders, arms and back. She brushed it back with her spread fingers. "Oh," she said. "I thought we'd get out before that started."

"Bub-Ba-*Ba-Ba*!"

"Settle down. We'll eat first then join them."

Samnang tugged harder. His good arm compensated in strength for his gawkish side. He nearly knocked her over.

"I'm hungry," Samol cried.

"Sophan." Su Livanh also cried and her crying feathered Samol's and the volume of the two little girls ascended until Samnang, frustrated, excited, just pushed them back to the mat and wrenched his mother up to follow.

"Bub-Bub-*Ba-Ba*."

"Yes. Yes. Show me, then let's get on the road. Perhaps in the old regions, where they're established, we'll find a better life."

Vathana followed the boy behind the hedge. Her eyes popped. Her heart plummeted. In the dusty rubble of dry stalks were piles of human parts. Torsos. Hundreds of headless, limbless torsos stacked vertically like broken pawns awaiting a chess match. Arms, neatly lined up, a hundred lefts, a hundred rights. Legs, footless in one pile like lumber, footed in another. Feet, in pairs. And heads. Hundreds of heads. Perfectly ordered, arranged by size in columns and rows. Vathana's body convulsed, then went limp. She sank to her knees. Her waist seemingly liquified. She fell to her hands. Her arms collapsed. "Bu-ba-ba-ba." Samnang shook her. Her body trembled. She hugged her son close to her, recovered enough to stand, to back away. She reached to her bosom, grasped the Buddha statuette Chhuon had given her so many years before. "Blessed One . . ." she exhaled. She said no more. Holding Samnang's hand she ran to the sleeping mat where the two girls were pilfering the bundle for cooked rice. Don't look back.

Again they walked, now in column with thousands of fleers. From time to time Vathana stopped, shaded her eyes from the sun with her hand and tried to look up the highway to ascertain what lay head.

"Don't stop, Sister," a kindly middle-aged man whispered to her.

"Eh! The little ones need to rest."

"There are soldiers in the trees. Don't look. Don't stop."

"Where should we go?"

"Go as far as you can."

"For how long?"

"For as long as you can." The man became silent as they neared a clump of palm trees at the shoulder of the highway. Vathana followed his lead though others about them chattered carelessly. A few cars crammed with families and belongings overtook them. On the next open stretch the middle-aged man asked quietly, without looking at her, "Do you have any money?"

"A little," Vathana said. In her mind she asked the Lord Buddha to forgive her for using such vagueness.

"Throw it away," the man whispered. "They'll say you're a capitalist."

"How do you know this?"

"Don't ask. Cut your hair."

"I'll roll it up."

"It would be better to cut it now. Angkar will demand it later."

"The Khmer Rouge?"

"The Organization. Is that baby yours?!"

"She's my daughter."

"She's not Khmer."

"I was married to an . . . a Frenchman. He was killed by the bombers in 1973 . . . before she was born."

"Tell no one of him. Blacken her hair. They'll think you're an agent or a spy."

"Who?"

"ssshh."

At midday a few armed yotheas joined the column. They were smaller than the troops who had taken Neak Luong but they too were without smiles, seemingly without emotions.

"More quick. Walk more quick." The yotheas scowled. "You, you don't go more quick." They singled out an elderly woman who shuffled by the road's edge.

"My legs," Vathana heard the woman say, "are too old to go more quickly, Nephew." The woman's manner was sweet and respectful.

"You run," one yothea screamed furiously.

"Run?!" The old woman stopped and smiled. "Me?" She laughed gently, gaily. "If I could run, I would have joined you in the forest years ago."

The angry yothea lifted his rifle. A shot cracked. Vathana saw the woman fly back as if a sudden gust had caught a leaf. Then she dropped without life. Vathana covered Su Livanh's head with a corner of her krama, pulled Samol tightly to her leg and doubled their pace. As they passed the body she kept her head down, her eyes on the road. With horror she saw Samnang's feet. From an aid package the boy had taken a pair of red, high-top sneakers. They were Samnang's pride. At the next stop they would go.

The road was now full of uprooted city dwellers and villagers and the roadside was littered with corpses. For all the walking their progress was painfully slow. It took them two days to reach the road junction which led to the villa where Vathana's father-in-law had been assassinated in 1971. How strange it looked on the rise. What had it seen? The NVA, the KVM, the return of FANK and the ARVN. American bombs had cratered the lawn yet someone had restored the landscaping. From the road Vathana could just see two groups of people standing amid bright bougainvillea and jacaranda blooms. As the column shuffled north, the grounds became clearer. Vathana noted one group of perhaps three hundred men, many in FANK officers' uniforms. The second group, from the hospital she thought—she recognized a nurse, then several, then an aide—was much smaller. Scattered about them were dark-clad yotheas. As she watched, the scene transformed soundlessly. The officers made four long neat ranks. Above them, by the arch from which Pech Lim Song and his old servant, Sambath, had been hung, a man was addressing the assembly. The civilian staff clumped to one side. Now Vathana saw children. They were on the villa's great veranda watching as if attending a parade. Vathana felt relief, joy. She thought to break from the road column, to join the people at the villa. It's a sign, she thought. An omen. Reconciliation. She placed a hand over Samnang's shoulder, turned him slightly and whispered, "Your grandpa built that house." Behind the children on the veranda were a few women but mostly the young appeared to be unattended. Vathana snatched a glance toward the rear of the column. Far back she saw three yotheas helping a family with small children. Again she thought it was a reconciliation. Again her hopes rose.

She stopped, stopped her son. She was about to step from the column when men in the rear rank began jolting, falling.

Vathana's eyes narrowed. From other ranks men bolted only to be seemingly upended in midstride. Then the sound. Explosive banging of a dozen automatic weapons. The civilians stood paralyzed. Children's screams reached the column. On the road refugees hung their heads, shuffled more quickly. Vathana clamped her hands over Su Livanh's ears and eyes but she could not turn away. Now hospital members attempted to run only to be toppled, to fall like rag dolls tossed casually down on soft verdant lawn. Red blotches burst upon the green. Vathana shook. Don't look back. Children were brought to find their dead parents then forced to watch as the bodies were disemboweled. Vathana froze. Evacuees behind her nudged her, pushed her. Still she was unable to turn.

"Bub-ba-ba!" Samnang pulled. He no longer found the scene of interest.

"Divine Buddha . . ." she whispered. "Say this," she said to her children, "it will protect you. 'Divine Buddha . . .' "

Late afternoon of the seventh day of their trek, Vathana was stopped at a checkpoint. The middle-aged man who'd warned her earlier had stayed with her for three days, had somehow obtained rice and water for their meals, and had disappeared leaving her with most of the ten-kilo sack of good rice. His last words to her were, "Try to appear ugly. Don't be the Angel. Some of them like beautiful girls."

"What is your name?" the checkpoint guard asked.

"Yani."

"Do you have any papers?"

"No."

"Read this." Vathana grabbed the page printed in French and English. She turned it clumsily sideways. Then upside down. "Read this one." The interviewer snatched the first page from her hand and handed her one printed in Khmer script.

Vathana held it for some moments. The interviewer fussed impatiently. "Kam—pu—che—a." She read slowly. She smiled at the interviewer, flashing blackened teeth.

"Angkar Leou wishes you to write who you are. Do you understand?" The man handed her a ballpoint pen and a pad and indicated that she should move to an area where others were scribbling furiously. Vathana leaned forward, over the table. Samnang leaned in. He stared at the page then blurted, "Bub-ba-ba-ba."

"Bu. Bu-bu." Vathana mimicked him lovingly.

"Ba. Ba-ba-ba-ba-ba." The boy laughed loudly.

In childish strokes Vathana marked the page. "Over there," the interviewer snapped. Her filthy appearance disgusted him.

And the baby, covered with muck. To the line behind her he called politely, "Angkar needs pilots. Engineers. Teachers. Anyone who speaks French." He moved to push Vathana from the table. "When you're finished bring it back."

"Done," Vathana said. She had written only, Yani. Mom: Sok. Home: Sath Din.

"I've never heard of it. Never mind. Get out of here. Take this pass and follow that group. You can plant. Next."

Vathana led the children to the end of a long line of women and children. "Where are we going, Sister?" she asked the woman ahead of her.

"To the reorganization center," the woman answered.

"What is that?"

"You!" a yothea called sternly. Vathana glanced at the armed boy. "You, Met Srei, comrade girl, Angkar forbids you to talk in line." The boy wandered up the line.

"they are sending us to the forest to work and to be educated," the woman whispered.

"with the children?" Vathana said without looking at her.

"they're taking the children to the child center. it's better, yes? one cannot watch them in the forest."

That night Vathana slipped from the group. If anyone noticed, if anyone missed her, she did not know. She did not care. All night she and her children headed east along a secondary road. Much of the way Samnang carried Su Livanh on his back while Vathana carried Samol. "We're going to see Grandpa and Grandma," she told them again and again. What had been at best a vague thought to give her direction the day she'd left Neak Luong now became both her tactical plan and her guiding spiritual strength. She would unite grandchildren and grandparents for at least a brief time and the Samsara, the Wheel of Life, would be fulfilled.

The secondary road led east, circumventing Prey Veng, then north through low fields. For a week they walked at night and hid in the treelines or hedges or in abandoned peasant homes by day. Food was not yet a problem. Many of the small village silos had at least handfuls of rice. Some had bushels. Water, also, was present, if not abundant. Many of the cisterns had cups. Some of the homes had jars. Only a few wells were putrid with decaying corpses. What was not abundant was people. Here and there a village seemed to have totally escaped the effects of the war. Farmers worked their fields preparing for the coming rains. Women repaired thatched roofs while children played in the shade beneath stilt houses. But mostly the land was empty. At each inhabited hamlet Samnang asked, "Bub-ba-ba?'' He wanted to enter, to be with the people. In Cambodia to live alone, separated from all others, was very rare. Growing up in the refugee camp he'd had a hundred friends, a thousand aunts and uncles. Always his mother stopped him.

"We cannot trust anyone. Not until we talk to your grandpa."

"Bub? Ba-ba-ba."

"Are we going to walk all the way?" Samol asked, her voice as petite as her carriage.

"If we must. A terrible evil has been unleashed, but so you will not be frightened, say, 'Divine Lord Buddha . . .' '' Each morning Vathana prayed with her children, prayed for protection, prayed for a successful journey to Phum Sath Din. Each night they walked. They spoke to no one. They avoided being seen. On 17 and 18 April the villages and camps they circled were ablaze with wanton rifle fire, music, even some skyrockets. They did not ask why. On the 19th the celebrations ceased. They had reached the Mekong at Tonle Bet across from Kompong Cham. To head north they would either have to cross the river or cross Highway 7 and follow the secondary roads through the Chup Plantation toward Kratie.

Vathana could not decide. For a day they stopped, hid. That night they did not move. Nor the next day. Don't look back, she told herself. How would Captain Sullivan solve this? What did he say to do? What did he do to escape? But he didn't have to carry children. Vathana worried. She moved their tiny camp to a small hollow below Highway 7. From there she could glimpse the roadway through a hundred meters of forest. The road was packed. Thousands of people. Where were they being sent? Chams by dress. The detritus of the evacuees was piled so high along the road's edge it blocked her view. How to cross? How to move north? How to get to Phum Sath Din?

"You must stay here. Do you understand?" The children were very frightened. "Mama will be back soon. You must not move. You must be very quiet."

At dusk she walked toward the road. The sides of the hollow converged like a funnel, the bottom rolled. From the small encampment she had not been able to see into the bottom of the rolls. She approached slowly, tree by tree. A radio played. A monkey whooped. Chills ran from arm to arm. She leaned into a tree for support. A headless corpse toppled from the other side. She stared at the base of the trees. Before her, beside her, dare she look back, sitting against the trunk of each tree was a body holding its head in its lap. Her heart ached. She wished to flee but she drove herself cautiously forward. Then a lap head moved. She froze. It was crying. No. A child. A child lay its head on the lap of its father, lay tightly holding, hugging the headless man's leg. Vathana pressed toward the road. She could smell the smoke and see the fires of the burning city across the river. She could hear the radio of a Krahom cadreman. The voice was Norodom Sihanouk's: ". . . in victory the Revolution will achieve genuine happiness . . ."

There was a break in the flow of people on the road. To get here, she thought, the evacuees must have been ferried across the river. ". . . we have attained our sovereignty, our independence . . ." Yes. They must come in groups, she thought. ". . . With the traitorous Lon Nol and his clique eliminated we shall defend and construct the most beautiful nation . . ." They won. Vathana felt nothing. Win. Lose. It made no difference now.

Quickly she scurried to her children. They were gone. Frantic she searched their rest area. Their belongings were gone. Then, whispered, she heard, "ba-ba-ba." They had hidden. How her heart leaped. How wonderfully they'd adapted.

At midnight they crossed the road, their first steps into the sparsely populated regions of the Northeast. In the dim light of a crescent moon they walked, stumbled along paths of the old rubber tree plantation. Vathana had not seen the trees with their silver bark since coming south to marry Teck. At that time, she recalled, the plantation forest had been perfectly ordered, row after row; the aisles between had been clear, clean, looking manicured. Now the aisles were ripped with craters, the trees splintered and felled. Dead branches cluttered the ground. Everywhere were signs of war. They moved slowly, fearing ambush by bandits or . . . or who? Forest spirits? "You are good trees," Vathana whispered as they entered an area devastated by American bombs searching for NVA tanks. "Be compassionate, trees. I know you won't harm my children." More trashed foliage: NVA artillery aiming for ARVN incursioners. Farther, the charred hulks of KK Chicom trucks, an old bivouac site, a burned-out clearing where FANK units had fallen. Oh, Vathana thought, if the trees could talk. She pulled Samnang closer to her side. All the misery, all the fear, the pain, ache, worry, disillusionment, all which had been put on hold, all which she'd steeled herself against, first to assist the refugees, then to help the associations and finally to flee, to walk home with her children, in the seemingly silent security of the shattered rubber tree forest—all cascaded to her heart.

"bu. bu-ba. bu-ba."

Vathana squatted, pulled the girls in, hugged all three. "Soon," she wept, "soon we will see Grandpa and he will fix all this. He loves you very much. He loves me."

That night they did not go far. With the seeming emptiness of the forest, and with the fear of wandering aimlessly in the dark, Vathana decided it would be best to travel mornings and evenings when she could be certain they were on a northerly course. They lay on the mat, covered themselves with the thin blanket. The children—how good they've been, she thought—slept. But Vathana could not. She prayed. She planned. She projected. She meditated. In so many ways the trip had been easier than she'd expected. Food had been plentiful. Twigs, straw, paper had been easy to collect for their daily cooking fire. But the sights. They had been beyond her wildest nightmares. As she recounted their trek she tallied the bodies, the human debris at roadsides, the neatly stacked corpses at the execution sites. A hundred here, a few there, four hundred . . . and on and on. She meditated on the tragedy which had struck her people and the sadness of the four thousand dead she'd seen since leaving Neak Luong. She cried for the murdered. She shuddered. She wept asking, "Why? Why, Teck, have you abandoned me? Why, Sophan? Why, John Sullivan, do you abandon your daughter?" By first light Vathana had convinced herself that the slaughter was an aberrant action, a part of the final offensive which had overflowed into the victory. Soon the country with its new army and new masters would settle back. Soon Samdech Euv would reign. Compassion would return.

The rubber plantation gave way to the wilds of the Srepok Forest and the lonely progress of the small family slowed further. Now there was no more rice. Daily patrols could be seen or heard on the main roads or in new camps being hacked from the jungle. Old villages had been abandoned, torched, the wells polluted with the carcasses of draft animals. Execution sites, small in comparison to the ones in the heavily populated area to the south, were not uncommon. The Srepok had become a no-man's-land. Even the animals had abandoned the region. There was no whoop of monkeys, no caw of birds. Only mosquitos and black flies flourished. By April's end when the first slight rains dampened the dusty earth, Vathana and her children had reached an area just east of Kratie. They had walked nearly three hundred kilometers in twenty-two days; they had nearly an equal distance yet to cover. Vathana's feet were raw from the constant walking, carrying Su Livanh. Samnang seemed to be thriving. Each day he became a better tree climber, here picking bananas, there a coconut, at five and a half, partially deaf, dumb, with one side of his body contorted and asthenic, the forager and provider. Occasionally they crossed old paddies which should now be being turned, readied for the May planting, but which lay fallow, abandoned. Occasionally they crossed the route taken by a column of deportees. Always it was the same, the road's edge littered with corpses—people who could not keep up, the aged, the very young, those previously wounded. Often they had not been killed but simply left to die of thirst. Here an elderly woman hung at a smashed water-supply pipe; there a man lay facedown in a puddle reached too late; bloated corpses emitting the stench of decay. Always now Vathana and the children were thirsty.

"In a few days it will rain," Vathana told them. "Maybe tomorrow. Divine Buddha . . . Say it with me. 'Divine Buddha, we are not frightened.' " Their progress slowed further as they spent ever-increasing amounts of time foraging for food, searching for clean water. From the modern conveniences of prewar Neak Luong through the refugee camp years to the first steps north to now, time had accelerated in reverse, dropping Vathana from an agricultural and early industrial era, through all the steps between, back 10,000 years to foraging subsistence. The rich ecosystem of the Srepok favored them. Edible plants were plentiful; damp-land newts and dry-wood efts were numerous. In order to preserve their walking time they cooked only in midafternoon, throwing into the pot all they had gathered in the morning. Still the foraging slowed them.

Still it did not rain. Their lips cracked. Their throats parched. Water became an obsession, yet Vathana dared neither turn west toward the Mekong nor tarry at any of the dry rills long enough to dig for wetness. "Soon. Soon. Grandpa will have water. Grandpa knows where. Grandpa knows how. He loves you very much. He loves me, too."

Cuts on Vathana's heels festered. The pain shot to her ankles, up the Achilles tendons to the base of her calves. She did not see Samol drink from the cistern with the two rotting heads. Had she seen, from a distance, she questioned whether she would have had the strength to stop her. By evening the child was ill. Vathana carried her. Samnang carried Su Livanh. Vathana was faint.

"ba. baba. ba! ba! ba!"

"what is it, precious heart?" Samnang pulled his mother, directed her. She had been tottering aimlessly. She knew it but she'd been unable to concentrate.

Samnang pulled hard. Vathana stumbled after him. She stumbled up a slight incline then down a sudden dip to the shallow valley of the small Kampi. Water trickled between rocks in the riverbed. Samnang pulled yet harder but Vathana held him back. She knelt and forced him to his knees.

Samol's stomach had been gurgling loudly for an hour. Now, as they said a prayer of thanksgiving, she heaved. Vathana startled. She cleaned her daughter's mouth. "slowly, precious heart," she whispered. "there may be soldiers."

"Bub-*bub*." The boy blurted his utterance as if saying, I couldn't care less. He bolted for the stream. Su Livanh, her little legs no match for the undergrowth, tumbled after him. Vathana followed. Before she drank she washed Samol's face and mouth and let the child drink her fill.

"mama, i don't feel good," Samol complained. She heaved the water she'd just swallowed.

For four days they stayed by the Kampi. Beneath rocks in the riverbed Samnang found tiny thin-shelled clams and hundreds of hermit crabs. Vathana's physical strength returned. She cleaned the sores on her heels, and the pains which had shot to her calves subsided. She washed the mud from Su Livanh's hair and skin and she washed all their clothes. Still she did not feel strong. Lethargy, depression, exhaustion grasped her mind.

Samol had not been able to keep anything in her stomach. She could barely walk from the sleeping mat to the river. The first hard rain fell in mid-May and the girl shook with chills all night. In the morning she'd woken with diarrhea squirts on her legs. Vathana washed her, bundled her in the blanket. The trek continued. Samol cried for hours. "It hurts, mama." She clamped her elbows to her sides, her tiny arms and hands tight to her chest. Through the blanket, from her face, Vathana could feel the girl's fever radiating. "It hurts so bad, mama." Then Samol lay limp, spent, in her mother's arms.

Now it rained every day. Vathana decided to head west, to find Highway 13, to find a village or camp. Despite the water Samol became lighter and lighter. "We must find a doctor," she told Samnang. "We must find medicine. What root would the *khrou* boil? What will stay down?"

They walked all night. They walked all the next day. They walked until dusk. Samnang never complained. He carried Su Livanh on his back. She whined about her legs being sore. He carried her on his hip as Sophan had carried him as an infant. They saw no one. The land was deserted. Highway 13 was empty. Not even a roadblock. They walked north hoping to be interdicted, to be captured. Samol's abdomen became hard. She shriveled. In the dark Vathana tried to force her to sip, to drink just a little water. It rolled from her mouth.

Now they rested. Now they foraged. Now they walked. Days passed. Vathana said little. She carried Samol. Samnang carried Su Livanh. They did not seek the security of the forest but walked the highway north. Several times they were stopped. The old people of the "liberated" zones had been forbidden to give aid to the deportees, yet in true Khmer tradition the family found small bundles of rice, a few vegetables, even a cooked eel in amongst their belongings. John, Vathana thought in mental flaccidity, why, why have you abandoned me? Why have you abandoned your daughter? Don't look back. Divine Buddha, I am not afraid. Sophan, will you carry Samol for me? She's not heavy. Teck would carry her if he weren't at the front.

South of Stung Treng where Highway 13 junctions with 19 they were stopped. A yothea demanded their papers, their passes. Vathana freely handed him the blue cards from her bundle. He screamed at her but the sharp words fell softly into the mush of her thoughts. He pulled the scarf from Su Livanh's head. Her light hair shocked him. Then he peeled back the blanket from Samol's face. The skin was black, wrinkled. "Leprosy," Vathana said softly.

The yothea jumped back. "Bu-ba-bah-bah," Samnang blurted.

"It's gotten into his ears," Vathana whispered. She pointed to Su Livanh. "Into her eyes and hair."

The soldier stepped back. He yelled to others along the road and they too backed away. "Go. Go now. Get away from here."

As they left they heard the radio, again Samdech Euv's voice: ". . . A general amnesty has been decreed. All soldiers and workers of the Lon Nol regime . . ."

It took them six more days to reach the bridge which crossed the Srepok to Phum Sath Din. Vathana no longer looked at Samol. Nor could she look upon her other children. It was midday. Through the canopy Vathana sensed that high clouds had gathered and that rain was imminent. She paused. She whispered the prayer to the spirit of the water which Chhuon had taught her as a child. The forest about her was very high, very dense, much denser than she remembered but, she vaguely thought, that is because I've lived in the city for many years.

"Bub-bub ba bub." Samnang was anxious to cross. They had reached their destination.

Vathana prayed against the evidence of her vision that what little she could view was a matter of war weariness. She dragged her feet. "Come here," she said to Samnang. "Let me straighten you." Methodically she preened her son.

"Grandpa," Su Livanh said. "Grandpa and Grandma."

"I want them to see how pretty you are," Vathana whispered. Tears dropped from her eyes.

"Mama." Su Livanh smiled. "Samol?"

Vathana did not uncover her other daughter. Instead she

straightened her own clothes, let down her hair and rewrapped it in her krama.

They crossed the bridge. The high trees made her feel very small. They walked the old street to where her home should have been. The jungle had encroached upon the clearing, had invaded the shattered structures and interned the memories of the village. Go to your home village, Vathana thought. Go to the village of your parents or your grandparents. That was the order. But what are we to do if the village is no longer there? Now she could not keep from crying openly. She collapsed, trembling on the dirt floor of the old orchard. She dropped Samol. "Papa," she cried. "Papa, I need you. You haven't seen your granddaughter. I can't carry her any farther." Vathana cried hysterically. "Mama. Mama, see my son. Oh, Mama. Mama, you have three beautiful grandchildren."

"Do not cry, child." There is a voice in the orchard. Vathana looks. Through her tears she sees nothing. She's not sure she heard the voice.

"Bub-ba. Bah-ba-ba-ba."

"Don't be frightened." It is an old woman. Perhaps not so old. She is in rags. "What's your name?"

"Cahuom Vathana." Vathana has not moved. From where she has fallen she sees the wraith standing by the angel house. The post is thick with vines but the little shrine is intact.

"Then you are my niece." The voice is lithesome.

"Who are you?" Vathana sees the woman has no eyes. "Where is the village?"

"Grandpa?" Su Livanh whispers.

"I came from the pile of the dead, Niece. But I am not dead. My husband wanted me to go with him but I told him it was better he go alone."

"Go? Go where?"

"They have all gone. Years now. You must go too. You can't . . ."

"How do you live, Auntie?"

"I find food." She laughs an ugly distorted cackle and Su Livanh crushes to her mother's side. "Bury the dead child here. In the orchard. Then you must go. Go west." Again the cackle. "You can't stay here. Go now. West. Otherwise they will send you to the ancestors."

The small paddies carved from the jungle in late 1973 and improved in 1974 by the inhabitants of Phum 117 had been abandoned. New jungle had been cut without leaving treelines. The people were roused at four in the morning and sent to

work moving the new dike, constructing the connectors, filling
the year-old feeder trenches which regulated the irrigation level.
Eight hundred people worked the new system, Chhuon amongst
them. He clawed at the laterite clods as he planned, prayed,
attempting to achieve the impossible, a viable agricultural system on a landscape as inviting as the moon. At seven the
workers stopped for a ten-minute breakfast of rice soup, then
they pushed on till noon. Again they rested, rested not the
traditional Cambodian siesta, 12 to 4, but broke for an hour.
The rains were coming. The new people were coming. They
worked through the heat of the afternoon and into the dusk.
Again they rested, again for but an hour. Then by the light of
bonfires built of new-cut jungle they pushed on until eleven,
even midnight.

"It must be done. It must be done. We must finish," Met Vong
pressed Chhuon. "When the dikes are complete the people can
rest."

"They'll be too tired to plant."

"New people can plant."

"Will they? Will they bring enough food to last until harvest?"

"Make the rice grow quickly. Angkar holds you responsible."

Chhuon's hut was still the one-man cocoon he'd rewoven after
Sok's death in December 1973. He had made several improvements. Heavy branches in the platform had been replaced with
hollow bamboo making the cocoon lighter, more easily moved.
Both ends could now be opened to catch the slightest breeze, or
closed for total privacy. In the walls were open pockets for his
few belongings and the hidden pocket for his notebooks.

At midnight, a week after the first city dwellers arrived, he
wearily crawled through the hatch, closed it, lay his head on a
flimsy straw pad and became the chrysalis of a future free man.
He listened carefully. Would a *chrops* crawl under the platform
tonight? For the informer who caught him, anyone with a notebook, Chhuon knew, it would mean extra rice or a day's rest. In
hunger, Chhuon also knew, people would do anything. He listened. He'd laid a few dried leaves beneath the platform. With
it low to the ground it would be difficult for a *chrops* to trick
him. Chhuon smiled. Very slowly he raised one hand. He let his
fingers find the side pocket, let two split the banana leaf and
snip to find the book. Slowly he removed it. Now he rolled
noisily, hacked, resettled as if asleep. The smoke from bonfires
hung on the ground amid the small huts and the one neary
dorm. All about people coughed. He coughed himself into position to scribble a few notes.

The hysterical know-nothingness of the enforcer, and thus of Angkar, is beyond description. All knowledge of cultivation is subordinate to Angkar's will. Yet one can live in a draconian land only if one follows the rules. Now we are Democratic Kampuchea. The rains come. New people come. Gone is the proper rhythm of life, the rhythm of rice. Gone is Khum 4, replaced by Sangkat 4. To earn merit by showing compassion is prohibited. Tonight I shall guide Mir and his family to the path to the border. I pray they find safety.

For a week they came. For a month. For two months. At first a trickle. Then a flow. Then a constant plodding procession. By July they numbered ten thousand. They had no food, few possessions. They were more battered, more emaciated than the residents of Phum Sath Din had been two and a half years earlier. New People. City dwellers. Four of five were women or small children.

This is your beautiful new village, Angkar says. If you close your eyes you can see it. Now build what you see. Build a hut. Tomorrow you will plant rice, weed rice, transplant rice. Make it grow quickly or you will starve. There's not enough paddy. Dig, build. The rains have been kind. The Old People have been kind. During the little dry season you shall increase the paddy tenfold. It is the will of Angkar. Work harder. The energy of the peasant is a hundredfold that which he knows. Tonight there will be a meeting to reflect upon our lives and our great fortune. Tonight there will be a meeting to learn from our work experience. Do not fall asleep or you will be disappeared. New People are prohibited from speaking to Old People. Angkar will use you as fertilizer. Boys are prohibited from talking to girls. Do not sit near one another. You will be invited to visit the forest. Enemies will be eliminated. Anyone attempting escape is an enemy. You cannot leave.

The commune of the New People was established on the hard laterite upheavals beyond the Old People's massive paddy. Quietly, covertly, communication between the groups was established. Chhuon and others tried to help, tried to advise. He felt overwhelmed. Those new wards of Sangkat 4 most likely to be identified by Angkar as ex–Lon Nol lackeys needed to be spirited onto the forest paths to the Thai border. But to be caught assisting meant immediate death. To be suspect of compassion could mean disappearance.
    "are you poh?"
    "voen?"
    "who are you?"

"voen!" Chhuon grasped his sister's hands. She pulled them back. Scabs broke. The thin fingers bled. "i am brother."

"brother is forbidden, eh?"

"no. your brother. chhuon."

Voen stared at the dark face in the dark jungle. She reached to touch it. Hesitated. Then reached, touched. Chhuon trembled. They had not seen each other since Vathana's wedding. Tears flooded her eyes. "is . . . is *meh* with you?" She used the rural word for "mom."

Chhuon dropped his head. "i buried her three years ago now."

"sok?"

"she i buried two dry seasons past."

"samay? sakhon?"

"i don't know. there was word that kdeb is not dead but with some resistance."

"samnang?!"

"i don't know if it's true. have you seen vathana? is she with you? is her child well?"

"there are three. three grandchildren for you."

"three!" Joy burst immediately on Chhuon's weathered face. "where?"

"i don't know. her city fell very early." Chhuon's heart dropped. "we need food," Voen whispered. "please, brother, tell us where to get rice."

"i don't know. i'll get some."

For an hour they talked. Voen related the horrors of the evacuation and march from Phnom Penh, the deaths she'd seen, the families separated, the march up the Northern Corridor past ghost cities, past rubble heaps, through the stink of rotting meat. Then time became critical and they fled to their respective huts. Twice more they met. The first time Voen brought a high-level functionary for Chhuon's underground roadway out. Chhuon brought two kilos of rice, enough to supplement her food ration for several weeks. The second time Chhuon brought all his notebooks but the original with the story of Plei Srepok. It was September. Norodom Sihanouk had returned to Phnom Penh. Rains were driving and continuous. The huge dikes were eroding, collapsing. Ten thousand hands could not plug the spillways ripping through everywhere. Seedlings and plants were sucked from their loose hold and washed through with the torrential current. Hundreds of workers were being bludgeoned to death for being lax. Their bodies were thrown in the gaps but floated with the rising waters and at best clogged the few transfer ditches and forced them, too, to collapse.

"there will be no food next year. the crop is gone."

"yes."

"can we escape?"

"i will take you."

"you will come. you are my brother."

"no. when i die i will die on this land. i am cambodia . . ."

"i too am khmer. we'll stay. we'll send others."

"a little resistance, it feeds the soul, eh?"

"aah."

"take these. there are *chrops* at my hut every night. hide them. someday the story must be told. I Am Cambodia . . ."

A week later Chhuon was taken from his cocoon. Vong was furious. "Angkar," Vong ranted, "holds Poh responsible for this failure. Angkar demands that conspirators expose their networks. Met Khieng, too, has confessed. Both of you are sent up to Site 169."

Nang squatted. About him a tribe of five- and six-year-olds sat, rapt, their eyes glued to his every gesture, their ears to his every word. "He was called Kambu," Nang said softly. "He was my father. He is yours. He is the father of all Khmers. From him came Kambuja." Nang shifted. His mind was not on his speech but on the unsolved problem. He had bathed, manicured his seven fingers, dressed in an immaculate light-gray uniform with a red-checked krama folded neatly and hung about his neck. Nang looked beyond the children, his children. Each had been separated from his or her parents by force or by the deaths of the parents. Each had been starving up to the moment they'd been taken in by Nang. To them he was not an ugly and scarred nineteen-year-old security controller but a substitute parent, family, a provider, a hero. Nang spoke softly. His eyes were consoling, gentle, lusterless, as if a matte finish had somehow been impressed upon the surface. From his eyes the most astute child concluded he was unassuming, sincere. Amongst themselves they called him Kindly Uncle Nang.

Nang's eyes fell back on the children. They too were spotless. Amid the filth which had exploded upon the land, amid the encroaching jungle, Nang's house was light, on clear days ablaze with sunshine reflecting off polished bamboo surfaces and confiscated rosewood furniture. The house sat alone in a small jungle clearing a kilometer north of the nearest commune perimeter, several kilometers east of the cliffs. From early morning to midafternoon sunbeams splashed on the veranda, swarmed through doors and windows. Then the shadow of the cliffs blanketed the house in premature dusk. Nang smiled a wisp of a smile. "From Kambuja came Angkar. Now you are all comrade children of Angkar. In Angkar we shall take the great leap forward. If others hesitate, we'll drag them with us."

The children loved Nang. They loved his gentle manner, his soft voice, his wonderful words. They loved his home, their home, the largest and best any had ever seen—a villa in thatch and bamboo. That they were totally surrounded by minefields meant nothing other than that they could not play or school beyond the yard.

Nang loved the children. He loved their potential. He loved their openness. To him they were a sounding board, an awestruck audience, an experiment in "the scientific application of security measures," his future army.

"The old society was very bad," Nang said. "Corrupt. Full of senseless values which made everyone slaves. On Glorious 17 April when the Americans fled in shame, we began anew. Every vestige of old Cambodia has been eliminated. Now it is year zero. Now we shall create a new Kampuchea in which Khmer purity will reign, a Kampuchea which will ensure the continuance of the Khmer race for the next thousand years.

"For us, comrade children, all things are possible. Only Khmers have overthrown the feudal regime and the capitalist warmongers. Only we have established true independence and national sovereignty." The children nodded, pleased in their importance.

"Now you must study the teachings of Pol Pot," Nang said. "Met Nem will help. All must learn to read and to count. Learn to construct yourselves in the proper mold. Someday, like me, you will be masters of the waters and of the land."

An hour later Nang said, "Have you identified any new children for me?" He stood with Met Ku, his site assistant, in a high observation tower at one corner of Site A-26.

"Yes. Several." Ku was not enthusiastic. "Also a new spy."

"Bring the children to my home." Nang raised the binoculars and scanned below. "They'll become our eyes where our eyes cannot see," he said.

Below them perfectly ordered huts stretched in two facing parallel lines. Between the rows was an unsided, roofed pavilion used for dining and nightly meetings. "They'll become our ears where our ears cannot hear," Nang continued. Beyond the huts perfectly ordered, seemingly perfectly irrigated paddies glowed a verdant iridescence. "In a year they'll train others."

"I don't see the need," Ku said. "We have the security force, and those children"—he gestured to the paddy—"spy for us. They come, they say, 'Mama speaks French.' They eat. Mama is disappeared."

"These all will be disappeared," Nang said softly. "They are the bourgeois of Kompong Chhnang. Undesirables."

"Then . . ."

"They'll spy in the *sangkats,* not the sites," Nang said. "The Chinese botched their revolution because they didn't attack all the foundations of culture. Children must be weaned from adults at two. Doors must be eliminated. We shall be the first people in history to achieve a pure communist society without time frittered on intermediate steps."

Again Nang raised the binoculars. From the tower he could see four of his isolated subsites. All were to his design—his contribution to Angkar. Instead of the massive communes of the controllers or chiefs he had established a network of more than twenty camps—not one larger than four hundred people—each isolated by mined jungle, each totally controlled by a permanent cadre, each containing a homogeneous group to be eliminated. Site A-26 now held middle-class Khmer families from Kompong Chhnang; B-26 ethnic Chinese from the Kompong Thom area; C-26 Chams; D-26 Mountaineers, and on and on. Surviving FANK officers with families were grouped together; those without families were housed at another site. Ethnic Viet Namese were clustered at the most remote subsite so as not to infect the air and pass their diseases. Small prisons had been hidden amid the camps. At night screams from the dark terrorized the peasants.

Nang's mouth broadened in a flat look of disdain as he observed his workers. The contortion forced the shrapnel scar and the napalm scar into ugly wrinkles. "They are the past," he said to Ku. "Until the rice is in, until we create a better system, let them believe. Let them tend rice." Nang's face creased deeper. His eyes glittered. "Reeducate them."

As the complex of Site 169 and the northern *sangkats* and *sroks* had burgeoned with the deluge of evacuees from Phnom Penh and much of northern Cambodia, Nang had realized platform elimination was too inefficient. It could not keep up with demand. Enemies were many, loyal cadre few. In June he'd had groups brought to the largest craters he could find. He let his yotheas shoot them, but ammunition was scarce and the method proved too costly. In July and August he'd scouted the wilderness for areas in which to dispose of bodies. With each find he'd directed a group be brought out and bludgeoned to death. The method was slow. The yotheas became bored. Worse, it gave useless elements time to react. Always one or two attempted escape and time was wasted in hunting them down, dragging them back to their group and finally bashing in their skulls.

At Site 169 emptied camps were reoccupied by a second wave

of refugees who moved into established huts and tended established fields. These people came from the hard life in the *sangkats*. Nang imagined them in his camps eating better, receiving better treatment. He worked them hard yet he was certain they were not being pushed to their limit. "They become lax," he told Ku. "Lax, they're easier to control. They write longer biographies."

Still the camps refilled faster than they could be emptied. New sites were constructed as controllers sent more and more traitors, agents and spies. After the first wave of eliminations, a record center was established. Biographies were referenced, cross-referenced and analyzed. Seditious networks were unmasked. More and more people were arrested.

"What's your estimate of per-hectare production?" Nang asked Ku.

"Three, four tons from the best paddies," Ku said. In reality his estimate was a tenfold exaggeration. "The people are proud of their work."

"Good. From the poorest?"

"One point four if you don't count the yuons. They're terrible workers."

"This will be a very big crop." Nang's mind was not on rice. He babbled yet his concentration was scattered. The unsolved problem vexed him. How? How to make it more efficient? He was running out of space. Criticism from the Center was rising. His biweekly death reports were not reaching expectations. "Next year," he muttered to Ku, "we double or triple crop."

"What is there to criticize, Met Vannah?" The brashness of the young woman's question was caustic to the cadreman's ears yet he did not correct her. The reeducation session was an hour old. The workers and peasants were tired. How many times did they need to hear the rantings against the three mountains of old power—the imperialists, the feudalists, the comprador capitalists? How many times did they need to be told that work was their sacred right? "Met Vannah," the young woman continued, "we have struggled in the paddies. We have vigorously attacked our labor. I managed a farm for my uncle under the old regime. This," she lied, "is the most wonderful crop I've seen."

"Yes. For me too. Ah . . . ah . . ."

"Bona."

"Yes, Met Bona. For me too. Thanks to Angkar the rice grows quickly, eh."

Bona talked on. Met Vannah agreed. Topics changed. Met Vannah explained how the state now owned all property, how individual rights were subservient to the rights of the state. He told the meeting that Angkar had ordered the national construction effort to be rapidly carried forth. Then he noted the most serious problems. "Angkar has been informed of heinous crimes committed in its name during the evacuations. These atrocities were inflicted not by Angkar but by enemy agents disguised as yotheas. The CIA wishes to discredit Democratic Kampuchea. The Viet Namese wish hegemony over Kampuchea. Work hard. Learn from Angkar. When the yuon threat is neutralized you will be returned to your homes. You will be addressed by Norodom Sihanouk. But first, the Viet Namese sickness must be eradicated. Work hard."

Again Bona stood. "If we are allowed more sleep, Met Vannah," she said, "we will have more energy to work."

Vannah laughed. "Yes, you're correct. All shall sleep now. You are dismissed. Ah, Met Bona . . ."

"Yes?"

"You are a manager, eh?"

"Yes. Well I . . . I helped."

"Do you wish to be invited to help the planner?"

"Out of the paddies?! Oh, yes!"

"Then tomorrow you should pack a small bag. I'll have you transferred to Met Nang's office where paddies are mapped and fertilizer needs established."

Bona first was led past ancient ruins. The guide forced her to stop and observe the bas-relief—a three-tiered sculpture where those at the top, plump with much merit, awaited reincarnation to better lives and those at the base, chained, with concave starving bellies, being beaten or lifted by the ankles, swung and smashed to the earth, expected to return as rodents or dogs.

"How far we have come, eh, Comrade Sister?" The young soldier snickered.

All day she waited for her assignment. By sunset she'd completed her biography; at midnight Nang arrived; at two she was brought to his chamber and left. She had been well treated yet she was afraid. Nang closed the door. Outside latches clacked. Nang slid the inner bolt. Then he picked up a switch. Bona tried to be brave, tried not to show the fear which had seized her. It was incomprehensible that this impeccably dressed scarred man her own age would truly harm her. She was to assist a planner. She'd done nothing wrong.

"You're very beautiful," Nang whispered. His voice was thick. Bona dropped her eyes respectfully. "You are not allowed to cry loudly," he said.

"To cry?" She forced the words.

Nang's hand flicked and the switch slapped her cheek. Immediately a welt raised. She didn't cry.

"Tell me the names of your contacts." Nang's eyes began to glaze.

"Contacts?" Bona was bewildered.

"Your American boss."

"What American boss . . ." Again the switch flicked, caught her neck. She backed to the wall.

"You're a spy. Do you work for Americans or yuons?"

"I don't work for anyone," Bona blurted.

Nang feigned a flick of the switch. Bona cringed, her arms snapped to cover her face. Then she lowered them. Instantaneously Nang stepped, whirled, smashed her face with a powerful kick. Her nose broke. Blood splattered, her head smacked the wall behind her. She collapsed.

Nang unlatched the door. From outside bolts clattered. The door opened. Two large boys entered. Both were dressed in rough black uniforms. Harshly, Nang said to Bona, "Your biography says you were a functionary for the old regime. Must I turn you over to Angkar's loyal men or will you tell me all?"

Bona wiped blood from her mouth. It smeared on her face and hand. Though there were now three men she felt more secure, as if none would assault her before the others. "I was not a 'functionary.' My father's oldest brother had a small plot. I helped with the rice."

"Angkar Leou"—Nang was in full control—"prohibits one to use words to hide the truth."

"This is the truth."

The switch snapped. It caught her eye. As she stumbled a yothea snatched her shirt at the shoulder. Violently he jerked her from the wall, flipped her toward Nang as if she were a rag doll, his hand clutching the shirt, the cloth shredding.

Nang grabbed her, held her, kept her from falling. Then his hands flew, clutching her tattered clothes, ripping downwards, exposing her breasts, throwing her to her knees. All three men laughed. "Hang her there." Nang indicated steel cuffs attached to the wall just above shoulder height.

"*No*," Bona screamed. "I'll . . . I'll tell you anything."

The yotheas laughed loudly as they grasped her, each grabbing one thin wrist and pulling her arms apart, displaying her chest to Nang who chuckled appreciatively. Then they hung her and left.

Again Nang latched the inner bolt. "Answer immediately." Though quiet, Nang's voice was severe. "Do not waste time reflecting. Do not fabricate lies." Nang grabbed the waistband of her skirt, ripped the material, pulled down. "Who is your boss?"

"An American . . . ?" The answer came quick, firm, but ended in a question.

"How do you contact him?" Nang rubbed the stubs of his cleaved fingers hard against Bona's vulva. She raised a knee to protect herself. Nang jabbed the quadriceps with one finger with such force that the muscle danced in spasm. Bona shuddered in pain, in fear, in loss of response. How could she tell him about a contact procedure which she'd never known? "How do you . . ." Nang screamed his righteous questions as he rammed his hand into her. Bona tried to think. Stuttered grunts dribbled from her mouth. Nang laughed uproariously. "You like it." Bona didn't answer. Nang pulled back, angry. He cocked the arm of his broken hand. "Where?" he screamed.

"At the cliff," she blurted. "At the base, near the border."

Nang smashed her mouth, shattering teeth. "I should throw you from the cliff," Nang screamed. He punched her chest trying to flatten Bona's breasts. Ribs broke. Nang punched wildly. The breasts sank into her lifeless torso.

For a month Nang searched for Bona's contact site at the base of the cliffs near the Thai border. For a month he had ambush teams lying in wait for the American. Every person from Bona's camp was interrogated, beaten. A hundred were *chap teuv bat*, taken away never to be seen again.

"Met Ku." Nang was frantic. "The enemy comes to the base of the cliffs. He must be caught. The Center must never know."

In order to solidify his position, Nang now took drastic measures. He directed Ku, Met Arn and Met Ro, his three most faithful underlings, to develop within each camp a core of unquestioning, second-level spies and police who could be used to carry out Nang's policies, whims and will.

His paranoia grew with each report of treachery. "Ku"—Nang banged his claw into his left palm—"we need a larger detention center for the POWs." Nang's eyes leaped from wall to wall. "I know," he whispered, pulling Ku close, "I know exactly where and how it's to be built."

Nang envisioned the new system. Within a year, he saw, he would not only have his own private security minions, his children spies and his secret police force to supplement the regional and national forces, but also three small, roving, gestapo-type platoons which would spy on the children, the minions, the police, the regional and national forces, on one another and on themselves. And all would feed a new facility. The slightest gesture, by anyone, could be interpreted as anti-Krahom, anti-Angkar, or anti–Met Nang. Immediately, he saw, he would be able to move to isolate any threat. That this might lead to the highest level of executions in any district of Democratic Kampuchea, he knew, would be a feather in his cap.

In November, when the main harvest was to be reaped, camps on subsites D-26, D-134, D-143 and A-39 had so few able-bodied people that Nang "sold" the unharvested fields to the director of Sector 4 of the northwest region who marched two thousand workers ninety kilometers in seven days. The harvest had been scant. Some rice had rotted, some was destroyed by late-season winds, some died in dry paddies because of faulty irrigation. When the harvest was in, Nang's pay was a mere twelve metric tons. All his rice and that of the director from Sector 4 was shipped to the Center's central collection point for further shipment to China. "They did not harvest the crop," Nang later said of the remaining inhabitants of those camps. "How could they expect to eat it?" The Sector 4 director was equally compassionate. "My people have simply and graciously contributed a few days to harvest the rice of an ill neighbor. In Angkar's eyes they have earned much praise and honor."

Nang scowled. Construction was behind schedule. In his mind he questioned Met Arn's loyalty. Openly he questioned Met Ro. Ro disappeared.

"Why is it so difficult to string a wire from here to there?" Nang demanded of Arn.

"The wire breaks with the weight of the fixture," Arn said. Quickly he added, "We've secured thicker cables. They're being joined and . . ."

Nang stamped out. In mid-October the Center had issued the following order: "Angkar Leou no longer requires prisoners of war. Local chiefs and controllers shall dispose of them. This is the wish of Angkar Leou." Nang walked to the railing of the new observation platform. It was a tree house in the upper limbs of the highest tree surrounded by other trees, a small box house built under the branches so as to be undetectable from above. To one side, down a four-hundred-foot cliff, was the new main detention facility and all of Democratic Kampuchea; to the other side was a broad ledge and then the fifteen-hundred-foot rising escarpment to the Thai border. Directly in front, the lower cliff curved to make a horseshoe-falls bowl. Beneath the vegetation of the ledge were a hundred small concrete-block cells—only a fraction completed and occupied. Nang stared across the horseshoe gap. He clenched his teeth, furrowed his nose. Already there was odor coming from the cells. How he hated those creatures. The cells were one and a half by two meters, by one and a quarter meters high. In each were a dozen or more squirming, disheveled, cowering, pathetic people. He saw them as his plight, his guilt, his banishment to the border. Without them his nation would never have suffered so. It was their fault, he told himself. They're to blame. Had they not been corrupt, had they been pure, never would Kampuchea have needed what Nang had now become. Had they been strong, he told himself, he would never have been reduced to being an eliminator. I am a soldier. No, "am" is not right. Being a yothea is honorable. Being a babysitter for this scum . . . being a trash disposer . . . He wanted to beat them for what he'd become. He wanted them vanished so no memory existed. He wanted . . .

"Ah . . . Met Nang." Met Ku topped the ladder. "There's a new ward in Camp E-26."

Nang glared at his assistant. Idiots, he thought. They are all idiots. "In every camp, every day, there are new wards." His face was blank.

"This one is very odd," Ku said. Nang's face remained empty. "He walked in carrying a cocoon on his back."

They found her unconscious with a small child rooted into the nest created by her curled body. She was wet, cool from exposure to the rains. Her breathing was shallow, almost imperceptible. The two men didn't speak. They had observed her for several hours without ever seeing the child. How she had gotten there, who she was, they did not know. One man had been living in the forest for more than three years, moving constantly, eating jungle fare—berries, leaves, roots—the other had been with him for two months. Between them they had seen much suffering and death along the back roads of South Viet Nam and Cambodia, had become yet more cautious, more patient. She might be bait, they'd thought. A trap. She was probably dead. Hours mattered little. Before they approached they scouted the road in both directions, scouted the forest deep to each side. Still they waited. Then quietly they approached. Slowly they prodded her with a long branch. Her head and torso fell back exposing the child who squirmed, shivered and faintly sobbed. They bent over her and the child, touched her to see if she were alive. One of them, the man without a left arm, cradled and lifted the child. The krama wrapped about the child's head fell back. In the dank grayness red hair shone. Shocked, the men's eyes met. They did not talk. The second man lifted the mother. He struggled. He heaved her up as he dropped to one knee. She collapsed over his shoulder. Then, seemingly from nowhere, exploding in the silence like a well-laid ambush, *"Bah! Bah-ba-ba-ba-ba-ba-ba-ba!"* Then *bam!* A small hard boy-child slammed like a locomotive into the man trying to lift his mother, splaying all three into the mud-dirt road.

"Bah! Ba! Bababa!" Samnang's gibber blasted, then tailed off in confusion. Then the boy leaped up, grabbed the man holding Su Livanh, kicked him, wrenched the girl from his arm.

"No hurt. No hurt." The man tried to calm the boy. His Khmer was broken.

"Bah! Ba! Ba-bababa!" The boy's eyes flashed.

"Ssshh!" The second man grabbed him. Samnang spun, swung his fists wildly, tried kicking. The man grabbed him firmly, turned him to face away, then squeezed him until he was unable to thrash. "ssshh! we're friends. let us help you. and her. she's very ill. divine buddha, he order us to help."

For an hour they followed ever-branching trails deeper and deeper into the forest. The trails became narrower, the vegetation lower. Samnang, suspicious, followed the man with his mother who walked behind the one-armed one with Su Livanh. They came to a stream. The trail ended. The water was dark, smooth. The men changed positions, stepped to the shallow edge at the bank, waded upstream. Occasionally the one-armed one turned to see if the boy still followed. After twenty minutes they came upon a small, V-shaped bamboo footbridge suspended from braided vines. The entire trek had been silent. Now, Samnang, afraid of the bridge, began a low monosyllabic babble. The one-armed man crossed with Su Livanh. Samnang's stammering became louder. The second man looked blankly at him. With Vathana over his shoulder he stepped onto the bridge. Samnang backed away, his "ba-ba" turning into a wheezing moan. The man backed off the bridge. He motioned the boy to him. "you ba-ba, eh? i am kpa. i am your friend. divine buddha say i am your friend."

The camp was tiny. A single hut with walls of vertical branches placed side to side and a roof of palm fronds. Inside there was a single bamboo platform. On it a third man lay wrapped in a quilt, shivering. Still without speaking the men laid Vathana and Su Livanh on the platform. Then they built a small fire. From a clay jar they produced rice, from a second a shriveled smoked bat. Soon they had hot bowls of rice and bat soup. Kpa

offered his to Samnang. The boy hesitated. Slowly he accepted
the bowl. Then he lunged at the food, sucking and slurping the
gruel, then loudly licking the wooden bowl trying to lap the
lingering flavor from the wooden pores. Kpa and the one-armed
man ate calmly. They fed the man coming out of his malarial
tremor, then Su Livanh.

Vathana, though still subconscious, sensed the loss of Su
Livanh's warmth. Her body curled tighter in a fetal squeeze. A
slight gasp escaped her lips.

"mama," Su Livanh whispered.

"You can talk, eh?" Kpa said quietly. Su Livanh stared at the
red-brown man. She tried to squirm back into her mother's
nest. "Don't be afraid." Kpa squatted by the edge of the platform, gently extended a hand and rubbed the back of Su Livanh's
arm. "What's your name?" Su Livanh dug her heels in and
pushed harder against Vathana. Vathana's curl eased. Again she
gasped. "Bring some water," Kpa said to the other man.

"ba, ba ba ba." Samnang sat on the platform beside his
sister.

"Ba ba," Kpa said gently. "Who is this?" He tapped Su
Livanh.

Su Livanh looked at the man squatting before her. "Su Livanh,"
she answered in a sweet little-girl voice. "We went to see Grandpa
Cahuom but he was gone."

"Cahuom? Cahuom Chhuon?"

"Grandpa." Su Livanh shuddered and again squirmed against
her mother.

"my baby," Vathana mumbled in delirium. "samol." Her
voice was very weak.

For weeks Kpa and the other two men nursed Vathana, fed
and sheltered the children. They spoke little, almost no words
at all, a habit they'd fallen into in their hiding. The children
responded well but Vathana remained weak and withdrawn.
She refused to eat. Slowly the men forced her to swallow, first
just water, then soup, then rice; a little more each day. All day,
all night, when conscious, she cried though she had no tears.
The man with malaria spoke softly to her. She remained withdrawn. He sang childhood songs to her. She was impassive.
When she slipped into subconsciousness she moaned for Samol.

"Who is Samol?" the malarial man asked Su Livanh.

"My sister," the little girl answered, using the form meaning
elder sister.

"Where is she?"

"The witch ate her. Mama says the blind witch ate her."

More weeks passed. Then came the little dry season. Heat and humidity were intolerable. Then the clouds broke with fierce monsoon rains. Vathana sat up. She hung her legs off the platform, placed her feet on the ground. Slowly she rocked to and fro humming the tune to a childhood song, rhythmically rocking, staring at the steady dripping from the palm-frond eave, staring as if her eye sockets were empty, her mind disgorged.

"You are my niece," said the man who suffered from malaria. "I sang that song to you when you were your daughter's age." Vathana stopped humming, stopped rocking. She leaned against the man. He put his arm around her, rocked gently, hummed. He fell silent. Then he said, "I wanted them all to stay. We were a strong force but when the village was liberated they rushed to join the new force. Some were marched west with the villagers. We found most of them in a grave on the trail to Phum Sath Nan. How I wanted to see your father. And your mother and Aunt Sita—your grandmother. I would have given up the resistance but Kpa knew. He saw into their hearts. Still we can't stay much longer. When the rains stop and all the people and their yotheas are consumed with the harvest, then we'll go out. Then we'll go to Thailand."

The rains continued to intensify throughout September. Foraging became more difficult. Food stores disappeared. Samnang roamed far and wide, alone. He alone seemed to thrive. Sam's recurring bouts with malaria weakened him and he spent the time between bouts fearing the next onset. Su Livanh, though she ate as much as the others, became more and more lethargic. Under her flesh she seemed to be melting away. Nothing she did caught her mother's attention.

On a wet evening in early October, after the three men had remapped and replanned the escape across the Mekong and west and north toward Preah Vihear and up the escarpment to the Thai border, the one-armed man sat with Vathana. "Can't you hug your child?" he asked her. His Khmer was poor. He dropped his eyes, embarrassed by the deficiency. "Can't you . . ." He repeated the question in French.

Vathana turned. She glared at him. Then for the first time in one hundred days she spoke. "Where's your other arm?" Her voice was accusing, in French, flat.

"The Communists took it," he answered in Viet Namese.

"You are yuon."

"Viet Namese. Call me Le." He switched back to French.

"Thmil."

"No."

"Lon Nol warned thmils would bring a dark age. Would bring an age where the ignorants would rule the educated and Buddha would be chased from the land; where only deaf-mutes would survive."

"Yes, I remember. His prophecy holds true for my country as well."

Vathana's glare widened. She leaned away from him. The stub of his left arm involuntarily jumped. "What country?" Vathana's tone remained flat.

"South Viet Nam," he said proudly. "My country. My people. They are not the *thmils*."

"Why aren't you there?"

"I escaped."

"Escaped?"

"The Communists, they're your *thmils*. In my country too they've ushered in a dark age. They took my arm in 1972. I was captured but released when the Khmer Rouge attacked the NVA base. I think they meant to kill me but your uncle's men assisted me to ARVN lines." Vathana stared uncomprehendingly. It was the first time she'd spoken. Le was afraid if he stopped she'd slip back into her remote void. He talked on. "I was medically discharged but even so . . . when . . . they put me in the Ka Tum Reeducation Camp west of An Loc. Then they told me, because I was an intelligence officer, I should go to Nghe Tinh, to Reeducation Camp Number 6 in Tanh Phnong, very very far north. I was sure they meant to kill me so I escaped and ran for days. West of Ban Me Thuot I jumped into the Krong River and I floated downstream until it became the Srepok and then I followed the river until I recognized the peak by the old NVA camp. Then your Uncle Sam found me again. Only he and Kpa remain from their . . ."

"You must take my children to Thailand."

"Uh . . . yes. Of course. We're all going."

"I will die here . . . The children, they are yours now." At that Vathana turned from Tran Van Le. She pulled her legs back up to the platform with her hands, fell to her side, curled and slept. As she did, in her mind, an old prayer unfolded.

> From great suffering comes great insight.
> From great insight comes great compassion.
> From great compassion comes a peaceful heart.
> From a peaceful heart comes a peaceful family.
> From a peaceful family comes a peaceful community.
> From a peaceful community comes a peaceful nation.
> From a peaceful nation comes a peaceful world.

The rains slowed. The winds shifted. The rains stopped. Kpa led the tiny column away from the camp toward the swollen stream and to the bamboo-and-vine suspension bridge. Each day in the month and a half since Tran Van Le had broken through to Vathana, he, Kpa and Sam had forced her to listen, to talk, to eat and to walk. Each day, though her health was fragile, she became a little stronger. Each night they told her their dream of Thailand. Each night she too dreamed. Each dream ended with her in Kampuchea and the children in Bangkok. Vathana was happy, happy as the day she raised the first medical tent for the refugees fleeing the border war, happy as the day Samol was born. She believed the dream.

Su Livanh, too, recouped much of her lost spirit. The lilt returned to her voice; flaccid muscle turned taut. Kpa and Samnang became almost inseparable, a hunting-foraging team able to supply the tiny unit with enough food if not to thrive, at least to heal and regain some weight. Only Sam remained weak. The malarial bouts which should have tempered remained a nagging constant, dragging him closer and closer to despair.

The bridge was intact but weather worn and flimsy. They spent an entire day laboring in its repair. Then they crossed it and camped. The trails had not been used since they'd come to the camp in July. In five months the jungle had nearly obliterated the trails and the going was painfully slow. What once had taken the best part of a day to traverse now took a week. Again food was scarce. Where for five years Vathana had viewed her scant diet as a religious precept or as an exercise in self-denial and self-control, now she saw it as starvation. It weakened and depressed her. She fought to move on. Her mind and body, so fragile, slowed. Her soul filled with dejection. Kpa pushed her. Le prodded. Samnang, bursting anew upon adventure, tugged her. Day by day they moved closer to the main road. Now Vathana wanted to burst from the jungle, to run, to scream, to surrender. Kpa forced a halt. Vathana seethed, mad, claustrophobic. Le restrained her. Sam held her. "Not now. Not now. Not until we know. Tomorrow."

"You will see my children reach Thailand."

"Yes. All of us."

"I must go."

"No."

Before dawn Kpa and Le crept from the night camp toward the roadway. In July there had been no villages in the area, yet now they sensed many inhabitants. Inhabitants would mean soldiers, guards. They proceeded cautiously. They stayed in the trees, moved slowly from concealment to concealment until they could distinguish the sounds of voices. They stopped. They moved parallel to the road to a clearing through which they saw the multitudes—thousands upon thousands of filthy emaciated wraiths in tattered black cloth dragging their unshod feet, limping forth, dazed. At the roadside, in view of the nearly unconscious parade, a dozen yotheas were gang-raping a young woman. Then they dug a hole and buried her to the neck, then they beat her head with clubs until she was dead. Not finished, two boys hacked at her neck with bayonets until they severed the head from the body. Then they put the head on a stake and planted it so the smashed face would greet the oncoming procession. They laughed and ran off, moving against the flow, knocking people down until they found another young woman whom they pulled from the roadway.

Kpa and Le turned back. Again they moved through the forest parallel to the road. All morning they traveled west. At varying intervals they reconnoitered the road. The procession was broken into units but the units seemed endless. By night they returned to find Vathana stir-crazy, Sam yet more anemic. They attempted to reason with both, to explain their sightings, their new plan to remain in the forest slowly moving west. Kpa was able to get nods only when he ordered, "Follow me."

Day fell to night, night rose to day, seemingly without end. One day they moved three kilometers, one day only a half. Always they were quiet. Snakes fell from the trees and frightened them. Spiders crawled over them at night. Ticks buried their heads into their flesh and leeches sucked precious moisture from their bodies. On and on. Wherever they approached roadways they spied starving processions. They crossed the Mekong south of Stung Treng by bribing a government ferryman who responded to every query, "Take care of your mouth, Brother," or "Don't talk of tigers, Sister, where tigers can overhear." Then they came to an area of unharvested golden paddies shimmering in the gentle December wind. Again they slowed, established a camp in a treeline. At night they crept into the fields, rasped their fingers over the grains, filling bags. By day they husked, separated and dried—cooking and eating half, saving half for the next phase.

In areas where few people had lived they'd seen multitudes. Now in areas of once dense habitation they saw no one. Vathana was heedless, indifferent. Kpa became disoriented on the flat plain. Sam remained weak. Le became lax. Only Samnang's natural visual vigilance and Su Livanh's fear of sounds remained intact.

With full rice bags they stepped onto the open empty road.

Suddenly there were shots. Kpa's hip erupted red. More shots. Le scooped Su Livanh in his arms, sprinted. Vathana froze, trembled. She turned, looked back. A hundred meters away a herd of young yotheas were stampeding down upon them. Samnang grabbed Sam. They fled toward scattered palms along the roadside. Vathana dropped her bag, knelt by Kpa. Rice splattered in the dirt.

"Go!" he screamed. *"Go!"*

She grasped his shoulders with her frail hands. "Please," she pleaded weakly.

Kpa struggled. He sat forward, up. Vathana pulled. She looked up. Le, Sam and the children were gone. More shots. Kpa rolled to the knee on his good side, Vathana wedged her hands in his armpits, pushed up. As she held him above her two more shots, very close, exploded. Kpa's face shattered. For a second he stood, to her weightless. Then he collapsed into her.

For two hours the yotheas raped her. Whatever purity the Krahom had claimed before victory was mocked in this taking of the spoils of war. "This is Angkar's rice, eh, Met Trollop? Angkar must be paid. Pay me. Pay my brothers." Again and again. Bang, bang bang—next. Bang, bang bang—next. Rough, crude, cruel. Not concerned with their own pleasures—strictly hate, conquest, control, humiliation. Then beating and interrogation and more beating and then a second day of rape and beating and perhaps a third or a fourth but at that point Vathana did not think of time. "Please," she begged. "Please, let me die. Let death release me." Still she feared death at their hands. She feared they'd dig her grave, bury her to the neck, then bludgeon her. And she feared the decapitation. What pain does the human spirit feel when the head is rammed upon a stake and hoisted, used even in death to terrorize other slaves?

They did not kill her but left her to die. Someone helped her. She did not know who. In mid-December she was given to a newly relocated phum. No one knew her. The *mekong* in charge threw her out. "You can't stay here," the *mekong* snapped angrily. "What's your village? Where's your family?" Vathana was forced to the road, alone, without food, without water, without shelter, without passes. For two weeks she wandered through the new wilderness zone begging for food at each settlement, sucking water from clawed hard dirt clumps at the bottom of dried puddles.

Then, "Phum Sath Din, eh, Sister? Those people are in Sangkat 117. That's where you must go. Here. Take these mangoes. And this. I'm sorry we have so little to give. In the old days . . ."

Then, "You will live with me. How did you get here?"

Vathana could barely answer.

"Who is she?" demanded Met Nem, a *mekong* of Sangkat 117.

"She is my daughter," the woman answered.

"Met Voen, if this is a lie, you'll be sent to Site 169."

"I tell you, she is my daughter. She is very ill. Let me treat her. She'll become strong and will struggle hard for Angkar's glory."

"Humph!" Nem left to report to the commune's enforcer.

"vathana," Voen whispered. It was their first of almost five hundred nights. "your father left a message for you." Vathana's body trembled. Dry sobs wracked her once-beautiful face. "you must live, little niece."

"auntie, where is papa?"

"they sent him to site 169."

"and mama?"

"i will tell you all, but first you must hear your father's words."

"yes."

" 'you must live to tell our story and the story of our people to the whole world.' he told me to make you promise that."

"i promise."

"for our people, vathana."

"i promise."

"i've hidden his notebooks. get them to thailand. he's been disappeared."

"There's a letter for you. From Washington," his father said over the phone.

"An official one?" he asked.

"No, John. Personal. Looks personal. That's why we didn't open it. Looks like a woman's hand. Return address says, R. Donaldson. Want me to forward it or are you coming home for Christmas?"

"I'll be home, Pop."

"Good. It's not right for you to stay away like this."

"I work, you know. For Mr. Pradesh. I'm essentially the ranch manager. It's hard to get away."

"What kind of name is that, anyway?"

"Pradesh? Indian. He . . ."

"Indian?! That doesn't sound like any Indian name I know."

"India Indian. He's a political exile."

"Ah, well, you come home for Christmas, okay? I'll keep the letter till you're here."

John Sullivan went home for Christmas, 1975. He arrived on Wednesday, the twenty-fourth, perfunctorily visited aunts, uncles, cousins, with his parents, sister and brother-in-law. He felt weird, out of it, as if he'd become an alien, but he kept it to himself. On his mind was Rita's letter and ranch business and his independent studies—nothing he felt he could share with his father or sister or any of the others. Christmas morning and through dinner Margie and Bob remained polite yet distant. By noon his Uncle Gus was drunk and wanted John to join him. His mother became furious but she too bottled it up. The day passed as holidays do. On the morning of the twenty-sixth he packed his one bag, carried it to his jeep, then went back in, made coffee and waited for his father to come down.

"Pre-desh, you say?" Henry Sullivan sat with his son.

"Pradesh," John corrected.

"Indian?"

"Um-hum."

"Them and the Arabs and the Japs are buying all the farms in this county. That's gotta stop."

"I don't know," John said. "I know Mister Pradesh runs the place better than the guy that had it before."

"Humph!"

"Look, Pop, I don't want to argue. There's nothing I can say— or do—that makes sense to any of you here. Some of it doesn't make sense to me."

Henry Sullivan squeezed his coffee cup. A thin wisp of white vapor swirled over the dark liquid. "John," he said. It was difficult for him to find the words. He looked at his son. "There's nothin you can say, or do, that'll keep us ... that'll ... you'll always be our son. You know that? Whether you're three or thirty, understand?"

"Thanks, Pop. Maybe, just now, it's better for me to be a few miles away."

"Maybe. But ... John, don't be away because you think no one agrees with you. That sister of yours and her husband, they don't think for all of us. Look, you go back to this Mister Pradesh. If that's what you want, be the best ranch manager there ever was. And ... John ... I'm fifty-seven ... I ... I, ah, got this letter for you from R. Donaldson. Do you have a girl out there on the ranch?"

"No." John laughed. "Not at the moment, Pop. There's a few women in town but no one I'm interested in."

"Who's this?" Henry took the letter from his shirt pocket. The envelope was cream colored, the script neat. He passed it to his son.

John looked at it a moment, gritted his teeth. He didn't want to open it before his father. He had no idea what it might contain. "She was a reporter in Cambodia," John said. "A real hard-nosed bitch."

"Why'd she write?"

"Beats me."

"Well, open the damned thing."

John slid the handle of his teaspoon beneath the flap, cleanly broke the glue. He glanced at the few lines, then read them aloud to his father. " 'John, if this reaches you, contact me. As you predicted, terrible things are happening in Cambodia. No one wants to hear about it. I would like your help in relieving what misery we can. You were the best 'advisor' I ever met there. Situation desperate. Let me send you our reports.' " The note was signed, simply, "Rita." Beneath the signature was written, "Director, Cambodian Crisis Relief."

Six weeks into the new year, John Sullivan received a packet, via his father, from Cambodian Crisis Relief. He had not answered Rita's letter. The packet seemed to be the rough draft of a yet-to-be-released report. Copies of news clippings with comments written in the margins were attached.

> The Khmer Rouge victory of 17 April 1975 has ushered in a new age, one which Khmers call *peal chur chat*, a sour and bitter time. It has not brought peace.

Sullivan dropped the packet on the coffee table in his small living room. He did not want to read it. He did not want to remember anymore. Indeed, he felt he had been quite successful at putting the memories, the bitterness and pain, behind him. He grabbed his jacket. There were fence lines to be checked, feed to be distributed. The words of the report stared up at him.

> Phnom Penh's nearly three million inhabitants were herded from the capital only hours after Khmer Rouge soldiers entered . . .

All towns! Sullivan said to himself. All? Those slimy scumbags.

> . . . bloodbaths . . . all officers of the old army, down to second lieutenant, are being executed. . . .

Three hundred thousand! Sullivan sat on the cheap convertible sofa behind the coffee table. Bloodbaths . . . ! How many . . . how many times did I tell them . . . ? Sullivan stood abruptly, shot an arm into one sleeve of his jacket.

Though these reports have been at least partially substantiated
. . . that is, figures indicating half this number of deaths have
been verified . . . President Ford, according to Press Secretary Ron
Nessen, is "disturbed" by the confirmation of the execution of
eighty to ninety of Lon Nol's officers and their wives. Is it any
wonder America isn't outraged? Is it any wonder America has
barely noticed these atrocities? Even the president of the United
States has hardly mentioned the slaughter of perhaps 10,000 unarmed human beings in that tiny country *each day*.

Sullivan sat, read the report. Then he reread it. He could no
longer ignore what was happening on the far side of the earth,
nor on the East Coast of his own country. His first response was
anger. To Rita Donaldson he wrote.

You know this Cambodian Crisis Relief of yours . . . Do you know
who was, who used to be Cambodian Crisis Relief? Me! That was
my job. It seems to me some people put major obstacles in my
path, some people kept me from helping the people of Cambodia.
Now they ask for my help!

He did not send that note, but ripped it to shreds. He began
again, tore up the pages again. He left, checked the fences,
gritting his teeth the whole time. His stomach felt empty. In the
evening, back in his room, he pored over the report. He pondered the meanings, projected the ramifications. For two days,
as he rode to distant grazing areas to check feed supplies for the
cattle, his anger built. Then he drove to town to begin a search
for materials he might purchase, bring back to the ranch and
study. For weeks he read, bringing to his study the same dedica-
tion and intensity he'd brought to his study of physics and
organic chemistry. Finally, in March 1976 he wrote an impersonal response to Rita Donaldson.

Do we need a new definition of peace, a new theoretical construct?
In the American mind it is not non-peace if a nation slaughters its
own people. War and Peace are not the only alternatives. The
paradigm needs expansion, otherwise incidents drop into categories which stimulate inappropriate responses. Holocaust is not
peace! Genocide is not peace! Pogroms and gulags are not peace!
Reeducation camps are not peace! Slavery is not peace! Fine! Stay
out of other nations' internal affairs—but when does a government lose its legitimacy? When does it forfeit its right to rule/
represent/serve its people? When does a neighbor have the right
or the responsibility to stop the guy next door from abusing his
child? Does a person from Massachusetts have the right to protest
a Texas legislative action which upholds capital punishment?

Why? Is there a line, and if so, when and how is crossing it justifiable?

That Phnom Penh was evacuated is, it seems to me, now well known and well documented. That it was *not* the first of the evacuations is also well documented if less well recognized (recall the entire Northern Corridor evacuations which I witnessed in 1971). That it seemingly will *not* be the last is deeply disturbing. Evacuations, forced migrations and purges are part and parcel of the Communist policy to remake the culture.

As to Gerry Ford, would a public tantrum over the murder of 300,000 have been seen as a sign of weakness or a sign of humanity, a sign of clumsiness or a sign of leadership? Is America now *unleadable*? Did Ford's golf handicap increase or decrease during this period? Can Carter jog beyond it? Is America guilty of mythological ostrichism? Is it easier to bury our heads in each other's asses (and call it a sexual revolution)?

History. Truth. As closely as we can achieve truth via neutral observation (which does not mean neutral conclusions) that truth must be our criterion for our moral judgment of past actions and present policies. Good and evil do exist. Between, there are shades of gray . . . but . . . recognizing ground between should not limit one from seeing and judging the ground at the ends!

I cannot help but think of a line from Eric Hoffer: "You can discover what your enemy fears most by observing the means he uses to frighten you."

Why didn't you see it coming?!

Yes, Rita, I will help. Contact me directly.

CHAPTER TWENTY

Nang's eyes were glazed. "Never forget our people's legacy," he said to the new group, "or the Path of the Revolution. When I was as small as you I learned that from my father."

"Met Nang." Kosal, Nang's bodyguard, escorted in a messenger.

"What is it? Can't you see I'm with my children?"

"The old peasant from E-26 . . ." The runner cowed under Nang's glare.

"Good fertilizer," Nang snapped. He rose to dismiss him.

"The one sent up from Sangkat 117. Very odd. The one who lives in the cocoon he carries on his back."

Nang turned cold eyes on the young man. He pointed, walked away from the children, hissed, "When his camp is scheduled for disposal, dispose of him."

"He said"—the runner rushed the words—"he knows the Center is disappointed."

"What?"

"With the crop. He said if the system was brought into harmony with the local terrain we would double the crop without additional effort. Met Arn had his plan. Arn thinks you might like to review it."

"Then show me."

"Ye . . . yes. Ah . . . one more . . ."

"*Yes!* Say it!"

"The new site . . ."

"More delays?"

". . . it's operational."

Chhuon untied his bundle of poles, relashed them into a bed frame and set the cocoon cover in place. Met Arn had ordered him to move again and he'd moved with grace, moved more easily than an occidental carrying a suitcase through an airport. His stomach no longer burned. It had made peace with the rest of his physical being. His knees ached worse than ever. Still he moved as if the body and the pain were not his, were not the carriers of his spirit, but as if they were needless though not burdensome adjuncts to his being. He crawled into the woven cocoon-house, closed the foot-door blocking the sun, cracked the head-door for light, and immediately set to work on his crude drawings. Perhaps, he thought, they would disappear him for drawing, but drawing was not writing and the need for proper planning was urgent if starvations were to be avoided.

Chhuon reviewed his sketches of the waterworks at Sangkat 117. He added details to the cross-section of the long dike which had turned to muck and melted and let the water wash out and destroy the lower fields as it drained and dried the upper. Then he reviewed his newer diagrams, his proposed dike cross-sections, his overall design based on smaller, more manageable paddies within the new monster fields. It is right, he thought, to aspire to feed the people. It is right to believe Angkar will listen. It is right to speak, to strive. He closed the sketch pad, closed the head-door, lay back. In him, always, refusing to abandon him, was the belief he could make it work, make any of it work, if he, Cahuom Chhuon, were only allowed to bring his mind and his effort to the it, and if he received even a modicum of cooperation, a morsel of others' belief. A morsel of others' . . . He let his mind slip. His fingers absently patted the hidden pocket where his notebooks were concealed, then dropped to his side. Soon, he thought, they will come for me. Soon . . . the thought would not stick. Perhaps he slept for an hour, perhaps only a few minutes. Within, below the eyelids, light stuttered, his being vibrated. Then all subsided into calm reasoning: they would accept his plan because it was common sense, because in light of the past disasters, his answer, when revealed, was obviously the correct solution. Then the old thought recurred, respawned, now faint, now sorrowful: He's alive. I know he's alive. Why? Why has Kdeb abandoned me?

Suddenly there was jarring. Ripping. Bright lights burning. His face shook. Eyes opened, bleary.

"Hey, Comrade Ancient One." A second-level cadre flung the head-door into the communal straw heap for cooking fires. The address used was not the old honorary form but an old derogatory idiom, a cross between "bum" and "derelict." "Behind closed doors people become devils. Comrade Nang has decreed, doors are no longer allowed." With that the foot-door was ripped from the cocoon.

*   *   *

Met Kosal, Nang's bodyguard, held Chhuon by a rope attached
to the old man's left ankle, held him a respectful six meters
from Nang. Chhuon's black trousers were worn through at the
knees, thin at the thighs and ass, tattered at the cuff. His
black shirt was frayed, patched in so many places it was a rag.
His krama was too thin, the cloth on the verge of disintegrating.
Physically—from imprisonment, from beatings, from malnutrition and slave labor—he had lost his former stature, had shrunk
in height a full twelve centimeters, had atrophied of muscle and
bone to the point that although he stood erect he appeared
slumped. At one end, his eyes had gone bad, his vision beyond
five paces blurry, closer than arm's length, dizzying; at the
other, his feet, the connective tissues deteriorated, splayed like
frog flippers on the polished floor.

Nang barely glanced at the pathetic creature. In his impeccable uniform, in his spotless house, in his well-fed condition and
in his iron-hard nineteen-year-old body, he could not imagine
his needing this *anoupracheachon*, this subhuman. It was only
an old rice farmer, like all old rice farmers. Nang did note the
filthy feet on his floor, made a mental note to have the floor
cleaned when the feet were removed.

"The people are hungry," Chhuon said simply. How horribly
scarred this one's face, he thought. Like the one who . . . on the
march from Phum Sath Din . . . Who saved . . . No . . . this one
is much worse. Nang scowled. "It is not necessary," Chhuon
continued. Suddenly the left corner of Nang's mouth jerked
down. "Minor changes will protect the soil and ensure adequate
yields for the Revolution."

The tic at Nang's mouth jumped again. He pushed it with his
fingers to make it cease. "Met Arn said you've drawn plans. Are
you an engineer?"

"No."

"Were you ever?"

"No. Just a farmer." Chhuon held out his bony callused
hands. "I've been told you are the master of the water."

"Humph."

"The water is out of control. Angkar's center is adrift. Half the
fields have washed out. Half the . . ."

Nang stopped him. "American agents sabotaged the dikes."
He clenched his teeth, paused, angry, then screamed, *"Don't
you know? Eh!? I'll show you!* At the border we'll catch them.
I'm sick and tired of grumbling. If you don't wish to live here"—a
quick laugh spurted—"you need not." Nang stamped away.
Then stamped back. "Bring him," Nang snapped at Met Kosal.

"We'll join a border patrol. Then"—he sneered at Chhuon—"you'll see. You'll see. Every night we catch them. Give me those drawings."

At dusk they set off. There was no opposition, no potential opposition. There was no need for noise or light discipline, no need for point or rear guards, or for flank security. Nang, Kosal and Arn rode the first mile in Nang's newly acquired Lada sedan. They drove slowly away from their destination on a road Nang had ordered built, the only auto road in Site 169, rode as Chhuon and a dozen yotheas trotted behind. Chhuon stumbled often. The yotheas lifted him, pushed him. The car stopped. Nang, Kosal and Arn emerged. Immediately they stepped to the footpath along the road and headed back in the direction they'd come. "I've looked at the drawings," Nang said pompously. "Tell me your plan."

For an hour they walked in circuitous approach toward the border. Three armed yotheas led, then Kosal and Nang, then Chhuon and Arn, then the others. Chhuon spoke easily, compassionately. Arn scribbled notes. Nang listened, pretended to be aloof. Chhuon spoke of the living fields, of the care they required. He punctuated his points with the phrases and goals of the Revolution. "It is necessary to return the straw to the earth. This retains soil moisture. The people burn the rice stalks to cook and the forest wood for nightly bonfires. Surely Angkar's wish for self-sufficiency is better served when we struggle to maximize the yields."

Chhuon was silent as they crossed a clearing. As they reentered the forest he offered an audible prayer to the spirits of the trees. Then, "When the water is properly controlled there is no drought in dry times, no floods under monsoon. The water runs and cleans itself and fish are abundant. Yet if Angkar's wishes are unfulfilled, the water loses its discipline. It washes away the soil, it leaves the high land bare. The feeder trenches and canals clog. It stagnates and becomes ill and dies. Nothing grows."

As Chhuon talked, Nang seethed. He had made a mistake hearing the old peasant in Kosal and Arn's presence. To simply eliminate him now would show weakness and lack of judgment.

"There are other problems," Chhuon said. "For Angkar to come to its center and for the fighters to launch an offensive to increase yields, crops must be chosen which will gain victory over famine. This area is better suited for military crops: yams, sugarcane, maize. Grow those here and rice downwater. Then . . ."

"Hush!" Nang had heard enough.

"Kampuchea must not depend solely on one crop." Chhuon

rushed to include a last thought. "That invites disaster. Systems are fragile. Humans too. Massive collectives steal from the peasant his control over his own well-being. It robs him of his pride as master of his own paddy. The system fails when . . ."

Nang turned on Chhuon. "Enemies make it fail," he whispered harshly. "Saboteurs. Even amongst the cadre there are agents. Two-faces want Angkar to fail. In failure America can justify its attacks. Viet Nam can launch a 'liberation' effort."

"High Comrade Nang," Chhuon said clearly, "Angkar is very great and very powerful. If an offensive is launched to improve the agricultural system, no enemy will be able to lure the cadre or the people."

"I'll see enemies at the base of my mountain. Bad cadre will be culled, replaced by loyal . . . Why do I talk to you? From here, silence."

Quietly they moved into the thicket and rendezvoused with a preestablished ambush team. The evening had turned soft-dark beneath a rising quarter moon. Before them Chhuon saw nothing but vegetation. "they call it the underground roadway," Nang whispered to Chhuon. "very structured. ha! we help them with baskets of food in the forest."

Chhuon could not speak. Then too loudly he blurted, "Underground roadwa . . ."

"ssssh, ha. ha. it funnels to here. ha, when we lived in the jungle, we were always wet and cold and hungry. so many caught malaria we often attacked with only half force. now our enemies run from a little hardship. ha. we kill them. tomorrow i'll show you a body dump. it's very good, eh! maybe you'll tell everyone and the enemies will not lure the people."

For hours they waited. The moon rose. Nang slept sporadically, lurched at each monkey's whoop or bird's cry. Chhuon quietly tapped a dried palm frond before him. He listened intently, but his hearing had worsened along with all his perceptory senses. How could he signal? He turned to Arn. "How do you catch them?"

"land mines," Arn whispered.

"But doesn't that mar the trail and give away the site for tomorrow?"

"ssshh. each day we move back a few meters."

"Oh."

"ssshh."

"What?" Chhuon tapped the side of his head. "I don't hear so well any . . ." Kosal clamped a hand over Chhuon's mouth.

Tick . . . Tick . . . Tick . . . Chhuon's fingernail on the palm frond. Then a rustling down trail. Tick . . . Tick . . . Tick . . .

Chhuon shifted, trying to see. The rustling stopped. Nang seized his old hand. "Are you awak . . ." Kosal's grip on Chhuon's mouth silenced him. More rustling on the animal path. A young man, two women. Between them a pole with young children hammocked in fishnet.

Suddenly, the first explosion. Fireball. Concussion. Roar. Then sniper fire and screams. Forty people running. Maybe more. Cries. "Help me." Anguished pleas, "Carry me." "I can't." Running. More rifle cracks. "Mama! Maaaaa-Maaa!"

Laughing. There is no counterfire. The "enemies of the people" are unarmed. Nang clicks on a powerful flashlight. Other beams crisscross the trail as yotheas review their kill. The atmosphere is festive. In the trees an escapee is caught, dragged back to the killing zone. "Please, Brothers!" The man is on his knees. His hands are together in a *lei*. Supplicant and beseeching he's reverted to traditional behavior, to the yotheas a sure sign of sedition. They laugh heinous laughs. Nang pulls Chhuon up. Pulls him forward. In the light beams Chhuon sees the carnage. A scream-shrill-cry pierces his frail back like a javelin. "Maaaa-Maaaa!" Billows of laughter burst from Kosal, others. Nang snickers. He flicks his claw at the pleading man. A yothea chops the man's skull with a hatchet, hits it low, behind, hard enough to damage the brainstem, not hard enough for an instantaneous kill. Death will take painful days. The method has been empirically tested and perfected by the yotheas.

"MaaaaaMaaaa!"

Two more rifle reports. More screams. More running in the forest. Chhuon spies a small boy trembling, silently hugging the trunk of a thick tree. Their eyes meet. In Chhuon there is terror, shock. He is not concerned for himself or his body. How to protect the child? He turns. A scrawny baby, perhaps two years old yet small and maldeveloped, is given to Nang. The infant's face distorts in fear. "MaaaaaMaaaa." All about, yotheas are stripping corpses, turning waistbands, ripping anuses, checking mouths. Here two links of gold chain are found, there a ruby.

Nang puts the infant to his shoulder. He pats her back gently with his right claw, supports her by holding her twig-thin ankles together with his left hand. "There, there," he consoles. The infant is shrieking unintelligibly. "There, there."

Agitated sorrow gushes from the depths of Chhuon's soul, yet seeing Nang with the infant wakens in Chhuon a memory of a time when he held his own children such. In this horror there is this tenderness. To hold him, Chhuon thinks. To hold my Kdeb. He will find me.

The infant arches her back. Jerks her legs against Nang's hardening grip. Blasts an ear-splitting *"Maaaa-Maaaaa!"* Pisses. "You . . ." Nang holds the infant away from his gray uniform. For a second she gasps, snivels, then again screams. *"Aaaaghhh!"* Nang shrieks. He lets go of the body, grasps the ankles with both hands, shoves the infant up. The body topples over his back. Then Nang swings hard as if holding an ax, whipping forward, down, smashing the child's head on the ground. Then immediately up, back down. The head cracks. Then up, like a hammer thrower, he swings, releases her into the forest.

For two days Chhuon cannot hold a thought. To have witnessed such evil, to have participated . . . his mind rejects every semblance of life. There is no ideology, no enemy, only evil, only torture for torture's sake, killing for killing's sake. Any instant the agitation abates, his consciousness floods with the images. He jabs at his eyes but cannot concentrate long enough to blind himself. Yet there is more. Nang is yet to bring him to the innermost circles of hell.

"You must tell me more of your plans for the fields." Nang leads Chhuon from his home. His speech is light. The sun is high. The sky clear. Dust lingers low in the listless ground air. The ground dries and cracks and the cracks widen. Fields look like the skin of spiny horned lizards. Moaning, like a low wind through forest trees, embraces them. Chhuon does not speak. Nang prattles. He feels satisfied, sated. His newest report to the Center is full of glowing figures, wonderful statistics; the number of double agents unmasked has soared; the number of undesirable elements eliminated has jumped tenfold. Only his crop figures are inadequate. But then, with this old one's knowledge, perhaps that could be fixed.

"Kampuchea is one nation, eh?" Nang feels cheerful as they walk the path toward Site 13. "It should have one language, the Khmer tongue; one people, Khmer people." He chuckles. That Chhuon has not responded means nothing to him. He wants to show the old man how the new site operates, he wants to brag, yet to him the old man is naught but a temporary anonymous audience. "Why should Khmers share Khmer soil with Thais, Chams, Chinks, *phnongs*, yuons, eh?" The trail begins to rise. The moaning is as constant as a waterfall's hum in a canyon; as deep as prayers chanted in Pali. "You talk of natural order. Of how man disrupted it. Ha! Now it's time to let the natural order return. They have no right here. The yuons had agents in the cities so we moved people to farms. If they had stayed in the cities the yuons or the imperialists would have stirred them to rebel. Did you know the yuons appealed to the KGB and the CIA to eliminate Pol Pot, Ieng Sary and Khieu Samphan? It's true. We have proof. My friend, Rin of Svay Rieng, has sent me proof."

As the trail snaked closer to the huge rocky escarpment the forest dropped away. Suddenly a long column of climbing men, women and children came into view. Chhuon could not make out details. He could not distinguish faces. But he could discern that people were climbing with heads down and hands behind their backs.

"Follow close after me," Nang instructed. "Don't stray. You needn't be purified."

The path with the long column circled to their right then disappeared in folds of the escarpment. Nang's path ran straight then zigzagged in a series of tight switchbacks and newly sculpted stairs. To their left was the four-hundred-foot horseshoe cliff. Directly above them, in a high tree on the wide ledge before the final thousand-foot escarpment which led to Thailand, Chhuon could make out the silhouette of a tree house. A woman screamed. Someone laughed. Nang laughed too. "Climb quicker, old man." Then not a laugh but a titter.

"What's that cable?" Chhuon's eyes followed the thick wire from the tree house out over the abyss toward a tower on the far side. At the center were various dark spheres but his eyes were too poor to discern their function. He climbed more slowly now. His skinny legs and decrepit feet cramping as he negotiated the steep narrow stairs. Each switchback brought him closer to the edge of the abyss until finally one took him so close the updraft hit him full in the face. He gasped, squeezed his old features attempting to block the wretched odor. He shook. His legs trembled, about to collapse. With the hot, rising, putrid updraft came the full volume of tormented moans. Chhuon stumbled. From above more laughs, more cries. Nang's arm shot toward the old peasant. His forefinger stabbed the pitching Chhuon, hooked his armpit, righted him as if he, Chhuon, were a weightless rag doll. "Not yet, old one," Nang said compassionately.

"Wha . . . wha . . ." Words would not form.

"They're only *Viet gian*." Nang chuckled. To him it was a pun, using the Viet Namese term for Viet Namese traitors. He smiled more broadly when he realized Chhuon understood the words. "We only kill Viets here," Nang boasted.

"The . . . other trail . . ."

"Oh, maybe some Thais. Or Chinese. They walk that way

thinking they're being expelled to Thailand. They're no trouble. Besides, if it's not one's fate to remain alive, this must be accepted, eh?"

Again the scream from the tree house. "What happens there?" Chhuon asked, dazed yet compelled to understand.

"Some of the ladies . . ." Nang's sentence was shattered by his titter. Then, "Come. You walk in front. I'll push you up."

"How many . . . ?" The words came hard to Chhuon. ". . . Why?"

"Just enough to purify the country," Nang said lightly. "When they get here, they know. They've elected to die. They are always quiet."

"But . . . but . . . People take refuge in silence."

Nang's voice snapped sharp. "They're all enemies."

"But . . ."

"*Viet gian.*"

They reached the ledge. A squad of yotheas sat beneath the large tree. Immediately upon seeing Nang they sprang up. In rapid conversation Chhuon watched this situation evolve. As two yotheas bitched quietly that they'd not gotten their turn, a naked and beaten young woman was pushed down the tree house ladder. Two soldiers held the prisoner as a third tied a red-checked krama about her head. Nang laughed caustically, stared into her blindfold and rasped his stubbed hand on her wet privates. Then he backed away. "Let the old one watch." Nang winked at the yotheas. Then loudly he scolded the soldiers and added, "I'll take her to clean up."

To the woman Nang spoke easily, softly, calling her "sister," as in the old days. At first she hesitated, then she freely let him guide her along a trail which brought them to the midpoint of the horseshoe.

Near Chhuon the yotheas chattered happily. "Four meters," said one. "Two," said another. "No, not Met Nang. He has much courage. Half a meter." "She'll grab him and pull him over," said the boy who'd guessed two.

"Why . . . What has she . . ." Chhuon knew what would happen but he did not believe his foreknowledge.

"She had a cooking pot," one of the yotheas explained.

"A pot . . ." Chhuon's words were weak.

"A bourgeois pot," the yothea said. "She must be an imperialist. Ooooo! Look!"

Nang stood not a half meter back but at the very edge of the cliff. His back was to the cliff, his claw arm stretched to her. Like a delicate flower he guided her toward him. Then she vanished.

                              *   *   *

That bastard, Nang thought. *Hysterical know-nothingness . . . of
Angkar . . .* Nang turned a page of the notebook labeled 7. He
skimmed, read a note here, a section there. *Tonight I shall guide
Mir and his family to the path to the border . . .* Nang slammed
the notebook closed. After all I have done for him. What tricks
do his field plans contain? Stupid. How could I have let him
trick me? *Ma is Meh, Pa is Poh.* He thinks that's wrong? Nang
grasped the two books, lifted them before him, shook them
violently. "Know-nothing enforcers, eh?" He seethed aloud then
seethed in silence. "Met Arn," Nang screamed. Then he muttered, "Perhaps the enforcers, even the chiefs and controllers,
but not me. I know everything. I'll show him. He'll reveal his
network. Every shred of evidence of seditious acts will be exposed." Nang glared at the books. "Arn," he shouted. "Read these.
I can't stand them."

"Why do you hate so?" Chhuon's mouth was swollen, distorted.
The words came garbled. "Hate does not cease by hatred, hatred ceases by love. This is an old rule." Again the torturer hit
him. How long the beating had lasted he didn't know. How long
he'd been in the detention camp he didn't know. Nor did he
know how many times he'd written his biography. He prayed
for the escape of loss of consciousness, for the peace of death.
Yet it had been Nang's orders that this one must not be killed,
must not die until he told all and in repentance killed himself.
How easy it had been to acquiesce to the first demand for a
biography. But the first had not been accepted. He wrote a
second, more detailed account of his life. The torturer filed the
papers and beat him. Standard Krahom procedure: by virtue of
the character of the enemy, the first and second writings were
necessarily false. The science of interrogation demanded beating to obtain truth. Chhuon's file grew. There was a mug photo
of him, his wrists tied behind his back. Then came his two
notebooks—the last and the first—Voen had concealed the others. Then the biographies, the first two unread. The third and
fourth analyzed along with the denials of confession. Nang had
personally chosen the torture specialists for their sadistic repertoire, had personally instructed them in the best tortures to
extract strategic information about enemy plots. For days on
end Chhuon was punched, kicked until unconscious, then revived with buckets of water, then tied to a metal cot and given
electric shocks, then revived and placed in solitary confinement
in a sheet-metal box which became an oven under the sun.

"You must not cry," the torturer snarled. "When you are hit, when you are lashed, when you receive electrification, you must remain silent. Tell us all your contacts."

Chhuon whimpered.

"Tell me!"

Physically he could bear no more.

"Tell me!"

He babbled. "Buddha says, 'To hold anger is to grasp an ember with the intent of throwing it at another. You are the one who gets burned.' "

"Ha!" Again the fists, the rope lashes. They broke a hand, a wrist. Then, "This is your last chance, buffalo shit. You will write a confession. You will tell all your contacts. They can't help you. No one knows you're here. You've been disappeared. Your cocoon made a splendid fire."

The next day, before they hung Chhuon by the neck, he was taken to witness a fresh kill. Hung and nailed to a torture shed wall was a man. His pants had been removed, his genitals had been impaled with spikes. "Ha." A yothea nudged Chhuon. "You see how Met Nang deals with special enemies, eh?"

"He . . ." Chhuon stuttered. "He . . . is a . . ."

"Ha! He was . . ."

"Met Khieng . . ."

"They say he stole the virtue of many workers."

"But . . . a cadre of . . ."

"No one, old man, is above the Will of Angkar."

Chhuon's frail body, covered with scabies, scars and scabs, barely pulled the kinks out of the thick rope. The specialists laughed, grabbed his feet and tugged down. The noose tightened. Blood to the brain stopped. Chhuon dropped toward unconsciousness. Yet the release of death was denied. They lifted him, lowered the rope, loosened the noose. An hour later they hung him again. Then again two days later.

Then for a month they left him alone in a clean cell, fed him yothea's meals twice a day through a slot opening, let him emerge to wash and clean his bucket once a week. Then they returned him to the hanging chamber, tied his hands behind his back, placed the noose about his neck and raised him to his toes.

"We know the truth. You have not told the whole truth." A yothea read the accusations. He smirked. "Why do you hide the truth from Angkar? Angkar does not wish anyone's death, yet your behavior proves you will not be converted."

Chhuon began meditating on his body rhythms. He would shut them out. Shut out the pain, the fear, the loss of self. Slowly they hoisted him. He could feel the blood of the carotid artery pulsing against the rope. He concentrated on the beating. Then in agitation his mind slipped. He felt the air squeezing through his constricted trachea. Then the thought, Kdeb! Why have you abandoned me? His strength snapped. His will to forgo life, to release himself from suffering evaporated. A wave of anguished desperation crashed upon his waning consciousness. Pulse. Kdeb! pulse. kdeb. pul . . . Then with immense concentration and effort, "Wait!"

The specialists smiled. Laughed. Lingered to allow Chhuon's frantic kicking to reach its zenith. Then they lowered him and loosened the noose. "Wait. There is . . ." Chhuon sobbed. He had been broken. "I will write it all."

"vathana, are you awake?"

"yes." Vathana lay between her Aunt Voen and her cousin Robona. Though the night was warm they huddled close. To Voen's other side was her second daughter, Amara, and Amara's three young children. Filling the one-room hut were ten more people—Voen's in-laws.

The moon had not yet risen. The air was still. "you must learn quickly," Voen whispered. Quietly she explained the lies they'd invented to secrete their background from the new masters, the cadre of Angkar. Voen tested Vathana, corrected her answers, asked again until Vathana gripped the tale as reality.

"what of my father?" Vathana finally asked.

Voen told her of the great evacuation from Phnom Penh and how on the tenth day her husband's soul left his body. Of how she had then begged him to close his eyes and go peacefully, of how he had lain staring at the sky and of how the soldiers had made her leave him. As Voen spoke she wept and Vathana wept too and said a prayer that her uncle's spirit would not torment them. Then Voen said, "here they are not so cruel. rama is very kind. yam, she is fair. beware nava, he's the one who disappears people. there is one, met soth, at the higher level, some say he cuts off heads and eats hearts and livers."

"auntie. what of my father? chhuon? you said . . ."

"ssshh. sometimes there are soldiers under the house. when it's safe, i'll tell you."

Nights and days passed before they were again able to speak securely. Met Rama, chairman of the tribunal of enforcers for Sangkat 117, interrogated Vathana on her second day. He accepted her story that she was Voen's daughter though Vathana suspected he knew it was a lie. Then he assigned her to work.

It was now Vathana's turn to live the life of the incarcerated in that Asian Sparta where since the second deportation the

distinction between new people and old, or base people and 17
April people, had blurred. Sangkats received orders via state
radio. The harvest season was ending. The radio became obsessed with building dikes and digging canals. "Hurry. Reap
the rice quickly. We must return to the dikes. We shall move
forward to master the water. It is year zero. The land is one vast
work site where night does not exist, where work is unending,
where workers labor in joy and enthusiasm without fear of
fatigue."

Vathana labored at a massive work site with thousands of
men, women and children, labored like a black ant with the
emaciated in their tattered black uniforms, with few tools and
with little expectation. On whatever scale previous projects had
been undertaken, they were now increased. Democratic Kampuchea
was ordered to rebuild the agricultural system of canals, dikes
and reservoirs that had existed during the golden age of the
Angkor Empire more than 900 years earlier. The entire nation
was to be blanketed with a network of rice paddies a thousand
meters square, and between the paddies ten-meter-wide irrigation canals were ordered dug. Feeder canals and minidikes were
to be built to subdivide the larger fields. The dikes around the
larger fields were each to be four feet high and ten feet wide.
Thus, a thousand-meter dike contained approximately 2,430
cubic yards of dirt—about three hundred pickup-truck loads!
And such a dike was merely one side of one paddy.

Vathana touched the node just above her elbow on the inside
of her left arm. It was as large as a plum. Her entire arm, her
entire body, ached. She dared not stop. Only one night earlier
Nava had come and questioned her as to why she had no
children. It hurt her to answer, to deny them. She did not sleep.
In her anguish she'd heard the soldiers roust the family of the
next hut "for a meeting." They were not at work the next day
and Met Nem, the *mekong* who was Nava's favorite, was seen
with the blouse of one of the women.

Without talking Vathana glanced to Amara and both lifted
the pole from which hung a pallet of earth. Up the path, out of
the canal, in line behind a hundred pairs of women like themselves, they carried the dirt to the ever-expanding dump point.
Then, in line, they walked back for the next load. Slowly the
canal lengthened, slowly the dike rose. Without shoes the wom-
en's feet callused but without sufficient food their bodies did
not replace the skin and their feet wore away.

Vathana shivered. She'd been hot all morning. Now she felt
cold and clammy. Again she felt her arm. A week earlier she'd
cut her thumb relashing the pallet to the shoulder pole. There

seemed to be little infection, only a small red ulcer, yet from it came a poison her body could not defeat. She looked up. On the dike top an older deformed man was staring at her. He held a red banner on a long pole, rocking it back and forth to some inner cadence. Their eyes met. Quickly she looked to the ground. He's Khmer Rouge, she thought. Wounded during the war. They're the most cruel.

Again the glance to Amara. Oh God, Vathana thought. What have they loaded us with? Amara led but after a few steps Vathana stumbled. The pallet skidded, dust rose, clumps of dirt fell off. "Ha!" The man with the banner laughed loud. "She's no farmer's daughter. One like you has never touched dirt."

Vathana coughed, quickly scooped the dirt back onto the pallet. The dust of the work site was thick in the air. At ground level it was nearly impenetrable. Her eyes filled. Quickly she rehoisted her end of the pole. The pain in her eyes was excruciating, as if someone had thrown slivers of glass against the cornea. She tried to blink, to squeeze her eyes but the dust implanted further. Behind her the line bunched. "amara," she whispered frantically. "i can't see."

"just follow," Amara whispered back.

They did not stop for lunch though late in the afternoon other workers came and fed each a cup of thin rice gruel while their pallet was being loaded. Seeing Vathana's eyes the worker whispered, "do not cry, sister. it is forbidden. they will take you to the forest to be educated."

"it's only the dust," Vathana whispered back.

"they'll think you criticize them," the woman said. She lifted the hem of her skirt and wiped Vathana's face.

The work continued until eight o'clock. Exhausted, Amara led Vathana back to the hut. Nebella, Voen's mother-in-law, greeted them with hugs and tears. She was old and had been spared from work in the fields. Her work was to make plaited mats, to cook for the hut and to watch over the children. Now there were new rules. The cooking pot had been confiscated. All would eat in a communal hall yet to be built. The children could watch over one another—five-year-olds could care for infants—Angkar so pronounced. Nebella, at sixty-six, would pack the dikes with a wooden tamper. It was Met Nem's pronouncement.

There was but one man in the family hut, Mey, Voen's husband's brother. The women beseeched him to go to Met Rama to plead for his mother. "i will," he told them, "but first i must get our food. until the hall is built, i'm to go for the hut. if i don't, no one will be given anything."

Mey was frightened. To him, seeking out Rama was like

asking to talk to Pol Pot. Instead he went to Met Khron. In Sangkat 117, there were about thirty *mekongs* (unarmed) and yotheas (armed). Perhaps half, though they strictly obeyed orders, were tolerant of the people's requests. Half of these were kind in a traditional Khmer sense. They seemed to recognize their charge of, and responsibility for, the wards of the commune and they took the responsibility seriously. This was particularly true of the older yotheas and those of the old Rumdoah (Sihanoukist) faction. To them the job was an adjunct to their lives. To the younger, more heavily indoctrinated, their jobs became their lives.

Mey told Khron of their hardships, of Vathana's arm and eyes, of Nebella's great age, of his infant son's need for palm sugar. Khron was cautious, yet helpful. "Boil the water. Save a little for the baby. Have the girl soak her hand in it as hot as possible, as long as possible."

"But we have no pot."

"I will give you a pot. Then you must go."

"You are very kind."

"hide it," Khron whispered. "even rama cannot protect you from the high organization if it is found."

That night as the others slept Vathana soaked her hand. Voen mixed the coals of the fire with mud then rolled two hot compresses and held them on the large node at Vathana's elbow and the now swelling ones at her armpit. "tonight," Voen whispered, "you must read chhuon's notebooks."

"yes, mama," Vathana whimpered.

"also, cut your hair."

"my hair?"

"amara says a yothea longs for you." With that Voen crept from the hut. Only because there were so many workers and so few fanatical cadre were people able to do anything other than as strictly ordered. Thus the people retained secret freedoms the new masters were never able to extinguish. Voen returned. "when the moon is up, read. now sleep."

Vathana removed her hand from the pot and dried it on her skirt. The notebooks were in her lap. She at once felt excited and terrified. It was still dark. How could she sleep? Would she awaken for the moon? If she slept until the 5 a.m. gong Met Nem or another cadre might find her with the books. Surely she would be disappeared. And she would not have read her father's words. She touched the spiral bindings. They too were warm. Oh Papa! Oh Papa! she thought. How I miss you. How I wish to be with you and Mama. How I wish to be your daughter once again. She opened the first page and gently tickled the paper.

No longer did her arm ache. No longer did her body cry. She closed her eyes. When she opened them the moon was high. Immediately her head snapped to the door, to the aisle between huts, checking. Then she listened for breathing below the floor. Often Nem hid below the platforms searching, always searching for evidence of seditious acts.

In Chhuon's orderly fashion the notebooks were numbered— two to six. There was no number one.

> Forgive me, my children, for not having seen all that has happened— for having seen it and for not having the vision or the courage to understand what I saw.

Oh Divine Buddha, Vathana prayed, help me. Give me the courage to read. She now read the story of her father and her Uncle Sam and the tinker and all that had happened to her mother and her home village while she had been languishing as the wife of Teck, then while she had flourished under the tutelage of Pech Lim Song. She read of the people who fled and the people who arrived, of Hang Tung and the first night booby trap which killed two soldiers as she rendezvoused with John Sullivan.

When the morning gong sounded Voen sprang up, whisked the notebooks from Vathana's lap, disappeared, reappeared empty-handed. Mey went to the communal kitchen for the hut's rice soup. The line was long. Before he returned, Amara and Vathana left for their distant work site. To be late meant to be disappeared.

Through February and March Vathana labored amid thousands of slaves at the massive site. Not once did she miss a day, though many others—weak, sick, starving—quit. Not when she read her father's account of his burying her grandmother; not when she read of her mother's death. Some who quit were allowed a day or two to rest, others were sent to the "hospital" to die, some were simply disappeared never to be seen again. Each night Vathana stole time to read more of Chhuon's words. When she finished the books, she reread them. Then she studied them. By April she had much of the story committed to memory and she contemplated burning the books but she could not. They were her father. Even had he been a stranger she would have guarded them with her life. It was the story of the Northeast and she had promised to live to deliver it to the world. Now at night she chanted the words aloud, in her mind, chanted them in the monotone of the sacred Pali prayers so as to ensure that every word would be exact.

And she made vows. I will not let them get me. I will obey. I will follow their rules. I will be a first-class peasant.

But the rules changed. Almost daily new directives came from the Center of Angkar Leou. And with them came The Purge. Met Khron, the kind yothea, was disappeared in mid-March, replaced by Met Deth. Rumors of mass defections of Krahom troops and of a second revolution swept the commune. The new masters tightened their grip. Yotheas, cadre and high chiefs of the northern zone were replaced by new officials from the eastern zone. With the communal "hall" erected, there no longer were family meals in family huts. No longer could a mother save a spoonful of her ration for her child. Then all the children except infants were taken to be reared at the children's center. "I will feed you better than your mother," the caretakers told them. "She did not love you. She kept your food for herself." The children were schooled to spy on their parents, on all adults, to sing Communist songs and to rampage through the peasant huts. Soon people began to fear the children and one another. Men and women were separated. Fathers were afraid to ask about the well-being of their offspring. No one mentioned those who had been disappeared. At night meetings, held in Sangkat 117 every tenth night, flirting was banned. It was punishable by death. People became afraid to speak, to even look at one another. Families were officially dissolved and the people regrouped into labor brigades of men or of women, into mobile task forces of teenaged boys, into production companies of teenaged girls. Boys of ten to twelve were sent to military training camps, those of eight and nine to the new schools of the cruel.

Khmer culture was to be destroyed. None of the old glues which had held people together were tolerated. Long gone was the monarchy. Its potential return had been a powerful source of strength for many people. In April, Norodom Sihanouk, with these words, resigned:

Today, my dream that Kampuchea would recover and strengthen forever its independence, sovereignty, territorial integrity, and neutrality, and acquire a system capable of giving the people and the nation true sovereignty and perfect social justice, and a national life that is absolutely clean, without stain, corruption, and other social ills, has been fulfilled beyond anything I could imagine, thanks to our fighting men and women, peasants, laborers, and other working people, under the enlightened leadership of our revolutionary Angkar.

. . . on March 18, 1970, I swore to myself and to the Kampuchean people that after I had accompanied my countrymen to complete victory over U.S. imperialism and the traitorous clique and after the opening of the new revolutionary era, I would retire completely and forever from the political scene, for my role would logically come to an end.

Thus, all my fondest wishes have come true.

Buddhism and all religions were further devastated. One day in a field near Vathana a peasant had broken and in desperation he'd pointed at the man next to him and screamed, "That man! He was a monk! In the old days he sapped the people." Immediately both men were whisked away. The screamer returned. About his head was a new krama.

Now there was no family. Everyone fell into one of three categories: workers, peasants, or soldiers; the new constitution so pronounced. Everyone was equal. Everyone worked. All work was matched to "the scientific distribution of labor." In the dry season eighty percent dug major canals and reservoirs and built the high dams and long dikes. Ten percent built the minidikes. Ten percent made tools and performed service functions like preparing food. One's nuclear family was now one's work unit; one's extended family became one's company, battalion, regiment and division. The Center's agricultural obsession with rice became ultrazealous. Work teams were forced to destroy small hut-side vegetable plots because only rice was necessary. That there was no science in their science meant nothing to the new masters. Science was rigid Communist ideology.

Again rations were cut.

When the rains came emphasis shifted from constructing fields to planting. For a month Vathana, Amara and Robona worked side by side in a flooded paddy picking and bundling rice seedlings for replanting. They worked barefoot, their black sarong skirts tied up, their legs exposed. At first the work was easy compared to carrying pallets of dirt but daily their production quota was increased until it was impossible to fulfill. The women worked quickly picking with both hands, knocking the root mud off against their feet, tying the bundles with reed leaves. The work was monotonous yet Vathana found a satisfaction in mastering it. Her fears now centered on the long orange and brown leeches which undulated in the water about her legs, the occasional snake which slashed between the seedlings fleeing her dashing hands, and the deformed ex-soldier with the red banner who now appeared wherever she worked, eyeing her continuously, perhaps even spending nights under the floor of her new hut.

In May her job changed. She was put on fertilizer detail

collecting human excrement to be mixed with rice chaff. Her ration was reduced. She did not know why. In June she was sent back to the fields to plant. Again the man with the red banner stalked her. For days she dared not raise her head. *Chrops* were everywhere. Vathana hated herself for it but she came to suspect Amara of colluding against her, of telling the deformed man of their conversations, perhaps even of the notebooks. At night she sought Voen's advice but her aunt had been transferred to a different unit.

Again Vathana was pulled from the fields. Now she was assigned to the job of collecting bodies of the dead, of searching them, removing their clothes, then bringing them to a central point for processing. From there they were carted away. How the work frightened her. The smell of death clung to her, and Amara and Robona shunned her. But it was the spirits of the dead which most terrified her. So many of the dead were freshly killed. From so many blood still oozed. And even here the teams had quotas which if unfilled meant a further reduction in rations—or worse. Some days it was easy. She and a partner were led to shallow holes with ten or twenty corpses clumped under pillows and clothing. Flies swarmed thickly, invading their nostrils, ears and eyes. Vathana and her partner descended into the pit, dragged one body up, performed the newly prescribed ritual of rape and robbery, then carted the stripped meat to the central point. All day, every day, Vathana prayed. Divine Buddha give me strength. Lord Buddha protect me. I will not let them get me. I will obey. Enlightened One, bring this soul to the one heaven for all people. Vathana prayed but she no longer cried for the dead.

Some days it was difficult to fill the quota and Vathana found herself waiting beside old and feeble bodies, waiting for the death rattle of collapsing lungs, waiting so she might cart the corpse to the central point. Divine Buddha, protect this spirit. Let it leave this swollen wretched body and pass to a new life of joy and peace.

One afternoon as she perched in a squat beside an old seemingly unconscious woman whose face was cloaked in open sores, perched like a vulture afraid to look at its prey, looking, staring the thousand-meter stare of tragedy, a voice hissed from the ulcerous lips, "is that you, angel?" Vathana tightened. Her face snapped to the noise. An urge to fly, to flee, swept over her. She covered her mouth with her hands. "from great suffering . . ." The voice was weak. ". . . pray with me. you are the angel, yes? of neak luong. i lived in your camp. you washed my face. you taught me the prayer."

Vathana's jaw trembled. She clenched her teeth. Then, "yes . . . yes, old mother. yes, dear old mother."

Together they prayed softly, "from great suffering comes great insight; from great insight comes great compassion . . ." The old woman began to wheeze. Vathana grasped her hands.

"it is the destiny of kampuchea," the old one said.

Vathana did not answer but continued the prayer. ". . . from great compassion comes a peaceful heart; from a peaceful heart comes a peaceful family . . ."

"i do not blame anyone," the woman whispered.

". . . from a peaceful family comes a peaceful community . . ."

"there is no fault, angel. no fault."

". . . from a peaceful community comes a peaceful nation, from a peaceful nation . . ." The old woman's body shuddered, then froze. Vathana's eyes teared as they had not in a long time. The woman's insides collapsed noisily, the rattle escaping through her open mouth. ". . . comes a peaceful world."

Vathana dragged the corpse from the small hut. The woman was light, as if there were no physical bulk at all under her dilapidated black clothes. Vathana checked the body for gold or gems then dragged it to the collection point. The oxcart was waiting. Driving it was the deformed ex-soldier who'd been ogling her.

"What are you called?" the man asked harshly.

"Met Hana." Vathana cowered with the corpse by one of the cart's large wheels.

"The old cart team has been moved forward. Put that in back."

"Lift her?"

"Yes! Are you stupid? You can see I can't bend. Do it, then get up here."

The bed of the cart was waist high but the cart was stacked with dead higher than Vathana's shoulders. Vathana propped the corpse upright against the heap, purposely struggling, attempting to delay, to give herself time to think. "Hurry!" the man shouted. He dragged himself back over the dead, grabbed the old woman's shoulder and jerked, flinging the light body up, almost over the pile. "Walk beside or ride," the deformed man ordered. "It's three kilometers."

He sat cross-legged at the front of the cart. One ankle and foot bent back on its leg and stuck up in front of him like a saddle horn. One arm and shoulder had also been broken and rehealed unset so the arm came not from his side but like a stiff triple-bent branch from his chest. The hand, too, was stiff. On it he rested the hemp rope reins to the noses of two water buffalo.

"Either come now or I'll bring you with them." He jerked his good hand at the back of the cart.

Vathana said nothing. She did not move. She was afraid to ride with the dead, afraid to offend the driver if she didn't. He snapped the reins. The buffalo began their lumbering gait. Vathana fell in behind, a funeral procession of one. At first he led her down a road between fields of workers, then down a narrow road into the forest. The wheel ruts deepened and became mud trenches. The mud clung to the wheels and the buffalo stopped. The man cursed. He flicked the beasts with a switch. "You," he yelled. "Push!" Vathana placed her hands on the cart. It rolled slowly. She closed her eyes. Her face bumped an outthrust arm, then a foot. She opened her eyes, averted her face to the road and the mud.

For half an hour she pushed deeper and deeper into the forest. Then they came to the pit. Thirty wraiths converged on the cart. Of all the horrors she'd seen she now faced a still more repugnant sight. The workers here were not men, not women, but some aberrant transformation of humanity—filthy, odious, mostly naked, starving, thin as reeds, sickly gray.

She stepped back. They had no eyes. They bumped and smashed one another, prodded by a single screaming yothea with a long bamboo rod. Frantically they tore the bodies from the cart. The yothea screamed, jabbed them, directed them to the central pit. One beast held Vathana's last corpse, the gentle old woman, by the lower jaw. He dragged her into the work site. In a minute the crater was filled with dead bodies and savage mutants. Then, by feel, the mutants ripped faces apart, snorting, laughing inhuman noises. Then the bodies were crushed, dismembered, shredded with small hatchets. One worker in her blind frenzy fell across a corpse and immediately was slashed by four others. It may have been moments, maybe hours—to Vathana time fled the universe—until the bodies were reduced to a red muck stew. Vathana saw one worker grab a hunk of meat, bite it. A yothea impaled him with a bamboo lance. Other workers hearing his scream scurried to him, reduced him to mush. Now other worker-pairs were brought forward carrying dirt pallets hanging from shoulder poles. They, too, had been blinded. Quickly, efficiently, they padded to the edge of the central pit and dumped in their loads. Then they disappeared and a third blind team came and descended into the pit with spades and poles. These were the stirrers. They mixed the bodies with the dirt until the central pit was a smooth bowl of purple-brown fertilizer. A fourth team, these with sight, shoveled the mixture into baskets until the pit was scraped clean. Then the baskets were carried to a storage shed for aging.

As Vathana and the deformed man turned the cart to go, a second cart arrived from another direction. At that Vathana noted the pit was a hub with eight spoke roads. Behind her the wraiths shrieked gleefully. The skin of Vathana's back tightened. She walked behind the cart, afraid they were behind her, afraid they would set upon her, rip her apart, afraid to look back, afraid to close her eyes, to keep them open, afraid she had now been chosen to progress, to move forward from collector to transporter to shoveler on down until starving, blind and crazy she was hacked to death while eating what she herself had dismembered.

"I've been trying to place it in perspective," John Sullivan said. He had been sitting across the table from her for a long time. Through the window of the small bistro he could see the last of Washington's cherry blossoms. Coolly she had laid out the humanitarian efforts she'd planned, his role as she saw it. To Rita he seemed relaxed, except that his fingernails methodically tore away the wet paper labels from his sweating beer bottles.

"Me too," she said.

Ever since he'd responded to her second correspondence—every day, almost all day—Cambodia and Vathana had been on his mind. The more he'd tried to bury himself in his work on the Pradesh ranch, or the more he'd sought to mask the intrusive thoughts by concentrating on difficult mathematics, physics or chemistry, the more he'd been drawn to the material he'd begun accumulating on Southeast Asia. And in his study of math and physics and chemistry he'd found a higher mental discipline, a greater ability to analyze the events he'd repressed but could no longer ignore.

"You know what I've been wondering?" he said. He was on his fourth beer; the alcohol, the enclosure, was giving him a headache. And Rita looked so different to him—a business suit, stockings and heels, her hair done up. Only her pale blue eyes were the same.

"What?" she said.

"When the Communists entered Phnom Penh and Saigon, the war ended—or that ended the war."

"Yes." She had turned sideways in her chair. His eyes caught a glimpse of her legs. "Ended the war, but not the suffering," she said.

"It's something I don't understand," he said, leaning back. He could not think and look at her legs. "If we were invaded, if we'd fought for a decade for our land, would we give up if Washington was occupied? The French didn't when Hitler held Paris. Why did Thieu order his divisions to cease resistance instead of ordering them into hiding? Why didn't he establish a jungle headquarters? Maybe down in the bewitched Seven Mountains by Tri Ton. Why didn't Lon Nol or Sirik Matak order FANK to establish bases in the Cardamom Mountains? Would Americans, if we were war weary, fall for those Communist ruses—there's only seven supertraitors who must answer for their crimes? Everybody else will be granted amnesty?"

"It's irrelevant, isn't it, John?" Rita said.

Sullivan ignored her attempt to limit the thought. "Not we Americans," he said too loudly. "We'd never fall for such blatant bovine excrement, eh?"

"Eh! . . .?" She chuckled. She wanted to defuse what she saw as growing anger. "Becomes a part of you, eh?"

"Not Americans," Sullivan continued. His head was back, his eyes toward the ceiling. "Not in the wake of having fought." He looked forward, at her. "I mean, we're too sophisticated for such tricks. We're too knowledgable. Eh? Of course we, *Americans*, war weary from a war not even near our homeland, did fall for that exact ruse, did accept that exact Communist propaganda, that promise of utopia if the imperialist pigs would just tuck tail and withdraw. Take their troops, their advisors, their material and moral support. Ha! It's one thing to accept defeat for someone else, another thing to accept one's own defeat. Eh?! We wouldn't do that, would we? We'd fight to the end. Wouldn't we? What do you think?"

"*John!*"

"What *do* you think?" he asked even more aggressively.

"I don't know," she snapped. "You chase your wild theories. I just want to stop that misery."

Sullivan gritted his teeth to keep from shouting. "You bitch," he growled. "Why were you against stopping it five years ago?"

"Look!" Rita stared him in the eyes, forcefully smacked the table with her index finger. "You can accuse me of anything you want. I can't turn time back. But right now I'm trying to correct a horrible situation. I thought I wanted your help."

"I'm . . . what the hell more could I have done?" He closed his eyes, squeezed them, squeezed his hands to fists on the table.

"I've got a letter," she said. Her voice was icy.

"Hum . . ." He opened his eyes. He didn't understand the reference.

"Do you remember a Khmer named Louis?"

Sullivan shook his head.

"From Neak Luong. He was a friend of Pech Chieu Teck's, Cahuom Vathana's husband."

"A little guy," Sullivan said. "Real small."

"Um-hum. He made it to a Thai camp."

Sullivan leaned forward. Words formed in his mind but would not come to his lips.

"You bastard," Rita said. "One thing you could have done is told me."

"Told you what?"

"You could have told me how beautiful that Cahuom woman was." Sullivan didn't answer. "Do you know about Amerasian children?"

"I know chil—" he began. "What kind of children?"

"Amerasian," Rita said. "Kids with American fathers and Asian mothers. Kids left behind."

"I'm not up on them."

"There was a little girl born in Neak Luong on the day it was bombed. You did know that the American B-52s bombed Neak Luong, didn't you?!"

"No, dammit. I haven't seen that. When? What happened? Was . . . Dammit! I told you I didn't read any papers for three years. What girl?"

"A little red-haired baby. You bastard! You don't even know, do you?"

"Vathana! A red-haired . . ."

"Cahuom Chhuon," Chhuon signed the document which stated that he had not been mistreated during his detention, that he freely and openly submitted his confession of espionage.

"That's very good," Met Ku whispered to the torturer as they watched him. Chhuon sat at a flimsy table, his head hanging, almost resting on the top. "Very good," Ku repeated. "Have you photographed him with it?"

"He's going now."

"Good. Met Nang will be pleased."

An underling grasped Chhuon by the elbow and pulled him up. The boy was young, plump, uncomfortable in his new job. "Eh," he said to Chhuon, "you escaped from the mouth of the crocodile. The rest is easy."

Chhuon did not look at the boy but instead turned to where Ku and the torturer stood. He glanced at them, turned away, shuffled slowly in the direction the boy pushed. The boy shoved. Still Chhuon shuffled. "When you escape from the crocodile," he muttered, speaking neither to the underling nor to himself, "you sometimes find yourself in the mouth of the tiger." Chhuon laughed. The saying was an old Khmer proverb. The boy, Chhuon was sure, did not understand. He repeated it louder. The boy paid no attention. "Are you a Buddhist?" Chhuon asked. Still the boy did not answer. "I am a Buddhist," Chhuon said. "Do you know your vows? No, eh? I will become enlightened for the sake of . . ." The boy shoved him harder. He stumbled and fell. "You do know them, don't you?" Chhuon rose. He felt sorry for the boy. How difficult, Chhuon thought, this is for him. He needs to be so strong and he has so little strength. ". . . all living things." Chhuon said the words disconnected from the beginning of the vow.

Again the boy shoved him. Again he fell. The boy jerked him to his feet. "Shut up . . . ee . . . en . . . enemy. You . . ." Agitation, fear and confusion showed in the boy's eyes. ". . . You . . . Enemies of the people voluntarily forfeit their humanity."

Chhuon was photographed with his hands tied, with a single cotton thread, behind his back. It would have been nothing to break the thread but he had been warned if his thread broke they would poke out an eye of the girl before him. The girl was similarly warned, as was the man after. About the photography hut there was a line of sixty people. Surrounding them were two squads of guards. As Chhuon joined the line of those completed he heard older yotheas in jolly debate. Was it better to put a child before a parent and thus force the parent to watch as they jabbed the child's eye with a bamboo needle—yes, said a few—or better to put the parent first, trip the child, scream blame at the child as they cut the mother's or father's eyeball? Empirically the guards had tested their hypotheses. Best was still debated, though certainly it was good to pair fathers with sons, mothers with daughters; good, too, to separate the members of those pairs with one unpaired enemy of the people. Thus if the unpaired fell and broke his thread causing a wife's eye to be impaled, the husband could retaliate by tripping, snapping his binding and causing the stabbing of the eye of the person between. How careful the Khmers were of their threads. How they tried to protect one another. How difficult it was to keep their wrists together standing for hours in line while one by one the enemies of the state were photographed. Keeping them docile was this promise: they were so despicable that the state had decided to expel them to Thailand. All they needed to do was follow the path and climb the escarpment without breaking their thread, and they would be allowed to cross into the imperialists' hell.

The last picture was taken. The column, five oozing from the left eyeball, began the thread march through the jungle toward the base of the cliff. A careful excitement fluttered in their souls. Expelled to Thailand! Lord Buddha, keep me from falling, keep the one behind me from falling too.

The trail rose slowly as it approached the foundation of the great escarpment, then it forked, veered left, and rose steeply. Quietly, slowly, the damned climbed. From somewhere above came music, then various announcements, then more patriotic songs. Chhuon recognized the trail, the ruse. He recognized the music and voice and knew that in the tree house soldiers were playing Radio Phnom Penh to mask the moaning from the abyss. He knew there would be no Thailand at the top of the climb. But he did not know what to do. His eyesight had continued to weaken in the months of torture and confinement and he felt cheated as he climbed that his insight had not improved. Was it better to yell, to scream, "It's a trick. They're going to kill us all," or was it better to remain quiet and allow his column mates a last hope, a last day before death? If he yelled and they broke and ran surely the soldiers would shoot everyone. If they didn't break but thought only that he, Chhuon, had cracked, gone mad, then the soldiers would beat him to death and the others would march on as if he'd never been one with them. Each step made the decision more difficult.

The column closed and opened like an accordion, depending on the difficulty of the climb at the lead. At one close a third of the way up Chhuon stopped, breathed deeply. His old legs were weak, rubbery. He could not fall. He could not break his thread. He stared at a boulder beside the trail. The front of the column began to move. His eyes searched the rock. Tell me, old one, he asked the rock spirit, tell me what to do. You are very old, you have been here for a very long time. Tell me, old one. A man lasts but half a century. You have endured a thousand centuries. Your spirit must know. Tell me.

"Move!" A yothea smacked the small of Chhuon's back with his rifle butt. Chhuon's abdomen snapped forward, his head jerked back, his feet stuck in the gravel. As he fell his arms snapped sideways. He forced his hands back, took the force of the fall on his face. Still the thread broke. Immediately three yotheas leaped on him, cussing, kicking, beating him with rifle butts. On his side he curled into a fetal position, his arms over his head. "You've blinded her! You son of a bitch, you've blinded her!" Again and again they screamed. One jerked his head up forcing him to watch as others clamped a frail and frightened young girl before him.

"No! Please! No!" A shriek. The girl's mother from a step above. "Do mine!"

"You've blinded that girl," a yothea spit, kicked Chhuon's ribs, held his face up. Chhuon saw another yothea jab the girl's eye with a bamboo stiletto, jab it just deep enough to collapse the eyeball. The mother leaped on the yotheas and they beat her. Then others grabbed the man who'd been above her and stabbed his eye. Somehow he managed to bear the pain without breaking his thread. The yotheas retied the mother and Chhuon. They allowed the girl to walk holding her face.

For Nang each day now became a chore, each chore a punishment. Each punishment he feared yet he bore them in silence, bore them, hating them, hating every element, every man, woman and child, yet cloaking hate, self-hate and fear in terms of wonderment and progress, in febrile enthusiasm, in praise of his *kang chrops*, his child-spies, in glowing reports of progress in the paddies and at the elimination sites. Every tenth day he filed a report for the Center. Every tenth day he boasted of the number of joyful workers toiling his lands, of the number of traitors he'd exposed, of the number of spies and useless elements he'd eliminated for others, of the confessions he'd obtained and the networks he'd exposed. And he bragged. *His* units were by far the best. *His* crops the densest, *his* slaves the most loyal, *his* zone the purest, *his* future the brightest. He basked in his righteous vengeance. His chest billowed when he thought of the difficulties he'd overcome, the enemies he'd beaten. But the satisfaction was shallow, fleeting, and in its void was the chore, the fear, and the hate.

Met Ku found him at home late afternoon on the day Chhuon was photographed. Ku reported the statistics and the two young men along with Met Arn chatted and ate heartily as they discussed the report for the next period. Finally Ku said as he scooped some hot curried rice from the serving dish to his bowl, "You remember that old peasant, the one who did the irrigation drawings?" Nang looked at Ku, then Arn. He shook his head. "The one you took to the border on ambush so he would tell the others and . . ."

"Yes." Nang said it without conviction.

"He's confessed," Ku said. "I brought his file."

"Eliminate him," Nang said. He plucked three thin skewered slices of spiced, smoked meat from a platter.

"His file's very interesting. Very complete." Ku looked at Arn, and Arn nodded confirmation. "Shall I leave it?"

Nang did not ponder. "Why?"

"For you to read. It's a shame to have shown him so much then not let him go back and tell the others. The stories help keep the people in line."

"Aahggh!" Nang pulled a bamboo skewer from his mouth. "It only makes them more rebellious. All we do for them, and they are ingrates." Nang threw the skewer. Harshly he rasped, "All Angkar provides . . . I hate them. I hate them all. They've earned their merit. They're getting the reward for such evil. Enemies must be utterly crushed. What's rotten must be excised." Nang sprang up. "Where's the file?"

"It's with . . ."

"Never mind. I can't read their lies. Their shit. Take me to that evil *phnong*. I'll see him."

The little dry season was upon the land. Days were intolerably hot and humid, evenings were no relief. Not until long after the sun descended, when the ground mist formed, was there some respite. Chhuon lay on his side in a concrete cell amid the rows of low cells atop the ledge of the lower cliff. Each small box held eight to ten people, people crammed onto one another so tightly they took turns inhaling. The air was putrid. A moaning came from the canyon like a wind from the underworld. Radio Phnom Penh, the Voice of Democratic Kampuchea, resounded off cell walls but was not enough to mask the gasping spirits of the chasm which filled the night wind for miles, which reverberated in the canyon like a low guitar string plucked within the sound box, vibrating the ground as if to shake the stones of the cliff loose, threatening an avalanche, tumbling and burying the misery below. All day the sounds had been punctuated with shrieks, screams, pleas, cries and the laughter of the yotheas. "When it's dark," Chhuon's cellmates whispered to one another, "when the Thais can't see, they'll send us up the last escarpment. I overheard them. All we have to do is not anger them." "But what's the yelling?" "Rape," Chhuon whispered. No one listened. The old one had been the only one to stumble on the climb. He'd caused them to blind the girl and the man.

Unseen, the soldiers indeed raped a few women, but the screams came not from that but from their games. Those with one eye blinded were taken for "treatment." There the right eye was poked, popped. Then they were brought, wrists lashed with wire, to the edge of the cliff. The soldiers spun them three or four times then left them to wander, jeering if they stumbled away from the edge, bashing them if they froze or fell to hug the ground. "Get up! Get up! Run!" One by one they found the edge, fell, bouncing off outcroppings, suffering mutilation and eventual death, landing on those still alive and those dead. Moaning in mass pain.

At midnight a generator came to life and added its drone to the noises on the ledge. In the darkness house lights glowed, seemingly an entire electrified village. On the ledge yotheas dimly lit the aisles between the cells with small torches.

"Bring the old one first." Nang snapped the order and the yothea squad jumped. Nang cursed them for being slow. When Chhuon was brought forth Nang addressed him. "Old Man," Nang lied, "this evening I read your confession."

"Yes," Chhuon mumbled.

"Are you sorry for the horrible atrocities you've brought upon the Khmer people?"

Chhuon did not answer. In the darkness and mist he was disoriented. Then he blurted, "What are those lights?"

"Come closer." Nang held a hand out to Chhuon. "You're too far back to make it out clearly." Chhuon hesitated. "Come," Nang urged. "Walk with me. When we're a little closer your eyes won't deceive you." Still Chhuon hesitated. "That's the way to Thailand, Old Man. You're being expelled. Remember?"

"I've been here before," Chhuon said clearly. "Remember? I know the cable over the canyon."

"Oh. Ha!" Nang laughed lightly. Gently he took Chhuon's hand in his right pincer. "Let me explain what you see. And I will walk ahead. When you're in Thailand don't speak badly of us. Come."

Quietly Chhuon said, "I shall become enlightened . . ." He too laughed lightly. Nang's mangled hand was warm and small and it reminded Chhuon of his son's hand when the boy was six or seven. ". . . May . . . may I say good-bye to you?"

Now Nang hesitated. Not a single victim had ever asked that. "Perhaps you'll rejoin us when you realize how terrible the imperialists are."

"It's okay. I know. You know I know. Don't pretend. I had a son who would be your age. Eight years ago he was taken from me in the mountains. Every night I've prayed for him. I heard he'd survived. Become part of the resistance. How I wish to live to see him. He was a good boy and I loved him so." Chhuon began to cry. "When they stole him my heart broke. I only wished to see him once more. To say good-bye. Let me say good-bye to you."

Nang did not answer. He walked the old man slowly toward the lights, which appeared to be a village in the distance. Somehow this repulsive creature with his gentle words had caused

him to choke up. He cleared his throat. "I wish," he uttered
quietly, "you were not an enemy of Kampuchea. Good-bye."
    With that Chhuon vanished from sight.

All night human beings were taken from the cells and told to
"walk to the light." Many screamed as they fell but, as had
happened every night since the site had become operational,
not one refused to go.
    Nang did not stay past the first dozen. The cliff no longer
thrilled him as it once had. Instead he returned to his home. He
attempted to sleep but could not. The moaning from the gorge
seemed particularly loud, as if the voices were trapped in by the
low clouds and mist. He arose. Turned on the radio. There was
no broadcast from Phnom Penh. He refused to tune in Hanoi.
Nang cleaned himself. He checked his closet for his best uniform and changed clothes. Then he went to the central room
where he had collected a number of books, but he could not
read. Instead he hefted the file of the old peasant. Nang sat,
looked at the photos, began to read. The last confession was
stilted, the work of coercion. Nang read only the beginning,
then he read the start of an earlier version. Then he put them
aside and lifted the spiral notebooks labeled #1 and #7. He
flipped through the last. This creature surely was a spy, an
agent of the Americans. Freely he'd written accounts of secret
meetings, of aiding escapees. Why he'd not been dealt the ultimate measure earlier Nang didn't know but he suspected collusion and bribery involving the cadre of Sangkat 117, the old
man's last site, perhaps even involving Arn or Ku.
    Nang put notebook #7 down. He sighed, rolled forward in his
chair, was about to return to bed. But his hand opened notebook #1. Immediately it grabbed him. Nang read quickly, reread carefully. He knew some of the people . . . this was the
story of the trip to Stung Treng, Lomphat and Plei Srepok.
Nang closed the book. His abdomen and chest burned. He swallowed hard to keep the bile down but immediately belched the
hot acid to the back of his throat. He closed his eyes. Into his
memory leaped a vision of a giant. He opened his eyes. Looked
about. "My father was Kambu," he said aloud. "The other
father is dead. Kambu. Kambu. He is the father of all."
    Again Nang opened the notebook. Again he read. Again he
shut the pages and closed his eyes. The written words jarred
loose all sorts of memories. Again the giant, now surrounded by
total village immolation. "Yiii . . ." the giant screams. "For all
eternity our blood will call for revenge." Whose words? "Watch
over Mayana." Who speaks to me? "Yiii-KA!" The head, the

neck split clean. Ears scraping naked body. *"I—"* Nang bolted up, erect, rigid, yelling, *"I am the giant!"*

"Huh?" Nang sees himself standing. He looks around. Met Nem, the house teacher, and Met Kosal, his bodyguard, have rushed to the room. "I must go." Nang barks the order at himself. He is feverish, frantic. He runs. Kosal runs with him, follows him to the path to the cliff. Nang is sprinting at a pace Kosal can't match. He reaches the fork of the path but takes neither way. Instead he bears left and crashes through the undergrowth. In the canyon along the base of the cliff he passes a set of stone stairs, then a three-tiered wall, then a large bust of Buddha. The three-tiered wall curves with the cliff base and in the apex there is a shrine. Splattered thickly over the shrine are the dead, the mutilated dying—thousands. Nang climbs the pile at the base of the lowest tier. He is certain he will not be there. Millions of flies swarm. First light has broken. The illumination is soft on the oily dripping pools of yellow, brown, red swirls, massive pockets of maggots. Black birds descend with the dawning. They pick at the carnage, the decomposing, the disfigured. Nang waddles maniacally into the depths of the offal. "papa? Papa?" He sloshes to the center and climbs the second tier. No stone can be seen beneath the body dump. "Papa!" Nang pulls through bodies of children, flipping them to the lowest level. As he grasps, one screams. The shriek amid the constant hum of flies and the thunderous groaning horrifies him. He lurches back, stumbles, falls cascading backward to the bottom. Again he climbs, to the first, the second, now to the third tier. "Papa! Papa, you didn't abandon me. I thought you left me. They lied. They lied to me. I thought you died. I thought you hated me. Papa!" Nang lifts face after face. Where? Where could the old peasant be? "Papa! Papa, I was such a disappointment to you. But . . . you . . . you didn't leave me." Oh . . . oh . . . oh, Lord Buddha, help me, help me find him. "Papa!" Nang is crying, frantic, distraught. "I tried to become all you could want . . . to become everything I could. I too will be enlightened. For your sake. Papa, please help me." Nang drooped, plopped down amid the corpses. "You," he said sadly to one. "Have you seen my father?" Then he looked up. The upper rim of the cliff looked to be a thousand kilometers high. "Papa! I'm so frightened . . . everything around me . . . there are ghosts everywhere."

Nang rolled to his knees. He crawled along the top tier, crying, blithering, unable to see through the clouds of insects he'd stirred up. Then he saw the face. The eyes were opened. It was not broken. The body too appeared intact. But it was without life. Nang moved to Chhuon. He sat the old body up, leaned it against other corpses, then sat next to it, lifted its arm and put it over his own shoulder. "Papa, what should I do? Should I have my children spy on one another, eliminate one another? Look at that child there. She didn't deserve to live. What of your life these eight years? Would it have been better to die at Plei Srepok? Look, Papa! Look at them all. *I am the giant now!* They were his enemies. These people, they're not enemies of the state!" Nang righted a head with his left foot. "You, old woman, did you love your children? This man"—Nang hugged his father—"he loved me."

From high above, the radio, the Voice of Democratic Kampuchea, turned to top volume, blasted urgent words. Yotheas scurried. Nang looked up. Amid the buzzing and moaning he could not at first make out the distant words. Then distinctly he heard the message. "Two Viet Namese divisions," the voice blared, "are advancing west along Highway 19 through the highlands of Ratanakiri. Soldiers of the Northeast Zone . . ."

Nang straightened up. They approach us here, eh? he thought. He removed Chhuon's arm from about his shoulders, looked into Chhuon's face. "I must go now, Papa. Good-bye."

CHAPTER TWENTY-ONE
March 1977

For more than a year Vathana had existed in the gulag of Sangkat 117. It was the time of the great starvation, the second famine. But to call it a year is very odd. Time crumbled. There is no time in a gulag. For a while Vathana made daily trips to the fertilizer factory but then she was allowed to return to the fields. She was expected to tell all. She told no one.

In the gulag all people were now to eat in the communal dining place, but there was room for only half and rations for only half. The healthiest people hustled from the fields to gain a place in line, the weakest stumbled and fell and died. Midline was a place of shoving, cutting, prodding. Yotheas encouraged it until it became tiresome. Then they bashed people with their clubs. Each day people became more desperate; each night the rice riot became worse. Some nights the yotheas announced there would be no rice and the people would have to "make do." Always they blamed enemies. "The rice shipment we expected was seized by imperialist saboteurs. Anyone caught hiding rice will be severely punished."

As the famine deepened cadre changed, first at *srok* level, then at *khum*. The newest cadre were the most cruel. The population of the commune rose with new deportees, then fell because of "natural causes." In August 250 people died of starvation in Sangkat 117; in September, 300. More people came, more died. Two communes were combined and together totaled 12,000 workers. Then a mobile youth brigade of 2,000 was force-marched toward Battambang or Siem Reap. No one knew for certain. With it went Mey's eldest daughter. In October rations were cut further. Now, in the center of thousands of hectares of rice fields, the ration for an adult full-time field worker was seventy kernels of corn per day. Other adult workers—mat weavers, tool

makers—received thirty-five. For nearly 10,000 people the enforcers, chiefs and controllers allowed but ten children to be on
fishing detail. Foraging was prohibited. October's death count
stopped at 400 but there were more.

Robona and Vathana were frail, Amara was the weakest. All
were distraught. "I went to Met Rama," Amara said to her
sister and cousin. The three lay on mats on the raised floor of
the hut. Everywhere about them, under them, falling on them,
was water. It was the time of the heaviest rains, the time the
sparsely manned cadres had the least control over the people.
"I said," Amara's lips quivered, "Brother, we must have food."

"Did he answer?" Vathana asked. Others in the hut took note
of their speech and the three women huddled closer and lowered their voices.

"he said it is his order to see each person has one milk can of
rice each day. but he said there is no rice. i said, 'then let us eat
the forest.' he answered he would not stop us but he was not the
security enforcer but nava was. i kissed his feet and left. tomorrow one of us must get food. you're the strongest. we'll tell the
mekong you are ill."

The next day the two sisters went to work. Vathana lay
moaning on her mat until all the women except the old mat
weavers left. Then she rolled to her knees and slowly crawled to
the doorless doorway. Purposely she made her belches loud as if
she were about to vomit. The old women eyed her, shied back,
pretended not to notice. Another one nauseous from overexer-
tion and starvation, from dysentery or other diseases. Another
one probably to die in a day or two. Best not to get to know her.
What could one do?

Vathana backed to the door, let herself slowly down into the
water. It came to midthigh. She rolled her skirt up and stumbled away. The area north of the hut was intermittent forest,
empty of fields, of people. She came upon a path and followed
it. The rain came hard all day. The sky and land and vegetation
blurred in their grayness. Here she picked a water lily stalk,
broke it, chewed it to mush though her gums seemed barely
able to keep her teeth in place. She swallowed it knowing it
would have been okay cooked, fearing raw it would make her
stomach swell. She came to a banana tree with no fruit. She
picked a young leaf and again chewed. Her experience with
Kpa, Le and Sam helped her forage but in her dazed and feeble
state the land seemed picked clean. Then attached to a large lily
she spied a snail. Her eyes darted about ensuring that no one
saw. She snatched it and stuck it in the waistband of her skirt.
Now she looked frantically for snails, for shrimp. In the water

were dozens of small fish. She tried again and again to snap one up. She caught one. The slower she moved her hand in the water, the more she was able to grab. These too she rolled in her waistband until she had several dozen. She caught three more and ate them on the spot, savored them, crunching their delicate bones between her few good molars. She caught another, was about to pop it in her mouth when she spied movement. She hid. Four girls stumbled toward her.They were filthy, covered with sores, as sickly as the sickest in her commune. The girls saw her but only one seemed to comprehend. Lowly the one muttered, "How much food do you get in your cooperative?" It had become the new idiomatic greeting of all Democratic Kampuchea.

In fear Vathana said nothing. The girls wandered on. Vathana trekked deeper into the forest. She came to a slight rise. The earth was saturated and the path was slick. She fell. She raised her head. This mud oasis, she thought, it could be a hideout. She rose. Now she walked more carefully, more afraid, as alert as her condition would permit. Months without proper nutrition affected her ability to concentrate. Swimming in her mind was the thought of ambush but it wouldn't coalesce. She stumbled down the rise into a small clearing, into a slime pit where blackbirds fed ravenously, where smaller birds chirped and dove on scraps dropped by the ravens. Before she saw it she sensed it, felt the restless spirits of souls not blessed with proper ceremony. Then she saw the bodies floating as if suspended in a viscous twilight, face up, facedown, no face at all, floating in the rain, swimming, struggling to the surface of the pool, the decomposition gases filling internal sacs, rising, muck wings for the departed who could neither kick nor stroke but only do the deadman's float until they broke the surface faceup, facedown, no face at all. Vathana fled. In her haste and dizziness she took a wrong path and ran into a clearing where a hundred low-lying objects were wrapped in opaque plastic bags. Again the feeling, again the hesitation, again the fixed eyes searching confirmation of a terror she wished not to confirm. A torn bag. A head crushed beyond recognition, the bag tied at the neck, the entire body buried. Vathana backpedaled, faster and faster. The fish in her waistband spilled. She spun, ran, fled, fled from the dark age of the *thmils,* but these were not *thmils,* not foreign atheists, but Khmer men and boys and girls turning the nation upon itself, turning it into a charnel house.

"You! Halt!"

Vathana stopped. A calm descended upon her. It would be better to die than to witness more. She turned to the voice. It

was Met Nava. With him was Nem. They were killing the girls
Vathana had seen earlier. Calm vanished. She ran hard. She
would have run on leg stubs had they cut off her feet; on hands
had they taken her legs. Her heart pumped wildly. She crashed
through brush, splashed in the low water, lunged, dove-rose-
dove in the deep.

That night there was an education session. The words changed
little, the people in their exhaustion barely heard. "You work
well," Met Nava told them. "You are strong. You don't need to
eat. Work. There is no need to think. Give yourselves to Angkar.
Angkar protects all, provides for all. Rebuild yourselves in the
spirit of Angkar Leou." Then came new orders. Do this, do that.
"Tomorrow all will double their production. Mothers may suckle
newborns only one month. Then they will be given to the lactaters
of the children's center." Do that. Do this. Not that. Not this.
This and this. People became confused. Confusion was punishable by death. Nava shouted, "Someone was seen stealing food
from the people. She entered the forest. That person must stand."
No one moved. "If she does not stand—we know who it is—her
family will fade away."

Vathana lightly shut her eyes. Lord Buddha, she thought, they
can only kill my body.

"Stand!"

Vathana rolled to her side but before she could rise seven
women were up. Others began to cry. Then a man stood. Then
another and another. Robona stood. Amara stood. Tears ran on
Vathana's cheeks. She stood. Everyone stood. To save face Met
Nava grasped the closest woman to him. She was never seen
again.

The rice gruel and the corn soup became yet thinner. One
six-ounce can of rice in water per day was issued to sustain
twenty adults. Met Nem teased the starving by letting them
watch her eat plates of pork ribs, large boiled fish, dishes of
vegetables. Some people went crazy. Others became apathetic.
Bodies consumed themselves. Muscles atrophied. Skin sagged
from bones without meat. Bones weakened as the minerals
were metabolized to keep the organism alive. When few people
could work and production fell below quotas, yotheas and *mekongs*
feared that their lies to the enforcers, the padded production
figures, would become sources of suspicion. Then they turned
their backs when people plucked and ate worms from the fields.
For many it was too little, too late. By the time the waters began
to recede a quarter of the people of Sangkat 117 had died.

The first of the new rice was picked early and eaten green.
This too caused problems because the grain was indigestible. A

thousand people fell ill. In her sickness Amara gave Vathana her three-year-old son. To Robona she gave her five-year-old daughter. Her baby was dead. "You will get well again," Vathana whispered to her cousin.

"No," Amara said. She was too weak and too ill to rise from her sleeping mat. "When the *mekong* allows, you must take him. If I see him again, I will eat him."

As Vathana brushed Amara's hair from her eyes, Amara, unseen, under a rag blanket, slit her wrist with a shard of glass. Her head drooped to one side. Vathana thought she slept. She brushed her hair, quietly singing a sweet lullaby. Then she knew Amara was dead. "Go, dear Sister," Vathana whispered in her ear. "Go to the true life."

As fast as the new crop came in the yotheas ordered it removed. People stole what they could but the famine did not stop. At night, after work, Vathana's mind ran terribly. She could not stop her thoughts. She was not yet ready to love her new son whom she was allowed to visit only one hour each week. For this she felt guilty. The guilt led to frustration and the frustration to anger. She was angry at Angkar. Angkar was lies. Angkar promised them food for work but though the crop was sufficient there was no food. She was angry at the cadre who now openly admitted to being Communists. She was angry at Pol Pot who now openly admitted to being head of Democratic Kampuchea. Now Robona was near death. Her body swelled, blood flow to her extremities stopped. She lay down and refused to rise up. Vathana's anger turned to Lon Nol, then to America. Shame, she thought. Shame on America for bringing on this misery. Shame on them for their indifference. Do they know? Do you know, John Sullivan? Does he know? How does he react? Does he cry for me? How does America react? Surely they know. Are there demonstrations in Washington? Maybe in Paris? Shame on them for their half-boiled policies. It would have been better to give no aid at all. None. Not just enough to keep us alive and suffering. They are as bad as the Khmer Rouge. Will they aid us again, bring us to life again, keep all Kampuchea suffering only to let us die again? John L., our daughter is lost. You didn't even see her.

Then came new demands. Angkar, all were told, wishes the population to double. Women no longer menstruate, Vathana thought, and Pol Pot wants the population to double! Men! Do you know this, John L.? Do your people cry for mine? Do they know of this bloodbath? You warned me. How I hate myself for not believing you. You wanted to teach me? I used to teach my brothers and sisters how to forgive. In Phum Sath Din I helped Samay with his schoolwork. Oh, how Papa had plans for the family. Between the extremes, he said. In a Buddhist-socialist state we would live well. But there is no state. Nothing can be done. All is lost. When I die I will go to my mother and to my children. Let us all die together. Let the Americans drop their atomic bomb. Then we can escape this life.

The night Robona died Vathana cried over her body. Beneath the platform a child spy heard her and the next day she was told she would not eat for a week. To cry was to criticize the regime.

In a few days Vathana's body swelled. Her hands and feet became cold. She could not urinate though her urge was constant. She lay down and like Robona refused to rise for morning work call. At midday an old mat weaver came to give her water but she had no desire to eat or drink. Her eyes dulled, her body bloated, her lungs became congested. She lost control of her anal sphincter and diarrhetic water fouled her skirt and mat. When conscious she thought to rise, to clean herself, prepare her body for death, but she did not care. Someone moved her from the hut. Someone forced palm sugar water down her throat. She vomited.

An entire month passed without her being aware of her treatment. Slowly she realized she was living in a house instead of a communal hut. What act of kindness had returned her from the dead she knew not, but she feared she was only being set up to be starved again. For a long time she remained morosely silent. Inside she wept. Another month passed. Each day the housekeeper brought three meals. At first she could not eat. Then she could not resist. She was brought new clothes, black, like all clothes, but clean and pressed. She saw no one except the housekeeper though she often heard a man's voice and at night she heard clunking and scraping. She was not allowed to go from the house or to peer from the windows or doors. Then one day she was told she would marry Met Leng at the 17 April celebration. "But who is Met Leng? I cannot marry . . ."

"He is a veteran of the war," the housekeeper interrupted. "You were dead, just as he was dead. He has given you life, just as Angkar had given him."

"But my husband . . . he is not dead."

"Your file said you never married."

"I have a son. At the center."

"He was your sister's. He's dead."

"I have a husba—"

"Have you not yet learned to tremble?! You'll see. Tomorrow night I will present you to the meeting. Angkar has decreed the people will produce more workers to advance the economy. Tomorrow you will marry my son."

That night Vathana had a dream. Her dead mother came to her and told her not to marry this man. In the dream Vathana beseeched her mother's spirit for a solution. The spirit said she would help and vanished.

All the next day Vathana was pampered by the housekeeper. The older woman brought her water and French soap to bathe, a small vial of perfume, new panties, a comb for her hair. She was given more new clothes, black; a sarong skirt, a shirt and a black krama. When night fell and the workers returned from the new excavation sites, there was a big meeting and a big celebration. For hours various chieftains boasted, bolstered or blasted the people. A cow was killed. Everyone was given a sliver of meat. Then names were called. From one side came fifty wisps of girl workers, from the other mostly yotheas though a few peasant men. The "betrothed" were not allowed to touch but simply stood across the center aisle from each other. Then Vathana was brought in to stand at the front of the line of women. In her new clothes with her regained weight she felt conspicuous. Compared to the others she was plump, beautiful. Her eyes shone. About her head she'd wrapped the black krama like an Egyptian goddess and in her clean hands she held a white chrysanthemum. Met Leng was helped to the head of the line of men. He could not stand without a crutch, for one foot pointed not sole to earth but sole to sky. From the middle of his chest stuck the deformed arm. He leered at Vathana. She showed no shock, indeed appeared at ease with the deformed transporter of the dead.

Met Rama had been purged. Met Yam had been disappeared. Met Nava conducted the ceremony. "Comrades being married," he said proudly, "today you accept the responsibility for each other as husband and wife until the end of your days. Assist each other in your service to Angkar. Never allow the other to falter. Now we will sing the national anthem. Then, eat soup. Then go back to work." Nava led the meeting in song:

Bright red Blood which covers towns and plains
Of Kampuchea, our Motherland,
Sublime Blood of workers and peasants,
Sublime Blood of revolutionary men and women fighters!
The Blood changing into unrelenting hatred
And resolute struggle,
On April 17th, under the Flag of the Revolution,
Frees from Slavery!

Long live, long live Glorious April 17th!
Glorious Victory with greater signification
Than the times of Angkor!

We are uniting to edify
Splendid and democratic new Kampuchea and new society
With equality and justice,
Firmly applying the line of independence, sovereignty and self-reliance.
Let us resolutely defend
Our Motherland, our sacred Soil
And our Glorious Revolution!

Long live, long live, long live,
Democratic and prosperous new Kampuchea!
Let us resolutely raise high
The red Flag of the Revolution!
Let us edify our Motherland!
Let us make her advance with great leaps,
So that She will be more glorious and more marvelous than ever!

Vathana brought her new husband a stool. She sat at his feet. Small straw fires lit the ceremonial arena. Children brought bowls of soup, one per couple, and a choir sang revolutionary songs.

"Do I please you?" Vathana's voice was sweet as she looked just below Leng's eyes.

"You do," he answered, reaching out to touch her. He put his good hand to her cheek, to her forehead. She pushed her head into it like a cat. He pushed his thumb up behind her ear. Her head . . . "Damn *you!*" he bellowed. He threw her to the ground ripping away the krama. Her head was bald, rough shaven, stubble and cuts everywhere. "You *whore!*" Leng screamed furiously. He kicked his broken leg, swung his bent arm. He roared, growled unintelligible noises.

Vathana scrambled up. "I am not your slave," she shouted back. "I am not your servant. None of us are slaves! What are you going to do, kill me? Do it. I wish only deliverance from this hell."

"Then"—Leng's face distorted—"build your house at . . . at . . . at 169."

People who have suffered multiple tortures and who have been starved for long periods do not scramble to elude additional inescapable torture but instead tend to set their minds and bodies for the impending punishment. So deep is the hopelessness of slavery that even when an opening for escape or resistance is presented, the tortured's eyes are shut. "Submit. Go along. All attempts to flee have ended in death." Thus it was, after Vathana's small rebellion against Met Leng sent her to Site 169, Vathana's spirit was in a greater state of depression than ever before. Only the promise to her father via Aunt Voen kept her from total submission and acquiescence to her own death. It did not, however, spark even the tiniest resistance to the tiger cage, nor did it cause her to object to all she was shown.

Life in the camp at 169 differed little from life at Sangkat 117. Vathana was immediately assigned a hut, given a tin plate, and put to work planting rice seedlings. Soon the monsoon rains began in earnest. The people at 169 were better fed than those at 117 yet still they were famished, frail, dropping from lack of food and long, tedious, strenuous slave labor. They were different in a way Vathana did not yet understand, more withdrawn, more suspicious. Constantly there was undertalk of the cliffs, of the body dumps and of an invasion force which soon would liberate them. Yet no sooner would Vathana hear someone whisper such than that person and those near her would be disappeared forever. Thus she too withdrew, spoke to no one, listened to no one. In June when the sun shone between rains she asked it, How can you shine on Cambodia? Why do you not weep until the land is washed clean? Indeed the rains were unusually hard that summer and the little dry season unusually short. The irrigation systems were chaotic. In one area water flowed too quickly and destroyed the earthworks, in another it stagnated to the point of putrifying. Flies flew in viscous swarms beneath the roofs of the huts without doors. Mosquitos, their buzzing constant, were so ravenous, ubiquitous, that when slaves were beaten they barely bled. Vathana tore small swabs from the hem of her skirt and plugged her ears. She wrapped her krama so it fit snugly at her eyebrows then loosely over and around her head, then doubling back to protect her neck and face. At night she slept beneath the cloth, pulled her ulcerated feet up into her skirt, her bony hands into the sleeves of her blouse. Still the flies and mosquitos got to her. Some of the less fortunate, some with no energy and no hope, let the insects feed and breed on them, calculating that death would thus liberate them sooner. From the eyes and open sores of those despondent souls squirmed maggots.

One night in July, forty-four women from a neighboring brigade, using their kramas, hung themselves. Seven were unsuccessful because the fabric of their scarves was too weak to hold their emaciated bodies. The next night eighteen more succeeded.

On the third night Vathana was awakened by mosquitos on her face and neck sucking her dry. Someone had stolen her krama. Slowly, as first light crept into the hut, the images of her hut mates emerged. All were hung by their necks from kramas tied to the rafters.

"Stand still!" The yothea was mean, stern. In three days seventy people had cheated Angkar of killing them. "You will answer immediately and fully all questions you are asked." Vathana stood perfectly still. Before she'd reported the suicides to her *mekong* she had regained her krama from a corpse and rewrapped her head and face. A young girl had evidently attempted to hang herself with her own scarf. When it shredded, she had quietly and gently removed Vathana's while she slept. Vathana had found the girl's tattered cloth near her sleeping mat. She had taken it and tied it about the girl's neck, then she'd placed the body in such position as to make it appear the krama had held until after death.

Vathana waited. The yothea waited. He strode back and forth. She did not know why. The camp's enforcer had been purged the day before. People were the property of Angkar Leou and only Angkar had the right to dispose of its property. As she stood she could feel her face heat up. She could feel sweat break out into the krama. Her entire body was warm and she thought the spirit of the dead girl must have been in her krama and now had entered her and was very angry. Then she felt chilled. Her jaw trembled. She tried to clench her teeth but they chattered out of control. Her head ached. Her breathing became rapid and shallow.

A car arrived. She had not seen an automobile in almost two years but her head hurt so badly she was not able to concentrate. A young man emerged. He was stiff and straight and strong, clad in the most beautiful gray uniform Vathana had ever seen. The yothea ran to him, snapped to attention, seemed ready to fall to the ground to kiss the man's polished boots. The young man barely noticed. Other men emerged. They marched straight to her. Her trembling was now very bad.

"Did you aid these criminals?" The young man's voice was even, professional.

Vathana tried to swallow but her throat had swelled; saliva and phlegm stuck at the epiglottis. She opened her mouth to speak but only the chattering of her teeth made sound. The man reached his hands to her krama, peeled it from her face then removed it completely. "Did you?"

"N . . . n . . . no."

"No, Met Nang," an aide corrected her.

"N . . . n . . . no, Me . . . et N . . ."

"That's all right." Nang smiled compassionately. "You are ill?" He snickered. If one claimed illness Angkar often interpreted it as a criticism. To criticize Angkar meant death. "Don't speak. I can see you are ill." He studied her face. "You didn't join them, eh? That took great strength." Nang turned to the local yothea. "See that she collects her belongings and comes to my house in the forest."

"Yes, Met Nang."

Nang smiled. He still held Vathana's krama. Now he looked at her more closely. Her hair stuck out like porcupine quills, her face was a massive welt of mosquito bites, yet her eyes, shrunk in the hollows in her face, were the darkest he had ever seen.

"Why didn't you join them?" Nang's small laugh was vile. Vathana only trembled. Nang approved of her submissiveness. "In two days"—he beamed to Met Kosol—"to my house."

To go build a house in the forest was a euphemism for being taken away to be murdered. Vathana was very frightened but her new sickness was so severe that for hours at a time she had no concentration for fear. She thought of the sickness—fevers and headaches and chills—and when she was lucid she knew it had been coming on for weeks, knew it was malaria, knew there was no one to help her, nowhere to get medicine. But in the hut where she had been condemned to stay amid the hanging dead she was seldom lucid.

She lay in delirium, thinking, I must live. I promised Papa. Tell them. No. You mustn't. Don't argue with them. They'll kill you. Go along. I will live to get out. Go along. I'll go to meet Mama. Sweet Mama. How I cry when I think of Papa's words when he buried you. Mama, I've lost my children. Samol. You would love Samol. Is she with you? Samnang. He's six now. Oh, what a wonderful boy. He is so strong. And Su Livanh. She had . . . no, Mama, she has red hair. She is so funny. What! Oh God, what's coming? Please. Get them away. They'll slash me. No! Don't make me fertilizer. Oh Divine Buddha . . . Oh! Teck! You . . . they killed you. I'm sorry. I don't want to lose your child. Don't be angry. Don't blame me. I would be a good wife if you . . . Samnang. Teck, leave Samnang . . . He . . . he's a good boy . . . I'll come to Phnom Penh. John? He . . . you know how I am ordered . . . I hate America . . . I hate Americans . . . you know how . . . I love Captain Sullivan. You cannot take him. You cannot take him in the night.

When the fever broke Vathana lay listless, exhausted, not yet asleep but in semiconsciousness, trying to hang on to the delirium dream, to analyze it, but usually losing it in the sleep that followed. For two days she lay in the hut of the hanging dead. Six times the fever spiked, six hours she spent feeling it coming, feeling her headache build to the point she knew her brains would burst, then six hours in delirium fevers trembling, moaning, then fifteen hours in postfever semiconsciousness or sleep.

In the few hours between she prepared her body for disappearance. Carefully she cleaned herself as best she could. Carefully she arranged her clothes, confiscating a single clean sarong skirt from the mat of a woman in her hut. There was but to wait, to pray. She did not eat. There was only green rice and only a little. It would be of better use for someone who was not to go to the forest.

The second day passed. No one came for her. Then passed the third, fourth and fifth. The fevers got worse. Now, in the time between, the headaches were so severe she could not rise. The sixth day passed. She was morose. Bodies began to fall, to break apart and fall. The smell was horrible. Inside she cried because she was all alone. She had no tears. Then someone came and told her there was war at the border and the Center had issued a new directive. Everyone with Viet Namese ancestry was to be killed immediately. Met Nang was very busy. The cliff was overloaded. She should return to work and live elsewhere.

Beat thyself, *America*, he thought, he screamed at them in his thoughts. Sullivan stood at the bar. Conklin would not make it to San Francisco for two more days. He had resisted drinking, but with Huntley backing out and Conklin's delay, he'd had a shot and a beer and his resistance had crumbled.

Flail thy back with the straps of Southeast Asian crimes ye committed, he yelled at the top of his lungs in his mind as he chased the Jack Daniel's with Bud. Forget all else. For what does it mean for a nation to gain all the world but to lose its soul, eh? Ay, ye decrepit fool, proclaim thy guilt and bury thyself in self-indulgence. Fornicate in BMWs. Masturbate in stone-washed dun-gar-ees. What matter? You've been proven guilty of the most heinous crimes—your young bucks have, in time of war, under great tension and less than great leadership, they have raped, murdered, plundered.

He glanced at the reports spewing from the borrowed attaché case onto the polyethylene surface. ". . . we must arrange the Party's history into something clean and perfect, in line with our policies of independence and self-mastery." They were Pol Pot's words, words from the Party's journal. Uck, he thought. In the dining room behind him people were picking at their food. He watched plate after plate being carried to the automatic dishwasher, heaped with untouched mashed potatoes, or enough steak to feed a village for a week.

Though it was against our law, his mental oration ran, though it was against our policy and against normal operating procedure, *Some* Americans committed atrocious crimes. That most were honorable, brave, honest and righteous, that their cause was one of freedom for a people assailed by the modern-day *Hun*, the *Hun* whose slaughter paralleled that of seventeenth-century Swedes in Poland, paralleled that of Stalinist Russia, is to no account. Or is it only my righteousness? Ay, ye *America*, condemn thyself before all the people of the world, tell them you are not worthy and abdicate all responsibility to all humanity. Fornicate in BMWs. Masturbate in stone-washed *dun-gar-ees*. Truckle thy principled manner to microwave ovens and world-class shopping sprees. Spread thy thighs for stereo-television, camcorder complexes projecting images of thy vile and hideous past, thy violent streets, thy corrupt and exploitive businesses. That most of you are decent means nothing.

Conklin, of all people! He had agreed to go back. Him with his lady. Divorced now. In January of 1976, one report said, the defection of Krahom troops was so high some referred to it as the second revolution. In Ratanakiri, only a few months back, the Krahom minister of defense led KK Regiment 703 in an open uprising against Pol Pot's local forces. Then there was an aborted rebellion in the eastern zone and a Colonel Rin and thousands of troops had escaped to Viet Nam and were forming a new Khmer Viet Minh.

Abdicate thy role, America, Sullivan snarled inside. I am not worthy. I am not worthy. To every nation: Know ye, America is not worthy.

A second famine is reported to be sweeping Democratic Kampuchea and upwards of half the population is estimated to be at risk of perishing. What the fuck, Sullivan thought. It ain't on TV. It can't be true. How did Elie Wiesel, the Nazi holocaust survivor, put it? ". . . if we forget, we are guilty, we are accomplices." Is it so painful to look at that we deny it? Forget it? Change the historical script? Or is it no such deep and hidden psychological defense mechanism but instead our hedonistic and narcissistic shallow selves attempting to entertain ourselves to death with the latest lust from the giggly-boob tube? Is it cover-up or just plain apathy?

Sullivan downed another shot. In his mind he blared to the world, Expect nothing if insurgents attack. We've nothing to offer. It is the lesson we've learned from Viet Nam. Lo, if thee shall fall behind the creeping curtain of restricted information flow—we know not your suffering. How can it be?! It's not on our TV.

"In the lee of world view," the report said, "Khmers *had* to march to their deaths even when they knew that was where they were marching." My daughter, marching to her death, he thought, and the anger in him was so immense, only another shot kept him from tearing the bar from the floor and thrashing the people behind him, beside him.

Fornicate in your BMWs, he screamed at them in his mind, while the filthy fat female sighs lewdly over your vehicular speakerphone, only three dollars per minute. Masturbate in stone-washed *dun*-gar-ees. You are not worthy to entertain the thought of assisting others. Abdicate thy responsibility with dry, stinkless armpits. You can be sure you are not worthy. You can feel soft as a gentle summer breeze—as Khmers toast.

Soft leather reclining bucket seats with six-speaker vehicular video-audio . . . Lao die under yellow rain from poison bee pollen shaken from bugs by PAVN high explosives and napalm. Peace at last in Southeast Asia!

Peace is at hand. Sullivan now drank directly from the beer bottle, purposely hoping it disgusted the well dressed about him. The domino theory has been disproven. Angola does not touch Kampuchea. I am not worthy. Abdicate thy responsibility to the people of the world. Do not give me your homeless. They probably carry disease. I am not worthy to even think I may be intelligent enough to sort out what is decent from what is foul. The insurgents have legitimate points, after all. World, you are not worthy of the sacrifice of even one American life. Have a bag of money. Let me sell you some bombs. It is the lesson of Viet Nam.

I have a daughter! She is the property of Angkar Leou! You bastards. Fornicate in thy Mercedes in your sealed, secure garage, behind your tight security system—in your stone-washed denim lacy lingerie from Freddie of HoBo Woods.

Why? Bastards! You devious, calculating . . . make a "new communist woman" of my daughter . . . Is that a manifestation of your "purity of purpose," your desire for pure communism?

What of our myths, our moral foundation, our history, my fellow Americans? In January 1961 John F. Kennedy said

> In the long history of the world, only a few generations have been granted the role of defending freedom in its hour of maximum danger. . . . The energy, the faith, the devotion which we bring to this endeavor will light our country and all who serve it—and the glow from that fire can truly light the world.

Was it not that spirit which propelled me, us, into the Viet Nam era? Change the word "spirit" to "purpose" or "motive." The spirit, purpose, and motive survived Lee Harvey Oswald's bullets. But it could not survive the icon busters. Revelations that JFK was boffing MM or whomever while Jackie was on hold tarnished the hero in the tabloid brains of America and that tarnish dulled his beautiful, altruistic and moralistic ideals. Results: the hero falls from grace and with him the mythical strength, his high ideals *and* with that, the motivation to emulate. Cultural idealism wanes. Society accepts less, standards fall, people emulate the mores of television vamps and me-generation gurus.

Lock your iron triangle on thy guilt, oh nation. I am not worthy of any good. Thus I am free from trying. Look out for number *one*! It is the lesson of Viet Nam.

Reexamine your viewpoints, your foresight and hindsight—*not, for most, your principles*. Fifty million people have been enslaved in Southeast Asia since the falls, fifty million political hostages. Around the world "free" nations are backing off to appease Soviet expansionism because of America's decline in power, not firepower but willpower. Oh, to lie you down, America. Right there. On that couch. Lie down, you big overstuffed oaf. Oh to be the guide on your psychoanalytic journey—not because you are nuts, but because you've got so much right with you, so much of positive value to offer the world. If only you weren't hung up on immediate gratification. If only you could cope with your insecurities and face reality. If only you had a sense of your own, and world, history.

Fuck it! Fornicate on the hood of your Ferrari. Nay, masturbate, America. No one wants to lie with the guilt ridden.

But know this, world, America may stay at home—but John Sullivan is coming.

CHAPTER TWENTY-TWO
March 1978

"I killed my father," Met Nang told Vathana. He had had her brought to his house, bathed, scrubbed raw, fed, given chloroquinine and tetracycline, and put in the cage in his room. "Well, not really," Nang continued. His words were quick though he tried to portray himself as detached. "He killed himself. I could have prevented it. Maybe not. He . . . he was so . . . I mean he confessed. He confessed to being infected with yuon disease. He confessed to many horrible and malicious acts against the people and against the state. Of course, he had to die."

"I killed my father," Nang repeated. Vathana said nothing. She was not expected to comment. She squatted in the low cage when Nang came, squatted, stared, listened. At times the young man babbled straight Krahom-Marxist cliché babble; at other times he referred to very intimate details of his personal life, yet all of it was scattered and out of context. For months Vathana had no idea what he was talking about. Always there was the one recurring theme: I killed my father.

When Nang was not home Met Nem, the housekeeper and teacher of Nang's children, often let Vathana out of the cage. Nem was severe yet, within her own system, consistent and just. She was given the task of remaking Vathana in the image of Angkar. It was serious business. Angkar was strong. Vathana must be strong. Angkar was powerful. Vathana must be powerful. Angkar was righteous, pure, single-minded. Vathana must hold only the beliefs of Angkar Leou. The skin of her feet and hands, which had looked like dried wax when she'd been chosen, began to moisten and fill. Her hair grew out. Clumps with scabs fell off leaving bald pink patches on the scalp but these were soon hidden beneath thickening new growth. Daily Nem coined Vathana, rubbing her back or shoulders or legs with a brass coin until the skin seemingly glowed red. Nem pulled her earlobes, her hair. Vathana, having twice been starved to the point where food was repulsive, was now again force-fed until she continuously craved food. In the cage her body filled out like a calf being fattened for veal.

Each day Nang made Nem undress Vathana before him so he could gauge the results. The sickly stick figure became curvaceous. Nang lifted her breasts—once nothing but shriveled nipples in a sunken chest, now, slowly, the lovely tissues of femininity—with his pincer. "It is," he told Nem, not even addressing Vathana, "the best way to assess the progress."

Then for days he would be gone and Vathana would sit or squat or lie in the small tiger cage in his room in his house in the forest isolated from the horrors, forced to listen to Radio Phnom Penh, to listen to Pol Pot's three-, four-, five-hour broadcasts. Then the winds shifted, the rains passed and the harvest season came. During daylight new winds carried a constant low moaning. At night, all night, the wind brought a ghastly, odorous cloud. There was a great thrust at the border, vicious fighting, constant reports of Khmer victories, each nearer to the heart of Democratic Kampuchea.

Nang returned. He was flushed, feverish, agitated. Again he babbled the nonsense about killing his father, but now to Vathana he seemed not to hear his own words. Then he said to her, "You are now loyal to Angkar." She, as always, did not respond. He turned on her, a harsh evil glare contorting his scarred features. "You are now one with Angkar."

"Yes, Met Nang." She did not know what he wanted. She wanted only more food.

"Yes. You had better say yes. We destroyed the foreign devils. Yes?"

"Yes, Met Nang."

"Where is Nem?"

"I'm not given to . . ."

"You," Nang exploded, "are *one* with *Angkar*! Angkar saved you. Angkar gave you life." Nang reached out, grasped her shirt, jerked it hard throwing her across the room. The shirt opened. He leaped toward her, grabbed the shirttail and ripped up, over her head. Vathana cringed. Nang seized her skirt, yanked it from her. "I fuck them," he shouted. "Do you doubt me?"

"N . . . no." Vathana rushed the answer.

"I fuck them and kill them because they are evil. Do you *doubt me?*"

"No."

"Should I fuck you?" he screamed. He stood over her, his

teeth clenched, his hands balled into rock-tight fists ready to smash her to death. Vathana looked into his eyes. Behind his insanity she saw his fear and she relaxed. "Should I?" Nang screamed. Vathana lay back. She touched her fingertips to her shoulders, above her breasts, her elbows at her side. She did not know why but she was not afraid. She resisted by offering no resistance.

"I fuck them all," Nang seethed again. He dropped to a knee, grasped her pants, ripped them apart. "Then I cover them with city evils." As he spoke he shoved his stubbed hand between her legs, rubbing, separating the labia. "Rouge, lipstick, necklaces." Nang laughed. Vathana stared at the roof. She shuddered from a stab of pain. Still she did not resist. "The yuons stuff women with rice stalks. Ha! But you are one with Angkar." His tone became less severe, his pressure softened. "You are not yet called to walk to Thailand. Struggle, Met Ana. Struggle courageously to be one with Angkar."

Now Nang smiled. He seemed relieved, then dizzy, then relieved again. It was very hot, the moaning was very loud. "I fucked you well, eh?"

"Yes, Met Nang."

"We must have faith in Met Sar, in Pol Pot, in Angkar. Angkar will crush all enemies."

"Yes, Met Nang."

"Now you must come with me. I will show you how enemies are crushed. Then we can fuck again. The CIA pays thousands of evildoers but we ferret them out. Everyone must be scrutinized. Anyone may be an agent. Anyone!"

In late December the Viet Namese launched a massive broad-front attack stretching from the Gulf of Siam to the high plateau of the Srepok Forest. Again fear of treachery set off a wave of killings in the interior and again Met Nang became very busy. Now he did not leave Vathana in the cage but brought her to witness his efficiency. First he showed her the prisons, the meticulous records room, the photography "studio," the confession chambers.

"You must read his confession," Nang told her one day.

"Whose?"

"My father's. He was very evil."

Vathana stared at Nang. She was reluctant to answer. This creature had total control of her. "If you wish me to see . . ."

"Ha! Maybe sometime, Met Ana. You are very brave. Tonight I will fuck you well. Very special. Now I will show you a platform ceremony."

The Viet Namese invasion fizzled in January 1978. The Krahom

armies drove the invaders back toward the border, and in celebration the Center launched a new purge. For two months
Vathana accompanied Nang to witness one atrocity after another. Some were small: a married couple stripped, the wife
raped by several yotheas before her husband—then his genitals
hacked off and given to her—then both disemboweled. Some
were large: platform ceremonies like the earliest ones, except
now the women and children were told they were being reunited with fathers or husbands who had disappeared years
earlier. They were lined up on the platform, given a speech,
given flowers to present to the men who would come shortly.
Till the very end the ruse continued. Bloodlines were being
eradicated. Some were massive: groups of a hundred or two
hundred were led, arms tied, to dikes of neighboring *sangkats*,
then they were bludgeoned to death with hardwood clubs. As
young children shrieked for their kin, yotheas bayoneted them
or grabbed them by the feet and used them as clubs to smash
the adults. The neighbors were called to bury the dead. Then
they were ordered to dig deep ponds which later became their
own mass graves.

Now as they traversed the northern part of the zone, Vathana
saw many empty phums. Many nights she lay limp and the
thought would come to her, come softly without intensity, come
to her emptied spirit, I have seen so much, too much, when this
ends, I shall never see again.

In the early months of 1978 she was so numb she followed
Nang like a beaten dog. He had taken to "fucking" her every
night. The sessions never lasted long and most often it was with
the stub of his damaged hand. Yet some nights were "very
special." These nights he penetrated her with various objects:
the femur of a long-dead victim, a long narrow ebony statuette
of Pol Pot carved by a prisoner to Nang's specifications, a
loaded American .45-caliber pistol. "This is how Americans
fuck," Nang would coo. "Very special, eh?"

Through it all Vathana remained submissive, passive, at times
praying, calling in her mind, Divine Buddha, Enchanted One,
Compassionate One! but most often not praying, attempting on
an inner plane to become nonexistent and thus to mask all
emotions. She was not totally successful. "Everything I see
takes a piece of my heart," she once told one of Nang's children.
"Soon I'll have no heart. You have a heart, eh? I've seen many
piles of dead. I've seen . . . one time he brought me to see a
forest ambush. Then he told me he brought his own father on
ambush and the old man tried to warn the people by ticking his
finger against a dry palm frond. Met Nang pretended to be

asleep. He is very tricky, eh?" The child liked the story and told the others and for a week Nang didn't fuck her because he was too angry.

Then he took her to the cliff. He was so proud. "Tonight," he told her, "will be very very special. This is where I killed my father." Nang was joyous. It was late March. The sun was high, the wind carried the sounds and smells away from the small tree house. A dozen yotheas were playing blindman's buff with the emaciated waste of political upheaval. Some people screamed when they fell, some seemed able to see beneath their blind-folds. Some of these ran, leaped from the precipice, attempting to deny the yotheas the enjoyment of their death. Most stumbled, half dead already, finally tripping at the edge, sliding down the short lip then silently falling; the sound of their bodies hitting denied the yotheas because of the odd wind. The boys became bored and left.

"He died very well for an enemy," Nang said. "I'll have Met Arn fetch his file. You'll see. You would do exactly what I did. When I was in school I was taught this."

The day moved slowly on, the sun seemed to linger. Nang told her about the school on Pong Pay Mountain and his jour-ney north. Between incidents he lambasted her for her weak-ness, for her improper background, for not having become a neary long before Lon Nol ousted Sihanouk. He raged about friends and foes. "We are betrayed by devious allies and hei-nous saboteurs," he shouted. Then, "But my security apparatus will get them. It will uncover them all." He paced, waiting for the sun to set, waiting for Arn, waiting to show her his Lakshmi, his own vision of the hell which awaits the treacherous and the evil ones. "More than eight hundred families in the district are under suspicion. There are twenty thousand ex–CIA agents in 169 alone. I will prove them all traitors, all."

As the sky darkened Vathana stood beside Nang. She watched the lines forming up out of sight of the cliff's edge. Arn brought the file Nang had requested. Agitated more then ever Nang ram-paged amongst the papers. His hand shook, his entire body was in near spasm. "Look!" he ordered, shaking the confession before her. "See!" He snatched it back. He read a line here, there, then found and read aloud the paragraph he wanted her to hear:

> . . . in appearance I am totally a revolutionary. I struggle to cultivate the paddies, I vigorously attack the forest, I courageously plow and rake. But deep in my mind I serve the imperialists. I can no longer hide my traitorous acts of toeing the American line. I am a feudalist. I stood with the establishment. I am not a human being. I am an animal . . .

"See! See! An animal! He wasn't human. See! He denied his humanity, therefore he could be killed. I was right. Kampuchea must be purified."

As Nang spoke the generator kicked on and lights appeared over the abyss. Vathana trembled but she could not turn away. The wind shifted. The smell was horrible but still she bore witness. Screams of those being murdered cut her like the hatchets of the fertilizer pit. She could not move. The screams, the low moaning, penetrated her veil of defensive numbness. She cried inwardly, afraid, aware again of fear, of her fear, fear of expressing an emotion. For hours she stood holding the railing, stood frozen, stood dying inside with each scream. Nang launched into a new harangue. "Today, ninety-five percent of the people live under better conditions than they did under the old regime." On and on he went. "Without the collective system we are defenseless. Without it the yuons would disappear the entire Khmer race." On and on went the killings. At first light the descending screams ceased. Now there was a new flurry of activity. The odor of gasoline enveloped them. "We must get down." Nang prodded her. In the dim light Vathana could see yotheas throwing hundreds of small bags of liquid over the cliff, the bags bursting onto the mass of broken screaming groaning bodies. Then a torch. Everyone standing fell flat. From the abyss came a long FaaAHHHH-WHHUUUMP, a blast of flame, an ear-splitting roar, a swirling wind. The screaming died. Below, the mutilated living suffocated as the conflagration sucked all air from around them. The bodies hardly burnt. Some charred in small secondary fires. Now there was no moaning.

Nang led Vathana down the steep path beside the cavern, across the small trail which brought them to the base of the cliff. "Before we used flame," Nang said, businesslike, a subordinate foreman explaining a process to a manufacturing CEO, "the flies were horrible. Now it's not so bad."

"This is how you murdered your father?" Vathana's voice for the first time was strong. Nang stepped back. "Like *this*!?"

"Well, not exactly. He really killed himself. He . . ."

"You've *murdered* all these *people*?!"

"No! They're enemies. Every one. Everyone's confessed. They're animals. Old grass must be burned for new grass to grow."

Vathana put her hands to her face but she did not hide her eyes. Black chunks of charred meat clung to bone shards which had been blown everywhere by the explosions. On the highest tier, evidently a pocket protected from the concussion, were thousands of decomposing bodies amid thousands of skeletons whose bones had been cleaned by insects and bleached by the sun. On the middle and lowest levels the bodies were mashed and macerated beyond recognition.

Nang began to back out. His joy at showing her the new system had been deflated. His anger had not yet risen. Vathana stopped him. She grabbed him by his disfigured hand, then turned back to the massacre. "Angkar has raped Cambodia." Her voice was as hard as his.

"What do you know?" Nang's anger finally caught. His eyes glazed. He cocked his arm to bludgeon her.

"You don't know how to fuck," she snarled. She stepped into him. One hand went straight to his groin. He squirmed backward. She held him. "You fuck with this." She squeezed him. "I'm going to teach you. I've fucked imperialists. I've fucked an American. Now I'm going to teach you and you'll know. Then you won't have to rape Cambodia."

"An . . . an . . . an American. You've . . . with an American. Raped! You can say Angkar has raped Kampuchea! Kampuchea's been raped. Raped by the French. Raped by the Thais, the Japanese, the yuons. Sihanouk raped Kampuchea. Lon Nol raped Kampuchea. Americans raped Kampuchea. Now yuons again." As he spoke his furry expanded. Vathana did not let go. He shoved fingers into her eyes. "There's nothing"—he stepped forward, she tripped back—"nothing we do which is not justified. All deserve to die. The rapers. The looters. The invaders. The bombers. I laugh at their deaths. I gorge myself on their blood. I should rape you. It is justified."

Vathana exploded into hysterical menacing laughter. "You're a little boy. Your father, ha! He didn't teach you to be a man." Again Nang cocked a fist to smash her but she skipped back. He shuffled forward, slipped on a human heart, fell. "Let me teach you," she taunted. "Let me make you a man." She laughed hysterically. "Fuck me very special! Ha!"

Nang stopped. He was trapped. He could kill her but then she wouldn't teach him. I'll kill her after, he thought. "Okay." His voice settled. "Tonight you teach me."

John Sullivan sat in a bath in the Royal Hotel in Bangkok, Thailand. The door to the small suite was open, and lounging on the bed reviewing the new reports was Ian Conklin. For almost a year they'd worked in the camps along the border, helping, by day, refugees as prescribed by the Cambodian Crisis Relief manual. At night they'd searched for clues to Vathana's whereabouts, asked every new refugee if they'd seen or heard of a small red-haired girl. Very few refugees from the East had reached Thailand, virtually none from the far Northeast. Their original intensity waned, their enthusiasm dwindled in the boredom of routine. Once a month they returned to Bangkok for self-authorized R&R.

" 'The Viet Namese invasion of December 1977 to January 1978 threw the interior into a great state of madness,' " Conklin read loudly enough for Sullivan to hear over the gurgle of water. " 'Although the entire front advanced, there were major blitzkrieg spearheads against which KK air power (nearly nonexistent) and artillery were ineffective. Major Khmer units were ill equipped and poorly led. In the North the PAVN rolled to the east bank of the Mekong River at Stung Treng; in the South they advanced to Neak Luong with little difficulty. Radio Hanoi claimed the drive freed 150,000 Khmers. Phnom Penh reported the Viet Namese forcibly conscripted 150,000 and sent them into battle against Pol Pot's forces.' "

"Probably ten times too high," Sullivan called out. "Neak Luong, huh?"

"Yeah. Yeah, probably. 'On 6 January 1978, the Viet Namese spearheads—with amphibious vehicles, ferry boats, helicopters, portable bridging, tanks and artillery—stopped. Phnom Penh claimed a glorious victory saying guerrilla tactics behind the PAVN lines forced the Viet Namese to withdraw. Some observers have concluded the problem was the new Viet Namese army was heavily comprised of ex-ARVN soldiers who purposefully sabotaged the invasion. On 6 February, its troops withdrawn to old border sanctuary bases, Hanoi publicly called for peace talks between the two nations—indicating that only by its good grace was the offensive canceled and Phnom Penh left standing. Pol Pot immediately rejected Hanoi's proposal.' "

"You know what I think?" Sullivan called. He didn't wait for an answer. "I think any observer who thinks the PAVN is full of ex-ARVNs is full of shit."

"Just listen, will ya. It says, 'The campaign resulted in the death of one third of Kampuchea's army, about thirty thousand soldiers. The PAVN suffered almost equal casualties, though this represented but five percent of its force. In the Kampuchean interior cadre in several western provinces "planned" or launched small rebellions against the Center. All were put down, most (even those which were imaginary) by preemptive massacres. In the East dissident factions have flocked to join the new Khmer Viet Minh. Politically the interior is polarized and fragmented. Pol Pot himself has drawn distinctions between the units of Takeo, Kampot, and Kompong Speu, who are his "unconditional troops," and all others, whom he suspects of double-dealing.' "

"Where do they get that stuff?" Sullivan asked.

"Same place we do, I'd guess."

"From refugee reports?"

"There and commie radio."

"Conk!"

"Yeah."

"I'm sick of these border camps. I haven't gotten to step one in a whole fuckin year."

"Yeah. You haven't gotten out of that tub yet, either. It's my turn."

"I want to go inside," Sullivan said.

"Inside?"

"Yeah. Inside."

Slowly Vathana unbuttoned Nang's gray tunic. It was in her mind that she would be killed the moment they finished but that did not matter. In this one way, by this one act, she would attempt to plant a seed of love in his sterile desiccated soul. Perhaps it would germinate. Perhaps, in time, long after her body had rotted, he would abandon this murdering.

"You have very big muscles," Vathana said. It was the first time she'd seen him without his uniform. "You have many scars."

"In the war . . ." He hesitated. He felt vulnerable without the tunic. He felt giddy. He felt foolish. ". . . I was stronger and quicker and more sure. I could pick a coin from a blind man's cup without him feeling or the monk seeing."

"Do you remember, before the war . . ." Vathana pulled her blouse tail from her skirt. ". . . I would collect *kathen* . . ." She looked upon Nang's face as never before, looked beyond the burn-scar, beyond the face of her master, her executioner. ". . . during the *bon* I would give the alms to the monks . . ." Vathana lightly laid a hand on Nang's belt. "Papa was very . . ."

Nang went rigid. A wave of humiliation swept over him. "Stop." Vathana stilled. "Before . . . I . . . I want you to read my father's confession. All of it. It is . . . you will understand then. Then we can proceed."

He forced her to the cage, left, returned with the file, released her, sat. Immediately, Vathana saw the notebooks. A shudder quaked her entire body, a tremor more severe than any malaria attack, more frightening than the errant bomb on Neak Luong.

". . . It . . ." Nang stuttered. "It was . . . an accident, really. He should have . . . What is it?"

"Those . . ."

"Those?"

"Notebooks. You have one and seven!" Vathana's hand flew. *Crack!* She slapped Nang's face, knocking him from the chair. "One and seven! You *murderer!*" Shock grabbed her, grabbed him. To her these meant Chhuon's death. She went beyond shock, beyond horror. Met Nang, executioner . . . She pounced on the file. The script was unmistakable. She glared, screamed, "Don't you wonder . . . why . . . one and seven?"

"Hum?" He was totally bewildered.

"I have two through six." She fell to her knees, wailed a terrible crying sobbing cackling wail.

Met Nem and Kosol broke into the room. "Get *out!*" Nang shrieked.

Vathana vomited. Again she glared at Nang. Still he sat on the floor. "Every day, every night, I see the dead parade before me and it's . . . *it's* . . . *it's* because of my own brother. *My brother!*"

"Who's your brother? Don't be stupid. I'm . . ."

"Cahuom Samnang. That's who you are. Little Samnang, son of Chhuon, lost at Plei Srepok . . . Oh! Oh . . . oh . . . oh . . ." She beat her fists on the floor, on her thighs. For a long time she cried. Nang sat stupefied. Then he rose, collected his tunic and left.

He did not return until long after the rains began. The monsoon rains of 1978 were heavier even than those of 1977, the worst in a hundred years. Everywhere fields washed out and people died but Vathana no longer was privileged to witness the genocide. No longer was she caged, but she did not flee. The house staff bitched constantly to her about betrayals, about new conditions, about Met Sar's ignoble abandonment. They treated her not like a prisoner but like the shadow queen, yet she knew she could not escape. By June yotheas were complaining about the lack of rice and other staples, about the renewed moaning because there was no gasoline, about the loathsome stench which even the heaviest rains in a century could not wash from the air.

Then Nang returned. He was insane. With the others he bitched about the odor and the moaning though daily he tabulated the progress Site 169 was making in the eradication of enemies and useless elements. Each tenth day he filed his report exactly as he had for three years. And if the progress was less than satisfactory Nang meted out punishment to cadre and subordinates as if none of his acts were tied to the moaning and the odor.

In July Nang took Vathana back toward the cliff. She had

read and memorized Chhuon's file, had sent Met Arn to unearth the middle notebooks.

At the base of the cliff Nang took an overgrown path she'd not seen. It led down a steep escarpment to a gushing, vine-cloaked stream which flowed from the cliff. "I found it when I came for my father." Nang's words were unconnected to previous utterances. The banks were red—from laterite soil or blood. He led her, in silence, downstream hundreds of meters. There, partially buried by jungle, was a small temple. "I've been cleaning it," Nang whispered. The stone walls were carved with hundreds of lingas, phallic symbols, the symbols of creative power of the Hindu god Siva. "He wished to bless the waters which flow to the paddies," Nang said. "This is where I am from. I came at the wrong time."

"Samnang," Vathana whispered, "for our father . . . your father . . . let me go. Let the people escape." Nang grasped her hand and pulled her to a second wall bedecked with ancient Apsarases, the heavenly maidens of Kambuja, and tortured slaves. "Samnang, you have a choice."

"Like them"—Nang rubbed a hand on the bas relief—"we are condemned to cycles of destruction and creation."

"Do you hear me? You can choose, right now. You can let the people live. They are not animals. Even animals, Samnang . . . Samnang . . ."

"Do you know why we call them yuons?"

"What? No. Listen. Please listen."

"When Chams attacked Kambuja in the tenth century they had Viet slaves. They were called *yavana*, evil foreigners."

"Samnang, you do not have to kill."

"Hum? Every Khmer must kill. Everyone must kill thirty yuons. The Center so decrees. We may sacrifice two million in combat but we will kill sixty million Viet Namese. There will still be millions of Kampucheans to repopulate all Southeast Asia. I will have them all work harder. Double our production."

"Samnang! Stop! Stop it! We don't need to wipe out the Viet Namese. They aren't devils. They're humans too."

"Ha! I know. Ha!" Nang turned to her, pulled her close, whispered so even the Apsarases couldn't hear, "i've had a meeting. ssshh! no one must know. first i must finish the killings. then . . . *ha!* i've met with them."

The interior of Democratic Kampuchea in mid- and late 1978 was more treacherous than anything Sullivan had seen in Viet Nam or Cambodia in the late '60s and early '70s. Ambushes were everywhere. The bodies of those who'd attempted escape lined the routes to the border. And of those who did not flee, the reports were numbing. The killings were the heaviest of the Pol Pot years. Like Nazi Germany in 1945, Angkar Leou seemed bent on stamping out the evidence of its own atrocities. It turned not only on the people but also upon itself, and the bloodbath leaped by logarithmic degrees up a vengeance scale. The Free World barely reacted.

New mass deportations struck some areas. Starvation continued everywhere. Reports claimed that up to 300,000 Khmers had fled to Viet Nam, that Krahom military units continued to mutiny, that forty thousand Khmer insurgents were "working the border" and that the Center had decreed a new offensive against the Viet Namese. The trickle of refugees to Thailand increased to a steady stream. Still the Free World barely reacted.

Sullivan and Conklin found penetration deeper than a few kilometers almost impossible. They were *phalangs,* tall white foreigners. No matter where they went, they stood out. Still they made their forays—into the South, the center, the North. Always they returned, sometimes empty-handed, sometimes with a fleeing family in tow, to a small house they'd rented near Aranyaprathet. The home was in the town where many of the relief agencies had field headquarters. They made their house their headquarters, their information center. They lined the walls with maps, concocted an elaborate file system of where they'd searched, what they'd learned, where the people they'd contacted originated from, and their route to that border point.

Newsweek magazine carried refugee stories in the 23 January issue. The articles concluded, "Some of the horror stories told by refugees about life in Cambodia are undoubtedly exaggerations. . . . Several prominent Indochina experts have recently disputed many of the refugees' charges, contending that a few thousand Cambodians at the most have died at the hands of Angkar Leou. They also maintain that it was a matter of economic necessity to relocate the population into rural areas because U.S. bombing forced too many people off the land during the Vietnam War."

"Damn!" Sullivan blurted, reading the old issue which had just arrived. "If one replaces the word Cambodia with Germany the statement could have been from Free World papers of 1943 or even '44 or '45. Will we ever learn? It's so much easier to deny the reports. Then they don't have to feel the guilt of apathy."

Conklin picked up the magazine. The article showed photos of "baby-faced executioners" and spoke of ghost towns. "Who the fuck are these 'experts'?"

"Can't you guess?" Sullivan snapped back.

In the same issue there was a story about Soviet expansionism into the Horn of Africa—the USSR can move three divisions to African supply sites in one day. Also noted was the assassination in Nicaragua of *La Prensa* editor Pedro Joaquin Chamorro-Cardenal. Allegedly he was murdered by Somoza-backed death squads though there was the possibility the killers were Sandinistas posing as Somoza men. The death touched off major street rioting. Both stories, Sullivan said to Conklin, smacked of standard insurgent tactics seen in Southeast Asia for the past three decades. "How come they don't suggest a connection?"

The two ex–Special Forces teammates crossed the border west of Preah Vihear in June. For three kilometers the area had been picked clean. Then they came upon an uncrossable swath of forest evidently so littered with land mines that even Khmer Rouge soldiers couldn't pick their way through. They moved cautiously west, trying to outflank the mined belt. For two days they saw nothing but the mutilated bodies of soldiers. On their return to Aranyaprathet Sullivan was more depressed than ever.

His new reading material did nothing to bolster his spirits. Columnist David Broder, speaking of U.S. involvement in Central America, simply said America was pursuing "the path of stupidity again." Quoting Senator Frank Church he said, ". . . we seem unable to learn from the failure of our Viet Nam policy . . . Somehow, someday, this country has got to learn to live with revolutions in the third world."

"Which stupid lessons shall we learn, Mister Broder?" Sullivan threw the article at Conklin. "Shall we learn to allow the Pol Pots of the world to slaughter their own people—as long as we don't see it? This morally depraved person thinks not. There are other lessons we should learn. To hide our heads is not one. To question why our Viet Nam policies failed is valid and essential, but to do so means to examine and analyze, not to accept flippant propaganda."

In June 1978, Viet Nam cracked down on its 1.5 million people of Chinese ancestry, confiscating their property and driving them from their homes. In Asia it was major news. From what Sullivan and Conklin saw of American press coverage, it was virtually ignored. "Hey." Conklin chuckled cynically. "What'd ya expect? There's no photos of the self-immolation protests. No photos, no story, right? Didn't happen!"

"Know what I think?" Sullivan countered. "I think we're seeing a new American society—one so convinced of its own evil, it seeks only to reinforce that image. What effect is that gonna produce down the line? How many Democratic Kampucheas is this world gonna have?"

"Fuck it, man," Conklin said.

"Fuck it is right," Sullivan said. "There's no chance, Conk. There's no chance they're alive."

"Yes there is."

"We haven't been able to trace anybody, nobody, back to Neak Luong. Ya know what?"

"Come on, J. L. We've still helped a lot of people."

"Fuck it. I'm sick of it. I'm gonna follow the American example. The American plan. That's what the travel agents call it, eh?"

"What American plan?"

"I'm gonna quit."

Met Kosal has been replaced by two ten-year-old boys; Met Nem by a nine-year-old girl. The boys carry AK-47 rifles which dwarf them. The girl is unarmed—even her eyes—a total emptiness. They do not have names. They are "Comrade Child." Nothing more. Today, Vathana is under casual house arrest. She sits in a large wicker chair in the central room watching these beautiful, relatively well nourished children. They speak Khmer though she finds she cannot understand them—their language is so different. These are the new people of Met Sar, of Pol Pot, of Mao Zedong, of Ho Chi Minh, of Lenin and Marx— the New Communist Man and Woman. Nang is not home, has not been in the house for a week. For a week he has not brought Vathana to the cliff. Vathana does not know why. She finds herself praying for him, her little brother, praying, hoping he will perish peacefully. Comrade Child, girl, brings Vathana's lunch on a tray. The food is sufficient—bland rice with some kind of meat dried to hard tack—but it is not good—prepared with little skill, little thought. Still it is more than the people get, much more. Vathana does not eat; does not move. Many children, very young, five to eight, come and go. The girl, Met Child, gives orders but Vathana cannot ascertain an orderliness. The moaning from the abyss comes and goes, too. For months it has been continuous, oscillating only in intensity. At the moment it is louder than ever before. The nightly burnings have been suspended because there is so little gasoline and what there is is being used at the front.

The children are abuzz. There are visitors. There are rumors. "The yuons are coming." Vathana doesn't move. Half a dozen little boys are running, playing. One steals some food from her tray. He dives behind her chair. Others are shooting at him with their fingers. Another takes food from the tray. Then another. Vathana doesn't move. She feels exposed, raw, as if she'd been skinned and all her nerve endings exposed. Even the wind currents from the moving children are painful. The food disappears. The little boys leave. The one from behind her chair slithers around to the front. Then he stands. He faces her, stares at her as if she is a stone object. He nudges her leg with his knee. Vathana watches him carefully, studies him. His eyes are bright, he is beautiful, more beautiful even than her own son, as beautiful as Samay when he was so small, almost as beautiful as Samnang. The little boy raises his hand, points his finger, cocks his thumb. "Bang! You're dead!" He runs out.

Vathana feels vulnerable, still she cannot move. She is not afraid of death, not afraid of torture. Everyone is vulnerable to those—no one escapes either—there are many forms of torture. But . . . Her brain refuses to carry the thought, to let it grow, blossom. Other thoughts germinate . . . to save her brother's soul . . . what did he mean, 'I've met with them'? . . . to get him to stop the killing . . . to let them all flee. . . . The ideas pull in so many directions that her core thoughts behind those large black eyes are unable to move, unable to decide on a thought to think, catatonic. Still the vulnerability to . . . to . . . not to be killed but to kill. Not to be tortured but to torture. If her own brother could become a mass executioner, why not she? Why not me? Why not you?

"Where is Little Rabbit?" Vathana can see a young man on the porch. He is Nang's height, perhaps slightly shorter. He's built powerfully like Nang, perhaps more powerfully. He wears a khaki tunic with a white shirt beneath, a symbol of his status. With him are a platoon of older yotheas—seventeen to twenty-two years old.

Comrade Child, girl, does not understand. "Rabbit Number Two?" the man says. "Night Rabbit! Met Nang!" Vathana is certain Comrade Child is playing dumb. Most of the children have disappeared. For one so young, Vathana thinks, she is very worthy. The rifles which usually stand in a central room rack are gone.

"Yes, we have here Met Nang. He is not here but he is here coming."

"Tell him Eng has come to assist him."

"Met Eng?" Met Child, girl, cracks an infinitesimal smile.

"Met Eng of Angkar Leou. Nang is my very long time friend."

For many days Met Eng stays at the house of Nang. His platoons, with Met Soth as an attaché, set up bivouac beyond the yard. Nang returns. The men meet privately. Their planning is detailed, far-reaching. Vathana knows none of it but every day she sees changes. No longer is the food sufficient. And Nang no longer looks healthy. His face sags, the scar tissue on the right side wrinkles, folds like soft wax. The scar on the left deepens as if it were a tightening cord burying itself into his head. Each day he is different. Each night he locks her in the tiger cage and prattles quietly. "Now Eng is here," he confides to Vathana, "now everything will be made right. He will not let me fail. All enemies will be utterly crushed." The next night he whispers, "The Viet Namese are coming. They've ten thousand troops in the East, a hundred and twenty thousand at the border. Soon they'll come. Eng will be disappeared. We shall lead them." Then the next, "Tomorrow get rice. Hide it where we can get it fast." Then, "If they conquer us, first we'll be their subjects, then slaves in their colony, then a minority in our own land. They'll kill every Kampuchean. Khmer will be no more."

One moment he is happy; one moment serious, thoughtful, pondering alternatives; then furious, raging uncontrollably; then very businesslike, controlled, detached. The periods in any mood grow shorter. The time arrives.

Vathana stands at the edge of the abyss. The rains had tapered off in late October. Now they have ceased entirely. Beside her is Nang. He is crazy. Eng is in the tree house, Soth has taken over Site 169. She feels them watching, feels Eng's empty eyes. Vathana glances down. The lip of the cliff hides the bloody tangled mass below but the rising wind is full of its agony and decay. "I've imprisoned every man, every woman, every child . . ." Nang's voice is conspiratorial. He does not look down. He moves as if there were not a four-hundred-foot drop only inches from his feet. ". . . in their communes. Ha! No, not there. In . . ." He grabs Vathana's arm, turns her, pulls her back away from the edge. ". . . in their own minds. Ha! They know nothing. Nothing exists but what I tell them, what I show them." To both sides Eng's yotheas have mothers with children. They are making the women play blindman's buff with their own offspring. One woman shrieks, tells a boy to run, jumps before she can see a yothea impale the boy with a bayonet. A second woman plays the game, tries to soothe her two daughters telling them it's just a game. Everything will be all right. Vathana is numb. At the moment she hates both these stupid women and the sickeningly naive children. Why not make them kill you? Why kill yourself? Yet as Nang turns her again she thinks she herself will leap and end his game. "For years they've known nothing of Kampuchea," he says. "The outside world does not exist. Only me. Only what I tell them."

From the cliff edge Vathana can see hundreds of square miles of Cambodian territory yet she cannot get a sense of the land. It rolls here, is lush there, is barren there, flat there. Somewhere, there must still be Khmer people but Vathana is not certain. She sees none other than those approaching the cliff in the line that disappears behind the escarpment to the east. The hot rising air is so foul her mind retches but she shows no emotion. Nang has switched topics. He is telling her about the creek bed beneath the canopy, about the small hidden temple. "there is an Apsaras on the east wall that has eyes like yours. follow her eyes. she looks to the cache. Now, one more step."

Vathana closes her eyes. It is time. "Divine Buddha . . ." she whispers. She lifts her left foot, advances it over the edge.

"Ha!" Nang spins her, pulls, walks her back. "you must be more careful. you promised chhuon you'd take our story to the world." He laughs loudly. Yotheas to each side smirk, laugh with him, at him. I . . . he thinks, they see me, they think I play the game better than them. Again he turns Vathana. "you must listen. there is the creek. there are mines on the west bank but not the east." They are thirty feet from the edge, walking slowly.

"Samnang." Vathana lays a hand on his arm. She is trembling. "Let me go. I want to go to Papa!"

"ach!" The noise of disgust is very quiet. "you go to chhuon, you are dead."

"Isn't that what . . ."

"Twenty-eight thousand in thirty days. That's the latest report. I'm the best. Sar must take notice. You tell the world. Then Sar will know, too. No one knows. They know only what they're told. Tell them, twenty-eight thousand in thirty days. Tell them no one is better than Nang. Yesterday I measured the fill, the drop is now less than three hundred feet. Can you survive that?"

"You can kill me. You can let me kill myself. Or you can let me go. Those are your choices. You make that choice for everyone. You make that choice, Kdeb."

Again they are at the edge. Vathana has grasped Nang's sleeve. "So many," she whispers. "So many have died. There is Chhuon, Sok, Grandmother. Let's go to Papa together."

"Ha! Haha!" Nang snatches grips at both her shirt sleeves. His laugh is loud. "Ha! You are crazier than me! Ha!" He pulls her down with his right pincer, pushes up with his good hand. Vathana resists, yet he is very strong and she leans face first over the edge. Her knee buckles. He releases. She slides head first down the lip. He grabs an ankle. She reaches out, down, digs her fingers into the dry crumbling stone, pulls herself down. He sits, pulls back, digs his heels in. She flails her arms, twists her body, attempts to kick his hand with her free foot. Her skirt flaps up over her back.

Half a dozen cliff yotheas converge, laughing, staring. One grabs Nang's shoulder and pulls. Then another assists. All are laughing. Nang lets her dangle, thrash. Three yotheas form a chain. One reaches out, grabs the waistband of her pants, pulls them back. "What an ass," one yells. "Look at her hump the cliff," another calls. "Hey, let's hump her first." "Yeah." They drag Nang, he drags Vathana. He lifts her by the ankles, pulls her over his back. "Me first," he shouts. "Me first." He runs away from the cliff. The yotheas follow. He runs beyond the row of cells. They cannot go there. "Hey, bring her back," they yell. He pays no heed.

Again Nang cages Vathana but now continuously, not just at night. "For safekeeping," he insists. He is morbid. He has fallen into a chasm of guilt and depression so deep that the violent acts occurring in the East are not new PAVN blitzkrieg spearheads but the righteous punishment of God, the lightning and sword of Vishnu striking through Viet Namese—aimed, Russian-made cannons, tanks and rockets. Radio Hanoi's broadcasts call for a general uprising, plot the advance in words.

Eng is incensed. He wants to go to the front. The front is coming to him. Mimot, Snuol, Svay Rieng have fallen. The PAVN is driving up Highway 1 toward Neak Luong, up U-shaped Highway 7 toward the Chup Plantation on one leg and toward Kratie on the other, and down out of Ratanakiri along Highway 19 through Andaung Pech, past the ruins of Phum Sath Din toward Stung Treng. Radio Phnom Penh reports resistance everywhere, reports brave victories ever closer to the Mekong. From Viet Nam there is announcement of the new Kampuchean United Front for National Salvation. It is headed by Heng Samrin.

Everywhere there is the whisper, "the viet namese are coming. the viet namese are coming." The whisper grows louder.

"Met Nang," Eng calls in a loud voice. There is no answer. Vathana can hear the commotion, the movement of squads of yotheas in and about the house, but she sees nothing. Nang has covered her cage as one covers a birdcage at night.

"Met Nang." Vathana recognizes the voice of Eng's underling, Soth. "You are accused of heinous crimes against the people . . ." More commotion, scuffling, shots, then running and quiet. Suddenly, beyond, there are explosions.

Vathana does not feel sorrow though she is sad. There is but one heaven, she thinks. It is what Chhuon taught her when she was very little. One death for all bodies, one heaven for all souls. But only to have lived better, only to have died with peace in his heart. It is now very quiet. The house is empty, she thinks. They have gone. She reaches through the slats of the cage and lifts the plastic tarp. It is dusk. She is alone. She has never before attempted a break from the cage and she thinks of Nang's words—I have imprisoned them in their own minds. She thinks it is disgusting yet she knows it is true. The latch is crude but strong. She cannot budge the pins. The cage is lashed together with vines and wires. She works on a joint. The wires are easy to untwist and unwrap but the vines have dried and are hard as wood. Methodically she picks at just one, at just the edge. She is able to break off a sliver. She works. She is frustrated by the resilience of the rattan. She quits. Holds her head. Pulls her hair. Then she attacks the vines again.

It is now dark. Vathana has broken two lashing joints. She thinks it will take five before she can separate the side from the top enough to force her head through. There is noise in the yard. She works frantically. There is noise in the house. She pulls the tarp down, freezes. She tries to stop breathing. Her chest aches. The noise stops. She is certain it—he?—who?—has not departed. She waits. Her head is hot. The air under the tarp is stale, the ambient odor from the abyss is caged with her. She hears a step, a creak of the floor. Then again all is silent. Still she doesn't move. More noise—outside. Something light scampers into the room with her. There are shouts. Yotheas. They've surrounded the house. Then the tarp flicks up. A knife blade slits the joints Vathana had been working on. "come." The voice is small. Vathana squeezes up, out to the waist. "quick." It is little Comrade Child, girl. The girl pulls her to the floor. Then she lies atop Vathana and covers them both with the crumpled tarp. Yotheas are stomping into the house, flashlight beams cross the central room, flick into Nang's room, into the cage.

"Damn it." The voice is hard, angry. "She's escaped. Go for the aunt. She'll go there." There is the noise of a squad rushing out.

Comrade Child, girl, waits only half a minute. Then she creeps from under the tarp, pulling Vathana with her. Quickly, quietly, she leads Vathana from the house, from the yard, out beyond the minefields to the trail to the cliff. She does not speak. Vathana follows, blind, dumb. Aunt, she thinks. Aunt Voen. Where is she? Comrade Child hustles on. The path is empty. At the cliff base the stink, the moaning air, the night gnats assault them. Still they stumble on. Above, Vathana senses the light show strung between the points of the horseshoe, but she does not look up. A shriek, a hundred shrieks fill the air. Thuds, thunks, moans, gasps. Vathana's senses close down. They slip off the path toward the cliff base. The falling, dying humans splat upon the dead and rotting so near they are sprayed with blood and fluids. Comrade Child descends into the creek. Her footing is sure. Vathana cannot see. She stumbles, falls, rises. Comrade Child stops. As Vathana reaches her the girl pulls her past. "you aren't . . . don't leave me."

"booby trap." The little girl removes the pin from a grenade and sets the trip wire. They move on. Three more times Comrade Child arms traps. In the ancient Hindu temple there is a faint light. All about are Nang's children. Comrade Child, girl, directs Vathana to enter as she goes to her post. The stones are cold and damp against her feet. The breasts of the Apsarases and the tips of the lingas have all been chipped. In the pale light Vathana sees a man. He is dressed in bloody tattered rags taken from a corpse. He bows to her, his hands together in an awkward *lei.* "Have you eaten rice today!" The old idiom.

"Samnang!"

"I am Eng Samron of Stung Treng."

"Samnang. I thought . . . Those clothes . . . How . . ."

"I am in the clothes of my people. Join my people. Nang is dead. When Eng sprang the trap, my children sprang theirs. Eng too is dead. And the most treacherous, Soth. You must change clothes. Then we will go."

Slowly Vathana edges forward. Gently she lays her left hand on the drooping waxlike scar. She runs her hand up to his forehead, across, down his other scarred cheek, down his neck, across his chest to his arm and to his mutilated hand. "You could have been such a fine younger brother."

"Quickly now," Nang says. "We have very far to go. I will go out. Put these on."

All night they travel west and south, deeper into Cambodia. At moments Vathana feels safe, free, then she feels very frightened. Much of the time they crawl through low, prepared tunnel trails through dense vegetation—trails like those made by a small rabbit. At dawn they hole up. At dusk they set off again. West farther, then north. Again they stop at dawn. They are hidden in a forested oasis of green amid a sea of ruined paddies. Quietly Nang points out minefields, ambush sites, sniper holes, death pits. He knows every inch of the landscape, every bone of the dead. "If I had been allowed to continue," Nang says matter-of-factly, "Kampuchea would be a land without Kampucheans, eh!" Then he laughs. "Now . . ." He laughs again. It is very funny. "Eng Samron shall go to Stung Treng. Papa is there. He's there with Uncle Cheam. I will go to school. He promised I could."

"Samnang . . ." Vathana begins, but he interrupts.

"I had a friend from Prey Veng. He is Rin, Met Rin. He is very impressed with Nang of Kompong Thom. A Gray Vulture. Why do you think I wore his uniform all these years? So he will know. Now there, you see, there is Thailand. At dusk you will take my children there."

"You'll come too."

"Me? No. I have a choice, eh? I am Eng Samron of the Khmer Viet Minh. I have valuable intelligence about the forces of Democratic Kampuchea. How can I go there?"

SULLIVAN'S EPILOGUE
DECEMBER 1986

One forgets joy, one never forgets sorrow.
> —Mihail Lermontov,
> *A Hero of Our Times*

Every man has a right to his opinion, but no
man has a right to be wrong in his facts.
> —Bernard Mannes Baruch

An aerogram!

I did not quit in June of 1978. Nor in 1979 after the Viet Namese overran Kampuchea. For two years I worked for Cambodian Crisis Relief. Then I quit. I returned to the United States in late 1980, returned, burned up and burned out. For a while I worked for Mr. Pradesh on the ranch, for a while I drifted doing odd jobs here and there. Through a contact I had made through Rita Donaldson, I worked for *The Washington News-Times* for almost a year. During this period I researched and prepared background files for the paper's reporters and editors. Then, last year, I returned to the Pradesh ranch, resumed my daily chores here while staying somewhat abreast of the situation in Southeast Asia. Some days it seems so far away and so long ago. Then, on days like today, it seems so immediate. Below is my last report before I close this account. An aerogram? That's how Mr. Pradesh pronounced it. He called down here from the main house. He says there is an aerogram for me from Bangkok.

The Cambodian holocaust has not stopped. There is so much more to tell. The camps; the expulsion from Thailand of more than 40,000 refugees, their forced march down the high escarpment of the Dang Rek Mountains near Preah Vihear into the maw of the Viet Namese army; the suicides caused by callous U.S. Immigration and Naturalization Service officers; the incredible *purposeful continuation of the starvation* which killed an estimated 600,000 Khmer in the first year of Hanoi's occupation; the occupation and colonialization of the Socialist Republic of Kampuchea by the hegemonic Hanoi warlords bowing before their own new emperor, the Soviets. That is history, not the story of Cahuom Chhuon's family.

Knowing that does not let me sleep. What is story, what is history?

The accelerated killings of late 1978 are well documented. They include the slaughter of thousands of Khmer Krahom cadre at the "security and interrogation" center of Tuol Sleng in the heart of Phnom Penh and the mass decapitation of 22,000 people at Prey Vong. For at least two months Angkar Leou knew a PAVN assault was imminent. By November 1978 the Viet Namese had massed 120,000 troops along the Viet Nam-Cambodia border plus 40,000 along the Laos-Cambodia border. In the interior the Khmer leadership began its frantic scrambling for scapegoats which set off the final wave of mass executions. In December Ieng Sary told Elizabeth Becker, "Frankly speaking, about the so-called slaughters, the massacres, 'we could not avoid the killings.'"

On 8 December 1978 (some accounts say 3 December)—only a few months after Viet Nam's prime minister, Pham Van Dong, completed a goodwill tour of noncommunist Southeast Asian nations and only a month after the USSR and Viet Nam signed a major friendship treaty (was this why on 8 January 1978 the PAVN ceased their offensive against Democratic Kampuchea—a bargaining chip for more military and financial aid from the Soviets in the Sino-Soviet dispute?)—the PAVN launched a seven-pronged blitzkrieg. Immediately the Viet Namese broke through and bypassed the heavy border fortifications. Using thousands of Soviet tanks, American- and Soviet-made fighter-bombers and heavy self-propelled artillery, Hanoi's troops (12 to 14 divisions) led Heng Samrin's new Khmer Viet Minh units (about the equivalent of one division) to topple the eastern third of the country. One should note the Communist tactic, used again with success, of "talking while fighting, fighting while talking." Norodom Sihanouk fled Phnom Penh, via China, bound for the United Nations in New York City. Hundreds of thousands of rag-cloaked slaves streamed west from every area of the country. For the second time in a year Ratanakiri, Mondolkiri and eastern Stung Treng fell. Then Kompong Cham and Kratie, Neak Luong, Takeo and Bokor. The launching points were all familiar: Duc Co, Bu Ntoll, Mimot-Krek, Svay Rieng and Chau Doc. Within days PAVN troops controlled Kompong Som, Cambodia's only deep-water port.

At the United Nations, Norodom Sihanouk assailed the Viet

Namese for attacking your "brother and comrade-in-arms during the war against the imperialists." He continued, blaming Moscow for Viet Nam's successes: "The Soviets methodically helped the Viet Namese make their preparations to topple Pol Pot." (Recall the November signing of the Soviet–Viet Namese friendship treaty which was followed by a major augmentation of Soviet advisors.) Then followed Sihanouk's request to the United States for military assistance for Pol Pot. Perhaps it is no wonder there is U.S. apathy. But isn't that caused by our looking at the governments and not seeing the people? En route to New York, Sihanouk had told correspondents, "I do not know why [Pol Pot's regime] imposed such a terrible policy. . . . They say this is genuine Communism and it must be so. But I am a Buddhist, and I will never understand Communism."

By 4 January ten of nineteen empty provincial capitals were in PAVN hands; five days later the blitzkrieg rolled through Phnom Penh and headed northwest up Highway 5 to Kompong Chhnang, Pursat and Battambang, and up 6 to Skoun, Pa Kham, Baray, Kompong Thom, Siem Reap and finally Sisophon. It is interesting to note, amongst the numerous pockets of resistance, that Cheon Ksar, near Preah Vihear and within twenty-five miles of Nang's cliff, held out until 17 January, perhaps longer. Also of interest to note (again): America's attention span (measured again by *Newsweek* magazine articles). Within two weeks of the fall of Phnom Penh (the week that Ayatollah Khomeini came to power in Iran), stories about Cambodia ceased. By the 5 February issue the story had been reduced to two letters to the editor. One (from C. R. Lotts, of Harrisonburg, Virginia) proclaimed that the local factions are not motivated "by outside international forces" and continues, "Fortunately, this time U.S. dollars and blood were not prostituted to either side."

Perhaps the second, from Ward A. Holcomb, of Quantico, Virginia, comes closest to what I see as the most common attitude in America: "The conquest of Cambodia by Vietnam affords a rare opportunity for America. It is a chance to keep our politicians silent, our money in the bank and our uniformed sons at home. *Let Southeast Asia stew in its own juice!*" (My emphasis.)

And stew it did. Without us. And were it only the Pol Pots or the Pham Van Dongs, I too would cheer. But it was not and is not. It is the Vathanas. It is the Chhuons. You must see that. Don't be duped by bread and circuses, by stone-washed (oops! now it's ice-washed) dungarees and video entertainment systems. Don't be so overentertained that you don't take the time to analyze our, your, world—to be skeptical, questioning, to help solve its problems, to feel its pain and help it heal!

By 1980, 500,000 Khmer had fled to the relative security of the Thai border region—perhaps twenty percent crossing to enter refugee camps for potential processing for shipment to third nations. Those who remained in Thailand—people without a land, listless, restless—will they become the new Palestinians?

Many world agencies responded to the famine in Cambodia in 1979. They asked for help, asked for 108,000 tons of rice or wheat flour, for oil and sugar, for trucks to help dispense the foodstuffs. Of four million surviving Khmers, it was estimated that fifty-five percent were threatened with starvation. But, by policy, the new regime blocked much of the distribution: ". . . We never received this aid. It went to Viet Nam at night by truck." (Prak Savath, Battambang district chief, 1980–1983, quoted from *To Bear Any Burden*, by Al Santoli.)

Again, secret, purposeful, government-sponsored starvation. While Viet Namese troops looted and pillaged the remnants of Khmer family culture, the United States, under the leadership of the Carter administration, generally took the attitude that as long as Communists are killing Communists, as long as the factions' respective patrons, China and the USSR, are bickering, it is in America's best interest. Yet even if one were to forget that the pawns were being trampled, the long-term results of political destabilization are *not* in America's best interest.

Truong Nhu Tang, in his book *A Vietcong Memoir*, noted this about earlier American mentalities:

> Along with their political forebears both Nixon and Kissinger suffered from a fundamental inability to enter into the mental world of their enemy and so to formulate policies that would effectively frustrate the strategies arrayed against them, the strategies of a people's war.

Do we, the people, of this representative democratic nation, still suffer from that very same fundamental inability—the inability to enter *not only* the mental world of our adversaries and thus effectively frustrate the strategies arrayed against us, *but also* the mental world of our friends and thus fail to formulate policies of mutual interest? Do we, the people, then instill those inabilities in our leaders—either by selection or by the pressure of public opinion?

Under Heng Samrin (ex–Khmer Krahom cadre "constitute the majority [eighty percent, says Douglas Pike] within the apparatus of the [new] party and state," as reported in *Indochina Report* in October 1984) the Viet Namization of Kampuchea has been a continuing model of the efficient extermination of a race. At first the new leaders decreed that everyone should return home. On the surface this matched the desires of the people. In reality it set off a new mass deportation without sustenance, a new disruption of the main crop as paddies were abandoned or left fallow. Thousands soon starved to death. Thousands more starved slowly. Then the new repression began. The new collective masters (the Khmer Viet Minh) invited people to form anti–Pol Pot associations, anti–Viet Namese associations, new leadership associations, ex–military men associations, and so on. Then the new association leaders were systematically rounded up and shipped for reeducation. Most simply disappeared. Schools were reopened. All teaching (the materials and content prepared in Viet Nam and approved in Hanoi) is conducted in Viet Namese. There are now a million Viet Namese civilians in Cambodia. Viet Namese "advisors," 12,000 strong, stand behind the Khmer puppet government at every level. "Behind them, even more discreetly . . . are the Soviet advisors," says French Red Cross worker (1984–1986) Doctor Esmeralda Luciolli. Doctor Luciolli further describes the Viet Namese Occupation Army's military plan SB-1785 (a.k.a. K-5), which forcibly conscripted 1.5 million Cambodians to build a fortified barrier and no-man's-land along the entire Thailand-Cambodia border: "a jungle equivalent of the communist-built Berlin Wall," according to the *Southeast Asia and Afghanistan Review*. The horror story goes on. Old torture centers were reopened, new ones built. Amnesty International and the Lawyers Committee for International Human Rights both labeled the new regime as a human rights violator that rivaled the Khmer Rouge. Amnesty International further noted the role of the Viet Namese advisory "experts" in the detention and torture centers.

Yet should we be surprised?

There is a PAVN occupation headquarters at Siem Reap. It is in the same locale as the old A-40 Office of the Central Office for Kampuchean Affairs (COKA). Indeed, COKA is alive and well and headed by the same Viet Namese warlords who were at its head in the late 1960s and early 1970s. But some things have changed. Le Duc Anh, who headed COKA and answered to Le Duc Tho of the Hanoi Politburo's Central Kampuchean Affairs

Commission, is now a full Politburo member as vice-minister of the Department of Defense.

American reaction still remains disgustingly minute. The looking-out-for-number-one generation has yet to throw a (oh God!) rock concert "to raise awareness" and perhaps money. (I'm not suggesting a rock concert would alleviate the suffering—there are times when only firepower works! In retrospect the time and opportunity to provide relief was in 1970 when instead of bombers Cambodia needed advisors to train a capable and honest defense force. Are we in our 1970 position anywhere in the world today?)

I would like to quote a thought from Herman Wouk's *War and Remembrance:* "One surmises that mankind has outgrown human sacrifice, human slavery and dueling, and thus shall or should outgrow war—particularly in light of the modern world's incredible destructive capabilities." Wouk writes about the end of World War Two. But mankind has not outgrown human sacrifice—the sacrifice has only become institutionalized on a grander scale. Nor has humanity outgrown slavery. That humanity shall outgrow war in our time, though a beautiful thought, is, I fear, a sentimental and overoptimistic idea. As imbecilic and abhorrent as war is, unopposed war is unquestionably more horrible. At the very least—and it is little—war brings hope that evil might be defeated. Appeasement equals hopelessness.

And yet, in the next breath, I say, evil cannot defeat evil. Evil can only multiply evil. Only good can defeat evil. Usually it doesn't. But it never loses either. Good and evil are weights on a scale. With each other they obey the laws of addition and subtraction; alone, each obeys the law of multiplication.

John Healey, executive director of Amnesty International, writes, "You and I and all decent people of this world must stand up as one and cry out: 'No one, anywhere, should ever be tortured by anybody.' I hope when you hear of torture . . . you want to cry out, 'How dare they!' " Elie Wiesel says, "The worst enemy of humankind is indifference."

And yet I feel a general malaise, an indifference, has settled over a large percentage of our population. It is as if America is in a depression, not economic but spiritual; as if its morale is terribly fragile. We are in a battle for our minds, a battle for history. When a person or a nation is depressed it selectively seeks out and concentrates on all its past errors and present faults and it ignores its present strengths and past achievements. It is as if it *wants* to believe the worst about itself. It becomes a sucker for other people's propaganda. Snap out of it,

America! There is something much worse than war and that is unopposed genocide! And the genocide goes on!

There is so much more—what the Hanoi despots have done in the North as well as the South brings another flood of pain . . .

I'm so sickened with what I now know, what I refused to learn thirteen years ago . . . I want to tell her that . . . I want to say, "Vathana, I'm sorry. I didn't know. I didn't know not knowing could hurt you. Did hurt you. Hurt your people so."

The aerogram from Bangkok. Mr. Pradesh has handed it to me and left. The parchment is thin.

John,
    Confirmed. Nang now secretary People's Republic Kampuchea, Eastern Zone, Neak Luong. A.k.a. Hnong Kieng. Voen found in Thai camp, Khao I Dang. *Has Su Livanh*. Is with Mey and Mey's sister, Ton, plus two children, plus Amara's son given to Vathana. Samnang or other d/d boy, reported in or near Battambang. To be checked out. Tran Van Le in Cambodia leading resistance unit. Vathana's uncle, Sam, ill, at Camp Site 7. Vathana rumored in camp north of Preah Vihear. I will continue search, struggle. Come at once. Or set up there a basecamp for refugees. Rita. PS: Conklin is great help. Many thanks.

ADDITIONAL READINGS

The author particularly wishes to recommend and acknowledge the following books and articles:

David A. Ablin and Marlowe Hood, editors. *The Cambodian Agony*. Armonk, New York: M. E. Sharpe, 1987.

The Amnesty International Report—1985. London, England: Amnesty International Publications, 1985.

Elizabeth Becker. *When the War Was Over: Cambodia's Revolution and the Voice of Its People*. New York: Simon & Schuster, 1986.

John S. Bowman, general editor. *The Vietnam War: An Almanac*. New York: World Almanac Publications, 1985.

David P. Chandler. *The Land and People of Cambodia*. New York: Lippincott, 1972.

David P. Chandler and Ben Kiernan, editors. *Revolution and Its Aftermath in Kampuchea: Eight Essays*. New Haven: Yale University Press, 1983.

David Chanoff and Doan Van Toai. *Portrait of the Enemy*. New York: Random House, 1986.

Georges Condominas. *We Have Eaten the Forest: The Story of a Montagnard Village in the Central Highlands of Vietnam*. (Translated by Adrienne Foulke.) New York: Hill and Wang, 1977. (French edition, 1957.)

Tom Dooley. *Dr. Tom Dooley's Three Great Books: Deliver Us from Evil [1956]: The Edge of Tomorrow [1958]; The Night They Burned the Mountain [1960]*. New York: Farrar, Straus and Cudahy.

William Faulkner. *The Unvanquished*. New York: Vintage Books (Random House), 1934.

Bruce Grant. *The Boat People, An "AGE" Investigation*. Ringwood, Victoria, Australia: Penguin Books, 1979.

Haing Ngor, with Roger Warner. *A Cambodian Odyssey*. New York: Macmillan, 1987.

Stuart A. Herrington. *Silence Was a Weapon: The Vietnam War in the Villages*. Novato, California: Presidio Press, 1982.

Martin F. Herz, assisted by Leslie Rider. *The Prestige Press and the Christmas Bombing, 1972: Images and Reality in Vietnam*. Washington, D.C.: Ethics and Public Policy Center, 1980.

Arnold R. Isaacs. *Without Honor: Defeat in Vietnam and Cambodia*. Baltimore: Johns Hopkins University Press, 1983.

Ben Kiernan. *How Pol Pot Came to Power: A History of Communism in Kampuchea, 1930–1975*. London, England: Verso, 1985.

Arthur Kleinman and Byron Good, editors. *Culture and Depression: Studies in the Anthropology and Cross-Cultural Psychiatry of Affect and Disorder*. Berkeley: University of California Press, 1985.

Nayan Chanda. *Brother Enemy: The War After the War*. San Diego: Harcourt Brace Jovanovich, 1986.

Nhat Tien, Duong Phuc, and Vu Thanh Thuy. *Pirates on the Gulf of Siam*. San Diego: The Boat People S.O.S. Committee, 1981.

Pham Kim Vinh. *Vietnam After 1975: Bamboo Gulags and Subtle Genocide*. San Diego: PKV Publications, 1982.

Pham Kim Vinh. *In Their Defense: U.S. Soldiers in the Vietnam War*. Phoenix: Sphinx Publishing, 1985.

Douglas Pike. *PAVN: People's Army of Vietnam*. Novato, California: Presidio Press, 1986.

Pin Yathay, with John Man. *Stay Alive, My Son*. New York: Free Press, 1987.

François Ponchaud. *Cambodia: Year Zero*. (Translated by Nancy Amphoux.) New York: Holt, Rinehart and Winston, 1978.

George C. Hildebrand and Gareth Porter. *Cambodia: Starvation and Revolution*. New York: Monthly Review Press. 1976.

Kenneth M. Quinn. "Political Change in Wartime: The Khmer Krahom Revolution in Southern Cambodia, 1970–1974." *Naval War College Review*, 1976.

Al Santoli. *To Bear Any Burden: The Vietnam War and Its Aftermath in the Words of Americans and Southeast Asians*. New York: E. P. Dutton, 1985.

Sidney H. Schanberg. *The Death and Life of Dith Pran*. New York: Viking, 1985.

Robert Shaplen. *Bitter Victory*. New York: Harper & Row, 1986.

William Shawcross. *Sideshow: Kissinger, Nixon, and the Destruction of Cambodia*. New York: Simon & Schuster, 1979.

William Shawcross. *The Quality of Mercy: Cambodia, Holocaust, and Modern Conscience*. New York: Simon & Schuster, 1984.

Norodom Sihanouk. *My War with the CIA: The Memoirs of Norodom Sihanouk*. (As related to Wilfred Burchett.) New York: Pantheon Books, 1973.

Norodom Sihanouk. *War and Hope: The Case for Cambodia*. (Translated by Mary Feeney.) New York: Pantheon Books, 1980.

Someth May. *Cambodian Witness: The Autobiography of Someth May*. (Edited by James Fenton). New York: Random House, 1986.

Shelby L. Stanton. *The Rise and Fall of an American Army: U.S. Ground Forces in Vietnam, 1965–1973*. Novato, California: Presidio Press, 1985.

Scott C. S. Stone and John E. McGowan. *Wrapped in the Wind's Shawl: Refugees of Southeast Asia and the Western World*. San Rafael, California: Presidio Press, 1980.

Harry G. Summers, Jr. *On Strategy: A Critical Analysis of the Vietnam War*. Novato, California: Presidio Press, 1982.

Harry G. Summers, Jr. *Vietnam War Almanac*. New York: Facts on File Publications, 1985.

Molyda Szymusiak. *The Stones Cry Out: A Cambodian Childhood, 1975–1980*. (Translated by Linda Coverdale.) New York: Hill and Wang, 1986.

Teeda Butt Mam and Joan D. Criddle. *To Destroy You Is No Loss: The Odyssey of a Cambodian Family*. New York: Atlantic Monthly Press, 1987.

Torture in the Eighties. London, England: Amnesty International Publications, 1984.

Truong Nhu Tang, with David Chanoff and Doan Van Toai. *A Vietcong Memoir: An Inside Account of the Vietnam War and Its Aftermath*. San Diego: Harcourt Brace Jovanovich, 1985.

The Vietnam Experience. (A 20-volume series.) Boston: Boston Publishing Company, 1981–1986.

Vo Nguyen Giap. *People's War, People's Army: The Viet Cong Insurrection Manual For Underdeveloped Countries.* New York: Bantam Books, 1962.

F. J. West, Jr. *The Village.* Madison: University of Wisconsin Press, 1985.

Donald P. Whitaker et al. *Area Handbook for the Khmer Republic (Cambodia).* Washington, D.C.: U.S. Government Printing Office, 1973. (DA Pam 550-50.)

Herman Wouk. *War and Remembrance.* New York: Pocket Books, 1978.

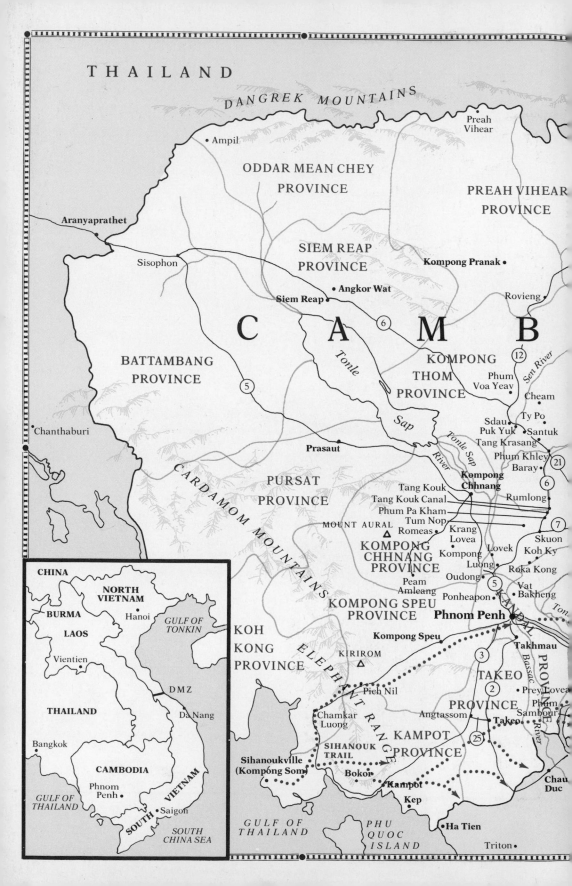